W9-DFP-584

Feb 4

DEMONS

DEMONS

A NOVEL IN THREE PARTS BY

Fyodor Dostoevsky

TRANSLATED AND ANNOTATED
BY RICHARD PEVEAR AND
LARISSA VOLOKHONSKY

ALFRED A. KNOPF   NEW YORK
1994

SOMERSET COUNTY LIBRARY
BRIDGEWATER, N. J. 08807

This Is a Borzoi Book
Published by Alfred A. Knopf, Inc.

Copyright © 1994
by Richard Pevear and Larissa Volokhonsky

All rights reserved under International and Pan-American Copyright Conventions. Published in the United States by Alfred A. Knopf, Inc., New York, and simultaneously in Canada by Random House of Canada Limited, Toronto. Distributed by Random House, Inc., New York.

This translation has been made from the Russian text of the Soviet Academy of Sciences edition, volumes ten and eleven (Leningrad, 1974).

Library of Congress Cataloging-in-Publication Data

Dostoevsky, Fyodor, 1821–1881.
　[Besy. English]
　Demons : a novel in three parts / by Fyodor Dostoevsky : translated and annotated by Richard Pevear and Larissa Volokhonsky.—1st ed.
　　p.　cm.
　ISBN 0-679-42314-1
　I. Pevear, Richard.　II. Volokhonsky, Larissa.　III. Title.
PG3326.B6　1994
891.73'3—dc20　　　　　　　　　　　　　　　　93-33367
　　　　　　　　　　　　　　　　　　　　　　　　　CIP

Manufactured in the United States of America
First Edition

SOMERSET COUNTY LIBRARY
BRIDGEWATER, N. J., 08807

Contents

Foreword

I N THE FALL of 1869, Dostoevsky was living in Dresden. That October, his brother-in-law, a student at the Petrov Agricultural Academy in Moscow, came for a visit. Dostoevsky had been following events in Russia through the foreign press, which often reported things that did not appear in Russian newspapers, and, guessing that there was going to be political trouble at the Academy, had invited the young man to stay in Dresden for fear he might otherwise become involved in the disturbances. In the course of their conversations, his brother-in-law told him about a fellow student at the Academy by the name of Ivan Ivanov, a man of intelligence and strong character, who had radically changed his convictions. The figure appealed to Dostoevsky, and he thought of writing a novel about the revolutionary movement of that time with Ivanov as one of the main heroes.

On November 21, 1869, this same Ivanov was murdered in the park of the Petrov Academy by a group consisting of two students, an older writer, and their leader, a hanger-on in university circles with credentials from the anarchist movement abroad, the twenty-two-year-old nihilist Sergei Nechaev. Ivanov had protested against Nechaev's dictatorial rule over their group and had eventually left the society. It was thought he might turn informer. Lured to an artificial grotto near the pond in the Academy park on the pretext of helping to recover a printing press hidden there, Ivanov was thrown to the ground, beaten, strangled, and finally shot in the head by Nechaev. The body, weighted with bricks prepared beforehand, was shoved through a hole in the ice.

Dostoevsky was deeply shocked by the news of the murder, but in part it was a shock of recognition that confirmed his sense of what was happening in Russia. In December 1869 he began to make notes for a story based on the confrontation of Ivanov, who in his mind represented the "new Russian man," with the nihilist Nechaev. This story, after three years of laborious transformation, became the novel *Demons*.

The events in the park of the Petrov Academy gave Dostoevsky the general outlines and many specific details for the characters we know as Ivan Shatov and Pyotr Verkhovensky (called "Nechaev" in the first sketches for the novel). Early in his work, however, in February 1870, Dostoevsky wrote to a friend in Russia asking for a recently published memoir on Timofei Granovsky, a historian and professor at Moscow University, who had died in 1855. "Material absolutely indispensable for my work," he said. Granovsky was an embodiment of the liberal idealism of the 1840s, the perfect "Westerner" (as those favoring the progressive intellectual and social views of the West were known in Russia, in opposition to the "Slavophils," who stood for the native traditions of tsar, Orthodox Church, and old Russian culture). "Nihilist sons are immediately linked . . . with idealist fathers," in the words of Dostoevsky's biographer and critic Konstantin Mochulsky. The theme of the two generations, of the moral responsibility of the men of the forties for the men of the sixties, had occurred to Dostoevsky at once. Taking details from the life of Granovsky, and from other leading liberals of the forties such as the critic Vissarion Belinsky and the publicist Alexander Herzen, Dostoevsky penned his composite portrait of the father of the nihilists—Stepan Trofimovich Verkhovensky.

The whole ideological nexus of the novel would seem to have been in place: the conflict of generations, the opposition of Westerners and Slavophils, dissent within the young revolutionary movement, the promising emergence of the "new Russian man," the sensational murder. At this stage in his work, Dostoevsky still considered the book a "novel-pamphlet," a topical piece on a contemporary theme, part documentary and part polemic, tangential to his real work. He spoke slightingly of it in letters to his friends: "What I'm writing is a tendentious piece, I want to speak out rather more forcefully. Here the nihilists and the Westerners will begin howling about me that I'm a *retrograde*! Well, to hell with them, but I'll say everything to the last word!" And so he would, though in a very different sense.

This urge to "say everything," even at the expense of art, came partly from Dostoevsky's deep concern for the fate of Russia, but partly also from more personal motives. He himself had been a liberal

idealist of the 1840s. His first book, *Poor Folk* (1846), had been championed by Belinsky. He had made the acquaintance of other literary
lights—Turgenev, Nekrasov, Herzen, Bakunin, Ogaryov. But he had
never been at ease with them, and they soon began to treat him contemptuously, laughed behind his back, wrote doggerel verses in which
they called him "a new pimple glowing on the nose of literature"
(Turgenev and Nekrasov were probably responsible for this poem,
entitled "Belinsky's Missive to Dostoevsky"). More significantly, it
was under Belinsky's tutelage that Dostoevsky had gone from a lingering social Christianity to atheist materialism. "I have acquired the
truth," he wrote to Herzen in 1845, "and in the words *God* and *religion*
I see darkness, obscurity, chains, and the knout." This negative conver-
sion out of love for suffering humanity was not an ideological affecta-
tion for Dostoevsky, it was the central crisis of his life and would
inform all his later work.

When Dostoevsky broke with Belinsky's group in 1847, it was not
to renounce the master's teachings, but to go deeper into revolutionary
activity. He began to attend meetings of the Petrashevsky circle, a
secret society of liberal utopians, and within it he joined the most
extreme faction, a group intent on preparing the Russian people for
a general uprising. The center of this group was a young man named
Nikolai Speshnyov, a rich and handsome aristocrat who, as Mochulsky
says, exercised "a vast and mysterious influence upon Dostoevsky."
Speshnyov had lived abroad, had caused the suicide of a young woman,
had been a great social success in Dresden. Ogaryova-Tuchkova, the
wife of Herzen, described him in her memoirs: "He attracted universal
attention by his sympathetic appearance. He was tall, had regular
features; dark blond locks fell in waves to his shoulders; his eyes, large
and gray, were clouded by some quiet sadness." Dostoevsky wrote of
him: "The wondrous fate of that man; wherever and however he
makes his appearance, the most unconstrained, the most impervious
people immediately surround him with devotion and respect." But
during the time of their acquaintance, just before Dostoevsky's arrest
in 1849, the writer's friend and physician, Dr. Yanovsky, noted that he
had become listless, irritable, and even complained of dizzy spells. He
told him this gloomy mood would pass, but Dostoevsky said, "No, it
won't pass, but will torment me for a long, long time, because I've

borrowed money from Speshnyov. Now I am with him and am his. I will never be able to pay back this sum, and besides he won't take it back in money, that's the sort of man he is. You understand, from now on I have my own Mephistopheles." A striking confession, particularly in his unexpected use of the instrumental case—"he won't *take it back in money.*" Dostoevsky had already begun to recognize the element of seduction in revolutionary behavior.

In 1873, when the final parts of *Demons* had been published, Dostoevsky returned to the question of personal responsibility and the link between generations in his *Diary of a Writer*: "I am an old 'Nechaevist' myself . . . I know that you, no doubt, will say in rebuttal that I am not a Nechaevist at all, and that I am only a 'Petrashevist.' All right—a Petrashevist . . . But how do you know that the Petrashevists could not have become Nechaevists, i.e. have taken the 'Nechaev' path, if things had turned that way? . . . Permit me to speak of myself alone: I probably could never have become a *Nechaev,* but a *Nechaevist* I cannot guarantee, perhaps I could have become one . . . in the days of my youth." He knew the conspiratorial milieu very well, and he knew what it had led him to—not only ten years of prison and exile (which in retrospect he may have welcomed), but a state of inner servitude that might have made him an accomplice in murder. His point is that Nechaev and the Nechaevists were not an exception—a group of "idlers and defectives"—within the revolutionary movement, but were of its essence. History has shown that he was right.

The novel-pamphlet was going to "say everything" in Dostoevsky's best (or worst) polemical style, settling some old scores, exposing the real nature of nihilism, and bringing forward the "new Russian man" in Slavophil trappings. Many elements of this proto-polemic remain in the finished novel, in its sharpness of tone, in its series of minor comic portraits, like a gallery of Daumier sculptures, and above all in the masterful caricature-parody of Turgenev as "the great writer Karmazinov." (Dostoevsky even seems to have granted Lenin a precocious appearance as the unnamed final speaker at the disastrous fête—a man of about forty, bald front and back, with a grayish little beard, who, while delivering his incomprehensible harangue, keeps raising his fist over his head and bringing it down as if crushing some adversary to dust.) But the center has shifted significantly.

When he began writing *Demons,* Dostoevsky had already been at work for several months on plans for an immense novel to be entitled *Atheism,* which by the end of 1869 had grown into an even more immense conception, a five-book *summa* with the general title of *The Life of a Great Sinner,* a "religious poem" which he thought would be his last and most important work. But as early as May 1870, the novel-pamphlet began to intrude on the *Life,* taking over some of its material and growing in the author's mind into a full-scale novel on its own. In July, another creative upheaval occurred; Dostoevsky threw out all he had written and started over from page one. "A genuine inspiration visited me," he wrote to a friend in October. In a letter written at the same time to his publisher, Mikhail Katkov, Dostoevsky explained what had happened. The letter is worth quoting at length:

One of the major events of my story will be the murder of Ivanov by Nechaev, which is well known in Moscow. I hasten to make a reservation: I do not know and never knew either Nechaev or Ivanov, or the circumstances of this murder, except from the newspapers. And even if I knew, I would not have started copying. I only take the accomplished fact. My fantasy may differ in the highest degree from the actual reality, and my Pyotr Verkhovensky may not resemble Nechaev in the least, but it seems to me that in my shocked mind imagination has created the person, the type, that corresponds to this evil-doing. No doubt it is not useless to present such a man: but he alone would not have tempted me. In my opinion, these pathetic freaks are not worthy of literature. To my own surprise, this character comes out with me as a half-comic character, and therefore, despite the fact that the event occupies one of the first planes of the novel, he is nevertheless only an accessory and circumstance for the action of another character, who really could be called the main character of the novel . . . This other character is also a dark character, also a villain, but it seems to me that he is a *tragic* character, although many will probably say upon reading, "What is this?" I sat down to write the poem of this character because I have long wished to portray him. I will feel very, very sad if it doesn't come out. I will be even sadder if I hear the judgment that this character is stilted. *I have taken him from my heart.*

This tragic character is Nikolai Stavrogin, the strongest of Dostoevsky's "strong personalities," handsome, rich, aristocratic, intelligent, fearless—the supremely autonomous man. His emergence from *The Life of a Great Sinner,* and from Dostoevsky's memories of his own "Mephistopheles," Nikolai Speshnyov, entailed a total reordering of the novel and a deepening of its motifs. Instead of the ideological opposition of Shatov and Verkhovensky, the new Russian man and the nihilist, the central place was taken by the tragic struggle of the autonomous man with his demon, brought to the point of revelation in Stavrogin's meeting with another character taken from the unfinished *Life*—the retired bishop Tikhon.

"Stavrogin is everything," Dostoevsky wrote in a note to himself dated August 16, 1870. Once the true protagonist appeared, the materials of the novel began to compose themselves around him. The result, neither pamphlet nor religious poem but a blending and recasting of both, cost him another two years of work. This groping procedure— "slipshod," one displeased critic called it—may seem surprising in so great a novelist, the assumption being that a good writer knows what he wants to write before he sets about writing it. In fact, the opposite is true, as René Girard, one of the most perceptive readers of Dostoevsky, and one of the very few to see his work whole, has said in his essay *Dostoïevski—du double à l'unité*: "This work is a means of knowledge, an instrument of exploration; it is thus always beyond the creator himself; it is in advance of his intelligence and of his faith." The novelist's "operational formalism," as Girard calls it, is a search for the form that will reveal meaning, a testing of truth by artistic embodiment. The form achieved grants the artist, and thus the reader, a knowledge of the world which is also self-knowledge, for the penetration of reality goes both ways. (Bishop Tikhon applies this same "aesthetic" testing to Stavrogin's written confession, whereas Stavrogin expected and even hoped for the reassurance of moral condemnation.) No other means of knowledge works in quite this way. And it is remarkable that Dostoevsky, constantly risking formal chaos, should arrive at such perfect formal unity as we find in *Demons.*

* * *

Stavrogin is everything. Yet *Demons* is the broadest and most multi-voiced of Dostoevsky's novels before *The Brothers Karamazov*. The "possession" it describes affects not one man or a few families, but an entire provincial town and all levels of its society. We have mentioned Stavrogin's struggle with his demon. To avoid romantic misunderstandings, we had better consider who or what the "demons" of Dostoevsky's title are. The answer is far from obvious.

It would be simpler if the title were indeed *The Possessed*, as it was first translated into English (and into French—a tradition to which Albert Camus contributed in his dramatization of the novel). This misrendering made it possible to speak of Dostoevsky's characters as demoniacs in some unexamined sense, which lends them a certain glamour and even exonerates them to a certain extent. We do see a number of people here behaving as if they were "possessed." The implications of the word are almost right, but it points in the wrong direction. And in any case it is not the title Dostoevsky gave his novel. Discovering that the Russian title *Besy* refers not to possessed but to possessors, we then apply this new term "demons" to the same set of characters in the same unexamined way—a surprising turnabout, if one thinks of it. Which characters, however, are the demons? Varvara Petrovna and Stepan Trofimovich, the mother and spiritual father of Nikolai Stavrogin? No, hardly. Stavrogin himself? If the title were singular, it might be taken as referring to him, with those very romantic overtones we are trying to avoid, because Dostoevsky avoids them entirely. But there is no odor of brimstone about Stavrogin. He is not a demon. On the contrary, he has a demon of his own, as we have already said, the one he sits staring at in the corner of his study, his "hallucination" (who finally becomes incarnate, not in this novel, but as Ivan Fyodorovich's devil in *The Brothers Karamazov*). And, besides, the title is plural. Could it refer to the first rank of Stavrogin's "disciples"? To Pyotr Verkhovensky, Shatov, Kirillov, all of whom claim him as the decisive force in their lives? Or to the second rank, to Pyotr Verkhovensky's crew—Liputin, Virginsky, Lyamshin, Tolkachenko, Erkel? To Fedka the Convict and long-eared Shigalyov? But the contagion of evil does not originate with any of them. Who, then, are the demons?

Dostoevsky's "expressive art," as Mochulsky aptly terms it, is all drama. He suppresses narrative commentary on his characters' words and feelings, explanation of their motives, examination of their thoughts, the broad "painting" of descriptive realism. All commentary comes from other characters, among whom is the narrator-chronicler himself. Dostoevsky renders only the words of his characters, their personal ways of speaking, facial expressions, gestures, in minimally detailed and often "naïvely" symbolic settings (mud, rain, mist, darkness). The absence of commentary intensifies the behavior of the characters and at the same time leaves it enigmatic. Hence the accusations of exaggeration and irrationalism often leveled at Dostoevsky, or, the same error in reverse, the praise bestowed upon his "mystical Russian soul." This expressive art relies on bold compositional arrangement, verbal emphasis, and revealing contradictions to make itself understood. And it relies on the memory of the reader, who thus participates in the unfolding drama. Aware that his artistic method left his work open to misunderstanding, Dostoevsky tried to include directives for the reader through the heightening of contrasts, the multiplying of contradictions and confrontations, and, in this case, the "mechanical" pointing of his title, supported by two epigraphs.

Dostoevsky called the novel *Demons,* we would suggest, precisely because the demons in it *do not appear,* and the reader might otherwise overlook them. The demons are visible only in distortions of the human image, the human countenance, and their force is measurable only by the degree of the distortion. What this means for an understanding of demonic possession in the novel may be elucidated by a passage from *The Brothers Karamazov.* Alyosha and Ivan Karamazov are talking about the murder of their father. Alyosha suddenly turns to his brother and says: "It was *not you* who killed father . . . You've accused yourself and confessed to yourself that you and you alone are the murderer. But it was not you who killed him, you are mistaken, the murderer was not you, do you hear, it was not you! God has sent me to tell you that." In fact, Ivan *was* their father's murderer, if only in an "intellectual" sense. But Alyosha is talking about something else. He seems to mean that the evil in Ivan is *not him,* is not identical with him, is not his essence. Ivan is in danger of taking it for his essence, of "damning" himself and losing himself entirely. He is on the verge of madness. Alyosha's message is truly meant to save him. The world of *Demons*—the provincial town with its society, its administration, its older and younger generations, its club members and revolutionaries— is in a condition similar to Ivan's. The title is perhaps Dostoevsky's message to us that "it is *not them.*"

Here, in what many consider the darkest of his novels, Dostoevsky inscribes the fundamental freedom of Judeo-Christian revelation—the freedom to turn from evil, the freedom to repent. His vision is not Manichaean; he does not see evil as co-eternal with good. Evil cannot be the essence of any living person. The "possessed" can at any moment be rid of their demons, which are wicked but also false. The devil is a liar and the father of lies. And the lie here is the same as in the beginning: "you will be like God . . ." It is what we have referred to as autonomy, embodied most fully in Stavrogin and most purely in Kirillov. The assertion of human autonomy is finally a revolt against God; it is also the final lie, the mystification behind all the demystifying critiques of modern times. It was in this light that Dostoevsky saw not only the political movements of his day, but the ideas that nourished them—ideas that came a bit late to Russia, but developed there at an accelerated pace. That acceleration makes itself felt very strongly in *Demons.*

The two epigraphs form a sharp contrast of the kind Dostoevsky's expressive art often employs. The first, a pair of fragments whirled out of the snowy night of Pushkin's poem "Demons," calls up the realm of spirits, goblins, witches. It is a spooky poem, not very serious, a phantasmagoria that touches lightly on the strings of Russian folk memory. Nevertheless, it is suggestive of much that we find in Dostoevsky's novel—the bewilderment, the whirlwind of events, the grotesquerie, the uncanny atmosphere. Underlying which there is also a richness of folk memory, articulated mainly through the figure of the lame and half-mad Marya Timofeevna, with her "other reality" and her marriage to the prince-impostor. She brings a current of half-pagan piety into the novel's symbolism, about which the Russian poet and philosopher Vyacheslav Ivanov has written most perceptively in *Freedom and the Tragic Life, a Study in Dostoevsky* (1916; English translation 1952). On the one hand, then, the demons of the title belong to the folkloric realm of spirits; they are devilish misleaders of men, tricksters, whose presence is deduced from the question: "We've lost our way, what shall we do?"

The second epigraph, which in a sense answers the first, shows the demons in a different light. It is the eschatological light of all the Gospel accounts of Christ's miracles and healings, which are not supernatural or magical but prefigure the coming of the Kingdom of God. Luke's account of the Gerasene demoniac is considerably longer than the passage Dostoevsky cites. His selection emphasizes two things: the self-destruction of the swine, and the healing of the man. This, highly abbreviated, is the plot of *Demons*.

In a letter to his friend Apollon Maikov, written when the design of the novel had finally become clear to him, Dostoevsky referred to the same passage from Luke in explaining his conception:

> The facts have shown us that the illness that seized civilized Russians was much stronger than we ourselves imagined, and that the matter did not end with Belinsky, Kraevsky, etc. But what occurred here is what is witnessed to by the evangelist Luke. Exactly the same thing happened with us: the demons came out of the Russian man and entered into a herd of swine, i.e. into the Nechaevs . . . etc.

Stepan Trofimovich repeats this comparison near the end of the novel, with small but significant changes:

> . . . you see, it's exactly like our Russia . . . But a great will and a great thought will descend to her from on high, as upon that insane demoniac, and out will come all these demons, all the uncleanness, all the abomination that is festering on the surface . . . and they will beg of themselves to enter into swine. And perhaps they already have! It is us, us and them, and Petrusha . . . and I, perhaps, first, at the head, and we will rush, insane and raging, from the cliff down into the sea, and all be drowned, and good riddance to us, because that's the most we're fit for. But the sick man will be healed and "sit at the feet of Jesus" . . .

The polemical, accusatory tone of the letter has given way to self-accusation and confession. The two impulses are always there in Dostoevsky; the former tends to predominate in his journalism, the latter in his artistic works. The penetration of his vision is linked to personal experience, to his recognition in himself of the forces at play in the world. The artist's struggle for adequate formal expression is at the same time a process of awakening. The "healing" of the sick man is, however, barely adumbrated in the novel; the intensity of the demonic paroxysm all but overshadows it; yet awakening does come *in extremis* to Stepan Trofimovich, whose end is the antithesis of Stavrogin's, but equally exemplary. On the other hand, the Nechaevs of the novel, Petrusha Verkhovensky and the rest, turn out in both comparisons to be, not demons, not demoniacs, but the herd of swine.

The demons, then, are ideas, that legion of isms that came to Russia from the West: idealism, rationalism, empiricism, materialism, utilitarianism, positivism, socialism, anarchism, nihilism, and, underlying them all, atheism. To which the Slavophils opposed their notions of the Russian earth, the Russian God, the Russian Christ, the "light from the East," and so on. In his journalism and letters, Dostoevsky often wielded these notions himself. In *Demons,* however, they are given to Shatov. And, as René Girard has observed, "the character of Shatov destroys the hypothesis of a simply reactionary Dostoevsky . . . Shatov is Dostoevsky meditating on his own ideological development, on his own powerlessness to escape negative modes of thinking. And it is in this meditation itself that Dostoevsky goes beyond Slavophil ideology" *(Mensonge romantique et vérité romanesque).* The key to this meditation is that Shatov's Slavophilism, no less than Kirillov's "man-godhood" and Pyotr Verkhovensky's revolutionary nihilism, has its source in Nikolai Stavrogin. *Stavrogin is everything.* At first he may not seem so to the reader. He says little in the novel. His doings are almost all in the past, and without his written confession, in the suppressed chapter "At Tikhon's," he would be even more enigmatic than Dostoevsky intended. Stavrogin is not identical with the contradictory "idea-demons" that have come from him, which he scarcely recognizes. His own struggle lies at a deeper level; his "idea" is a more subsuming one.

Is it not an exaggeration, even a sort of mystification, to give the status of "demons" to mere ideas? But, in the first place, there are no mere ideas in Dostoevsky, there are what Mikhail Bakhtin, in his *Problems in Dostoevsky's Poetics,* calls "voice-ideas," "voice-viewpoints," "idea-images," "idea-forces," "idea-heroes." There is no neutral, impersonal truth. "It is not the idea itself that is the 'hero of Dostoevsky's works' . . . but rather the *person born of that idea.*" Bakhtin pretends to a scientific analysis and therefore avoids evaluation of the "ideological content" of Dostoevsky's works, but implicit at least in his analysis is the possibility of an evil or alien idea coming to inhabit a person, misleading him, perverting him ontologically, driving him to crime or insanity. Dostoevsky portrays this phenomenon time and again. It even becomes a topic of discussion between two experts— Ivan Fyodorovich and the devil—in *The Brothers Karamazov.* We see it in almost all the characters of *Demons.* "It was not you who ate the idea, but the idea that ate you," Pyotr Verkhovensky says to Kirillov. Later Kirillov notes, "Stavrogin was also eaten by an idea." At one point Shatov cries out: "Kirillov! If . . . if you could renounce your terrible fantasies and drop your atheistic ravings . . . oh, what a man you'd be, Kirillov!" These unguarded observations imply that the person is not one with the idea; there is play here, a loose fit, a mismatch. Marya Shatov is a normal girl who has been invaded by a "voice-idea" totally alien to her, which leaves her quite suddenly once she has given birth. Stepan Trofimovich confesses in the end, after the book-hawker reads the Sermon on the Mount to him: "My friend, I've been lying all my life. Even when I was telling the truth."

The person born of the idea may be distorted and even destroyed by it. But to make such a judgment, one must have some way of measuring the distortion, some image of the undistorted person. And, again, if Dostoevsky is to be true to his poetics, this cannot be an abstract idea or principle. Bakhtin acknowledges the existence of this "measure" in a passage that is rather obliquely worded, but is crucial for an understanding of his own concept of "polyphony," not to mention Dostoevsky's novel:

> . . . what unfolds before Dostoevsky is not a world of objects, illuminated and ordered by his monologic thought, but a world of consciousnesses mutually illuminating one another . . . Among them Dostoevsky seeks the highest and most authoritative orientation, and he perceives it not as his own true thought, but as another authentic human being and his discourse. The image of the ideal human being or the image of Christ represents for him

the resolution of ideological quests. This image or this highest voice must crown the world of voices, must organize and subdue it. Precisely the image of a human being and his voice, a voice not the author's own, was the ultimate artistic criterion for Dostoevsky: not fidelity to his own convictions and not fidelity to convictions themselves taken abstractly, but precisely a fidelity to the authoritative image of a human being.

The openness of Dostoevsky's novels is an openness *to* this image; his polyphony has no other aim than the silent indication of its presence. Ideas that deface or distort this "authoritative image of a human being" in a person are indeed acting like demons, and are them.

In the second place, judging by their own consistency and the results of their realization in the world, these are ideas of a peculiar sort. They behave strangely. Their chief peculiarity is summed up by Shigalyov, the leading theoretician in *Demons,* commenting on his own system: ". . . my conclusion directly contradicts the original idea I start from. Starting from unlimited freedom, I conclude with unlimited despotism. I will add, however, that apart from my solution to the social formula, there is no other." Here we have the voice of the demonic idea in its pure state. Shigalyov is a doggedly honest man. He admits the contradiction in his thinking, but asserts that there can be no other solution. He is a man blinded by his own lucidity, in René Girard's terms. It is a lucidity produced by elimination; there is an absence at the center of his thought, a *golfo mistico* through which the demons enter, turning his idea into its opposite. And it is not just any idea, but the one dearest to us all—the idea of freedom. Dostoevsky was accused in his own time, and is often accused in ours, of producing only caricatures of revolutionaries in *Demons.* Readers of the tracts written by Bakunin and Nechaev will recognize the voice of Shigalyov, as will readers of the works of Lenin. Or of their ideological opponents in the hollow rivalries that have continued throughout our century and spread to every corner of the world. Shigalyov's words are a paradigm of the operation of demonic ideas. As for the realization of these ideas in the world, historical examples are to be found everywhere, perhaps most appallingly in the sixty million victims of such ideas in Shigalyov's own country. "It was only towards the middle of the twentieth century that the inhabitants of many European countries came, in general unpleasantly, to the realization that their fate could be influenced directly by intricate and abstruse books of philosophy," Czesław Miłosz wrote in the opening sentence of *The Captive Mind*. Books written by Shigalyovs, of course.

The opposite of blind lucidity was Dostoevsky's clear-sightedness about the historical situation of his time and its implications. Writing to his publisher some years after completing *Demons,* he spoke of the "blasphemy" he was then representing in "The Grand Inquisitor" as "the seed of the idea of destruction in our time, in Russia, in the milieu of the young people who have lost touch with reality," and he defined this blasphemy as the "denial not of God, but of the meaning of His creation. The whole of socialism emerged and began with the denial of the meaning of historical reality and went on to a program of destruction and anarchism." In another letter from the same time, he wrote: ". . . the scientific and philosophical refutation of the existence of God has already been abandoned, present-day *practical socialists* are not occupied with it at all (as they were for the whole past century and the first half of the present one), instead they deny with all their might God's creation, God's world, and its meaning. Here in this alone does modern civilization find nonsense." The "seed of the idea of destruction" is the revolt against God; but that is over and done with, it is already forgotten, no one is concerned with it anymore. What follows is man's replacement of God and the correction of His creation. This amounts to a declaration of the absurdity and meaninglessness of history, of historical reality as the unfolding of God's will in time, but also as the lived life of mankind—that is, to a separation from the historical body of mankind. Reality itself, physical reality, begins to drain out of this radical "idea," leaving only the drab abstraction of materialism. This Dostoevsky felt and realized, and it is one reason why his heroes, when they begin to save themselves, kiss the earth and "water it with their tears." The third stage of the revolt in the name of unlimited freedom is destruction and anarchism, represented by Pyotr Verkhovensky. This whole "development" is a continuous fall, and its thrust is towards sheer fantasy, which our century has witnessed in its bloodiest and most senseless forms. Dostoevsky explored, tested, represented these three stages with extraordinary prescience in *Demons*.

Everything is inverted here: freedom ends in despotism, adoration turns to hatred, lucidity increases blindness, the first real act of the liberator of mankind—Nechaev or Verkhovensky—is the murder of his human brother. Seeking the greatest good, we do the greatest evil. The demons parody God's world and invert its ends, playing for its loss. And the source of all these inversions, the primordial parody, is the replacement of the "authoritative image of a human being" by the would-be autonomous human will. Demons are unoriginal. They cannot come up with anything new or real. Their lies are copied from sacred truths. They introduce a dreadful buffoonery into the world. This brings us to the question of humor and parody in the novel. Because if *Demons* is the darkest of Dostoevsky's novels, it is also the most hilarious. We have said that Dostoevsky's expressive art relies on heightened contrasts: the contrasts here are more extreme, the antitheses are more marked, than in any other of his works. Alongside what one critic has called "the most harrowing scene in all fiction" (Kirillov's suicide), there are scenes filled with wild laughter. The role of laughter is complex here, and that, too, is owing to the unseen presence of the demons.

The world reflected in the novel is already in a state of parody. The "great writer Karmazinov" did exist and was Turgenev. Turgenev did write his *Phantoms* and *Enough*, the models for Karmazinov's *Merci*. The absurd "quadrille of literature" in *Demons* does represent the rivalries of various literary-political factions and their publications. The revolutionaries we are introduced to at Virginsky's name-day party stepped into the novel from the transcripts of the trial of the Nechaevists, which took place in the summer of 1871, just when Dostoevsky returned to Petersburg and while he was still at work on the book. (This was the first public political trial in Russia; stenographic records of the proceedings were published daily in the official *Government Messenger.*) The issues, the passions, the oppositions, the polemics, the conspiracies are serious, all too serious. It may be said that this world is in a very serious state of parody (demons always want to be taken seriously). Dostoevsky unmasks this serious parodic condition by means of comic parody, that is, by reinserting it in the great tradition of irreverent laughter, overturning the inversion. But together with this sharp, flensing laughter there is a broader laughter that saves, a comedy that is the embodiment of true freedom, in the portrait of Stepan Trofimovich, who, after standing as "reproach incarnate" for twenty years, finally begins to move.

A few words about this translation. With regard to the style of the original, we can do no better than quote Konstantin Mochulsky:

> Dostoevsky's verbal mastery deserves special study. *Demons* is built on the subtlest stylistic effects. Each of the dramatis personae is immersed in his own verbal element, and the comparing and contrasting of the characters permits the author to trace intricate designs in the fabric of his narrative . . . Each character inscribes himself in this chronicle by his personal manner of speech, his own peculiar diction. Stepan Trofimovich is characterized by his French-Russian speech, gentlemanly intonations, and elegant quips . . . The monomaniac and fanatic Kirillov, who has fallen out of human society, is defined by his odd, agrammatical speech. He talks in some abstract, universal Volapük. Marya Timofeevna is shown in the fairy-tale light of her folk-monastic speech; Bishop Tikhon in the stern splendor of Church-Orthodox language; Shatov in the fiery inspiration of a prophet; Pyotr Verkhovensky in the abrupt, deliberately rude and vulgar remarks of the "nihilistic style"; Shigalyov in the dead heaviness of scientific jargon; Stavrogin in the formlessness and artificiality of his "omni-human tongue." The clashing and interweaving of these verbal styles and rhythms form the intricate counterpoint of the novel's stylistics.

The narrator, too, though he claims that "as a chronicler, I limit myself simply to presenting events in an exact way, exactly as they occurred," is capable of all sorts of little jokes, as if language were mocking itself: someone, for instance, finds "a florin on the floor"; there is "Virginsky . . . overpowering the maiden"; there is the governor's wife "obliged to get up from her bed of rest, in indignation and in curlers"; there is "the fat but tea-bypassed monk from the monastery"; there is Officer Filibusterov, whose name alone sends the governor finally out of his mind. These voices and details make for the delight as well as the difficulty of translating Dostoevsky.

The terms "smooth" and "natural" are used almost automatically in praise of what are thought to be good translations. Their appropriateness is not self-evident. Dostoevsky's prose is all movement and life, it has great forward momentum, but there is nothing smooth about it. A smooth translation of Dostoevsky would be what Paul Valéry called a "résumé that annuls resonance and form." The question of "naturalness" is more complicated. Kirillov, for instance, does not speak in a naturally low-class or careless manner. His speech is very deliberate, but precisely agrammatical. Language seems to be dying out in him. The result is totally unnatural in Russian, and in this case our translation actually reads more naturally than the original. Stepan Trofimovich speaks much of the time in French, but his Russian also often sounds like French, coming out in French word order or in words calked from the French. The mixture produces some memorable, but hardly natural, absurdities. Fedka the Convict has a peasant manner of speaking and a peasant love of long, biblical-sounding words, which he often uses incorrectly; some of his talk is also a special thieves' jargon. And so on. In each case, with each voice of this many-voiced composition, we have sought "natural" English equivalents for the richly unnatural languages of the original. The scholastic philosopher Duns Scotus thought that *haecceitas,* or "thisness," was the final perfection of any creature. So it is of any good book, and, it should follow, of any good translation.

—RICHARD PEVEAR

Translators' Note

RUSSIAN NAMES are composed of first name, patronymic (from the father's first name), and family name. Formal address requires the use of first name and patronymic; diminutives are commonly used among family and intimate friends; a shortened form of the patronymic (e.g., Yegorych instead of Yegorovich), used only in speech, also suggests a certain familiarity. Among the aristocracy, who spoke French at least as readily as Russian, the French forms of names were frequently used, such as Julie in place of Yulia. The following list gives the names of the novel's main characters, with their variants. Accented syllables of Russian names are italicized.

Ale*xei* Ye*go*rovich, or Ye*go*rych (no family name)
Dro*zdov*, Mav*riky* Niko*la*evich (Maurice)
_____, Pras*kovya* I*va*novna (Dro*zdikha*)
*Er*kel (no first name or patronymic)
*Fyo*dor *Fyo*dorovich, called "*Fed*ka the Convict" (no family name)
Ga*ga*nov, *Ar*temy *Pav*lovich
_____, *Pavel* *Pav*lovich
G——v, An*ton* Lav*ren*tievich
Karma*zi*nov, Sem*yon* Ye*go*rovich
Ki*ri*llov, Ale*xei* *Ni*lych
Le*byad*kin, Ig*nat* (patronymic "Timo*fee*vich" never used)
_____, *Mar*ya Timo*fee*vna, or Timo*fev*na
Li*pu*tin, Ser*gei* Ye*go*rovich (or Va*sil*yich)
*Lyam*shin (no first name or patronymic)
Matr*yo*sha (no patronymic or family name)
Sem*yon* *Yak*ovlevich (no family name)
*Sha*tov, *Dar*ya *Pav*lovna (*Da*sha)
_____, *Ivan* *Pav*lovich (*Sha*tushka)
_____, *Mar*ya Ig*na*tievna (Marie)

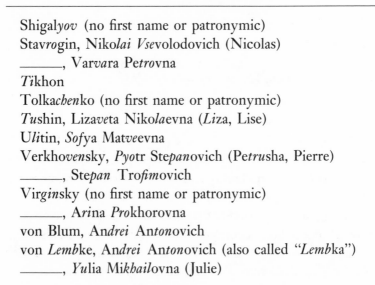

Shigal*yov* (no first name or patronymic)
Stav*rog*in, Niko*lai Vse*volodovich (Nicolas)
———, Var*v*ara Pe*trov*na
*Ti*khon
Tolka*chen*ko (no first name or patronymic)
*Tu*shin, Liza*v*eta Niko*lae*vna (*Liza*, Lise)
U*li*tin, *Sof*ya Mat*v*eevna
Verkho*ven*sky, *Pyo*tr Ste*pan*ovich (Pe*tru*sha, Pierre)
———, Ste*pan* Tro*fim*ovich
Vir*gin*sky (no first name or patronymic)
———, A*ri*na *Pro*khorovna
von Blum, An*drei* Anto*nov*ich
von *Lemb*ke, An*drei* Anto*nov*ich (also called "*Lemb*ka")
———, *Yu*lia Mik*hail*ovna (Julie)

The name "Stavrogin" comes from the Greek word *stavros,* meaning "cross." "Shatov" comes from the Russian verb *shatat'sya,* "to loosen, become unsteady, wobble," and, by extension, "to waver, vacillate." The name "Verkhovensky" is rich in suggestions for the Russian ear: *verkh* means "top, head, height"; *verkhovny* means "chief, supreme"; *verkhovenstvo* means "command, leadership."

We include as an appendix the chapter "At Tikhon's," which was suppressed by M. N. Katkov, editor of the *Russian Messenger,* where *Demons* first appeared serially. Dostoevsky valued this chapter highly, but after efforts to salvage it, none of which satisfied his editor, he was forced to eliminate it. Since he never restored it to later editions of the novel, we have chosen, as most editors have, to print it as an appendix, rather than put it back in its rightful place as Chapter Nine of the second part.

The chapter has survived in two forms, neither of which can be considered finished. The first version is in printer's proofs for the December 1871 issue of the *Russian Messenger,* corresponding to the manuscript Dostoevsky originally submitted to Katkov. The fifteenth page of these proofs is missing, however, and the proofs themselves are covered with additions and alterations made at different times and representing Dostoevsky's attempts to rework the chapter. The second version is a fair copy written out by Anna Grigorievna Dostoevsky, the author's wife, from an unknown manuscript. It differs considerably from the proof text, and essentially constitutes a distinct version. It, too, was never finished or published. Our translation of "At Tikhon's" has been made from the proof text, reproduced in volume II of the Soviet Academy of Sciences edition of Dostoevsky's works (Leningrad, 1974), omitting later additions and alterations, and with the lost fifteenth page restored from the corresponding passage in Anna Grigorievna's manuscript.

DEMONS

Upon my life, the tracks have vanished,
We've lost our way, what shall we do?
It must be a demon's leading us
This way and that around the fields.

.   .   .   .

How many are there? Where have they flown to?
Why do they sing so plaintively?
Are they burying some household goblin?
Is it some witch's wedding day?

A. S. PUSHKIN, "Demons"

Now a large herd of swine was feeding there on the hillside; and they begged him to let them enter these. So he gave them leave. Then the demons came out of the man and entered the swine, and the herd rushed down the steep bank into the lake and were drowned.

When the herdsmen saw what had happened, they fled, and told it in the city and in the country. Then people went out to see what had happened, and they came to Jesus, and found the man from whom the demons had gone, sitting at the feet of Jesus, clothed and in his right mind; and they were afraid. And those who had seen it told them how he who had been possessed with demons was healed.

LUKE 8:32–36 (RSV)

PART ONE

1

Instead of an Introduction

I

IN SETTING OUT to describe the recent and very strange events that took place in our town, hitherto not remarkable for anything, I am forced, for want of skill, to begin somewhat far back—namely, with some biographical details concerning the talented and much esteemed Stepan Trofimovich Verkhovensky. Let these details serve merely as an introduction to the chronicle presented here, while the story itself, which I am intending to relate, still lies ahead.

I will say straight off: Stepan Trofimovich constantly played a certain special and, so to speak, civic role among us, and loved this role to the point of passion—so much so that it even seems to me he would have been unable to live without it. Not that I equate him with a stage actor: God forbid, particularly as I happen to respect him. It could all have been a matter of habit, or, better, of a ceaseless and noble disposition, from childhood on, towards a pleasant dream of his beautiful civic stance. He was, for example, greatly enamored of his position as a "persecuted" man and, so to speak, an "exile."[1] There is a sort of classical luster to these two little words that seduced him once and for all, and, later raising him gradually in his own estimation over the course of so many years, brought him finally to some sort of pedestal, rather lofty and gratifying to his vanity. In a satirical English novel of the last century, a certain Gulliver, having returned from the land of the Lilliputians, where people were only some three inches tall, had grown so accustomed to considering himself a giant among them that even when walking in the streets of London, he could not help shouting at passers-by and carriages to move aside and take care that he not somehow crush them, imagining that he was still a giant and they were little. For which people laughed at him and abused him, and rude coachmen even struck the giant with their whips—but was that fair? What will habit not do to a man? Habit brought Stepan Trofimovich to much the same thing, but in a still more innocent and inoffensive form, if one may put it so, for he was a most excellent man.

I even think that towards the end he was forgotten by everyone everywhere; but it is by no means possible to say that he had been completely unknown earlier as well. It is unquestionable that he, too, belonged for a while to the famous pleiad of some renowned figures of our previous generation, and for a time—though only for one brief little moment—his name was uttered by many hurrying people of that day almost on a par with the names of Chaadaev, Belinsky, Granovsky, and Herzen, who was just beginning abroad.[2] But Stepan Trofimovich's activity ended almost the moment it began—due, so to speak, to a "whirlwind of concurrent circumstances."[3] And just think! It turned out later that there had been not only no "whirlwind" but not even any "circumstances," at least not on that occasion. Just the other day I learned, to my great surprise, but now with perfect certainty, that Stepan Trofimovich had lived among us, in our province, not only not in exile, as we used to think, but that he had never even been under surveillance. Such, then, is the power of one's own imagination! He himself sincerely believed all his life that he was a cause of constant apprehension in certain spheres, that his steps were ceaselessly known and numbered, and that each of the three governors who succeeded one another over the past twenty years, in coming to rule our province, brought along a certain special and worrisome idea of him, inspired from above and before all, upon taking over the province. Had someone then convinced the most honest Stepan Trofimovich, on irrefutable evidence, that he had nothing at all to fear, he would no doubt have been offended. And yet he was such an intelligent man, such a gifted man, even, so to speak, a scholar—though as a scholar, however . . . well, in a word, he did very little as a scholar, nothing at all, apparently. But with scholars here in Russia that is ever and always the case.

He returned from abroad and shone briefly as a lecturer at the university back at the end of the forties. But he managed to give only a few lectures, apparently on the Arabians; he also managed to defend a brilliant thesis on the nearly emerged civic and Hanseatic importance of the German town of Hanau, in the period between 1413 and 1428,[4] together with the peculiar and vague reasons why that importance never took place. This thesis cleverly and painfully needled the Slavophils[5] of the day, and instantly gained him numerous and infuriated enemies among them. Later—though by then he had already lost his lectureship—he managed to publish (in revenge, so to speak, and to show them just whom they had lost), in a monthly and progressive journal, which translated Dickens and preached George Sand,[6] the beginning of a most profound study—having to do, apparently, with the reasons for the remarkable moral nobility of some knights in some epoch, or something of the sort. At any rate, some lofty and remarkably noble idea was upheld in it. Afterwards it was said that the sequel of the study was promptly forbidden, and that the progressive journal even suffered for having printed the first part. That could very well have happened, because what did not happen back then? But in the present case it is more likely that nothing happened, and that the author himself was too lazy to finish the study. And he stopped his lectures on the Arabians because someone (evidently from among his retrograde enemies) somehow intercepted a letter to someone giving an account of some "circumstances," as a result of which someone demanded some explanations from him. I do not know if it is true, but it was also asserted that in Petersburg at the same time they unearthed a vast anti-natural, anti-state society of some thirteen members which all but shook the foundations. It was said that they supposedly intended to translate Fourier himself.[7] As if by design, at the same time in Moscow they seized a poem by Stepan Trofimovich, written six years earlier in Berlin, in his first youth, which circulated in manuscript among two amateurs and one student. This poem is now also sitting in my desk drawer; I received it just last year, in a quite recent copy, handwritten by Stepan Trofimovich himself, with his inscription, and bound in magnificent red morocco. Incidentally, it is not lacking in poetry, or even in a certain talent; it is a strange piece, but in those days (that is, more precisely, in the thirties) that kind of thing was not uncommon. I find it difficult to give the plot, because to tell the truth I understand nothing of it. It is some sort of allegory, in lyrical-dramatic form, resembling the second part of *Faust*. [8] The scene opens with a chorus of women, then a chorus of men, then of some powers, and it all ends with a chorus of souls that have not lived yet but would very much like to live a little. All these choruses sing about something very indefinite, mostly about somebody's curse, but with a tinge of higher humor. Then suddenly the scene changes and some sort of "Festival of Life" begins, in which even insects sing, a turtle appears with some sort of sacramental Latin words, and, if I remember, a mineral—that is, an altogether inanimate object—also gets to sing about something. Generally, everyone sings incessantly, and if they speak, they squabble somehow indefinitely, but again with a tinge of higher meaning. Finally, the scene changes again, and a wild place appears, where a civilized young man wanders among the rocks picking and sucking at some wild herbs, and when a fairy asks him why he is sucking these herbs, he responds that he feels an overabundance of life in himself, is seeking oblivion, and finds it in the juice of these herbs, but that his greatest desire is to lose his reason as quickly as possible (a perhaps superfluous desire). Suddenly a youth of indescribable beauty rides in on a black horse, followed by a terrible multitude of all the nations. The youth represents death, and all the nations yearn for it. Finally, in the very last scene, the Tower of Babel suddenly appears and some athletes finally finish building it with a song of new hope, and when they have built to the very top, the proprietor of, shall we say, Olympus flees in comical fashion, and quick-witted mankind takes over his place and at once begins a new life with a new perception of things. Well, this is the poem that was found so dangerous then. Last year I proposed to Stepan Trofimovich to publish it, in view of its perfect innocence nowadays, but he declined the proposal with obvious displeasure. My opinion as to its perfect innocence he did not like, and I even ascribe to it a certain coolness towards me on his part, which lasted for a whole two months. And just think! Suddenly, almost at the same time as I proposed publishing it here, our poem was published *there*—that is, abroad, in one of the revolutionary miscellanies, and absolutely without Stepan Trofimovich's knowledge. He was frightened at first, rushed to the governor, and wrote a most noble letter of vindication to Petersburg, read it to me twice, but did not send it, not knowing to whom to address it. In short, he was worried for a whole month; but I am convinced that in the hidden turnings of his heart he was remarkably flattered. He all but slept with the copy of the miscellany that had been sent to him, hid it under the mattress during the day, and even would not allow the woman to make his bed, and though he expected any day some telegram from somewhere, his look was haughty. No telegram came. And then he reconciled with me, which testifies to the extreme kindness of his gentle and unresentful heart.

II

I AM BY NO MEANS claiming that he never suffered at all; only I am now fully convinced that he could have gone on with his Arabians as much as he liked, if he had simply given the necessary explanations. But at the time he made a grand gesture, and with particular hastiness took care to convince himself once and for all that his career had been ruined for the whole of his life by a "whirlwind of circumstances." Though, if one were to tell the whole truth, the real reason for this change of career was a most delicate offer, made once before and now renewed by Varvara Petrovna Stavrogin, the wife of a lieutenant general and a woman of considerable wealth, to take upon himself the upbringing and the whole intellectual development of her only son, in the capacity of a superior pedagogue and friend, to say nothing of a splendid remuneration. This offer had first been made to him in Berlin, and precisely at the time when he had first been left a widower. His first wife was a flighty girl from our province whom he had married in his very first and still reckless youth, and it seems he suffered much grief from this—incidentally attractive—person, for lack of means to support her, and for other, somewhat delicate reasons as well. She died in Paris, having been separated from him for the previous three years, leaving him a five-year-old son, "the fruit of a first, joyful, and still unclouded love," as once escaped the sorrowing Stepan Trofimovich

in my presence. The nestling was from the very start sent back to
Russia, where he was brought up all the while in the hands of some
distant aunts, somewhere in a remote corner. Stepan Trofimovich had
declined Varvara Petrovna's offer at that time and quickly got married
again, even before the year was out, to a taciturn little German woman
from Berlin, and that, moreover, without any special need. But there
turned out to be other reasons, besides, for declining the position of
tutor: he was tempted by the then resounding glory of one unforgettable professor, and in his turn flew to the chair for which he had been
preparing himself, to try out his own eagle's wings. And so now, with
his wings singed, he naturally recalled the offer that had already once
made him hesitate. The sudden death of his second wife, who did not
live even a year with him, finally settled it all. I will say straight out:
it was all resolved through Varvara Petrovna's fervent sympathy and
precious, so to speak, classical friendship for him, if one may thus
express oneself about friendship. He threw himself into the embrace
of this friendship, and the thing got set for more than twenty years.
I have used the expression "threw himself into the embrace," but God
forbid that anyone should think anything idle and unwarranted; this
embrace should be understood only in the highest moral sense. The
most subtle and delicate bond united these two so remarkable beings
forever.

The position of tutor was accepted also because the bit of an estate
left by Stepan Trofimovich's first wife—a very small one—happened
to be just next to Skvoreshniki, the splendid suburban estate of the
Stavrogins in our province. Moreover, it was always possible, in the
quiet of one's study and no longer distracted by the vastness of university employment, to dedicate oneself to the cause of learning and
enrich the literature of one's fatherland with the most profound research. No research resulted; but what did result instead was the possibility of standing for the rest of his life, for more than twenty years,
as, so to speak, a "reproach incarnate" to his fatherland, to use the
expression of a people's poet:[9]

Reproach incarnate you did stand

.   .   .   .

Before the fatherland,
O liberal idealist.

Perhaps the person of whom the people's poet so expressed himself did have the right to pose all his life in this vein, if he wanted, boring though it is. But our Stepan Trofimovich in truth was only an imitator compared with such persons; then, too, he used to get tired of standing and would often recline. But, even then, the incarnateness of the reproach was still preserved in that reclining position—the more so, speaking in all fairness, as even that was quite sufficient for our province. You should have seen him when he sat down to play cards in our club. His whole look seemed to say: "Cards! Me sit down to play whist with you! Is it compatible? Who must answer for it? Who broke up my activity and turned it into whist? Ah, perish Russia!" and he would trump majestically with a heart.

And to tell the truth he was terribly fond of a little game of cards, for which, especially of late, he had frequent and unpleasant skirmishes with Varvara Petrovna, the more so as he was forever losing. But of that later. I will merely note that he was even a man of tender conscience (sometimes, that is) and therefore often sorrowful. In the course of his twenty-year-long friendship with Varvara Petrovna he used to fall regularly, three or four times a year, into a state known among us as "civic grief"[10]—that is, simply a fit of spleen, but our much respected Varvara Petrovna liked the expression. Later on, besides civic grief, he also began falling into champagne; but the alert Varvara Petrovna guarded him all his life against all trivial inclinations. And he did need a nurse, because he would sometimes become quite strange: in the midst of the loftiest grief he would suddenly start laughing in a most plebeian manner. Moments came over him when he would start talking about himself in a humorous vein. And there was nothing Varvara Petrovna feared more than a humorous vein. This was a woman-classic, a woman-Maecenas, whose acts presupposed only the loftiest considerations. Supreme was the twenty-year-long influence of this lofty lady upon her poor friend. One ought to speak of her separately, and so I shall.

III

THERE ARE strange friendships: two friends are almost ready to eat each other, they live like that all their lives, and yet they cannot part. Parting is even impossible: the friend who waxes capricious and breaks it off will be the first to fall sick and die, perhaps, if it should happen. I know positively that several times, occasionally even after his most intimate outpourings tête-à-tête with Varvara Petrovna, Stepan Trofimovich suddenly jumped up from the sofa when she had gone and started pounding the wall with his fists.

This occurred without a trace of allegory, so that once he even broke some plaster from the wall. Perhaps I shall be asked how I could have learned of such a fine detail. And what if I myself witnessed it? What if Stepan Trofimovich himself sobbed many a time on my shoulder while portraying in vivid colors all his innermost secrets? (And what, oh, what did he not tell me then!) But here is what almost always happened after such weepings: the very next day he would be ready to crucify himself for his ingratitude; he would hurriedly send for me, or come running to me himself, with the sole purpose of announcing to me that Varvara Petrovna was "an angel of honor and delicacy, while he was just the opposite." He not only came running to me, but he described it more than once to her in the most eloquent letters, and confessed, over his full signature, that no more than a day ago, for instance, he had been telling some outsider that she kept him out of vanity, that she envied his learning and talents, that she hated him and was only afraid to show her hatred openly for fear he would leave her and thereby damage her literary reputation; that he despised himself on account of that and had resolved to die a violent death, and was only waiting for a last word from her that would decide it all, and so on, and so on, in the same vein. You can imagine after that how hysterical the nervous outbursts of this most innocent of all fifty-year-old infants could become! I once read one of these letters, after some quarrel between them, venomously acted out, though the cause was a trifling one. I was horrified and implored him not to send the letter.

"Impossible . . . honor . . . duty . . . I shall die if I do not confess everything to her, everything!" he answered all but deliriously, and he did send the letter.

And here lay the difference between them—Varvara Petrovna would never have sent such a letter. True, he loved writing to distraction, wrote to her even while living in the same house, and on hysterical occasions even two letters a day. I know positively that she always read these letters in a most attentive way, even in the event of two letters a day, and, having read them, lay them away in a special drawer, marked and sorted; what's more, she laid them up in her heart. Then, having kept her friend all day without an answer, she would meet him as if nothing had happened, as if nothing special had taken place the day before. She gradually drilled him so well that he himself did not dare to remind her of the previous day and only kept peeking into her eyes for some time. But she forgot nothing, and he sometimes forgot much too quickly, and, often that same day, encouraged by her composure, would laugh and frolic over the champagne, if friends stopped by. What venom there must have been in her eyes at those moments, yet he noticed nothing! Maybe after a week, or a month, or even half a year, at some special moment, having chanced to recall some expression from such a letter, and then the whole letter with all its circumstances, he would suddenly burn with shame, and suffered so much that he would come down with one of his attacks of cholerine. These special attacks of his, resembling cholerine, were on certain occasions the usual outcome of his nervous shocks and represented a certain rather interesting peculiarity of his organism.

Indeed, Varvara Petrovna undoubtedly and quite frequently hated him; but there was one thing he failed to notice in her to the very end, that for her he finally became her son, her creation, even, one might say, her invention, became flesh of her flesh, and that she maintained and sustained him not at all out of "envy of his talents" alone. And how insulted she must have been by such suppositions! Some unbearable love for him lay hidden in her, in the midst of constant hatred, jealousy, and contempt. She protected him from every speck of dust, fussed over him for twenty-two years, would lie awake whole nights from worry if his reputation as a poet, scholar, or civic figure were in question. She invented him, and she was the first to believe in her invention. He was something like a sort of dream of hers . . . But for that she indeed demanded a lot of him, sometimes even slavery. And she was incredibly resentful. Here, incidentally, I will relate two anecdotes.

IV

ONCE, back in the time of the first rumors about the emancipation of the serfs,[11] when the whole of Russia suddenly became exultant and all ready to be reborn, Varvara Petrovna was visited by a traveling Petersburg baron, a man with the highest connections and who stood quite close to these matters. Varvara Petrovna greatly valued such visits, because her connections with high society had grown weaker and weaker since her husband's death, and finally had ceased altogether. The baron stayed for an hour and had tea. No one else was there, but Varvara Petrovna invited Stepan Trofimovich and put him on display. The baron had even heard something about him before, or pretended he had, but he spoke little with him over tea. Of course, Stepan Trofimovich could not fall on his face, and his manners were most refined. Though his origins, it seems, were not high, it so happened that he had been brought up from a very early age in an aristocratic house in Moscow, and, therefore, decently; he spoke French like a Parisian. Thus the baron was to understand from the very first glance what sort of people Varvara Petrovna surrounded herself with, even in provincial seclusion. However, it did not turn out that way. When the baron positively confirmed the complete reliability of the first rumors then just spreading about the great reform, Stepan Trofimovich suddenly could not restrain himself and shouted "Hurrah!" and even made some sort of gesture with his hand signifying delight. His shout was not loud and was even elegant; it may even be that the delight was premeditated and the gesture was rehearsed on purpose in front of the mirror half an hour before tea; but something here must not have come out right, so that the baron allowed himself a little smile, though he at once, with remarkable courtesy, put in a phrase about the general and appropriate tender feeling of all Russian hearts in view of the great event. He left shortly after that and, as he was leaving, did not forget to hold out two fingers to Stepan Trofimovich as well. On returning to the drawing room, Varvara Petrovna remained silent for about three minutes, as if she were looking for something on the table; then she turned suddenly to Stepan Trofimovich, pale, her eyes flashing, and whispered through her teeth:

"I will never forgive you for that!"

The next day she met her friend as if nothing had happened; she never recalled the incident. But thirteen years later, at a tragic moment, she did recollect it, and she reproached him and became pale in just the same way as thirteen years before, when she had reproached him the first time. Only twice in her whole life did she say to him: "I will never forgive you for that!" The occasion with the baron was already the second occasion; the first occasion, for its part, was so characteristic and, it seems, had such significance in Stepan Trofimovich's destiny, that I am resolved to mention it as well.

It was the year 'fifty-five, in springtime, the month of May, just after news reached Skvoreshniki of the demise of Lieutenant General Stavrogin, a frivolous old man who had died of a stomach disorder on his way to the Crimea, where he was hastening on assignment to active duty. Varvara Petrovna was left a widow and clad herself in deep mourning. True, she could not have grieved very much, because for the last four years she had lived completely separately from her husband, owing to the dissimilarity of their characters, and had provided him with an allowance. (The lieutenant general himself had only a hundred and fifty souls and his salary, along with nobility and connections; all the wealth and Skvoreshniki belonged to Varvara Petrovna, the only daughter of a very rich tax farmer.) Nevertheless, she was shaken by the suddenness of the news and withdrew into complete seclusion. Of course, Stepan Trofimovich never left her side.

May was in full bloom; the evenings were remarkable. The bird cherry was blossoming. The two friends came together in the garden every evening and stayed until nightfall in the gazebo, pouring out their feelings and thoughts to each other. There were poetic moments. Under the effect of the change in her destiny, Varvara Petrovna talked more than usual. She seemed to be clinging to her friend's heart, and so it continued for several evenings. A strange thought suddenly dawned on Stepan Trofimovich: "Is the inconsolable widow not counting on him and expecting a proposal from him at the end of the year of mourning?" A cynical thought; but loftiness of constitution sometimes even fosters an inclination towards cynical thoughts, if only because of the versatility of one's development. He began to go more deeply into it and concluded that it did look that way. "True, it's an immense fortune," he pondered, "but . . ." Indeed, Varvara Petrovna in no way resembled a beauty: she was a tall, yellow, bony woman with an exceedingly long face recalling something horselike. Stepan Trofimovich hesitated more and more; he was tortured by doubts, and even shed a few tears now and then from indecision (he wept rather often). But in the evenings—that is, in the gazebo—his face somehow involuntarily began to express something capricious and mocking, something coquettish and at the same time haughty. This happens somehow inadvertently, involuntarily, and is all the more noticeable the nobler the person is. God knows how to judge here, but most likely nothing was awakening in Varvara Petrovna's heart that could fully have justified Stepan Trofimovich's suspicions. And she would not have exchanged her name of Stavrogin for his name, however glorious it might be. Perhaps it was only a feminine game on her part, the manifestation of an unconscious feminine need, so natural on certain extraordinary feminine occasions. However, I would not vouch for it; inscrutable even to this day are the depths of the feminine heart. But, to continue.

One may suppose that within herself she soon understood the strange expression on her friend's face; she was alert and observant, whereas he was sometimes too innocent. But the evenings went on as before, and the conversations were as poetic and interesting. And then once, as night was falling, after a most animated and poetic conversation, they parted in a friendly manner, warmly shaking hands at the porch of the cottage Stepan Trofimovich occupied. Every summer he moved from the huge manor house of Skvoreshniki to this little cottage which stood almost in the garden. He had just walked into his room and, having taken a cigar, before he managed to light it, troubled by thoughts, had stopped, weary and motionless, by the open window, observing some white clouds, light as down, gliding past the bright crescent moon, when suddenly a faint rustle made him start and turn around. Varvara Petrovna, whom he had left only four minutes earlier, was again standing before him. Her yellow face was almost blue, her lips were pressed together and twitched at the corners. For a full ten seconds she looked silently into his eyes with a firm, implacable gaze, and then suddenly whispered rapidly:

"I will never forgive you for that!"

When, ten years later, Stepan Trofimovich told me this sad story in a whisper, having locked the door first, he swore he had been so dumbfounded then and there that he had not heard or seen how Varvara Petrovna disappeared. Since she never once alluded afterwards to what had taken place, and everything went on as if nothing had happened, he was inclined all his life to think it was just a hallucination before illness, all the more so as he actually did fall ill that same night for two whole weeks—which, incidentally, also put an end to the meetings in the gazebo.

But despite his fancy about the hallucination, he seemed every day of his life to be waiting for the sequel and, so to speak, the denouement of this event. He did not believe it could have ended just like that! And if so, what strange looks he must sometimes have given his friend.

V

S HE HERSELF even invented a costume for him, in which he went about all his life. It was an elegant and characteristic costume: a long-skirted black frock coat, buttoned almost to the top, but with a dapper look; a soft hat (a straw one for summer) with a wide brim; a white batiste cravat with a big knot and hanging ends; a cane with a silver knob; and shoulder-length hair to go with it all. His hair was dark brown and only recently had begun to go a bit gray. He shaved his beard and moustache. He was said to have been extremely handsome as a young man. But, in my opinion, as an old man he was also remarkably imposing. And how old is fifty-three? Still, out of a certain civic coquetry, he not only did not try to look younger, but seemed to flaunt the solidity of his years, and in his costume, tall, lean, with hair falling to his shoulders, he resembled a patriarch, as it were, or, more precisely, the portrait of the poet Kukolnik[12] in a lithograph from some edition of the thirties, especially when he sat in the garden in summer, on a bench, under a flowering lilac bush, leaning with both hands on his cane, an open book beside him, poetically pondering the sunset. Speaking of books, I will note that towards the end he began somehow to withdraw from reading. That, however, was towards the very end. The newspapers and magazines Varvara Petrovna subscribed to in great numbers, he read constantly. He was also constantly interested in the successes of Russian literature, though without in the least losing his dignity. At some point he became involved in a study of the higher modern politics of our internal and external affairs, but soon abandoned the enterprise with a wave of the hand. And there was this, too: he would take Tocqueville with him to the garden, but with Paul de Kock tucked in his side pocket.[13] That, however, is a trifle.

I will also note parenthetically about Kukolnik's portrait, that Varvara Petrovna had first chanced upon this picture while still a young girl at an upper-class boarding school in Moscow. She at once fell in love with the portrait, as is customary for all young girls in boarding schools, who fall in love with anything at all including their teachers, mainly of drawing and calligraphy. What is curious here is not the young girl's feelings, but that even at the age of fifty Varvara Petrovna still kept this picture among her most intimate treasures, so that perhaps only because of it had she invented a costume for Stepan Trofimovich somewhat resembling the one in the picture. But, of course, that is also a small thing.

For the first years, or, more precisely, for the first half of his residence at Varvara Petrovna's, Stepan Trofimovich still had thoughts of some sort of a work, and was seriously preparing every day to write it. But for the second half he must even have forgotten what it had all been about. More and more often he would say to us: "It seems I'm ready to work, the materials have all been collected, yet the work doesn't come! Nothing gets done!" And he would hang his head dejectedly. No doubt this was supposed to give him even more grandeur in our eyes as a martyr of learning; but he himself wanted something else. "I'm forgotten, no one needs me!" escaped him more than once. This intense spleen took particular hold of him at the end of the fifties. Varvara Petrovna finally understood that it was a serious matter. And she also could not bear the thought that her friend was forgotten and not needed. To distract him, and to patch up his fame at the same time, she then took him to Moscow, where she had a few refined literary and learned connections; but, as it turned out, Moscow was not satisfactory either.

It was a peculiar time; something new was beginning, quite unlike the former tranquillity, something quite strange, but felt everywhere, even in Skvoreshniki. Various rumors arrived. The facts were generally more or less known, but it was obvious that, besides the facts, certain accompanying ideas also appeared, and, what's more, in exceeding numbers. That was what was bewildering: there was no way to adapt and find out just exactly what these ideas meant. Varvara Petrovna, owing to the feminine makeup of her character, certainly wanted to suppose some secret in them. She herself began reading newspapers and magazines, prohibited foreign publications, and even the tracts that were beginning then (she had it all sent to her); but it only made her head spin. She started writing letters: the replies were few, and the longer it went on, the more incomprehensible they became. Stepan Trofimovich was solemnly invited to explain "all these ideas" to her once and for all; but she remained positively displeased with his explanations. Stepan Trofimovich's view of the general movement was scornful in the highest degree; with him it all came down to his being forgotten and not needed by anyone. Finally he, too, was remembered, first in foreign publications, as an exiled martyr, and immediately after that in Petersburg, as a former star in a noted constellation; he was even compared for some reason with Radishchev.[14] Then someone printed that he had died, and promised an obituary. Stepan Trofimovich instantly resurrected and reassumed his majesty. All the scornfulness of his views of his contemporaries dropped away at once, and a dream began burning in him: to join the movement and show his powers. Varvara Petrovna instantly believed again and in everything, and started bustling about terribly. It was decided that they should go to Petersburg without the least delay, to find out everything in reality, to go into it all personally, and, if possible, to involve themselves wholly and undividedly in the new activity. Among other things, she announced that she was prepared to found her own magazine and dedicate her whole life to it from then on. Seeing it had even come to that, Stepan Trofimovich became more scornful than ever, and during the trip began treating Varvara Petrovna almost patronizingly, which she immediately laid up in her heart. However, she also had another quite important reason for going—namely, the renewal of her high connections. She needed as far as possible to remind the world of herself, or at least to make the attempt. And the avowed pretext for the trip was a meeting with her only son, who was then finishing his studies at a Petersburg lycée.

VI

THEY WENT and stayed in Petersburg for almost the whole winter season. By Lent, however, everything burst like an iridescent soap bubble. The dreams scattered, and the jumble not only was not clarified, but became even more repellent. First, the high connections all but failed, except perhaps in microscopic form, and with humiliating strain. The insulted Varvara Petrovna threw herself wholly into the "new ideas" and began holding evenings. She invited writers, and they were immediately brought to her in great numbers. Afterwards they took to coming on their own, without invitation, each one bringing another. Never before had she seen such writers. They were impossibly vain, but quite openly so, as if thereby fulfilling a duty. Some (though by no means all) even came drunk, but it was as if they perceived some special, just-yesterday-discovered beauty in it. They were all proud of something to the point of strangeness. It was written on all their faces that they had just discovered some extremely important secret. They were abusive, and considered it to their credit. It was rather difficult to find out precisely what they had written; but there were critics, novelists, playwrights, satirists, exposers among them. Stepan Trofimovich even penetrated their highest circle, the place from which the movement was directed. It was an immensely steep climb to reach the directors, but they met him cordially, though none of them, of course, knew or had heard anything about him except that he "represented an idea." He maneuvered among them so far that he even managed to invite them a couple of times to Varvara Petrovna's salon, despite all their olympianity. These were very serious and very polite people; they bore themselves well; the others were evidently afraid of them; but it was obvious that they had no time. Two or three former literary celebrities who then happened to be in Petersburg, and with whom Varvara Petrovna had long maintained the most refined relations, also came. But, to her surprise, these real and indisputable celebrities were meek as lambs, and some of them simply clung to all this new rabble and fawned on them shamefully. At first Stepan Trofimovich was in luck; they seized on him and began displaying him at public literary gatherings. When he came out on the platform for the first time as a reader at one of these public literary readings, there was a burst of wild applause that continued for about five minutes. He recalled it with tears nine years later—rather more because of his artistic nature than out of gratitude. "I swear to you and will wager," he himself said to me (but only to me, and as a secret), "that no one in that whole audience knew a blessed thing about me!" A remarkable confession: indeed he must have possessed keen intelligence if he could understand his position so clearly, right there on the platform, despite all his rapture; and indeed he must not have possessed very keen intelligence if even nine years later he could not recall it without feeling offended. He was made to sign two or three collective protests (against what, he himself did not know); he signed. Varvara Petrovna was also made to sign some "outrageous act," and she signed.[15] However, though the majority of these new people had been Varvara Petrovna's guests, they for some reason considered it their duty to look upon her with contempt and unconcealed derision. Stepan Trofimovich hinted to me afterwards, in bitter moments, that it was then that she had begun to envy him. Of course, she understood that she ought not to associate with these people, but still she received them avidly, with all of a woman's hysterical impatience, and, above all, kept expecting something. At her evenings she spoke little, though she could speak, but rather listened. They talked about the abolition of censorship, about spelling reform, about replacing Russian letters with Roman, about someone's exile the day before, about some scandal in the Passage, about the advantages of dividing Russia into a free federation of nationalities, about abolishing the army and navy, about restoring Poland up to the Dnieper, about peasant reform and tracts, about the abolition of inheritance, the family, children, and priests, about women's rights, about Kraevsky's house, for which no one would ever forgive Mr. Kraevsky, and so on and so forth.[16] It was clear that among this rabble of new people there were many swindlers, but it was also unquestionable that there were many honest and even quite attractive persons, despite certain nonetheless surprising nuances. The honest ones were far more incomprehensible than the rude and dishonest ones; but it was not clear who was making use of whom. When Varvara Petrovna announced her idea of publishing a magazine, still more people came flocking to her, but accusations also immediately flew in her face that she was a capitalist and an exploiter of labor. The unceremoniousness of the accusations was equaled only by their unexpectedness. The elderly general Ivan Ivanovich Drozdov, a former friend and fellow officer of the late general Stavrogin, a most worthy man (though in his own way), known to all of us here, extremely obstinate and irritable, who ate terribly much and was terribly afraid of atheism, began arguing at one of Varvara Petrovna's evenings with a famous young man. The latter said straight off: "Well, you're a general if you talk like that," meaning that he could not even find any worse abuse than a general. Ivan Ivanovich got extremely fired up: "Yes, sir, I am a general, a lieutenant general, and I've served my sovereign, and you, sir, are a brat and an atheist!" An impossible scandal took place. Next day the incident was exposed in the press and signatures were gathered under a collective letter against the "outrageous act" of Varvara Petrovna in not wishing to throw the general out at once. A caricature appeared in an illustrated magazine, caustically portraying Varvara Petrovna, the general, and Stepan Trofimovich together as three retrograde cronies; the picture was accompanied by some verses written by a people's poet solely for the occasion. I will add, for my part, that in fact many persons with the rank of general have the habit of saying ludicrously: "I have served my sovereign . . ." as if they did not have the same sovereign as the rest of us, the sovereign's ordinary subjects, but their own special one.

To remain any longer in Petersburg was, of course, impossible, the more so in that Stepan Trofimovich also suffered a final fiasco. He could not help himself and started proclaiming the rights of art, and they started laughing at him all the louder. At his last reading he decided to employ civic eloquence, fancying he would touch people's hearts and counting on their respect for his "exile." He unquestioningly agreed that the word "fatherland" was useless and comical; he also agreed with the notion of the harmfulness of religion; but he loudly and firmly proclaimed that boots are lower than Pushkin, even very much so.[17] He was hissed so mercilessly that he burst into tears right there, publicly, before he even got off the platform. Varvara Petrovna brought him home more dead than alive. *"On m'a traité comme un vieux bonnet de coton!"** he babbled senselessly. She spent the whole night looking after him, gave him laurel water, and kept telling him until dawn: "You are still useful; you will still make your appearance; you will be appreciated . . . elsewhere."

The very next day, early in the morning, five writers called on Varvara Petrovna, three of them complete strangers whom she had never set eyes on before. They announced to her with stern faces that they had looked into the case of her magazine and had brought her their decision about it. Varvara Petrovna had decidedly never asked anyone to look into or decide anything about her magazine. The decision was that, after founding the magazine, she should at once turn it over to them, along with the capital, under the rights of a free co-operative; and she herself should leave for Skvoreshniki, and not forget to take along Stepan Trofimovich, "who was obsolete." From delicacy they agreed to acknowledge her right of ownership and to send her one sixth of the net income annually. Most touching of all was that, of these five people, four certainly had no mercenary motive, but were busying themselves only for the sake of the "common cause."

"We left as if in a daze," Stepan Trofimovich used to say. "I was unable to sort anything out and, I remember, kept muttering to the click-clack of the wheels:

> Vek and Vek and Lev Kambek,
> Lev Kambek and Vek and Vek . . .[18]

and devil knows what else, all the way to Moscow. It was only in Moscow that I came to my senses—as if indeed I could have found anything different there! Oh, my friends," he sometimes exclaimed, inspired, "you cannot imagine what sorrow and anger seize one's whole soul when a great idea, which one has long and piously revered, is picked up by some bunglers and dragged into the street, to more

---

*"They treated me like an old cotton bonnet!"

fools like themselves, and one suddenly meets it in the flea market, unrecognizable, dirty, askew, absurdly presented, without proportion, without harmony, a toy for stupid children! No! It was not so in our day, that is not what we strove for. No, no, not that at all. I recognize nothing . . . Our day will come once more, and once more turn all this wavering, all this present, onto a firm path. Otherwise what will there be? . . ."

VII

IMMEDIATELY AFTER their return from Petersburg, Varvara Petrovna sent her friend abroad—to "rest"; besides, they needed to be apart for a time, so she felt. Stepan Trofimovich was delighted to go. "I shall resurrect there!" he kept exclaiming. "There I shall finally take up my studies!" But with his first letters from Berlin he struck his perennial note. "My heart is broken," he wrote to Varvara Petrovna. "I can forget nothing! Here in Berlin everything reminds me of the old days, of my past, my first raptures, and my first torments. Where is she? Where are they both? Where are you, my two angels, of whom I was never worthy? Where is my son, my beloved son? Where, finally, am I, I myself, my former self, strong as steel and unshakable as rock, while now some *Andrejeff, un* Orthodox clown in a beard, *peut briser mon existence en deux,*"* etc., etc. As for Stepan Trofimovich's son, he had seen him only twice in his life, the first time when he was born, and the second time recently in Petersburg, where the young man was preparing to enter the university. The boy, as has already been mentioned, had been brought up all his life by his aunts (at Varvara Petrovna's keeping), in O—— province, five hundred miles from Skvoreshniki. And as for *Andrejeff*—that is, Andreev—he was simply one of our local merchants, a shopkeeper, a great eccentric, a self-taught archaeologist and passionate collector of Russian antiquities, who had occasional altercations with Stepan Trofimovich on learned matters, but above all to do with trends. This venerable merchant, with a gray beard and big silver spectacles, still owed Stepan Trofimovich

*"can break my existence in two"

four hundred roubles for the purchase of several acres of timber on his little estate (near Skvoreshniki). Though Varvara Petrovna lavishly provided her friend with means on sending him to Berlin, Stepan Trofimovich had still been counting especially on getting those four hundred roubles before he left, probably for his secret expenses, and nearly wept when *Andrejeff* asked him to wait a month—which, by the way, he had the right to do, since he had paid the first installment almost half a year ahead of time, because Stepan Trofimovich had had special need of it then. Varvara Petrovna read this first letter greedily and, having underlined in pencil the exclamation: "Where are you both?" dated it and locked it away in a box. He was, of course, recalling his two deceased wives. In the second letter that came from Berlin there was a variation in the tune: "I work twelve hours a day ["Or maybe just eleven," Varvara Petrovna grumbled], burrowing in the libraries, checking, taking notes, rushing about; have called on professors. Renewed my acquaintance with the excellent Dundasov family. How charming Nadezhda Nikolaevna is, even now! She sends her regards. Her young husband and all three nephews are in Berlin. In the evenings I converse with the young people till dawn, and we have almost Athenian nights,[19] though only in terms of refinement and elegance; it is all quite noble: there is a lot of music, Spanish airs, dreams of universal renewal, the idea of eternal beauty, the Sistine Madonna,[20] a light shot through with darkness, but then there are spots even on the sun! Oh, my friend, my noble, faithful friend! In my heart I am with you and am yours, always with you alone, *en tout pays,* even *dans le pays de Makar et de ses veaux,* * of which you remember we so often spoke, trembling, in Petersburg, before our departure. I recall it with a smile. Having crossed the border, I felt myself safe—a strange, new feeling, the first time after so many years . . ." etc., etc.

"Well, it's all nonsense!" Varvara Petrovna decided, folding up this letter, too. "If it's Athenian nights until dawn, then he's not sitting twelve hours over books. Was he drunk when he wrote it, or what? This Dundasov woman, how dare she send me her regards? Oh, well, let him have a good time . . ."

The phrase *"dans le pays de Makar et de ses veaux"* meant: "where

---

*"in every land, [even] in the land of Makar and his calves"

Makar never drove his calves."²¹ Stepan Trofimovich sometimes deliberately translated Russian proverbs and popular sayings into French in
a most stupid way, though he undoubtedly understood and could have
translated them better. He did it from a special sort of chic, and found
it witty.

But his good time was not long. He did not hold out even four
months, and came rushing back to Skvoreshniki. His last letters consisted of nothing but outpourings of the most tenderhearted love for
his absent friend and were literally wet with the tears of separation.
There are natures that become extremely attached to home, like lap-
dogs. The reunion of the two friends was rapturous. In two days
everything was back the old way, and even more boring than the old
way. "My friend," Stepan Trofimovich told me two weeks later, as the
greatest secret, "my friend, I've discovered something new and . . .
terrible for me: *je suis un* mere sponger *et rien de plus! Mais r-r-rien
de plus!*"*

VIII

THEN CAME a lull which continued almost unbroken for all these
nine years. Hysterical outbursts and weepings on my shoulder,
which regularly recurred, did not hinder our prosperity in the least.
I am surprised how it could have been that Stepan Trofimovich did
not put on weight during that time. His nose only became a little
redder, and he grew more benign. Gradually a circle of friends established itself around him, though a perpetually small one. Varvara
Petrovna, who had little contact with this circle, was nevertheless
acknowledged by us all as our patroness. After the Petersburg lesson,
she settled herself permanently in our town; the winters she spent in
her town house, and the summers on her suburban estate. Never before
had she enjoyed so much importance and influence in our provincial
society as during the last seven years, that is, right up to the appointment of our present governor. Our former governor, the mild and
unforgettable Ivan Osipovich, was a close relation of hers and had once

---

*"I am a [mere sponger] and nothing more! Yes, nothing more!"

been the object of her benefactions. His wife trembled at the very thought of displeasing Varvara Petrovna, and the reverence of provincial society even went so far as to resemble something sinful. It was, consequently, good for Stepan Trofimovich as well. He was a member of the club, lost majestically at cards, and earned himself esteem, though many looked upon him as merely a "scholar." Later on, when Varvara Petrovna permitted him to live in a separate house, we felt even more free. We gathered at his place about twice a week; it used to get quite merry, especially when he was generous with the champagne. The wine came from the shop of that same Andreev. Varvara Petrovna paid the bill every six months, and the day of payment was almost always a day of cholerine.

The most long-standing member of the circle was Liputin, a provincial official, no longer a young man, a great liberal and known around town as an atheist. He got married for the second time to a young and pretty woman, took her dowry, and had, besides, three adolescent daughters. He kept his whole family in fear of God and under lock and key, was exceedingly stingy, and had set aside a little house and some capital for himself from his service. He was a restless person, and of low rank besides, little respected in town, and not received in higher circles. Moreover, he was an undisguised gossip and had more than once been punished, and punished painfully, for it—once by some officer, and another time by a landowner, the respectable head of a family. But we loved his sharp wit, his inquisitiveness, his peculiar wicked gaiety. Varvara Petrovna did not like him, but somehow he was always able to get in good with her.

She also did not like Shatov, who became a member of the circle only in the last year. Shatov had been a student, but was expelled from the university after some student incident; as a child he had been Stepan Trofimovich's pupil, and he had been born Varvara Petrovna's serf, the son of her late valet Pavel Fyodorov, and had been the object of her benefactions. She disliked him for his pride and ingratitude, and simply could not forgive him for not coming to her at once after he was expelled from the university; on the contrary, he did not even reply to the letter she specially sent him then, and preferred putting himself in bondage to some civilized merchant as teacher of his children. He went abroad with this merchant's family, more as a babysitter than as a tutor; but at the time he wanted very much to go abroad. The children had a governess as well, a pert Russian girl who also joined the household just before their departure and was taken mainly for her cheapness. About two months later the merchant threw her out for "free thoughts." Shatov went trudging after her and soon married her in Geneva. They lived together for about three weeks, and then parted as free people not bound by anything; also, of course, because of poverty. For a long time afterwards he wandered around Europe alone, living God knows how; they say he shined shoes in the streets and worked as a stevedore in some port. Finally, about a year ago, he came back to his own nest here and stayed with an old aunt, whom he buried within a month. His communications with his sister Dasha, who was also Varvara Petrovna's ward and lived with her as her favorite on the most noble footing, were very rare and distant. With us he was perpetually glum and taciturn; but occasionally, when his convictions were touched upon, he became morbidly irritated and quite unrestrained in his language. "Shatov should be tied up before you try reasoning with him," Stepan Trofimovich sometimes joked; yet he loved him. Abroad, Shatov had radically changed some of his former socialist convictions and leaped to the opposite extreme. He was one of those ideal Russian beings who can suddenly be so struck by some strong idea that it seems to crush them then and there, sometimes even forever. They are never strong enough to master it, but they are passionate believers, and so their whole life afterwards is spent in some last writhings, as it were, under the stone that has fallen on them and already half crushed them. In appearance Shatov corresponded completely to his convictions: he was clumsy, blond, shaggy, short, with broad shoulders, thick lips, bushy, beetling white eyebrows, a scowling forehead, and unfriendly eyes stubbornly downcast and as if ashamed of something. There was this one lock of his hair that simply refused to lie flat and was eternally sticking up. He was twenty-seven or twenty-eight years old. "It no longer surprises me that his wife ran away from him," Varvara Petrovna once allowed, after studying him intently. He tried to dress neatly, despite his extreme poverty. He again refused to turn to Varvara Petrovna for help, but got by on whatever God sent him; he also had some doings with shopkeepers. One time he sat in a shop; then he almost left altogether on a trading ship as a salesman's assistant, but fell ill just before the departure. It is hard to imagine what poverty he was able to endure without even giving it a thought. After his illness, Varvara Petrovna secretly and anonymously sent him a hundred roubles. He found out the secret, however, pondered, accepted the money, and went to Varvara Petrovna to thank her. She received him warmly, but here, too, he shamefully deceived her expectations: he sat for only five minutes, silent, staring dully at the floor and smiling stupidly, and suddenly, without letting her finish speaking and at the most interesting point of the conversation, got up, bowed somehow sideways, hulkily, dissolved in shame, incidentally brushed against her expensive inlaid worktable, which went crashing to the floor and broke, and walked out nearly dead from disgrace. Liputin later upbraided him strongly, not only for accepting the hundred roubles instead of rejecting them with contempt as coming from his former despot-landowner, but for dragging himself there to thank her on top of it. He lived solitarily on the outskirts of town, and did not like it when anyone, even one of us, stopped to see him. He regularly came to Stepan Trofimovich's evenings, and borrowed newspapers and books to read from him.

There was yet another young man who used to come to the evenings, a certain Virginsky, a local official, who bore some resemblance to Shatov, though he was also apparently his complete opposite in all respects; but he was a "family man" as well. A pathetic and extremely quiet young man, already about thirty, however, with considerable education, but mainly self-taught. He was poor, married, in the civil service, and supported his wife's sister and an aunt. His spouse and all the ladies were of the latest convictions, but with them it all came out somewhat crudely—here, precisely, was "an idea that ended up in the street," as Stepan Trofimovich put it once on a different occasion. They got everything out of books, and even at the first rumor from our progressive corners in the capital were prepared to throw anything whatsoever out the window, provided they were advised to throw it out. Madame Virginsky practiced the profession of midwife in our town; as a young girl, she had lived for a long time in Petersburg. Virginsky himself was a man of rare purity of heart, and rarely have I encountered a more honest flame of the soul. "Never, never shall I abandon these bright hopes," he used to say to me, his eyes shining.

Of these "bright hopes" he always spoke softly, with sweetness, in a half-whisper, as if secretly. He was quite tall but extremely skinny and narrow-shouldered, and had remarkably thin hair of a reddish hue. He bore meekly all of Stepan Trofimovich's scornful jibes at some of his opinions, and his objections to him were sometimes very serious and in many ways nonplussed him. Stepan Trofimovich treated him benignly, and generally took a fatherly attitude towards us all.

"You are all 'half-baked,' " he observed jokingly to Virginsky, "all your sort; though in you, Virginsky, I have not noticed that nar-row-mind-ed-ness that I met with in Petersburg *chez ces séminaristes,* *[22] but still you're 'half-baked.' Shatov would very much prefer to have been fully baked, but he, too, is half-baked."

"And me?" asked Liputin.

"And you are simply the golden mean that will get along anywhere . . . in your own fashion."

Liputin was offended.

It was told of Virginsky, unfortunately on quite good grounds, that his wife, after less than a year of lawful wedlock, suddenly announced to him that he was being retired and that she preferred Lebyadkin. This Lebyadkin, who was some sort of transient, later turned out to be a rather suspicious character, and was even not a retired captain at all, as he styled himself. He only knew how to twirl his moustaches, drink, and spout the most uncouth nonsense imaginable. The man quite indelicately moved in with them at once, being glad of another man's bread, ate and slept with them, and finally began treating the master of the house with condescension. It was asserted that when his wife announced his retirement, Virginsky said to her: "My friend, up to now I have only loved you, but now I respect you," but it is hardly possible that such an ancient Roman utterance was actually spoken; on the contrary, they say he wept and sobbed.[23] Once, about two weeks after his retirement, all of them, the whole "family," went to a grove in the countryside to have tea with friends. Virginsky was somehow feverishly merry and took part in the dancing; but suddenly and without any preliminary quarrel he seized the giant Lebyadkin—who was dancing a cancan solo—by the hair with both hands, bent him down,

*"among these seminarians"

and began dragging him around with shrieks, shouts, and tears. The giant was so frightened that he did not even defend himself and hardly broke silence all the while he was being dragged around; but after the dragging he became offended with all the fervor of a noble man. Virginsky spent the whole night on his knees begging his wife's forgiveness; but forgiveness was not granted, since he still would not consent to go and apologize to Lebyadkin; he was denounced, besides, for paucity of convictions and stupidity—the latter because he knelt while talking with a woman. The captain soon vanished and reappeared in our town only quite recently, with his sister and with new purposes; but more will be said of him later. No wonder the poor "family man" needed our company to ease his heart. Though he never spoke of his domestic affairs with us. Only one time, as we were returning together from Stepan Trofimovich's, did he begin speaking remotely about his situation, but at once, seizing me by the hand, he exclaimed ardently:

"It's nothing; it's just a particular case; in no way, in no way will it hinder the 'common cause'!"

Chance guests used to visit our circle; a little Jew named Lyamshin used to come. Captain Kartuzov used to come. For a while we had a certain inquisitive old man, but he died. Liputin started bringing an exiled Polish priest named Slonzevsky, and for a time we received him on principle, but later we even stopped receiving him.

IX

FOR A WHILE there was talk of us around town, that our circle was a hotbed of freethinking, depravity, and godlessness; and this rumor has always persisted. Yet what we had was only the most innocent, nice, perfectly Russian, jolly liberal chatter. "Higher liberalism" and the "higher liberal"—that is, a liberal without any aim—are possible only in Russia. Stepan Trofimovich, like any witty man, needed a listener, and, besides, he needed an awareness that he was fulfilling the high duty of the propaganda of ideas. And, finally, one also needs someone to drink champagne with, over the wine exchanging jolly little thoughts of a certain sort about Russia and the "Russian spirit," about God in general and the "Russian God" in particular; for the hundredth time repeating scandalous Russian anecdotes known to everyone and repeated by everyone. We were not above local gossip either, and here sometimes reached the point of stern and highly moral verdicts. We also fell into general human things, sternly discussed the future destiny of Europe and of mankind, prophesied doctrinarily that after Caesarism France would fall at once to the level of a secondary state, which we were quite sure could come about terribly quickly and easily. For the Pope we had long ago prophesied the role of mere metropolitan in a united Italy, and were quite convinced that this whole thousand-year-old question was, in our age of humaneness, industry, and railroads, but a trifling matter. Indeed, "higher Russian liberalism" has no other way of treating things. Stepan Trofimovich sometimes used to speak about art, and rather well, too, though somewhat abstractly. He sometimes recalled the friends of his youth—all noted persons in the history of our development—recalled them with tenderness and reverence, but somewhat enviously, as it were. If things got too boring, the little Jew Lyamshin (a petty postal clerk), a good hand at the piano, would sit down to play, and in the intermissions would do mimicries of a pig, a thunderstorm, a mother giving birth with the first cry of the baby, and so on and so forth; that was the sole reason for inviting him. If there was too much tippling—and it did happen, though not often—we would grow rapturous, and once even sang the "Marseillaise"[24] in chorus to Lyamshin's accompaniment, though I do not know that it came out very well. The great day of February nineteenth[25] we celebrated with raptures and even began emptying toasts in its honor way ahead of time. That was long, long ago when there was as yet no Shatov and no Virginsky, and Stepan Trofimovich still lived in the same house with Varvara Petrovna. Some time prior to the great day, Stepan Trofimovich took to muttering to himself the well-known though somewhat unnatural verses, written most likely by some former liberal landowner:

> Peasants come, they're bringing axes,
> Something terrible will happen.[26]

I believe it went something like that, I do not remember it literally. Varvara Petrovna overheard it once, shouted "Nonsense! Nonsense!"

at him, and angrily walked out. Liputin, who happened to be present, remarked caustically to Stepan Trofimovich:

"What a pity if the former serfs get so joyful as to really cause some unpleasantness for their gentleman landowners."

And he drew his index finger across his throat.

"*Cher ami,*" Stepan Trofimovich remarked to him good-humoredly, "believe me, *this*" (he repeated the gesture across his throat) "will be of no use whatsoever either to our landowners or to the rest of us in general. Even without heads, we will not be able to arrange anything, though it's our heads that hinder our understanding most of all."

I should note that many among us thought something extraordinary, such as Liputin predicted, would take place on the day of the proclamation, and they were all so-called knowers of the people and the state. It seems Stepan Trofimovich also shared these thoughts, so much so that almost on the eve of the great day he suddenly began asking Varvara Petrovna to let him go abroad; in short, he began to worry. But the great day went by, and more time went by, and the scornful smile again appeared on Stepan Trofimovich's lips. In our presence he gave utterance to several remarkable thoughts on the character of the Russian man in general and of the Russian peasant in particular.

"We, being hasty people, were in too great a hurry with our dear little peasants," he concluded his series of remarkable thoughts. "We brought them into fashion, and for several years in a row the whole literary sector fussed over them as over some newly discovered treasure. We placed laurels upon lousy heads. In all its thousand years, the Russian village has given us only the 'komarinsky.'[27] A remarkable Russian poet, and one not wanting in wit, when he saw the great Rachel[28] on stage for the first time, exclaimed in rapture: 'I'd never trade Rachel for a peasant!' I am prepared to go further: I will trade all Russian peasants for one Rachel. It is time to take a more sober look and stop mixing our lumpish native tar with *bouquet de l'impératrice.*"[29]

Liputin agreed at once, but observed that for the moment it was still necessary to play the hypocrite and praise peasants for the sake of the trend; that even high-society ladies flooded themselves with tears reading *Anton the Wretch,*[30] and some even wrote from Paris to their managers in Russia that henceforth they were to treat the peasants with all possible humaneness.

And, as if by design, just after the rumors about Anton Petrov,[31] it so happened that in our province, too, and only ten miles from Skvoreshniki, a certain misunderstanding occurred, so that in the heat of the moment troops had to be sent. This time Stepan Trofimovich became so excited that he even frightened us. He shouted in the club that more troops were needed, that they should be summoned by telegraph from another district; he ran to the governor and assured him that he had nothing to do with it, begged that he not be somehow mixed up in the affair by force of habit, and suggested that his statement be communicated at once to the proper quarters in Petersburg. It was good that it all passed quickly and ended in nothing; but at the time I simply marveled at Stepan Trofimovich.

About three years later, as everyone knows, there began to be talk of nationhood, and "public opinion" was born. Stepan Trofimovich had a good laugh.

"My friends," he would instruct us, "if our nationhood has indeed been 'born,' as they assure us nowadays in the newspapers, it is still sitting at school, in some German *Peterschule*,[32] over a German book, grinding out its eternal German lesson, and its German teacher makes it go on its knees when necessary. All praise to the German teacher; but most likely nothing has happened, and nothing of the sort has been born, and everything is still going on as before, that is, by the grace of God. In my opinion, that should be enough for Russia, *pour notre sainte Russie.** Besides, all these panslavisms and nationhoods—it's all too old to be new. Nationhood, if you like, has never appeared among us otherwise than as a gentlemen's clubroom fancy—a Moscow one at that! To be sure, I'm not talking about Igor's time.[33] And, finally, it all comes of idleness. With us everything comes of idleness, even what is fine and good. It all comes of our dear, cultivated, whimsical, gentlemanly idleness. I've been repeating it for thirty thousand years. We are unable to live by our own labor. And what is all this fuss nowadays about some public opinion being 'born'—did it just drop from the sky, suddenly, for no rhyme or reason? Don't they understand that in order to acquire an opinion what is needed first of all is labor, one's own labor, one's own initiative and experience! Nothing can ever be ac-

*"for our holy Russia."

quired gratis. If we labor, we shall have our own opinion. And since we shall never labor, those who have been working for us all along will have the opinion instead—that is, Europe again, the Germans again, our teachers from two hundred years back. Besides, Russia is too great a misunderstanding for us to resolve ourselves, without the Germans and without labor. For twenty years now I've been ringing the alarm and calling to labor! I've given my life to this call, and—madman—I believed! Now I no longer believe, but I still ring and shall go on ringing to the end, to my grave; I shall pull on the rope until the bells ring for my funeral!"

Alas, we simply yessed him! We applauded our teacher, and with what ardor! But after all, gentlemen, even now do we not at times hear all around us the same "dear," "intelligent," "liberal" old Russian nonsense?

Our teacher believed in God. "I do not understand why everyone here makes me out to be a godless man," he used to say occasionally. "I believe in God, *mais distinguons,* * I believe as in a being who is conscious of himself in me. Why, I cannot go believing like my Nastasya" (the servingwoman) "or like some grand sir who believes 'just in case'—or like our dear Shatov—but, no, Shatov doesn't count, Shatov believes *perforce,* like a Moscow Slavophil. So far as Christianity is concerned, for all my sincere respect for it, I am not a Christian. I am rather an ancient pagan, like the great Goethe,[34] or like an ancient Greek. Take this one thing alone, that Christianity has never understood woman—as has been so splendidly developed by George Sand in one of her brilliant novels.[35] As for the bowings, the fasts, and the rest of it, I do not see why anyone should care about me. However our informers may bustle about here, I have no wish to become a Jesuit. In the year 'forty-seven Belinsky, while abroad, sent his famous letter to Gogol, in which he hotly reproached him with believing 'in some sort of God.'[36] *Entre nous soit dit,* † I can imagine nothing more comical than the moment when Gogol (the Gogol of that time!) read this expression and . . . the whole letter! But, ridiculousness aside, since I still agree with the essence of the matter, I will point to them and

---

*"but let us distinguish"
†"Just between us"

proclaim: These were men! They knew how to love their people, they knew how to suffer for them, they knew how to sacrifice everything for them, and they knew at the same time how to disagree with them when necessary, not to indulge them in certain notions. Indeed, Belinsky could hardly seek salvation in Lenten oil or turnips and peas! . . ."

But here Shatov would interrupt.

"These men of yours never loved the people, never suffered for them or sacrificed anything for them, no matter what they themselves imagined for their own good pleasure!" he growled gloomily, looking down and turning impatiently on his chair.

"Never loved the people, did they!" Stepan Trofimovich yelled. "Oh, how they loved Russia!"

"Neither Russia nor the people!" Shatov also yelled, flashing his eyes. "One cannot love what one does not know, and they understood nothing about the Russian people! All of them, and you along with them, turned a blind eye and overlooked the Russian people, and Belinsky especially; it's clear in that same letter to Gogol. Belinsky was just like Krylov's Inquisitive Man,[37] who didn't notice the elephant in the museum, but gave all his attention to French socialist bugs; and that's where he ended up. Yet he was maybe more intelligent than all of you! Not only have you overlooked the people—you have treated them with loathsome contempt, which is enough to say that by people you meant only the French people, and even then only the Parisians, and were ashamed that the Russian people are not like them. And this is the naked truth! And those who have no people, have no God! You may be sure that all those who cease to understand their people and lose their connection with them, at once, in the same measure, also lose the faith of their fathers, and become either atheists or indifferent. It's right, what I'm saying! The fact will be borne out. That is why all of you, and all of us now, are either vile atheists or indifferent, depraved trash, and nothing more! And you, too, Stepan Trofimovich, I do not exclude you in the least, I've even said it on your account, be it known to you!"

Usually, after delivering such a monologue (and this often happened with him), Shatov would seize his cap and rush to the door, completely certain that it was all over now and that he had broken his friendly relations with Stepan Trofimovich utterly and forever. But the latter always managed to stop him in time.

"Why not make peace, Shatov, after all these nice little words?" he would say, offering his hand good-naturedly from his chair.

Clumsy but bashful Shatov did not like tendernesses. On the surface he was a crude man, but inwardly, it seems, a most delicate one. Though he often lost his sense of measure, he was the first to suffer for it. Having growled something under his nose to Stepan Trofimovich's appeal, and shuffling in place like a bear, he would suddenly grin, lay his cap aside, and sit down in his former chair, stubbornly staring at the ground. Of course, wine would be brought out, and Stepan Trofimovich would pronounce some appropriate toast—say, for example, to the memory of one of the old activists.

2

Prince Harry. Matchmaking

I

THERE WAS one other person on earth to whom Varvara Petrovna was attached no less than to Stepan Trofimovich—her only son, Nikolai Vsevolodovich Stavrogin. It was for him that Stepan Trofimovich had been invited as a tutor. The boy was then about eight years old, and the frivolous General Stavrogin, his father, was at the time already living separately from his mama, so that the child grew up in her care alone. One must do Stepan Trofimovich justice: he knew how to win his pupil over. The whole secret lay in his being a child himself. I was not around then, and he was constantly in need of a true friend. He did not hesitate to make a friend of such a small being, once he had grown up a bit. It somehow came about naturally that there was not the least distance between them. More than once he awakened his ten- or eleven-year-old friend at night only to pour out his injured feelings in tears before him, or to reveal some domestic secret to him, not noticing that this was altogether inadmissible. They used to throw themselves into each other's embrace and weep. The boy knew that his mother loved him very much, but he hardly had much love for her. She spoke little to him, rarely hindered him in anything, but he always somehow morbidly felt her eyes fixed upon him, watching him. However, in the whole business of education and moral development, his mother fully trusted Stepan Trofimovich. She still fully believed in him then. One may suppose that the pedagogue somewhat unsettled his pupil's nerves. When he was taken to the lycée in his sixteenth year, he was puny and pale, strangely quiet and pensive. (Later on he was distinguished by his extraordinary physical strength.) One may also suppose that when the friends wept, throwing themselves into their mutual embrace at night, it was not always over some little domestic anecdotes. Stepan Trofimovich managed to touch the deepest strings in his friend's heart and to call forth in him the first, still uncertain sensation of that age-old, sacred anguish which the chosen soul, having once tasted and known it, will never exchange for any cheap satisfaction. (There are lovers of this anguish who cherish it more than the most radical satisfaction, if that were even possible.) But in any event it was good that the youngling and the mentor, though none too soon, were parted in different directions.

For the first two years the young man came home from the lycée for vacations. While Varvara Petrovna and Stepan Trofimovich were in Petersburg, he was sometimes present at his mother's literary evenings, listening and observing. He spoke little, and was quiet and shy as before. He treated Stepan Trofimovich with the former tender attentiveness, but now somehow more reservedly: he obviously refrained from talking with him about lofty subjects or memories of the past. In accordance with his mama's wish, after completing his studies he entered military service and was soon enrolled in one of the most distinguished regiments of the Horse Guard. He did not come to show himself to his mama in his uniform and now rarely wrote from Petersburg. Varvara Petrovna sent him money without stint, in spite of the fact that the income from her estates fell so much after the reform that at first she did not get even half of her former income. However, through long economy she had saved up a certain not exactly small sum. She was very interested in her son's successes in Petersburg high society. The young officer, rich and with expectations, succeeded where she had not. He renewed acquaintances of which she could no longer even dream, and was received everywhere with great pleasure. But very soon rather strange rumors began to reach Varvara Petrovna: the young man, somehow madly and suddenly, started leading a wild life. Not that he gambled or drank too much; there was only talk of some savage unbridledness, of some people being run over by horses, of some beastly behavior towards a lady of good society with whom he had had a liaison and whom he afterwards publicly insulted. There was something even too frankly dirty about this affair. It was added, furthermore, that he was some sort of swashbuckler, that he picked on people and insulted them for the pleasure of it. Varvara Petrovna was worried and anguished. Stepan Trofimovich assured her that these were merely the first stormy impulses of an overabundant constitution, that the sea would grow calm, and that it all resembled Shakespeare's description of the youth of Prince Harry, carousing with Falstaff, Poins, and Mistress Quickly.[1] This time Varvara Petrovna did not shout "Nonsense, nonsense!" as it had lately become her habit to shout quite often at Stepan Trofimovich, but, on the contrary, paid great heed to him, asked him to explain in more detail, herself took Shakespeare and read the immortal chronicle with extreme attention. But the chronicle did not calm her down, nor did she find all that much resemblance. She waited feverishly for answers to certain of her letters. The answers were not slow in coming; soon the fatal news was received that Prince Harry had almost simultaneously fought two duels, was entirely to blame for both of them, had killed one of his opponents on the spot and crippled the other, and as a consequence of such deeds had been brought to trial. The affair ended with his being broken to the ranks, stripped of his rights, and exiled to service in one of the infantry regiments, and even that only by special favor.

In the year 'sixty-three he somehow managed to distinguish himself; he was awarded a little cross, promoted to noncommissioned officer, and then, somehow quite soon, to officer. Throughout this time Varvara Petrovna had sent perhaps as many as a hundred letters to the capital with requests and pleas. She allowed herself to be somewhat humiliated in so extraordinary a case. After his promotion, the young man suddenly retired, once again did not come to Skvoreshniki, and stopped writing to his mother altogether. It was learned in some roundabout way that he was back in Petersburg, but was not seen at all in the former society; he seemed to have hidden somewhere. It was discovered that he was living in some strange company, had become associated with some castoffs of the Petersburg populace, with some down-at-the-heel officials, retired military men who nobly begged for alms, drunkards, that he visited their dirty families, spent days and nights in dark slums and God knows what corners, that he had gone to seed, gone ragged, and that he apparently liked it. He did not ask money of his mother; he had his little estate—a former village of General Stavrogin's, which did bring at least some income and which, according to rumors, he had rented out to a German from Saxony. At last his mother begged a visit out of him, and Prince Harry appeared in our town. It was then that I first had a close look at him, for before then I had never seen him.

He was a very handsome young man, about twenty-five years old, and I confess I found him striking. I expected to see some dirty ragamuffin, wasted away from depravity and stinking of vodka. On the contrary, this was the most elegant gentleman of any I had ever happened to meet, extremely well dressed, of a behavior such as is to be found only in a gentleman accustomed to the most refined decorum. I was not alone in my surprise: the whole town was surprised, having already been informed, of course, of the whole of Mr. Stavrogin's biography, and even in such detail that it was impossible to imagine where it could have come from, and, what is most surprising, half of which turned out to be true. All our ladies lost their minds over the new visitor. They were sharply divided into two parties—one party adored him, the other hated him to the point of blood vengeance; but both lost their minds. Some were especially fascinated by the possibility of some fatal mystery in his soul; others positively liked his being a killer. It also turned out that he was quite well educated, and even rather knowledgeable. Of course, it did not take much knowledge to surprise us; but he could reason about vital and rather interesting issues as well, and, what was most precious, with remarkable reasonableness. I will mention as an oddity that everyone here, almost from the very first day, found him to be an extremely reasonable man. He was not very talkative, was elegant without exquisiteness, surprisingly modest, and at the same time bold and confident like no one else among us. Our dandies looked at him with envy and were totally eclipsed in his presence. I was also struck by his face: his hair was somehow too black, his light eyes were somehow too calm and clear, his complexion was somehow too delicate and white, his color somehow too bright and clean, his teeth like pearls, his lips like coral—the very image of beauty, it would seem, and at the same time repulsive, as it were. People said his face resembled a mask; however, they said much else as well, about his great physical strength, among other things. He was almost a tall man. Varvara Petrovna looked at him with pride, but also with constant uneasiness. He spent about half a year with us—listless, quiet, rather morose; he appeared in society and observed all our provincial etiquette with unswerving attention. He was related to our governor through his father, and was received in his house as a close relative. But several months passed, and the beast suddenly showed its claws.

By the way, I will note parenthetically that dear, mild Ivan Osipovich, our former governor, had something of the woman about him, but was from a good and well-connected family—which explains how he could sit with us for so many years constantly brushing all business aside. With his openhandedness and hospitality he should have been a marshal of nobility of the good old days, and not a governor in such a worrisome time as ours. There was eternal talk in town that it was not he but Varvara Petrovna who ruled the province. It was caustically put, of course, but nonetheless decidedly a lie. And much wit was wasted among us on account of it. On the contrary, in recent years Varvara Petrovna had specifically and consciously withdrawn from any higher destiny, despite the extreme respect accorded her by the whole of society, and voluntarily confined herself within the strict limits she set for herself. Instead of a higher destiny, she suddenly turned to the management of her estate, and in two or three years brought its income up almost to the former level. Instead of the former poetic impulses (visits to Petersburg, plans for publishing a magazine, and so on), she started scrimping and saving. She even removed Stepan Trofimovich from herself, allowing him to rent an apartment in another house (which he himself, under various pretexts, had been pestering her to do for a long time). Stepan Trofimovich gradually began referring to her as a prosaic woman, or, even more jocularly, as his "prosaic friend." To be sure, he allowed himself such jokes not otherwise than in the most highly respectful form and after a long selection of the appropriate moment.

All of us who were close to them understood—and Stepan Trofimovich more sensitively than any of us—that her son appeared to her then as if in the guise of a new hope and even in the guise of some new dream. Her passion for her son dated from the time of his successes in Petersburg society, and had increased especially from the moment she received the news that he had been broken to the ranks. And yet she was obviously afraid of him and seemed like a slave before him. One could see that she was afraid of something indefinite, mysterious, which she herself would have been unable to explain, and oftentimes she studied Nicolas unobtrusively and attentively, pondering and puzzling over something . . . and then—the beast suddenly put out its claws.

II

OUR PRINCE SUDDENLY, for no reason at all, committed two or three impossibly brazen acts upon various persons—that is, the main thing lay in their being so unheard-of, so utterly unlike anything else, so different from what is usually done, so paltry and adolescent, and devil knows why, with no pretext whatsoever. One of the most respectable senior members of our club, Pavel Pavlovich Gaganov, an elderly man and even a decorated one, had acquired the innocent habit of accompanying his every word with a passionately uttered: "No, sir, they won't lead me by the nose!" And so what. But one day in the club, when he uttered this aphorism at some heated moment to a small group of club guests gathered around him (none of them inconsequential), Nikolai Vsevolodovich, who was standing apart by himself and whom no one was addressing, suddenly came up to Pavel Pavlovich, seized his nose unexpectedly but firmly with two fingers, and managed to pull him two or three steps across the room. He could not have felt any anger towards Mr. Gaganov. One might think it was merely a childish prank, a most unpardonable one, of course; yet it was re-counted later that at the very moment of the operation he was almost in a reverie, "just as if he had lost his mind"; but this was recalled and grasped long afterwards. At first, in the heat of the moment, everyone recalled only what happened next, by which time he certainly under-stood how things really were and not only did not become embarrassed but, on the contrary, smiled gaily and maliciously, "without the least repentance." There was a terrible uproar; he was surrounded. Nikolai Vsevolodovich kept turning and looking around, not answering any-one, gazing with curiosity at the exclaiming faces. At last he seemed suddenly to lapse into reverie again—so they said, at least—frowned, stepped firmly up to the insulted Pavel Pavlovich, and with obvious vexation muttered rapidly:

"Forgive me, of course . . . I really don't know why I suddenly wanted . . . silly of me . . ."

The casualness of the apology amounted to a fresh insult. There was even more shouting. Nikolai Vsevolodovich shrugged and walked out.

All this was very silly, to say nothing of its ugliness—a calculated and deliberate ugliness, as it seemed at first sight, and therefore constituting a deliberate and in the highest degree impudent affront to our entire society. And that is how everyone understood it. First of all, Mr. Stavrogin was immediately and unanimously expelled from membership in the club; then it was decided on behalf of the whole club to appeal to the governor and ask him at once (without waiting for the affair to be taken formally to court) to restrain the pernicious ruffian, the big-city "swashbuckler, through the administrative power entrusted to him, and thereby protect the peace of all decent circles in our town from pernicious encroachments." It was added with malicious innocence that "some law may perhaps be found even for Mr. Stavrogin." This phrase was prepared for the governor precisely in order to sting him on account of Varvara Petrovna. They delighted in smearing it around. As if by design, the governor happened to be out of town then; he had gone somewhere nearby to baptize the baby of a certain interesting and recent widow who had been left in a certain condition by her husband; but it was known that he would soon return. Meanwhile they arranged a real ovation for the esteemed and offended Pavel Pavlovich: they embraced and kissed him; the whole town came to call on him. They even planned a subscription dinner in his honor, and abandoned the idea only at his urgent request—perhaps realizing finally that the man had after all been dragged by the nose, and therefore there was no reason to be quite so triumphant.

And yet how had it happened? How could it have happened? The remarkable thing was precisely that no one in the whole town ascribed this wild act to madness. Which meant that they were inclined to expect such acts from Nikolai Vsevolodovich even when sane. For my own part, to this day I do not know how to explain it, even despite the event that soon followed, which seemed to explain everything and, apparently, to pacify everyone. I will also add that, four years later, to my cautious question concerning this past event in the club, Nikolai Vsevolodovich responded, frowning: "Yes, I was not quite well then." But there is no point in rushing ahead.

I also found curious the explosion of general hatred with which everyone here fell upon the "ruffian and big-city swashbuckler." They insisted on seeing an insolent deliberateness and calculated intention to insult our whole society at once. In truth, the man pleased no one and, on the contrary, got everyone up in arms—but how, one wonders? Until the last occasion, he had not once quarreled with anyone, or insulted anyone, and was as courteous as a gentleman in a fashion plate, if the latter were able to speak. I suppose he was hated for his pride. Even our ladies, who had begun with adoration, now cried against him still more loudly than the men.

Varvara Petrovna was terribly struck. She confessed later to Stepan Trofimovich that she had long been foreseeing it all, during that entire half year, every day, and even precisely "of that very sort"—a remarkable confession on the part of one's own mother. "It's begun!" she thought with a shudder. The next morning after the fatal evening in the club, she set out cautiously but resolutely to have a talk with her son, and yet the poor woman was all atremble despite her resolution. She had not slept all night and had even gone early in the morning to confer with Stepan Trofimovich and wept while she was there, which had never happened to her in public before. She wished that Nicolas would at least say something to her, at least deign to talk with her. Nicolas, always so courteous and respectful with his mother, listened to her for some time, scowling but very serious; suddenly he got up without a word of response, kissed her hand, and walked out. And that same day, in the evening, as if by design, there came another scandal which, though a bit more mild and ordinary than the first, nevertheless, owing to the general mood, considerably increased the town outcry.

Namely, our friend Liputin turned up. He called on Nikolai Vsevolodovich immediately after his talk with his mama, and earnestly requested the honor of his presence that same evening at a party on the occasion of his wife's birthday. Varvara Petrovna had long looked with a shudder at the low orientation of Nikolai Vsevolodovich's acquaintances, but never dared to remark on it. He had already struck up several other acquaintances in this third-rate stratum of our society, and even lower—but such was his inclination. However, he had not yet visited Liputin's house, though he had met Liputin himself. He realized that Liputin was inviting him as a result of the scandal in the club the day before, that as a local liberal he was delighted by the scandal, sincerely thought it was the proper way to treat senior club members, and that it was all very good. Nikolai Vsevolodovich laughed and promised to come.

Many guests assembled; they were unsightly but rollicksome people. The vain and jealous Liputin invited guests only twice a year, but on those occasions he did not stint. The most honored guest, Stepan Trofimovich, did not come for reason of illness. Tea was served; there was an abundance of appetizers and vodka; cards were being played at three tables, and while waiting for supper the young people started dancing to the piano. Nikolai Vsevolodovich chose Madame Liputin—a very pretty little lady, who was terribly shy of him—took two turns with her, sat down beside her, made her talk, made her laugh. Finally, after remarking on how pretty she was when she laughed, he suddenly put his arm around her waist, in front of all the guests, and kissed her on the lips, three times in a row, to the full of his heart's content. The poor frightened woman fainted. Nikolai Vsevolodovich took his hat, went up to her husband, who stood dumbstruck amid the general commotion, looked at him, became confused himself, muttered hastily "Don't be angry," and walked out. Liputin ran after him to the front hall, helped him into his fur coat with his own hands, and, bowing, saw him down the stairs. And the very next day there came a rather amusing addition to this, comparatively speaking, essentially innocent story—an addition which thereafter even brought Liputin a sort of honor, which he was able to exploit to his full advantage.

Around ten o'clock in the morning, Liputin's servant Agafya, a bold, pert, and red-cheeked wench of about thirty, appeared at Mrs. Stavrogin's house, sent by him with a message for Nikolai Vsevolodovich, saying she absolutely had "to see the master himself, ma'am." He had a very bad headache, but he came out. Varvara Petrovna managed to be present when the message was delivered.

"Sergei Vasilyich" (that is, Liputin), Agafya rattled out pertly, "asked me first of all to bring you his greetings and inquire about your health, sir, how you slept yesterday, and how you feel now after yesterday, sir."

Nikolai Vsevolodovich grinned.

"Bring him my greetings and thanks, and tell your master from me, Agafya, that he is the most intelligent man in the whole town."

"And he told me to answer you on that," Agafya picked up even more pertly, "that he knows it even without you, and he wishes you the same, sir."

"Well, now! And how could he have found out what I was going to tell you?"

"I really don't know what way he found out, sir, but when I'd left and was already at the other end of the lane, I heard him running after me without his cap, sir. 'Agafyushka,' he said, 'if it perhappens he says to you: "Tell your master he's the smartest man in town," then be sure to say at once: "We know that ver-ry well ourselves, and the same to you, sir . . ."' "

III

THE TALK with the governor also finally took place. Our dear, mild Ivan Osipovich had just returned and had just had time to hear the club's hot complaint. Without a doubt something had to be done, but he was perplexed. Our hospitable old man also seemed a bit afraid of his young relative. He decided, however, to persuade him to apologize to the club and to the offended man, but in satisfactory form, and if necessary even in writing, and then gently talk him into leaving us and going to Italy, say, for the interest of it, or generally somewhere abroad. In the reception room, where he came out this time to meet Nikolai Vsevolodovich (who on other occasions, as a relative, wandered freely all over the house), the well-bred Alyosha Telyatnikov, an official and also a familiar of the governor's house, was opening envelopes in the corner at a table; and in the next room, by the window nearest the door, a visitor had placed himself, a fat and healthy colonel, a friend and former colleague of Ivan Osipovich's, who was reading the *Voice*, paying no attention, of course, to what was going on in the reception room; he even sat with his back turned. Ivan Osipovich began in a roundabout way, almost in a whisper, but kept getting slightly confused. Nicolas had an ungracious look, not at all like a relative, was pale, sat staring at the floor, and listened with knitted brows, as if overcoming great pain.

"You have a kind heart, Nicolas, and a noble one," the old man included among other things, "you are quite an educated man, you have moved in the highest circles, and here, too, your behavior up to now has been exemplary and you have set at ease the heart of your mother, who is dear to us all . . . And now everything has again taken on a coloring so mysterious and dangerous for everyone! I speak as a friend of your family, as an elderly man who is your relative and loves you sincerely, in whom you can take no offense . . . Tell me, what prompts you to such unbridled acts, so beyond all convention and measure? What might be the meaning of such escapades, as if in delirium?"

Nicolas listened with vexation and impatience. Suddenly something as if sly and mocking flashed in his eyes.

"Perhaps I'll tell you what prompts me," he said sullenly, and, looking around, he leaned towards Ivan Osipovich's ear. The well-bred Alyosha Telyatnikov withdrew another three steps towards the window, and the colonel coughed over the *Voice*. Poor Ivan Osipovich hastily and trustfully offered his ear; he was an extremely curious man. And here something utterly impossible occurred, which, on the other hand, was all too clear in one respect. The old man suddenly felt that, instead of whispering some interesting secret to him, Nicolas had suddenly caught the upper part of his ear in his teeth and clamped it quite firmly. He trembled and his breath failed.

"Is this a joke, Nicolas?" he moaned mechanically, in a voice not his own.

Alyosha and the colonel had no time to realize anything; besides, they could not see and thought all along that the two were whispering to each other; and yet the old man's desperate face worried them. They looked goggle-eyed at each other, not knowing whether to rush to his assistance, as agreed, or to wait longer. Nicolas noticed it, perhaps, and bit harder on the ear.

"Nicolas! Nicolas!" the victim moaned again, "so . . . you've had your joke, that's enough . . ."

Another moment and the poor man would, of course, have died of fright; but the monster had mercy on him and released his ear. This whole mortal terror lasted a full minute, and after it the old man had a sort of fit. But half an hour later Nicolas was arrested and taken for the time being to the guardhouse, where he was locked in a separate cell with a separate guard at the door. The decision was a harsh one, but our mild superior was so angry that he decided to take the responsibility upon himself even in the face of Varvara Petrovna. To the general amazement, this lady, who arrived at the governor's in haste and displeasure for an immediate explanation, was turned away at the porch; whereupon, without getting out of the carriage, she went back home, hardly able to believe it herself.

And finally everything was explained! At two o'clock in the morning, the arrested man, who until then had been surprisingly quiet and had even fallen asleep, suddenly raised a clamor, began beating violently on the door with his fists, with unnatural force tore the iron grating from the little window in the door, broke the glass, and cut his hands all over. When the officer of the guard came running with a detachment of men and the keys and ordered the cell to be opened so as to fall upon the raging man and bind him, it turned out that he was in an acute state of brain fever. He was brought home to his mama. At once everything was explained. All three of our doctors gave the opinion that the sick man could already have been in delirium three days earlier, still in possession of consciousness and cunning, but not of common sense and will—which, by the way, was confirmed by the facts. Thus it turned out that Liputin had been the first to guess right. Ivan Osipovich, a delicate and sensitive man, was extremely embarrassed; but, curiously, that meant that he, too, considered Nikolai Vsevolodovich capable of any crazy act while in his right mind. In the club they were also ashamed and puzzled at how they had failed to notice the elephant and had missed the only possible explanation of all these wonders. Skeptics turned up as well, of course, but they did not hold out for long.

Nicolas spent more than two months in bed. A famous doctor was invited from Moscow for consultation; the whole town came to call on Varvara Petrovna. Forgiveness was granted. Towards spring, when Nicolas had completely recovered and had assented without any objections to his mother's proposal that he go to Italy, she also persuaded him to pay farewell visits to everyone and, while doing so, to make apologies as far as possible and wherever necessary. Nicolas assented quite readily. It became known in the club that he had a most delicate talk with Pavel Pavlovich Gaganov in his own home, which left the man perfectly satisfied. Going around on his visits, Nicolas was very serious, even somewhat gloomy. Everyone received him, apparently, with complete sympathy, but everyone was also embarrassed for some reason and glad that he was going to Italy. Ivan Osipovich even shed a tear, but for some reason did not dare to embrace him even at this final parting. Indeed, some among us remained convinced that the scoundrel was simply laughing at us all, and that his illness was beside the point. He also stopped by at Liputin's.

"Tell me," he asked him, "how could you guess beforehand what I was going to say about your intelligence, and provide Agafya with an answer?"

"I'll tell you how," laughed Liputin. "It's because I also regard you as an intelligent man, and therefore could divine your answer before-hand."

"Still, it's a remarkable coincidence. Excuse me, however, but does it mean that you regarded me as an intelligent man and not a crazy one when you sent Agafya over?"

"As a most intelligent and reasonable man, and I only pretended to believe that you were not in your right mind . . . And you immediately guessed my thoughts then and sent me a patent for my wit through Agafya."

"Well, there you're slightly mistaken. I really . . . wasn't well . . ." Nikolai Vsevolodovich muttered, frowning. "Bah!" he cried out, "do you really think I'm capable of throwing myself on people when I'm in my right mind? Why would I do that?"

Liputin cringed and was unable to answer. Nicolas became some-what pale, or at least it seemed so to Liputin.

"In any case, you have a very amusing turn of mind," Nicolas continued, "and as for Agafya, I realize, of course, that you sent her to abuse me."

"Could I have challenged you to a duel, sir?"

"Ah, yes, right! I did hear something about your dislike of duels . . ."

"Why translate from the French!" Liputin cringed again.

"You adhere to native things?"

Liputin cringed even more.

"Hah, hah! What's this I see?" Nicolas cried out, suddenly noticing a volume of Considérant[2] in a most conspicuous place on the table. "Do you mean you're a Fourierist? Good for you! But isn't this also a translation from the French?" he laughed, tapping the book with his finger.

"No, it's not a translation from the French!" Liputin jumped up, even with some sort of spite. "It's a translation from the universal human language, sir, and not just from the French! From the language of the universally human social republic and harmony, that's what, sir! Not just from the French! . . ."

"Pah, the devil, but there is no such language!" Nicolas went on laughing.

Sometimes even a little thing strikes one's attention exceptionally and for a long time. Though the whole main story about Mr. Stavrogin still lies ahead, I will note here, as a curiosity, that of all his impressions during all the time he spent in our town, the sharpest stamp was left in his memory by the homely and almost mean little figure of the little provincial official, the jealous husband and crude family despot, the miser and moneylender, who locked up candle ends and the leftovers from dinner, and who was at the same time a fierce sectarian of God knows what future "social harmony," who reveled by night in ecstasies over fantastic pictures of the future phalanstery,[3] in the coming realization of which, in Russia and in our province, he believed as firmly as in his own existence. And that in a place where he himself had set aside "a little house," where he had married a second time and picked up a bit of cash as a dowry, where perhaps for a hundred miles around there was not a single person, beginning with himself, who even outwardly resembled a future member of the "universally all-human social republic and harmony."

"God knows how these people get made!" Nicolas thought in bewilderment, occasionally recalling the unexpected Fourierist.

I V

O UR PRINCE TRAVELED for more than three years, so that he was
almost forgotten in town. But we knew through Stepan Trofimovich that he had been all over Europe, had even gone to Egypt and
stopped off at Jerusalem; then he had stuck himself onto some scientific
expedition to Iceland and actually visited Iceland. It was also reported
that during one winter he attended lectures at some German university. He seldom wrote to his mother—once in six months or even less
often; but Varvara Petrovna was not angry or offended. She accepted
the once-established relationship with her son submissively and without a murmur; but, of course, every day of those three years she
worried about her Nicolas, pined for him, and dreamed of him contin-
ually. She did not tell anyone about her dreams or complaints. Apparently she even withdrew somewhat from Stepan Trofimovich. She
formed some plans within herself and, it seemed, became even stingier
than before, and began saving even more and getting all the more
angry over Stepan Trofimovich's losses at cards.

Finally, in April of this year, she received a letter from Paris, from
Praskovya Ivanovna, General Drozdov's widow and her childhood
friend. In the letter Praskovya Ivanovna—whom Varvara Petrovna
had not seen or corresponded with for about eight years—informed
her that Nikolai Vsevolodovich had become a familiar of her house and
was friends with Liza (her only daughter), and intended to accompany
them to Switzerland in the summer, to Vernex-Montreux, despite the
fact that he was received like a son and was almost living in the family
of Count K. (quite an influential person in Petersburg), who was now
staying in Paris. It was a brief letter and its object was perfectly clear,
though apart from the above-mentioned facts it contained no conclusions. Varvara Petrovna did not think long, made her mind up instantly, got ready, took her ward Dasha (Shatov's sister) with her, and
in the middle of April went off to Paris and then to Switzerland. She
returned alone in July, having left Dasha with the Drozdovs; the
Drozdovs themselves, according to the news she brought, promised to
come to us at the end of August.

The Drozdovs were also landowners of our province, but the duties of General Ivan Ivanovich (a former friend of Varvara Petrovna's and a colleague of her husband's) constantly prevented them from ever visiting their magnificent estate. After the general's death, which occurred last year, the inconsolable Praskovya Ivanovna went abroad with her daughter, with the intention among other things of trying the grape cure, which she planned to undergo at Vernex-Montreux in the latter half of the summer. On her return to the fatherland she intended to settle in our province for good. She had a big house in town, which for many years had stood empty with its windows boarded up. They were rich people. Praskovya Ivanovna, Mrs. Tushin by her first marriage, was also, like her school friend Varvara Petrovna, the daughter of an old-time tax farmer and had also married with a very large dowry. The retired cavalry captain Tushin was himself a man of means and of some ability. At his death he bequeathed a goodly capital to his seven-year-old and only daughter Liza. Now that Lizaveta Nikolaevna was about twenty-two, her own money could safely be reckoned at no less then 200,000 roubles, to say nothing of the fortune that would come to her in time from her mother, who had no children from her second marriage. Varvara Petrovna was apparently quite pleased with her trip. In her opinion, she had managed to come to a satisfactory understanding with Praskovya Ivanovna, and immediately upon her arrival she told everything to Stepan Trofimovich; she was even quite expansive with him, something which had not happened to her in a long time.

"Hurrah!" Stepan Trofimovich cried and snapped his fingers.

He was perfectly delighted, the more so as he had spent the whole time of separation from his friend being extremely dejected. She had not even said a proper good-bye to him as she was leaving, and did not mention any of her plans to "that old woman," fearing, perhaps, that he might blurt something out. She was angry with him then for the loss of a considerable sum at cards, which had suddenly been discovered. But while still in Switzerland she had felt in her heart that her abandoned friend should be rewarded on her return, the more so as she had long been treating him severely. The abrupt and mysterious separation struck and tormented the timid heart of Stepan Trofimovich, and, as if by design, other perplexities also came along at the same time.

He suffered over a certain rather considerable and long-standing financial obligation, which could by no means be met without Varvara Petrovna's help. Moreover, in May of this year came the end of our kindly, mild Ivan Osipovich's term as governor; he was replaced, and not without some unpleasantness. Then, in Varvara Petrovna's absence, the entrance of our new superior, Andrei Antonovich von Lembke, also took place; with that there at once began to be a noticeable change in the attitude of almost all our provincial society towards Varvara Petrovna, and, consequently, towards Stepan Trofimovich as well. At least he had already managed to gather a few unpleasant though valuable observations and, it seems, had grown very timid on his own without Varvara Petrovna. He had an alarming suspicion that the new governor had already received reports on him as a dangerous man. He learned positively that some of our ladies intended to stop calling on Varvara Petrovna. It was said repeatedly of the future governor's wife (who was expected here only in the autumn) that though she was, one heard, a haughty woman, at least she was a real aristocrat, not like "our wretched Varvara Petrovna." Everyone knew from somewhere, certainly and with details, that the new governor's wife and Varvara Petrovna had already met once in society and had parted in enmity, so that the mere reminder of Mrs. von Lembke supposedly produced a morbid impression on Varvara Petrovna. Varvara Petrovna's bright and victorious look, the contemptuous indifference with which she heard about the opinions of our ladies and the agitation in society, resurrected the fallen spirits of timid Stepan Trofimovich and cheered him up at once. With a special joyfully fawning humor he began to elaborate upon the new governor's arrival.

"You undoubtedly know, *excellente amie,*" he spoke, drawing the words out fashionably and coquettishly, "what is meant by a Russian administrator, generally speaking, and what is meant by a new Russian administrator—that is, newly baked, newly installed . . . *Ces interminables mots russes!** . . . But it is unlikely that you can have learned in practice what administrative rapture means and what sort of thing it is!"

"Administrative rapture? I have no idea."

*"These interminable Russian words!"

"That is . . . *Vous savez, chez nous . . . En un mot,** set some utter nonentity to selling some paltry railroad tickets, and this nonentity will at once decide he has the right to look at you like Jupiter when you come to buy a ticket, *pour vous montrer son pouvoir.*† 'Come,' he thinks, 'I'll show my power over you . . .' And it reaches the point of administrative rapture with them . . . *En un mot,* I've just read that some beadle in one of our churches abroad—*mais c'est très curieux*‡ —chased out, I mean literally chased out of the church, a wonderful English family, *les dames charmantes,* just before the start of the Lenten service—*vous savez ces chants et le livre de Job* §—on the sole pretext that 'it is not in order for foreigners to hang about in Russian churches and they should come at the proper time . . .' and he sent them all into a faint . . . This beadle was in a fit of administrative rapture *et il a montré son pouvoir* ‖ . . ."

"Abbreviate if you can, Stepan Trofimovich."

"Mr. von Lembke is now touring the province. *En un mot,* this Andrei Antonovich, though he is a Russian German of Orthodox faith and even—I will grant him that—a remarkably handsome man, of the forty-year-old sort . . ."

"Where did you get that he's a handsome man? He has sheep's eyes."

"In the highest degree. But, very well, I yield to the opinion of our ladies . . ."

"Let's move on, Stepan Trofimovich, I beg you! By the way, since when have you been wearing a red necktie?"

"I . . . only today . . ."

"And do you take your exercise? Do you go for a four-mile walk every day, as the doctor prescribed?"

"Not . . . not always."

"Just as I thought! I felt it even in Switzerland!" she cried irritably. "You are now going to walk not four but six miles a day! You've gone terribly to seed, terribly, ter-ri-bly! You're not just old, you're decrepit . . . I was struck when I saw you today, in spite of your red

---

*"You know, with us . . . In a word"
†"in order to show you his power."
‡"no, it's very curious"
§"you know that singing and the book of Job"
‖"and he showed his power"

necktie . . . *quelle idée rouge!** Go on about von Lembke, if there really
is anything to say, but let it end somewhere, I beg you, I'm tired."

"*En un mot,* I merely wanted to say that he is one of those administrators who start out at the age of forty, who vegetate in insignificance
until they're forty and then suddenly make their way by means of
an unexpectedly acquired wife or by some other no less desperate
means . . . That he is away now . . . that is, I mean to say that he at
once had it whispered in both ears that I am a corrupter of youth and
a fomenter of provincial atheism . . . He began making inquiries at
once."

"Can it be true?"

"I've even taken measures. When it was 're-por-ted' that you 'ruled
the province,' *vous savez,* † he allowed himself to say that 'such things
will not continue.' "

"Is that what he said?"

"That 'such things will not continue,' and *avec cette morgue* ‡ . . . His
spouse, Yulia Mikhailovna, we shall behold here at the end of August,
direct from Petersburg."

"From abroad. I met her there."

"*Vraiment?*"§

"In Paris and in Switzerland. She's related to the Drozdovs."

"Related? What a remarkable coincidence! They say she's ambitious
and . . . supposedly has good connections?"

"Nonsense! Nothing to speak of! She sat a spinster without a kopeck
until she was forty-five, then she went and married her von Lembke,
and now, of course, her whole goal is to pull him up. A pair of
intriguers."

"And they say she's two years older than he is."

"Five. Her mother wore out the train of her dress on my doorstep
in Moscow; she used to get herself invited to my balls out of charity
when Vsevolod Nikolaevich was alive. And the girl used to sit alone
in the corner all evening with a turquoise fly on her forehead, no one
would dance with her, so when it got to be past two I'd take pity on

---

*"what an idea, red!" *or* "what a red idea!"
†"you know"
‡"with such pomposity"
§"Really?"

her and send her her first partner. She was already twenty-five then, and they still took her out in short skirts like a schoolgirl. It became indecent to invite them."

"That fly, I can just see it!"

"I tell you, I arrived and stumbled right onto an intrigue. You've just read Drozdov's letter—what could be clearer? And what did I find? That fool Drozdov herself—she's never been anything but a fool—suddenly looked at me as if she were asking why I had come. You can imagine how surprised I was! I looked and there was this finagling Lembke woman, and this cousin with her, old Drozdov's nephew—it was all clear! Of course, I undid it all at once, and Praskovya is on my side again; but the intrigue, the intrigue!"

"Which you overcame, however! Oh, you Bismarck!"[4]

"Bismarck or not, I'm still able to see through falseness and stupidity when I meet them. Lembke is falseness, and Praskovya—stupidity. I've rarely met a more flaccid woman, and moreover her legs are swollen, and moreover she's kind. What could be stupider than someone who is stupid and kind?"

"The wicked kind, *ma bonne amie,* the wicked kind are even stupider," Stepan Trofimovich parried nobly.

"Perhaps you're right, but do you remember Liza?"

*"Charmante enfant!"**

"And no longer an *enfant* now, but a woman, and a woman of character. Noble and passionate, and what I love in her is that she stands up to her gullible fool of a mother. The whole story took place because of that cousin."

"Hah, but in fact he's not related to Lizaveta Nikolaevna at all . . . Does he have intentions or something?"

"You see, he's a young officer, very taciturn, even modest. I wish always to be just. It seems to me that he's against the whole intrigue himself and doesn't want anything, and the only finagler was Lembke. He had great respect for Nicolas. You understand, it all depends on Liza, but I left her on excellent terms with Nicolas, and he himself promised me that he would certainly come to us in November. So Lembke alone is intriguing here, and Praskovya is simply a blind

*"Charming child!"

woman. She suddenly told me that my suspicions were all a fantasy, and I told her to her face that she was a fool. I'm ready to repeat it at the Last Judgment. And if it weren't for Nicolas, who asked me to let it be for a while, I would never have gone away without exposing that false woman. She paid court to Count K. through Nicolas, she tried to come between a mother and her son. But Liza is on our side, and I came to an understanding with Praskovya. You know she's related to Karmazinov."

"Who? Madame von Lembke?"

"Why, yes. Distantly."

"Karmazinov, the novelist?"

"The writer, yes—why are you surprised? Of course, he considers himself great. A puffed-up creature! She'll bring him with her, and now she's fussing over him there. She intends to introduce something here, some sort of literary gatherings. He'll come for a month, he wants to sell his last estate here. I very nearly met him in Switzerland, not that I really wanted to. However, I hope he will deign to recognize me. In the old days he used to write me letters, he used to visit our house. I wish you were better dressed, Stepan Trofimovich; you're getting more slovenly by the day . . . Oh, how you torment me! What are you reading now?"

"I . . . I . . ."

"I understand. Friends, drinking parties, club and cards, as usual—and the reputation of an atheist. I don't like this reputation, Stepan Trofimovich. I'd rather you weren't called an atheist, especially now. I've never liked it, in fact, because it's all just empty talk. It must finally be said."

"*Mais, ma chère* . . ."

"Listen, Stepan Trofimovich, compared with you I am, of course, an ignoramus in all matters of learning, but on the way here I was thinking a lot about you. I've arrived at a conviction."

"And what is it?"

"It is that you and I alone are not smarter than everyone else in the world, but that some people are smarter than we are."

"Witty and apt. Some are smarter, meaning some are more right than we are, and therefore we, too, can be mistaken, isn't that so? *Mais, ma bonne amie,* suppose I am mistaken, but do I not have my all-human, all-time, and supreme right of free conscience? Do I not have the right not to be a bigot and a fanatic if I choose? And for that I shall naturally be hated by various gentlemen till the end of time. *Et puis, comme on trouve toujours plus de moines que de raison,** and since I am in perfect agreement with that . . ."

"What? What did you say?"

"I said: *on trouve toujours plus de moines que de raison,* and since I am in . . ."

"That can't be yours; you must have gotten it somewhere."

"Pascal said it."[5]

"Just as I thought . . . it wasn't you! Why don't you ever say anything like that, so brief and so apt, instead of dragging it all out so? It's much better than what you said earlier about administrative rapture . . ."

"*Ma foi, chère†* . . . why? First, probably, because I'm not Pascal, after all, *et puis* . . . second, we Russians cannot say anything in our own language . . . At least we haven't yet . . ."

"Hm. Perhaps that's not quite true. You ought at least to write down such words and remember them, you know, in the event of a conversation . . . Ah, Stepan Trofimovich, on my way I thought of talking with you seriously, seriously!"

"*Chère, chère amie!*"

"Now that all these Lembkes, all these Karmazinovs . . . Oh, God, how you've gone to seed! Oh, how you torment me! . . . I wished these people to feel respect for you, because they're not worth your finger, your little finger, and look how you carry yourself! What will they see? What am I going to show them? Instead of standing nobly as a witness, of continuing to be an example, you've surrounded yourself with some riffraff, you've acquired some impossible habits, you've grown decrepit, you cannot live without wine and cards, you read nothing but Paul de Kock, and you write nothing, while there they all write; you waste all your time on chatter. Is it possible, is it permissible to be friends with such riffraff as your inseparable Liputin?"

---

*"And then, since one always finds more monks than reason"
†"My word, dear"

"But why *my* and why *inseparable?*" Stepan Trofimovich timidly protested.

"Where is he now?" Varvara Petrovna went on, sternly and sharply.

"He . . . he has boundless respect for you, and has gone to S——k to collect his inheritance from his mother."

"Getting money seems to be the only thing he does. What about Shatov? Same as ever?"

"Irascible, mais bon."

"I can't bear your Shatov; he's angry and thinks too much of himself!"

"How is Darya Pavlovna's health?"

"You mean Dasha? Why her all of a sudden?" Varvara Petrovna looked at him curiously. "She's well, I left her with the Drozdovs . . . I heard something about your son in Switzerland, something bad, not good."

*"Oh, c'est une histoire bien bête! Je vous attendais, ma bonne amie, pour vous raconter . . ."**

"Enough, Stepan Trofimovich, let me rest; I'm exhausted. We'll have time to talk our fill, especially about bad things. You're beginning to splutter when you laugh—there's decrepitude for you! And how strangely you laugh now . . . God, you're so full of bad habits! Karmazinov will never come to call on you! And they're gleeful over everything here even without that . . . You've revealed yourself completely now. Well, enough, enough, I'm tired! You might finally spare a person!"

Stepan Trofimovich "spared a person," but he withdrew in perplexity.

V

OUR FRIEND had indeed acquired not a few bad habits, especially of late. He had visibly and rapidly gone to seed, and it was true that he had become slovenly. He drank more, grew more tearful and

*"Oh, it's a very stupid story! I was waiting for you, my good friend, in order to tell you . . ."

nervous; became overly sensitive to refinement. His face acquired a strange ability to change remarkably quickly, for instance, from the most solemn expression to the most ridiculous and even silly. He could not endure solitude and constantly longed for someone to entertain him at once. He had an absolute need for gossip, for some local anecdote, and it had to be new each day. If no one came for a long time, he wandered dejectedly about his rooms, went up to the windows, pensively chewed his lips, sighed deeply, and finally all but whimpered. He kept having presentiments of something, being afraid of something unexpected, inevitable; he became timorous; began paying great attention to his dreams.

He spent that whole day and evening in extreme dejection, sent for me, was very agitated, talked for a long time, narrated for a long time, but it was all quite incoherent. Varvara Petrovna had long known that he concealed nothing from me. It seemed to me, finally, that he was concerned about something particular, something that he perhaps could not imagine to himself. As a rule, when we were alone together and he began complaining to me, a little bottle was almost always brought out after a while, and things would become more heartening. This time there was no wine, and he obviously suppressed in himself the recurring desire to send for it.

"Why is she so angry all the time!" he complained every moment, like a child. *"Tous les hommes de génie et de progrès en Russie étaient, sont et seront toujours des* card players *et des* drunkards *qui boivent en zapoï** . . . and I'm not such a card player and drunkard yet . . . She reproaches me, asks me why I don't write anything. Strange notion! . . . And why am I lying down? You must stand 'as an example and a reproach,' she says. *Mais, entre nous soit dit,* † what else can a man destined to be a standing 'reproach' do but lie down—doesn't she see that?"

And finally the main, the particular anguish that was then tormenting him so persistently became clear to me. Many times that evening he went up to the mirror and stood before it for a long while. Finally,

---

*"All men of genius and progress in Russia were, are and always will be [card players] and [drunkards] who drink in *zapoï* [bouts]"
†"But, just between us"

he turned from the mirror to me and said with some strange despair:
"*Mon cher, je suis un* man gone to seed!"

Yes, indeed, until then, until that very day, he had always remained
certain of just one thing—namely, that despite all Varvara Petrovna's
"new views" and "changes of ideas," he still had charms over her
woman's heart, that is, not only as an exile or as a famous scholar, but
also as a handsome man. For twenty years this flattering and comfort-
ing conviction had been rooted in him, and of all his convictions it was
perhaps the hardest to part with. Did he anticipate that evening what
a colossal ordeal was being prepared for him in the nearest future?

VI

I WILL NOW set out to describe the somewhat amusing incident with
which my chronicle really begins.

At the very end of August the Drozdovs finally returned. Their
appearance slightly preceded the arrival of their relative, our new
governor's wife, long expected by the whole town, and generally made
a remarkable impression on society. But I will speak of these curious
events later; now I will confine myself to the fact that Praskovya
Ivanovna brought Varvara Petrovna, who was expecting her so impatiently, a most worrisome riddle: Nicolas had parted with them in July
and, meeting Count K. on the Rhine, had gone to Petersburg with him
and his family. (*N.B.* All three of the count's daughters were of mar-
riageable age.)

"I could get nothing from Lizaveta because of her pride and her
testiness," Praskovya Ivanovna concluded, "but I saw with my own
eyes that something had happened between her and Nikolai Vsevolodovich. I do not know the reasons, my dear Varvara Petrovna, but
it seems you will have to ask your Darya Pavlovna what the reasons
were. I think Liza was offended. I'm only too glad to bring you your
favorite at last and hand her over to you: to get her off my back."

These venomous words were spoken with extraordinary vexation.
It was obvious that the "flaccid woman" had prepared them in advance
and had relished their effect beforehand. But Varvara Petrovna was not
one to be taken aback by sentimental effects and riddles. She sternly

demanded the most precise and satisfactory explanations. Praskovya Ivanovna lowered her tone at once and even ended by bursting into tears and launching into the most friendly effusions. Like Stepan Trofimovich, this irritable but sentimental lady was in constant need of true friendship, and her chief complaint against her daughter Lizaveta Nikolaevna was precisely that "her daughter was not her friend."

But of all her explanations and effusions the only certainty turned out to be that some sort of a falling-out had indeed taken place between Liza and Nicolas, but what sort of falling-out—of this Praskovya Ivanovna was apparently unable to form any definite idea. As for the accusations she had brought against Darya Pavlovna, in the end she not only renounced them altogether, but even asked especially that her previous words not be given any importance because she had spoken them "in irritation." In short, everything was left rather vague, even suspicious. According to her account, the falling-out arose because of Liza's "testy and derisive" character, and "the proud Nikolai Vsevolodovich, though very much in love, could not endure her derision and became derisive himself."

"Shortly afterwards we made the acquaintance of a young man, the nephew of your 'professor,' I believe, and with the same last name . . ."

"His son, not his nephew," Varvara Petrovna corrected. Praskovya Ivanovna had never been able to remember Stepan Trofimovich's last name and always called him "professor."

"Well, his son, then, and so much the better; it's all the same to me. An ordinary young man, very lively and easygoing, but there's nothing to him. Well, here Liza herself behaved wrongly, she allowed the young man some closeness, intending to make Nikolai Vsevolodovich jealous. I don't condemn that too much: it's a girl's business, quite usual, even charming. Only instead of being jealous, Nikolai Vsevolodovich, on the contrary, became friendly with the young man himself, as if he didn't notice a thing, or as if it made no difference to him. Liza blew up at that. The young man soon left (he was in a great hurry to get somewhere), and Liza started picking on Nikolai Vsevolodovich at every opportunity. She noticed that he sometimes talked with Dasha and she began to get frantic, at which point, dearest, my life became impossible. The doctors forbade me to be irritated, and I was so sick from that much-vaunted lake of theirs, it gave me toothaches, and such rheumatism! They've even published somewhere that Lake Geneva causes toothaches, it has that property. And then Nikolai Vsevolodovich suddenly received a letter from the countess and left us at once, packed up in a day. They parted in a friendly way, and as she was seeing him off, Liza became very gay and carefree and laughed loudly all the time. Only it was all put on. He left, and she became very pensive, stopped mentioning him completely, and wouldn't let me. And I'd advise you, my dear Varvara Petrovna, not to bring up the subject with Liza, you will only make things worse. If you keep silent, she'll start talking with you first; then you'll learn more. I believe they'll get back together, if only Nikolai Vsevolodovich does not put off coming as he promised."

"I shall write to him at once. If that's how it was, it's just an empty falling-out; all nonsense! And I know Darya only too well. Nonsense!"

"About Dashenka I confess . . . my sin. They were just ordinary conversations, and aloud, too. But, dearest, it all upset me so at the time. And Liza herself became close to her again as affectionately as before, I saw it . . ."

That same day Varvara Petrovna wrote to Nicolas, begging him to come at least a month earlier than the time he had fixed. But for her there still remained something unclear and unknown in it. She spent the whole evening and the whole night thinking. Praskovya's opinion seemed too innocent and sentimental to her. "Praskovya has been too emotional all her life, ever since boarding school," she thought. "It's not like Nicolas to run away because of a girl's taunts. There's some other reason, if indeed there was a falling-out. That officer is here, however, they've brought him with them, and he's living in their house like a relative. And Praskovya confessed much too quickly about Darya; she must have left something out, something she didn't want to tell . . ."

By morning a project had ripened in Varvara Petrovna for putting an immediate end to at least one perplexity—a project remarkable for its unexpectedness. What was in her heart when she created it? It is difficult to say, and I will not undertake to explain beforehand all the contradictions that went into it. As a chronicler I limit myself simply to presenting events in an exact way, exactly as they occurred, and it is not my fault if they appear incredible. Nevertheless, I must testify once again that by morning she had no remaining suspicions about Dasha, and, in truth, there had been none to begin with—she was too sure of her. And she could not admit the idea that her Nicolas could take a fancy to her . . . "Darya." In the morning, while Darya Pavlovna was pouring tea at the tea table, Varvara Petrovna studied her long and fixedly and, perhaps for the twentieth time since the day before, said confidently to herself:

"It's all nonsense!"

She only noticed that Dasha looked somehow tired and that she was even quieter than before, even more apathetic. After tea, following a custom established once and for all, they both sat down to needlework. Varvara Petrovna told her to make a full report of her impressions abroad, mainly of nature, the inhabitants, the towns, their art and industry—everything she had managed to notice. Not one question about the Drozdovs or her life with the Drozdovs. Dasha, who was sitting next to her at the worktable helping her with some embroidery, had already been talking for about half an hour in her even, monotonous, but somewhat weak voice.

"Darya," Varvara Petrovna suddenly interrupted her, "is there anything special you wish to tell me?"

"No, nothing," Darya thought for a moment and looked at Varvara Petrovna with her light eyes.

"Nothing on your soul, on your heart, on your conscience?"

"Nothing," Dasha repeated softly, but with a sort of sullen firmness.

"So I thought! Believe me, Darya, I shall never have doubts of you. Now sit and listen. Come and sit on this chair, facing me, I want to see all of you. So. Listen—do you want to be married?"

Dasha responded with a long, questioning, though not too surprised look.

"Wait, don't speak. First of all there is a difference in age, a very great difference; but you know better than anyone what nonsense that is. You're a reasonable girl, and there should be no mistakes in your life. He is still a handsome man, by the way . . . In short, Stepan Trofimovich, whom you have always respected. Well?"

Dasha looked even more questioningly, and this time was not only surprised, but even blushed visibly.

"Wait, don't speak, don't be hasty! You have money left to you in my will, but if I should die, what will become of you even with money? They will deceive you and take your money—well, and that's the end of you. But with him you will be the wife of a noted man. Now look at it from the other side: if I were to die now—even if I provide for him—what will become of him? But on you I can truly rely. Wait, I haven't finished: he is light-minded, a maunderer, cruel, an egoist, with base habits, but you will appreciate him, first of all, because there are much worse. I'm not trying to get you off my hands by marrying you to some scoundrel, you're not thinking that! And above all because I ask it of you, that's why you will appreciate him," she broke off irritably all of a sudden. "Do you hear? Why are you staring?"

Dasha listened and kept silent.

"Wait, one more thing. He's an old granny—but so much the better for you. A pitiful old granny, by the way; it's not worthwhile a woman's loving him. But it is worthwhile loving him for his defenselessness, and you will love him for his defenselessness. Do you understand me? Do you?"

Dasha nodded affirmatively.

"I just knew you would, I expected nothing less of you. He will love you, because he must, he must; he must adore you!" Varvara Petrovna shrieked with some peculiar irritation. "And in any case he will fall in love with you even without any duty, I know him. Besides, I will be here myself. Don't worry, I will always be here. He will start complaining about you, he will begin to slander you, he will whisper about you with the first person he meets, he will whine, whine eternally; he will write letters to you from one room to another, two letters a day, but still he won't be able to live without you, and that is the main thing. Make him obey; if you can't, you're a fool. He will want to hang himself, he will threaten to—don't believe him; it's just nonsense! Don't believe him, but still keep your ears pricked up; who knows, maybe he will: it does happen with his kind; they hang themselves not out of strength but out of weakness; so you must never push it to the last limit—that is the first rule of married life. Remember also that he is a poet. Listen, Darya: there is no higher happiness than to sacrifice yourself. Besides, you will give me great pleasure, and that is the main thing. Don't think I'm just blathering out of foolishness; I understand what I'm saying. I am an egoist, and you be an egoist, too. I'm not forcing you; it's all your will; as you say, so it shall be. Well, why are you sitting there? Say something!"

"It makes no difference to me, Varvara Petrovna, if it's necessary for me to be married," Dasha said firmly.

"Necessary? What are you hinting at?" Varvara Petrovna looked sternly and fixedly at her.

Dasha was silent, poking the needle into her embroidery.

"Though you're an intelligent girl, that's just blather. Though it's true that I've firmly decided to get you married now, it's not from necessity, but only because the thought occurred to me, and only because it's Stepan Trofimovich. If it weren't for Stepan Trofimovich, I wouldn't have thought of getting you married now, though you're already twenty years old . . . Well?"

"I'll do as you please, Varvara Petrovna."

"So you consent! Wait, don't speak, there's no rush, I haven't finished: in my will I've left you fifteen thousand roubles. I will hand them over to you at once, after the wedding. You will give him eight thousand—that is, not him, but me. He has a debt of eight thousand; I will pay it, but he should know that the money is yours. Seven thousand will remain in your hands; by no means give him a single rouble, ever. Never pay his debts. Once you pay, you'll never see the end of it. Anyway, I'll always be here. The two of you will receive an annual allowance of twelve hundred roubles, fifteen hundred with extras, besides room and board, which I will also provide, just as I do for him now. Only you will have to hire your own servants. I will give you your annual money all at once, right into your own hands. But be kind: give something to him, too, occasionally; and allow his friends to visit once a week, but if they come more often, chase them out. But I will be here myself. And if I die, your pension will not stop until his death, do you hear, only until *his* death, because it's his pension, not yours. And besides the seven thousand which you will have left intact, unless you're going to be stupid yourself, I will leave you another eight thousand in my will. And you will get nothing more from me; you should know that. Well, do you consent, eh? Will you finally say something?"

"I already did, Varvara Petrovna."

"Remember that it is entirely your will; as you wish, so it shall be."

"Only, forgive me, Varvara Petrovna, has Stepan Trofimovich said anything to you?"

"No, he has not said anything, he doesn't know yet, but . . . he'll start saying something now!"

She jumped up instantly and threw on her black shawl. Dasha again blushed a little and was following her with a questioning look. Varvara Petrovna suddenly turned to her with a face burning with wrath.

"You fool!" she fell upon her like a hawk, "you ungrateful fool! What's in your mind? Do you think I would compromise you in any way, even the slightest bit? Why, he himself will come crawling on his knees and begging, he must die from happiness—that is how it will be arranged! Don't you know that I would never allow you to be offended? Or do you think he'll take you for the eight thousand, and that I'm running now to sell you? Fool, fool, you're all ungrateful fools! Give me my umbrella!"

And she flew on foot over the wet brick walks and wooden planks to Stepan Trofimovich.

VII

IT WAS TRUE that she would not allow Darya to be offended; on the contrary, she considered that she was now acting as her benefactress. The most noble and blameless indignation flared up in her soul when, putting on her shawl, she caught the embarrassed and mistrustful glance of her ward fixed upon her. She had sincerely loved her from her very childhood. Praskovya Ivanovna had justly called Darya Pavlovna her favorite. Long ago Varvara Petrovna had decided once and for all that "Darya's character is not like her brother's" (that is, like the character of her brother Ivan Shatov), that she was quiet and meek, capable of great self-sacrifice, unusually devoted, remarkably modest, possessed of rare reasonableness and, above all, of gratitude. So far

Dasha had apparently justified all her expectations. "There will be no mistakes in this life," Varvara Petrovna had said when the girl was just twelve years old, and as she had the quality of clinging stubbornly and passionately to any dream that captivated her, and to any new design, to any idea that seemed bright to her, she had decided at once to bring Dasha up like her own daughter. She at once set a sum of money aside for her and sent for a governess, Miss Criggs, who lived in her house until the ward was sixteen years old, but for some reason was suddenly dismissed. Teachers also came from the high school, among them a real Frenchman who taught Darya her French. He, too, was dismissed suddenly, as if thrown out. One poor lady who came to town, a widow of gentle birth, taught her to play the piano. But the chief pedagogue remained Stepan Trofimovich. In fact, he was the first to discover Dasha: he began teaching the quiet child before Varvara Petrovna had even thought about her. Again I repeat: it was remarkable how children took to him! Lizaveta Nikolaevna Tushin studied with him from the age of eight to eleven (of course, Stepan Trofimovich taught her without fee, and would not have taken one from the Drozdovs for anything). But he fell in love with the lovely child and told her some sort of poetic tales about the order of the world, the earth, the history of mankind. His lectures on primitive peoples and primitive man were more engaging than Arabian tales. Liza, who used to be thrilled by these stories, would imitate Stepan Trofimovich at home in a very funny way. He found out about it, and once caught her unawares. Embarrassed, Liza threw herself into his arms and burst out crying. So did Stepan Trofimovich, from rapture. But Liza soon left, and only Dasha remained. When teachers started coming to Dasha, Stepan Trofimovich abandoned his lessons with her and gradually ceased paying attention to her. It went on like that for a long time. Once, when she was already seventeen, he was suddenly struck by her comeliness. This happened at Varvara Petrovna's table. He got into conversation with the young woman, was very pleased with her responses, and in the end suggested that he give her a serious and extensive course in the history of Russian literature. Varvara Petrovna praised and thanked him for the wonderful idea, and Dasha was delighted. Stepan Trofimovich set about making special preparations for the lectures, and finally they began. He started with the ancient period; the first lecture proved fascinating; Varvara Petrovna was present. When Stepan Trofimovich finished and announced to his pupil, upon leaving, that next time he would begin analyzing *The Song of Igor's Campaign*,[6] Varvara Petrovna suddenly stood up and announced that there would be no more lectures. Stepan Trofimovich winced, but said nothing. Dasha blushed. However, that was the end of the enterprise. This happened exactly three years before Varvara Petrovna's present unexpected fantasy.

Poor Stepan Trofimovich was sitting alone and had no presentiment of anything. In sad pensiveness he had long been glancing out the window to see if some acquaintance was coming. But no one would come. It was drizzling outside; it was getting cold; the stove needed lighting; he sighed. Suddenly a dreadful apparition appeared before his eyes: Varvara Petrovna was coming to see him in such weather and at such an odd hour! And on foot! He was so struck that he forgot to change his costume and received her just as he was in his usual pink quilted dressing jacket.

"*Ma bonne amie!* . . ." he cried weakly in greeting.

"You're alone, I'm glad: I cannot bear your friends! It's always so smoky here! Lord, what air! You haven't finished your tea yet, and it's past eleven! Disorder is bliss to you. Messiness is a delight! What are these torn papers doing on the floor? Nastasya, Nastasya! What is your Nastasya up to? Open the windows, my dear, open the vents, the doors, everything should be wide open. And we will go to the drawing room; I've come to you on business. And sweep the floor, my dear, at least once in your life!"

"It does get messy, ma'am," Nastasya squeaked in an irritably plaintive little voice.

"Sweep up, then, sweep fifteen times a day! A wretched drawing room you've got" (when they had come to the drawing room). "Shut the door properly; she'll eavesdrop. You must change this wallpaper. Didn't I send you a paperhanger with samples? Why didn't you choose something? Sit down and listen. Sit down, finally, I beg you. Where are you going? Where are you going?"

"I . . . just a moment," Stepan Trofimovich cried from the other room, "here I am again!"

"Ah, you've changed your costume!" she looked him up and down mockingly. (He had put on his frock coat over the dressing jacket.) "That is certainly more fitting for . . . our conversation. Sit down, finally, I beg you."

She explained everything to him at once, abruptly and convincingly. Hinted at the eight thousand he so desperately needed. Spoke in detail of the dowry. Stepan Trofimovich sat wide-eyed and trembled. He heard everything, but could not understand it clearly. Wanted to speak, but his voice kept failing. He knew only that everything would be as she was saying, that to object or disagree would be a futile undertaking, and that he was irretrievably a married man.

"Mais, ma bonne amie, a third time, and at my age . . . and to such a child!" he said at last. *"Mais c'est une enfant!"**

"A child who, thank God, is twenty years old! Please stop rolling your eyes, you're not on stage. You are very intelligent and learned, but you understand nothing of life, you need a nanny constantly looking after you. I will die, and what will become of you? And she will be a good nanny for you; she's a modest girl, firm, reasonable; besides, I will be here myself, I won't die right away. She's a homebody, an angel of meekness. This happy thought kept occurring to me still in Switzerland. Do you understand, since I myself am telling you she's an angel of meekness!" she suddenly cried out fiercely. "Your place is a mess, she'll make it clean, she'll put everything in order, it will be like a mirror . . . Ah, but do you still fancy I should bow and scrape before you with such a treasure, enumerating all the benefits, playing the matchmaker? No, you yourself should . . . on your knees . . . Oh, empty, empty, pusillanimous man!"

"But . . . I'm old!"

"So what if you're fifty-three! Fifty isn't the end, it's the middle of life. You're a handsome man, and you know it yourself. You also know how she respects you. If I were to die, what would become of her? But with you she will be at ease, and I will be at ease. You have distinction, a name, a loving heart; you receive a pension, which I regard as my duty. You may even save her, save her! In any case, you will do her an honor. You will shape her life, develop her heart, guide her thoughts. So many people perish nowadays because their thoughts are

---

*"But she's a child!"

misguided! By then your work will be ready, and all at once you will remind the world of yourself."

"I was just . . ." he mumbled, flattered now by Varvara Petrovna's clever flattery, "I was just going to sit down and write my *Stories from Spanish History* . . ."

"There, you see, everything is falling into place."

"But . . . her? Have you told her?"

"Don't worry about her, and there's no need for you to be curious. Of course, you must ask her yourself, beg her to do you the honor, understand? But don't worry, I will be here. Besides, you love her . . ."

Stepan Trofimovich became dizzy; the walls began spinning around. There was one dreadful idea here which he was unable to cope with.

"*Excellente amie!*" his voice suddenly trembled, "I . . . I could never have imagined that you would decide to give me in marriage . . . to some other . . . woman!"

"You're not a young maiden, Stepan Trofimovich; only young maidens are given in marriage, and you yourself are doing the marrying," Varvara Petrovna hissed venomously.

"*Oui, j'ai pris un mot pour un autre. Mais . . . c'est égal,*"* he stared at her with a lost look.

"I see that *c'est égal,*" she said through her teeth, contemptuously. "Lord! he's fainted! Nastasya, Nastasya! Water!"

But it did not get as far as water. He revived. Varvara Petrovna took her umbrella.

"I see there's no point in talking to you now . . ."

"*Oui, oui, je suis incapable.*"†

"But by tomorrow you will have rested and thought it over. Stay home, and if anything happens, let me know, even during the night. Don't write letters, I won't read them. Tomorrow at this time I will come myself, alone, for a final answer, and I hope it will be satisfactory. Try to see that no one is here, and that there's no mess, because just look at this! Nastasya, Nastasya!"

---

*"Yes, I mistook one word for another. But . . . it's all the same"
†"Yes, yes, I'm incapable."

Of course, the next day he accepted; and he could not have done otherwise. There was one special circumstance here . . .

VIII

S TEPAN TROFIMOVICH'S estate, as we used to call it (about fifty souls by the old way of reckoning,[7] and adjoining Skvoreshniki), was not his at all, but had belonged to his first wife, and so now to their son, Pyotr Stepanovich Verkhovensky. Stepan Trofimovich was merely the trustee, and thus, once the nestling was fully fledged, acted through a formal warrant as manager of the estate. For the young man it was a profitable deal: he received up to a thousand roubles a year from his father as income from the estate, while under the new regulations it did not yield as much as five hundred (and perhaps even less). God knows how such arrangements were set up. However, the entire thousand was sent by Varvara Petrovna, and Stepan Trofimovich did not contribute a single rouble to it. On the contrary, he pocketed all the income from this bit of land, and, furthermore, ruined it altogether by leasing it to some dealer and, in secret from Varvara Petrovna, selling the timber that was its main valuable asset. He had been selling this timber piecemeal for a long time. Its total worth was about eight thousand at least, yet he got only five for it. But he sometimes lost too much at the club, and was afraid to ask Varvara Petrovna. She ground her teeth when she finally learned of it all. And now the boy suddenly notified him that he was coming himself to sell his property at all costs, and charged his father with promptly arranging for the sale. It was clear that Stepan Trofimovich, being a lofty and disinterested man, felt ashamed before *ce cher enfant* (whom he had last seen as a student in Petersburg all of nine years earlier). Originally, the entire estate might have been worth some thirteen or fourteen thousand, but now it was unlikely that anyone would give five for it. Stepan Trofimovich undoubtedly had every right, in terms of the formal warrant, to sell the timber, and taking into account the impossible annual income of a thousand roubles, which had been sent punctually for so many years, could make a good defense of himself in any final settlement. But

Stepan Trofimovich was noble and had lofty aspirations. A remarkably beautiful thought flashed in his head: to lay out nobly on the table, when Petrusha came, the highest maximum of the price—that is, even fifteen thousand—without the slightest hint at the sums that had been sent previously, and then firmly, very firmly, with tears, to press *ce cher fils** to his heart, and so settle all accounts. He began remotely and cautiously unfolding this picture before Varvara Petrovna. He hinted that it would even add some special, noble tinge to their friendly connection . . . to their "idea." It would show former fathers and former people generally in such a disinterested and magnanimous light, as compared with the new frivolous and social youth. He said many other things, but Varvara Petrovna kept silent. At last she dryly informed him that she would agree to buy their land and would pay the maximum price for it—that is, six or seven thousand (even four would have been enough). Of the remaining eight thousand that had flown away with the timber, she did not say a word.

That was a month before the matchmaking. Stepan Trofimovich was struck and began to ponder. Before then there could still have been a hope that the boy might perhaps not come at all—a hope, that is, judging from outside, in the opinion of some third person. Stepan Trofimovich, as a father, would have rejected indignantly the very notion of such a hope. In any case, up to then all sorts of strange rumors kept reaching us about Petrusha. At first, after finishing his studies at the university about six years before, he had hung about Petersburg with nothing to do. Suddenly there came news that he had taken part in the composing of some anonymous tract and was implicated in the case. Then he suddenly turned up abroad, in Switzerland, in Geneva—might have fled there for all we knew.

"It is surprising to me," Stepan Trofimovich, deeply embarrassed, preached to us then. "Petrusha *c'est une si pauvre tête!*† He is kind, noble, very sensitive, and I was so glad then, in Petersburg, comparing him with modern young people, but *c'est un pauvre sire tout de même‡* . . . And, you know, it all comes from that same

*"this dear son"
†"he's such a poor mind!"
‡"he's a poor specimen all the same"

half-bakedness, from sentimentality! They're fascinated not by realism, but by the sensitive, ideal aspect of socialism, its religious tinge,
so to speak, its poetry . . . to someone else's tune, of course. And yet
me, what about me! I have so many enemies here, and even more
there, it will all be put down to his father's influence . . . God! Petrusha—a moving force! What times we live in!"

Petrusha, by the way, very soon sent his exact address from Switzerland, so that his money could be sent as usual: therefore he was not
entirely an émigré. And now, after spending about four years abroad,
he suddenly reappeared in his fatherland and sent word of his imminent arrival: therefore he had not been accused of anything. Moreover,
someone had supposedly even taken an interest in him and become his
patron. He wrote now from the south of Russia, where he was on a
private but important mission for someone and was making arrangements for something. This was all wonderful, but still, how get hold
of the remaining seven or eight thousand to make up a decent maximum of the price for the estate? And what if there were an outcry, and
instead of that majestic picture it should all wind up in court? Something told Stepan Trofimovich that the sensitive Petrusha would not
relinquish his interests. "Why is it, as I've noticed," Stepan Trofimovich once whispered to me at the time, "why is it that all these desperate socialists and communists are at the same time such incredible
misers, acquirers, property-lovers, so much so that the more socialist
a man is, the further he goes, the more he loves property . . . why is
it? Can that, too, come from sentimentality?" I do not know what truth
there is in Stepan Trofimovich's observation; I only know that Petrusha had obtained some information about the sale of the timber and the
rest of it, and that Stepan Trofimovich knew he had obtained this
information. I also happened to read Petrusha's letters to his father; he
wrote extremely rarely, once a year or even less often. But just recently
he had sent two letters, almost one after the other, giving notice of his
imminent arrival. All his letters were short, dry, consisting only of
directives, and as the father and son, ever since Petersburg, had been
addressing each other on familiar terms, according to the fashion,
Petrusha's letters looked decidedly like those letters of instruction that
old-time landowners used to send from the capital to the house-serfs
appointed to manage their estates. And now suddenly the eight thou-

sand that would resolve the situation came flying out of Varvara Petrovna's proposal, and with that she let him understand clearly that it could not come flying from anywhere else. Naturally, Stepan Trofimovich accepted.

As soon as she left he sent for me, and locked the door to everyone else for the whole day. Of course, he wept a little; he spoke much and well, got much and badly mixed up, accidentally made a pun and remained pleased with it; then came a slight cholerine—in short, everything took place in due order. After which he brought out a portrait of his little German wife, now twenty years deceased, and began calling to her plaintively: "Will you forgive me?" Generally, he was somehow befuddled. And we had a bit to drink in our grief. Soon, however, he fell fast asleep. Next morning he expertly knotted his tie, dressed with care, and went frequently to look at himself in the mirror. He sprayed perfume on his handkerchief—just a tiny bit, by the way— and then, as soon as he caught sight of Varvara Petrovna through the window, he quickly took another handkerchief and hid the perfumed one under the pillow.

"That's splendid!" Varvara Petrovna praised, after hearing his consent. "A noble determination, first of all, and, second, you've heeded the voice of reason, which you so rarely heed in your private affairs. However, there's no need to rush things," she added, examining the knot of his white tie, "say nothing for the time being, and I will say nothing. It will soon be your birthday; I will come to see you with her. Prepare an evening tea and, please, no wine or appetizers; however, I'll see to everything myself. Invite your friends—you and I will make the selection, however. You may have a talk with her the day before if need be; and during your evening we will not really make an announcement or some sort of betrothal, but simply hint or let it be known without any solemnity. And then in two weeks or so you'll be married, with as little noise as possible . . . You both might even go away for a while, right after the ceremony, let's say to Moscow, for instance. Perhaps I'll go with you as well . . . And, above all, say nothing till then."

Stepan Trofimovich was surprised. He tried to murmur that it was impossible that way, that he must have a talk with the fiancée, but Varvara Petrovna fell upon him irritably:

"And what for? First, it's still possible that nothing will happen . . ."

"What? Nothing?" the fiancé muttered, now totally flabbergasted.

"Just so. I still have to see . . . However, everything will be as I've said, and don't worry, I'll prepare her myself. There's no need for you at all. Everything necessary will be said and done, and there's no need of you for that. Why? In what role? Do not come yourself and do not write letters. Not a breath, not a whisper, I beg you. I, too, will say nothing."

She was decidedly unwilling to explain herself and left visibly upset. It seemed she was struck by Stepan Trofimovich's excessive readiness. Alas, he decidedly did not understand his position, and the question had not yet presented itself to him from any other point of view. On the contrary, some new tone emerged, something triumphant and frivolous. He swaggered.

"I like that!" he exclaimed, standing before me and spreading his arms. "Did you hear? She wants to push me so far that I finally will stop wanting it. Because I, too, can lose my patience and . . . stop wanting it! 'Sit still, there's no need for you to go there'—but why, finally, must I get married? Just because of her ridiculous fantasy? But I am a serious man and may not want to submit to the idle fantasies of a whimsical woman! I have duties towards my son and . . . towards myself! I am making a sacrifice—does she understand that? Perhaps I agreed because I'm tired of life and it makes no difference to me. But she may provoke me, and then it will make a difference; I will get offended and refuse. *Et enfin, le ridicule** . . . What will they say at the club? What will . . . what will Liputin say? 'It's still possible that nothing will happen'—fancy that! But that's the limit! That's . . . I don't know what! *Je suis un forçat, un Badinguet,*[8] *un*† man pushed to the wall! . . ."

And at the same time a certain capricious smugness, something frivolously playful, peeped out through all these plaintive exclamations. In the evening we drank some more.

---

*"And finally, the ridicule"
†"I am a galley slave, a Badinguet, a"

3

Someone Else's Sins

I

ABOUT A WEEK went by, and the affair began to expand itself somewhat.

I will observe in passing that I endured much anguish during this unfortunate week, staying almost constantly at the side of my poor matchmade friend in the quality of his closest confidant. It was mainly shame that oppressed him, though during this week we did not see anyone and sat by ourselves all the time; but he was ashamed even before me, and to such an extent that the more he revealed to me, the more vexed he was with me for it. In his insecurity he suspected that everyone already knew everything, all over town, and was afraid to show himself not only at the club but in his own circle as well. Even for a stroll, to get the necessary exercise, he would go out only at full dusk, when it was already quite dark.

A week went by, and he still did not know whether he was engaged or not, and had no way of finding out for certain, however much he tried. He still had not seen the fiancée; did not even know if she was his fiancée; did not even know if there was anything serious in it all! Varvara Petrovna for some reason decidedly did not want to admit him to the house. She replied to one of his first letters (and he wrote her a great many) with a direct request that he spare her any relations with him for the time being, because she was busy, and as she herself had much of the greatest importance to tell him, she was deliberately waiting for a freer moment than the present, and would *in time* let him know herself when he could come to her. And she vowed to send his letters back unopened, because it was all "just sheer indulgence." I myself read this note; he showed it to me.

And yet all of it, all this rudeness and uncertainty, was nothing compared with his chief care. This care tormented him greatly, relentlessly; he kept losing weight over it, and his spirits declined. It was something he was ashamed of most of all, and which he by no means wished to speak about even with me; on the contrary, whenever the occasion arose, he lied and hedged before me like a little boy; and yet he himself would send for me every day, he was unable to be without me even for two hours, needing me like water or air.

Such behavior wounded my pride somewhat. Needless to say, I had long since guessed this chief secret for myself and seen through it all. According to my deepest conviction then, the revealing of this secret, this chief care of Stepan Trofimovich's, would not have added to his credit, and therefore, being still a young man, I was somewhat indignant at the coarseness of his feelings and the ugliness of some of his suspicions. In the heat of passion—and, I confess, finding it boring to be a confidant—I perhaps blamed him too much. In my cruelty, I tried to obtain a full confession from him, though, by the way, I did allow that to confess certain things might prove embarrassing. He, too, understood me thoroughly; that is, he clearly saw that I understood him thoroughly, and that I was even angry with him, and was himself angry with me for being angry with him and for understanding him thoroughly. Perhaps my irritation was petty and stupid; but shared isolation is sometimes extremely damaging to true friendship. From a certain angle he understood some aspects of his position correctly, and even defined it quite subtly in those points about which he did not find it necessary to be secretive.

"Oh, is this how she was then?" he would sometimes let slip about Varvara Petrovna. "Is she the same woman she once was, when she and I used to talk . . . Do you know that she was still able to talk then? Can you believe that she had thoughts then, her own thoughts! That's all changed now! She says it was all just the same old blather! She despises the former times . . . She's become some sort of steward, an economist, a hard person, and she's angry all the time . . ."

"What is there for her to be angry about, since you've done what she demanded?" I objected to him.

He gave me a subtle look.

"*Cher ami*, if I hadn't consented she would have been terribly angry, ter-ri-bly! But still less than she is now that I have consented."

He remained pleased with this phrase of his, and we finished a little bottle that evening. But it was only momentary; the next day he was more terrible and morose than ever.

But I was vexed with him most of all because he could not even bring himself to go and pay the necessary call on the just-arrived Drozdovs, to renew the acquaintance, which it was heard they themselves desired, for they had already asked about him, and which grieved him daily. He spoke of Lizaveta Nikolaevna with a sort of rapture which was incomprehensible to me. No doubt he remembered in her the child he had once loved so much; but, besides that, for some unknown reason he fancied that near her he would at once find relief from all his present torments and would even resolve his most important doubts. He hoped to find some extraordinary being in Lizaveta Nikolaevna. And yet he would not go to her, though he made ready to do so every day. The main thing was that at the time I myself wanted terribly to be introduced and recommended to her, for which I had only Stepan Trofimovich to count on. I had been greatly impressed then by my frequent meetings with her—in the street, of course, when she went for an outing on horseback, dressed in a riding habit and mounted on a beautiful horse, accompanied by her so-called relative, a handsome officer, the late General Drozdov's nephew. My blindness lasted only a moment, and soon afterwards I understood all the impossibility of my dream—but it really did exist, if only for a moment, and therefore it may be imagined how indignant I occasionally became with my poor friend at that time for his persistent seclusion.

Our group was officially notified from the very beginning that Stepan Trofimovich would not be receiving for a while and asked to be left in perfect peace. He insisted on a circular notification, though I advised against it. And so I went around, at his request, and gave out to everyone that Varvara Petrovna had charged our "old man" (as we all referred to Stepan Trofimovich among ourselves) with some urgent work putting in order some correspondence from several years past; that he had locked himself in, and I was helping him, and so on and so forth. Only I had no time to go to Liputin and kept postponing it—or, rather, I was afraid to go. I knew beforehand that he would not believe a single word I said, would certainly imagine that there was some secret which we wanted to keep strictly hidden from him alone, and as soon as I left him would at once scuttle off inquiring and gossiping all over town. It so happened that while I was picturing all this to myself, I accidentally ran into him in the street. It turned out that he had already learned everything from the friends I had just notified. But, strangely, he was not only not curious, and asked nothing about Stepan Trofimovich, but, on the contrary, he himself interrupted me when I tried to apologize for not coming to him sooner, and skipped at once to another subject. True, he had stored up a lot to say; he was in an extremely excited state of mind, and was glad to have caught me as a listener. He began talking about town news, about the arrival of the governor's wife "with her new conversations," the opposition that had already formed in the club, how everyone was shouting about the new ideas, and how well it suited them all, and so on and so forth. He talked for nearly a quarter of an hour, and was so amusing that I was unable to tear myself away. Though I could not stand him, I confess that he had a gift for making one listen to him, especially when he was very angry about something. The man was, in my opinion, a natural-born spy. He knew at any moment all the latest news and all the innermost secrets of our town, mostly of the nasty sort, and one marveled at the degree to which he took things to heart that sometimes did not concern him at all. I always thought that the main feature of his character was envy. When, that same evening, I told Stepan Trofimovich about my morning meeting with Liputin and about our conversation, to my surprise he became extremely agitated and asked me a wild question: "Does Liputin know or not?" I started proving to him that he could not possibly have found out so soon, and had no one to find out from; but Stepan Trofimovich held his own.

"Believe it or not, then," he finally concluded unexpectedly, "but I am convinced that he not only knows all about *our* position in all its details, but also knows something beyond that, something you and I do not know yet, and perhaps will never know, or will find out only when it's already too late, when there will be no turning back! . . ."

I said nothing, but these words hinted at a lot. After that we did not so much as mention Liputin for five days; it was clear to me that Stepan Trofimovich very much regretted having displayed such suspicions before me and having talked too much.

II

ONE MORNING—that is, on the seventh or eighth day after Stepan Trofimovich had consented to become engaged—at about eleven o'clock, when I was rushing as usual to my sorrowful friend, I had an adventure on the way.

I met Karmazinov, the "great writer," as Liputin styled him.[1] I had been reading Karmazinov since childhood. His novellas and stories were known to the whole of the previous generation and even to ours; as for me, I reveled in them; they were the delight of my adolescence and youth. Later I grew somewhat cold to his pen; the tendentious novellas he had been writing lately I liked less than his first, original creations, in which there was so much ingenuous poetry; and his most recent works I even did not like at all.

Generally speaking, if I dare express my own opinion in such a ticklish matter, all these gentlemen talents of the average sort, who are usually taken almost for geniuses in their lifetime, not only vanish from people's memory almost without a trace and somehow suddenly when they die, but it happens that even in their lifetime, as soon as a new generation grows up to replace the one in whose time they were active—they are forgotten and scorned by everyone inconceivably quickly. This happens somehow suddenly with us, like a change of sets in the theater. Oh, it is quite another matter than with the Pushkins, Gogols, Molières, Voltaires,[2] with all these figures who came to speak their new word! It is also true that these gentlemen talents of the average sort, in the decline of their venerable age, usually write themselves out in a most pathetic way, without even noticing it at all. Not infrequently it turns out that a writer to whom an extreme profundity of ideas had long been attributed, and from whom an extreme and serious influence upon the movement of society was expected, in the end displays such thinness and puniness in his basic little idea that no one is even sorry that he has managed to write himself out so quickly. But the old graybeards do not notice this and get angry. Their vanity, precisely towards the end of their career, sometimes takes on proportions worthy of wonder. God knows who they begin to think they are—gods, at the least. It was said of Karmazinov that he valued his connections with influential people and with higher society almost more than his soul. It was said that he would meet you, show you kindness, seduce you, charm you with his ingenuousness, especially if he needed you for some reason, and most certainly if you had been recommended to him beforehand. But at the first prince, at the first countess, at the first person he was in fear of, he would regard it as his sacred duty to forget you with the most insulting disdain, like a speck, like a fly, then and there, even before you had time to leave him; he seriously considered it the most lofty and beautiful tone. In spite of his complete self-possession and perfect knowledge of good manners, he was said to be so vain, to the point of such hysterics, that he was simply unable to conceal his authorial petulance, even in those social circles where there was little interest in literature. And if someone chanced to confound him with their indifference, he would be morbidly offended and seek to revenge himself.

About a year before, I had read an article of his in a magazine, written with a terrible pretension to the most naïve poetry and, at the same time, to psychology. He described the wreck of a steamer somewhere on the English coast, of which he himself had been a witness and had seen how the perishing were being saved and the drowned dragged out. The whole article, quite a long and verbose one, was written with the sole purpose of self-display. One could simply read it between the lines: "Pay attention to me, look at how I was in those moments. What do you need the sea, the storm, the rocks, the splintered planks of the ship for? I've described it all well enough for you with my mighty pen. Why look at this drowned woman with her dead baby in her dead arms? Better look at me, at how I could not bear the sight and turned away. Here I am turning my back; here I am horrified and unable to look again; I've shut my eyes—interesting, is it not?" I told Stepan Trofimovich my opinion of Karmazinov's article, and he agreed with me.

When rumors began to spread recently that Karmazinov was coming, I, of course, wanted terribly to see him and, if possible, to make his acquaintance. I knew that I could do so through Stepan Trofimovich; they had been friends once upon a time. And now I suddenly met him at an intersection. I recognized him at once; he had already been pointed out to me three days earlier as he rode past in a carriage with the governor's wife.

He was quite a short, prim little old man, though no more than fifty-five, with a rather red-cheeked little face, with thick gray locks emerging from under his round cylindrical hat and curling behind his clean, pink little ears. His clean little face was not exactly handsome, with its thin, long, slyly compressed lips, its somewhat fleshy nose, and its sharp, intelligent little eyes. He was dressed somehow shabbily, with a sort of cloak thrown over his shoulders such as would have been worn at that season somewhere in Switzerland, say, or the north of Italy. But at least all the minor accessories of his costume—the little cuff links, collar, studs, the tortoiseshell lorgnette on its narrow black ribbon, the little signet ring—were most assuredly just as they are with people of irreproachably good tone. I am sure that in summer he certainly went around in bright prunella bootikins with mother-of-pearl buttons at the side. When we ran into each other, he had stopped for a moment at the street corner and was looking around with attention. Noticing that I was looking at him curiously, he asked me in a honeyed, though somewhat shrill, little voice:

"Would you be so good as to tell me the shortest way to Bykov Street?"

"Bykov Street? But it's here, right here," I cried out in unusual excitement. "Keep straight on this way, then second turn to the left."

"I am much obliged to you."

Cursed be that moment: I seemed to have grown timid and looked fawning! He instantly noticed everything, and, of course, understood everything at once—that is, understood that I already knew who he was, that I had read him and revered him since childhood, and that I had just grown timid and looked fawning. He smiled, nodded his head once more, and went straight on as I had directed him. I do not know why I turned to follow him; I do not know why I went running alongside him for about ten paces. He suddenly stopped again.

"And might you be able to tell me where the nearest cabstand is located?" he shouted to me again.

A nasty shout; a nasty voice!

"Cabstand? The nearest cabstand . . . is by the cathedral, that's where they always stand"—and I almost turned and ran to fetch a cab. I suspect that that was precisely what he expected of me. Of course, I came to my senses at once and stopped, but he had made good note of my movement and went on watching me with the same nasty smile. What happened then I shall never forget.

He suddenly dropped a tiny satchel that he was holding in his left hand. It was not a satchel, by the way, but a sort of little box, or rather a sort of briefcase, or, better still, a little reticule such as ladies once used to carry, but I do not know what it was, I only know that it seems I rushed to pick it up.

I am perfectly convinced that I did not pick it up, but my initial movement was unquestionable; it was too late to conceal it, and I blushed like a fool. The cunning fellow at once derived all that could be derived from this circumstance.

"Don't trouble, I'll do it myself," he said charmingly—that is, once he had fully noted that I was not going to pick up his reticule—picked it up as if forestalling me, nodded his head once more, and went on his way, having made a fool of me. It was the same as if I had picked it up myself. For about five minutes I considered myself disgraced utterly and forever; but coming up to Stepan Trofimovich's house, I suddenly burst out laughing. The encounter seemed so funny to me that I immediately decided to amuse Stepan Trofimovich by telling him about it and even acting out the whole scene.

III

BUT THIS TIME, to my surprise, I found him in an extreme change. True, he fell upon me with a sort of greediness as soon as I entered, and began listening to me, but with such a lost look that at first he appeared not to understand what I was saying. But as soon as I uttered the name of Karmazinov, he suddenly flew into a complete frenzy.

"Don't tell me, don't utter!" he exclaimed, all but in a rage. "Here, here, look, read! read!"

He pulled open the drawer and threw onto the table three small scraps of paper, hastily written on in pencil, all of them from Varvara Petrovna. The first note was from two days ago, the second from yesterday, and the last had come today, just an hour earlier; they were all of the most vapid content, to do with Karmazinov, betraying Varvara Petrovna's vain and ambitious concern for fear that Karmazinov might forget to call on her. Here is the first one, from two days ago (there had probably also been one from three days ago, and perhaps one from four days ago):

> If he finally honors you today, not a word about me, I beg you. Not the slightest hint. No mention, no reminder.
>
> V.S.

And yesterday's:

> If he finally decides to call on you this morning, I think the most noble thing would be not to receive him at all. That is my opinion, I don't know what yours is.
>
> V.S.

And today's, the latest:

> I'm sure you have a whole heap of litter there and clouds of tobacco smoke. I'll send you Marya and Fomushka; they'll tidy up in half an hour. And don't get in their way, just sit in the kitchen while they're tidying up. I'm sending you a Bukhara rug and two Chinese jars—I've long been meaning to give them to you—and also my Teniers[3] (for a time). You can put the vases on the windowsill and hang the Teniers to the right above Goethe's portrait, it's a more conspicuous place and always light in the morning. If he finally appears, receive him with refined courtesy, but try to talk about trifles, about something learned, and make it seem as if you parted only yesterday. Not a word about me. Perhaps I'll stop by for a look this evening.
>
> V.S.
>
> P.S. If he doesn't come today, he won't come at all.

I read and was surprised that he was so agitated over such trifles. Glancing at him questioningly, I suddenly noticed that he had had time, while I was reading, to change his usual white tie for a red one. His hat and stick lay on the table. He was pale, and his hands were even trembling.

"I won't hear of her worries!" he cried out frenziedly, in response to my questioning glance. *"Je m'en fiche!** She has the heart to worry about Karmazinov, and yet she doesn't answer my letters! Here, here is a letter she returned to me unopened yesterday, here on the table, under the book, under *L'Homme qui rit.*[4] What do I care if she's grieving over Ni-ko-lenka! *Je m'en fiche et je proclame ma liberté. Au diable le Karmazinoff! Au diable la Lembke!*† I put the vases away in the front hall, and Teniers into the chest, and demanded that she receive me at once. Do you hear: demanded! I sent her an identical scrap of paper, in pencil, unsealed, through Nastasya, and I am waiting. I want Darya Pavlovna herself to tell me with her own lips, and before the face of heaven, or at least before you. *Vous me seconderez, n'est-ce pas, comme ami et témoin.*‡ I do not want to blush, I do not want to lie, I do not want secrets, I will not allow secrets in this matter! Let them confess everything to me sincerely, guilelessly, nobly, and then . . . then perhaps I'll surprise the whole generation with my magnanimity! . . . Am I a scoundrel or not, my dear sir?" he concluded suddenly, giving me a menacing look, as though it were I who considered him a scoundrel.

I suggested that he drink some water; I had never before seen him like this. All the while he was speaking, he kept running from one corner of the room to the other, but suddenly he stopped before me in some extraordinary attitude.

"Can you really think," he began again, with morbid haughtiness, looking me up and down, "can you really suppose that I, Stepan Verkhovensky, will not find moral strength enough to take my box— my beggar's box—and, heaving it onto my weak shoulders, go out the gate and disappear from here forever, if honor and the great principle

---

*"I don't give a damn!"
†"I don't give a damn and I proclaim my freedom. To the devil with Karmazinov! To the devil with the Lembke woman!"
‡"You will second me, won't you, as friend and witness."

of independence demand? This is not the first time that Stepan Verkhovensky will have to repel despotism with magnanimity, be it only
the despotism of a crazy woman—that is, the most offensive and cruel
despotism that can possibly exist in the world, despite the fact that you
now permit yourself, it seems, to smile at my words, my dear sir! Oh,
you do not believe that I can find enough magnanimity in myself to
be able to end my life as a tutor in some merchant's house, or die of
hunger in a ditch! Answer me, answer me at once: do you believe it,
or do you not?"

But I purposely held my tongue. I even pretended that I did not dare
to offend him with a negative answer, but could not answer positively
either. There was something in all this irritation that decidedly offended me, and not personally—oh, no! But . . . I will explain myself
later.

He even turned pale.

"Perhaps you're bored with me, G——v" (that is my last name),
"and would prefer . . . not to come to me at all?" he said, in that tone
of pale composure that usually precedes some extraordinary explosion.
I jumped up in fright; at the same moment, Nastasya walked in and
silently handed Stepan Trofimovich a piece of paper with something
written on it in pencil. He glanced at it and threw it over to me. On
the piece of paper, in Varvara Petrovna's hand, were written just two
words: "Stay home."

Stepan Trofimovich silently grabbed his hat and stick and went
quickly to the door; I followed him mechanically. Suddenly voices and
the sound of someone's rapid footsteps came from the hallway. He
stopped as if thunderstruck.

"That's Liputin, and I am a lost man!" he whispered, seizing my
arm.

At the same moment, Liputin entered the room.

IV

W HY HE SHOULD be a lost man as the result of Liputin I did not
know, nor did I attach much importance to his words; I ascribed

it all to nerves. But even so his fright was extraordinary, and I decided to watch closely.

By his look alone the entering Liputin already announced that this time he had a special right to enter, in spite of all prohibitions. He led in an unknown gentleman who must have been a newcomer to town. In reply to the senseless stare of the dumbfounded Stepan Trofimovich, he at once loudly proclaimed:

"I bring you a visitor, and a special one! I make so bold as to break in upon your seclusion. Mr. Kirillov, a remarkable structural engineer. And the main thing is that he knows your boy, the much respected Pyotr Stepanovich; very closely, sir; and he has an errand from him. He has just arrived, if you please."

"You added that about the errand," the visitor remarked curtly, "there was never any errand, but it's true I know Verkhovensky. I left him in Kh—— province, ten days before here."

Stepan Trofimovich mechanically held out his hand and pointed to the seats; he looked at me, looked at Liputin, and suddenly, as if coming to his senses, hastened to sit down, still holding his hat and stick without noticing it.

"Hah, but you were about to go out! And I was told that your studies had left you quite indisposed."

"Yes, I'm ill, I was just intending to go for a walk, I . . ." Stepan Trofimovich stopped, quickly threw his hat and stick on the sofa, and—blushed.

Meanwhile, I made a hurried examination of the visitor. He was still a young man, about twenty-seven years old, decently dressed, trim and lean, dark-haired, with a pale face of a somewhat muddy tinge and black, lusterless eyes. He seemed somewhat pensive and absentminded, spoke abruptly and somehow ungrammatically, somehow strangely shuffling his words, and became confused when he had to put together a longer phrase. Liputin noticed very well how extremely frightened Stepan Trofimovich was, and this apparently pleased him. He sat on a wicker chair, which he pulled almost into the middle of the room so as to be at an equal distance from the host and the visitor, who had installed themselves facing each other on two opposing sofas. His sharp eyes darted curiously into every corner.

"I . . . haven't seen Petrusha for a long time now . . . Did you meet abroad?" Stepan Trofimovich barely muttered to the visitor.

"Both here and abroad."

"Alexei Nilych himself has just returned from abroad, after a four-year absence," Liputin picked up. "He went to advance himself in his profession, and came here having reasons to hope he could obtain a position for the building of our railroad bridge, and is now awaiting an answer. He knows Mrs. Drozdov and Lizaveta Nikolaevna through Pyotr Stepanovich."

The engineer sat looking ruffled and listened with awkward impatience. It seemed to me that he was angry about something.

"He knows Nikolai Vsevolodovich, too, sir."

"You know Nikolai Vsevolodovich, too?" Stepan Trofimovich inquired.

"Him, too."

"I . . . I haven't seen Petrusha for an extremely long time, and . . . I find I have so little right to be called a father . . . *c'est le mot;* * I . . . how did you leave him?"

"I just left him . . . he'll be coming himself," Mr. Kirillov again hastened to get off. He was decidedly angry.

"He'll be coming! At last I . . . you see, I haven't seen Petrusha for so very long!" Stepan Trofimovich had gotten mired in this phrase. "I'm now awaiting my poor boy, before whom . . . oh, before whom I am so guilty! That is, as a matter of fact, I mean to say, when I left him then in Petersburg, I . . . in short, I regarded him as nothing, *quelque chose dans ce genre.* † A nervous boy, you know, very sensitive and . . . fearful. Before going to sleep, he'd bow to the ground and make a cross over his pillow, so as not to die in the night . . . *je m'en souviens. Enfin,* ‡ no sense of refinement whatsoever, that is, of anything lofty, essential, of any germ of a future idea . . . *c'était comme un petit idiot.* § However, I seem to be confused myself, excuse me, I . . . you have caught me . . ."

---

*"that's the word"
†"something of that sort."
‡"I remember it. Finally"
§"he was like a little idiot."

"You're serious about him crossing his pillow?" the engineer suddenly inquired with some special curiosity.

"Yes, he crossed . . ."

"No, never mind. Go on."

Stepan Trofimovich looked questioningly at Liputin.

"I thank you very much for your visit, but, I confess, right now I'm . . . unable . . . However, allow me to ask, where are you staying?"

"In Bogoyavlensky Street, at Filippov's house."

"Ah, the same place where Shatov lives," I remarked involuntarily.

"Precisely the same house," Liputin exclaimed, "only Shatov is staying upstairs in the garret, and he is downstairs, at Captain Lebyadkin's. He also knows Shatov, and he knows Shatov's wife. He met her very closely abroad."

"*Comment!** Do you really know something about this unfortunate marriage *de ce pauvre ami*,† and this woman?" Stepan Trofimovich exclaimed suddenly, carried away by emotion. "You are the first one I've met who knows her personally; and if only . . ."

"What nonsense!" the engineer snapped, blushing all over. "How you add on, Liputin! Nohow did I see Shatov's wife; just once far off, not close at all . . . Shatov I know. Why do you add on various things?"

He turned sharply on the sofa, seized his hat, then put it down again, and, having settled himself as before, fixed his black and now flashing eyes on Stepan Trofimovich with some sort of defiance. I was quite unable to understand such strange irritability.

"Excuse me," Stepan Trofimovich remarked imposingly, "I understand that this may be a most delicate matter . . ."

"There's no most delicate matter here, and it's even shameful, and I shouted 'nonsense' not at you but at Liputin, because he adds on. Excuse me if you took it to your name. I know Shatov, but I don't know his wife at all . . . not at all!"

"I understand, I understand, and if I insisted, it was only because I love our poor friend, *notre irascible ami*,‡ very much, and have always

---

*"How's that!"
†"of this poor friend"
‡"our irascible friend"

taken an interest . . . In my opinion, the man changed his former, perhaps too youthful, but still correct ideas too abruptly. And now he shouts various things about *notre sainte Russie,** so much so that I've long attributed this break in his organism, for I do not want to call it anything else, to some strong family shock—namely, to his unsuccessful marriage. I, who have come to know my poor Russia like my own two fingers, and have given my whole life to the Russian people, can assure you that he does not know the Russian people,[5] and what's more . . ."

"I don't know the Russian people either, and . . . there's no time to study!" the engineer snapped again, and again turned sharply on the sofa. Stepan Trofimovich broke off in the middle of his speech.

"He's studying, he's studying," Liputin picked up, "he's already begun studying, and is composing a most curious article on the reasons for the increasing number of suicides in Russia and generally on the reasons for the increase or restriction of the spread of suicides in society. He's reached some surprising results."

The engineer became terribly agitated.

"You have no right about that," he began to mutter angrily. "Not an article. No such foolishness. I asked you confidentially, quite by chance. Not an article at all; I don't publish, and you have no right . . ."

Liputin was obviously enjoying himself.

"I beg your pardon, perhaps I was mistaken in calling your literary work an article. He only collects observations, and as for the essence of the question, or its moral side, so to speak, he doesn't touch on that at all, he even rejects morality itself outright, and holds to the newest principle of universal destruction for the sake of good final goals. He's already demanding more than a hundred million heads in order to establish common sense in Europe, much more than was demanded at the last peace congress. In this sense, Alexei Nilych goes further than anyone."

The engineer listened with a contemptuous and pale smile. For half a minute or so everyone was silent.

"This is all stupid, Liputin," Mr. Kirillov said finally, with a certain

*"our holy Russia"

dignity. "If I accidentally told you a few points, and you picked them up, it's as you like. But you have no right, because I never tell anyone. I despise about telling . . . If one has convictions, it's clear to me . . . and you've acted stupidly. I don't reason about these points that are done with. I can't stand reasoning. I never want to reason . . ."

"And perhaps it's quite wonderful that you don't," Stepan Trofimovich could not help saying.

"I excuse myself to you, but I am not angry with anyone here," the visitor continued in an ardent patter. "For four years I've seen little of people . . . For four years I've spoken little and tried to meet no one, for my own purposes, which don't matter, for four years. Liputin found out and laughs. I understand and do not regard. I'm not easy to offend, it's just vexing because of his liberty. And if I don't explain thoughts with you," he concluded unexpectedly, looking around at us with a firm look, "it is not at all as I'm afraid of being denounced to the government, no, not that; please do not think any trifles in that sense . . ."

None of us made any reply to these words, we merely exchanged glances. Even Liputin himself forgot to titter.

"Gentlemen, I'm very sorry," Stepan Trofimovich rose from the sofa, "but I'm feeling unwell and upset. Excuse me."

"Ah, about us leaving," Mr. Kirillov suddenly recollected, seizing his cap. "It's good you said; I'm forgetful."

He stood up and with a simplehearted look went over to Stepan Trofimovich, holding out his hand.

"Sorry you're not well and I came."

"I wish you all success here," Stepan Trofimovich replied, shaking his hand well-wishingly and unhurriedly. "I understand that if you have lived so long abroad, as you say, avoiding people for your own purposes, and—have forgotten Russia, then, of course, whether you will or no, you must look at us dyed-in-the-wool Russians with surprise, and, in the same measure, we at you. *Mais cela passera.** Only one thing puzzles me: you want to build our bridge, and at the same time you declare yourself for the principle of universal destruction. They'll never let you build our bridge!"

*"But that will pass."

"What? What did you say . . . ah, the devil!" Kirillov exclaimed, amazed, and suddenly burst into the most gay and bright laughter. For a moment his face took on a most childlike expression, which I found very becoming to him. Liputin was rubbing his hands, delighted with Stepan Trofimovich's little witticism. Meanwhile, I kept wondering to myself why Stepan Trofimovich was so afraid of Liputin, and why he had cried out, "I am a lost man," when he heard him coming.

V

WE WERE STILL standing on the threshold, in the doorway. It was that moment when hosts and guests hasten to exchange their last and most amiable words and then happily part.

"He's so sullen today just because," Liputin suddenly put in as he was leaving the room and, so to speak, on the wing, "just because of some row he had earlier with Captain Lebyadkin over his dear sister. The captain whips that beautiful sister of his, the crazy one, with a quirt, a real Cossack quirt, sir, every day, morning and evening. So Alexei Nilych has even moved to another wing of the house so as to have no part of it. Well, sir, good-bye."

"Sister? Ill? With a quirt?" Stepan Trofimovich cried out, as if he himself had suddenly been lashed with a quirt. "What sister? What Lebyadkin?"

His former fear instantly returned.

"Lebyadkin? He's a retired captain; only he used to call himself a captain junior-grade . . ."

"Eh, what do I care about his rank! What sister? My God . . . Lebyadkin, you say? But we had a Lebyadkin . . ."

"That's the very one, *our* Lebyadkin—remember, at Virginsky's?"

"But that one was caught with bogus banknotes?"

"And now he's back, since three weeks ago, and under the most peculiar circumstances."

"But he's a scoundrel!"

"What, can't we have any scoundrels around here?" Liputin suddenly grinned, as if he were feeling Stepan Trofimovich all over with his thievish little eyes.

"Ah, my God, I don't mean that . . . though, by the way, I quite agree with you about the scoundrel, with you precisely. But go on, go on! What did you mean by that? . . . You must have meant something by that!"

"It's all really such trifles, sir . . . that is, this captain, in all likelihood, left us then not from the bogus banknotes, but just so as to find this sister of his, and she was allegedly hiding in some unknown place; well, and now he's brought her, that's the whole story. Why is it you seem so frightened, Stepan Trofimovich? I'm only repeating his drunken babble, anyway; when he's sober he keeps mum about it. He's an irritable man and, shall we say, of military aesthetics, only in bad taste. And this sister is not only mad, but even lame. She supposedly had her honor seduced by somebody, and for that Mr. Lebyadkin has supposedly been taking an annual tribute from the seducer for many years, in reward for a noble offense, so at least it comes out from his babble—but I think it's just drunken talk, sir. He's simply boasting. Such things are handled more cheaply. But that he has money—that is completely correct: a week and a half ago he was walking around without socks, and now I've seen for myself he has hundreds in his hands. His sister has some kind of fits every day, she shrieks, and he 'puts her in order' with a quirt. One has to instill respect into a woman, he says. Only I don't understand how Shatov can go on living near them. Alexei Nilych stayed just three days, he's known them since Petersburg, and now he's living in the wing on account of the disturbance."

"Is this all true?" Stepan Trofimovich turned to the engineer.

"You're babbling too much, Liputin," the latter muttered angrily.

"Mysteries! Secrets! Where did we get so many mysteries and secrets all of a sudden!" Stepan Trofimovich exclaimed, not restraining himself.

The engineer frowned, blushed, heaved his shoulders, and started out of the room.

"Alexei Nilych even snatched away his quirt, sir, broke it, and threw it out the window, and there was a big quarrel," Liputin added.

"What are you babbling for, Liputin, it's stupid, what for?" Alexei Nilych at once turned back again.

"And why conceal out of modesty the noblest impulses of one's soul—your soul, that is, sir, I'm not talking about mine."

"How stupid this is . . . and quite unnecessary . . . Lebyadkin is stupid and completely empty—useless for action and . . . completely harmful. Why do you babble various things? I'm leaving."

"Ah, what a pity!" Liputin exclaimed, with a bright smile. "Otherwise I'd get you to laugh, Stepan Trofimovich, with yet another little anecdote. I even came with that in mind, though anyway you must have heard it yourself. Well, let's wait till next time, Alexei Nilych is in such a hurry . . . Good-bye, sir. The anecdote is about Varvara Petrovna, she really made me laugh the day before yesterday, she sent for me on purpose, it's really killing! Good-bye, sir."

But here Stepan Trofimovich simply fastened on to him: he seized him by the shoulders, turned him sharply back into the room, and sat him on a chair. Liputin even got scared.

"But it really is, sir!" he began, looking cautiously at Stepan Trofimovich from his chair. "She suddenly sent for me and asked 'confidentially' what I think in my own opinion: is Nikolai Vsevolodovich crazy, or in his right mind? Isn't that surprising?"

"You're out of your mind!" Stepan Trofimovich muttered, and suddenly seemed beside himself: "Liputin, you know perfectly well that you came here only in order to tell me some abomination of that sort and . . . something worse still!"

I instantly recalled his surmise that Liputin not only knew more about our situation than we did, but even knew something that we ourselves would never know.

"For pity's sake, Stepan Trofimovich!" Liputin muttered, as if terribly frightened, "for pity's sake . . ."

"Keep still and begin! I beg you, too, Mr. Kirillov, to come back and be present, I beg you! Sit down. And you, Liputin, begin directly, simply . . . and without any little excuses!"

"If I'd only known you'd be so astounded by it, I wouldn't have begun at all, sir . . . But I really did think you already knew everything from Varvara Petrovna herself!"

"You didn't think anything of the kind! Begin, begin, I tell you!"

"Only do me a favor, sit down yourself, or else I'll be sitting and you'll be . . . running about in front of me all agitated. It will be awkward, sir."

Stepan Trofimovich restrained himself and sank imposingly into an armchair. The engineer sullenly fixed his eyes on the ground. Liputin looked at them with wild delight.

"How shall I begin . . . you've got me so confused . . ."

VI

"ALL OF A SUDDEN, the day before yesterday, she sent her servant to me: 'You are requested,' he says, 'to visit tomorrow at twelve o'clock.' Can you imagine? I dropped what I was doing, and yesterday at twelve sharp was there ringing the bell. I'm taken straight to the drawing room; I wait for a minute—she comes in, sits me down, sits down facing me. I sit and just can't believe it; you know how she's always treated me! The lady begins directly, without dodging, in her usual way: 'You remember,' she says, 'that four years ago Nikolai Vsevolodovich, while ill, committed several strange acts, so that the whole town was puzzled until everything became clear. One of these acts concerned you personally. Nikolai Vsevolodovich then came to see you after he recovered and at my request. I am also informed that he had spoken with you several times before. Tell me, frankly and straightforwardly, how did you . . .' (here she hesitated a little) 'how did you find Nikolai Vsevolodovich then . . . how did you regard him generally . . . what opinion were you able to form of him . . . and do you have of him now? . . .'

"Here she really hesitated, so that she even stopped for a whole minute and suddenly blushed. I got scared. She begins again, not so much in a moving tone—that wouldn't be like her—but so imposingly:

" 'I wish you,' she says, 'to understand me fully and correctly,' she says. 'I sent for you now because I consider you a perspicacious and sharp-witted man, capable of forming an accurate observation' (such compliments!). 'You,' she says, 'will also understand, of course, that this is a mother speaking to you . . . Nikolai Vsevolodovich has experienced certain misfortunes and many upheavals in his life. All this,' she says, 'could influence his frame of mind. Of course,' she says, 'I am not talking about madness—that could never be!' (spoken firmly and with pride). 'But there could be something strange, peculiar, a certain turn of thought, an inclination towards certain special views' (these are all her exact words, and I marveled, Stepan Trofimovich, at how exactly Varvara Petrovna is able to explain the matter. A lady of high intelligence!). 'I myself, at least,' she says, 'have noticed a certain constant restlessness in him, and an urge towards peculiar inclinations. But I am a mother, while you are an outsider and are therefore capable, given your intelligence, of forming a more independent opinion. I implore you, finally' (uttered just like that: 'I implore'), 'to tell me the whole truth, without any contortions, and if at the same time you give me your promise never to forget in future that I have spoken with you confidentially, you may expect of me a complete and henceforth permanent readiness to show my gratitude at every opportunity.' Well, what do you think of that, sir!"

"You . . . you astound me so . . ." Stepan Trofimovich stammered, "that I don't believe you . . ."

"No, but observe, observe," Liputin picked up, as if he had not even heard Stepan Trofimovich, "how great the trouble and worry must be, if such a question is addressed from such a height to such a man as me, and if she stoops so far as to beg for secrecy. What can it be, sir? Has she received some unexpected news about Nikolai Vsevolodovich?"

"I don't know . . . any news . . . it's some days since I've seen . . . but I must observe to you . . ." Stepan Trofimovich went on stammering, apparently barely able to master his thoughts, "but I must observe to you, Liputin, that if this was told you confidentially, and now, in front of everyone, you . . ."

"Absolutely confidentially! God strike me dead if I . . . And so what if now . . . what of it, sir? Are we strangers here, even taking Alexei Nilych?"

"I do not share such a view; no doubt the three of us here will keep the secret; it is you, the fourth, that I am afraid of, and I do not believe you in anything!"

"Oh, come now, sir! I'm the one who has most to gain, it's to me the eternal gratitude was promised! And, in this same connection, I precisely wanted to mention an extremely strange occurrence—or more psychological, so to speak, than simply strange. Yesterday evening, under the influence of that conversation at Varvara Petrovna's (you can imagine what an impression it made on me), I addressed Alexei Nilych with a distant question: 'You,' I say, 'used to know

Nikolai Vsevolodovich even before, abroad and in Petersburg; what do you think,' I say, 'regarding his intelligence and abilities?' So this gentleman answers laconically, as his way is, that he is a man 'of refined mind and sound judgment,' he says. 'And didn't you ever notice over the years,' I say, 'some deviation of ideas, as it were, or a peculiar turn of thought, or as if some madness, so to speak?' In short, I repeated Varvara Petrovna's own question. And just imagine, Alexei Nilych suddenly turned thoughtful and scowled, just as he's doing now. 'Yes,' he says, 'at times it seemed to me there was something strange.' Note, besides, that if there could seem something strange even to Alexei Nilych, then what might turn out in reality, eh?"

"Is this true?" Stepan Trofimovich turned to Alexei Nilych.

"I wish not to speak of it," Alexei Nilych replied, suddenly raising his head and flashing his eyes. "I want to contest your right, Liputin. You have no right to this occurrence about me. I by no means told my whole opinion. Though I was acquainted in Petersburg, that was long ago, and though I met him now, I still know Nikolai Stavrogin very little. I ask that you remove me and . . . and this all resembles gossip."

Liputin spread his arms in the guise of oppressed innocence.

"A gossip, am I! And maybe also a spy? It's easy for you to criticize, Alexei Nilych, since you remove yourself from everything. But you wouldn't believe it, Stepan Trofimovich, take even Captain Lebyadkin, sir, one might think he's stupid as a . . . that is, it's even shameful to say as what—there's a Russian comparison signifying the degree— but he, too, considers himself offended from Nikolai Vsevolodovich, though he bows to his sharp wits. 'The man amazes me,' he says, 'a wise serpent' (his very words). So I asked him (still under yesterday's same influence and after talking with Alexei Nilych), 'And what do you think for your own part, Captain, is your wise serpent crazy, or not?' And, can you believe, it was as if I'd given him a lash from behind without asking permission; he simply jumped in his seat. 'Yes,' he says . . . 'Yes,' he says, 'only that,' he says, 'cannot affect . . .' but affect what—he didn't finish saying; and then he turned so ruefully thought-ful, so thoughtful that even his drunkenness dropped off him. We were sitting in Filippov's tavern, sir. And only maybe half an hour later he suddenly banged his fist on the table: 'Yes,' he says, 'maybe he is crazy, only that cannot affect . . .' and again he didn't finish saying what it

couldn't affect. Of course, I'm telling you only an extract of the conversation, but the thought is clear; whoever you ask, they all come up
with the same thought, even if it never entered anybody's head before:
'Yes,' they say, 'crazy—very intelligent, but maybe also crazy.' "

Stepan Trofimovich sat deep in thought, his mind working in-
tensely.

"And why does Lebyadkin know?"

"Be so good as to make that inquiry of Alexei Nilych, who has just
called me a spy. I am a spy, yet I don't know—while Alexei Nilych
knows all the innermost secrets and keeps silent, sir."

"I know nothing, or little," the engineer replied, with the same
irritation. "You pour drink into Lebyadkin in order to find out. You
also brought me here in order to find out, and to get me to say. So you
are a spy!"

"I've never yet poured any drink into him, sir, and he's not worth
the money, with all his secrets—that's how much he means to me, I
don't know about you. On the contrary, he's throwing money around,
though twelve days ago he came to beg me for fifteen kopecks, and he's
pouring champagne into me, not I into him. But you've given me an
idea, and if need be I will get him drunk, precisely in order to find
things out, and perhaps I will learn, sir . . . all your little secrets, sir,"
Liputin snarled back spitefully.

Bewildered, Stepan Trofimovich observed the two quarreling men.
They were giving themselves away and, moreover, were being quite
unceremonious about it. It occurred to me that Liputin had brought
this Alexei Nilych to us precisely so as to draw him into the conversation he wanted through a third person—his favorite maneuver.

"Alexei Nilych knows Nikolai Vsevolodovich only too well," he
went on irritably, "but he conceals it. And as for your question about
Captain Lebyadkin, he met him before any of us, in Petersburg, five
or six years ago, in that little-known epoch, if I may put it so, of Nikolai
Vsevolodovich's life when he had not yet even thought of doing us the
happiness of coming here. Our prince, one can only conclude, surrounded himself at that time in Petersburg with a very odd choice of
acquaintances. It was then, I believe, that he became acquainted with
Alexei Nilych."

"Beware, Liputin, I warn you that Nikolai Vsevolodovich is intending to be here in person soon, and he knows how to stand up for himself."

"And how do I deserve this, sir? I am the first one to shout that he's a man of the most refined and elegant mind, and I set Varvara Petrovna completely at ease yesterday in that regard. 'Only,' I said to her, 'I cannot vouch for his character.' Yesterday Lebyadkin said it in so many words: 'I've suffered from his character,' he said. Ah, Stepan Trofimovich, it's fine for you to shout about gossiping and spying, and that, notice, when you yourself have already extorted everything from me, and with such exceeding curiosity besides. And Varvara Petrovna, she really put her finger on it yesterday: 'You had a personal interest in the matter,' she says, 'that's why I'm turning to you.' And what else, sir! Why talk about purposes, when I swallowed a personal offense from His Excellency in front of a whole gathering! It would seem I have reasons to be interested, not just for the sake of gossip. Today he shakes your hand, and tomorrow, for no reason at all, to repay your hospitality, he slaps your face in front of a whole honorable gathering, the moment he pleases. From fat living, sir! And the main thing with them is the female sex: butterflies and strutting roosters! Landowners with little wings like antique cupids, lady-killer Pechorins![6] It's easy for you, Stepan Trofimovich, an inveterate bachelor, to talk this way and call me a gossip on account of His Excellency. But if you, being the fine fellow you still are, were to marry a pretty and young one, you might just keep your door bolted against our prince, and build barricades in your own house! But why go far: if this Mademoiselle Lebyadkin, who gets whipped with knouts, weren't mad and bow-legged, by God, I'd think it was she who was the victim of our general's passions, and that this is what Captain Lebyadkin has suffered 'in his familial dignity,' as he himself puts it. Only maybe it contradicts his refined taste, but that's no great trouble to him. Any berry will do, so long as it comes his way while he's in a certain mood. You talk about gossip, but I'm not shouting about it, the whole town is clattering, while I just listen and yes them—yessing's not forbidden, sir."

"The town is shouting? What is it shouting about?"

"That is, it's Captain Lebyadkin, in a drunken state, who's shouting for the whole town to hear—well, and isn't that the same as if the whole marketplace was shouting? How am I to blame? I'm interested only as among friends, sir, because I still consider myself among friends here." He looked around at us with an innocent air. "There was an incident here, sirs, just think: it seems His Excellency, while still in Switzerland, supposedly sent three hundred roubles by a most noble girl and, so to speak, humble orphan, whom I have the honor of knowing, to be given to Captain Lebyadkin. But a little later Lebyadkin received most precise information, I won't say from whom, but also from a most noble and therefore most reliable person, that the sum sent was not three hundred roubles, but a thousand! . . . 'That means,' Lebyadkin is shouting, 'that the girl filched seven hundred roubles from me,' and he wants to demand it back even if it's through the police, at least he's threatening to, and he's clattering all over town . . ."

"That is mean, mean of you!" the engineer suddenly jumped up from his chair.

"But you yourself are that most noble person who confirmed to Lebyadkin on Nikolai Vsevolodovich's behalf that it was not three hundred but a thousand roubles that were sent. The captain himself told me in a drunken state."

"That . . . that is an unfortunate misunderstanding. Someone made a mistake and it came out . . . that is nonsense, and you are mean! . . ."

"But I also want to believe that it's nonsense, and I listen to it with regret, because, whether you like it or not, a most noble girl is mixed up, first of all, with the seven hundred roubles and, second, in some obvious intimacy with Nikolai Vsevolodovich. It's nothing for His Excellency to disgrace the noblest girl or to defame another man's wife, just as in that mishap with me, sir! He'll come across some man full of magnanimity and make him cover up someone else's sins with his honorable name. Just the same way as I suffered, sir; I'm talking about myself, sir . . ."

"Beware, Liputin!" Stepan Trofimovich rose from his chair and turned pale.

"Don't believe it, don't believe it! Someone made a mistake, and Lebyadkin is drunk . . ." the engineer exclaimed in inexpressible agitation. "It will all be made clear, but I can no longer . . . it's baseness . . . and enough, enough!"

He ran out of the room.

"What's the matter? I'm going with you!" Liputin, all aflutter, jumped up and ran after Alexei Nilych.

VII

STEPAN TROFIMOVICH stood in thought for a moment, glanced at me somehow without looking, took his hat and stick, and slowly walked out of the room. I went after him as before. Passing through the gate, he noticed that I was following him and said:

"Ah, yes, you can serve as a witness . . . *de l'accident. Vous m'accompagnerez; n'est-ce pas?*"*

"Stepan Trofimovich, are you really going there again? Think what may come of it!"

With a pathetic and lost smile—a smile of shame and utter despair, and at the same time of some strange rapture—he whispered to me, stopping for a moment:

"I really cannot marry 'someone else's sins'!"

This was just the phrase I had been waiting for. At last this little phrase, cherished, concealed from me, had been spoken, after a whole week of hedging and contortions. I decidedly lost my temper.

"And such a dirty, such a . . . base thought could come to you, to Stepan Verkhovensky, to your lucid mind, to your kind heart, and . . . even prior to Liputin!"

He looked at me, made no reply, and continued on his way. I did not want to lag behind. I wanted to testify before Varvara Petrovna. I would have forgiven him if, in his womanish faintheartedness, he had simply believed Liputin, but it was clear now that he had conceived it all even long before Liputin, and Liputin had merely confirmed his suspicions and added fat to the fire. He had not hesitated to suspect the girl from the very first day, still without any grounds, not even Liputin's. He had explained Varvara Petrovna's despotic actions to himself only by her desperate wish to paint over the aristocratic peccadilloes of her priceless Nicolas by a marriage with an honorable man! I certainly wanted to see him punished for it.

*"to the accident. You will accompany me, won't you?"

"*O Dieu qui est si grand et si bon!*"* Oh, who will comfort me!" he exclaimed, having gone another hundred steps or so and suddenly stopped.

"Let's go home now, and I'll explain everything to you!" I cried out, forcing him to turn back towards his house.

"It's him! Stepan Trofimovich, is it you? You?" a fresh, playful young voice, like a sort of music, was heard beside us.

We had not noticed anything, but suddenly there beside us was Lizaveta Nikolaevna, on horseback, with her usual companion. She stopped her horse.

"Come, come quickly!" she called loudly and gaily. "I haven't seen him for twelve years and I recognized him, but he . . . Don't you recognize me?"

Stepan Trofimovich seized the hand she offered him and kissed it reverently. He looked at her as if in prayer and could not utter a word.

"He recognizes me, and he's glad! Mavriky Nikolaevich, he's delighted to see me! Then why haven't you come for two whole weeks? Auntie kept persuading us you were sick and couldn't be disturbed; but I know auntie lies. I stamped my feet and abused you, but I absolutely, absolutely wanted you to be the first to come, that's why I didn't send for you. God, he hasn't changed in the least!" she examined him, leaning down from her saddle, "It's funny how he hasn't changed! Ah, no, there are wrinkles, lots of little wrinkles around the eyes, and on the cheeks, and some gray hair, but the eyes are the same! And have I changed? Have I? But why don't you say something?"

I remembered at that moment having been told of how she was almost ill when she was taken to Petersburg at the age of eleven; during her illness she had allegedly cried and asked for Stepan Trofimovich.

"You . . . I . . ." he babbled now, in a voice breaking with joy, "I just cried out, 'Who will comfort me!' and then heard your voice . . . I regard it as a miracle *et je commence à croire.*"†

"*En Dieu? En Dieu qui est là-haut et qui est si grand et si bon?*‡ You

---

*"O God who is so great and so good!"
†"and I am beginning to believe."
‡"In God? In God who is on high and who is so great and so good?"

see, I remember all your lectures by heart. Mavriky Nikolaevich, how he taught me then to believe *en Dieu, qui est si grand et si bon!* And do you remember your story of how Columbus discovered America and everybody shouted: 'Land, land!' My nurse Alyona Frolovna says that I raved during the night after that and shouted 'Land, land!' in my sleep. And do you remember telling me the story of Prince Hamlet? And do you remember describing to me how poor emigrants were transported from Europe to America? It was all untrue, I learned it all later, how they were transported, but how well he lied to me then, Mavriky Nikolaevich, it was almost better than the truth! Why are you looking at Mavriky Nikolaevich that way? He is the best and most faithful man on the whole earth, and you must come to love him as you do me! *Il fait tout ce que je veux.* * But, dear Stepan Trofimovich, it must mean you're unhappy again, if you're crying out in the middle of the street about who will comfort you? Unhappy, is it so? Is it?"

"I am happy now . . ."

"Does auntie offend you?" she went on without listening, "that same wicked, unjust, and eternally priceless auntie of ours! And do you remember how you used to throw yourself into my arms in the garden, and I'd comfort you and weep—don't be afraid of Mavriky Nikolaevich; he has known everything about you, everything, for a long time; you can weep on his shoulder as much as you like, and he'll stand there as long as you like! . . . Lift your hat, take it all the way off for a moment, raise your head, stand on tiptoe, I'm going to kiss you on the forehead now, as I kissed you that last time, when we were saying good-bye. See, that young lady is admiring us through the window . . . Well, closer, closer. God, how gray he's become!"

And, leaning down from her saddle, she kissed him on the forehead.

"Well, now to your house! I know where you live. I'll join you presently, in a moment. I'll pay you the first visit, you stubborn man, and then I'll drag you to our place for the whole day. Go, now, get ready to receive me."

And she rode off with her cavalier. We came back. Stepan Trofimovich sat down on the sofa and wept.

---

*"He does everything I want."

"Dieu! Dieu!" he kept exclaiming, *"enfin une minute de bonheur!"**

Not more than ten minutes later she appeared as promised, accompanied by her Mavriky Nikolaevich.

"Vous et le bonheur, vous arrivez en même temps!"† He rose to meet her.

"Here is a bouquet for you; I've just been to Madame Chevalier's, she'll have bouquets for birthday parties all winter. Here is Mavriky Nikolaevich as well, please become acquainted. I almost wanted to get a cake instead of a bouquet, but Mavriky Nikolaevich insists that it's not the Russian spirit."

This Mavriky Nikolaevich was an artillery captain, about thirty-three years old, a tall gentleman, of handsome and impeccably decent appearance, with an imposing and, at first glance, even stern physiognomy, in spite of his remarkable and most delicate kindness, of which everyone became aware almost from the moment of making his acquaintance. However, he was taciturn, appeared rather cool, and did not force his friendship upon anyone. Many in our town said afterwards that he was none too bright; that was not quite correct.

I will not describe the beauty of Lizaveta Nikolaevna. The whole town was already shouting about her beauty, though some of our ladies and young girls indignantly disagreed with the shouters. There were some among them who already hated Lizaveta Nikolaevna, in the first place for her pride: the Drozdovs had hardly even begun to pay any visits, which was insulting, though in fact the cause of the delay was Praskovya Ivanovna's ailing condition. In the second place, she was hated because she was a relative of the governor's wife; and in the third place, because she went for daily outings on horseback. There had never been any horsewomen in our town before; it was natural that the appearance of Lizaveta Nikolaevna, going for her outings on horseback without having paid any visits, was bound to insult society. Incidentally, everyone knew already that she went riding on doctor's orders, and spoke caustically of her poor health. She was indeed ill. One thing that was obvious about her from the first glance was her morbid, nervous, unceasing restlessness. Alas! the poor girl was suffer-

*"God! God! . . . at last a minute of happiness."
†"You and happiness, you arrive at the same time!"

ing very much, and everything became clear afterwards. Recalling the past now, I will not say that she was the beauty she seemed to me then. Perhaps she was even not good-looking at all. Tall, slender, but lithe and strong, the irregularity of the lines of her face was even striking. Her eyes were set somehow in Kalmuck fashion, slantingly; her face was pale, with high cheekbones, swarthy and thin; yet there was in this face something so conquering and attracting! Some sort of power told itself in the burning look of her dark eyes; she appeared "as a conqueror, and to conquer." She seemed proud, and sometimes even bold; I do not know if she succeeded in being kind; but I know that she wanted terribly and suffered over forcing herself to be a little bit kind. In her nature there were, of course, many beautiful yearnings and very just undertakings; but it was as if everything in her were eternally seeking its level without finding it, everything was chaos, restlessness, agitation. Perhaps she made too severe demands on herself, never finding herself strong enough to satisfy them.

She sat down on the sofa and looked around the room.

"Why is it that I always feel sad at such moments—can you solve that, my learned man? All my life I thought I'd be God knows how glad to see you and remember everything, and now I don't seem to be glad at all, though I do love you . . . Ah, God, he's got my portrait hanging here! Give it to me, I remember it, I remember!"

An excellent miniature watercolor portrait of the twelve-year-old Liza had been sent to Stepan Trofimovich by the Drozdovs from Petersburg nine years before. Since then it had always hung on his wall.

"Was I really such a pretty child? Is that really my face?"

She got up and, holding the portrait in her hand, looked at herself in the mirror.

"Take it, quickly!" she exclaimed, giving the portrait back. "Don't hang it up now, later, I don't even want to look at it." She sat down on the sofa again. "One life passed, another began, then that passed and a third began, and there's still no end. All the ends are cut off as if with a pair of scissors. See what old things I'm saying, and yet so true!"

She grinned and looked at me; she had already glanced at me several times, but Stepan Trofimovich, in his excitement, even forgot that he had promised to introduce me.

"And why is my portrait hanging under those daggers? And why do you have so many daggers and swords?"

Indeed, he had hanging on the wall, I do not know why, two crossed yataghans and, above them, a real Circassian sabre. She looked at me so directly as she asked that I was just about to make some reply, but cut myself short. Stepan Trofimovich finally realized and introduced me.

"I know, I know," she said, "I'm very glad. Maman has also heard a lot about you. And let me also introduce you to Mavriky Nikolaevich, he is a wonderful man. I've already formed a funny idea of you: you're Stepan Trofimovich's confidant, aren't you?"

I blushed.

"Ah, forgive me, please, I used the completely wrong word—not funny at all, but just . . ." She blushed and became embarrassed. "However, why be ashamed of being a wonderful man? Well, it's time to go, Mavriky Nikolaevich! Stepan Trofimovich, in half an hour you must be at our place. God, how we're going to talk! Now I am your confidante, in everything, *everything,* understand?"

Stepan Trofimovich immediately became frightened.

"Oh, Mavriky Nikolaevich knows everything, don't be embarrassed because of him!"

"What does he know?"

"But can it be, really?" she cried out in amazement. "Hah, so it's true they're hiding it! I didn't want to believe it. They're hiding Dasha, too. Auntie wouldn't let me see Dasha just now, said she had a headache."

"But . . . but how did you find out?"

"Ah, my God, the same way everyone else did. What could be simpler!"

"But does everyone . . . ?"

"Well, and what else? Mama, it's true, was the first to find out, through my old nurse Alyona Frolovna; your Nastasya came running to tell her. And you did tell Nastasya, didn't you? She says you told her yourself."

"I . . . I once said . . ." Stepan Trofimovich stammered, blushing all over, "but . . . I only hinted . . . *j'étais si nerveux et malade et puis . . .*"*

---

*"I was so nervous and sick and then . . . ."

She burst out laughing.

"And the confidant wasn't around, and Nastasya turned up—and that was it! And the woman's got herself a whole town full of busybodies. Well, good heavens, what difference does it make? Let them know, it's even better. Come for dinner as quickly as you can, we dine early . . . Oh, yes, I forgot," she sat down again, "listen, what is this Shatov?"

"Shatov? He is Darya Pavlovna's brother . . ."

"I know he's her brother, what's the matter with you, really!" she interrupted impatiently. "I want to know what he is, what sort of man?"

"*C'est un pense-creux d'ici. C'est le meilleur et le plus irascible homme du monde . . .*"*

"I've heard he's somehow odd. Anyway, that's not the point. I've heard he knows three languages, English, too, and can do literary work. If so, I have a lot of work for him; I need an assistant, and the sooner the better. Will he take work, or not? He was recommended to me . . ."

"Oh, most certainly, *et vous fairez un bienfait . . .*"†

"It's not for the sake of a *bienfait*; I myself need assistance."

"I know Shatov quite well," I said, "and if you charge me with telling him, I'll go this minute."

"Tell him to come tomorrow morning at twelve o'clock. Wonderful! Thank you. Mavriky Nikolaevich, are you ready?"

They left. Of course, I ran at once to Shatov.

"*Mon ami!*" Stepan Trofimovich overtook me on the porch, "you must be here at ten or eleven o'clock, when I come back. Oh, I am guilty, all too guilty before you, and . . . before everyone, everyone."

VIII

I DID NOT FIND Shatov at home; I ran by two hours later—again no one home. Finally, after seven o'clock, I went hoping either to find

---

*"He's a local dreamer. He's the best and most irascible man in the world . . ."
†"and you will do a good deed . . ."

him or to leave a note; again I did not find him. His apartment was locked, and he lived alone without any servant. It occurred to me to try knocking downstairs at Captain Lebyadkin's, to ask about Shatov; it was locked there, too, and there was not a sound, not a glimmer, as if the place were empty. I passed Lebyadkin's door with curiosity, being under the influence of the stories I had just heard. Finally, I decided to come back early the next day. Indeed, I did not count very much on the note; Shatov might ignore it, he was so stubborn, so shy. Cursing my bad luck and already going out the gate, I suddenly ran into Mr. Kirillov; he was going into the house and recognized me first. Since he began questioning me himself, I told him all the essentials, and that I had a note.

"Let's go," he said, "I'll do everything."

I remembered that according to Liputin's words he had been occupying the wooden wing in back since morning. This wing, which was too spacious for him, he shared with some old deaf woman who also served him. The owner of the house lived in another, new house, on another street, where he ran a tavern, and this old woman, apparently his relative, stayed to look after the whole of the old house. The rooms in the wing were quite clean, but the wallpaper was dirty. In the room we entered, the furnishings were random, ill-sorted, utter rejects: two card tables, an alder-wood chest, a big plank table brought from some peasant cottage or kitchen, chairs and a sofa with lattice backs and hard leather cushions. In the corner there was an old icon in front of which the woman had lighted an oil lamp before we came, and on the walls there hung two big, dark oil portraits—one of the late emperor Nikolai Pavlovich, painted back in the twenties by the look of it; the other of some bishop.

Mr. Kirillov, having entered, lit a candle, and from his suitcase, which stood in the corner and was still unpacked, took an envelope, a piece of wax, and a crystal seal.

"Seal your note and address the envelope."

I tried to protest that there was no need for that, but he insisted. Having addressed the envelope, I took my cap.

"And I thought perhaps some tea," he said. "I bought tea. Want some?"

I did not refuse. The woman soon brought in the tea—that is, a great big kettle of hot water, a small teapot full of strongly brewed tea, two large, crudely painted stoneware cups, a kalatch,[7] and a whole soup plate of crumbled loaf sugar.

"I like tea," he said, "at night; a lot: I walk and drink; till dawn. Tea at night is awkward abroad."

"You go to bed at dawn?"

"Always; a long time. I eat little; mainly tea. Liputin is cunning, but impatient."

I was surprised that he wanted to talk; I decided to make use of the moment.

"There were some unpleasant misunderstandings today," I observed.

He frowned deeply.

"It's foolishness; great trifles. It's all trifles, because Lebyadkin is drunk. I told Liputin nothing, I just explained the trifles, because the other one gets it all wrong. Liputin has a lot of fantasy; in place of the trifles he made mountains. I trusted Liputin yesterday."

"And me today?" I laughed.

"But you already know everything from this morning. Liputin is either weak, or impatient, or harmful, or . . . envious."

The last little word struck me.

"Anyway, you've set up so many categories, it would be surprising if he didn't fit into one of them."

"Or into all together."

"Yes, you're right about that, too. Liputin is—a chaos! Is it true what he was blathering today, that you're planning to write something?"

"Why blathering?" he frowned again, staring at the floor.

I apologized and began assuring him that I was not trying to get it out of him. He blushed.

"He was telling the truth; I am writing. Only it makes no difference."

We were silent for a moment; suddenly he smiled the same childlike smile as that morning.

"He invented about the heads himself, from books, and told me first, and he understands badly, but I'm only looking for the reasons why people don't dare to kill themselves, that's all. And it makes no difference."

"What do you mean, don't dare? Do we have so few suicides?"

"Very few."

"You really think so?"

He did not answer, got up, and began pacing back and forth pensively.

"And what, in your opinion, keeps people from suicide?" I asked.

He looked at me distractedly, as if trying to recall what we were talking about.

"I . . . I still know little . . . two prejudices keep them, two things; just two; one very small, the other very big. But the small one is also very big."

"What is the small one?"

"Pain."

"Pain? Is it really so important . . . in this case?"

"The foremost thing. There are two sorts: those who kill themselves from great sorrow, or anger, or the crazy ones, or whatever . . . they do it suddenly. They think little about pain and do it suddenly. But the ones who do it judiciously—they think a lot."

"Are there any who do it judiciously?"

"Very many. If it weren't for prejudice, there'd be more; very many; everybody."

"Really? Everybody?"

He did not reply.

"But aren't there ways of dying without pain?"

"Imagine," he stopped in front of me, "imagine a stone the size of a big house; it's hanging there, and you are under it; if it falls on you, on your head—will it be painful?"

"A stone as big as a house? Naturally, it's frightening."

"Fright is not the point; will it be painful?"

"A stone as big as a mountain, millions of pounds? Of course, it wouldn't be painful at all."

"But go and stand there in reality, and while it's hanging you'll be very much afraid of the pain. Every foremost scientist, foremost doctor, all, all of them will be very afraid. They'll all know it won't be painful, but they'll all be very afraid it will be."

"Well, and the second reason, the big one?"

"The other world."

"Punishment, you mean?"

"That makes no difference. The other world; the one other world."

"Aren't there such atheists as don't believe in the other world at all?"

Again he did not reply.

"You're judging by yourself, perhaps."

"Each man cannot judge except by himself," he said, blushing. "There will be entire freedom when it makes no difference whether one lives or does not live. That is the goal to everything."

"The goal? But then perhaps no one will even want to live?"

"No one," he said resolutely.

"Man is afraid of death because he loves life, that's how I understand it," I observed, "and that is what nature tells us."

"That is base, that is the whole deceit!" his eyes began to flash. "Life is pain, life is fear, and man is unhappy. Now all is pain and fear. Now man loves life because he loves pain and fear. That's how they've made it. Life now is given in exchange for pain and fear, and that is the whole deceit. Man now is not yet the right man. There will be a new man, happy and proud. He for whom it will make no difference whether he lives or does not live, he will be the new man. He who overcomes pain and fear will himself be God. And this God will not be."

"So this God exists, in your opinion?"

"He doesn't, yet he does. There is no pain in the stone, but there is pain in the fear of the stone. God is the pain of the fear of death. He who overcomes pain and fear will himself become God. Then there will be a new life, a new man, everything new . . . Then history will be divided into two parts: from the gorilla to the destruction of God, and from the destruction of God to . . ."

"To the gorilla?"

". . . to the physical changing of the earth and man. Man will be God and will change physically. And the world will change, and deeds will change, and thoughts, and all feelings. What do you think, will man then change physically?"

"If it makes no difference whether one lives or does not live, then everyone will kill himself, and perhaps that will be the change."

"It makes no difference. They will kill the deceit. Whoever wants the main freedom must dare to kill himself. He who dares to kill himself knows the secret of the deceit. There is no further freedom;

here is everything; and there is nothing further. He who dares to kill himself, is God. Now anyone can make it so that there will be no God, and there will be no anything. But no one has done it yet, not once."

"There have been millions of suicides."

"But all not for that, all in fear and not for that. Not to kill fear. He who kills himself only to kill fear, will at once become God."

"He may not have time," I observed.

"It makes no difference," he replied softly, with quiet pride, almost with scorn. "I'm sorry you seem to be laughing," he added half a minute later.

"And I find it strange that you were so irritated earlier today, and are now so calm, though you talk heatedly."

"Earlier? Earlier today it was funny," he replied with a smile. "I don't like to abuse, and I never laugh," he added sadly.

"Well, you do spend your nights rather cheerlessly over your tea." I rose and took my cap.

"You think so?" he smiled, somewhat surprised. "But why? No, I . . . I don't know," he suddenly became confused, "I don't know how it is with others, and my feeling is that I cannot be like any other. Any other thinks, and then at once thinks something else. I cannot think something else, I think one thing all my life. God has tormented me all my life," he suddenly concluded, with surprising expansiveness.

"And tell me, if I may ask, why do you speak Russian not quite correctly? Can it be you forgot in your five years abroad?"

"Do I, really, incorrectly? I don't know. No, not because of abroad. I've spoken this way all my life . . . it makes no difference to me."

"Another question, a more delicate one: I fully believe that you are not inclined to meet people and that you speak little with them. Why did you get into conversation with me now?"

"With you? You sat there nicely this morning, and you . . . anyway it makes no difference . . . you very much resemble my brother, a lot, extremely," he said, blushing. "He died seven years ago—the older one—very, very much."

"He must have greatly influenced your way of thinking."

"N-no, he spoke little; he said nothing. I'll deliver your note."

He walked me to the gate with a lantern, to lock up after me. "He's crazy, of course," I decided to myself. At the gate a new encounter took place.

IX

JUST AS I LIFTED my foot to step over the high sill of the gate, someone's strong hand grabbed me by the chest.

"Who's this?" someone's voice bellowed, "friend or foe? Confess!"

"He's one of us, one of us!" Liputin's little voice squealed nearby. "It's Mr. G——v, a young man of classical upbringing and connected with the highest society."

"I love it, if it's society, clas-si . . . that means high-ly ed-u-ca-ted . . . retired captain Ignat Lebyadkin, at the world's and his friends' service . . . if they're faithful, faithful, the scoundrels!"

Captain Lebyadkin, over six feet tall, fat, beefy, curly-haired, red, and extremely drunk, could barely stand up in front of me and had difficulty articulating. I had, incidentally, seen him even before, from a distance.

"Ah, and this one, too!" he bellowed again, noticing Kirillov, who was still standing there with his lantern. He raised his fist, but lowered it at once.

"I forgive him on account of his learning! Ignat Lebyadkin—the high-ly ed-u-ca-ted . . .

A cannonball with hot love loaded
In Ignat's noble breast exploded.
Again with bitter torment groaned
Sebastópol's armless one.

Though I was never at Sebastopol,[8] nor am I armless—but what rhymes!" He thrust himself at me with his drunken mug.

"He has no time, no time, he's going home," Liputin tried to reason with him. "He'll tell Lizaveta Nikolaevna all about it tomorrow."

"Lizaveta!" he shouted again. "Wait, don't move! A variation:

A star on horseback she flies free
In Amazonian round-dance wild

And then from horseback smiles on me,
The aris-to-crat-ic child.

'To a Star-Amazon.' This is a hymn, see! It's a hymn, or else you're an ass! The slobs, they don't understand! Wait!" he grabbed at my coat, though I was trying with all my might to pass through the gate. "Tell her I'm a knight of honor, and Dashka . . . With two fingers I'll . . . She's a serf slave and won't dare . . ."

At this point he fell over, because I forcibly tore myself from his grip and ran off down the street. Liputin tagged along.

"Alexei Nilych will pick him up. Do you know what I just found out from him?" he babbled, huffing and puffing. "Did you hear that jingle? Well, he's sealed those same verses 'To a Star-Amazon' in an envelope, and is going to send them to Lizaveta Nikolaevna tomorrow with his full signature. How about that!"

"I bet you put him up to it yourself."

"You lose!" Liputin guffawed. "He's in love, in love like a tomcat, and, you know, it actually started with hatred. He hated Lizaveta Nikolaevna at first for riding around on horseback, so much so that he almost abused her out loud in the street; in fact, he did abuse her! Only the day before yesterday he abused her when she rode by—fortunately she didn't hear; and suddenly today—verses! Do you know he means to venture a proposal? Seriously, seriously!"

"I'm surprised at you, Liputin; wherever there's some such trash to be found, you're always there as a leader!" I said in a rage.

"Now, that's going too far, Mr. G——v; hasn't your little heart skipped a beat for fear of a rival, eh?"

"Wha-a-at?" I cried, stopping.

"So, just to punish you, I'm not going to say anything more! And you'd love to hear more, wouldn't you? Just this one thing: that that nitwit is no longer merely a captain, but a landowner of our province, and quite a significant one at that, because Nikolai Vsevolodovich sold him his entire estate, his former two hundred souls, the other day, and by God I'm not lying! I only just found it out, but from a most reliable source. So now go groping around for the rest yourself; I won't tell you anything more; good-bye, sir!"

X

STEPAN TROFIMOVICH was waiting for me with hysterical impatience. He had been back for an hour. He was as if drunk when I found him; at least for the first five minutes I thought he was drunk. Alas, his visit to the Drozdovs had knocked the last bit of sense out of him.

"*Mon ami*, I've quite lost the thread . . . Lise . . . I love and respect the angel as before, exactly as before; but it seems they were both waiting for me only in order to find something out, that is, quite simply, to wheedle it out of me, and then—off you go, and God be with you . . . It's really so."

"Shame on you!" I cried out, unable to help myself.

"My friend, I am completely alone now. *Enfin, c'est ridicule.* * Imagine that there, too, it's all crammed with mysteries. They simply fell on me with these noses and ears and other Petersburg mysteries. It was only here that the two of them found out about those local stories to do with Nicolas four years ago: 'You were here, you saw, is it true that he's mad?' And where this idea came from, I don't understand. Why is it that Praskovya must absolutely have Nicolas turn out to be mad? The woman wants it, she does! *Ce Maurice,* or what's his name, Mavriky Nikolaevich, *brave homme tout de même,* † but can it be for his benefit, after she herself was the first to write from Paris to *cette pauvre amie . . . Enfin,* this Praskovya, as *cette chère amie* calls her, is a type, she's Gogol's Korobochka,[9] Mrs. Littlebox, of immortal memory, only a wicked Littlebox, a provoking Littlebox, and in an infinitely enlarged form."

"That would make her a trunk! Enlarged, really?"

"Well, diminished then, it makes no difference, only don't interrupt me, because it all keeps whirling around. They had a final spat there, except for Lise; she still says 'auntie, auntie,' but Lise is sly, and there's something more to it. Mysteries. But she did quarrel with the old

*"Anyhow, it's ridiculous."
†"a worthy man all the same"

woman. *Cette pauvre* auntie, it's true, is despotic with everyone . . . and
there's also the governor's wife, and the disrespect of society, and the
'disrespect' of Karmazinov; and then suddenly this notion of craziness,
ce Liputine, ce que je ne comprends pas, * and . . . and they say she put
vinegar to her head, and then you and I come along with our complaints and letters . . . Oh, how I've tormented her, and at such a time!
Je suis un ingrat!† Imagine, I come back and find a letter from her—
read it, read it! Oh, how ignoble it was on my part."

He handed me the just-received letter from Varvara Petrovna. She
seemed to have repented of her morning's "Stay home." It was a polite
little letter, but nonetheless resolute and laconic. She invited Stepan
Trofimovich to call on her the day after tomorrow, Sunday, at twelve
o'clock sharp, and advised him to bring along some one of his friends
(my name appeared in parentheses). She, for her part, promised to
invite Shatov, as Darya Pavlovna's brother. "You can receive a final
answer from her; will this suffice you? Is this the formality you've been
striving for?"

"Note that irritated phrase at the end about formality. Poor, poor
woman, the friend of my whole life! I confess, this *sudden* deciding of
my fate crushed me, as it were . . . I confess, I was still hoping, but
now *tout est dit*, I know it's finished; *c'est terrible.* ‡ Oh, if only there
were no Sunday at all, and everything could go on as before: you
would visit me, and I would . . ."

"You're bewildered by all that nasty gossip of Liputin's today."

"My friend, you have just put your friendly finger on another sore
spot. These friendly fingers are generally merciless, and sometimes
muddled, *pardon,* but would you believe that I almost forgot about it
all, I mean that nasty gossip—that is, I by no means forgot, but, in my
foolishness, all the while I was at Lise's I tried to be happy and kept
assuring myself that I was happy. But now . . . oh, now it's this
woman—magnanimous, humane, patient with my mean shortcom-
ings—that is, perhaps not quite patient, but what am I myself, with my
bad, empty character! I am a whimsical child, with all the egoism of

*"this Liputin, which I do not understand"
†"I am an ungrateful man!"
‡"all has been said . . . it's terrible."

a child, but with none of the innocence. For twenty years she's been looking after me like a nurse, *cette pauvre* auntie, as Lise graciously calls her ... And suddenly, after twenty years, the child decides to get married—get me married, get me married, in letter after letter—and she sits putting vinegar to her head and ... and here I've done it, on Sunday I'll be a married man, no joking ... And why did I insist, why did I write letters? Ah, yes, I forgot: Lise idolizes Darya Pavlovna, at least she says she does. '*C'est un ange,* '* she says of her, 'only a rather secretive one.' They both advised it, even Praskovya ... though Praskovya didn't advise it. Oh, how much venom is locked up in that Littlebox! And, as a matter of fact, Lise did not advise it either: 'What do you need to get married for; the pleasures of learning are enough for you.' Gales of laughter. I forgave her the laughter, because she herself is sick at heart. All the same, they said, it is impossible for you to be without a woman. Infirmity is coming upon you, and she will cover you, or whatever ... *Ma foi,* all this time I've been sitting here with you, I, too, have been thinking to myself that providence was sending her in the decline of my stormy days and that she would cover me, or whatever ... *enfin,* would be useful around the house. My place is a mess, look, over there, everything's scattered about, I just ordered it to be tidied up, and there's a book lying on the floor. *La pauvre amie* has always been angry at the mess in my place ... Oh, no longer will her voice be heard here! *Vingt ans!*† And—and it seems they've got anonymous letters, imagine, Nicolas has supposedly sold his estate to Lebyadkin. *C'est un monstre; et enfin,* ‡ who is this Lebyadkin? Lise listens, listens, ohh, how she listens! I forgave her the laughter, I saw the look on her face as she listened, and *ce Maurice* ... I wouldn't want to be in his present role, *brave homme tout de même,* but somewhat shy; God help him though ..."

He fell silent; he was tired and bewildered, and sat downcast, his tired eyes fixed on the floor. I took advantage of the pause to tell him about my visit to Filippov's house, expressing curtly and dryly my opinion that Lebyadkin's sister (whom I had not seen) might indeed

*"She's an angel"
†"Twenty years!"
‡"He's a monster; and anyhow"

have been some sort of victim of Nicolas's during the mysterious period of his life, as Liputin put it, and that it was quite possible that Lebyadkin was for some reason receiving money from Nicolas, but that was all. As for the gossip about Darya Pavlovna, it was all nonsense, it had all been stretched by the blackguard Liputin, or so at least Alexei Nilych, whom there was no reason to doubt, hotly insisted. Stepan Trofimovich listened to my assurances with a distracted look, as if it did not concern him. I also mentioned, incidentally, my conversation with Kirillov, and added that Kirillov was possibly mad.

"He's not mad, but these people have short little thoughts," he mumbled listlessly and as if unwillingly. *"Ces gens-là supposent la nature et la société humaine autre que Dieu ne les a faites et qu'elles ne sont réellement.* * They are flirted with, but not at any rate by Stepan Verkhovensky. I saw them when I was in Petersburg, *avec cette chère amie* (oh, how I used to insult her then!), and I was frightened neither of their abuse—nor even of their praise. I will not be frightened now either, *mais parlons d'autre chose* † . . . I seem to have done some terrible things; imagine, I sent Darya Pavlovna a letter yesterday, and . . . how I curse myself for it!"

"What did you write about?"

"Oh, my friend, believe me, it was all done so nobly. I informed her that I had written to Nicolas five days before, also nobly."

"Now I understand!" I cried out hotly. "And what right did you have to put them together like that?"

"But, *mon cher,* don't crush me finally, don't yell at me; I am quite crushed as it is, like . . . like a cockroach, and, finally, I think it is all so noble. Suppose there had indeed been something there . . . *en Suisse* . . . or there was beginning to be. Oughtn't I to question their hearts first, so as . . . *enfin,* so as not to hinder their hearts or stand in their way like a post . . . solely out of nobility?"

"Oh, God, what a stupid thing to do!" burst from me involuntarily.

"Stupid, stupid!" he picked up, even greedily. "You've never said anything more intelligent, *c'était bête, mais que faire, tout est dit.* ‡ I am

---

*"These people imagine that nature and human society are otherwise than God made them and than they actually are."
†"but let's speak of other things"
‡"it was stupid, but what can be done, all has been said."

getting married anyway, even if it's to 'someone else's sins,' and so what was the point of writing? Isn't that so?"

"You're at it again!"

"Oh, you won't frighten me with your shouting now, it's not the same Stepan Verkhovensky you see before you; that one is buried; *enfin, tout est dit.* And why are you shouting? Only because it's not you who is getting married, and it's not you who is going to wear a certain ornament on your head. You're cringing again? My poor friend, you don't know women; as for me, all I've ever done is study them. 'If you want to overcome the whole world, overcome yourself'—the only thing that other romantic like yourself, Shatov, my spouse's dear brother, ever managed to say well. I gladly borrow the utterance from him. Well, now I, too, am prepared to overcome myself and am getting married, and yet what am I conquering in place of the whole world? Oh, my friend, marriage is the moral death of any proud soul, of any independence. Married life will corrupt me, will rob me of my energy, my courage in serving the cause; there will be children, perhaps not even mine, that is, certainly not mine—a wise man is not afraid to face the truth . . . Liputin suggested today that I save myself from Nicolas with barricades; he's stupid, Liputin. A woman will deceive the all-seeing eye itself. *Le bon Dieu* knew, of course, what he was letting himself in for when he created woman, but I'm sure she herself interfered with him and forced him to make her this way and . . . with these attributes; otherwise who would want to get himself into such troubles for nothing? Nastasya, I know, will probably be angry with me for freethinking, but . . . *Enfin, tout est dit.*"

He would not have been himself if he could have done without the cheap, quibbling freethinking that had flourished so much in his day, but at least he had comforted himself this time with his little quibble, though not for long.

"Oh, why couldn't there simply not be this day after tomorrow, this Sunday!" he suddenly exclaimed, now in utter despair. "Why couldn't just this one week be without a Sunday—*si le miracle existe*?* What would it cost providence to cross out just this one Sunday from the

*"if miracles exist?"

calendar, just to prove its power to an atheist, *et que tout soit dit*!* Oh, how I loved her! Twenty years, all these twenty years, and she never, never understood me!"

"But who are you talking about? I also don't understand you!" I asked in surprise.

"*Vingt ans!* And she never once understood me—oh, this is cruel! Can she really think I'm getting married out of fear, out of need? Oh, shame! Auntie, auntie, it is for you that I . . . Oh, may she know, this auntie, that she is the only woman I have adored for these twenty years! She must know it, otherwise it will not be, otherwise they will have to drag me by force to this *ce qu'on appelle le*† altar!"

It was the first time I had heard this confession, and so energetically expressed. I will not conceal that I had a terrible urge to laugh. I was wrong.

"Alone, he alone is left to me, my only hope!" he clasped his hands all at once, as if suddenly struck by a new thought. "Now only he alone, my poor boy, can save me, and—oh, why does he not come! Oh, my son, oh, my Petrusha . . . and though I am not worthy to be called a father, but a tiger rather, still . . . *laissez-moi, mon ami,*‡ I'll lie down for a while to collect my thoughts. I'm so tired, so tired, and I suppose it must be time for you to go to bed, *voyez-vous,* § it's twelve o'clock . . ."

*"and let all be said!"
†"what is known as the"
‡"leave me, my friend"
§"you see"

4

The Lame Girl

I

SHATOV PROVED not to be stubborn and, following my note, came at noontime to call on Lizaveta Nikolaevna. We entered at almost the same time; I, too, was paying my first call. All of them—that is, Liza, maman, and Mavriky Nikolaevich—were sitting in the big drawing room, arguing. Maman had requested that Liza play some waltz for her on the piano, and when she began the requested waltz, started insisting that it was the wrong one. Mavriky Nikolaevich, in his simplicity, interceded for Liza and insisted that it was the right one; the old woman got so angry that she burst into tears. She was ill, and even had difficulty walking. Her legs were swollen, and already for several days she had done nothing but wax capricious and find fault with others, despite the fact that she had always been slightly afraid of Liza. They were glad that we came. Liza blushed with pleasure and, after saying *merci* to me, for Shatov of course, went up to him, looking at him curiously.

Shatov stopped clumsily in the doorway. Having thanked him for coming, she led him over to maman.

"This is Mr. Shatov, of whom I spoke to you, and this is Mr. G——v, a great friend of mine and of Stepan Trofimovich's. Mavriky Nikolaevich also made his acquaintance yesterday."

"And which one is the professor?"

"There isn't any professor, maman."

"Yes, there is, you were saying yourself there would be a professor; it must be this one," she pointed squeamishly at Shatov.

"I never told you there would be a professor. Mr. G——v is in the civil service, and Mr. Shatov is a former student."

"Student, professor, anyway it's from the university. You just want to argue. And the Swiss one had a moustache and a little beard."

"It's Stepan Trofimovich's son that maman keeps calling a professor," Liza said, and she led Shatov to a sofa at the other end of the drawing room.

"She's always like that when her legs are swollen—ill, you know," she whispered to Shatov, still studying him with the same extreme curiosity, especially his lock of hair.

"Are you military?" the old woman, to whom I had been so mercilessly abandoned by Liza, addressed me.

"No, madam, I am in the civil service . . ."

"Mr. G——v is a great friend of Stepan Trofimovich's," Liza echoed at once.

"You serve at Stepan Trofimovich's? But isn't he a professor, too?"

"Ah, maman, you must even dream about professors in your sleep," Liza cried in vexation.

"There are quite enough of them in reality. And you are eternally contradicting your mother. Were you here when Nikolai Vsevolodovich came four years ago?"

I replied that I was.

"And was there some Englishman here with you?"

"No, there wasn't."

Liza laughed.

"Ah, you see, there wasn't any Englishman, so it's all a pack of lies. Varvara Petrovna and Stepan Trofimovich are both lying. And everyone else is lying, too."

"That's because yesterday auntie and Stepan Trofimovich found some resemblance between Nikolai Vsevolodovich and Prince Harry from Shakespeare's *Henry the Fourth,* and in answer to that maman says there was no Englishman," Liza explained to us.

"If there was no Harry, then there was no Englishman either. Nikolai Vsevolodovich was playing pranks all by himself."

"I assure you that maman does it on purpose," Liza found it necessary to explain to Shatov, "she knows perfectly well about Shake-speare. I myself read her the first act of *Othello;* but she's suffering very much now. Maman, do you hear, it's striking twelve, time for you to take your medicine."

"The doctor is here," a chambermaid appeared in the doorway.

The old woman raised herself and began calling her dog: "Zemirka, Zemirka, you come with me at least."

The nasty little old dog Zemirka did not obey and hid under the sofa where Liza was sitting.

"You don't want to? Then I don't want you either. Good-bye, dearie, I don't know your name," she turned to me.

"Anton Lavrentievich . . ."

"Well, it makes no difference, it goes in one ear and out the other. Don't see me out, Mavriky Nikolaevich, I was only calling Zemirka. Thank God, I can still walk by myself, and tomorrow I shall go for a drive."

She angrily walked out of the drawing room.

"Anton Lavrentievich, talk for a while with Mavriky Nikolaevich. I assure you, you'll both gain from a closer acquaintance," Liza said, and she gave a friendly smile to Mavriky Nikolaevich, who simply beamed all over from her look. There was no help for it, I was left to talk with Mavriky Nikolaevich.

II

THE BUSINESS Lizaveta Nikolaevna had with Shatov turned out, to my surprise, to be indeed only literary. I don't know why, but I had been thinking that she had summoned him for something else. We—that is, Mavriky Nikolaevich and myself—seeing that they were not concealing anything from us and were talking quite loudly, began to listen; then we, too, were invited to join the council. The whole thing was that Lizaveta Nikolaevna had long since conceived of publishing a—in her opinion useful—book, but being completely inexperienced, she needed a collaborator. I was even amazed at the seriousness with which she began to explain her plan to Shatov. "Must be one of the new sort," I thought, "it's not for nothing she was in

Switzerland." Shatov listened attentively, his eyes fixed on the ground, not surprised in the least that an idle society girl should undertake affairs seemingly so unsuitable for her.

The literary undertaking was of the following sort. A multitude of metropolitan and provincial newspapers and other journals is published in Russia, and these report daily on a multitude of events. The year goes by, the newspapers are everywhere stacked up in bookcases, or turned into litter, torn up, used for wrapping things or for hats. Many of the facts published produce an impression and remain in the public memory, but are then forgotten over the years. Many people would like to refer to them later, but what an effort it is to search through that sea of pages, often without knowing the day, or the place, or even the year when the event occurred. And yet, if all these facts for a whole year were brought together in one book, with a certain plan and a certain idea, with a table of contents, an index, a classification by month and day—such a combined totality could present a whole characterization of Russian life for that whole year, notwithstanding the extremely small portion of facts as compared with all that had happened.

"Instead of many pages there will be a few fat books, that's all," observed Shatov.

But Lizaveta Nikolaevna hotly defended her project in spite of its difficulty and her inexperience in talking about it. There should be one book, and not even a very fat one, she insisted. But even supposing it were a fat one, still it would be a clear one, because the main thing was the plan and the way the facts were presented. Of course, not everything was to be collected and reproduced. Government decrees and acts, local directives, laws—all facts of that sort, though important, could be entirely omitted from the proposed volume. A great deal could be omitted, and the choice could be limited only to events that more or less expressed the personal moral life of the people, the personality of the Russian people at a given moment. Of course, anything could be included: curiosities, fires, donations, all sorts of good and bad deeds, all sorts of pronouncements and speeches, perhaps even news about flooded rivers, perhaps even some government decrees as well, but with the choice only of those things that portrayed the epoch; everything would be included with a certain view, a direction, an intention, an idea, throwing light on the entire whole, the totality. And, finally, the book should be interesting even as light reading, to say nothing of its being an indispensable reference work! It would be, so to speak, a picture of the spiritual, moral, inner life of Russia over an entire year. "Everyone should want to buy it, the book should become a household item," Liza kept affirming. "I realize that the whole thing depends on the plan, and that is why I'm turning to you," she concluded. She was quite flushed, and though her explanations were obscure and incomplete, Shatov began to understand.

"So the result would be something with a tendency, a selection of facts with a certain tendency," he muttered, still without raising his head.

"Not at all, there's no need to select with a tendency, there's no need for any tendency. Just impartiality—that's the only tendency."

"But there's nothing wrong with a tendency," Shatov stirred, "and it's impossible to avoid, as soon as at least some selection reveals itself. The selection of facts will in itself indicate how they are to be understood. Your idea isn't bad."

"So that means such a book is possible?" Liza rejoiced.

"We'll have to see and think. It's a huge matter. One cannot invent something all at once. Experience is necessary. Even when the book is published, we'll still hardly know how to publish it. Maybe only after many trials; but the idea is nearly there. A useful idea."

He finally raised his eyes, and they even shone with pleasure, so interested he was.

"Did you think it up yourself?" he asked Liza, gently and as if bashfully.

"But it's not hard to think it up, it's the plan that's hard," Liza smiled. "I don't understand much, and I'm not very smart, I only pursue what is clear to me . . ."

"Pursue?"

"Maybe not the right word?" Liza inquired quickly.

"It's a possible word; never mind."

"It seemed to me even abroad that I, too, could be useful in some way. I have my own money, and it just sits there, so why couldn't I, too, work for the common cause? Besides, the idea came somehow suddenly, by itself; I didn't sit thinking it up, and I was very glad when it came; but I saw at once that I couldn't do it without a collaborator, because I don't know how to do anything myself. The collaborator will, of course, become co-editor of the book. We'll go half and half: your plan and work, my original idea and the means for publishing it. The book will pay for itself, won't it?"

"If we hit on the right plan, the book will go over."

"I warn you that it's not for the sake of profit, but I wish very much for the book to sell, and I'll be proud of the profit."

"Well, and what does it have to do with me?"

"But it's you I'm asking to be my collaborator . . . half and half. You will work out the plan."

"What makes you think I'm capable of working out the plan?"

"I was told about you, and I heard here . . . I know you're very intelligent and . . . occupied with important things . . . and you think a lot; I was told about you by Pyotr Stepanovich Verkhovensky in Switzerland," she added hastily. "He's a very intelligent man, isn't he?"

Shatov gave her a momentary oblique glance, but at once lowered his eyes.

"And Nikolai Vsevolodovich also told me a lot about you . . ."

Shatov suddenly blushed.

"Anyway, here are the newspapers," Liza hastily snatched up from a chair a stack of prepared and tied-up newspapers, "here, I've tried to mark some choice facts, to make a selection, and add numbers . . . you'll see."

Shatov took the bundle.

"Take it home and have a look—where is it you live?"

"On Bogoyavlensky Street, in Filippov's house."

"I know. I've heard there's also some captain who, it seems, lives next to you—a Mr. Lebyadkin?" Liza went on hastily as before.

Shatov, holding the stack of papers in his still outstretched hand, sat there for a whole minute without replying, staring down.

"Why don't you choose someone else for this business, I won't be of any use to you," he said finally, lowering his voice somehow terribly strangely, almost to a whisper.

Liza blushed.

"What business are you talking about? Mavriky Nikolaevich!" she cried, "that letter, please."

I went up to the table together with Mavriky Nikolaevich.

"Look at this," she suddenly turned to me, unfolding the letter in great agitation. "Have you ever seen anything like it? Please read it aloud; I want Mr. Shatov to hear it, too."

With no little astonishment I read aloud the following epistle:

To the Perfection of the Young Miss Tushin.

Dear lady, Elizaveta Nikolaevna!

Oh, what a lovely vision
Is Elizaveta Tushin.
When she flies sidesaddle with her relation
And her locks share the wind's elation,
Or when with her mother in church she bows
And the blush of reverent faces shows,
Then matrimonial and lawful delights I do desire,
And after her, and her mother, send my tear.

Composed by an unlearned man in an argument.

Dear lady!

I pity myself most of all for having not lost an arm at Sebastopol in the cause of glory, not having been there at all, but served the whole campaign managing vile provisions, considering it baseness. You are a goddess in antiquity, and I am nothing but have guessed about the boundlessness. Consider it as verse and no more, for verse is nonsense after all and justifies what is considered boldness in prose. Can the sun be angry at an infusorian if it composes from its drop of water, where there is a multitude of them, as seen in a microscope? Even the very club of human kindness towards big cattle in Petersburg of high society, rightly commiserating with the dog and the horse, scorns the brief infusorian, not mentioning it at all, because it has not grown big enough. I have not grown big enough either. The thought of marriage might seem killing; but soon I will possess a former two hundred souls through a hater of mankind whom you should scorn. I can tell much, and volunteer it according to documents— enough for Siberia. Do not scorn the offer. The letter from the infusorian is to be understood in verse.

Captain Lebyadkin, a humble friend,
with much free time to spend.

"This was written by a man in a drunken state and a scoundrel!" I cried out indignantly. "I know him!"

"I received this letter yesterday," Liza began to explain to us, blushing and hurrying, "and I myself understood at once that it was from some fool, and if I have not yet shown it to maman, it's because I didn't want to upset her still more. But if he continues again, I don't know what to do. Mavriky Nikolaevich wants to go and forbid him. Since I regarded you as my collaborator," she turned to Shatov, "and since you live there, I wanted to ask you, so as to be able to judge what more can be expected from him."

"He's a drunk man and a scoundrel," Shatov muttered, as if reluctantly.

"And is he always such a fool?"

"Oh, no, he's not a fool at all, when he's not drunk."

"I knew a general who wrote exactly the same kind of verses," I observed, laughing.

"Even from this letter you can see that he keeps his own counsel," the taciturn Mavriky Nikolaevich unexpectedly put in.

"They say there's some sister there?" Liza asked.

"Yes, a sister."

"They say he tyrannizes over her—is it true?"

Shatov again glanced at Liza, scowled, and grumbling "What do I care?" moved towards the door.

"Ah, wait," Liza cried out worriedly, "where are you going? We still have so much to talk about . . ."

"What is there to talk about? I'll let you know tomorrow . . ."

"But the main thing, the printing! Believe me, I'm not joking, I seriously want to do it," Liza went on assuring him, with ever increasing alarm. "If we decide to publish it, where will we have it printed?

That is the most important question, because we won't go to Moscow for it, and the local printer is impossible for such a publication. I made up my mind long ago to start my own press, in your name, let's suppose, and I know maman would allow it if it was in your name . . ."

"And how do you know I can be a printer?" Shatov asked sullenly.

"But Pyotr Stepanovich, still in Switzerland, pointed me precisely to you, as one who could run a press and was familiar with the business. He even wanted to give me a note for you, but I forgot."

Shatov, as I recall now, changed countenance. He stood there for a few more seconds and then suddenly walked out of the room.

Liza got angry.

"Does he always walk out like that?" she turned to me.

I shrugged, but Shatov suddenly returned, went straight up to the table, and placed on it the bundle of newspapers he had taken:

"I won't be your collaborator, I have no time . . ."

"But why, why? You seem to have become angry?" Liza asked in an upset and pleading voice.

The tone of her voice seemed to strike him; for a few moments he studied her attentively, as if wishing to penetrate to her very soul.

"It makes no difference," he muttered softly, "I don't want to . . ."

And he left for good. Liza was completely struck, somehow even excessively, or so it seemed to me.

"A remarkably strange man!" Mavriky Nikolaevich loudly observed.

III

"Strange," certainly, yet there was in all this a great deal of obscurity. Something was implied in it. I decidedly did not believe in this publication; then there was this stupid letter, which all too clearly offered some sort of denunciation "with documents," which they all said nothing about, and instead talked of something entirely different; finally, there was this press, and Shatov's sudden departure precisely because they began to speak of a press. All this led me to think

that something had already happened here before me of which I knew
nothing; that, consequently, I was not wanted, and that it was all none
of my business. Besides, it was time to go, it was enough for a first
visit. I went up to Lizaveta Nikolaevna to say good-bye.

She seemed to have forgotten I was in the room and continued
standing in the same place by the table, deep in thought, her head
bowed, staring fixedly at one chosen spot in the carpet.

"Ah, you, too? Good-bye," she prattled, in a habitually sweet voice.
"Give my greetings to Stepan Trofimovich and persuade him to come
to me soon. Mavriky Nikolaevich, Anton Lavrentievich is leaving. I'm
sorry maman cannot come and say good-bye to you . . ."

I walked out and had even gone down the stairs when a servant
suddenly overtook me on the porch.

"My lady begs you very much to come back . . ."

"The lady, or Lizaveta Nikolaevna?"

"That's the one, sir."

I found Liza no longer in that big drawing room where we had been
sitting, but in the adjoining reception room. The door to the drawing
room, where Mavriky Nikolaevich now remained alone, was tightly
shut.

Liza smiled at me, but she was pale. She stood in the middle of the
room, obviously undecided, obviously struggling with herself; but all
at once she took me by the hand and silently, quickly led me to the
window.

"I want to see *her* at once," she whispered, turning to me her ardent,
strong, impatient gaze, not allowing for a shadow of contradiction. "I
must see *her* with my own eyes, and I ask your help."

She was in a complete frenzy and—in despair.

"Who is it you wish to see, Lizaveta Nikolaevna?" I asked in fright.

"This Lebyadkin woman, the lame one . . . Is it true that she's lame?"

I was astounded.

"I've never seen her, but I've heard that she's lame, I heard it only
yesterday," I murmured with hasty readiness and also in a whisper.

"I absolutely must see her. Could you arrange it for this same day?"

I felt terribly sorry for her.

"That is impossible, and, besides, I wouldn't have any idea how to
do it," I began persuading her. "I'll go to Shatov . . ."

"If you don't arrange it by tomorrow, I shall go to her myself, alone, because Mavriky Nikolaevich has refused. I'm counting only on you, I have no one else; I spoke stupidly with Shatov . . . I'm sure you are a completely honest man and, perhaps, completely devoted to me, only do arrange it."

A passionate desire to help her in everything came over me.

"Here is what I'll do," I thought a bit, "I'll go myself and see her today for certain, *for certain*! I'll make it so that I see her, I give you my word of honor; only—allow me to confide in Shatov."

"Tell him that I have this wish and that I can wait no longer, but that I was not deceiving him just now. He left, perhaps, because he's a very honest man and did not like it that I seemed to be deceiving him. I wasn't deceiving him; I really want to publish and to start a press . . ."

"He is honest, honest," I confirmed with fervor.

"However, if it doesn't get arranged by tomorrow, then I will go myself, whatever may come of it, and even if everyone finds out."

"I cannot come to you before three o'clock tomorrow," I observed, recollecting myself somewhat.

"At three o'clock, then. I guessed right, then, at Stepan Trofimovich's yesterday, that you are somewhat devoted to me?" she smiled, pressing my hand in parting and hurrying to the abandoned Mavriky Nikolaevich.

I left, oppressed by my promise, and not understanding what had happened. I had seen a woman in real despair, who was not afraid to compromise herself by confiding in a man who was almost a stranger. Her feminine smile in a moment so difficult for her, and the hint that she had already noticed my feelings yesterday, simply stabbed my heart; yet I felt pity, pity—that was all! Her secrets suddenly became something sacred for me, and even if they had been revealed to me right then, I think I would have stopped my ears and refused to hear any more. I only had a foreboding of something . . . And yet I had absolutely no idea how I was going to arrange anything here. What's more, even then I still did not know precisely what had to be arranged: a meeting, but what sort of meeting? And how bring them together? All my hopes lay in Shatov, though I might have known beforehand that he would not help with anything. But I rushed to him anyway.

IV

O NLY IN THE EVENING, past seven, did I find him at home. To
my surprise, he had visitors—Alexei Nilych, and another gentleman I was half acquainted with, a certain Shigalyov, the brother of
Virginsky's wife.

This Shigalyov must already have spent about two months in our
town; I do not know where he came from; the only thing I had heard
about him was that he had published some article in a progressive
Petersburg magazine. Virginsky introduced us by chance in the street.
Never in my life have I seen a more grim, gloomy, glowering face on
a man. He looked as if he were expecting the destruction of the world,
and not just sometime, according to prophecies which might not be
fulfilled, but quite definitely, round about morning, the day after tomorrow, at ten twenty-five sharp. Incidentally, we said almost nothing
then, but only shook hands, looking like a pair of conspirators. I was
struck most of all by the unnatural size of his ears—long, broad, and
thick, sticking out somehow peculiarly. His movements were clumsy
and slow. If Liputin ever did dream that a phalanstery might be realized in our province, this man was sure to know the day and hour
when it would come about. He made a sinister impression on me;
meeting him now at Shatov's, I was surprised, all the more so in that
Shatov generally had no love of visitors.

Even from the stairs they could be heard talking very loudly, all
three at once, and apparently arguing; but as soon as I appeared, they
all fell silent. They had been arguing standing up, and now suddenly
they all sat down, so that I, too, had to sit down. The stupid silence
would not get broken for about three full minutes. Shigalyov, though
he recognized me, pretended he did not know me—certainly not from
hostility, but just so. Alexei Nilych and I bowed slightly to each other,
but silently, and for some reason did not shake hands. Shigalyov finally
began looking at me sternly and gloweringly, in the most naïve conviction that I would suddenly get up and leave. Finally, Shatov rose from
his chair, and everyone else suddenly jumped up. They walked out

without saying good-bye; only Shigalyov, already in the doorway, said to Shatov, who was seeing them out:

"Remember, you're obliged to report."

"I spit on your reports, and the devil if I'm obliged to anybody." Shatov saw him out and fastened the door with a hook.

"Snipe!" he said, glancing at me and grinning somehow crookedly.

His face was angry, and I felt it strange that he had begun talking. Usually, whenever I had come to see him before (very rarely, by the way), he would sit glowering in the corner, responding angrily, and only after a long time would become quite animated and begin talking with pleasure. On the other hand, each time he said good-bye, he would unfailingly glower again and let you out as if he were getting rid of a personal enemy.

"I had tea yesterday with this Alexei Nilych," I remarked. "He seems to have gone crazy over atheism."

"Russian atheism has never gone further than a pun," Shatov growled, replacing the burnt-down candle with a new one.

"No, the man doesn't seem to be a punster to me; he seems unable to speak even plainly, to say nothing of punning."

"They're paper people; it all comes from lackeyishness of thinking,"[1] Shatov observed calmly, sitting down in the corner on a chair and placing both palms on his knees.

"And there's hatred there, too," he said, after a moment's silence. "They'd be the first to be terribly unhappy if Russia somehow suddenly got reconstructed, even if it was in their own way, and somehow suddenly became boundlessly rich and happy. They'd have no one to hate then, no one to spit on, nothing to jeer at! All that's there is an endless animal hatred of Russia that has eaten into their organism . . . And there are no tears invisible to the world under the visible laughter![2] Nothing more false has ever been said in Russia than this phrase about invisible tears!" he cried out, almost with fury.

"Well, God knows what it's all about!" I laughed.

"And you, you're a 'moderate liberal,'" Shatov also grinned. "You know," he suddenly picked up, "maybe that was just silly talk about 'lackeyishness of thinking'; you'll probably say to me at once: 'It's you who were born of a lackey, but I'm no lackey.'"

"Not at all . . . how could you think such a thing!"

"Don't apologize, I'm not afraid of you. Once I was simply born of a lackey, but now I've become a lackey myself, just like you. Our Russian liberal is first of all a lackey and is only looking for someone's boots to polish."

"What boots? What kind of allegory is that?"

"I wouldn't call it an allegory! You're laughing, I see . . . Stepan Trofimovich was right to say that I'm lying under a stone, crushed but not crushed to death, I'm just writhing—it's a good comparison."

"Stepan Trofimovich assures us that you've gone crazy over the Germans," I went on laughing. "In fact, we did filch something or other from the Germans and stick it in our pocket."

"We took twenty kopecks, and gave away a hundred roubles of our own."

We were silent for about a minute.

"No, he got it from lying there in America."

"Who? Got what from lying there?"

"Kirillov, I mean. He and I spent four months there, lying on the floor of a hut."

"Have you really been to America?" I was surprised. "You never talk about it."

"What's there to tell? The year before last, three of us went to the American States on an emigrant steamer, on our last pennies, 'in order to try the life of the American worker for ourselves, and thus by *personal* experience to test on ourselves the condition of man in his hardest social position.'[3] That was the goal we set out with."

"Lord!" I laughed, "but for that it would have been better to go somewhere in our province at harvest time, if you wanted to 'test by personal experience'—why on earth go to America!"

"We got hired to work there for an exploiter; six of us Russians were gathered there in all—students, even landowners from their estates, even officers were there, all with the same grand purpose. So we worked, got wet, suffered, wore ourselves out, and finally Kirillov and I left—got sick, couldn't stand it anymore. Our employer-exploiter cheated us when he paid us off; instead of thirty dollars as agreed, he paid me eight and him fifteen; they also beat us there, more than once.

So, without work then, Kirillov and I spent four months lying side by side on the floor in some little town; he thought of one thing, and I of another."

"Can it be that your employer really beat you? In America? How you must have cursed at him!"

"Not in the least. On the contrary, Kirillov and I decided at once that 'we Russians are mere kids next to Americans, and that one must be born in America, or at least live for long years with Americans, to be on the same level with them.'[4] Not only that: when they asked us to pay a dollar for something worth a penny, we paid it, not just with pleasure, but even with enthusiasm. We praised everything: spiritualism, lynching, six-shooters, hoboes. Once, on a train, a man went into my pocket, took my hairbrush, and began brushing his hair with it; Kirillov and I just looked at each other and decided that it was good and we liked it very much . . ."

"Strange that with us such things not only enter our heads, but even get carried out," I observed.

"Paper people," Shatov repeated.

"But, all the same, to cross the ocean on an emigrant steamer to an unknown land, even if it's with the purpose of 'learning by personal experience' and so forth, by God, that seems to have some big-hearted staunchness about it . . . But how did you get out of there?"

"I wrote to a man in Europe, and he sent me a hundred roubles."

All the while he talked, Shatov stared stubbornly at the ground, as was his custom even when excited. But here he suddenly raised his head.

"And do you want to know the man's name?"

"Who was it?"

"Nikolai Stavrogin."

He suddenly rose, turned to his limewood desk, and began rummaging around on it. There was a vague but trustworthy rumor among us that his wife had for some time had a liaison with Nikolai Stavrogin in Paris, and precisely about two years ago, that is, when Shatov was in America—though, true, long after she had left him in Geneva. "If so, what on earth possessed him now to volunteer the name and smear it about?" the thought came to me.

"I still haven't paid him back," he suddenly turned to me again, looked at me intently, went and sat down in his former place in the corner, and asked abruptly, now in a completely different voice:

"You came for something, of course; what do you want?"

I at once told him everything, in exact historical order, and added that though by now I had had time to think better after today's fever, I had become all the more confused: I understood that there was something very important here for Lizaveta Nikolaevna, I greatly wished to help her, but the whole trouble was that I not only did not know how to keep the promise I had given her, but I no longer even understood what precisely I had promised her. Then I repeated to him imposingly that she did not want and had not intended to deceive him, that there had been some misunderstanding there, and that she had been very upset by his remarkable departure today.

He listened very attentively.

"Maybe I did something stupid today, as my custom is . . . Well, if she herself didn't understand why I left like that, it's . . . so much the better for her."

He rose, went to the door, opened it, and began listening on the stairs.

"Do you want to see this person yourself?"

"That's just what I need, but how?" I jumped up, delighted.

"Let's simply go down while she's sitting alone. He'll beat her up when he comes back, if he finds out we were there. I often go to see her on the quiet. I attacked him today when he began beating her again."

"What do you mean?"

"Precisely that; I dragged him away by the hair; he was on the point of thrashing me for it, but I frightened him, and it ended there. I'm afraid if he comes back drunk and remembers, he'll give her a bad thrashing for it."

We went downstairs at once.

V

THE DOOR TO the Lebyadkins' place was just closed but not locked, and we walked in freely. Their entire apartment consisted of two ugly little rooms with sooty walls on which the dirty wallpaper hung literally in tatters. There had been a tavern there for a few years, until the owner, Filippov, moved it to his new house. The other rooms once occupied by the tavern were now locked, and these two had fallen to Lebyadkin. The furniture consisted of simple benches and plank tables, except for just one old armchair with a missing arm. In the second room, in the corner, there was a bed with a cotton blanket, which belonged to Mlle. Lebyadkin, while the captain, when he settled down for the night, would collapse each time on the floor, often just as he was. Everywhere there were crumbs, litter, puddles; a big, thick, soaking-wet rag lay in the middle of the floor in the first room, and in the same pool sat an old, worn-out boot. One could see that no one did anything here; no one lit the stoves, cooked the meals; they did not even have a samovar, as Shatov detailed. When the captain arrived with his sister, he was completely destitute and, as Liputin said, went around to certain houses begging; but, having unexpectedly received money, he at once began drinking and went completely off his head from wine, so that he could not be bothered with housekeeping.

Mlle. Lebyadkin, whom I wished so much to see, was sitting placidly and inaudibly in the second room, in the corner, at a wooden kitchen table, on a bench. She did not call out to us when we opened the door, she did not even move from her place. Shatov told me that their door to the front hall even could not be locked, and had once stood wide open for a whole night. By the light of a dim, slender candle in an iron candlestick I made out a woman of perhaps thirty, sickly thin, wearing a dark old cotton dress, her long neck not covered with anything, her scanty dark hair twisted at the nape into a small knot no bigger than a two-year-old child's fist. She looked at us quite gaily. Besides the candlestick, she had on the table before her a small rustic mirror, an old deck of cards, a tattered songbook, and a little roll of white German bread from which one or two bites had been taken. It was obvious that

Mlle. Lebyadkin used white makeup and rouge on her face, and wore lipstick. She also blackened her eyebrows, which were long, thin, and dark even without that. Her narrow and high forehead, in spite of the makeup, was marked rather sharply by three long wrinkles. I knew already that she was lame, but this time she did not get up and walk in our presence. Some time ago, in early youth, this thin face might have been not unattractive; but her quiet, tender gray eyes were remarkable even now; something dreamy and sincere shone in her quiet, almost joyful look. This quiet, serene joy, also expressed in her smile, surprised me after everything I had heard about the Cossack quirt and all the outrages of her dear brother. Strangely, instead of the heavy and even fearful repulsion one usually feels in the presence of such God-afflicted creatures, I found it almost pleasant to look at her from the very first moment, and it was only pity, and by no means repulsion, that came over me afterwards.

"She just sits like that, alone as can be, literally for days on end, without moving; she reads the cards and looks at herself in the mirror," Shatov pointed to her from the threshold. "He doesn't even feed her. The old woman brings her something from the wing every once in a while, for the love of Christ. How can they leave her alone like this with a candle!"

To my surprise, Shatov spoke aloud, as if she were not in the room.

"Good evening, Shatushka!" Mlle. Lebyadkin said affably.

"I've brought you a guest, Marya Timofeevna," said Shatov.

"Honor to the guest, then. I don't know who it is you've brought, I don't seem to remember this one." She looked at me attentively from behind the candle and at once turned to Shatov again (and concerned herself no further with me during the whole conversation, as if I were not there beside her).

"Got bored, did you, pacing your little garret alone?" she laughed, revealing two rows of excellent teeth.

"Got bored, and I also wanted to come and see you."

Shatov moved a bench up to the table, sat down, and sat me down beside him.

"I'm always glad for some talk, only you make me laugh anyhow, Shatushka, you're so like a monk. When did you last comb your hair?

Let me comb it again," she took a comb from her pocket, "you must not have touched it since I combed it that other time."

"But I don't even have a comb," laughed Shatov.

"Really? Then I'll give you mine, not this one, but another, only remind me to do it."

She began combing his hair with a most serious expression, even parted it on one side, drew back a little to see if it was good, and then put the comb back in her pocket.

"You know what, Shatushka," she shook her head, "you may be a sensible man, but you're bored. It's strange for me looking at you all, I don't understand how it is that people are bored. Sorrow isn't boredom. I'm of good cheer."

"And with your brother, too?"

"You mean Lebyadkin? He's my lackey. It makes no difference to me whether he's here or not. I shout at him: 'Lebyadkin, fetch water, Lebyadkin, bring my shoes,' and off he runs. I sin sometimes thinking how funny he is."

"And that's exactly so," Shatov again addressed me aloud and without ceremony, "she treats him just like a lackey; I myself have heard her shouting at him: 'Lebyadkin, fetch water,' and laughing loudly; the only difference is that he doesn't go running for water, but beats her for it; yet she's not afraid of him in the least. She has some sort of nervous fits almost every day, and they take away her memory, so that after them she forgets everything that's just happened and always gets mixed up about time. You think she remembers how we came in, and maybe she does, but she's certainly changed it all in her own way and takes us for someone other than we are, even if she remembers that I'm Shatushka. It doesn't matter that I'm talking out loud; if the talk isn't addressed to her, she immediately stops listening and immediately plunges into dreaming within herself; precisely plunges. She's an extraordinary dreamer; she sits in one place for eight hours, for a whole day. Here's her roll, she may have taken only one bite of it since morning, and won't finish it until tomorrow. And now she's begun reading the cards . . ."

"Reading the cards I am, Shatushka, only it comes out wrong somehow," Marya Timofeevna suddenly joined in, catching the last words, and without looking she reached for the roll with her left hand (having probably heard about the roll, too). She finally got hold of it, but after keeping it for a while in her left hand, being distracted by the newly sprung-up conversation, she put it back on the table without noticing, and without having taken a single bite. "It keeps coming out the same: a journey, a wicked man, someone's perfidy, a deathbed, a letter from somewhere, unexpected news—it's all lies, I think. Shatushka, what's your opinion? If people lie, why shouldn't cards lie?" She suddenly mixed up the cards. "It's the same thing I said once to Mother Praskovya, a venerable woman she is, she used to stop by my cell to read the cards, in secret from the mother superior. And she wasn't the only one who stopped by. They'd 'oh' and 'ah,' shake their heads, say one thing and another, and I'd just laugh. 'Mother Praskovya,' I said, 'how are you going to get a letter if it hasn't come for twelve years?' Her daughter's husband took her daughter to Turkey somewhere, and for twelve years there wasn't a word or a peep from her. Only the next day I was sitting in the evening having tea at the mother superior's (and our mother superior is of a princely family), and there was also a lady visitor sitting there, a great dreamer, and some little monk from Athos,[5] rather a funny man in my opinion. And just think, Shatushka, that same monk had brought Mother Praskovya a letter from her daughter in Turkey that same morning—there's the knave of diamonds for you—unexpected news! So we're having tea there, and this monk from Athos says to the mother superior: 'Most of all, blessed Mother Superior, the Lord has blessed your convent because you keep such a precious treasure in its depths.' 'What treasure?' the mother superior asked. 'Mother Lizaveta the blessed.' Now, this blessed Lizaveta was set into our convent wall, in a cage seven feet long and five feet high, and for seventeen years she's been sitting there behind the iron bars, winter and summer, in nothing but a hempen shift, and she keeps poking at the shift, at the hempen cloth, all the time, with a straw or some twig, whatever she finds, and she says nothing, and she hasn't combed her hair or washed for seventeen years. In winter they'd push in a sheepskin coat for her, and every day a cup of water and a crust of bread. Pilgrims look, say 'Ahh,' sigh, give money. 'A nice treasure for you,' the mother superior replied (she was angry; she disliked Lizaveta terribly). 'Lizaveta sits there only out of spite, only out of stubbornness, and it is all a sham.' I didn't like that; I myself was thinking then about shutting myself away. 'And in my opinion,' I said, 'God and nature are all the same.' And they all said to me in one voice: 'There now!' The mother superior laughed, whispered something to the lady, called me to her, was ever so nice, and the lady gave me a pink bow, want me to show it to you? And the little monk right away began reading me a lesson, and he spoke so tenderly and humbly, and, it must be, with such intelligence. I sat and listened. 'Did you understand?' he asked. 'No,' I said, 'I didn't understand a thing, and just leave me completely in peace,' I said. So since then they've left me completely in peace, Shatushka. And meanwhile one of our old women, who lived with us under penance for prophesying,[6] whispered to me on the way out of church: 'What is the Mother of God, in your view?' 'The great mother,' I answered, 'the hope of the human race.' 'Yes,' she said, 'the Mother of God is our great mother the moist earth, and therein lies a great joy for man. And every earthly sorrow and every earthly tear is a joy for us; and when you have watered the earth under you a foot deep with your tears, then you will at once rejoice over everything. And there will be no more, no more of your grief from then on,' she said, 'and such,' she said, 'is the prophecy.' And this word sank into me then. After that I began to kiss the earth when I prayed, each time I bowed to the ground, I kissed it and wept. And I'll tell you this, Shatushka: there's no harm, no harm in these tears; and even if you have no grief, your tears will flow all the same from joy alone. The tears flow by themselves, that's the truth. I used to go away to the shore of the lake—on the one side is our convent, on the other our Pointed Mountain, for so they've named it—Pointed Mountain. I would go up this mountain, turn my face to the east, fall and press myself to the ground, and weep and weep, and I wouldn't remember how long I'd been weeping, and I wouldn't remember or know anything then. After that I'd get up, turn around, and the sun would be setting, so big, so splendid, so fair—do you like looking at the sun, Shatushka? It's nice, but sad. I'd turn back to the east, and the shadow from our mountain would run like an arrow far out on the lake, thin and long, so long, half a mile out, to the very island in the lake, and it would cut right across that stone island, and as soon as it cut across it, the sun would set altogether, and everything would suddenly die out. Now I, too, would be filled with sorrow, now my memory would come back, I'm afraid of the dark, Shatushka. And most of all I weep for my baby . . ."

"Was there one?" Shatov, who had been listening all the while with extreme attention, nudged me with his elbow.

"But, of course: little, pink, with such tiny fingernails, only my whole sorrow is that I don't remember whether it was a boy or a girl. One time I remember a boy, and another time a girl. And as soon as I gave birth to it then, I wrapped it in cambric and lace, tied it round with pink ribbons, strewed flowers, made it ready, prayed over it, and took it unbaptized, and as I was carrying it through the forest, I'd get frightened of the forest, and I'd be afraid and weeping most of all because I gave birth to it and did not know a husband."

"And might there have been one?" Shatov asked cautiously.

"You make me laugh, Shatushka, with your reasoning. There might have been one, but what of it, if it's the same as if there wasn't? There's an easy riddle for you—try and guess!" she smiled.

"Where did you take your baby?"

"To the pond," she sighed.

Shatov nudged me with his elbow again.

"And what if you never had any baby and all this is just raving, eh?"

"That's a hard question you're asking me, Shatushka," she replied pensively, and without being the least surprised at such a question. "I'll tell you nothing on that account, maybe there wasn't any; I think it's just your curiosity; but anyway I won't stop weeping over him, I didn't just see it in a dream, did I?" And big tears shone in her eyes. "Shatushka, Shatushka, is it true that your wife ran away from you?" She suddenly put both hands on his shoulders and looked at him with pity. "Don't be angry, I feel wretched myself. You know, Shatushka, I had such a dream: he comes to me again, beckons to me, calls me. 'Kitty,' he says, 'here, kitty, come out to me!' I was glad of that 'kitty' most of all: he loves me, I thought."[7]

"Maybe he really will come," Shatov muttered under his breath.

"No, Shatushka, it's a dream . . . he won't really come. Do you know the song:

> I need no high new house,
> I'll keep to this little cell.
> Saving my soul I'll be,
> And praying to God for thee.[8]

"Ah, Shatushka, Shatushka, my dear, why do you never ask me about anything?"

"But you won't tell, that's why I don't ask."

"I won't tell, I won't tell, put a knife into me, but I won't tell," she chimed in quickly, "burn me, but I won't tell. And however much I suffer, I won't say anything, people will never find out!"

"So you see, to each his own," Shatov said even more softly, bowing his head more and more.

"But if you asked, maybe I'd tell you; maybe I'd tell you!" she repeated rapturously. "Why won't you ask? Ask me, ask me well, Shatushka, and maybe I'll tell you; beg me, Shatushka, so that I myself consent . . . Shatushka, Shatushka!"

But Shatushka was silent; the general silence lasted for about a minute. Tears quietly flowed down her white made-up cheeks; she sat with both hands forgotten on Shatov's shoulders, but no longer looking at him.

"Eh, what do I care about you, it's even sinful," Shatov suddenly got up from the bench. "Get yourself up!" he angrily jerked the bench out from under me, took it and put it back where it had been. "So that he won't guess when he comes back; and it's time we left."

"Ah, you're still talking about my lackey!" Marya Timofeevna suddenly laughed. "You're afraid! Well, good-bye, dear guests; only listen for a moment to what I'm going to tell you. Today this Nilych came here with Filippov, the landlord, the big red-beard, just as my man was flying at me. The landlord, he grabbed him, he dragged him across the room, and my man was shouting: 'It's not my fault, I'm suffering for someone else's fault!' And would you believe it, we all just fell down laughing right there . . ."

"Eh, Timofevna, it was me, not the red-beard, I pulled him away from you by the hair; and the landlord came the day before yesterday to have a row with you, you've got it all mixed up."

"Wait, I really did mix it up, maybe it was you. Well, why argue over trifles; isn't it all the same for him who pulls his hair?" she laughed.

"Let's go," Shatov suddenly tugged my arm, "the gate is creaking; if he finds us here, he'll beat her."

Before we had time to run up the stairs, there came a drunken shout from the gateway and a flood of curses. Shatov let me into his room and locked the door.

"You'll have to sit here for a moment, if you don't want to get into some whole story. Just listen to him squealing like a pig, he must have stumbled over the sill; he goes sprawling every time."

However, we did not get away without a story.

VI

SHATOV STOOD at his locked door and listened down the stairs; suddenly he jumped back.

"He's coming here, I just knew it!" he whispered furiously. "Now he won't leave us alone before midnight."

There came several heavy thumps of a fist on the door.

"Shatov, Shatov, open up!" yelled the captain. "Shatov, my friend! . . .

> I have come to you with greeting,
> To tell you that the sun has r-r-risen,
> And that its hot light down is beating
> Upon the . . . for-r-rest . . . as it glistens,
> To tell you that I have awakened, devil take you,
> All awa-a-akened 'neath . . . the boughs . . .

Just like 'neath the blows, ha, ha!

> And every bird . . . is stirred . . . with thirst,
> To tell you I will dr-r-rink my fill,
> Drink . . . lord knows what, but dr-r-rink my fill.[9]

So, devil take this foolish curiosity! Shatov, do you understand how good it is to live in the world!"

"Don't answer!" Shatov whispered to me again.

"Open up now! Do you understand that there's something higher than fistfights . . . among mankind; there are moments of a no-o-oble person . . . I'm kind, Shatov; I'll forgive you . . . To hell with tracts, eh, Shatov?"

Silence.

"Do you understand, you ass, that I'm in love, I've bought a tailcoat, look, a tailcoat of love, fifteen roubles; a captain's love calls for social decency . . . Open up!" he suddenly bellowed wildly, and again pounded violently with his fists.

"Go to hell!" Shatov suddenly bellowed back.

"Ser-r-rf! Slave! And your sister is a ser-r-rf and a slave woman . . . a thief!"

"And you, you sold your sister."

"Lies! I'm a victim of slander, though . . . with one explanation I could . . . do you understand who she is?"

"Who is she?" Shatov, curious, suddenly went up to the door.

"But do you understand?"

"I will, just tell me who she is!"

"I dare to tell! I always dare to tell everything among the public! . . ."

"Well, that's hardly true," Shatov taunted him and motioned for me to listen.

"I don't dare?"

"I say you don't."

"I don't dare?"

"Go on, speak, if you're not afraid of the master's rod . . . You're a coward, captain or no!"

"I . . . I . . . she . . . she's . . ." the captain babbled in a trembling, agitated voice.

"Well?" Shatov put his ear to the door.

There was silence for at least half a minute.

"Sco-o-oundrel!" finally came from beyond the door, and the captain quickly retreated down the stairs, puffing like a samovar and stumbling noisily on each step.

"No, he's cunning, he won't let it out even when he's drunk," Shatov stepped away from the door.

"But what is all this?" I asked.

Shatov waved his hand, opened the door, and again began to listen down the stairs; he listened for a long time, he even went quietly down a few steps. Finally he came back.

"I don't hear anything, there was no fight; he must have dropped off at once. It's time for you to go."

"Listen, Shatov, what am I to conclude from all that?"

"Eh, conclude whatever you like," he answered in a weary and disgusted voice, and sat down at his desk.

I left. An incredible idea was growing stronger and stronger in my imagination. In anguish I thought of the next day . . .

VII

THAT "NEXT DAY"—that is, the same Sunday on which Stepan Trofimovich's fate was to be irrevocably decided—was one of the most portentous days in my chronicle. It was a day of the unexpected, a day of the unraveling of the old and the raveling up of the new, a day of sharp explanations and of a still greater muddle. In the morning, as the reader already knows, I was obliged to accompany my friend to Varvara Petrovna's, at her own stipulation, and by three in the afternoon I had to be at Lizaveta Nikolaevna's, in order to tell her—about what I did not know, and to assist her—in what I did not know. And yet it all resolved itself in a way no one could have imagined. In short, it was a day of surprisingly converging accidents.

It all began when Stepan Trofimovich and I, having come to Varvara Petrovna's at exactly twelve o'clock, as she herself had stipulated, did not find her at home; she had not yet returned from the Sunday liturgy. My poor friend was so disposed, or, better, so indisposed, that this circumstance instantly crushed him: almost powerlessly he lowered himself into an armchair in the drawing room. I offered him a glass of water; but, despite his paleness and even the trembling of his hands, he declined it with dignity. Incidentally, his outfit this time was distinguished by its remarkable elegance: a shirt almost fit for a ball, cambric, embroidered, a white tie, a new hat in his hand, fresh straw-colored gloves, and even just a touch of perfume. No sooner had we sat down than Shatov entered, shown in by the valet, also clearly on official invitation. Stepan Trofimovich rose slightly to offer him his hand, but Shatov, after looking at the two of us attentively, turned to the corner, sat down there, and did not even nod to us. Stepan Trofimovich again looked at me timorously.

We sat for a few more minutes in complete silence. Stepan Trofimovich suddenly began to whisper something to me very quickly, but I did not hear, and he himself was so agitated that he dropped it without finishing. The valet came in again to straighten something on the table—or, rather, to have a look at us. Shatov suddenly addressed him with a loud question:

"Alexei Yegorych, do you know whether Darya Pavlovna went with her?"

"Varvara Petrovna went to the cathedral alone, if you please, sir, and Darya Pavlovna stayed in her room upstairs, as she is feeling somewhat unwell," Alexei Yegorych reported didactically and decorously.

My poor friend again glanced at me furtively and anxiously, so that I finally began to turn away from him. Suddenly a carriage clattered up to the entrance, and a certain distant commotion in the house informed us that the hostess had come back. We all jumped up from our chairs—then another unexpected thing: the sound of many steps was heard, which meant that the hostess had not come back alone, and that was indeed somewhat strange, since she herself had stipulated this hour to us. Finally, there came the sound as of someone entering with a strange quickness, almost running, a way in which Varvara Petrovna could not have entered. And suddenly she all but flew into the room, breathless and extremely excited. Following a little behind her, and much more slowly, Lizaveta Nikolaevna came in, and arm in arm with Lizaveta Nikolaevna—Marya Timofeevna Lebyadkin! If I had seen it in a dream, even then I would not have believed it.

To explain this totally unexpected thing, it is necessary to go back an hour and tell in more detail than usual about the remarkable adventure that had befallen Varvara Petrovna in the cathedral.

First of all, nearly the whole town had gathered for the liturgy, meaning, that is, the upper stratum of our society. It was known that the governor's wife would be coming, for the first time since her arrival here. I will note that there were already rumors among us that she was a freethinker and of "the new principles." It was also known to all the ladies that she would be dressed magnificently and with remarkable elegance, and therefore our ladies' costumes this time were distinguished by their refinement and splendor. Varvara Petrovna alone was, as usual, modestly dressed all in black; she had dressed thus invariably over the last four years. Coming to the cathedral, she settled in her usual place, to the left, in the first row, and the liveried footman placed in front of her a velvet cushion for kneeling; in short, all was as usual. But it was also noticed that this time, all through the service, she prayed somehow extremely zealously; it was even affirmed later, when everything was recalled, that tears even brimmed her eyes. Finally the liturgy ended, and our priest, Father Pavel, came out to deliver a solemn sermon. In our town his sermons were loved and highly valued; he had even been urged to publish them, but he could not make up his mind. This time the sermon came out somehow especially long.

And so it was that, during the sermon, a certain lady drove up to the cathedral in a light, hired droshky of the old style, the kind on which a lady could only sit sideways, holding on to the driver's belt and swaying with the jolting of the carriage like a blade of grass in the wind. Such cabbies are still driving about in our town. Stopping at the corner of the cathedral—for there were many carriages and even mounted police standing by the gates—the lady jumped down from the droshky and handed the driver four silver kopecks.

"What, isn't that enough for you?" she cried out, seeing the face he made. "It's all I have," she added pitifully.

"Well, God be with you, I took you without bargaining," the cabbie waved his hand, looking at her as if thinking: "And it would be a sin to offend you." Then he stuffed his leather purse into his bosom, touched up his horse, and drove off, followed by the jeers of the nearby cabbies. Jeers and even surprise also accompanied the lady all the while she was making her way to the cathedral gates, amid the carriages and lackeydom awaiting their soon-to-emerge masters. And indeed there was something unusual and unexpected for everyone in such a person suddenly appearing out of nowhere, in the street, among people. She was sickly thin and limped a little, her face was painted with white makeup and rouge, her long neck was completely bared, with no kerchief or cloak, and she was wearing only a dark old dress, despite the cold, windy, though clear September day; her head was completely uncovered, her hair tied at the nape in a tiny knot, into the right side of which a single artificial rose was stuck, of the sort used to decorate Palm Sunday cherubs. I had noticed precisely such a Palm Sunday cherub with a wreath of paper roses in the corner under the icons the day before, when I was sitting at Marya Timofeevna's. To crown it all, the lady, though she walked with modestly lowered eyes, was at the same time smiling gaily and coyly. If she had lingered a bit longer, she might not have been allowed into the cathedral . . . But she managed to slip in and, entering the church, pushed her way inconspicuously to the front.

Though the sermon was at its midpoint and the entire packed crowd that filled the church was listening with full and hushed attention, nevertheless a few eyes glanced sideways, with curiosity and bewilderment, at the woman who had just entered. She dropped down on the church dais, lowered her whitened face to it, and lay there for a long time, apparently weeping; but, having raised her head and gotten up from her knees, she very soon recovered and became distracted. Gaily, with obviously extreme pleasure, she let her eyes roam from face to face and around the cathedral walls; she stared with special curiosity at some of the ladies, even standing on tiptoe to do so, and even laughing a couple of times with a sort of strange giggle. But the sermon came to an end, and the cross was brought out. The governor's wife was the first to go up to the cross, but within two steps of it she stopped, apparently wishing to give way to Varvara Petrovna, who was approaching it from her own side all too directly and as if not noticing anyone ahead of her. The extraordinary courtesy of the governor's wife undoubtedly contained an obvious and, in its way, witty barb; so everyone understood it; so Varvara Petrovna must have understood it; but, as before, not noticing anyone, and with a most unshakable air of dignity, she kissed the cross and at once headed for the exit. The liveried footman cleared the way, though people were all parting before her even without that. But right at the exit, on the porch, her way was momentarily blocked by a closely packed crowd. Varvara Petrovna paused, and suddenly a strange, extraordinary being, a woman with a paper rose in her hair, squeezed through the people and knelt in front of her. Varvara Petrovna, who was not easily perplexed by anything, especially in public, looked at her imposingly and sternly.

I hasten to note here, as briefly as possible, that although Varvara

Petrovna had in recent years become exceedingly economical, as they said, and even a bit stingy, still she could on occasion be unsparing of money for charity proper. She was a member of a charitable society in the capital. In a recent famine year she had sent five hundred roubles to Petersburg, to the main committee for the receipt of aid for the victims, and this was talked about in town. Finally, quite recently, before the appointment of the new governor, she had all but established a local ladies' committee to aid the poorest new mothers in our town and in the province. She was severely reproached among us for being ambitious; but the notorious impetuousness of Varvara Petrovna's character, together with her persistence, nearly triumphed over the obstacles; the society was almost set up, and the initial idea broadened more and more in the delighted mind of the foundress: she was already dreaming of establishing a similar committee in Moscow, of gradually expanding its activities through all the provinces. And then, with the sudden change of governors, everything came to a halt; and the new governor's wife, it was said, had already managed to utter in society a few pointed and, above all, apt and sensible objections regarding the supposed impracticability of the basic idea of such a committee, which—with embellishments, of course—had already been passed on to Varvara Petrovna. God alone knows what's hidden in men's hearts, but I suppose it was even with a certain pleasure that Varvara Petrovna now paused at the very gates of the cathedral, knowing that the governor's wife would pass by presently, and then everyone else, and "let her see for herself how it makes no difference to me what she thinks or what further witticisms she may produce concerning the vanity of my charitable works. Take that, all of you!"

"What is it, my dear, what do you ask?" Varvara Petrovna looked more attentively at the petitioner kneeling before her. The latter looked at her with terribly timid, abashed, but almost adoring eyes, and suddenly smiled with the same strange giggle.

"What is she? Who is she?" Varvara Petrovna glanced around at everyone there with a peremptory and inquisitive look. They were all silent.

"You are unfortunate? You are in need of assistance?"

"I need . . . I've come . . ." the "unfortunate" woman prattled, in a voice breaking with excitement. "I've come just to kiss your hand . . ." and she giggled again. With a most childlike look, as when children are being affectionate in order to beg for something, she reached out to seize Varvara Petrovna's hand, but suddenly, as though frightened, she jerked her hands back.

"You've come just for that?" Varvara Petrovna smiled a compassionate smile, but at once quickly took her mother-of-pearl purse from her pocket, took a ten-rouble bill from it, and gave it to the unknown woman. The latter took it. Varvara Petrovna was very interested, and apparently did not consider the unknown woman as some common petitioner.

"Ten roubles she gave her," someone said in the crowd.

"Your hand, please," prattled the "unfortunate" woman, firmly grasping with the fingers of her left hand the corner of the received ten-rouble bill, which was twirling in the wind. Varvara Petrovna frowned slightly for some reason, and with a serious, almost stern, look held out her hand; the woman kissed it adoringly. Her grateful eyes even shone with some sort of rapture. Just at that moment the governor's wife drew near, and the whole crowd of our ladies and senior dignitaries came pouring after her. The governor's wife had unwillingly to stop for a moment in the crush; many people stopped.

"You're shivering; are you cold?" Varvara Petrovna suddenly noticed, and throwing off her cloak, which was caught in midair by the footman, she took from her shoulders her black (far from inexpensive) shawl and with her own hands wrapped it around the bare neck of the still kneeling petitioner.

"But do get up, get up from your knees, I beg you!" The woman got up.

"Where do you live? Doesn't anyone at least know where she lives?" Varvara Petrovna again glanced around impatiently. But the former little crowd was no longer there; she saw familiar society faces gazing at the scene, some with stern surprise, others with sly curiosity and, at the same time, with an innocent desire for a bit of scandal, while still others even began to titter.

"Seems she's one of the Lebyadkins, ma'am," one good man finally stepped forward to answer Varvara Petrovna's question—our venerable and widely respected merchant Andreev, gray-bearded, bespectacled, in Russian dress, and with a round cylindrical hat which he was now holding in his hands. "She lives at Filippov's house, on Bogoyav-lensky Street."

"Lebyadkin? Filippov's house? I've heard something . . . thank you, Nikon Semyonych, but who is this Lebyadkin?"

"They call him a captain—an imprudent man, I'd have to say. And this is his sister right enough. It seems she's escaped from under super-vision," Nikon Semyonych said, lowering his voice and giving Var-vara Petrovna a significant look.

"I understand; thank you, Nikon Semyonych. So, my dear, you are Miss Lebyadkin?"

"No, I'm not Miss Lebyadkin."

"Then perhaps your brother is Lebyadkin?"

"My brother is Lebyadkin."

"Here's what I'll do, I'll take you with me, my dear, and from my house you will be driven to your family; would you like to come with me?"

"Ah, yes, I would!" Miss Lebyadkin clapped her hands.

"Auntie, auntie! Take me with you, too!" cried the voice of Lizaveta Nikolaevna. I will note that Lizaveta Nikolaevna had come to the liturgy with the governor's wife, and that Praskovya Ivanovna, on doctor's orders, had meanwhile gone for a ride in the carriage, taking Mavriky Nikolaevich along for diversion. Liza suddenly abandoned the governor's wife and sprang over to Varvara Petrovna.

"My dear, you know I'm always glad to have you, but what will your mother say?" Varvara Petrovna began imposingly, but suddenly became confused, seeing Liza's extraordinary agitation.

"Auntie, auntie, I must come with you now," Liza begged, kissing Varvara Petrovna.

"*Mais qu'avez vous donc, Lise!*"* the governor's wife said with em-phatic surprise.

"Ah, forgive me, my dear, *chère cousine,* I am going to my aunt's," Liza turned in midflight to her unpleasantly surprised *chère cousine* and kissed her twice.

"And tell maman to come at once to fetch me at auntie's; maman really, really wanted to come, she told me so today, I forgot to tell

*"But what is the matter with you, Liza!"

you," Liza kept on rattling, "it's not my fault, don't be angry, Julie . . . *chère cousine* . . . auntie, I'm ready!"

"If you don't take me with you, auntie, I'll run screaming after your carriage," she whispered, quickly and desperately, right into Varvara Petrovna's ear; luckily no one else heard it. Varvara Petrovna even started back a step and gave the mad girl a piercing look. This look decided everything: she resolved definitely to take Liza with her!

"We must put an end to this," escaped from her. "Very well, Liza, I shall take you with pleasure," she at once added loudly, "if Yulia Mikhailovna consents to let you go, of course," she turned directly to the governor's wife, with an open look and straightforward dignity.

"Oh, I certainly would not want to deprive her of that pleasure, the less so in that I myself . . ." Yulia Mikhailovna suddenly began prattling with surprising amiability, "I myself . . . well know what a fantastic, domineering little head we have on our pretty shoulders" (Yulia Mikhailovna smiled charmingly) . . .

"I thank you greatly," Varvara Petrovna thanked her, with a polite and imposing bow.

"And it is all the more pleasant," Yulia Mikhailovna went on with her prattling, now almost enraptured, even blushing all over with pleasant excitement, "that, besides the delight of visiting you, Liza has been carried away by such a beautiful, such a—I might say—lofty feeling . . . compassion . . ." (she glanced at the "unfortunate" woman) "and . . . right on the porch of the church . . ."

"Such a view does you honor," Varvara Petrovna approved magnificently. Yulia Mikhailovna impetuously offered her hand, and Varvara Petrovna with perfect readiness touched it with her fingers. The general impression was excellent, the faces of some of those present began to beam with pleasure, several sweet and fawning smiles appeared.

In short, it was suddenly revealed clearly to the whole town that it was not Yulia Mikhailovna who had scorned Varvara Petrovna all along and had not paid her a visit, but, on the contrary, it was Varvara Petrovna herself who had "kept Yulia Mikhailovna within bounds, when she would perhaps have run on foot to visit her, if only she had been sure that Varvara Petrovna would not chase her away." Varvara Petrovna's prestige rose in the extreme.

"Do get in, my dear," Varvara Petrovna motioned Mlle. Lebyadkin to the carriage that had driven up; the "unfortunate" woman ran joyfully to the door, where a footman caught her up.

"What! You're lame!" Varvara Petrovna cried out, as if totally frightened, and turned pale. (Everyone noticed it at the time but did not understand . . .)

The carriage drove off. Varvara Petrovna's house was quite near the cathedral. Liza told me later that Miss Lebyadkin laughed hysterically for all three minutes of the ride, while Varvara Petrovna sat "as if in some magnetic sleep"—Liza's own expression.

5

The Wise Serpent

I

VARVARA PETROVNA rang the bell and threw herself into an armchair by the window.

"Sit down here, my dear," she motioned Marya Timofeevna to a seat in the middle of the room, by the big round table. "Stepan Trofimovich, what is this? Here, here, look at this woman, what is this?"

"I . . . I . . ." Stepan Trofimovich began to stammer . . .

But the footman came.

"A cup of coffee, now, specially, and as quickly as possible! Don't unhitch the carriage."

"Mais, chère et excellente amie, dans quelle inquiétude . . ."* Stepan Trofimovich exclaimed in a sinking voice.

"Ah! French! French! You can see right off it's high society!" Marya Timofeevna clapped her hands, preparing rapturously to listen to a conversation in French. Varvara Petrovna stared at her almost in fright.

We were all silent, awaiting some denouement. Shatov would not raise his head, and Stepan Trofimovich was in disarray, as if it were all his fault; sweat stood out on his temples. I looked at Liza (she was sitting in the corner, almost next to Shatov). Her eyes kept darting keenly from Varvara Petrovna to the lame woman and back; a smile

---

*"But, my dear and excellent friend, in what agitation . . ."

twisted on her lips, but not a nice one. Varvara Petrovna saw this smile. And meanwhile Marya Timofeevna was completely enthralled: with delight and not the least embarrassment she was studying Varvara Petrovna's beautiful drawing room—the furniture, the carpets, the paintings on the walls, the old-style decorated ceiling, the big bronze crucifix in the corner, the porcelain lamp, the albums and knickknacks on the table.

"So you're here, too, Shatushka!" she suddenly exclaimed. "Imagine, I noticed you long ago, but I thought: It's not him! How could he have come here!"—and she laughed gaily.

"Do you know this woman?" Varvara Petrovna turned to him at once.

"I do, ma'am," Shatov mumbled, stirred on his chair, but remained sitting.

"And what do you know? Quickly, please!"

"But what . . ." he grinned an unnecessary smile and faltered . . . "You can see for yourself."

"What can I see? Go on, say something!"

"She lives in that house where I . . . with her brother . . . an officer."

"Well?"

Shatov faltered again.

"There's no point talking . . ." he grunted, and resolutely fell silent. He even blushed at his own resoluteness.

"Of course, nothing more could be expected of you!" Varvara Petrovna cut him off indignantly. It was clear to her now that everyone knew something, and at the same time that everyone was afraid of something and was evading her questions, wishing to conceal something from her.

The footman entered and offered her the specially ordered cup of coffee on a small silver tray, but at once, on a sign from her, went over to Marya Timofeevna.

"You got very cold just now, my dear, drink it quickly to warm yourself."

"*Merci,*" Marya Timofeevna took the cup, and suddenly burst out laughing at having said *merci* to a footman. But, meeting Varvara Petrovna's menacing gaze, she became timid and set the cup on the table.

"You're not angry, auntie?" she prattled, with some sort of frivolous playfulness.

"Wha-a-at?" Varvara Petrovna reared and sat straight up in her chair. "What sort of aunt am I to you? What are you suggesting?"

Marya Timofeevna, who had not expected such wrath, began trembling all over with convulsive little shivers, as if in a fit, and recoiled against the back of her chair.

"I . . . I thought that's how it should be," she prattled, staring at Varvara Petrovna, "that's what Liza called you."

"Which Liza?"

"But, this young lady," Marya Timofeevna pointed her finger.

"So she's already Liza to you?"

"You yourself just called her that," Marya Timofeevna regained some courage. "And I saw a beauty just like her in a dream," she chuckled as though inadvertently.

Varvara Petrovna understood and calmed down somewhat; she even smiled slightly at Marya Timofeevna's last phrase. The latter, having caught this smile, rose from her chair and, limping, went timidly up to her.

"Take it, I forgot to give it back, don't be angry at my impoliteness," she suddenly took from her shoulders the black shawl Varvara Petrovna had put on her earlier.

"Put it back on at once, and keep it for good. Go and sit down, drink your coffee, and please do not be afraid of me, my dear, calm yourself. I'm beginning to understand you."

"*Chère amie* . . ." Stepan Trofimovich allowed himself again.

"Ah, Stepan Trofimovich, one loses all sense here even without you; you at least might spare us . . . Please ring that bell, there beside you, to the servingwomen's quarters."

There was a silence. Her eyes ran suspiciously and irritably over all our faces. Agasha, her favorite maid, came in.

"Bring me the checkered kerchief, the one I bought in Geneva. What is Darya Pavlovna doing?"

"She does not feel very well, ma'am."

"Go and ask her to come here. Add that I want it very much, even if she isn't feeling well."

At that moment some unusual noise of footsteps and voices, similar to the previous one, was heard again from the adjacent rooms, and suddenly, breathless and "upset," Praskovya Ivanovna appeared on the threshold. Mavriky Nikolaevich was supporting her arm.

"Oh, dear me, I barely dragged myself here; Liza, you mad girl, what are you doing to your mother!" she shrieked, putting into this shriek, as is customary with all weak but very irritable people, all her pent-up irritation.

"Varvara Petrovna, dearest, I've come to fetch my daughter!"

Varvara Petrovna gave her a dark look, rose slightly to greet her, and, barely concealing her vexation, said:

"Good day, Praskovya Ivanovna, kindly sit down. I just knew you would come."

II

FOR PRASKOVYA IVANOVNA there could be nothing unexpected in such a reception. Ever since childhood, Varvara Petrovna had always treated her former boarding-school friend despotically and, under the guise of friendship, with all but contempt. In this case, however, the circumstances were also unusual. Over the last few days things had been tending towards a complete break between the two households, a fact I have already mentioned in passing. For Varvara Petrovna the reasons behind this incipient break remained mysterious and, consequently, were all the more offensive; but the main thing was that Praskovya Ivanovna had managed to assume a certain remarkably haughty position regarding her. Varvara Petrovna was wounded, of course, and meanwhile certain strange rumors began to reach her as well, which also annoyed her exceedingly, precisely by their vagueness. Varvara Petrovna was of a direct and proudly open character, a swooping character, if I may put it so. Least of all could she endure secret, lurking accusations; she always preferred open war. Anyhow, it was five days since the ladies had seen each other. The last visit had been paid by Varvara Petrovna, who had left "Drozdikha" offended and confounded. I can say without being mistaken that Praskovya Ivanovna walked in this time with the naïve conviction that Varvara Petrovna for some reason would quail before her; this could be seen even from the look on her face. But, apparently, the demon of the most arrogant pride took possession of Varvara Petrovna precisely when she had the slightest suspicion that she was for some reason considered humiliated. And Praskovya Ivanovna, like many weak people who allow themselves to be offended for a long time without protesting, was notable for being remarkably passionate in the attack the moment events turned in her favor. It is true that she was not well then, and illness always made her more irritable. I will add, finally, that the presence of the rest of us in the drawing room would not have hindered the two childhood friends if a quarrel had flared up between them; we were considered familiars and almost subordinates. I realized this just then, not without alarm. Stepan Trofimovich, who had not sat down since Varvara Petrovna's arrival, sank exhausted into his chair upon hearing Praskovya Ivanovna's shriek, and in despair began trying to catch my eye. Shatov turned sharply on his chair and even grunted something to himself. I think he wanted to get up and leave. Liza rose a little but sat down again at once, without even paying proper attention to her mother's shriek, not because of her "testy character," but because she was obviously all under the sway of some other powerful impression. Now she was looking off somewhere into the air, almost absentmindedly, and had even stopped paying her former attention to Marya Timofeevna.

III

"OOF, HERE!" Praskovya Ivanovna pointed to an armchair by the table and sank heavily into it with the help of Mavriky Nikolaevich. "I wouldn't sit down in your house, dearest, if it weren't for my legs!" she added in a strained voice.

Varvara Petrovna raised her head slightly, and with a pained look pressed the fingers of her right hand to her right temple, evidently feeling an acute pain there (a *tic douloureux*).

"Why so, Praskovya Ivanovna, why wouldn't you sit down in my house? I always enjoyed the genuine sympathy of your late husband, and as girls you and I played with dolls together in boarding school."

Praskovya Ivanovna waved her hands.

"I just knew it! You always start talking about boarding school when you're going to reproach me—that's your trick. In my view it's just fancy talk. I cannot abide this boarding school of yours."

"You seem to have come in particularly low spirits; how are your legs? Here, they're bringing you coffee; be my guest, drink it, and don't be angry."

"Dearest Varvara Petrovna, you treat me just as if I were a little girl. I don't want any coffee, so there!"

And she petulantly waved away the servant who was offering her coffee. (Incidentally, the others also declined coffee, with the exception of myself and Mavriky Nikolaevich. Stepan Trofimovich took a cup, but then set it on the table. Marya Timofeevna, though she very much wanted another cup, and had already reached for it, thought better of it and decorously declined, apparently pleased with herself for doing so.)

Varvara Petrovna smiled wryly.

"You know, Praskovya Ivanovna, my friend, you must have imagined something again and come here with it. You've lived by imagination all your life. You just got angry about boarding school; but do you remember how you came once and convinced the whole class that the hussar Shablykin had proposed to you, and how Madame Lefebure immediately exposed you in your lie? And you weren't even lying, you simply imagined it all for your own amusement. Well, speak: what is it now? What else have you imagined, what else are you displeased with?"

"And you fell in love with the priest who taught us religion in boarding school—take that, since you still have such a good memory—ha, ha, ha!"

She burst into bilious laughter and coughing.

"Ahh, so you haven't forgotten about the priest . . ." Varvara Petrovna gave her a hateful look.

Her face turned green. Praskovya Ivanovna suddenly assumed a dignified air.

"I'm in no mood for laughing now, dearest; why have you mixed my daughter up in your scandal before the eyes of the whole town—that is what I've come for!"

"My scandal?" Varvara Petrovna suddenly drew herself up menacingly.

"And I beg you to be more moderate, maman," Lizaveta Nikolaevna suddenly said.

"What did you say?" the maman was ready to shriek again, but suddenly withered under her daughter's flashing eyes.

"How can you talk of scandal, maman?" Liza flared up. "I came myself, with Yulia Mikhailovna's permission, because I wanted to know this unfortunate woman's story, so as to be useful to her."

" 'This unfortunate woman's story'!" Praskovya Ivanovna drawled with a spiteful laugh. "Is it fitting for you to get mixed up in such 'stories'? Ah, dearest! We've had enough of your despotism!" she turned furiously to Varvara Petrovna. "They say, whether it's true or not, that you've got the whole town marching to your orders, but now it seems your time has come!"

Varvara Petrovna sat straight as an arrow about to fly from the bow. For some ten seconds she looked sternly and fixedly at Praskovya Ivanovna.

"Well, Praskovya, thank God we're among our own here," she spoke at last, with ominous calm, "you've said a great deal that wasn't necessary."

"And I, my dear, am not so afraid of the world's opinion as some are; it's you who, under the guise of pride, are trembling before the world's opinion. And if there are only our own people here, it's so much the better for you than if strangers heard it."

"Have you grown smarter this week, or what?"

"I haven't grown smarter this week, it must be that the truth came out this week."

"What truth came out this week? Listen, Praskovya Ivanovna, don't vex me, explain this very minute, I ask you honestly: what truth came out, what do you mean by that?"

"But here it is, the whole truth, sitting right here!" Praskovya Ivanovna suddenly pointed her finger at Marya Timofeevna, with that desperate resolution which no longer considers the consequences but seeks only to strike at once. Marya Timofeevna, who had been looking at her all the while with gay curiosity, laughed joyfully at the sight of the wrathful guest's finger directed at her, and gaily fidgeted in her chair.

"Lord Jesus Christ, have they all lost their minds, or what!" Varvara Petrovna exclaimed and, turning pale, threw herself against the back of her chair.

She grew so pale that it even caused a commotion. Stepan Trofimovich was the first to rush to her; I also approached; even Liza rose from her place, though she remained standing by her chair; but it was Praskovya Ivanovna herself who was most frightened: she gave a cry, raised herself as much as she could, and almost wailed in a tearful voice:

"Varvara Petrovna, dearest, forgive me my spiteful foolishness! But, at least give her some water, someone!"

"Don't blubber, Praskovya Ivanovna, I beg you, please, and do move back, gentlemen, be so kind, there's no need for water!" Varvara Petrovna pronounced firmly, though softly, with her pale lips.

"Dearest!" Praskovya Ivanovna went on, calming down a little, "Varvara Petrovna, my friend, perhaps I am guilty of imprudent words, but, really, I'm so vexed, by these nameless letters most of all, which some paltry people are bombarding me with; I don't know why they don't write to you, since it's you they're writing about, and I, dearest, have a daughter!"

Varvara Petrovna silently gazed at her with wide-open eyes and listened in astonishment. At that moment a side door in the corner opened inaudibly and Darya Pavlovna appeared. She stopped and looked around; she was struck by our commotion. She must not immediately have noticed Marya Timofeevna, of whom no one had warned her. Stepan Trofimovich caught sight of her first, made a quick movement, blushed, and for some reason loudly announced: "Darya Pavlovna!" so that all eyes immediately turned to her.

"So, this is your Darya Pavlovna!" exclaimed Marya Timofeevna. "Why, Shatushka, your sister doesn't resemble you at all! How is it my man calls such loveliness the serf wench Dashka!"

Darya Pavlovna meanwhile had already gone up to Varvara Petrovna; but, struck by Marya Timofeevna's exclamation, she quickly turned around and remained thus in front of her chair, staring at the blessed fool with a long, riveted look.

"Sit down, Dasha," Varvara Petrovna said with horrifying calm, "closer, like so; you can see the woman as well sitting down. Do you know her?"

"I've never seen her," Dasha replied softly and, after a pause, added at once: "She must be the ailing sister of one Mr. Lebyadkin."

"And I, my soul, am only now seeing you for the first time, though I've long wished curiously to make your acquaintance, for I can see good breeding in your every gesture," Marya Timofeevna cried enthusiastically. "And that lackey of mine goes around swearing, but can it be that you took his money, and you so well bred and so nice? For you are nice, nice, nice, it's I who tell you so!" she concluded rapturously, waving her hand in front of her.

"Do you understand any of that?" Varvara Petrovna asked with proud dignity.

"I understand all of it, ma'am . . ."

"Did you hear about the money?"

"It must be the money that I undertook, while I was in Switzerland, to bring to Mr. Lebyadkin, her brother, at the request of Nikolai Vsevolodovich."

Silence ensued.

"Did Nikolai Vsevolodovich himself ask you to bring it?"

"He wanted very much to send this money, just three hundred roubles, to Mr. Lebyadkin. And since he didn't know his address, but only knew that he would be coming to our town, he charged me to give it to Mr. Lebyadkin in case he should come."

"And what money is . . . missing? What was this woman saying just now?"

"That I really don't know, ma'am; it has also reached me that Mr. Lebyadkin is saying aloud of me that I supposedly did not give him all of it, but I don't understand these words. There were three hundred roubles, and I gave him three hundred roubles."

Darya Pavlovna was now almost completely calm. And I will note that generally it was difficult to astonish this girl or to perplex her for long with anything—whatever she might feel inside herself. She now gave all her answers unhurriedly, responding to each question promptly and with precision, quietly, evenly, with no trace of her first sudden agitation, and with no embarrassment such as might betray the awareness of any guilt in herself. Varvara Petrovna did not tear her eyes from her all the while she was speaking. For a moment, Varvara Petrovna pondered.

"If," she finally said firmly, and evidently for the spectators, though she looked only at Dasha, "if Nikolai Vsevolodovich did not turn even to me with this charge, but asked you, he of course had his own reasons for doing so. I do not think I have any right to be curious about it, if it has been kept secret from me. But the fact alone of your participation in this affair sets me completely at ease about it all, that you should know, Darya, first of all. But you see, my friend, even with a pure conscience you might commit some imprudence, not knowing the world; and this you did, by agreeing to have dealings with some scoundrel. The rumors this blackguard has spread confirm your error. But I shall make inquiries about him and, being your protectress, I shall know how to intercede for you. And now all this must be ended."

"Best of all, when he comes to you," Marya Timofeevna suddenly joined in, leaning forward in her armchair, "send him to the lackeys' room. Let him sit there and play his trumps with them on a bench, and we'll sit here and have coffee. A cup of coffee might be sent to him, too, but I deeply despise him."

And she shook her head emphatically.

"This must be ended," Varvara Petrovna repeated, having carefully heard out Marya Timofeevna. "Ring, please, Stepan Trofimovich."

Stepan Trofimovich rang, and then suddenly stepped forward, all excited.

"If . . . if I . . ." he babbled hotly, blushing, faltering, and stammering, "if I, too, have heard a most repulsive account, or, better to say, slander, then . . . in perfect indignation . . . *enfin, c'est un homme perdu et quelque chose comme un forçat évadé . . .*"*

He broke off and did not finish; Varvara Petrovna, narrowing her eyes, looked him up and down. The decorous Alexei Yegorovich came in.

"The carriage," Varvara Petrovna ordered, "and you, Alexei Yegorych, get ready to take Miss Lebyadkin home, wherever she tells you."

"Mr. Lebyadkin himself has been waiting downstairs for some time, ma'am, and wishes very much to be announced."

---

*"anyhow, he is a depraved man and something like an escaped convict . . ."

"That is impossible, Varvara Petrovna," Mavriky Nikolaevich, who had been imperturbably silent all the while, suddenly stepped forward in alarm. "If you will allow me, this is not the sort of man who can enter society, this . . . this . . . this is an impossible man, Varvara Petrovna."

"Hold off," Varvara Petrovna turned to Alexei Yegorych, and he disappeared.

"*C'est un homme malhonnête et je crois même que c'est un forçat évadé ou quelque chose dans ce genre,*"* Stepan Trofimovich again muttered, again blushed, and again broke off.

"Liza, it's time to go," Praskovya Ivanovna announced squeamishly and rose from her seat. She seemed already to regret that, in her fright a little earlier, she had called herself a fool. While Darya Pavlovna was speaking, she had already begun listening with haughtily pursed lips. But I was struck most of all by the look of Lizaveta Nikolaevna from the moment Darya Pavlovna came in: hatred and contempt, much too unconcealed, flashed in her eyes.

"Hold off for a moment, Praskovya Ivanovna, I beg you," Varvara Petrovna stopped her with the same excessive calm. "Kindly sit down, I intend to speak everything out, and your legs hurt you. There, thank you. I lost my temper just now and said several impatient things to you. Kindly forgive me; it was foolish of me, and I'll be the first to repent, because I love justice in all things. Of course, you also lost your temper and mentioned some anonymous writer. Any anonymous calumny is deserving of contempt, if only because it is unsigned. If you think otherwise, I do not envy you. In any event, if I were in your place I would not drag such trash out of my pocket, I would not dirty myself. But you have dirtied yourself. However, since you started it, I will tell you that some six days ago I, too, received a letter, also anonymous and clownish. In it some scoundrel tries to persuade me that Nikolai Vsevolodovich has lost his mind and that I should beware of some lame woman who 'will play an extraordinary role in my fate'—I remember the expression. I thought it over and, knowing that Nikolai Vsevolodovich has an extraordinary number of enemies, I sent at once for one

*"He is a dishonest man and I believe he is even an escaped convict or something of the kind"

man here, a secret enemy of his and one of the most vengeful and contemptible of all, and my conversation with him at once convinced me of the contemptible source of the anonymous letter. If you, too, my poor Praskovya Ivanovna, have been bothered *because of me* with the same sort of contemptible letters, and have been 'bombarded,' as you put it, then, of course, I'll be the first to regret having been the innocent cause. That is all I wanted to tell you by way of explanation. I'm sorry to see that you are so tired and are now beside yourself. Furthermore, I am absolutely determined now to *admit* this suspicious man of whom Mavriky Nikolaevich said, in a not quite suitable phrase, that it was impossible to *receive* him. Liza, especially, has no reason to be here. Come, Liza, my friend, and let me kiss you once more."

Liza crossed the room and stopped silently in front of Varvara Petrovna. The latter kissed her, took her by the hands, moved her back a little, looked at her with feeling, then made a cross over her and kissed her again.

"So, good-bye, Liza" (tears almost sounded in Varvara Petrovna's voice), "believe that I shall never cease to love you, whatever your fate promises hereafter . . . God be with you. I have always blessed his holy right hand . . ."

She was going to add something, but checked herself and fell silent. Liza started walking back to her place, still in the same silence and as if pondering, but suddenly stopped before her mother.

"I won't go yet, maman, I'll stay with auntie a while longer," she spoke in a soft voice, but in those soft words there sounded an iron resolution.

"Oh, my God, what is it!" Praskovya Ivanovna cried out, feebly clasping her hands. But Liza did not answer, and did not even seem to hear; she sat down in her former corner and again began looking somewhere into the air.

Something proud and triumphant shone in Varvara Petrovna's face.

"Mavriky Nikolaevich, I have an extraordinary request: kindly go and have a look at that man downstairs, and if it is at all possible to *admit* him, bring him here."

Mavriky Nikolaevich bowed and went out. A minute later he brought in Mr. Lebyadkin.

IV

I HAVE SPOKEN before about the appearance of this man: a tall, curly, thick-set fellow of about forty, with a purple, somewhat bloated and flabby face, with cheeks that shook at every movement of his head, with small, bloodshot, at times quite cunning eyes, with a moustache and side-whiskers, with a nascent, fleshy, rather unpleasant-looking Adam's apple. But the most striking thing about him was that he appeared now wearing a tailcoat and clean linen. "There are people for whom clean linen is even indecent, sir," as Liputin once objected when Stepan Trofimovich jestingly reproached him for being slovenly. The captain also had black gloves, of which the right one, not yet put on, was held in his hand, while the left one, tightly stretched and refusing to be buttoned, half covered the fleshy left paw in which he held a brand-new, shiny, and probably never-before-sported round hat. It followed, therefore, that yesterday's "tailcoat of love," of which he had shouted to Shatov, actually existed. All this—that is, the tailcoat and linen—had been prepared (as I learned later) on Liputin's advice, for some mysterious purposes. There was no doubt that his arrival now (in a hired carriage) must also have been at someone's instigation and with someone's help; on his own he would never have managed to figure it out, along with getting dressed, ready, and resolved in some three quarters of an hour, even supposing that the scene on the church porch had become known to him immediately. He was not drunk, but was in the heavy, leaden, foggy state of a man who suddenly wakes up after many days of drinking. It seemed you would only have to shake him a couple of times by the shoulder and he would immediately become drunk again.

He all but flew into the drawing room, but suddenly stumbled over the carpet in the doorway. Marya Timofeevna simply died laughing. He gave her a ferocious look and suddenly took several quick steps towards Varvara Petrovna.

"I have come, madam . . ." he boomed, as if through a trumpet.

"Be so kind, my dear sir," Varvara Petrovna drew herself up, "as to take a seat over there on that chair. I will hear you from there just as well, and from here I will see you better."

The captain stopped, staring dully before him, but turned even so and sat in his appointed place, just by the door. The expression of his physiognomy betrayed extreme insecurity and, at the same time, insolence and some ceaseless irritation. He was terribly scared, one could see that, but his vanity also suffered, and one could guess that out of irritated vanity, despite his fear, he might venture any sort of insolence if the occasion arose. He apparently feared for every movement of his clumsy body. For all such gentlemen, as is known, when by some odd chance they appear in society, the worst suffering comes from their own hands and the constant awareness of the impossibility of somehow decently disposing of them. The captain froze in his chair, his hat and gloves in his hands, not taking his senseless eyes from Varvara Petrovna's stern countenance. He might have liked to take a better look around, but he did not dare yet. Marya Timofeevna, probably again finding his figure terribly funny, burst into another gale of laughter, but he did not stir. Varvara Petrovna kept him in that position for a mercilessly long time, a whole minute, studying him pitilessly.

"First, allow me to learn your name from you yourself," she spoke evenly and expressively.

"Captain Lebyadkin," boomed the captain. "I have come, madam . . ." he stirred again.

"I beg your pardon!" Varvara Petrovna again stopped him. "This pitiful person, who has so much attracted my interest, is she indeed your sister?"

"My sister, madam, who has escaped from under supervision, for she's in a certain condition . . ."

He suddenly faltered and turned purple.

"Don't take it perversely, madam," he became terribly disconcerted, "a brother's not going to soil . . . in a certain condition—that's not to say that sort of condition . . . in the sense that would stain one's reputation . . . at this late stage . . ."

He suddenly broke off.

"My dear sir!" Varvara Petrovna raised her head.

"This sort of condition!" he continued suddenly, tapping the middle of his forehead with his finger. Silence ensued.

"And has she been suffering from it for a long time?" Varvara Petrovna drawled somewhat.

"Madam, I have come to thank you for the generosity you displayed on the church porch, as a Russian, as a brother . . ."

"As a brother?"

"I mean, not as a brother, but solely in the sense that I'm my sister's brother, madam, and believe me, madam," he went on pattering, turning purple again, "I'm not as uneducated as I may seem at first sight in your drawing room. My sister and I are nothing, madam, compared with the splendor we can observe here. Having our slanderers, besides. But as concerning his reputation, Lebyadkin is proud, madam, and . . . and . . . I've come to thank . . . Here is the money, madam!"

At this point he snatched the wallet from his pocket, tore a wad of bills from it, and began going through them with trembling fingers in a frenzied fit of impatience. One could see that he wanted to explain something as soon as possible, and needed very much to do so; but, probably feeling himself that this fumbling with the money made him look even more foolish, he lost the last of his self-possession; the money refused to be counted, his fingers got entangled, and, to crown the disgrace, one green bill[1] slipped out of the wallet and fluttered zigzag to the carpet.

"Twenty roubles, madam," he suddenly jumped up with the wad in his hand, his face sweaty from suffering; noticing the escaped bill on the floor, he bent down to pick it up, but for some reason felt ashamed and waved his hand.

"For your servants, madam, for the footman who picks it up—let him remember Miss Lebyadkin!"

"I cannot possibly allow that," Varvara Petrovna said hastily and with some fright.

"In that case . . ."

He bent down, picked it up, turned purple, and, suddenly approaching Varvara Petrovna, held the counted money out to her.

"What is this?" she finally became altogether frightened and even shrank back in her armchair. Mavriky Nikolaevich, myself, and Stepan Trofimovich all stepped forward.

"Don't worry, don't worry, I'm not mad, by God, I'm not mad!" the captain assured excitedly in all directions.

"No, my dear sir, you are out of your mind."

"Madam, it's not at all what you think! I, of course, am a negligible link . . . Oh, madam, rich are your halls, but poor are those of Marya the Unknown, my sister, born Lebyadkin, but for now we will call her Marya the Unknown, for now, madam, only *for now,* for God himself will not allow it to be forever! Madam, you gave her ten roubles, and she accepted them only because they came from *you,* madam! Do you hear, madam! From no one else in the world would this Unknown Marya take, otherwise her grandfather, an officer killed in the Caucasus before the eyes of Ermolov himself,[2] would shudder in his grave, but from you, madam, from you she will take anything. She will take with one hand, but with the other she will now offer you twenty roubles, as a donation to one of the charitable committees in the capital, where you, madam, are a member . . . since you yourself, madam, have been published in the *Moscow Gazette,* that you are the keeper of this town's local book for this charitable society, where anyone can subscribe . . ."

The captain suddenly broke off; he was breathing heavily, as though after some difficult feat. All that about the charitable committee had probably been prepared beforehand, and perhaps edited by Liputin as well. He became even more sweaty; beads of sweat literally stood out on his temples. Varvara Petrovna scrutinized him sharply.

"This book," she said sternly, "is always downstairs, with the doorkeeper of my house, you may enter your donation in it if you like. And therefore I ask you now to put your money away and not to wave it in the air. That's right. I also ask you to take your former seat. That's right. I am very sorry, my dear sir, that I was mistaken with regard to your sister, and gave to her as to the poor when she is so rich. One thing only I fail to understand—why it is that she can take money from me alone and not from anyone else. You insisted on it so much that I should like a perfectly precise explanation."

"Madam, that is a secret that can only be buried in the grave!" the captain replied.

"Why so?" Varvara Petrovna asked, somehow less firmly now.

"Madam, madam! . . ."

He fell glumly silent, looking down, his right hand pressed to his heart. Varvara Petrovna waited, not taking her eyes off him.

"Madam!" he suddenly bellowed, "allow me to ask you one question, just one, but openly, directly, in the Russian way, from the soul."

"Kindly do."

"Have you, madam, ever suffered in your life?"

"You merely want to say that you have suffered or are suffering because of someone."

"Madam, madam!" he suddenly jumped up again, probably without noticing it, and struck himself on the chest. "Here, in this heart, so much has built up, so much that God himself will be surprised when it's revealed at the Last Judgment!"

"Hm, that's putting it strongly."

"Madam, I am speaking, perhaps, in irritable language . . ."

"Don't worry, I know myself when you will need to be stopped."

"May I pose one more question, madam?"

"Do pose one more question."

"Can one die solely from the nobility of one's own soul?"

"I don't know, I've never asked myself such a question."

"You don't know! Never asked yourself such a question!" he cried with pathetic irony. "In that case, in that case—

'Be silent, hopeless heart!' "[3]

and he struck himself fiercely on the chest.

By now he was pacing the room again. A trait of such people—this total incapacity to keep their desires to themselves; this uncontrollable urge, on the contrary, to reveal them at once, even in all their untidiness, the moment they arise. When he steps into society not his own, such a gentleman usually begins timidly, but yield him just a hair and he will at once leap to impertinence. The captain was already excited; he paced, waved his arms, did not listen to questions, spoke of himself rapidly, so rapidly that his tongue sometimes tripped, and without finishing he would leap on to the next phrase. True, he could hardly have been completely sober; then, too, Lizaveta Nikolaevna was sitting there, and though he did not glance at her even once, her presence seemed to make him terribly giddy. However, that is only a surmise. There must therefore have been some reason why Varvara Petrovna, overcoming her loathing, decided to listen to such a man. Praskovya Ivanovna was simply quaking with fear, though, to tell the truth, I don't think she quite understood what was going on. Stepan Trofimovich was also trembling, but, on the contrary, because he was always inclined to understand everything to excess. Mavriky Nikolaevich stood in the attitude of universal protector. Poor Liza was pale and was staring fixedly, with wide-open eyes, at the wild captain. Shatov went on sitting in the same attitude; but, what was strangest of all, Marya Timofeevna not only stopped laughing, but became terribly sad. She leaned her right elbow on the table and gazed at her declaiming brother with a long, sad look. Darya Pavlovna alone seemed calm to me.

"These are all nonsensical allegories," Varvara Petrovna finally became angry, "you have not answered my question—'Why?' I am insistently awaiting an answer."

"I didn't answer your 'why'? You're awaiting an answer to your 'why'?" the captain reiterated, winking. "This little word 'why' has been poured all over the universe since the very first day of creation, madam, and every moment the whole of nature cries out 'Why?' to its creator, and for seven thousand years[4] has received no answer. Is it for Captain Lebyadkin alone to answer, and would that be just, madam?"

"That's all nonsense, that's not the point!" Varvara Petrovna was growing wrathful and losing her patience. "These are allegories, and, besides, you choose to speak too floridly, my dear sir, which I regard as impertinence."

"Madam," the captain was not listening to her, "I might wish to be called Ernest, yet I am forced to bear the crude name of Ignat—why is that, do you think? I might wish to be called Prince de Monbars,[5] yet I'm only Lebyadkin, from *lebed*, the swan—why is that? I am a poet, a poet in my soul, and could be getting a thousand roubles from a publisher, yet I'm forced to live in a tub—why, why? Madam! In my opinion Russia is a freak of nature, nothing else!"

"You decidedly cannot say anything more definite?"

"I can recite you a piece called 'The Cockroach,' madam!"

"Wha-a-at?"

"Madam, I am not crazy yet! I will be crazy, I will be, that's certain, but I am not crazy yet! Madam, a friend of mine—a most no-o-oble person—has written a Krylov's fable entitled 'The Cockroach'—may I recite it?"

"You want to recite some fable of Krylov's?"

"No, it's not Krylov's fable I want to recite, it's my own fable, mine, I wrote it! Believe me, madam—no offense to you—but I'm not uneducated and depraved to such an extent as not to realize that Russia possesses the great fable-writer Krylov, to whom the minister of education erected a monument in the Summer Garden for childhood playing.[6] Now then, madam, you ask me, 'Why?' The answer is at the bottom of this fable, in flaming letters!"

"Recite your fable."

> " 'Tis of a cockroach I will tell,
> And a fine cockroach was he,
> But then into a glass he fell
> Full of fly-phagy . . ."

"Lord, what is this?" Varvara Petrovna exclaimed.

"It's in the summertime," the captain hurried, waving his arms terribly, with the irritated impatience of an author whose recitation is being hindered, "in the summertime, when lots of flies get into a glass, then fly-phagy takes place, any fool can understand that, don't interrupt, don't interrupt, you'll see, you'll see . . ." (he kept waving his arms).

> "The cockroach took up so much room
> It made the flies murmúr.
> 'A crowded glass, is this our doom?'
> They cried to Jupiter.
>
> But as the flies did make their moan
> Along came Nikifor,
> A kind, old, no-o-oble man . . .

I haven't quite finished here, but anyway, in plain words!" the captain rattled on. "Nikifor takes the glass and, in spite of their crying, dumps the whole comedy into the tub, both flies and cockroach, which should have been done long ago. But notice, madam, notice, the cockroach does not murmur! This is the answer to your question, 'Why?' " he cried out triumphantly. " 'The cock-roach does not mur-mur!' As for Nikifor, he represents nature," he added in a quick patter, and began pacing the room self-contentedly.

Varvara Petrovna became terribly angry.

"And to do with what money—allow me to ask you—supposedly received from Nikolai Vsevolodovich, and supposedly not given to you in full, have you dared to accuse a person belonging to my household?"

"Slander!" bellowed Lebyadkin, raising his right hand tragically.

"No, it is not slander."

"Madam, there are circumstances that make one rather endure family disgrace than proclaim the truth aloud. Lebyadkin will not let on, madam!"

He was as if blind; he was inspired; he felt his significance; he must have been imagining some such thing. He already wanted to offend, to do something dirty, to show his power.

"Ring the bell, please, Stepan Trofimovich," Varvara Petrovna requested.

"Lebyadkin is cunning, madam!" he winked, with a nasty smile, "he's cunning, but he, too, has his stumbling block, he, too, has his forecourt of passions! And this forecourt is the old hussar's war-bottle, sung by Denis Davydov.[7] And so, when in this forecourt, madam, it may happen that he sends a letter in verse, a mag-ni-fi-cent one, but which afterwards he might wish to bring back with the tears of his whole life, for the sense of beauty is violated. But the bird has flown, you can't catch it by the tail! It is in this forecourt, madam, that Lebyadkin could also talk about a noble young lady, by way of the noble indignation of a soul resenting its offenses, which fact has been made use of by his slanderers. But Lebyadkin is cunning, madam! And in vain does the sinister wolf sit over him, pouring more every moment and waiting for the end: Lebyadkin will not let on, and after two bottles what turns up each time, instead of the expected thing, is— Lebyadkin's Cunning! But enough, oh, enough! Madam, your magnificent halls might belong to the noblest of persons, but the cockroach does not murmur! Notice, yes, notice finally that he does not murmur, and know the great spirit!"

At that moment the bell rang from the doorkeeper's room downstairs, and almost at once Alexei Yegorych, who had been rather slow in responding to Stepan Trofimovich's ring, appeared. The decorous old servant was somehow unusually excited.

"Nikolai Vsevolodovich has been pleased to arrive just this minute and is on his way here, ma'am," he said in reply to Varvara Petrovna's inquiring look.

I especially remember her at that moment: at first she became pale, but suddenly her eyes flashed. She drew herself up in her chair with a look of extraordinary resolution. Everyone else was also astounded. The totally unexpected arrival of Nikolai Vsevolodovich, who was due to be here perhaps no sooner than in another month, was strange not only in its unexpectedness, but precisely in some fatal coincidence with the present moment. Even the captain stopped like a post in the middle of the room, openmouthed, staring at the door with a terribly stupid look.

And then, from the adjacent hall, a long and large room, came the sound of quickly approaching footsteps, small steps, extremely rapid, as if someone were rolling along, and suddenly into the drawing room flew—not Nikolai Vsevolodovich at all, but a young man totally unknown to anyone.

V

I WILL ALLOW MYSELF to pause and depict, if only in cursory strokes, this suddenly appearing person.

This was a young man of twenty-seven or thereabouts, a little taller than average, with thin, rather long blond hair and a wispy, barely evident moustache and beard. Dressed in clean and even fashionable clothes, but not foppishly; a bit hunched and slack at first sight, and yet not hunched at all, even easygoing. Seemingly a sort of odd man, and yet everyone later found his manners quite decent and his conversation always to the point.

No one would call him bad-looking, but no one likes his face. His head is elongated towards the back and as if flattened on the sides, giving his face a sharp look. His forehead is high and narrow, but his features are small—eyes sharp, nose small and sharp, lips long and thin. The expression of his face is as if sickly, but it only seems so. He has a sort of dry crease on his cheeks and around his cheekbones, which makes him look as if he were recovering from a grave illness. And yet he is perfectly healthy and strong, and has never even been ill.

He walks and moves very hurriedly, and yet he is not hurrying anywhere. Nothing, it seems, can put him out of countenance; in any circumstances and in any society, he remains the same. There is great self-satisfaction in him, but he does not take the least note of it himself.

He speaks rapidly, hurriedly, but at the same time self-confidently, and is never at a loss for words. His thoughts are calm, despite his hurried look, distinct and final—and that is especially noticeable. His enunciation is remarkably clear; his words spill out like big, uniform grains, always choice and always ready to be at your service. You like it at first, but later it will become repulsive, and precisely because of this all too clear enunciation, this string of ever ready words. You somehow begin to imagine that the tongue in his mouth must be of some special form, somehow unusually long and thin, terribly red, and with an extremely sharp, constantly and involuntarily wriggling tip.

Well, so this was the young man who had just flown into the drawing room, and, really, even now it seems to me that he started talking in the next room and came in that way, already talking. Instantly he was standing before Varvara Petrovna.

". . . And imagine, Varvara Petrovna," the beads spilled out of him, "I came in thinking to find he'd already been here for a quarter of an hour; it's an hour and a half since he arrived; we met at Kirillov's; he left half an hour ago to come straight here, and told me to come here, too, in a quarter of an hour . . ."

"But, who? Who told you to come here?" Varvara Petrovna questioned.

"But, Nikolai Vsevolodovich, of course! You don't mean you're only learning of it this minute? His luggage at least should have arrived long ago, didn't they tell you? So I'm the first to announce it. By the way, we could send for him somewhere, but, anyhow, he'll certainly come himself presently and, it would seem, precisely at a moment that answers to some of his expectations and, at least so far as I can judge, to some of his calculations." Here he looked around the room and rested his eyes especially on the captain. "Ah, Lizaveta Nikolaevna, how glad I am to meet you first thing, I'm very glad to shake your hand," he quickly flew over to take the hand which the gaily smiling Liza offered him, "and I notice that the much esteemed Praskovya Ivanovna also seems to remember her 'professor,' and is not even angry with him, as she always was in Switzerland. But, by the way, how do your legs feel here, Praskovya Ivanovna, and were the Swiss consultants right in sentencing you to the climate of the fatherland? . . . what's that, ma'am? wet compresses? that must be very good for you. But how sorry I was, Varvara Petrovna" (he quickly turned again), "that I was too late to find you abroad and pay my respects in person, and I had so much to tell you besides . . . I notified my old man here, but he, as is his custom, seems to . . ."

"Petrusha!" Stepan Trofimovich cried, instantly coming out of his stupor; he clasped his hands and rushed to his son. *"Pierre, mon enfant,* and I didn't recognize you!" He embraced him tightly, and tears poured from his eyes.

"There, there, don't be naughty, no need for gestures, there, enough, enough, I beg you," Petrusha hastily muttered, trying to free himself from the embrace.

"I have always, always been guilty before you!"

"Now, that's enough; save it for later. I just knew you were going to be naughty. Be a bit more sober, I beg you."

"But I haven't seen you for ten years!"

"The less reason for any outpourings . . ."

"Mon enfant!"

"So, I believe, I believe you love me, take your arms away. You're disturbing the others . . . Ah, here is Nikolai Vsevolodovich, now don't be naughty, I beg you, finally!"

Nikolai Vsevolodovich was indeed already in the room; he had come in very quietly, and stopped for a moment in the doorway, quietly looking around at the gathering.

Just as four years ago, when I saw him for the first time, so now, too, I was struck at the first sight of him. I had not forgotten him in the least; but there are, it seems, such physiognomies as always, each time they appear, bring something new, as it were, which you have not noticed in them before, though you may have met them a hundred times previously. Apparently he was still the same as four years ago: as refined, as imposing, he entered as imposingly as then, even almost as youthful. His faint smile was as officially benign and just as self-satisfied; his glance as stern, thoughtful, and as if distracted. In short, it seemed we had parted only yesterday. But one thing struck me:

before, even though he had been considered a handsome man, his face had indeed "resembled a mask," as certain vicious-tongued ladies of our society put it. Whereas now—now, I don't know why, but he appeared to me, at very first sight, as decidedly, unquestionably hand-some, so that it could in no way be said that his face resembled a mask. Was it because he had become a bit paler than before, and seemed to have lost some weight? Or was there perhaps some new thought that now shone in his eyes?

"Nikolai Vsevolodovich!" Varvara Petrovna cried, drawing herself up straight but not quitting her armchair, stopping him with an imperi-ous gesture, "stop for one moment!"

But to explain the terrible question that suddenly followed this gesture and exclamation—a question I could not have supposed possi-ble even in Varvara Petrovna herself—I shall ask the reader to recall what Varvara Petrovna's character had been all her life and the remark-able impetuousness she had shown in certain extraordinary moments. I also ask him to bear in mind that, despite the remarkable firmness of soul and the considerable amount of reason, and of practical, even, so to speak, managerial tact she possessed, there was no lack of moments in her life in which she would give all of herself suddenly, entirely, and, if it is permissible to say so, totally without restraint. I also ask him, finally, to consider that for her the present moment could indeed have been one of those in which the whole essence of a life—all that has been lived through, all the present, and perhaps the future—is suddenly focused. I shall also remind him in passing of the anonymous letter she had received, as she had just so irritably let on to Praskovya Ivanovna, though I think she kept silent about the further contents of the letter; and precisely in it, perhaps, lay the key to the possibility of that terrible question which she suddenly addressed to her son.

"Nikolai Vsevolodovich," she repeated, rapping out the words in a firm voice in which a menacing challenge sounded, "I ask you to tell me right now, without moving from that spot: is it true that this unfortunate lame woman—there she is, over there, look at her!—is it true that she is . . . your lawful wife?"

I remember that moment only too well; he did not even blink an eye, but looked intently at his mother; not the slightest change in his face ensued. At last he smiled slowly, a sort of condescending smile, and, without a word of reply, quietly went up to his mother, took her hand, brought it reverently to his lips, and kissed it. And so strong was his ever irresistible influence on his mother that even then she did not dare snatch her hand away. She simply stared at him, all question, and her whole look confessed that she could not endure the uncertainty a moment longer.

But he continued to be silent. Having kissed her hand, he glanced all around the room once again and, still as unhurriedly as before, went straight to Marya Timofeevna. It is very difficult to describe people's physiognomies at certain moments. It has remained in my memory, for example, that Marya Timofeevna, all numb with fear, rose to meet him and clasped her hands before her as if entreating him; and at the same time I also remember there was rapture in her eyes, a sort of insane rapture that almost distorted her features—a rapture hard for people to bear. Perhaps both were there, both fear and rapture; but I remember myself quickly moving closer (I was standing just next to her), for I fancied she was about to faint.

"You cannot be here," Nikolai Vsevolodovich spoke to her in a caressing, melodious voice, and an extraordinary tenderness shone in his eyes. He stood before her in a most reverent attitude, and his every movement expressed the most sincere respect. In an impetuous half-whisper the poor woman breathlessly murmured to him:

"And may I . . . kneel to you . . . now?"

"No, you certainly may not," he smiled magnificently at her, so that she, too, suddenly gave a joyful little smile. In the same melodious voice, and tenderly reasoning with her, as with a child, he added imposingly:

"Consider that you are a girl, and I, though your most faithful friend, am nevertheless a stranger to you, not a husband, not a father, not a fiancé. Now give me your hand and let us go; I will see you to the carriage and, if you permit, will take you to your house myself."

She listened and bent her head as if pondering.

"Let us go," she said, sighing, and gave him her hand.

But then a small mishap befell her. She must have turned somehow awkwardly and stepped on her bad, shorter leg—in a word, she fell full sideways on the armchair, and if it had not been for the armchair, she would have fallen to the floor. He instantly caught her up, supported her, holding her firmly under the arm, and led her carefully and sympathetically to the door. She was obviously distressed by her fall, became embarrassed, blushed, and was terribly ashamed. Silently looking down, limping badly, she hobbled after him, almost hanging on his arm. They walked out like that. Liza, I noticed, for some reason suddenly jumped up from her chair as they were walking out, and followed them with a fixed stare to the very door. Then she silently sat down again, but there was some convulsive movement in her face, as if she had touched some viper.

While this whole scene was taking place between Nikolai Vsevolodovich and Marya Timofeevna, everyone was hushed with amazement; one could have heard a fly buzz; but as soon as they walked out, everyone suddenly began talking.

VI

O R NOT TALKING so much as exclaiming. I have somewhat forgotten now the order in which it all happened, because there was a tumult. Stepan Trofimovich exclaimed something in French and clasped his hands, but Varvara Petrovna could not be bothered with him. Even Mavriky Nikolaevich muttered something abruptly and rapidly. But most excited of all was Pyotr Stepanovich; he was desperately convincing Varvara Petrovna of something, with big gestures, but for a long time I could not understand it. He addressed Praskovya Ivanovna and Lizaveta Nikolaevna as well; in the heat of the moment he even shouted something in passing to his father—in short, he whirled all around the room. Varvara Petrovna, all flushed, jumped up from her seat and cried to Praskovya Ivanovna: "Did you hear, did you hear what he just said to her?" But the latter could no longer even reply, and merely mumbled something, waving her hand. The poor woman had her own troubles: she kept turning her head towards Liza, looking at her in unaccountable fear, and no longer dared even to think of getting up and leaving before her daughter rose. Meanwhile, the captain certainly wanted to slip away, this I noticed. He had been in a great and unquestionable fright from the moment Nikolai Vsevolodovich appeared; but Pyotr Stepanovich seized him by the arm and did not let him leave.

"This is necessary, necessary," he spilled out his beads at Varvara Petrovna, still trying to convince her. He was standing in front of her, and she by then had already sat back down in the armchair and, I remember, listened to him greedily; he had succeeded in holding her attention.

"This is necessary. You can see for yourself, Varvara Petrovna, that there's a misunderstanding here, and much that looks odd, and yet the thing is clear as a candle and simple as a finger. I realize only too well that no one has authorized me to tell about it, and that I perhaps look ridiculous in inviting myself. But, first of all, Nikolai Vsevolodovich himself attaches no great importance to this thing, and, finally, there are still cases when it is difficult for a man to bring himself to explain things personally, and it must be undertaken by a third person, for whom it is easier to express certain delicate matters. Believe me, Varvara Petrovna, Nikolai Vsevolodovich is not in the least to blame for not giving your question a radical explanation at once, even though the matter is a trifling one; I've known of it since Petersburg. Besides, the whole anecdote only does honor to Nikolai Vsevolodovich, if it's necessary to use this vague word 'honor' . . ."

"You mean to say that you were a witness to some occurrence that gave rise to . . . this misunderstanding?" asked Varvara Petrovna.

"A witness and a participant," Pyotr Stepanovich hastened to confirm.

"If you give me your word that this will not offend Nikolai Vsevolodovich's delicacy in certain of his feelings towards me, from whom he does not conceal an-y-thing . . . and if you are so sure, besides, that it will even give him pleasure . . ."

"Pleasure, most certainly; that's why I regard it as a particular pleasure for me. I'm convinced he would ask me himself."

It was rather strange, and outside the usual ways, this importunate desire on the part of this gentleman who had suddenly fallen from the sky to tell other people's anecdotes. But he caught Varvara Petrovna with his bait, having touched her sorest spot. I did not know the man's character fully then, and still less did I know his intentions.

"You may speak," Varvara Petrovna announced reservedly and cautiously, suffering somewhat from her indulgence.

"It's a short matter; in fact, if you like, it's not even an anecdote," the beads began spilling out. "However, a novelist might cook up a novel from it in an idle moment. It's quite an interesting little matter, Praskovya Ivanovna, and I'm sure Lizaveta Nikolaevna will listen with curiosity, because there are many things here which, if not queer, are at least quaint. About five years ago, in Petersburg, Nikolai Vsevolodovich got to know this gentleman—this same Mr. Lebyadkin who is standing here with his mouth hanging open and, it seems, was just about to slip away. Forgive me, Varvara Petrovna. Incidentally, I'd advise you not to take to your heels, mister retired official of the former supply department (you see, I remember you perfectly). Both I and Nikolai Vsevolodovich are all too well informed of your local tricks, of which, don't forget, you will have to give an accounting. Once again I ask your forgiveness, Varvara Petrovna. Nikolai Vsevolodovich used to call this gentleman his Falstaff[8]—that must be some former character," he suddenly explained, "some burlesque everyone laughs at and who allows everyone to laugh at him, so long as they pay money. The life Nikolai Vsevolodovich then led in Petersburg was, so to speak, a jeering one—I cannot define it by any other word, because he was not a man to fall into disillusionment, and he scorned then to do anything serious. I'm talking only about that time, Varvara Petrovna. This Lebyadkin had a sister—the very one who was just sitting here. This nice brother and sister had no corner of their own, and wandered about staying with various people. He loitered under the arcades of the Gostiny Dvor,[9] unfailingly wearing his former uniform, and stopped the cleaner-looking passers-by, and whatever he collected he would spend on drink. His sister lived like the birds of the air. She helped out in those corners and served in exchange for necessities. It was a most terrible Sodom; I'll pass over the picture of this corner life—the life to which Nikolai Vsevolodovich then gave himself out of whimsicality.[10] This was only then, Varvara Petrovna; and as for 'whimsicality,' the expression is his. There is much that he does not conceal from me. Mademoiselle Lebyadkin, who at a certain period happened to run into Nikolai Vsevolodovich all too often, was struck by his appearance. He was, so to speak, a diamond set against the dirty background of her life.

I'm a poor describer of feelings, so I'll pass that over; but rotten little people immediately made fun of her, and she grew sad. They generally laughed at her there, but before she didn't notice it. She was already not right in the head then, but less so than now. There's reason to think that in childhood, through some benefactress, she almost received an education. Nikolai Vsevolodovich never paid the slightest attention to her, and rather spent his time playing old greasy cards, the game of preference for quarter-kopeck stakes, with some clerks. But once when she was being mistreated, he, without asking why, grabbed one clerk by the scruff of the neck and chucked him out the second-story window. There wasn't any chivalrous indignation in favor of offended innocence in it; the whole operation took place amid general laughter, and Nikolai Vsevolodovich himself laughed most of all; everything eventually came to a good end, they made peace and began drinking punch. But oppressed innocence herself did not forget it. Of course, it ended with the final shaking of her mental faculties. I repeat, I'm a poor describer of feelings, but the main thing here was the dream. And Nikolai Vsevolodovich, as if on purpose, aroused the dream even more; instead of just laughing at it, he suddenly began addressing Mademoiselle Lebyadkin with unexpected esteem. Kirillov, who was there (an exceedingly original man, Varvara Petrovna, and an exceedingly abrupt one; perhaps you'll meet him one day, he's here now), well, so this Kirillov, who ordinarily is always silent, but then suddenly got excited, observed to Nikolai Vsevolodovich, as I remember, that his treating this lady as a marquise was finally going to finish her off. I will add that Nikolai Vsevolodovich had a certain respect for this Kirillov. And how do you think he answered him? 'You assume, Mr. Kirillov, that I am laughing at her; let me assure you that I do indeed respect her, because she is better than any of us.' And, you know, he said it in such a serious tone. Though, in fact, during those two or three months he hadn't said a word to her except 'hello' and 'good-bye.' I, who was there, remember for a certainty that she finally reached the point of regarding him as something like her fiancé, who did not dare to 'abduct' her solely because he had many enemies and family obstacles, or something of the sort. There was much laughter over that! In the end, when Nikolai Vsevolodovich had to come here that time, as he was leaving he arranged for her keep, and it seems it was quite a substantial yearly pension, at least three hundred roubles, if not more. In short, let's say it was all self-indulgence, the fancy of a prematurely weary man—let it be, finally, as Kirillov was saying, a new étude by a jaded man, with the object of finding out what a mad cripple can be brought to. 'You chose on purpose,' he said, 'the very least of beings, a cripple covered in eternal shame and beatings—and knowing, besides, that this being is dying of her comical love for you—and you suddenly start to flummox her on purpose, solely to see what will come of it!' Why, finally, is a man so especially to blame for the fantasy of a mad woman to whom, notice, he had hardly spoken two sentences during that whole time! There are things, Varvara Petrovna, of which it is not only impossible to speak intelligently, but of which it is not intelligent even to begin speaking. Well, let it be whimsicality, finally—but that's all one can say; and yet quite a story has been made of it now . . . I'm partly informed, Varvara Petrovna, of what is going on here."

The narrator suddenly broke off and was turning to Lebyadkin, but Varvara Petrovna stopped him; she was in the greatest exaltation.

"Have you finished?" she asked.

"Not yet; for completeness, I would have to put some questions on certain matters to this gentleman, with your permission . . . You will see presently what it's about, Varvara Petrovna."

"Enough, later, stop for a moment, I beg you. Oh, how good it is that I allowed you to speak!"

"And observe, Varvara Petrovna," Pyotr Stepanovich roused himself, "how could Nikolai Vsevolodovich have explained all this to you himself just now, in answer to your question, which was perhaps much too categorical?"

"Oh, much too much!"

"And was I not right to say that in certain cases it is much easier for a third person to explain than for the interested person himself!"

"Yes, yes . . . But in one thing you are mistaken, and I regret to see that you continue to be mistaken."

"Really? What's that?"

"You see . . . And, incidentally, why don't you sit down, Pyotr Stepanovich?"

"Oh, if you like, and I am tired, thank you."

He at once pulled out a chair and turned it in such a way that he wound up between Varvara Petrovna on the one side and Praskovya Ivanovna at the table on the other, and facing Mr. Lebyadkin, whom he would not take his eyes off for a moment.

"You are mistaken in calling it 'whimsicality' . . ."

"Oh, if that's all . . ."

"No, no, no, wait," Varvara Petrovna stopped him, obviously preparing herself to speak much and ecstatically. As soon as he noticed it, Pyotr Stepanovich became all attention.

"No, this was something higher than whimsicality and, I assure you, even something holy! A man, proud and early insulted, who had arrived at that 'jeering' which you mentioned so aptly—in short, a Prince Harry, to use Stepan Trofimovich's magnificent comparison at the time, which would be perfectly correct if he did not resemble Hamlet even more, at least in my view."

"*Et vous avez raison,*"* Stepan Trofimovich echoed, weightily and with feeling.

"Thank you, Stepan Trofimovich, you I thank especially, and precisely for your constant faith in Nicolas, in the loftiness of his soul and calling. You even strengthened this faith in me when I was losing spirit . . ."

"*Chère, chère* . . ." Stepan Trofimovich was already making a step forward, but stopped, realizing that it would be dangerous to interrupt.

"And if Nicolas had always had at his side" (Varvara Petrovna was half singing now) "a gentle Horatio, great in his humility—another beautiful expression of yours, Stepan Trofimovich—he would perhaps have been saved long ago from the sad and 'sudden demon of irony' that has tormented him all his life. (The phrase about the demon of irony is again an astonishing expression of yours, Stepan Trofimovich.) But Nicolas never had a Horatio, or an Ophelia. He had only his mother, but what can a mother do alone and in such circumstances? You know, Pyotr Stepanovich, I can even understand, and quite well, how a being such as Nicolas could appear even in such dirty slums as those you were telling about. I can imagine so clearly now this 'jeering' life (your remarkably apt expression!), this insatiable thirst for contrast,

*"And you are right"

this dark background of the picture, against which he appears like a diamond—again according to your comparison, Pyotr Stepanovich. And so he meets there a creature offended by everyone, a cripple, half crazy, and perhaps at the same time with the noblest feelings!"

"Hm, yes, presumably."

"And after all that you still do not understand that he is not laughing at her like everyone else! Oh, people! You do not understand that he should protect her from her offenders, surround her with respect 'like a marquise' (this Kirillov must have a remarkably deep understanding of people, though he did not understand Nicolas!). If you like, it was precisely through this contrast that the trouble came; if the unfortunate woman had been in different circumstances, she might not have arrived at such a delirious dream. A woman, it takes a woman to understand this, Pyotr Stepanovich, and what a pity that you . . . that is, not that you are not a woman, but at least for this once, so as to understand!"

"You mean, in a sense, the worse the better—I understand, I understand, Varvara Petrovna. It's like with religion: the worse a man's life is, or the more downtrodden and poor a whole people is, the more stubbornly they dream of a reward in paradise, and if there are a hundred thousand priests fussing about at the same time, inflaming the dream and speculating on it, then . . . I understand you, Varvara Petrovna, rest assured."

"I don't suppose that's quite so, but tell me, can it really be that in order to extinguish the dream in this unfortunate organism" (why Varvara Petrovna used the word "organism" here, I could not understand), "Nicolas, too, should have laughed at her and treated her as the other clerks did? Can it really be that you reject that lofty compassion, that noble tremor of the whole organism with which Nicolas suddenly so sternly answered Kirillov: 'I do not laugh at her.' A lofty, a holy answer!"

"*Sublime,*" muttered Stepan Trofimovich.

"And, note, he is not at all as rich as you think; it is I who am rich, not he, and at that time he was taking almost nothing from me."

"I understand, I understand all that, Varvara Petrovna," Pyotr Stepanovich was now stirring somewhat impatiently.

"Oh, it is my character! I recognize myself in Nicolas! I recognize that youth, that possibility of stormy, awesome impulses . . . And, Pyotr Stepanovich, if one day you and I become close, which I for my part sincerely wish, all the more so in that I already owe you so much, perhaps then you will understand . . ."

"Oh, believe me, I wish it for my own part," Pyotr Stepanovich muttered abruptly.

"Then you will understand the impulse with which, in this blindness of nobility, one suddenly takes a man in all respects even unworthy of one, profoundly lacking in understanding of one, who is ready to torment one at the first opportunity, and, contrary to everything, makes such a man into some sort of ideal, one's dream, concentrates on him all one's hopes, worships him, loves him all one's life, absolutely without knowing why, perhaps precisely because he is unworthy of it . . . Oh, how I've suffered all my life, Pyotr Stepanovich!"

Stepan Trofimovich, with a pained look, tried to catch my eyes, but I dodged just in time.

". . . And even recently, recently—oh, how guilty I am before Nicolas! You would not believe how they torment me from all sides, all, all of them, enemies, paltry people, friends—friends perhaps more than enemies. When I received the first contemptible anonymous letter, Pyotr Stepanovich, you will not believe it but I did not have enough contempt, finally, to answer all this malice . . . Never, never will I forgive myself for my faintheartedness!"

"I've already heard something, generally, about anonymous letters here," Pyotr Stepanovich suddenly perked up, "and I'll find them for you, rest assured."

"But you cannot imagine what intrigues have begun here! They've even tormented our poor Praskovya Ivanovna—and why do that to her? I am perhaps all too guilty before you today, my dear Praskovya Ivanovna," she added, in a magnanimous impulse of tender feeling, but not without a certain triumphant irony.

"That'll do, dearest," the other lady muttered reluctantly, "and in my opinion all this should be brought to an end—too much talking . . ." and she again glanced timidly at Liza, but she was looking at Pyotr Stepanovich.

"And this poor, this unfortunate being, this insane woman who has lost everything and kept only her heart, I now intend to adopt,"

Varvara Petrovna suddenly exclaimed. "This is a duty which I intend to fulfill sacredly. From this day on I shall take her under my protection!"

"And that will even be very good, madam, in a certain sense," Pyotr Stepanovich became thoroughly animated. "Excuse me, I didn't finish just now. Precisely to do with patronage. Can you imagine, when Nikolai Vsevolodovich left then (I'm starting precisely from where I left off, Varvara Petrovna), this gentleman, this same Mr. Lebyadkin, at once fancied he had the right to dispose of the pension that had been allotted to his sister, the whole of it; and so he did. I don't know exactly how it was all arranged by Nikolai Vsevolodovich, but a year later, from abroad now, having found out what was going on, he was forced to make different arrangements. Again, I don't know the details, he will tell you himself, all I know is that the interesting person was placed somewhere in a remote convent, quite comfortably, even, but under friendly supervision—you understand? And what do you think Mr. Lebyadkin decides to do? First, he makes every effort to find out where the quitrent item—that is, his dear sister—has been hidden from him, achieves his goal just recently, takes her from the convent, having presented some sort of rights over her, and brings her straight to this town. Here he doesn't feed her, he beats her, tyrannizes over her, and finally in some way obtains a significant sum from Nikolai Vsevolodovich, immediately starts drinking, and instead of gratitude ends with brazen defiance of Nikolai Vsevolodovich, senseless demands, threatening to go to court in case of the nonpayment of the pension directly into his hands. So he takes Nikolai Vsevolodovich's voluntary gift as his due—can you imagine that? Mr. Lebyadkin, is *everything* I've said here just now true?"

The captain, who up to then had been standing silently and looking down, quickly stepped two steps forward and turned all purple.

"Pyotr Stepanovich, you have dealt harshly with me," he said abruptly.

"How and why is it harsh, sir? But, excuse me, we will talk about harshness and mildness later, and for now I only ask you to answer the first question: is *everything* I said true, or not? If you find it is not true, you may make your declaration at once."

"I . . . you yourself know, Pyotr Stepanovich . . ." the captain muttered, stopped short, and fell silent. It should be noted that Pyotr Stepanovich was sitting in an armchair, his legs crossed, while the captain stood before him in a most reverent attitude.

Pyotr Stepanovich seemed to be very displeased with Mr. Lebyadkin's hesitations; his face twitched in a sort of malicious contortion.

"Perhaps you really do want to make some declaration?" he gave the captain a subtle glance. "Go right ahead, then, we're waiting."

"You yourself know, Pyotr Stepanovich, that I cannot declare anything."

"No, I do not know that; it's the first time I've even heard of it; why can you not declare anything?"

The captain was silent, staring at the ground.

"Allow me to leave, Pyotr Stepanovich," he said resolutely.

"Not before you give me some answer to my first question: is *everything* I said true?"

"It's true, sir," Lebyadkin said dully, glancing up at his tormentor. Sweat even came to his temples.

"*Everything?*"

"*Everything*, sir."

"You can think of nothing to add, to observe? If you feel we are being unjust, declare as much; protest, declare your dissatisfaction aloud."

"No, I can think of nothing."

"Did you recently threaten Nikolai Vsevolodovich?"

"That . . . that was drink more than anything, Pyotr Stepanovich!" (He suddenly raised his head.) "Pyotr Stepanovich! If family honor and the heart's undeserved disgrace cry out among men, then—can a man be to blame even then?" he bellowed suddenly, forgetting himself as before.

"And are you sober now, Mr. Lebyadkin?" Pyotr Stepanovich gave him a piercing look.

"I . . . am sober."

"What is the meaning of this family honor and the heart's undeserved disgrace?"

"It's about nobody, I didn't mean anybody. It's me myself . . ." the captain crumbled again.

"You seem to have been very offended by the way I spoke about you and your conduct? You are very irritable, Mr. Lebyadkin. Excuse me, but I haven't even begun to say anything about your conduct in its real aspect. I shall begin to talk about your conduct in its real aspect. I shall begin, that may very well be, but so far I haven't even begun in any *real* aspect."

Lebyadkin gave a start and stared wildly at Pyotr Stepanovich. "Pyotr Stepanovich, I am only now beginning to awaken!"

"Hm. And it's I who have awakened you?"

"Yes, it's you who have awakened me, and I've been sleeping for four years under a dark cloud. May I finally withdraw, Pyotr Stepanovich?"

"Now you may, unless Varvara Petrovna finds it necessary . . ."

But she waved him on his way.

The captain bowed, walked two steps towards the door, suddenly stopped, put his hand to his heart, was about to say something, did not say it, and quickly rushed out. But in the doorway he ran right into Nikolai Vsevolodovich; the latter stood aside; the captain somehow shrank before him and simply froze on the spot, without tearing his eyes from him, like a rabbit in front of a snake. Nikolai Vsevolodovich, having paused briefly, brushed him aside with his arm and walked into the drawing room.

VII

HE WAS CHEERFUL and calm. Perhaps something very nice had just happened to him, as yet unknown to us; but he seemed to be even especially pleased with something.

"Will you forgive me, Nicolas?" Varvara Petrovna could not help herself and rose hastily to meet him.

But Nicolas positively burst out laughing.

"Just as I thought!" he exclaimed good-naturedly and jokingly. "I see you already know everything. And I, once I'd walked out of here, began thinking in the carriage: 'I ought at least to have told them the anecdote, it's not right to go off like this.' But then I remembered that you'd been left with Pyotr Stepanovich, and my care dropped away."

As he spoke he looked cursorily around.

"Pyotr Stepanovich told us an old Petersburg story from the life of one whimsical fellow," Varvara Petrovna rapturously joined in, "one mad and capricious fellow, though always lofty in his feelings, always chivalrously noble . . ."

"Chivalrously? Can it have gone as far as that?" Nicolas laughed. "Anyhow, this time I'm very grateful to Pyotr Stepanovich for his hastiness" (here he exchanged a momentary glance with him). "Be it known to you, maman, that Pyotr Stepanovich is a universal peacemaker; that is his role, his disease, his hobbyhorse, and I especially recommend him to you on that point. I can guess what he dashed off for you here. He precisely dashes off when he talks; he's got an office in his head. Note that being a realist he cannot lie, and truth is dearer to him than success . . . save, naturally, on those special occasions when success is dearer than truth." (He kept looking around as he was saying this.) "So you can clearly see, maman, that it is not you who should ask forgiveness of me, and if there is madness here anywhere, it is, of course, first of all on my part, and so, finally, I am crazy after all—just to keep up my local reputation . . ."

Here he embraced his mother tenderly.

"Anyhow, everything is said and done, and so we can finish with it," he added, and some dry, hard little note sounded in his voice. Varvara Petrovna understood this note; yet her exaltation would not leave her, even quite the contrary.

"I really didn't expect you before another month, Nicolas!"

"I will of course explain everything to you, maman, but now . . ."

And he went towards Praskovya Ivanovna.

But she barely turned her head to him, stunned though she had been by his first appearance half an hour earlier. Now, however, she had some new trouble: from the very moment the captain had gone out and run into Nikolai Vsevolodovich in the doorway, Liza had suddenly begun to laugh—at first softly, fitfully, but then her laughter increased more and more, becoming louder and more obvious. She was flushed. The contrast with her recent gloomy look was extreme. While Nikolai Vsevolodovich was speaking with Varvara Petrovna, she beckoned a couple of times to Mavriky Nikolaevich, as if wishing to whisper something to him; but as soon as he bent down to her, she would dissolve in laughter; one might have concluded that she was laughing precisely at poor Mavriky Nikolaevich. However, she made a visible effort to restrain herself, and put her handkerchief to her lips. Nikolai Vsevolodovich, with a most innocent and guileless air, addressed her in greeting.

"Excuse me, please," she answered in a patter, "you . . . you have seen Mavriky Nikolaevich, of course . . . My God, Mavriky Nikolaevich, how inadmissibly tall you are!"

And again laughter. Mavriky Nikolaevich was indeed tall, but not inadmissibly so.

"Did you . . . arrive long ago?" she murmured, again restraining herself, even embarrassed, but with flashing eyes.

"A little over two hours ago," Nicolas replied, studying her intently. I will observe that he was remarkably restrained and polite, but, politeness aside, he looked totally indifferent, even listless.

"And where will you be living?"

"Here."

Varvara Petrovna was also watching Liza, but a thought suddenly struck her.

"And where have you been all this time, Nicolas, for more than two hours?" she ventured. "The train comes at ten o'clock."

"I first took Pyotr Stepanovich to Kirillov. And Pyotr Stepanovich I met at Matveevo" (three stations away), "we came here in the same car."

"I'd been waiting at Matveevo since dawn," Pyotr Stepanovich picked up. "Our rear cars got derailed in the night; we almost broke our legs."

"Broke their legs!" Liza cried out. "Maman, maman, you and I were going to go to Matveevo last week, so we could have broken our legs, too!"

"Lord have mercy!" Praskovya Ivanovna crossed herself.

"Maman, maman, dear ma, don't be afraid if I really break both my legs; it's quite likely to happen to me, you yourself say I gallop around at breakneck speed every day. Mavriky Nikolaevich, will you lead me about when I'm lame?" she laughed aloud again. "If it happens, I won't have anyone else but you lead me about, you may safely count on that. Well, say I'll just break one leg . . . Well, be so kind, tell me you'll consider it a blessing."

"Where's the blessing in having one leg?" Mavriky Nikolaevich frowned gravely.

"But you will lead me about, you alone, I won't let anyone else!"

"You'll lead me about even then, Lizaveta Nikolaevna," Mavriky Nikolaevich murmured even more gravely.

"God, he wanted to make a pun!" Liza exclaimed, almost horrified. "Mavriky Nikolaevich, don't you ever dare to set out on that path! What a great egoist you are after that! No, I'm convinced, to your credit, that you're slandering yourself now; on the contrary, you'll be assuring me from morning till night that I've become even more interesting minus a leg! But one thing is irremediable—you are immensely tall, and I'll become so very tiny minus a leg, how will you be able to take my arm, what sort of couple will we make!"

And she laughed morbidly. Her hints and witticisms were flat, but she apparently no longer cared about quality.

"Hysterics!" Pyotr Stepanovich whispered to me. "A glass of water, quickly!"

He had guessed right; a minute later everyone was bustling about, water was brought. Liza embraced her maman, kissed her fervently, wept on her shoulder, and then, drawing back and peering into her face, at once began laughing loudly again. Finally, the maman also began to whimper. Varvara Petrovna hustled them off to her rooms, through the same door by which Darya Pavlovna had come out to us earlier. But they did not stay away long, about four minutes, no more . . .

I am now trying to recall every detail of these last moments of that memorable morning. I remember that when we were left alone, without the ladies (except for Darya Pavlovna, who did not move from her place), Nikolai Vsevolodovich went around and greeted each of us, except for Shatov, who continued to sit in his corner, bending towards the ground even more than before. Stepan Trofimovich had just begun talking about something extremely witty with Nikolai Vsevolodovich, but he hastily went towards Darya Pavlovna. On the way he was intercepted almost forcibly by Pyotr Stepanovich, who dragged him to the window and began whispering to him about something evidently very important, judging by the expression on his face and the gestures that accompanied the whisper. But Nikolai Vsevolodovich listened very languidly, even distractedly, with his official smile, even impatiently towards the end, and kept making as if to leave. He stepped away from the window precisely as our ladies came back; Varvara Petrovna sat Liza down in her former place, insisting that it was absolutely necessary to wait and rest for at least ten minutes, and that it was unlikely that fresh air would be good just then for her upset nerves. She really was being awfully attentive to Liza, and herself sat down beside her. The now free Pyotr Stepanovich sprang over to them at once and began a rapid, merry conversation. It was then that Nikolai Vsevolodovich finally went up to Darya Pavlovna with his unhurried gait; Dasha became all aflutter on her seat as he approached, and quickly jumped up in visible confusion, her whole face flushed red.

"I gather you are to be congratulated . . . or not yet?" he said, with a sort of peculiar wrinkle on his face.

Dasha made some reply, but it was hard to hear.

"Forgive my indiscretion," he raised his voice, "but, you know, I was specially notified. Do you know that?"

"Yes, I know you were specially notified."

"Anyway, I hope I haven't interfered in anything with my congratulations," he laughed, "and if Stepan Trofimovich . . ."

"Congratulations for what, for what?" Pyotr Stepanovich suddenly sprang over. "What are you to be congratulated for, Darya Pavlovna? Bah! You mean for that? The blush on your face tells me I've guessed right. Indeed, what else can our beautiful and well-behaved young ladies be congratulated for, and what sort of congratulations makes them blush the most? Well, miss, accept mine as well, if I've guessed right, and pay what you owe me—remember, in Switzerland you bet me that you would never get married . . . Ah, yes, about Switzerland—what's the matter with me? Imagine, that's half the reason I'm here, and I almost forgot: tell me," he turned quickly to Stepan Trofimovich, "when are you going to Switzerland?"

"I . . . to Switzerland?" Stepan Trofimovich was surprised and embarrassed.

"What? You're not going? But aren't you also getting married . . . as you wrote?"

"Pierre!" exclaimed Stepan Trofimovich.

"Pierre, nothing . . . You see, if it pleases you, I came flying here to announce to you that I am not at all against it, since you insisted on having my opinion, and as soon as possible; and if" (he went on spilling) "you need to be 'saved,' as you say and implore right there in the same letter, then again I'm at your service. Is it true that he's getting married, Varvara Petrovna?" he quickly turned to her. "I hope I'm not being indiscreet; he himself writes that the whole town knows and everyone's congratulating him, so that, to avoid it, he goes out only at night. The letter is in my pocket. But, would you believe, Varvara Petrovna, I understand nothing in it! Tell me just one thing, Stepan Trofimovich, are you to be congratulated or 'saved'? You won't believe me, but next to the happiest lines there are the most desperate ones. First of all, he asks my forgiveness; well, let's say that's just his way . . . Still, I can't help observing: imagine, the man has seen me twice in his life, and that by accident, and now suddenly, marrying for the third time, he imagines that in doing so he's violating some sort of parental duties towards me, and entreats me, from a thousand miles away, not to be angry and to grant him permission! Please don't go getting offended, Stepan Trofimovich, it's a feature of your time, I take a broad view and do not condemn, and let's say it does you honor, etc., etc., but again, the main thing is that I don't understand the main thing. There's something here about some 'sins in Switzerland.' I'm getting married, he says, on account of some sins, or because of someone else's sins, or however he puts it—'sins,' in short. 'The girl,' he says, 'is a pearl and a diamond,' well, and naturally 'he is unworthy'—that's his style; but because of some sins or circumstances, 'I am forced to go to the altar, and then to Switzerland,' and therefore 'drop everything and fly here to save me.' Can you understand anything after all that? However . . . however, I notice from the look on your faces" (he kept turning around, holding the letter in his hand, peering into their faces with an innocent smile) "that I seem to have committed a blunder, in my usual fashion . . . because of my foolish frankness, or hastiness, as Nikolai Vsevolodovich says. I thought we were among our own here—I mean, your own, Stepan Trofimovich, your own—but I, in fact, am a stranger, and I see . . . I see that everyone knows something, and something that I precisely do not know."

He still kept looking around him.

"Did Stepan Trofimovich really write to you that he was marrying 'someone else's sins committed in Switzerland,' and that you should fly to 'save him,' in those very expressions?" Varvara Petrovna suddenly went up to him, all yellow, her face distorted, her lips quivering.

"I mean, you see, madam, if there's something here I didn't understand," Pyotr Stepanovich became as if frightened, and hurried on even more, "then of course it's his fault, since that's the way he writes. Here's the letter. You know, Varvara Petrovna, his letters are endless and ceaseless, and in the past two or three months it was simply one letter after another, and, I confess, towards the end I sometimes didn't finish them. Forgive me my foolish confession, Stepan Trofimovich, but do please admit that, though you addressed them to me, you were still writing more for posterity, so it's all the same to you . . . Now, now, don't be offended; after all, we're no strangers! But this letter, Varvara Petrovna, this letter I did read to the end. These 'sins'—these 'someone else's sins'—these are surely some little sins of our own, and most innocent ones I'll bet, yet because of them we've suddenly decided to start a terrible story, with a noble tinge—it's for the sake of this noble tinge that we started it. You see, something must have gone lame here in the accounting department—one must finally admit. We're very fond of a little game of cards, you know . . . but, anyway, this is unnecessary, quite unnecessary, excuse me, I babble too much, but, by God, Varvara Petrovna, he put a scare into me, and I really got myself half ready to 'save' him. After all, I'm ashamed myself. Am I holding a knife to his throat, or what? Am I some implacable creditor, or what? He writes something here about a dowry . . . And, anyway, Stepan Trofimovich, are you really getting married, for pity's sake? It would be just like us, we talk and talk, and it's all more for style . . . Ah, Varvara Petrovna, but I'm sure you perhaps disapprove of me now, and also precisely for my style . . ."

"On the contrary, on the contrary, I see that you have lost patience, and you most certainly had reasons to," Varvara Petrovna picked up maliciously.

She had listened with malicious pleasure to the whole "truthful" torrent of words from Pyotr Stepanovich, who was obviously playing a role (I did not know then what it was, but it was obviously a role, played even much too crudely).

"On the contrary," she went on, "I am only too grateful to you for having spoken; without you I would never have found out. For the first time in twenty years I am opening my eyes. Nikolai Vsevolodovich, you just said that you, too, had been specially notified: did Stepan Trofimovich also write in the same manner to you?"

"I received from him a quite innocent and . . . and . . . a very noble letter . . ."

"You're embarrassed, fishing for words—enough! Stepan Trofimovich, I expect a great favor from you," she suddenly turned to him, her eyes flashing, "please be so good as to leave us right now, and henceforth never step across the threshold of my house."

I must ask you to bear in mind her recent "exaltation," which still had not passed. True, Stepan Trofimovich really was to blame! But this is what amazed me at the time: that he stood up with remarkable dignity both under Petrusha's "exposures," not even trying to interrupt them, and under Varvara Petrovna's "curse." Where did he get so much spirit? One thing I discovered was that he had been undoubtedly and deeply insulted by his first meeting with Petrusha earlier, namely, by that embrace. This was a deep, *real* grief, at least in his eyes, for his heart. He had yet another grief at that moment, namely, his own morbid awareness that he had acted basely; this he confessed to me later in all frankness. And a *real*, undoubted grief is sometimes capable of making a solid and steadfast man even out of a phenomenally light-minded one, if only for a short time; moreover, real and true grief has sometimes even made fools more intelligent, also only for a time, of course; grief has this property. And, if so, then what might transpire with a man like Stepan Trofimovich? A whole revolution—also, of course, only for a time.

He made a dignified bow to Varvara Petrovna without uttering a word (true, there was nothing else left for him to do). He was about to walk out altogether, just like that, but could not help himself and went over to Darya Pavlovna. She seemed to have anticipated it, because she began speaking at once, all in a fright, as if hastening to forestall him:

"Please, Stepan Trofimovich, for God's sake, don't say anything," she began, in an ardent patter, with a pained look on her face, and hurriedly giving him her hand. "Be assured that I respect you all the same . . . and value you all the same, and . . . you think well of me, too, Stepan Trofimovich, and I will appreciate it very, very much . . ."

Stepan Trofimovich gave her a low, low bow.

"As you will, Darya Pavlovna, you know that this whole matter is entirely at your will! It was and it is, both now and hereafter," Varvara Petrovna concluded weightily.

"Bah, but now I, too, understand it all!" Pyotr Stepanovich slapped himself on the forehead. "But . . . but in that case what position have I been put in? Darya Pavlovna, please forgive me! . . . What have you done to me in that case, eh?" he turned to his father.

"Pierre, you might express yourself differently with me, is that not so, my friend?" Stepan Trofimovich said, even quite softly.

"Don't shout, please," Pierre waved his hands, "believe me, it's all your old, sick nerves, and it won't help anything if you shout. Better tell me, couldn't you have supposed I'd start speaking the moment I came in? How could you not warn me?"

Stepan Trofimovich gave him a searching look.

"Pierre, you know so much about what is going on here, how can it be that you really didn't know anything, that you hadn't heard anything?"

"Wha-a-at? Such people! So we're not only an old child, but a wicked child as well? Varvara Petrovna, did you hear what he said?"

A hubbub ensued; but suddenly an incident broke out which no one could have expected.

VIII

First of all I will mention that during the last two or three minutes some new emotion had taken possession of Lizaveta Nikolaevna; she was quickly whispering something to her maman and to Mavriky Nikolaevich, who was bending down to her. Her face was anxious, but at the same time had a look of determination. Finally, she rose from her seat, obviously hurrying to leave and hurrying her maman, whom Mavriky Nikolaevich began helping up from her chair. But clearly they were not fated to leave without seeing everything to the end.

Shatov, who had been completely forgotten by all in his corner (not far from Lizaveta Nikolaevna), and who apparently did not know himself why he was sitting there and would not go away, suddenly rose from his chair and walked across the entire room, with unhurried but firm steps, towards Nikolai Vsevolodovich, looking him straight in the face. The latter noticed him approaching from afar and grinned slightly; but when Shatov came up close to him, he ceased grinning.

When Shatov stopped silently in front of him, without taking his eyes off him, everyone suddenly noticed it and became hushed, Pyotr Stepanovich last of all; Liza and her maman stopped in the middle of the room. Thus about five seconds went by; the expression of bold perplexity on Nikolai Vsevolodovich's face turned to wrath, he frowned, and suddenly . . .

And suddenly Shatov swung his long, heavy arm and hit him in the face with all his might. Nikolai Vsevolodovich swayed badly on his feet.

Shatov hit him even somehow peculiarly, not at all as people ordinarily slap someone in the face (if it is possible to put it so), not with his palm, but with his whole fist, and his was a big, heavy, bony fist, covered with red hair and freckles. If he had hit the nose, he would have broken it. But the blow landed on the cheek, touching the left corner of the lip and the upper teeth, which immediately started to bleed.

I think there was a momentary cry, perhaps Varvara Petrovna cried out—I do not recall, because everything at once froze again, as it were. In any case, the whole scene lasted no more than some ten seconds.

Nevertheless, terribly much happened in those ten seconds.

I will remind the reader once more that Nikolai Vsevolodovich was one of those natures that knows no fear. In a duel he would stand cold-bloodedly before his adversary's fire, take aim himself, and kill with brutal calm. If anyone had slapped him in the face then, I think he would not even have challenged the offender to a duel, but would have killed him at once, on the spot; he was precisely that sort, and would kill with full awareness and not at all in rage. I even think that he never knew those blinding fits of wrath that make one unable to reason. For all the boundless anger that would occasionally take possession of him, he was always able to preserve complete self-control, and therefore to realize that for killing someone otherwise than in a duel he would certainly be sent to hard labor; nevertheless, he would still have killed the offender, and that without the slightest hesitation.

I have been studying Nikolai Vsevolodovich all this recent time, and, owing to special circumstances, I know a great many facts about him as I now write. I might perhaps compare him with some past gentlemen, of whom certain legendary memories are still preserved in our society. It was told, for example, of the Decembrist L——n,[11] that all his life he deliberately courted danger, reveled in the sensation of it, turned it into a necessity of his nature; when young he would fight duels over nothing; in Siberia he would go against a bear armed only with a knife, liked meeting up with escaped convicts in the Siberian forests—and they, I will note in passing, are more dangerous than any bear. There is no doubt that these legendary gentlemen were capable of experiencing, even to an intense degree, the sensation of fear— otherwise they would have been much calmer, and would not have made the sense of danger into a necessity of their nature. No, but overcoming their own cowardice—that, of course, was what tempted them. A ceaseless reveling in victory and the awareness that no one can be victorious over you—that was what attracted them. Even before his exile, this L——n had struggled with starvation for some time and earned his bread by hard work, solely because he absolutely refused to submit to the demands of his rich father, which he found unjust. His understanding of struggle was thus many-sided; he valued his own staunchness and strength of character not only with bears or in duels.

However, since then many years have passed, and the nervous, tormented, and divided nature of people in our time no longer even admits of the need for those direct and integral sensations which were once so sought after by certain gentlemen of the good old days in their restless activity. Nikolai Vsevolodovich would perhaps have looked down on L——n, would even have called him an eternally strutting coward, a cock—though, true, he would not have expressed it aloud. He would shoot his adversary in a duel, and go against a bear if need be, and fight off a robber in the forest—all as successfully and fearlessly as L——n, yet without any sense of enjoyment, but solely out of unpleasant necessity, listlessly, lazily, even with boredom. Anger, of course, constituted a progress over L——n, even over Lermontov.[12] There was perhaps more anger in Nikolai Vsevolodovich than in those two together, but this anger was cold, calm, and, if one may put it so, *reasonable,* and therefore the most repulsive and terrible that can be. I repeat once more: I considered him then and consider him still (now that everything is over) to be precisely the sort of man who, if he received a blow in the face or some equivalent offense, would immediately kill his adversary, right there on the spot, and without any challenge to a duel.

And yet, in the present case, something different and wondrous occurred.

As soon as he straightened up, after having swayed so disgracefully to one side, almost as much as half his height, from the slap he had received, and before the mean, somehow as if wet, sound of a fist hitting a face seemed to have faded away in the room, he immediately seized Shatov by the shoulders with both hands; but immediately, at almost the same moment, he jerked both hands back and clasped them behind him. He said nothing, looked at Shatov, and turned pale as a shirt. But, strangely, his eyes seemed to be dying out. Ten seconds later his look was cold and—I'm convinced I'm not lying—calm. Only he was terribly pale. Of course, I do not know what was inside the man, I only saw the outside. It seems to me that if there were such a man, for example, as would seize a red-hot bar of iron and clutch it in his hand, with the purpose of measuring his strength of mind, and in the course of ten seconds would be overcoming the intolerable pain and would finally overcome it, this man, it seems to me, would endure something like what was experienced now, in these ten seconds, by Nikolai Vsevolodovich.

The first to lower his eyes was Shatov, obviously because he was forced to lower them. Then he slowly turned and walked out of the room, but not at all with the same gait as he had just had when approaching. He was walking softly, his shoulders hunched up somehow especially awkwardly, his head bowed, and as if he were reasoning something out with himself. He seemed to be whispering something. He made his way carefully to the door, without brushing against anything or knocking anything over, and he opened the door only a very little way, so as to be able to squeeze through the crack almost sideways. As he was squeezing through, the lock of hair standing up at the back of his head was especially noticeable.

Then, before all cries there came one terrible cry. I saw Lizaveta Nikolaevna seize her maman by the shoulder and Mavriky Nikolaevich by the hand and pull them two or three times, drawing them out of the room, but suddenly she cried out and fell full-length on the floor in a swoon. To this day it is as if I can still hear the back of her head hit the carpet.

PART TWO

1

Night

I

EIGHT DAYS PASSED. Now, when everything is past and I am writing my chronicle, we know what it was all about; but then we still knew nothing, and, naturally, various things seemed strange to us. Stepan Trofimovich and I, at least, first locked ourselves in and watched timorously from afar. Though I did go out here and there as before and bring him all sorts of news, without which he could not even exist.

Needless to say, the most diverse rumors spread around town—that is, concerning the slap, Lizaveta Nikolaevna's swoon, and the rest of what happened that Sunday. The surprising thing for us was: through whom could it all have come out so quickly and accurately? None of the persons then present would seem to have found any need or profit in breaking the secrecy of what had happened. No servants had been there; Lebyadkin alone might have blabbed something, not so much from malice, because he had left then in great fright (and fear of an enemy destroys any malice against him), but solely from lack of restraint. But Lebyadkin, together with his sister, disappeared without a trace the very next day; he was not in Filippov's house, he had moved to some unknown place, as if he had vanished. Shatov, of whom I wanted to inquire about Marya Timofeevna, locked himself in and, it seems, spent all those eight days sitting in his apartment, and even stopped his lessons in town. He would not receive me. I came to see him on Tuesday and knocked at the door. There was no answer, but being convinced by indubitable evidence that he was at home, I knocked once more. Then he, evidently having jumped off the bed, came up to the door with big strides and shouted to me at the top of his lungs: "Shatov's not home." With that I left.

Stepan Trofimovich and I, not without fearing for the boldness of such a suggestion, but mutually encouraging each other, finally arrived at this thought: we decided that the one and only person who could be to blame for spreading the rumors was Pyotr Stepanovich, though sometime later, in a conversation with his father, he himself asserted that he had found the story already on everyone's lips, predominantly at the club, and perfectly known in the smallest detail to the governor's wife and her husband. Another remarkable thing: on the very next day, Monday evening, I met Liputin and he already knew everything to the last word, which meant that he had doubtless been one of the first to find out.

Many of the ladies (and of the best society) were also curious about the "mysterious lame girl"—as they called Marya Timofeevna. There were some who even insisted on seeing her in person and making her acquaintance, so that those gentlemen who had hastened to tuck the Lebyadkins away had obviously acted opportunely. But in the forefront still stood Lizaveta Nikolaevna's swoon, and "all society" was interested in that, if only because the matter directly concerned Yulia Mikhailovna, as Lizaveta Nikolaevna's relation and patroness. And the chattering that went on! The mysteriousness of the situation was conducive to chatter: both homes were shut tight; Lizaveta Nikolaevna was said to be lying in brain fever; the same was also asserted of Nikolai Vsevolodovich, with repugnant details about a tooth that had supposedly been knocked out and a swollen cheek. In some little corners it was even said that there would perhaps be a murder, that Stavrogin was not a man to bear with such an offense, and that he would kill Shatov, but secretly, as in a Corsican vendetta. This idea was liked; but the majority of our young society people listened to it all with disdain and an air of the most scornful indifference—assumed, of course. In general, the ancient hostility of our society towards Nikolai Vsevolodovich was markedly evident. Even the most solid people were eager to accuse him, though they themselves did not know of what. It was whispered that he

had supposedly ruined Lizaveta Nikolaevna's honor, and that there had
been an affair between them in Switzerland. Of course, cautious people
restrained themselves, and yet everyone listened with appetite. There
was talk of other sorts, not general but private, rare, and almost covert—
extremely strange talk, the existence of which I mention just to warn the
reader, solely with a view to further events in my story. Namely: some
said, frowningly and God knows on what grounds, that Nikolai Vsevolodovich had some special business in our province, that in Petersburg,
through Count K., he had entered into certain high relations, that he
was perhaps even in government service and had been all but entrusted
with some mission by someone. When very solid and restrained people
smiled at this rumor, observing reasonably that a man who lived by
scandals and had begun among us with a swollen jaw did not look like
an official, it was observed to them in a whisper that he was serving not
quite officially but, so to speak, confidentially, in which case the service
itself required that the servant look as little as possible like an official.
This observation produced its effect; it was known among us that the
zemstvo[1] of our province was looked upon with somewhat special
attention in the capital. I repeat, these rumors only flashed and then
disappeared without a trace, for a time, at Nikolai Vsevolodovich's first
appearance; yet I will note that the cause of many of these rumors was
in part several brief but spiteful remarks uttered vaguely and abruptly in
the club by Artemy Pavlovich Gaganov, a retired captain of the Guard,
recently returned from Petersburg, a rather big landowner of our
province and district, a man of society in the capital, and son of the late
Pavel Pavlovich Gaganov, that same venerable senior member with
whom, over four years before, Nikolai Vsevolodovich had had a confrontation remarkable for its rudeness and suddenness, which I have
already mentioned above, at the beginning of my story.

It immediately became known to everyone that Yulia Mikhailovna
had paid an extraordinary visit to Varvara Petrovna, and that it had
been announced to her on the porch that "the mistress was ill and not
receiving." Also that two days or so after her visit, Yulia Mikhailovna
sent a messenger to inquire about Varvara Petrovna's health. Finally,
she started "defending" Varvara Petrovna everywhere, of course only
in the loftiest—that is, the vaguest possible—sense. To all the first hasty
hints about Sunday's story she had listened sternly and coldly, so that

in the following days they were not renewed in her presence. And thus the idea came to be held everywhere that Yulia Mikhailovna knew not only the whole mysterious story but also its whole mysterious meaning in the minutest detail, and not as an outsider but as a participant. I will observe, incidentally, that she had already begun little by little to acquire that lofty influence among us which she was so undoubtedly striving and thirsting for, and she was already beginning to see herself "surrounded." Part of society acknowledged her as having practical sense and tact . . . but of that later. Her patronage also partly explained Pyotr Stepanovich's rather rapid success in our society—a success which at the time particularly struck Stepan Trofimovich.

Perhaps we were both exaggerating. First of all, Pyotr Stepanovich became acquainted with the whole town almost instantly, in the first four days after his appearance. He appeared on Sunday, and already on Tuesday I met him in a carriage with Artemy Pavlovich Gaganov, a proud man, irritable and overbearing, despite all his worldly polish, and with whom, owing to his character, it was quite difficult to get along. Pyotr Stepanovich was also very well received at the governor's, so much so that he stepped at once into the position of an intimate or, so to speak, a much favored young man; he dined at Yulia Mikhailovna's almost daily. He had already made her acquaintance in Switzerland, but there was indeed something curious about his rapid success in His Excellency's house. After all, whether it was true or not, he was once reputed to have been a foreign revolutionary, to have participated in some foreign publications and conferences, "which can even be proved from the newspapers," as it was spitefully put in my presence by Alyosha Telyatnikov, now, alas, a retired petty official, but formerly also a much favored young man in the old governor's house. Still, the fact remained that the former revolutionary appeared in his beloved fatherland not only without any trouble, but almost with inducements; so perhaps there was nothing to it. Liputin once whispered to me that, according to rumors, Pyotr Stepanovich had supposedly made his repentance somewhere, and had received absolution, after disclosing a few other names, and had thus perhaps already managed to make good his guilt, also promising to be useful in future to the fatherland. I conveyed this venomous remark to Stepan Trofimovich, and he, though he was almost incapable of reflection, lapsed into deep thought. Later on it was disclosed that Pyotr Stepanovich had come to us with extremely respectable letters of recommendation, at least he had brought one to the governor's wife from an extremely important little old lady of Petersburg, whose husband was one of the most distinguished little old men of Petersburg. This little old lady, Yulia Mikhailovna's godmother, mentioned in her letter that Count K. also knew Pyotr Stepanovich quite well through Nikolai Vsevolodovich, had shown him favor, and found him "a worthy young man, in spite of his former errors." Yulia Mikhailovna valued exceedingly her scant and so difficultly maintained connections with the "high world," and was of course very glad of the important little old lady's letter; but there still remained something peculiar here, as it were. She even put her husband into almost familiar relations with Pyotr Stepanovich, which caused Mr. von Lembke to complain . . . but of that, too, later. I will observe, too, so as not to forget, that the great writer also treated Pyotr Stepanovich quite benignly and immediately invited him to visit. Such haste on the part of such a self-inflated man stung Stepan Trofimovich most painfully, but I explained it to myself otherwise: in courting a nihilist,[2] Mr. Karmazinov most certainly had in mind his relations with the progressive young men of both capitals. The great writer trembled morbidly before the newest revolutionary young men, and, imagining in his ignorance of the matter that the keys to the Russian future were in their hands, sucked up to them humiliatingly, the more so since they paid no attention at all to him.

II

Pyotr Stepanovich also ran by a couple of times to see his father, but, to my misfortune, I was absent both times. He visited him for the first time on Wednesday, that is, only on the fourth day after that first meeting, and even then on business. Incidentally, the settling of accounts for the estate was concluded between them in some unseen and unheard way. Varvara Petrovna took it all upon herself and paid for everything, acquiring the little piece of land, to be sure, and Stepan Trofimovich was simply informed that it had all been concluded, and Varvara Petrovna's agent, her valet Alexei Yegorovich, presented him with something to sign, which he proceeded to perform silently and with extreme dignity. Speaking of dignity, I will observe that I hardly recognized our former old man in those days. He behaved as never before, became surprisingly taciturn, did not write even one letter to Varvara Petrovna from that Sunday on, which I would consider a miracle, and, above all, became calm. He had settled upon some final and extraordinary idea which enabled him to be calm, one could see that. He found this idea, sat and waited for something. At first, however, he was sick, especially on Monday—an attack of cholerine. He also could not do without news all that time; but whenever, leaving facts aside, I moved on to the essence of the matter and voiced some suggestions, he would at once begin waving his hands at me to stop. The two meetings with his boy still had a painful effect on him, though they did not sway him. On both days after these meetings he lay on the sofa, his head wrapped in a handkerchief moistened with vinegar; but he continued to remain calm in the lofty sense.

Occasionally, however, he did not wave his hands at me. Occasionally it also seemed to me that the mysterious resoluteness he had acquired was abandoning him, as it were, and that he had begun to struggle with some new, tempting flood of ideas. These were just moments, but I make note of them. I suspected that he wanted very much to come out of seclusion and declare himself, to put up a fight, to wage his last battle.

"*Cher*, I would crush them!" escaped him on Thursday evening, after the second meeting with Pyotr Stepanovich, as he lay stretched out on the sofa with his head wrapped in a towel.

Until that moment he had not spoken a word to me all day.

" '*Fils, fils chéri,*' and so on—I agree, all these phrases are nonsense, kitchen-maidish vocabulary, but let it be, I see it now myself. I did not give him food and drink, I sent him off from Berlin to ——— province, a nursling, by mail, well, and so forth. I agree . . . 'You did not give me drink,' he says, 'and sent me off by mail, and here, on top of that, you've robbed me.' But, wretched man, I cry to him, my heart ached for you all my life, even if it was by mail! *Il rit.** But I agree, I agree . . . say it was by mail," he ended, as if in delirium.

*"He laughs."

"*Passons,*" he began again five minutes later. "I don't understand Turgenev. His Bazarov is some sort of false character, who doesn't exist at all; they were the first to reject him as having no resemblance to anything. This Bazarov is some vague mixture of Nozdryov and Byron,[3] *c'est le mot.* * Look at them attentively: they cavort and squeal with joy like puppies in the sun, they're happy, they're the victors! Forget Byron! . . . And besides, how mundane! What kitchen-maidish, irritable vanity, what a trite little desire to *faire du bruit autour de son nom,* † without noticing that *son nom* . . . Oh, caricature! For pity's sake, I cry to him, but do you really want to offer yourself to people, just as you are, in place of Christ? *Il rit. Il rit beaucoup, il rit trop.* His smile is somehow strange. His mother didn't have such a smile. *Il rit toujours.*"‡

Again there was silence.

"They're cunning; they had it all set up on Sunday . . ." he suddenly blurted out.

"Oh, no doubt," I cried, pricking up my ears, "it was all patched together, with the seams showing, and so badly acted."

"I don't mean that. You know, they left the seams showing on purpose, so that it would be noticed by . . . the right people. Do you understand?"

"No, I don't."

"*Tant mieux.* § *Passons.* I'm very irritated today."

"But why did you argue with him, Stepan Trofimovich?" I said reproachfully.

"*Je voulais convertir.* ‖ Laugh, of course, go on. *Cette pauvre* auntie, *elle entendra de belles choses!*¶ Oh, my friend, would you believe, I felt like a patriot today! But, in fact, I've always considered myself a Russian . . . yes, a true Russian cannot but be like you and me. *Il y a là-dedans quelque chose d'aveugle et de louche.*"**

---

* "that's it exactly."
† "to cause a sensation around his name"
‡ "He laughs. He laughs a lot, he laughs too much . . . He laughs all the time."
§ "So much the better."
‖ "I wanted to convert."
¶ "This poor [auntie,] she's going to hear some pretty things!"
** "There's something blind and shifty [or cross-eyed] in him."

"Absolutely," I replied.

"My friend, the real truth is always implausible, did you know that? To make the truth more plausible, it's absolutely necessary to mix a bit of falsehood with it. People have always done so. Perhaps there's something here that we don't understand. What do you think, is there something in this victorious squealing that we don't understand? I wish there was. I do wish it."

I kept my silence. He, too, was silent for a very long time.

"They say that the French mind . . ." he began babbling suddenly, as if in a fever, "but that's a lie, it has always been so. Why slander the French mind? It's simply Russian laziness, our humiliating impotence to produce an idea, our disgusting parisitism among the nations. *Ils sont tout simplement des paresseux,* * and not the French mind. Oh, Russians ought to be exterminated for the good of mankind, like harmful parasites! It was not for that, it was not at all for that that we strove; I don't understand any of it. I've ceased to understand! But do you understand, I cry to him, do you understand that if you have the guillotine in the forefront, and with such glee, it's for the sole reason that cutting heads off is the easiest thing, and having an idea is difficult! *Vous êtes des paresseux! Votre drapeau est une guenille, une impuissance.* † Those carts—or how does it go?—'the rumble of carts bringing bread to mankind' is more useful than the Sistine Madonna,⁴ or however it goes . . . *une bêtise dans ce genre.* ‡ But do you understand, I cry to him, do you understand that along with happiness, in the exact same way and in perfectly equal proportion, man also needs unhappiness! *Il rit.* You're tossing off bon mots here, he says, while 'pampering your members on a velvet sofa' (he put it more nastily) . . . And note our new custom of familiar speech between father and son: it's very well when the two agree, but what if they're quarreling?"

We were silent again for about a minute.

"*Cher,*" he suddenly concluded, rising quickly, "do you know that this will most certainly end with something?"

"That it will," I said.

---

*"They are quite simply lazybones"
†"You're lazy. Your banner is a rag, an impotence."
‡"some stupidity of the sort."

"*Vous ne comprenez pas.* * *Passons.* But . . . in this world things usually end with nothing, but here there will be an end, most certainly, most certainly!"

He got up, paced the room in the greatest agitation, and, coming to the sofa again, strengthlessly collapsed on it.

On Friday morning, Pyotr Stepanovich went somewhere in the district and was gone until Monday. I learned of his departure from Liputin, and just then, somehow in conversation, found out from him that the Lebyadkins, brother and sister, were both somewhere across the river, in the potters' quarter. "It was I who took them across," Liputin added, and, dropping the Lebyadkin subject, suddenly declared to me that Lizaveta Nikolaevna was going to marry Mavriky Nikolaevich, and though it had not been announced yet, there had been an engagement and the matter was concluded. The next day I met Lizaveta Nikolaevna on horseback, accompanied by Mavriky Nikolaevich, venturing out for the first time after her illness. She flashed her eyes at me from afar, laughed, and gave me a very friendly nod. All this I conveyed to Stepan Trofimovich; he paid some attention only to the news about the Lebyadkins.

And now, having described our puzzled situation during those eight days, when we still did not know anything, I will set out to describe the subsequent events of my chronicle, this time knowingly, so to speak, as they have now been revealed and explained. I will begin precisely from the eighth day following that Sunday, that is, from Monday evening, because it was essentially from that evening that the "new story" began.

III

IT WAS SEVEN O'CLOCK in the evening, and Nikolai Vsevolodovich was sitting alone in his study—his favorite room from long past, lofty, spread with carpets, filled with somewhat heavy, old-fashioned furniture. He sat in the corner on the sofa, dressed as if to go out, but he did not seem to be going anywhere. On the table before him stood

*"You don't understand."

a lamp with a shade. The sides and corners of this big room remained in shadow. His look was pensive and concentrated, not altogether at ease; his face was tired and had grown somewhat thin. He was indeed suffering from a swollen cheek; but the rumor about the knocked-out tooth was exaggerated. The tooth had been loosened, but was now firm again; the lower lip had also been cut inside, but this, too, had healed. It had taken a whole week for the swelling to go down only because he did not want to receive the doctor and have him lance the abscess, but waited until it broke of itself. Not just the doctor, he would scarcely even admit his mother, and then only for a moment, once a day, and inevitably at dusk, when it was already dark but before the lights had been brought in. He did not receive Pyotr Stepanovich either, who nevertheless ran by two or three times a day, while he was still in town, to see Varvara Petrovna. And then at last, on Monday, having returned in the morning from his three-day absence, having run all over town, and having dined at Yulia Mikhailovna's, Pyotr Stepanovich came at last in the evening to Varvara Petrovna, who was awaiting him impatiently. The ban had been lifted, Nikolai Vsevolodo-vich was receiving. Varvara Petrovna herself led the guest to the door of the study; she had long wanted this meeting, and Pyotr Stepanovich gave her his word that he would run to her from Nicolas and recount it all. She timidly knocked for Nikolai Vsevolodovich and, getting no answer, ventured to open the door a couple of inches.

"Nicolas, may I bring Pyotr Stepanovich in?" she asked softly and restrainedly, trying to make Nikolai Vsevolodovich out behind the lamp.

"You may, you may, of course you may!" Pyotr Stepanovich him-self cried loudly and gaily, opened the door with his own hand, and walked in.

Nikolai Vsevolodovich had not heard the knock on the door, he heard only his mother's timid question, but had no time to answer it. At that moment there lay before him a letter he had just read, over which he was pondering deeply. Hearing Pyotr Stepanovich's sudden cry, he started and quickly covered the letter with a paperweight that happened to be there, but not quite successfully: a corner of the letter and almost the entire envelope could be seen.

"I cried as loud as I could on purpose, to give you time to get ready,"

Pyotr Stepanovich whispered hastily, with surprising naïvety, running over to the desk and instantly fixing his eyes on the paperweight and the corner of the letter.

"And of course you had time to spy me hiding this just-received letter under the paperweight," Nikolai Vsevolodovich said calmly, without stirring from his seat.

"A letter? For heaven's sake, what's your letter to me!" the guest exclaimed. "But . . . the main thing," he whispered again, turning towards the door, now closed, and nodding in that direction.

"She never eavesdrops," Nikolai Vsevolodovich observed coolly.

"I mean, what if she did eavesdrop!" Pyotr Stepanovich picked up at once, raising his voice gaily and sitting down in an armchair. "I've got nothing against it, I just ran by to have a private chat with you . . . So I've got you at last! First of all, how is your health? I see, it's excellent, and perhaps you'll come tomorrow—eh?"

"Perhaps."

"But, release them, finally, release me!" he was gesticulating frantically, with a jocular and agreeable air. "If you knew the babble I've had to produce for them. But, then, you do know." He laughed.

"I don't know everything. I've only heard from mother that you've been very much . . . on the move."

"I mean, it wasn't anything specific," Pyotr Stepanovich suddenly heaved himself up, as if he were defending himself against some terrible attack, "you know, I pulled out Shatov's wife, I mean rumors about your liaison in Paris, which, of course, explained Sunday's incident . . . you're not angry?"

"I'm sure you tried very hard."

"Ah, just what I was afraid of. Incidentally, what does 'tried very hard' mean? It's a reproach. You put it straight, however; what I was most afraid of when I was coming here was that you wouldn't want to put it straight."

"I don't want to put anything straight," Nikolai Vsevolodovich said, with some irritation, but he grinned at once.

"I don't mean that, not that, don't take me wrong, not that!" Pyotr Stepanovich waved his hands, spilling the words out like peas, delighting at once in the master's irritability. "I won't irritate you with *our* thing, especially in your present situation. I ran by only to talk about

Sunday's incident, and that only so far as necessary, because it's really impossible. I've come with the most open explanations, and it's mainly I who need them, not you—that's for your vanity, but all the same it's the truth. I've come so as always to be frank from now on."

"So you weren't frank before?"

"And you know it yourself. I was cunning a lot of the time . . . you smile; I'm very glad of your smile, as a pretext for an explanation; I evoked your smile on purpose with the boastful word 'cunning,' so that you'd immediately get angry at my daring to think I could be cunning, and so as to explain myself at once. See, see how frank I've become now! Well, sir, will you kindly hear me out?"

The expression of Nikolai Vsevolodovich's face, contemptuously calm and even derisive, despite all the obviousness of the guest's wish to annoy his host with the insolence of his crude naïveties, prepared beforehand and intentionally, expressed at last a somewhat uneasy curiosity.

"Listen, now," Pyotr Stepanovich began to fidget more than ever. "When I set out to come here, I mean, here generally, to this town, ten days ago, I decided, of course, to adopt a role. The best would be no role at all, just one's own person, isn't that so? Nothing is more cunning than one's own person, because no one will believe you. To be frank, I wanted to adopt the silly fool, because the silly fool is easier than one's own person; but since the silly fool is, after all, an extreme thing, and extreme things arouse curiosity, I finally chose my own person. Well, sir, and what is my own person? The golden mean—neither stupid nor smart, rather giftless, and dropped from the moon, as sensible people here say, isn't that so?"

"Well, maybe it is," Nikolai Vsevolodovich smiled slightly.

"Ah, you agree—I'm very glad; I knew beforehand that these were your own thoughts . . . Don't worry, don't worry, I'm not angry, and I didn't define myself in that way to provoke your reverse praises: 'No, you're not giftless, no, you're smart . . .' Ah, you're smiling again! . . . I've been caught again. You wouldn't say 'you're smart'—well, all right, I accept all that. *Passons,* as papa says, and, in parenthesis, don't be angry at my verbosity. Incidentally, here's an example for you: I always speak a lot, I mean, a lot of words, and I rush, and it always comes out wrong. And why is it that I speak a lot of words and it comes out wrong? Because I don't know how to speak. Those who know how to speak well, speak briefly. So, there you have my giftlessness—isn't it true? But since this gift of giftlessness is natural to me, why shouldn't I use it artificially? And so I do. True, as I was preparing to come here, I first had the thought of being silent; but to be silent is a great talent, and is therefore not fitting for me, and, second, it's dangerous to be silent, after all; well, so I finally decided that it would be best to talk, but precisely in a giftless way, I mean, a lot, a lot, a lot, to be in a great rush to prove something, and towards the end to get tangled up in one's own proofs, so that the listener throws up his hands, or, best of all, just spits and walks away without any end. The result will be, first, that you've convinced him of your simpleheartedness, have been very tiresome, and haven't been understood—all three profits at once! For pity's sake, who is going to start suspecting you of mysterious designs after that? No, there's not one of them who wouldn't be personally offended with anybody who said I had mysterious designs. And, what's more, I sometimes make them laugh—and that is priceless. No, they'll forgive me everything for this alone, that the wise man who published tracts there has turned out here to be stupider than they are, isn't that so? I can see by your smile that you approve."

Incidentally, Nikolai Vsevolodovich was not smiling at all, but, on the contrary, was listening frowningly and somewhat impatiently.

"Eh? What? Did I hear you say 'Who cares?'" Pyotr Stepanovich rattled on (Nikolai Vsevolodovich had not said anything at all). "Of course, of course; I assure you it's not at all so as to compromise you with comradeship. And, you know, you're terribly jumpy today; I came running to you with an open and cheerful soul, and you pick up every dropped stitch; I assure you I won't talk about anything ticklish today, I give you my word, and I accept all your conditions beforehand!"

Nikolai Vsevolodovich was obstinately silent.

"Eh? What? Did you say something? I see, I see, it seems I've blundered again; you didn't offer any conditions, and you're not going to, I believe it, I believe it, but don't worry; I know it's not worth my while offering them myself, right? I'll answer for you beforehand, and—from giftlessness, of course; giftlessness, giftlessness . . . You're laughing? Eh? What?"

"Nothing," Nikolai Vsevolodovich finally grinned, "I just remembered that I did once call you giftless, but you weren't there, so you must have been told . . . I might ask you to get down to business quickly."

"But I am down to business, it precisely has to do with Sunday!" Pyotr Stepanovich babbled. "So, what, what was I on Sunday, in your opinion? Precisely a hasty, giftless mediocrity, and I took over the conversation by force in the most giftless way. But I was forgiven everything, because first of all I'm from the moon, that seems to have been decided on by everyone now; and, second, because I told a lovely little story and rescued the lot of you—right? right?"

"That is, you told it precisely so as to leave doubts and show our patching and shuffling, when there wasn't any patching and I never asked you to do anything at all."

"Precisely, precisely!" Pyotr Stepanovich picked up, as if in rapture. "I precisely did it that way, so that you would notice the whole spring; I was clowning mainly for you, because I was trying to catch you and wanted to compromise you. I mainly wanted to find out how afraid you were."

"Curious, why are you so frank now?"

"Don't be angry, don't be angry, don't flash your eyes . . . But, then, you're not flashing them. You're curious why I'm so frank? But, precisely because everything's changed now, finished, passed, and overgrown with sand. I've suddenly changed my thinking about you. The old way is completely finished; I'll never compromise you in the old way now; now it's the new way."

"Changed your tactics?"

"There aren't any tactics. Now it's entirely your will in everything—I mean, say *yes* if you want, or *no* if you want. That's my new tactic. And about *our* business I won't even make a peep until you yourself tell me to. You're laughing? Be my guest; I'm laughing myself. But I'm serious now, serious, serious, though anyone who is in such a hurry is naturally giftless, no? Never mind, let it be giftless, but I'm serious, serious."

He was indeed speaking seriously, in quite a different tone and in some special agitation, so that Nikolai Vsevolodovich glanced at him curiously.

"You say you've changed your thinking about me?" he asked.

"I changed my thinking about you the moment you took your hands back after Shatov—and enough, enough, please, no questions, I won't say anything now."

He jumped up, in fact, waving his hands as if he were waving the questions away; but since there were no questions, and there was no reason for him to leave, he sat down in the chair again, somewhat calmer.

"Incidentally, in parenthesis," he went rattling on at once, "some people here are babbling that you're going to kill him, and are making bets, so that Lembke even thought of jogging the police, but Yulia Mikhailovna forbade it . . . Enough, enough of that, I was just letting you know. Incidentally, again: I had the Lebyadkins moved that same day, you know; did you get my note with their address?"

"I got it right then."

"That wasn't out of 'giftlessness,' it was done sincerely, out of willingness. If it came out as giftless, anyway it was sincere."

"Yes, never mind, maybe it had to be so . . ." Nikolai Vsevolodovich said pensively. "Only don't write me any more notes, I beg you."

"Couldn't help it, just that once."

"So Liputin knows?"

"Couldn't help it, but you know yourself that Liputin doesn't dare . . . Incidentally, you ought to go and see our people—I mean, them, not *our* people—otherwise you'll be picking up my dropped stitches again. Don't worry, not now, but someday. It's raining now. I'll let them know, they'll get together, and we'll come in the evening. They're waiting with their mouths open, like baby jackdaws in a nest, to see what sort of treat we've brought them. A fervent lot. Got their books out, all ready to argue. Virginsky—an omni-man;[5] Liputin—a Fourierist, with a strong propensity for police dealings; a valuable man, I must tell you, in one respect, but requiring strictness in all others; and, finally, that one with the long ears, he'll read us his own system. And, you know, they're offended that I treat them casually and pour cold water on them, heh, heh! But to go is certainly a must."

"You've presented me there as some sort of chief?" Nikolai Vsevolodovich let escape as casually as he could. Pyotr Stepanovich glanced quickly at him.

"Incidentally," he picked up, as if he had not heard, and quickly glossing it over, "I did call two or three times a day on the much esteemed Varvara Petrovna, and was again forced to talk a lot."

"I can imagine."

"No, don't imagine, I simply said that you won't kill anybody, and, well, all sorts of sweet things. And, imagine, she already knew the next day that I'd had Marya Timofeevna moved across the river—did you tell her?"

"Never occurred to me."

"I just knew it wasn't you. But who could have, besides you? Interesting."

"Liputin, of course."

"N-no, not Liputin," Pyotr Stepanovich muttered, frowning. "I know who. It looks like Shatov . . . Nonsense, though, let's drop it! Though it's terribly important . . . Incidentally, I kept waiting for your mother suddenly to blurt out the main question . . . Ah, yes, all those first days she was terribly glum, and suddenly when I came today— she's beaming all over. What's that about?"

"It's because I gave her my word today that I'd propose to Lizaveta Nikolaevna in five days," Nikolai Vsevolodovich suddenly said with unexpected frankness.

"Ah, well . . . yes, of course," Pyotr Stepanovich babbled, hesitating, as it were, "there are these rumors about an engagement, you know? It's true, though. But you're right. She'll come running from the foot of the altar, you only have to call. You're not angry that I'm like this?"

"No, I'm not."

"I've been noticing that it's terribly difficult to make you angry today, and I'm beginning to be afraid of you. I'm terribly curious about how you'll appear tomorrow. You must have a lot of tricks ready. You're not angry that I'm like this?"

Nikolai Vsevolodovich made no reply at all, which thoroughly vexed Pyotr Stepanovich.

"Incidentally, were you serious with your mother about Lizaveta Nikolaevna?" he asked.

Nikolai Vsevolodovich looked at him intently and coldly.

"Ah, I understand, it was just to calm her down, that's what."

"And if I was serious?" Nikolai Vsevolodovich asked firmly.

"Well, then God be with you, as they say in such cases, it won't harm anything (you see, I didn't say our thing; you don't like the word *our*), and I . . . well, as for me, I'm at your service, you know that."

"You think so?"

"I think nothing, nothing," Pyotr Stepanovich rushed on, laughing, "because I know you've thought over your affairs beforehand, and you have it all thought out. I'm just saying that I am seriously at your service, always and everywhere and in any event—I mean any, understand?"

Nikolai Vsevolodovich yawned.

"You're tired of me," Pyotr Stepanovich suddenly jumped up, seizing his round, quite new hat as if he were leaving, yet still remaining and continuing to talk ceaselessly, though he was standing, pacing the room from time to time and slapping himself on the knee with his hat at animated points in the conversation.

"I still hoped to amuse you with the Lembkes," he cried gaily.

"No, don't, maybe later. How is Yulia Mikhailovna's health, by the way?"

"You all have this social manner, really: you care as much about her health as you do about a gray cat's, and yet you ask. I praise that. She's well, and respects you to the point of superstition, and, also to the point of superstition, expects a lot of you. Concerning Sunday's incident she says nothing and is certain that you yourself will overcome everything with your appearance alone. By God, she imagines you can do God knows what. Anyhow, you're a mysterious and romantic figure, now more than ever—an extremely advantageous position. How they're waiting for you—it's incredible. It was hot enough when I was leaving, but now it's even more so. Incidentally, thanks again for that letter. They're all afraid of Count K. You know, they seem to look on you as a spy? I yes them—you're not angry?"

"It's all right."

"It is all right; it will be necessary in the future. They have their own customs here. I encourage them, of course; Yulia Mikhailovna is at the head, Gaganov also . . . You're laughing? But I have a tactic: I blab and blab, then suddenly I say some intelligent word, precisely when they're all searching for it. They surround me, and I start blabbing again. They've all waved me away by now—'has abilities,' they say, 'but dropped from the moon.' Lembke's inviting me to go into the service, to straighten me out. You know, I tyrannize, I mean, I compromise him terribly—he just goggles his eyes. Yulia Mikhailovna encourages me. Ah, incidentally, Gaganov is terribly angry with you. Yesterday, in Dukhovo, he spoke quite nastily about you. I immediately told him the whole truth—I mean, of course, not the whole truth. I spent the day at his place. A fine estate, a nice house."

"Can he still be in Dukhovo?" Nikolai Vsevolodovich suddenly heaved himself up, almost jumped, and made a strong move forward.

"No, it was he who drove me here this morning, we came back together," Pyotr Stepanovich said, as if he had not noticed Nikolai Vsevolodovich's momentary agitation at all. "Look at that, I've dropped a book." He bent down to pick up the keepsake[6] he had brushed against. *"Balzac's Women,* with illustrations"—he suddenly opened the book—"I haven't read it. Lembke also writes novels."

"Really?" Nikolai Vsevolodovich asked, as if interested.

"In Russian—secretly, of course. Yulia Mikhailovna knows and lets him. A duffer, but he has his ways; they've got it all worked out. What strictness of form, what self-possession! We could use some of that."

"You're praising the administration?"

"And why not? The only thing in Russia that's natural and achieved . . . I'll stop, I'll stop," he suddenly heaved himself up, "I didn't mean it, not a word about anything delicate. Anyhow, goodbye, you look a bit green."

"It's a fever."

"I believe it; you should go to bed. Incidentally, there are castrates in the district, curious people[7] . . . Later, though. Here, though, is another little anecdote: there's an infantry regiment in the district. Friday evening I was drinking with the officers in B——tsy. We have three friends there, *vous comprenez?* There was talk about atheism, and, of course, we cashiered God well and good. They were delighted, squealing. Incidentally, Shatov insists that to start a rebellion in Russia one must inevitably begin with atheism. Maybe he's right. One grayhaired boor of a captain sat and sat, silent, not saying a word; suddenly he stands up in the middle of the room and says, so loudly, you know, as if to himself: 'If there's no God, then what sort of captain am I?'—took his cap, threw up his arms, and walked out."

"Having uttered a rather well rounded thought," Nikolai Vsevolodovich yawned for the third time.

"Really? I didn't understand it; I was going to ask you. Well, what else have I got for you? The Shpigulins' factory is interesting; five hundred workers there, as you know, a hotbed of cholera, they haven't cleaned the place in fifteen years, and they cheat their employees; the owners are millionaires. I can assure you some of the workers have a notion of what the Internationale[8] is. Did you smile? You'll see for yourself, just give me a tiny, tiny bit of time! I've already asked you for some time, and now I'm asking for more, and then . . . sorry, though, I won't, I won't, I don't mean that, don't scowl. Anyhow, good-bye. Ah, what's the matter with me?" he suddenly turned back. "I completely forgot the main thing: I was just told that our box has come from Petersburg."

"Meaning?" Nikolai Vsevolodovich looked at him uncomprehendingly.

"Meaning your box, your things, tailcoats, trousers, linen—has it come? Is it true?"

"Yes, I heard something earlier."

"Ah, might it be possible, now! . . ."

"Ask Alexei."

"Then tomorrow? Tomorrow? In with your things there are also my jacket, my tailcoat, and three pairs of trousers, from Charmeur's,[9] on your recommendation, remember?"

"I've heard you're playing the gallant around here?" Nikolai Vsevolodovich grinned. "Is it true you're going to take lessons from a riding-master?"

Pyotr Stepanovich smiled a crooked smile.

"You know," he suddenly hurried excessively, in a quivering and faltering voice, "you know, Nikolai Vsevolodovich, with regard to persons, we'll drop that once and for all, right? You may, of course, despise me as much as you like, if you find it so amusing, but still it would be better not to be personal for a while, right?"

"Very well, I won't do it again," said Nikolai Vsevolodovich. Pyotr

Stepanovich grinned, slapped his knee with his hat, shifted from one foot to the other, and assumed his former expression.

"There are some here who even consider me your rival with Lizaveta Nikolaevna, so how can I not think of my appearance?" he laughed. "Who has been informing you, though? Hm. It's precisely eight o'clock; well, I'm off; I promised to call on Varvara Petrovna, but I'll pass that up; you go to bed and tomorrow you'll feel more chipper. It's dark and raining outside, I have a cab, though, because the streets aren't quiet here at night . . . Ah, incidentally: there's a certain Fedka the Convict wandering around town and hereabouts, a fugitive from Siberia, imagine, my former household serf, whom papa packed off to the army fifteen years ago, to make some money.[10] A very remarkable man."

"Have you . . . talked with him?" Nikolai Vsevolodovich glanced up.

"I have. He's not hiding from me. A man ready for anything, anything—for money, naturally, but there are convictions there, too, of his own kind, of course. Ah, yes, again incidentally: if you were serious just now about that plan, remember, to do with Lizaveta Nikolaevna, then I repeat once more that I, too, am a man ready for anything, in all senses, whatever you like, and am completely at your service . . . What, are you reaching for your stick? Ah, no, it's not your stick . . . Imagine, I thought you were looking for your stick."

Nikolai Vsevolodovich was not looking for anything and did not say anything, but he did indeed rise a little, somehow suddenly, with some strange movement in his face.

"Or if you need something in connection with Mr. Gaganov," Pyotr Stepanovich suddenly blurted out, this time nodding directly at the paperweight, "I can, of course, arrange everything, and I'm sure you won't pass me up."

He suddenly walked out without waiting for a reply, but then stuck his head back in through the doorway.

"Because," he cried in a patter, "Shatov, for example, also had no right to risk his life on Sunday when he went up to you, right? I wish you to make note of that."

He disappeared again, without waiting for a reply.

IV

H E MAY HAVE THOUGHT, as he disappeared, that when Nikolai Vsevolodovich was left alone he would start pounding the wall with his fists, and no doubt he would have been glad to peek in, if only it had been possible. But he would have been very disappointed: Nikolai Vsevolodovich remained calm. For a couple of minutes he stood by the desk in the same position, apparently deep in thought; but soon a cold, listless smile forced itself to his lips. He slowly sat down on the sofa, in his former place in the corner, and closed his eyes as if from fatigue. The corner of the letter was still peeking out from under the paperweight, but he made no move to put it right.

Soon he became totally oblivious. Varvara Petrovna, who had worn herself out with cares during those days, could not restrain herself, and after Pyotr Stepanovich, who had promised to stop and see her, left without keeping his promise, she herself ventured to visit Nicolas, though it was not her appointed time. She kept imagining: what if he were finally to say something definite? Softly, as before, she knocked on the door and, again receiving no reply, opened it herself. Seeing Nicolas sitting there somehow too motionlessly, she cautiously approached the sofa, her heart pounding. She was as if struck that he had fallen asleep so quickly and that he could sleep like that, sitting so straight and so motionlessly; even his breathing was almost imperceptible. His face was pale and stern, but as if quite frozen, motionless; his eyebrows were slightly knitted and frowning; he decidedly resembled an inanimate wax figure. She stood over him for three minutes or so, scarcely breathing, and was suddenly overcome with fear; she went out on tiptoe, paused in the doorway, hastily made a cross over him, and withdrew unnoticed, with a new heavy feeling, and a new anguish.

He slept for a long time, more than an hour, still in the same torpor; not a muscle in his face moved, not the slightest movement appeared in his whole body; his eyebrows remained as sternly knitted. If Varvara Petrovna had stayed another three minutes, she would certainly have been unable to bear the oppressive feeling of this lethargic motionlessness and would have wakened him. But suddenly he opened his eyes himself and, still without stirring, sat for another ten minutes as if peering persistently and curiously at some startling object in the corner of the room, though there was nothing there either new or unusual.

Finally there came the quiet, deep sound of the big wall clock striking once. With a certain uneasiness he turned his head to look at the face of the clock, but at almost the same moment the far door, giving onto the corridor, opened, and the valet Alexei Yegorovich appeared. He was carrying a warm coat, a scarf, and a hat in one hand, and in the other a little silver salver on which a note was lying.

"Half past nine," he announced in a soft voice and, placing the clothing he had brought on a chair in the corner, held out to him the salver with the note—a small piece of paper, unsealed, with two penciled lines on it. Having glanced over these lines, Nikolai Vsevolodovich took a pencil from the desk, scribbled a couple of words at the end of the note, and put it back on the salver.

"To be delivered right after I leave, and now—to dress," he said, getting up from the sofa.

Noticing that he was wearing a light velvet jacket, he thought a bit and asked for a different, woolen frock coat to be brought, the one he wore on more formal evening visits. Finally, having dressed completely and put on his hat, he locked the door through which Varvara Petrovna had come to him and, taking the hidden letter from under the paperweight, silently walked out into the corridor, accompanied by Alexei Yegorovich. They went along the corridor to a narrow, stone back stairway, and went down to a hall that gave directly onto the garden. In a corner of the hall a lantern and a big umbrella stood ready.

"The rain being exceedingly heavy, the mud in our streets is intolerable," Alexei Yegorovich reported, in a last remote attempt to deflect his master from the journey. But the master opened his umbrella and silently walked out into the sodden and dripping old garden, dark as a cellar. The wind howled and swayed the tops of the half-bare trees, the narrow sand paths were swamped and slippery. Alexei Yegorovich went just as he was, in a tailcoat and bareheaded, lighting the way for some three steps ahead with the lantern.

"Won't we be noticed?" Nikolai Vsevolodovich asked suddenly.

"Not from the windows, what with everything having been foreseen beforehand," the servant replied softly and evenly.

"Mama has retired?"

"The mistress locked herself in, as she regularly has over the past few days, at nine o'clock sharp, and it's impossible for her to find out anything now. At what time should I expect you?" he added, making so bold as to pose a question.

"At one, or half past one, no later than two."

"Very good, sir."

Having passed through the garden along the winding paths they both knew by heart, they reached the stone garden wall, and there, in the far corner of the wall, they found a little door which led to a narrow and deserted lane and was almost always locked, but the key to which now turned up in Alexei Yegorovich's hands.

"Won't the door creak?" Nikolai Vsevolodovich questioned again.

But Alexei Yegorovich reported that it had been oiled just yesterday, "and today as well." He was now thoroughly soaked. Having opened the door, he gave the key to Nikolai Vsevolodovich.

"If you should be pleased to be undertaking a long trip, then I must report my being uncertain of the local folk, especially in the out-of-the-way lanes, and most of all across the river," he again could not restrain himself. He was an old servant, who had formerly taken care of Nikolai Vsevolodovich and used to dandle him in his arms, a serious and stern man, who liked hearing and reading about things divine.

"Don't worry, Alexei Yegorych."

"God bless you, sir, but only setting out upon good deeds."

"How's that?" Nikolai Vsevolodovich paused with one foot already in the lane.

Alexei Yegorovich firmly repeated his wish; never before would he have ventured to express it in such words, aloud, to his master.

Nikolai Vsevolodovich locked the door, put the key in his pocket, and went off down the lane, sinking several inches into the mud at every step. He finally came out onto a paved street, long and deserted. He knew the town like the back of his hand; but Bogoyavlensky Street was still a long way off. It was past ten o'clock when he finally stopped before the locked gate of Filippov's dark old house. Now that the

Lebyadkins had moved out, the ground floor was left completely empty, with the windows boarded up, but there was light in Shatov's garret. As there was no bell, he began rapping on the gate with his fist. The little window opened and Shatov peeked out; it was pitch-dark, and hard to distinguish anything; Shatov peered for a long time, about a minute.

"Is it you?" he asked suddenly.

"Yes," the uninvited guest replied.

Shatov slammed the window, went down, and unlocked the gate. Nikolai Vsevolodovich stepped across the high sill and, without saying a word, walked past him straight to Kirillov's wing.

V

HERE NOTHING was locked, or even closed. The entryway and the first two rooms were dark, but in the last room, where Kirillov lived and took his tea, light was shining and laughter could be heard, along with some strange little cries. Nikolai Vsevolodovich went towards the light, but stopped on the threshold without going in. Tea was on the table. In the middle of the room stood the old woman, the landlord's relative, bareheaded, wearing only a skirt, a rabbit-skin jacket, and shoes over her bare feet. She was holding in her arms a one-and-a-half-year-old baby, dressed only in a little shirt, with bare legs, flushed cheeks, tousled white hair, fresh from the crib. It must have been crying; tears still clung to its eyes; but at that moment it was reaching out its arms, clapping its hands, and laughing, as little children do, with a choke in its voice. Kirillov was bouncing a big, red rubber ball on the floor in front of it; the ball bounced up to the ceiling, came down again, the baby shouted: "Ba, ba!" Kirillov caught the "ba" and gave it to the baby, the baby threw the ball itself with its clumsy little hands, and Kirillov ran to pick it up again. Finally, the "ba" rolled under the wardrobe. "Ba, ba!" shouted the baby. Kirillov bent down to the floor and reached out, trying to get the "ba" from under the wardrobe with his hand. Nikolai Vsevolodovich entered the room; the baby, seeing him, clutched at the old woman and dissolved in a long, infantile cry; she carried it out at once.

"Stavrogin?" said Kirillov, raising himself from the floor a little, the ball in his hands, without the least surprise at the unexpected visit. "Want some tea?"

He stood up all the way.

"Very much, I won't refuse, if it's warm," said Nikolai Vsevolodovich. "I'm soaked through."

"Warm, even hot," Kirillov confirmed with pleasure. "Sit down: you're muddy; never mind; I'll mop later with a wet rag."

Nikolai Vsevolodovich sat down and drank the full cup almost at one gulp.

"More?" asked Kirillov.

"No thanks."

Kirillov, who had not sat down yet, at once seated himself across from him and asked:

"What have you come for?"

"Business. Here, read this letter, from Gaganov—remember, I told you in Petersburg."

Kirillov took the letter, read it, put it on the table, and looked up expectantly.

"As you know," Nikolai Vsevolodovich began to explain, "I met this Gaganov a month ago in Petersburg, for the first time in my life. We ran into each other about three times in public. Without making my acquaintance or speaking with me, he still found an opportunity for being very impudent. I told you at the time; but here is something you don't know: at that time, leaving Petersburg before I did, he suddenly sent me a letter which, though unlike this one, was still improper in the highest degree, and strange if only in that it contained no explanation of why it had been written. I replied to him at once, also with a letter, in which I stated quite frankly that he was probably angry with me for the incident with his father four years earlier, here at the club, and that for my part I was prepared to give him every possible apology, on the grounds that my action had been unintentional and caused by illness. I asked him to take my apologies into consideration. He did not reply, and left; and now I find him here completely enraged. I've been told of his several public comments about me, utterly abusive and with astounding accusations. Finally, today comes this letter—such as no one, surely, has ever received, with curses and such expressions as: 'your beaten mug.' I've come in hopes that you will not refuse to be my second."

"You say a letter no one received," Kirillov remarked. "In rage it's possible; written more than once. Pushkin wrote to Heeckeren.[11] All right, I'll go. Tell me how."

Nikolai Vsevolodovich explained that he wanted it to be tomorrow, and that he would certainly begin with the renewal of his apologies, and even with the promise of a second letter of apology, but with the understanding that Gaganov, for his part, should also promise not to write any more letters. The letter in hand would be regarded as never having existed.

"Too many concessions; he won't agree," Kirillov said.

"I've come primarily to find out whether you will agree to take these conditions to him."

"I will. It's your affair. But he won't agree."

"I know he won't."

"He wants to fight. Tell how you'll fight."

"The point is that I'd like to finish it all tomorrow for certain. You'll be at his place around nine in the morning. He'll listen and not agree, but he'll get you together with his second—say at around eleven. You'll arrange things, and by one or two everyone should be on the spot. Please try to do it that way. The weapon is pistols, of course, and I especially ask you to arrange it like this: the barriers should be ten paces apart; then you place each of us ten paces from the barrier, and at a sign we start walking towards each other. Each must be sure to reach his barrier, but he can fire before, as he's walking. That's all, I believe."

"Ten paces between barriers is too close," Kirillov observed.

"Twelve, then, only not more, you understand, he seriously wants to fight. Do you know how to load a pistol?"

"I do. I have pistols; I'll give my word that you've never fired them. His second will also give his word about his; two pair, and we'll do odds and evens, his or ours."

"Fine."

"Want to see the pistols?"

"Why not?"

Kirillov squatted down in front of his suitcase in the corner, which was still not unpacked, but from which he took things as he needed them. He pulled from the bottom a boxwood case lined with red velvet, and took from it a pair of elegant, extremely expensive pistols.

"I have everything: powder, bullets, cartridges. I also have a revolver, wait."

He again went into the suitcase and pulled out another case, with a six-chambered American revolver.

"You've got plenty of weapons, and very expensive ones."

"Very. Extremely."

The poor, almost destitute Kirillov—who, incidentally, never noticed his destitution—was now obviously boasting as he displayed the treasures of his weaponry, no doubt acquired at great sacrifice.

"You're still of the same mind?" Stavrogin asked, after a moment's silence, and somewhat cautiously.

"The same," Kirillov answered curtly, guessing at once by the tone what he was being asked about, and he began to remove the weapons from the table.

"When?" Nikolai Vsevolodovich asked even more cautiously, again after some silence.

Kirillov meanwhile put both cases into the suitcase and sat down in his former chair.

"That's not up to me, as you know; when they say," he muttered, as if the question were somewhat burdensome, but at the same time with an obvious readiness to answer all other questions. He looked at Stavrogin, not tearing his black, lusterless eyes away, with a certain calm but kind and affable feeling.

"I, of course, understand shooting oneself," Nikolai Vsevolodovich began again, frowning somewhat, after a long, three-minute-long, thoughtful silence. "I myself have sometimes imagined, and there's always some new thought here: if one did some villainy or, worse, some shame, that is, disgrace, only very mean and . . . ludicrous, so that people would remember it for a thousand years and spit on it for a thousand years, and suddenly comes the thought: 'One blow in the temple, and there will be nothing.' What do I care then about people and how they'll be spitting for a thousand years, right?"

"You call that it's a new thought?" Kirillov said, after some reflection.

"I . . . don't call . . . once, when I reflected, I felt quite a new thought."

" 'Felt a thought'?" Kirillov repeated. "That's good. Many thoughts are there all the time, and suddenly become new. That's right. I see much now as if for the first time."

"Suppose you lived on the moon," Stavrogin interrupted, not listening and continuing his thought, "suppose that there you did all those ludicrous, nasty things . . . From here you know for certain that there they'll laugh and spit on your name for a thousand years, eternally, all over the moon. But you are here now, and you're looking at the moon from here: what do you care here about all you've done there, or that they'll spit on you there for a thousand years, isn't it true?"

"I don't know," Kirillov answered. "I haven't been on the moon," he added, without any irony, solely to note the fact.

"Whose baby was that just now?"

"The old woman's mother-in-law came; no, daughter-in-law . . . it makes no difference. Three days. She's lying sick, with the baby; cries a lot at night—stomach. The mother sleeps, and the old woman brings it; I give it the ball. The ball's from Hamburg. Bought in Hamburg, to throw and catch: strengthens the back. A girl."

"You love children?"

"I love them," Kirillov echoed—quite indifferently, however.

"So, you also love life?"

"Yes, I also love life, what of it?"

"Yet you've resolved to shoot yourself."

"So what? Why together? Life's separate, and that's separate. Life is, and death is not at all."

"You've started believing in the future eternal life?"

"No, not future eternal, but here eternal. There are moments, you reach moments, and time suddenly stops, and will be eternal."

"You hope to reach such a moment?"

"Yes."

"It's hardly possible in our time," Nikolai Vsevolodovich responded, also without any irony, slowly and as if thoughtfully. "In the Apocalypse the angel swears that time will be no more."[12]

"I know. It's quite correct there; clear and precise. When all mankind attains happiness, time will be no more, because there's no need. A very correct thought."

"And where are they going to hide it?"

"Nowhere. Time isn't an object, it's an idea. It will die out in the mind."

"Old philosophical places, the same since the beginning of the ages," Stavrogin muttered with a certain squeamish regret.

"The same! The same since the beginning of the ages, and no others, ever!" Kirillov picked up with flashing eyes, as if this idea held nothing short of victory.

"You seem to be very happy, Kirillov?"

"Yes, very happy," the latter replied, as if making the most ordinary reply.

"But you were upset still so recently, angry with Liputin?"

"Hm . . . now I'm not scolding. Then I didn't know I was happy yet. Have you seen a leaf, a leaf from a tree?"

"I have."

"I saw one recently, a yellow one, with some green, decayed on the edges. Blown about by the wind. When I was ten years old, I'd close my eyes on purpose, in winter, and imagine a leaf—green, bright, with veins, and the sun shining. I'd open my eyes and not believe it, because it was so good, then I'd close them again."

"What's that, an allegory?"

"N-no . . . why? Not an allegory, simply a leaf, one leaf. A leaf is good. Everything is good."

"Everything?"

"Everything. Man is unhappy because he doesn't know he's happy; only because of that. It's everything, everything! Whoever learns will at once immediately become happy, that same moment. This mother-in-law will die, and the girl will remain—everything is good. I discovered suddenly."

"And if someone dies of hunger, or someone offends and dishonors the girl—is that good?"

"Good. And if someone's head gets smashed in for the child's sake, that's good, too; and if it doesn't get smashed in, that's good, too. Everything is good, everything. For all those who know that everything is good. If they knew it was good with them, it would be good with them, but as long as they don't know it's good with them, it will not be good with them. That's the whole thought, the whole, there isn't any more!"

"And when did you find out that you were so happy?"

"Last week, on Tuesday, no, Wednesday, because it was Wednesday by then, in the night."

"And what was the occasion?"

"I don't remember, just so; I was pacing the room . . . it makes no difference. I stopped my clock, it was two thirty-seven."

"As an emblem that time should stop?"

Kirillov did not reply.

"They're not good," he suddenly began again, "because they don't know they're good. When they find out, they won't violate the girl. They must find out that they're good, then they'll all become good at once, all, to a man."

"Well, you did find out, so you must be good?"

"I am good."

"With that I agree, incidentally," Stavrogin muttered frowningly.

"He who teaches that all are good, will end the world."

"He who taught it was crucified."

"He will come, and his name is the man-god."

"The God-man?"

"The man-god—that's the whole difference."[13]

"Can it be you who lights the icon lamp?"

"Yes, I lit it."

"You've become a believer?"

"The old woman likes the icon lamp . . . she's busy today," Kirillov muttered.

"But you don't pray yet?"

"I pray to everything. See, there's a spider crawling on the wall, I look and am thankful to it for crawling."

His eyes lit up again. He kept looking straight at Stavrogin, his gaze firm and unflinching. Stavrogin watched him frowningly and squeamishly, but there was no mockery in his eyes.

"I bet when I come the next time you'll already believe in God," he said, getting up and grabbing his hat.

"Why?" Kirillov also rose.

"If you found out that you believe in God, you would believe; but since you don't know yet that you believe in God, you don't believe," Nikolai Vsevolodovich grinned.

"It's not that," Kirillov thought it over, "you've inverted my thought. A drawing-room joke. Remember what you've meant in my life, Stavrogin."

"Good-bye, Kirillov."

"Come at night. When?"

"Why, you haven't forgotten about tomorrow?"

"Ah, I forgot, don't worry, I won't oversleep; at nine o'clock. I can wake up whenever I want to. I go to bed and say: at seven o'clock, and I wake up at seven; at ten o'clock, and I wake up at ten."

"You have remarkable qualities," Nikolai Vsevolodovich looked at his pale face.

"I'll go and unlock the gate."

"Don't bother. Shatov will unlock it."

"Ah, Shatov. Very well, good-bye."

VI

THE PORCH of the empty house where Shatov lodged was not locked; but on going into the entryway, Stavrogin found himself in complete darkness and began feeling with his hand for the stairway to the attic. Suddenly the door opened upstairs and light appeared; Shatov did not come out himself, but only opened his door. When Nikolai Vsevolodovich stood on the threshold of the room, he made him out in the corner by the table, standing expectantly.

"Will you receive me on business?" he asked from the threshold.

"Come in and sit down," Shatov replied, "lock the door—wait, I'll do it."

He locked the door with a key, went back to the table, and sat down facing Nikolai Vsevolodovich. During that week he had lost weight and now seemed to be in a fever.

"You've been tormenting me," he said, looking down, in a soft half-whisper, "why didn't you come?"

"Were you so certain I'd come?"

"Yes, wait, I was delirious . . . maybe I'm delirious now . . . Wait."

He stood up and got hold of something on the topmost of his three bookshelves, on the edge. It was a revolver.

"One night I had a delirium that you would come and kill me, and early in the morning I bought a revolver with my last money, from that worthless Lyamshin; I didn't want to give in to you. Later I came to my senses . . . I have no powder or bullets; it's been lying on the shelf ever since. Wait . . ."

He rose and opened the vent window.[14]

"Don't throw it out, what for?" Nikolai Vsevolodovich stopped him. "It cost money, and tomorrow people will start saying there are revolvers lying around under Shatov's window. Put it back, so, and sit down. Tell me, why are you as if repenting before me for thinking I would come and kill you? And I haven't come now to make peace, but to talk about necessary things. Explain to me, first of all: you didn't hit me because of my liaison with your wife?"

"You know I didn't," Shatov looked down again.

"And not because you believed the stupid gossip about Darya Pavlovna?"

"No, no, of course not! Stupid! My sister told me from the very beginning . . ." Shatov said impatiently and sharply, even stamping his foot slightly.

"Then I guessed right, and so did you," Stavrogin continued in a calm tone. "It's true: Marya Timofeevna Lebyadkin is my lawful wife, married to me in Petersburg about four and a half years ago. You hit me on account of her, didn't you?"

Shatov, totally astounded, listened and said nothing.

"I guessed, but didn't believe it," he finally muttered, looking strangely at Stavrogin.

"And you hit me?"

Shatov blushed and began to mutter almost incoherently:

"For your fall . . . for the lie. I didn't go up to you in order to punish you; as I was going I didn't know I would hit you . . . It was for your having meant so much in my life . . . I . . ."

"I understand, I understand, save your words. It's too bad you're in a fever; I've come with the most necessary business."

"I've been waiting too long for you," Shatov somehow nearly shook all over and rose slightly from his seat. "Tell me your business, I'll tell you, too . . . afterwards . . ."

He sat down.

"The business isn't of that kind," Nikolai Vsevolodovich began, studying him with curiosity. "Owing to certain circumstances, I was obliged to choose this hour, today, to come and warn you that it's possible you will be killed."

Shatov stared wildly at him.

"I knew I could be in danger," he said in measured tones, "but you, how can you know it?"

"Because I, too, belong to them, as you do, and am a member of their society, as you are."

"You . . . you are a member of the society?"

"I see by your eyes that you expected anything but that from me," Nikolai Vsevolodovich grinned slightly. "But, I beg your pardon, so you already knew there was to be an attempt against you?"

"I never thought so. And don't think so now, either, in spite of your words, though . . . though who could vouch for anything with those fools!" he suddenly cried out in fury, banging his fist on the table. "I'm not afraid of them! I've broken with them. That one ran by four times and said it was possible . . . but," he looked at Stavrogin, "what do you actually know about it?"

"Don't worry, I'm not deceiving you," Stavrogin went on rather coldly, with the air of a man who was merely fulfilling his duty. "You're testing what I know? I know that you joined this society abroad, two years ago, still under the old organization, just before your trip to America, and, I believe, right after our last conversation, of which you wrote me so much in your letter from America. By the way, forgive me for not answering with a letter of my own, and limiting myself to . . ."

"To sending money—wait," Shatov stopped him, hastily pulled open a drawer in the table, and took an iridescent banknote from under some papers, "here, take it, the hundred roubles you sent me; without you I'd have perished there. I wouldn't have paid it back for a long time if it weren't for your mother: she gave me that hundred roubles nine months ago, on account of my poverty, after my illness. But go on, please . . ."

He was breathless.

"In America you changed your thinking and, on returning to Switzerland, wanted to renounce. They gave no answer, but charged you to receive some printing press here in Russia from somebody, and to keep it until you turned it over to a person who would come to you from them. I don't know it all with complete precision, but that seems right in the main? And you undertook it in the hope, or on the condition, that it would be their last demand, and that after that they would let you go entirely. All this, right or wrong, I learned not from them but quite accidentally. But what you don't seem to know yet is that these gentlemen have no intention of parting with you."

"That's absurd!" Shatov yelled. "I declared honestly that I disagree with them in everything! It's my right, my right of conscience and thought . . . I won't have it! There is no power that could . . ."

"You know, you shouldn't shout," Nikolai Vsevolodovich stopped him very seriously. "This little Verkhovensky is the kind of man who could be eavesdropping on us now, with his own or someone else's ear, maybe in your own entryway. Even the drunkard Lebyadkin was all but obliged to keep watch on you, and perhaps you on him, right? Better tell me: has Verkhovensky accepted your arguments now, or not?"

"He's accepted; he says it's possible, and I have the right . . ."

"Well, then he's deceiving you. I know that even Kirillov, who hardly belongs to them at all, has furnished information on you; as for agents, they have a lot of them, some who don't even know they're serving the society. You've always been watched. Among other things, Pyotr Verkhovensky came here to resolve your case finally, and is authorized to do so—namely, by destroying you at an opportune moment, as someone who knows too much and may inform. I repeat that this is certain; and allow me to add that for some reason they are fully convinced that you are a spy, and that if you haven't informed yet, you will. Is that true?"

Shatov twisted his mouth on hearing such a question, uttered in such a matter-of-fact tone.

"Even if I were a spy, where would I go to inform?" he said spitefully, without giving a direct answer. "No, enough about me, to hell with me!" he cried, suddenly grasping his original thought, which had shaken him so much, by all evidence incomparably more strongly than the news of his own danger. "You, you, Stavrogin, how could you mix yourself in with such shameless, giftless, lackeyish absurdity! You a member of their society! And this is Nikolai Stavrogin's great exploit!" he cried out, all but in despair.

He even clasped his hands, as though nothing could be more bitter and dismal to him than such a discovery.

"Forgive me," Nikolai Vsevolodovich really was surprised, "but you seem to look upon me as some sort of sun, and upon yourself as some sort of bug compared with me. I noticed it even in your letter from America."

"You . . . you know . . . Ah, better let's drop me altogether, altogether!" Shatov suddenly cut himself short. "If you can explain anything about yourself, explain it . . . Answer my question!" he kept repeating feverishly.

"With pleasure. You ask how I could mix myself in with such a slum? After my communication, I even owe you a certain frankness in this matter. You see, in a strict sense I don't belong to this society at all, never did belong, and have far more right than you to leave them, since I never even joined them. On the contrary, from the very beginning I announced to them that I was no friend of theirs, and if I chanced to help them, it was just so, as an idle man. I participated partly in the reorganization of the society according to the new plan, and that's all. But now they've thought better of it, and have decided among themselves that it's also dangerous to let me go, so it seems that I, too, am under sentence."

"Oh, with them it's capital punishment for everything, and everything's on instructions, with sealed orders, signed by three and a half men. And you believe they're capable!"

"There you're partly right and partly not," Stavrogin went on with the same indifference, even listlessness. "No doubt there's considerable fantasy, as always in such cases: the crew exaggerates its size and significance. In my opinion, if you like, Pyotr Verkhovensky is the only one they have, and it's much too nice of him to consider himself merely the agent of his own society. However, the basic idea is no more stupid than others of the sort. They have connections with the Internationale; they've succeeded in placing agents in Russia, they've even stumbled onto a rather original method . . . but, of course, only in theory. As for their intentions here, the activities of our Russian organization are such an obscure affair, and almost always so unexpected, that anything might actually be tried. Note that Verkhovensky is a persistent man."

"He's a bedbug, an ignoramus, a tomfool, who doesn't understand a thing about Russia!" Shatov cried spitefully.

"You know him very little. It's true that they all generally understand little about Russia, but perhaps only slightly less than you and I; and, besides, Verkhovensky is an enthusiast."

"Verkhovensky an enthusiast?"

"Oh, yes. There's a point where he ceases to be a buffoon and turns half crazy. I ask you to recall an expression of yours: 'Do you know how strong one man can be?' Please don't laugh, he's quite capable of pulling a trigger. They're sure that I, too, am a spy. For lack of skill in conducting their own affairs, they're all terribly fond of accusations of spying."

"But you're not afraid, are you?"

"N-no . . . I'm not much afraid . . . But your case is quite different. I've warned you so that you can at least keep it in mind. I don't think you should be offended that you're being threatened by fools; their intelligence is not the point: they've raised their hand against better than you and me. However, it's a quarter past eleven," he looked at his watch and got up from his chair. "I'd like to ask you one quite unrelated question."

"For God's sake!" Shatov exclaimed, jumping up impetuously from his seat.

"Meaning what?" Nikolai Vsevolodovich looked at him questioningly.

"Do ask, ask me your question, for God's sake," Shatov repeated, in inexpressible agitation, "only I'm also going to ask you a question. I beg you to allow me . . . I can't . . . ask me your question!"

Stavrogin waited a little and then began:

"I've heard you had some influence here on Marya Timofeevna, and that she liked seeing and listening to you. Is it so?"

"Yes . . . she did listen . . ." Shatov was somewhat embarrassed.

"I have the intention of announcing my marriage to her one of these days, publicly, here in town."

"Can it be possible?" Shatov whispered, almost horrified.

"In what sense do you mean? There are no difficulties about it; the witnesses to the marriage are here. It all took place back in Petersburg in a completely calm and lawful manner, and if it hasn't been revealed before now, that is simply because the only two witnesses to the marriage, Kirillov and Pyotr Verkhovensky, and, finally, Lebyadkin himself (whom I now have the pleasure of regarding as my relation), gave their word at the time to keep silent."

"I don't mean that . . . You talk so calmly . . . but go on! Listen, you weren't forced into this marriage, were you?"

"No, no one forced me," Nikolai Vsevolodovich smiled at Shatov's provocative haste.

"And what's all this talk of hers about her baby?" Shatov hurried on, feverishly and disconnectedly.

"About her baby? Hah! I didn't know, it's the first time I've heard of it. She had no baby, and couldn't have: Marya Timofeevna is a virgin."

"Ah! Just as I thought! Listen!"

"What's the matter with you, Shatov?"

Shatov hid his face in his hands, turned away, but suddenly seized Stavrogin firmly by the shoulder.

"Do you know, do you at least know," he shouted, "why you did it all, and why you've decided on such a punishment now?"

"Your question is intelligent and caustic, but I am also going to surprise you: yes, I do almost know why I got married then, and why I've decided on such a 'punishment,' as you put it, now."

"Let's leave that . . . of that later, don't say yet; but about the main thing, the main thing: I've been waiting two years for you."

"Really?"

"I've been waiting too long a time for you, I've been thinking ceaselessly about you. You are the only man who could . . . I wrote you about it still in America."

"I remember well your long letter."

"Too long to read? I agree: six sheets of writing paper. Keep still, keep still! Tell me: can you give me ten more minutes, but right now, at once? . . . I've been waiting too long for you!"

"I can give you half an hour, if you like, but not more, if that's possible for you."

"And with this, by the way," Shatov went on fiercely, "that you change your tone. Do you hear? I demand, when I ought to implore . . . Do you understand what it means to demand when one ought to implore?"

"I understand that you thereby rise above common things for the sake of higher purposes," Nikolai Vsevolodovich grinned slightly. "I also regret to see that you are in a fever."

"I ask, I demand to be respected!" Shatov went on shouting. "Not for my person—to hell with it—but for something else, just for now, for a few words . . . We are two beings, and we have come together in infinity . . . for the last time in the world. Abandon your tone and take a human one! At least for once in your life speak in a human voice. Not for my sake, but for your own. Do you understand that you should forgive me that slap in the face if only because with it I gave you an opportunity to know your infinite power . . . Again you smile that squeamish, worldly smile. Oh, when will you understand me! Away with the young squire! Understand that I demand it, I do, otherwise I'm not going to speak, not for anything!"

His frenzy was reaching the point of raving; Nikolai Vsevolodovich frowned and seemed to become more guarded.

"If I have agreed to stay for half an hour," he said imposingly and seriously, "when time is so precious to me, then you may believe that I intend to listen to you with interest at least, and . . . and I am sure I shall hear much that is new from you."

He sat down on a chair.

"Sit down!" Shatov cried, and somehow suddenly sat down himself.

"Allow me to remind you, however," Stavrogin recalled once again, "that I had begun a whole request to you concerning Marya Timofeevna, a very important one, for her at least . . ."

"Well?" Shatov suddenly frowned, looking like someone who has suddenly been interrupted at the most important point, and who, though he is looking at you, has still not quite managed to grasp your question.

"And you didn't let me finish," Nikolai Vsevolodovich concluded with a smile.

"Eh, well, nonsense—later!" Shatov waved his hand squeamishly, having finally understood the claim, and went straight on to his main theme.

VII

"DO YOU KNOW," he began almost menacingly, leaning forward a little on his chair, flashing his eyes and raising the forefinger of his right hand in front of him (obviously without noticing it), "do you know which is now the only 'god-bearing' nation[15] on the whole earth, come to renew and save the world in the name of a new God, and to whom alone is given the keys of life and of a new word . . . Do you know which nation it is, and what is its name?"

"By the way you put it, I must inevitably conclude, and, I suppose, as quickly as possible, that it is the Russian nation . . ."

"And you're laughing already—oh, what a tribe!" Shatov reared up.

"Calm yourself, I beg you; on the contrary, I precisely expected something of this sort."

"Expected something of this sort? And are these words not familiar to you?"

"Quite familiar; I see only too well what you're driving at. Your whole phrase and even the expression 'god-bearing' nation is simply the conclusion of our conversation that took place more than two years ago, abroad, not long before your departure for America . . . At least as far as I now recall."

"The phrase is entirely yours, not mine. Your own, and not merely the conclusion of our conversation. There wasn't any 'our' conversation: there was a teacher uttering immense words, and there was a disciple who rose from the dead. I am that disciple and you are the teacher."

"But, if you recall, it was precisely after my words that you joined that society, and only then left for America."

"Yes, and I wrote to you about it from America; I wrote to you about everything. Yes, I could not all at once tear myself bloodily from what I had grown fast to since childhood, to which I had given all the raptures of my hopes and all the tears of my hatred . . . It is hard to change gods. I did not believe you then because I did not want to believe, and I clung for the last time to this filthy cesspool . . . But the seed remained and grew. Seriously, tell me seriously, did you read to the end of my letter from America? Perhaps you didn't read it at all?"

"I read three pages of it, the first two and the last, and glanced quickly over the middle as well. Though I kept meaning to . . ."

"Eh, it makes no difference, to hell with it!" Shatov waved his hand. "If you've now renounced those words about the nation, how could you have uttered them then? . . . That's what weighs on me now."

"But I was not joking with you then, either; in persuading you, I was perhaps more concerned with myself than with you," Stavrogin said mysteriously.

"Not joking! In America I lay on straw for three months next to a certain . . . unfortunate man, and I learned from him that at the very same time as you were planting God and the motherland in my heart— at that very same time, perhaps even in those very same days, you were pouring poison into the heart of this unfortunate man, this maniac, Kirillov . . . You confirmed lies and slander in him and drove his reason to frenzy . . . Go and look at him now, he's your creation . . . You've seen him, however."

"First, I shall note for you that Kirillov himself has just told me he is happy and he is beautiful. Your assumption that all this happened at one and the same time is almost correct; well, and what of it? I repeat, I was not deceiving either one of you."

"You are an atheist? An atheist now?"

"Yes."

"And then?"

"Exactly the same as then."

"I wasn't asking your respect for myself when I began this conversation; with your intelligence, you should have understood that," Shatov muttered indignantly.

"I didn't get up at your first word, didn't close the conversation, didn't walk out on you, but have sat here all the while humbly answering your questions and . . . shouts, which means that my respect for you is still intact."

Shatov interrupted him, waving his hand:

"Do you remember your expression: 'An atheist cannot be Russian, an atheist immediately ceases to be Russian'—remember that?"

"Really?" Nikolai Vsevolodovich seemed to want the question repeated.

"You ask? You've forgotten? And yet this is one of the most precise indications of one of the main peculiarities of the Russian spirit, which you figured out. You can't have forgotten it? I'll remind you of more— you said at the same time: 'He who is not Orthodox cannot be Russian.' "

"A Slavophil notion, I suppose."

"No, the Slavophils nowadays disavow it. People have grown smarter nowadays. But you went even further: you believed that Roman Catholicism was no longer Christianity; you affirmed that Rome proclaimed a Christ who had succumbed to the third temptation of the devil, and that, having announced to the whole world that Christ cannot stand on earth without an earthly kingdom, Catholicism thereby proclaimed the Antichrist, thus ruining the whole Western world. You precisely pointed out that if France is suffering, Catholicism alone is to blame, for she rejected the foul Roman God but has not found a new one. That is what you were able to say then! I remember our conversations."[16]

"If I had belief, I would no doubt repeat it now as well; I wasn't lying, speaking as a believer," Nikolai Vsevolodovich said very seriously. "But I assure you that this repetition of my past thoughts produces an all too unpleasant impression on me. Couldn't you stop?"

"If you had belief?" Shatov cried, paying not the slightest attention to the request. "But wasn't it you who told me that if someone proved to you mathematically that the truth is outside Christ, you would better agree to stay with Christ than with the truth?[17] Did you say that? Did you?"

"But allow me also to ask, finally," Stavrogin raised his voice, "what this whole impatient and . . . spiteful examination is leading to?"

"This examination will end forever and you will never be reminded of it."

"You keep insisting that we are outside space and time . . ."

"Be silent!" Shatov suddenly shouted. "I'm stupid and clumsy, but let my name perish in ridiculousness! Will you permit me to repeat before you your main thought of that time . . . Oh, only ten lines, just the conclusion."

"Repeat it, if it's just the conclusion . . ."

Stavrogin nearly made a move to look at his watch, but refrained and did not look.

Shatov again leaned forward a little on his chair, and even raised his finger again for a moment.

"Not one nation," he began, as if reciting line by line, and at the same time still looking menacingly at Stavrogin, "not one nation has ever set itself up on the principles of science and reason; there has never been an example of it, unless perhaps only for a moment, out of foolishness. Socialism by its very essence must be atheism, because it has precisely declared, from the very first line, that it is an atheistic order, and intends to set itself up on the principles of science and reason exclusively. Reason and science always, now, and from the beginning of the ages, have performed only a secondary and auxiliary task in the life of nations; and so they will to the end of the ages. Nations are formed and moved by another ruling and dominating force, whose origin is unknown and inexplicable. This force is the force of the unquenchable desire to get to the end, while at the same time denying the end. It is the force of a ceaseless and tireless confirmation of its own being and a denial of death. The Spirit of life, as Scripture says, the 'rivers of living water,' whose running dry is so threatened in the Apocalypse.[18] The aesthetic principle, as philosophers say, the moral principle, as they also identify it. 'Seeking for God'—as I call it in the simplest way. The aim of all movements of nations, of every nation and in every period of its existence, is solely the seeking for God, its own God, entirely its own, and faith in him as the only true one. God is the synthetic person of the whole nation, taken from its beginning and to its end. It has never yet happened that all or many nations have had one common God, but each has always had a separate one. It is a sign of a nation's extinction when there begin to be gods in common. When there are gods in common, they die along with the belief in them and with the nations themselves. The stronger the nation, the more particular its God. There has never yet been a nation without a religion, that is, without an idea of evil and good. Every nation has its own idea of evil and good, and its own evil and good. When many nations start having common ideas of evil and good, then the nations die out and the very distinction between evil and good begins to fade and disappear. Reason has never been able to define evil and good, or even to separate evil from good, if only approximately; on the contrary, it has always confused them, shamefully and pitifully; and science has offered the solution of the fist. Half-science has been especially distinguished for that—the most terrible scourge of mankind, worse than plague, hunger, or war, unknown till our century. Half-science is a despot such as has never been seen before. A despot with its own priests and slaves, a despot before whom everything has bowed down with a love and superstition unthinkable till now, before whom even science itself trembles and whom it shamefully caters to. These are all your own words, Stavrogin, all except the words about half-science; those are mine, because I myself am only half-science, and therefore I especially hate it. As for your thoughts and even your very words, I haven't changed anything, not a word."

"I wouldn't say you haven't," Stavrogin remarked cautiously. "You took it ardently, and have altered it ardently without noticing it. The fact alone that you reduce God to a mere attribute of nationality . . ."

He suddenly began to observe Shatov with increased and particular attention, not so much his words as the man himself.

"I reduce God to an attribute of nationality?" Shatov cried. "On the contrary, I raise the nation up to God. Has it ever been otherwise? The nation is the body of God. Any nation is a nation only as long as it has its own particular God and rules out all other gods in the world with no conciliation; as long as it believes that through its God it will be victorious and will drive all other gods from the world. Thus all have believed from the beginning of time, all great nations at least, all that were marked out to any extent, all that have stood at the head of mankind. There is no going against the fact. The Jews lived only to wait for the true God, and left the true God to the world. The Greeks deified nature, and bequeathed the world their religion, that is, philosophy and art. Rome deified the nation in the state, and bequeathed the state to the nations. France, throughout her whole long history, has simply been the embodiment and development of the idea of the

Roman God, and if she has finally flung her Roman God down into the abyss and plunged into atheism, which for the time being they call socialism, that is solely because atheism is, after all, healthier than Roman Catholicism. If a great nation does not believe that the truth is in it alone (precisely in it alone, and that exclusively), if it does not believe that it alone is able and called to resurrect and save everyone with its truth, then it at once ceases to be a great nation, and at once turns into ethnographic material and not a great nation. A truly great nation can never be reconciled with a secondary role in mankind, or even with a primary, but inevitably and exclusively with the first. Any that loses this faith is no longer a nation. But the truth is one, and therefore only one among the nations can have the true God, even if the other nations do have their particular and great gods. The only 'god-bearing' nation is the Russian nation, and . . . and . . . do you, do you really regard me as such a fool, Stavrogin," he suddenly cried out frenziedly, "who cannot even tell whether his words now are old, decrepit rubbish, ground up in all the Slavophil mills of Moscow, or a completely new word, the last word, the only word of renewal and resurrection, and . . . what do I care about your laughter at this moment! What do I care that you don't understand me at all, not at all, not a word, not a sound! . . . Oh, how I despise your proud laughter and look at this moment!"

He jumped up from his place; there was even foam on his lips.

"On the contrary, Shatov, on the contrary," Stavrogin said, with remarkable seriousness and restraint, without rising from his place, "on the contrary, with your ardent words you've revived many extremely powerful recollections in me. I recognize in your words my own state of mind two years ago, and I shall no longer say to you, as I just did, that you have exaggerated my thoughts of that time. It even seems to me that they were still more exceptional, still more absolute, and I assure you for the third time that I would wish very much to confirm everything you've said, even to a word, but . . ."

"But you need a hare?"

"Wha-a-at?"

"Your own vile expression," Shatov laughed spitefully, sitting down again. " 'To make sauce from a hare, you need a hare; to have belief in God, you need a God,' you went around saying in Petersburg, I'm told, like Nozdryov, who wanted to catch a hare by its hind legs."[19]

"No, he was precisely boasting that he'd already caught it. Incidentally, though, allow me to trouble you with a question as well, the more so as it seems to me I now have full right to ask. Tell me about your hare—have you caught it, or is it still running around?"

"Do not dare to ask me in such words; use others, others!" Shatov suddenly trembled all over.

"As you wish, here are your others," Nikolai Vsevolodovich looked at him sternly. "I simply wanted to know: do you yourself believe in God, or not?"

"I believe in Russia, I believe in her Orthodoxy . . . I believe in the body of Christ . . . I believe that the new coming will take place in Russia . . . I believe . . ." Shatov babbled frenziedly.

"But in God? In God?"

"I . . . I will believe in God."

Not a muscle moved in Stavrogin's face. Shatov looked at him fierily, defiantly, as if he wanted to burn him with his eyes.

"But I didn't tell you I don't believe at all!" he finally cried. "I'm only letting you know that I am a wretched, boring book, and nothing more so far, so far . . . But perish my name! The point is in you, not me . . . I'm a man without talent, and can only give my blood, and nothing more, like any other man without talent. Perish my blood as well! I'm talking about you, I've been waiting here two years for you . . . I've just been dancing naked for you for half an hour. You, you alone could raise this banner! . . ."

He did not finish, but leaned his elbows on the table and propped his head in both hands, as if in despair.

"I'll merely note, incidentally, as a strange thing," Stavrogin suddenly interrupted, "why is it that everyone is foisting some banner on me? Pyotr Verkhovensky is also convinced that I could 'raise their banner,' or so at least his words were conveyed to me. He's taken it into his head that I could play the role of Stenka Razin[20] for them, 'owing to my extraordinary capacity for crime'—also his words."

"How's that?" Shatov asked. " 'Owing to your extraordinary capacity for crime'?"

"Precisely."

"Hm. And is it true that you," he grinned spitefully, "is it true that in Petersburg you belonged to some secret society of bestial sensualists? Is it true that the Marquis de Sade[21] could take lessons from you? Is it true that you lured and corrupted children? Speak, do not dare to lie," he cried, completely beside himself, "Nikolai Stavrogin cannot lie before Shatov who hit him in the face! Speak everything, and if it's true, I'll kill you at once, right here, on the spot!"

"I did speak those words, but it was not I who offended children," said Stavrogin, but only after too long a silence. He turned pale, and his eyes lit up.

"But you spoke of it!" Shatov went on imperiously, not taking his flashing eyes from Stavrogin. "Is it true that you insisted you knew no difference in beauty between some brutal sensual stunt and any great deed, even the sacrifice of life for mankind? Is it true that you found a coincidence of beauty, a sameness of pleasure at both poles?"

"It's impossible to answer like this . . . I won't answer," muttered Stavrogin, who could very well have gotten up and left, but did not get up and leave.

"I don't know why evil is bad and good is beautiful either, but I do know why the sense of this distinction is faded and effaced in such gentlemen as the Stavrogins," Shatov, trembling all over, would not let go. "Do you know why you married so disgracefully and basely then? Precisely because here the disgrace and senselessness reached the point of genius! Oh, you don't go straying along the verge, you boldly fly down headfirst. You married out of a passion for torture, out of a passion for remorse, out of moral sensuality. It was from nervous strain . . . The challenge to common sense was too enticing! Stavrogin and a scrubby, feebleminded, beggarly lame girl! When you bit the governor's ear, did you feel the sensuality of it? Did you? Idle, loafing young squire—did you feel it?"

"You're a psychologist," Stavrogin was turning paler and paler, "though you are partly mistaken about the reasons for my marriage . . . And who, incidentally, could have given you all this information?" he forced himself to grin. "Could it be Kirillov? But he had no part in it . . ."

"You're turning pale?"

"What do you want, anyway?" Nikolai Vsevolodovich finally raised his voice. "I've sat for half an hour under your lash, you could at least politely let me go . . . if you indeed have no reasonable purpose in acting this way with me."

"Reasonable purpose?"

"Undoubtedly. It was your duty at least to announce your purpose to me finally. I kept waiting for you to do so, but all I've found is frenzied spite. I ask you to open the gate for me."

He got up from the chair. Shatov rushed frantically after him.

"Kiss the earth, flood it with tears, ask forgiveness!" he cried out, seizing him by the shoulder.

"Anyhow, I didn't kill you . . . that morning . . . I put both hands behind my back . . ." Stavrogin said, almost with pain, looking down.

"Say it all, say it all! You came to warn me about the danger, you allowed me to speak, you want to announce your marriage publicly tomorrow! . . . Can't I see by your face that you're at grips with some awesome new thought? . . . Stavrogin, why am I condemned to believe in you unto ages of ages? Would I be able to talk like this with anyone else? I have chastity, yet I wasn't afraid of my nakedness, for I was speaking with Stavrogin. I wasn't afraid to caricature a great thought by my touch, for Stavrogin was listening to me . . . Won't I kiss your footprints when you've gone? I cannot tear you out of my heart, Nikolai Stavrogin!"

"I'm sorry I cannot love you, Shatov," Nikolai Vsevolodovich said coldly.

"I know you cannot, and I know you're not lying. Listen, I can set everything right: I'll get you that hare!"

Stavrogin was silent.

"You're an atheist because you're a squire, an ultimate squire. You've lost the distinction between evil and good because you've ceased to recognize your own nation. A new generation is coming, straight from the nation's heart, and you won't recognize it, neither will the Verkhovenskys, son or father, nor will I, for I, too, am a squire—I, the son of your serf and lackey Pashka . . . Listen, acquire God by labor; the whole essence is there, or else you'll disappear like vile mildew; do it by labor."

"God by labor? What labor?"

"Peasant labor. Go, leave your wealth . . . Ah! you're laughing, you're afraid it will turn out to be flimflam."

But Stavrogin was not laughing.

"You suppose God can be acquired by labor, and precisely by peasant labor?" he repeated, after a moment's thought, as if he had indeed encountered something new and serious which was worth pondering. "Incidentally," he suddenly passed on to a new thought, "you've just reminded me: do you know that I'm not rich at all, so there's nothing to leave? I'm hardly even able to secure Marya Timofeevna's future . . . Another thing: I came to ask you if it's possible for you not to abandon Marya Timofeevna in the future, since you alone may have some influence on her poor mind . . . I say it just in case."

"All right, all right, you and Marya Timofeevna," Shatov waved his hand, holding a candle in the other, "all right, later, of itself . . . Listen, go to Tikhon."

"Who?"

"Tikhon. Tikhon, a former bishop, retired for reasons of health, lives here in town, within town limits, in our Saint Yefimi-Bogorodsky monastery."

"What's it all about?"

"Never mind. People go and see him. You should go to him; what is it to you? Well, what is it to you?"

"First time I've heard of him, and . . . I've never seen that sort of people before. Thank you, I'll go."

"This way," Shatov walked downstairs with the light. "Go," he flung open the gate to the street.

"I won't come to you anymore, Shatov," Stavrogin said softly, stepping through the gate.

Darkness and rain continued as before.

2

Night (Continued)

I

He walked the whole length of Bogoyavlensky Street; at last the road went downhill, his feet slid in the mud, a wide, misty, as if empty space opened out suddenly—the river. Houses turned to hovels, the street vanished into a multitude of disorderly lanes. For a long time Nikolai Vsevolodovich made his way along the fences without straying from the bank, but finding his way surely and without even thinking much about it. He was occupied with something else, and looked about him in surprise when suddenly, coming out of deep thought, he found himself almost in the middle of our long, wet pontoon bridge. There was not a soul around, so that it seemed strange to him when all at once, almost at his elbow, he heard a politely familiar, incidentally rather pleasant voice, with that sweetly drawn-out intonation flaunted among us by overcivilized tradesmen or young, curly-headed salesclerks from the shopping arcade.

"Will you allow me, dear mister, to borrow a bit of your umbrella for myself?"[1]

In fact some figure crept, or merely meant to make a pretense of creeping, under his umbrella. The tramp walked along beside him, almost elbow to elbow, as soldier boys say. Slowing his pace, Nikolai Vsevolodovich bent down to see, as well as he could in the dark: the man was not tall and looked like some little tradesman on a spree; his clothes were neither warm nor sightly; a wet flannel cap with a torn-off peak perched on his shaggy, curly head. He seemed to be very dark-haired, lean, and swarthy; his eyes were large, undoubtedly black, very shiny, and had a yellow cast, like a Gypsy's—that could be guessed even in the dark. He must have been about forty, and was not drunk.

"Do you know me?" asked Nikolai Vsevolodovich.

"Mister Stavrogin, Nikolai Vsevolodovich; you were pointed out to me at the station the moment the train stopped two Sundays ago. Besides from the fact that I heard about you before."

"From Pyotr Stepanovich? You . . . are you Fedka the Convict?"

"I was baptized Fyodor Fyodorovich; I've still got a natural parent here in these parts, sir, an old woman, God love her, growing right into the ground, prays to God for me daily, day and night, so as thereby not to waste her old woman's time lying on the stove."

"You're a fugitive from hard labor?"

"Changed my destiny. Handed over books and bells and everything else, because they aimed to settle my hash with that hard labor, sir, and for me it was far-r-r too long a wait."

"What are you doing here?"

"Watching the clock go round. Then, too, my uncle died here last week in prison, on account of bad money, so in his memory I threw a couple of dozen stones at the dogs—that's all my doings so far. Besides from that, Pyotr Stepanovich is kindly promising me a passport, good for all of Russia—a merchant's, for example—so I'm also waiting on his favor. Because, he says, papa lost you at cards in the Engullish club, and I, he says, find this inhumanness unjust. Maybe you could stoop to three roubles, sir, for tea, to warm up?"

"So you've been watching for me here; I don't like that. On whose orders?"

"As for orders, there was no such thing from anybody, sir, it's solely from knowing your loving-kindness, so famous to the whole world. Our income, you know yourself, is either a handful of rye or a poke in the eye. Granted, last Friday I stuffed myself with pie like nobody's business, but after that I gave up eating for a day, starved for another, and fasted for a third. There's plenty of water in the river, I'm breeding carp in my belly . . . So maybe Your Honor will be generous; and, as it happens, I've got a lady friend waiting not far from here, only one had better not come to her without a rouble."

"And what has Pyotr Stepanovich promised you from me?"

"It's not that he promised anything, sir, he just said in words, sir, that I could maybe be of use to Your Honor, if such a spell comes, for example, but what it might actually be he didn't exactly explain, because Pyotr Stepanovich is testing my Cossack patience, shall we say, and doesn't feel any confidentiality towards me."

"Why's that?"

"Pyotr Stepanovich is an astrominer, and has learned all God's planids, but even he is subject to criticism. Before you, sir, it's like I'm before the True One, because I've heard a lot about you. Pyotr Stepanovich is one thing, and you, sir, are maybe something else. With him, once he says a man is a scoundrel, then except from the scoundrel he knows nothing about him. And if it's a fool, then he's got no other title for him except fool. But maybe I'm only a fool on Tuesdays and Wednesdays, and on Thursdays I'm smarter than he is. So now he knows about me that it's real bad for me without a passport—because there's no way to be in Russia without a document—so he thinks he's got my soul captive. I tell you, sir, it's very easy for Pyotr Stepanovich to live in the world, because he imagines a man and then lives with him the way he imagined him. And besides from that, he's way too stingy. He's of the opinion that apart from him I won't dare disturb you, but before you, sir, it's like I'm before the True One—it's four nights now I've been waiting for Your Honor on this bridge, which goes to show that with quiet steps I can find my own way even apart from him. Better, I'd say, bow down to a boot than to a bast shoe."

"And who told you I'd be crossing this bridge at night?"

"That, I confess, came by the way, mostly on account of Captain Lebyadkin's foolishness, because he can't keep things to himself . . . So, then, three roubles from Your Honor, let's say, for three days and three nights, I'd have it coming for my boredom. And as for my wet clothes, that's an offense I won't speak of."

"I go left, you go right; the bridge is ended. Listen, Fyodor, I like my words to be understood once and for all: I won't give you a kopeck, don't meet me on the bridge or anywhere else from now on, I don't and won't have any need of you, and if you refuse to obey—I'll tie you up and hand you over to the police. March!"

"Ah, well, at least throw me something for my company, it was more fun walking, sir."

"Off with you!"

"And do you know your way around here, sir? There'll be such back alleys . . . I could lead you, because this town here is like the devil took and shook it from a sack."

"Hey, I'll tie you up!" Nikolai Vsevolodovich turned around threateningly.

"You might consider, sir; it's easy enough to wrong an orphan."

"Well, you certainly are sure of yourself!"

"I'm sure of you, sir, not so much of myself."

"I don't need you at all, I told you!"

"But I need you, sir, that's what. All right, then, I'll wait till you come back."

"On my word of honor, if I meet you I'll tie you up."

"And I'll prepare the belt, sir. Have a good journey, sir, anyway you warmed an orphan under your umbrella, for that alone I'll thank you till my dying day."

He dropped behind. Nikolai Vsevolodovich was preoccupied as he came to the place. This man who had fallen from the sky was fully convinced that he was necessary to him, and hastened to declare it all too insolently. Generally, he was being treated unceremoniously. But it could also be that the tramp was not altogether lying, and was offering to be of service just on his own and precisely in secret from Pyotr Stepanovich; now that was the most curious thing of all.

II

THE HOUSE that Nikolai Vsevolodovich came to stood in a deserted nook between fences, beyond which stretched kitchen gardens, literally on the very edge of town. It was quite a solitary little wooden house, built only recently and not yet clapboarded. The shutters of one of the windows were purposely not closed, and a candle stood on the windowsill—evidently meant to serve as a beacon for a late visitor who was expected that night. From thirty paces away Nikolai Vsevolodovich could make out the figure of a tall man standing on the porch, probably the master of the house, who had come out impatiently to look down the road. His voice could also be heard, impatient and as if timid:

"Is it you, sir? Is it?"

"It's me," Nikolai Vsevolodovich replied, but not before he had actually come to the porch, folding his umbrella.

"At last, sir!" Captain Lebyadkin—for it was he—fussed and fidgeted. "Your umbrella, please; it's very wet, sir; I'll open it here on the floor in the corner—welcome, welcome."

The door from the entryway to a room lighted by two candles stood wide open.

"If it hadn't been for your word that you'd certainly come, I'd have stopped believing it."

"A quarter to one," Nikolai Vsevolodovich looked at his watch as he went into the room.

"And in this rain, and such an interesting distance . . . I don't have a watch, and there are just kitchen gardens out the window, so . . . one lags behind events . . . but, as a matter of fact, not to murmur, for I wouldn't dare, I wouldn't dare, but solely from impatience consumed all week, in order to finally . . . be released."

"How's that?"

"To hear my fate, Nikolai Vsevolodovich. Welcome."

He bent forward, indicating a place by the little table in front of the sofa.

Nikolai Vsevolodovich looked around; the room was tiny, low; the furniture was the most necessary, wooden chairs and a sofa, also of quite new manufacture, without upholstery or pillows, two limewood tables, one by the sofa and the other in the corner, covered with a tablecloth, all cluttered with things, over which a very clean napkin had been spread. The whole room was also obviously kept extremely clean. Captain Lebyadkin had not been drunk for some eight days; his face had become somehow bloated and yellow; his look was restless, curious, and obviously bewildered; it was all too noticeable that he himself did not yet know in what tone he should begin to speak or it would be most profitable for him to strike straight off.

"Here, sir," he pointed around him, "I live like Zossima.[2] Sobriety, solitude, and poverty—the vow of the knights of old."

"You think the knights of old used to make such vows?"

"Maybe I've got it muddled. Alas, no development for me! I've ruined everything! Believe me, Nikolai Vsevolodovich, here for the first time I've recovered from my shameful predilections—not a glass, not a drop! I have a corner to live in, and for six days I've been feeling a well-being of conscience. Even the walls smell of resin, reminding one of nature. And what was I, who was I?

> I blow about by night unhoused,
> By day with my tongue hanging out,

in the poet's ingenious expression![3] But . . . how wet you are . . . Wouldn't you like some tea?"

"Don't bother."

"The samovar was boiling since before eight, but . . . went out . . . like everything in this world. And the sun, they say, will go out in its turn . . . Still, if you want, I can come up with it. Agafya's not asleep."

"Tell me, Marya Timofeevna is . . ."

"Here, here," Lebyadkin at once picked up, in a whisper. "Would you like to have a look?" he pointed towards the closed door to the other room.

"Not asleep?"

"Oh, no, no, how could she be? On the contrary, she's been waiting since evening, and as soon as she learned of it today, she immediately saw to her toilette," he twisted his mouth for a moment into a playful little smile, but instantly checked himself.

"How is she, generally?" Nikolai Vsevolodovich asked, frowning.

"Generally? That, sir, you know yourself" (he shrugged regretfully), "and now . . . now she sits reading the cards . . ."

"Very well, later; first we must finish with you."

Nikolai Vsevolodovich sat down on a chair.

The captain did not dare to sit on the sofa, but at once pulled another chair over for himself and bent forward to listen in trembling expectation.

"And what is it you've got there in the corner under the cloth?" Nikolai Vsevolodovich suddenly paid attention.

"That, sir?" Lebyadkin also turned around. "That is from your own generosities, by way of housewarming, so to speak, also taking into account the further way and natural fatigue," he tittered sweetly, then rose from his seat and, tiptoeing over, reverently and carefully took the cloth from the table in the corner. Under it a light supper turned out to have been prepared: ham, veal, sardines, cheese, a small greenish carafe, and a tall bottle of Bordeaux; everything had been laid out neatly, expertly, and almost elegantly.

"Was it you who saw to that?"

"Me, sir. Since yesterday, and whatever I could do to honor . . . And Marya Timofeevna, you know yourself, is indifferent in this respect. And, above all, it's from your generosity, it's yours, since you are the master here, not me, and I'm only by way of being your steward, so to speak, for all the same, all the same, Nikolai Vsevolodovich, all the same I am independent in spirit! You won't take away this last possession of mine, will you?" he ended sweetly.

"Hm! . . . why don't you sit back down."

"With gra-a-atitude, gratitude and independence!" (He sat down.) "Ah, Nikolai Vsevolodovich, so much has been stewing in this heart that I couldn't wait for you to come! So you will now decide my fate, and . . . that unfortunate woman's, and then . . . then, as I used to, in the old days, I'll pour everything out to you, as four years ago! You did deign to listen to me then, you read my stanzas . . . And though you used to call me your Falstaff from Shakespeare, you meant so much in my fate! . . . I have great fears now, and wait for counsel and light from you alone. Pyotr Stepanovich acts terribly with me!"

Nikolai Vsevolodovich listened with curiosity, studying him closely. It was obvious that Captain Lebyadkin, though he had stopped drinking, was still far from being in a harmonious state. Something incoherent, dazed, something damaged and crazy, as it were, finally settles for good into such long-term drunkards, though, by the way, they can cheat, dodge, and sham almost no worse than anyone else if need be.

"I see you haven't changed at all, Captain, in these four years," Nikolai Vsevolodovich said, as if somewhat more kindly. "It must be true that the whole second half of a man's life is most often made up only of habits accumulated during the first half."

"Lofty words! You've solved the riddle of life!" the captain cried, half shamming and half really in genuine delight, because he was a great lover of little sayings. "Of all your sayings, Nikolai Vsevolodovich, there's one I remember especially; you uttered it back in Petersburg: 'One must be a great man indeed to be able to hold out even against common sense.' There, sir!"

"Or else a fool."

"Yes, sir, or else a fool, I suppose, but you've poured out witticisms all your life, while they . . . Let Liputin, let Pyotr Stepanovich try uttering anything like that! Oh, how cruelly Pyotr Stepanovich acted with me! . . ."

"But what about you, Captain, how did you act?"

"A drunken state, and the myriads of my enemies besides! But now all, all has gone past, and I renew myself like the serpent. Nikolai Vsevolodovich, do you know that I'm writing my will, and have already written it?"

"Curious. What is it you're leaving, and to whom?"

"To the fatherland, to mankind, and to students. Nikolai Vsevolodovich, in the newspapers I read a biography about an American. He left his whole huge fortune to factories and for the positive sciences, his skeleton to the students at the academy there, and his skin to make a drum so as to have the American national anthem drummed on it day and night. Alas, we're pygmies compared to the soaring ideas of the North American States; Russia is a freak of nature, but not of mind. If I were to try and bequeath my skin for a drum, to the Akmolinsk infantry regiment, for example, where I had the honor of beginning my service, so as to have the Russian national anthem drummed on it every day in front of the regiment, it would be regarded as liberalism, my skin would be forbidden . . . and so I limited myself only to students. I want to bequeath my skeleton to the academy, on condition, however, that a label be pasted to its forehead unto ages of ages, reading: 'Repentant Freethinker.' There, sir!"

The captain spoke ardently and, to be sure, already believed in the beauty of the American bequest, but he was also a knave and wanted very much to make Nikolai Vsevolodovich laugh, having for a long time been in the position of his buffoon. Yet he did not even smile, but, on the contrary, asked somehow suspiciously:

"So you intend to make your will public in your lifetime, and get rewarded for it?"

"And what if it were so, Nikolai Vsevolodovich, what if it were so?" Lebyadkin peered at him cautiously. "For just you look at my fate! I've even stopped writing poetry, and there was a time when even you were amused by my little verses, Nikolai Vsevolodovich, remember, over a bottle? But it's all finished with my pen. I've written only one poem, like Gogol's 'Last Story,' remember, how he announced to Russia then that it 'sang itself' out of his breast.⁴ Well, it's the same with me, I sang it and basta!"

"And what is this poem?"

" 'In Case If She Broke Her Leg'!"

"Wha-a-at?"

This was just what the captain had been waiting for. He respected and valued his poems beyond measure, but besides, through some knavish duplicity of soul, he also liked it that Nikolai Vsevolodovich had always made merry over his little poems in the past, and had sometimes roared with laughter at them, holding his sides. Thus two objects were achieved—one poetic, the other subservient; but now there was also a third, special and quite ticklish object: the captain, by bringing poetry onto the scene, hoped to justify himself on one point, about which for some reason he had great apprehensions, and in which he felt himself at fault most of all.

" 'In Case If She Broke Her Leg,' that is, in case of horseback riding. A fantasy, Nikolai Vsevolodovich, raving, but a poet's raving: I was struck once, in passing, when I encountered a girl on horseback, and asked a material question: 'What would happen then?'—that is, in such case. The answer is clear: all pretenders back out, all wooers vanish, so it goes and wipe your nose, the poet alone will be left with his heart squashed in his breast. Nikolai Vsevolodovich, even a louse, even he can be in love, even he is not forbidden by any laws. And yet the person was offended by both the letter and the poem. I hear even you got angry—is it so, sir; that's regrettable; I didn't even want to believe it. Who could I harm with just my imagination? Besides, I swear on my honor, it was Liputin: 'Send it, send it, every man deserves the right of correspondence'—so I sent it."

"I believe you proposed yourself as a fiancé?"

"Enemies, enemies, enemies!"

"Recite the poem," Nikolai Vsevolodovich sternly interrupted.

"Raving, raving, above all."

Nevertheless, he drew himself up, raised his hand, and began:

> "The beauty of beauties broke her member
> And twice more intriguing she became,
> And twice more burning was love's ember
> In him who already felt the same."

"Well, enough," Nikolai Vsevolodovich waved his hand.

"I dream of Petersburg," Lebyadkin skipped quickly on, as if there never had been any poem, "I dream of regeneration . . . Benefactor! Can I count on not being denied the means for the journey? I've been waiting for you all week as for the sun."

"Ah, no, sorry, I have almost no means left, and, besides, why should I give you money? . . ."

It was as if Nikolai Vsevolodovich suddenly became angry. Dryly and briefly he listed all the captain's crimes: drinking, lying, spending money intended for Marya Timofeevna, taking her from the convent, insolent letters with threats to make the secret public, his conduct with Darya Pavlovna, and so on and so forth. The captain heaved, gesticulated, tried to object, but each time Nikolai Vsevolodovich imperiously stopped him.

"And, I beg your pardon," he finally observed, "but you keep writing about a 'family disgrace.' Why is it so disgraceful for you that your sister is legally married to Stavrogin?"

"But the marriage is kept covered up, Nikolai Vsevolodovich, covered up, a fatal secret. I get money from you, and suddenly I'm asked the question: What is this money for? My hands are tied, I can't answer, to the detriment of my sister, to the detriment of my family dignity."

The captain raised his tone: he loved this theme and was counting firmly on it. Alas, he in no way anticipated how dashed he was going to be. Calmly and precisely, as if it were a matter of the most ordinary household instructions, Nikolai Vsevolodovich informed him that one of those days, perhaps even the next day or the day after, he intended to make his marriage known everywhere, "to the police as well as to society," and, consequently, the question of family dignity would end of itself, and along with it the question of subsidies. The captain goggled his eyes; he did not even understand; he had to have it explained to him.

"But isn't she a . . . half-wit?"

"I'll make certain arrangements."

"But . . . what about your mother?"

"Well, that's as she likes."

"But won't you have to bring your wife into your house?"

"Perhaps so. That, however, is in the fullest sense none of your business and does not concern you at all."

"How does it not concern me!" cried the captain. "And what am I to do?"

"Well, you certainly will not enter the house."

"But am I not a relation?"

"One flees such relations. Consider for yourself, then, why should I give you any money?"

"Nikolai Vsevolodovich, Nikolai Vsevolodovich, this cannot be, perhaps you'll still consider, you don't want to lay hands on . . . what will the world think, what will it say?"

"Much I fear your world. Didn't I marry your sister then, when I wanted to, after a drunken dinner, on a bet for wine, and why shouldn't I now proclaim it aloud . . . if it now amuses me?"

He uttered this somehow especially irritably, so that Lebyadkin, with horror, began to believe it.

"But me, what about me, I'm the main thing here! . . . Perhaps you're joking, Nikolai Vsevolodovich, sir?"

"No, I am not joking."

"Be it as you will, Nikolai Vsevolodovich, but I don't believe you . . . I'll file a petition then."

"You are terribly stupid, Captain."

"Maybe so, but this is all I've got left!" the captain was totally muddled. "Before, we were at least given lodging for the work she did in those corners, but now what will happen if you drop me altogether?"

"But don't you want to go to Petersburg and change your career?

Incidentally, is it true what I've heard, that you intended to go and make a denunciation, hoping to obtain a pardon by naming all the others?"

The captain gaped, goggle-eyed, and did not reply.

"Listen, Captain," Stavrogin suddenly began to speak with extreme seriousness, leaning slightly across the table. Up to then he had spoken somehow ambiguously, so that Lebyadkin, experienced in the role of buffoon, remained a bit uncertain until the last moment whether his master was really angry or was only teasing, whether he really had the wild idea of announcing his marriage or was only playing. But now the unusually stern look of Nikolai Vsevolodovich was so convincing that a chill even ran down the captain's spine. "Listen and tell the truth, Lebyadkin: have you made any denunciation yet, or not? Have you managed to really do anything? Did you send some letter out of foolishness?"

"No, sir, I haven't managed . . . and wasn't thinking of it," the captain stared.

"Well, that you weren't thinking of it is a lie. That's why you were begging to go to Petersburg. If you haven't written, you must have blabbed something to somebody. Tell the truth, I've heard a thing or two."

"To Liputin, while drunk. Liputin is a traitor. I opened my heart to him," the poor captain whispered.

"Heart or not, there's no need to be a tomfool. If you had a notion, you should have kept it to yourself; smart people are silent nowadays, they don't talk."

"Nikolai Vsevolodovich!" the captain started to tremble. "You had no part in anything, it's not you that I . . ."

"Of course, you wouldn't dare denounce your milch cow."

"Nikolai Vsevolodovich, consider, consider! . . ." and in despair, in tears, the captain began hurriedly telling his story over all those four years. This was a most stupid story of a fool who had been drawn into something that was not his business, and the importance of which he scarcely understood until the very last minute, being occupied with drinking and carousing. He told how, while still in Petersburg, he "firstly got carried away just out of friendship, like a loyal student, though not being a student," and, knowing nothing, "guilty of nothing," was spreading various papers in stairways, leaving them by the dozens in doorways, behind bellpulls, sticking them in instead of newspapers, bringing them to theaters, tucking them into hats, slipping them into pockets. And later he had started taking money from them, "for my means, just think of my means, sir!" He had spread "all sorts of rubbish" over the districts of two provinces. "Oh, Nikolai Vsevolodovich," he went on exclaiming, "what made me most indignant was its being completely against all civic and predominantly fatherland laws! It would suddenly be printed to go out with pitchforks, and remember that he who goes out poor in the morning may come home rich in the evening—just think, sir! I myself used to get the shudders, but I kept spreading them around. Or else suddenly, five or six lines, to the whole of Russia, out of the blue: 'Quick, lock the churches, destroy God, break up marriages, destroy the rights of inheritance, grab your knives'—that's all, and God knows what next. It was with that piece, the one with the five lines, sir, that I almost got caught; the officers of the regiment gave me a beating, but, God bless them, they let me go. And then last year they almost got me when I gave French counterfeit fifty-rouble bills to Korovaev; but, thank God, just then Korovaev drowned in the pond while drunk, and they didn't have time to expose me. Here at Virginsky's I proclaimed the freedom of the social wife. In June I again did some spreading around the ———— district. They say they'll make me do more of it . . . Pyotr Stepanovich suddenly let me know that I have to obey; he's been threatening me for a long time. And how he treated me on that Sunday, really! Nikolai Vsevolodovich, I am a slave, I am a worm, but not a god—that is my only difference from Derzhavin.[5] But my means, just think of my means!"

Nikolai Vsevolodovich listened to it all with curiosity.

"Much of that I knew nothing about," he said. "Of course, anything could happen with you . . . Listen," he said, after some reflection, "if you like, tell them—well, you know whom—that Liputin was lying, and that you only meant to scare me a bit with a denunciation, thinking that I, too, was compromised, so as to extract more money from me that way . . . Understand?"

"Nikolai Vsevolodovich, my dear, can I really be threatened with such a danger? I've been waiting only so I could ask you."

Nikolai Vsevolodovich grinned.

"You certainly won't be allowed to go to Petersburg, even if I give you money for the trip . . . but, anyhow, it's time I went to Marya Timofeevna," and he got up from his chair.

"And, Nikolai Vsevolodovich, what about Marya Timofeevna?"

"Just as I said."

"Can that also be true?"

"You still don't believe it?"

"Can it be that you'll cast me off like an old, worn-out boot?"

"We'll see," laughed Nikolai Vsevolodovich. "Well, let me go."

"Wouldn't you like to order me to stay out on the porch, sir . . . so as not to overhear something somehow, by chance . . . because the rooms are tiny."

"That's a good idea; stay out on the porch. Take the umbrella."

"Your umbrella . . . am I worth it, sir?" the captain oversweetened.

"Every man is worth an umbrella."

"At one stroke you define the minimum of human rights . . ."

But he was now babbling mechanically; he was too overwhelmed by the news, and became totally bewildered. And yet, almost at once, as soon as he stepped out onto the porch and opened the umbrella over him, the usual soothing notion began to hatch in his frivolous and knavish head, that he was being cheated and lied to, and, if so, it was not he who should fear, but he who was feared.

"If they're lying and cheating me, what precisely is the gist of it?" buzzed in his head. The announcement of the marriage seemed absurd to him: "True, anything can happen with such a wonder-worker; he lives for people's evil. And what if he's afraid himself, after Sunday's affront, and more so than ever before? So he comes running to assure me he's going to announce it himself, for fear I'll announce it. Eh, don't miss your mark, Lebyadkin! And why then come by night, by stealth, if he wants the publicity himself? And if he's afraid, it means he's afraid now, precisely at this moment, precisely in these few days . . . Eh, don't slip up, Lebyadkin! . . .

"He frightens me with Pyotr Stepanovich. Aie, it's scary, aie, it's scary; no, that's where it's really scary! What ever made me blab about it to Liputin! Devil knows what these devils are cooking up, I never could make it out. They've begun to stir again, like five years ago. True, whom could I denounce them to? 'You didn't write to anybody out of foolishness?' Hm. So one could write as if it was out of foolishness? Is he advising me? 'That's why you're going to Petersburg.' The rogue, I just had a dream, and he's already guessed it! As if he himself was pushing me to go. There can only be one of two things here: either he's afraid, again, because he got into some mischief, or . . . or he's not afraid himself and is only prompting me so that I'll denounce them all! Oh, scary, Lebyadkin, oh, just don't let me miss my mark! . . ."

He fell to thinking so deeply that he even forgot to eavesdrop. Anyhow, eavesdropping was difficult; the door was a thick, single-leafed one, and they were speaking very softly; some indistinct sounds could be heard. The captain even spat and went back out, thoughtful, to whistle on the porch.

III

MARYA TIMOFEEVNA'S ROOM was twice the size of the one occupied by the captain, and furnished with the same crude furniture; but the table in front of the sofa was covered with a bright, festive tablecloth; a lamp was burning on it; a beautiful carpet was spread over the whole floor; the bed was set apart behind a green curtain that ran the whole length of the room; and there was, besides, one big, soft armchair by the table, in which, however, Marya Timofeevna never sat. In the corner, as in her former lodgings, there was an icon with an icon lamp burning in front of it, and on the table the same indispensable little things were laid out: the deck of cards, the little mirror, the songbook, even the sweet roll. In addition to which there had also appeared two books with colored pictures, one of extracts from popular travel writings adapted for young readers, the other a collection of light didactic tales, mostly about knights, intended for Christmases and boarding schools. There was also an album of various photographs. Marya Timofeevna was, of course, expecting her visitor, as the captain had said; but when Nikolai Vsevolodovich entered her room, she was asleep, half reclining on the sofa, leaning on an embroidered pillow. The visitor closed the door inaudibly behind him and, without moving from the spot, began to study the sleeping woman.

The captain had stretched things a bit when he said that she had seen to her toilette. She was wearing the same dark dress as on Sunday at Varvara Petrovna's. Her hair was done up in the same way, in a tiny knot at the nape; her long and dry neck was bared in the same way. The black shawl given her by Varvara Petrovna lay on the sofa, carefully folded. As usual, she was crudely made up with white and rouge. Nikolai Vsevolodovich had not been standing there even a minute when she suddenly awoke, as if she had felt his gaze on her, opened her eyes, and quickly sat up straight. But something strange must also have happened with the visitor: he went on standing in the same spot by the door; with a fixed and piercing look he stared silently and persistently into her face. Perhaps this look was excessively stern, perhaps it expressed loathing, even a malicious delight in her fear—unless the half-awake Marya Timofeevna was simply imagining it—but suddenly, after almost a minute-long pause, the poor woman's face took on an expression of complete horror; spasms ran across it, she raised her hands, shaking them, and suddenly began to cry, exactly like a frightened child; another moment and she would have screamed. But the visitor came to his senses; in an instant his face changed, and he approached the table with a most amiable and tender smile.

"I'm sorry I frightened you, Marya Timofeevna, by coming in unexpectedly while you were asleep," he said, giving her his hand.

The sound of these tender words produced its effect, her fright vanished, though she still looked at him with fear, apparently trying to understand something. Fearfully, she also gave him her hand. At last a smile stirred timidly on her lips.

"Greetings, Prince," she whispered, peering at him somehow strangely.

"You must have been having a bad dream?" he went on smiling with ever more amiability and tenderness.

"And how did you know I was dreaming *about that*? . . ."

And she suddenly trembled again and recoiled, raising her hand in front of her as if to protect herself, and preparing to cry again.

"Pull yourself together, enough, there's nothing to fear, didn't you recognize me?" Nikolai Vsevolodovich tried to persuade her, but this time it took him some while to persuade her; she looked at him silently, with the same tormenting bewilderment, with a heavy thought in her poor head, still straining to think her way through to something. She would drop her eyes, then suddenly look him over with a quick, embracing glance. Finally, she seemed not so much to calm down as to reach a decision.

"Sit here, next to me, I beg you, so that I can have a good look at you afterwards," she said quite firmly, with some new and obvious purpose. "And don't worry now, I won't look at you, I'll look down. And don't you look at me either, until I myself ask you to. Do sit," she added, even impatiently.

A new sensation seemed to be taking more and more possession of her.

Nikolai Vsevolodovich sat down and waited; there was quite a long silence.

"Hm! It seems all strange to me," she muttered suddenly, almost in disgust. "I am full of bad dreams, of course; only why should you come into my dreams in such a way?"

"Well, let's leave dreams out of it," he said impatiently, turning to her despite her prohibition, and perhaps the former expression flashed in his eyes again. He saw that several times she would have liked, and liked very much, to glance at him, but that she stubbornly resisted and looked down.

"Listen, Prince," she raised her voice suddenly, "listen, Prince . . ."

"Why did you turn away, why don't you look at me, what is this comedy about?" he cried, unable to help himself.

But it was as if she had not heard him at all.

"Listen, Prince," she repeated for the third time, in a firm voice, with an unpleasant, preoccupied look on her face. "When you told me in the carriage then that the marriage would be announced, I felt afraid right then that the secret would be over. Now I really don't know; I kept thinking, and I see clearly that I'm not fit at all. I could dress up, I could receive people, too, perhaps—it's not so hard to invite people for a cup of tea, especially if there are servants. But, still, how will they look at it from outside? I noticed a lot in that house then, that Sunday morning. That pretty young lady watched me all the time, especially when you came in. It was you who came in then, eh? Her mother's just a funny little old society lady. My Lebyadkin also distinguished himself; so as not to burst out laughing, I had to keep looking up at the ceiling; the ceiling there is nicely decorated. *His* mother ought to be the superior of a convent; I'm afraid of her, though she gave me her black shawl. It must be they all attested me then from an unexpected side; I'm not angry, only I was sitting there then and thinking: what kind of relation am I to them? Of course, what's required of a countess is only qualities of soul—because for housekeeping she has lots of servants—and some bit of worldly coquetry besides, so as to be able to receive foreign travelers. But, still, that Sunday they looked at me hopelessly. Only Dasha is an angel. I'm very afraid they may upset *him* with some imprudent comment on my account."

"Don't be afraid or worried," Nikolai Vsevolodovich twisted his mouth.

"Anyway, for me it won't matter much even if he should be a little ashamed of me, because there's always more pity in it than shame, depending on the person, of course. He does know that I ought rather to pity them than they me."

"You seem to be very offended with them, Marya Timofeevna?"

"Who, me? No," she smiled simpleheartedly. "Not a bit. I looked at you all then: you're all angry, you're all quarreling; you get together and can't even laugh from the heart. So much wealth and so little joy—it's all loathsome to me. But, anyway, I don't pity anyone now except my own self."

"I've heard your life with your brother was bad without me?"

"Who told you so? Nonsense; it's much worse now; my dreams are not so good now, and they became not so good because you arrived. Why, tell me, please, did you appear, if I may ask?"

"And don't you want to go back to the convent?"

"Well, I could just feel they were going to offer me the convent again! As if I haven't seen your convent! And why should I go there, what will I bring with me? I'm as alone as can be now! It's too late for me to begin a third life."

"You are very angry about something, perhaps you're afraid I've stopped loving you?"

"I don't care about you at all. I'm afraid I myself may well stop loving someone."

She grinned contemptuously.

"I must be guilty before *him* in some very big way," she added suddenly, as if to herself, "only I don't know what I'm guilty of, that is my whole grief forever. Always, always, for all these five years I've feared day and night that I'm guilty before him for something. I've prayed sometimes, prayed and kept thinking about my great guilt before him. And so it's turned out to be true."

"But what is it?"

"I'm only afraid there may be something on *his* part," she went on without answering his question, not even hearing it at all. "Again, he couldn't really become close with such paltry people. The countess would gladly eat me, even though she put me in her carriage. They're all in the conspiracy—is he, too? Has he, too, betrayed me?" (Her lips and chin began to tremble.) "Listen, you: have you read about Grishka Otrepev, who was cursed at the seven councils?"[6]

Nikolai Vsevolodovich did not answer.

"Anyway, I'll now turn and look at you," she suddenly seemed to make up her mind. "You also turn and look at me, only look more intently. I want to make sure for the last time."

"I've been looking at you for a long time."

"Hm," said Marya Timofeevna, studying him closely, "you've grown fatter . . ."

She wanted to say something more, but then again, for the third time, the same fright instantly distorted her face, and she again recoiled, raising her hand in front of her.

"What's the matter with you?" Nikolai Vsevolodovich cried out, almost in rage.

But the fright lasted only an instant; her face twisted into some strange smile, suspicious, unpleasant.

"I beg you, Prince, to get up and come in," she suddenly said, in a firm and insistent voice.

"How, *come in*? Come in where?"

"All these five years I've only been imagining how *he* would come in. Get up now and go out the door, into the other room. I'll sit here as if I'm not expecting anything and take a book in my hands, and suddenly you will come in after five years of traveling. I want to see how it will be."

Nikolai Vsevolodovich gnashed his teeth to himself and growled something incomprehensible.

"Enough," he said, slapping the table with his palm. "I beg you to listen to me, Marya Timofeevna. Kindly collect all your attention, if you can. You're not completely mad, after all!" he burst out impatiently. "Tomorrow I am announcing our marriage. You will never live in a mansion, don't deceive yourself. Would you like to live with me all your life, only very far from here? It's in the mountains, in Switzerland, there's a place there . . . Don't worry, I'll never abandon you or send you to the madhouse. I have enough money to live without begging. You'll have a maid; you won't do any work. Everything you want that's possible, you will be given. You will pray, go wherever you like, and do whatever you like. I won't touch you. I also won't stir from the place all my life. If you want, I won't speak to you all my life; if you want, you can tell me your stories every evening, as you did in those corners in Petersburg. I'll read books to you if you wish. But realize that it will be so all your life, in one place, and the place is a gloomy one. Do you want to? Are you resolved? You won't repent, you won't torment me with tears, curses?"

She heard him out with great curiosity, and thought silently for a long time.

"It's all incredible to me," she said at last, mockingly and disgustedly. "I might live like that for forty years in those mountains." She laughed.

"Well, so we'll live there for forty years," Nikolai Vsevolodovich scowled deeply.

"Hm. I won't go for anything."

"Not even with me?"

"And what are you that I should go with you? To sit with him on a mountain for forty years on end—I see what he's up to! Really, what patient people we've got nowadays! No, it can't be that my falcon has turned into an owl. My prince is not like that!" She raised her head proudly and solemnly.

Something seemed to dawn on him.

"Why do you call me prince, and . . . whom do you take me for?" he asked quickly.

"What? You're not a prince?"

"And I never have been."

"So you, you yourself, admit right to my face that you're not a prince?"

"I tell you, I never have been."

"Lord!" she clasped her hands, "I expected anything from *his* enemies, but such boldness—never! Is he alive?" she cried out in a frenzy, moving upon Nikolai Vsevolodovich. "Have you killed him, or not? Confess!"

"Whom do you take me for!" he jumped up from his seat, his face distorted; but by now it was difficult to frighten her, she was triumphant:

"Who knows who you are or where you popped up from! Only my heart, my heart sensed the whole intrigue all these five years! And I'm sitting here, wondering: what's this blind owl up to? No, my dear, you're a bad actor, even worse than Lebyadkin. Go bow as low as you can to the countess for me, and tell her to send someone cleaner than you. Did she hire you? Speak! Does she keep you in the kitchen for charity? I see through your whole deception, I know you all, to a man!"

He seized her firmly by the arm, above the elbow; she was laughing loudly in his face:

"You look very much like him, you do, maybe you might be his relative—sly people! Only *mine* is a bright falcon and a prince, and you are a barn owl and a little merchant! Mine will bow to God if he wishes, and won't if he doesn't, and you have had your face slapped by Shatushka (he's a dear, a sweet man, my darling!), my Lebyadkin told me. And why did you get scared then, as you walked in? Who frightened you then? As soon as I saw your mean face, when I fell and you picked me up—it was as if a worm crept into my heart: not *him*, I thought, it's not *him*! My falcon would never be ashamed of me in front of a fashionable young lady! Oh, Lord! but this alone has kept me happy all these five years, that my falcon lives and flies somewhere beyond the mountains, and gazes on the sun . . . Tell me, impostor, how much did you get? Did you agree for a big sum? I wouldn't give you a kopeck. Ha, ha, ha! Ha, ha, ha!"

"Ohh, idiot!" rasped Nikolai Vsevolodovich, still firmly holding her arm.

"Away, impostor!" she cried commandingly. "I am my prince's wife, your knife doesn't frighten me!"

"Knife!"

"Yes, knife! you have a knife in your pocket. You thought I was asleep, but I saw it: tonight, as you came in, you pulled out your knife!"

"What are you saying, wretched woman, is this the sort of dreams you have?" he cried out, and pushed her away from him with all his might, so that her head and shoulders even struck painfully against the sofa. He bolted; but she jumped up at once and went after him, limping and hopping, trying to overtake him, and from the porch, while the frightened Lebyadkin tried with all his might to restrain her, she managed to shout after him into the darkness, shrieking and laughing:

"Grishka Otrepev, anathema!"

IV

"A KNIFE, a knife!" he repeated, in unquenchable spite, striding broadly over mud and puddles without looking where he was going. True, at moments he wanted terribly to laugh, loudly, furiously; but for some reason he controlled himself and restrained his laughter. He came to his senses only on the bridge, just at the spot where he had previously met Fedka; the very same Fedka was again waiting for him there, and, seeing him, took off his cap, gaily bared his teeth, and at once began jabbering about something, perkily and gaily. Nikolai Vsevolodovich at first walked past without stopping, and for some time did not even listen at all to the tramp, who again tagged after him. He was suddenly struck by the thought that he had completely forgotten about him, and forgotten precisely at the time when he was repeating every moment to himself: "A knife, a knife!" He seized the tramp by the scruff of the neck and, with all his pent-up anger, dashed him against the bridge as hard as he could. For a moment the man thought

of putting up a fight, but realizing almost at once that he was something like a straw compared with his adversary, who, moreover, had
attacked unexpectedly—he quieted down and fell silent, without offering the least resistance. On his knees, pressed to the ground, his elbows
wrenched behind his back, the sly tramp calmly waited for the denouement, apparently not believing there was any danger at all.

He was not mistaken. Nikolai Vsevolodovich had already taken off
his warm scarf with his left hand, to tie his captive's arms, but suddenly, for some reason, abandoned him and pushed him away. The
man jumped to his feet at once, turned around, and a short, broad
cobbler's knife, which instantly appeared from somewhere, flashed in
his hand.

"Away with the knife, put it away, now!" Nikolai Vsevolodovich
ordered, with an impatient gesture, and the knife vanished as instantly
as it had appeared.

Nikolai Vsevolodovich went on his way again, silently and without
turning around; but the stubborn scoundrel still did not leave him
alone, though, true, he no longer jabbered, and even respectfully observed a distance of one full step behind. Thus they crossed the bridge
and came out on the bank, turning left this time into another long and
obscure back lane, which was a shorter way to the center of town than
the previous way down Bogoyavlensky Street.

"Is it true what they say, that you robbed a church the other day,
somewhere here in the district?" Nikolai Vsevolodovich suddenly
asked.

"Well, I mean, as a matter of fact, I stopped in firstly to pray, sir,"
the tramp answered sedately and deferentially, as if nothing had happened; not even sedately, but almost dignifiedly. There was no trace
of the former "friendly" familiarity. One glimpsed a practical and
serious man, who, though unjustly offended, was capable of forgetting
offenses.

"Then, once the Lord had brought me there," he went on, "I
thought, ah, what a heavenly blessing! It's owing to my being an
orphan that this thing has happened, because in my destiny it's quite
impossible without assistance. And then, by God, sir, it was my loss,
the Lord punished me for my sins: all I got for the swinger and the
swatter and the deacon's girth was twelve roubles. Nicholas the

Wonder-worker's pure silver getup went for nothing: they said it was similor."[7]

"You killed the beadle?"

"I mean, we bagged it together, me and that beadle; it was only towards morning, by the river, we got to quarreling mutually, who should carry the sack. I sinned, I lightened his load for him."

"Kill more, steal more."

"That's the same thing Pyotr Stepanovich advises me, sir, word for word just what you say, because he's an extremely stingy and hard-hearted man when it comes to assistance, sir. Besides from the fact that he doesn't have even a straw of belief in the heavenly creator who made us out of earthly dust, sir, but says nature alone arranged it all, supposedly even to the last beast, and what's more he doesn't understand that in my destiny it's quite impossible to do entirely without beneficent assistance, sir. I start explaining it to him, and he stares like a sheep at water, you can only wonder at him. Now, would you believe it, sir, with this Captain Lebyadkin, where you just visited, if you please, sir, when he was still living at Filippov's before you, sir, his door sometimes stood wide open all night, sir, he himself lying dead drunk and money spilling out of all his pockets onto the floor. I happened to observe it with my own eyes, because the way my life is, it's quite impossible without assistance, sir . . ."

"How, with your own eyes? Did you go in there at night, or what?"

"Maybe I did, only nobody knows."

"Why didn't you put a knife in him?"

"After making a reckoning, I steadied myself, sir. Because once I knew for sure that I could take out about a hundred and fifty roubles anytime, then how should I venture into such a thing when I can take out the whole fifteen hundred, provided I just wait a bit? Since Captain Lebyadkin (I heard it with my own ears, sir) always had gr-r-reat hopes of you in his drunken state, sir, and there's no such tavern establishment around here, not even the lowest pot-house, where he wouldn't announce as much, being in that same state, sir. So that, hearing about it from many lips, I, too, began to place all my hopes in Your Excellency. I'm telling it to you, sir, as I would to my own father or brother, because Pyotr Stepanovich will never find it out from me, and neither will a single soul else. So then, how about three little roubles, Your Excellency, would you be so kind, sir, or not? You'd unbind me, sir, so that I'd know the real truth, I mean, because it's quite impossible for me without assistance, sir."

Nikolai Vsevolodovich guffawed loudly, and taking from his pocket a wallet that contained as much as fifty roubles in small bills, he pulled one out of the wad for him, then another, a third, a fourth. Fedka caught them in the air, rushed about, the bills rained down into the mud, Fedka caught at them with little cries: "Ah, ah!" Nikolai Vsevolodovich finally threw the whole wad at him, and, still guffawing, set off down the lane, this time alone. The tramp stayed behind, fussing on his knees in the mud, picking up the bills that had scattered on the wind or sunk in puddles, and for a whole hour one could hear his abrupt little cries from the darkness: "Ah, ah!"

3

The Duel

I

THE NEXT DAY, at two o'clock in the afternoon, the proposed duel took place.[1] The speedy outcome of the affair was furthered by Artemy Pavlovich Gaganov's indomitable desire to fight at all costs. He did not understand his adversary's conduct, and was furious. For a whole month he had been insulting him with impunity, and was still unable to make him lose patience. He needed a challenge from Nikolai Vsevolodovich, because he had no direct pretext for a challenge himself. And for some reason he was embarrassed to admit his secret motive—that is, simply a morbid hatred of Stavrogin for the family insult of four years ago. And he himself considered this pretext impossible, especially in view of the humble apologies already twice offered by Nikolai Vsevolodovich. Inwardly he set Stavrogin down as a shameless coward; he simply could not understand how he could suffer a slap from Shatov; and thus he finally resolved to send that letter, remarkable in its rudeness, which finally prompted Nikolai Vsevolodovich to suggest a meeting himself. Having sent this letter the day before, and awaiting the challenge with feverish impatience, morbidly reckoning up his chances for it, now hopeful, now despairing, he provided himself, just in case, on the previous evening, with a second—namely, Mavriky Nikolaevich Drozdov, his friend from school days and a man he particularly respected. So it was that when Kirillov came with his errand the next day at nine o'clock in the morning, he found the ground quite prepared. All the apologies and unheard-of concessions of Nikolai Vsevolodovich were rejected at once, from the first word, and with remarkable vehemence. Mavriky Nikolaevich, who had learned only the day before of the course the affair had taken, gaped in astonishment at such unheard-of offers, and wanted to insist at once on a reconciliation, but noticing that Artemy Pavlovich, who guessed his intentions, almost started shaking in his chair, he kept silent and said nothing. Had it not been for the word he had given his friend, he would have walked out immediately; he stayed solely in hopes of helping at least with something in the outcome of the affair. Kirillov conveyed the challenge; all the conditions stipulated for the meeting by Stavrogin were accepted at once, literally, without the least objection. Only one addition was made, albeit a very cruel one—namely, that if nothing decisive occurred at the first shots, they would begin over again; if it ended with nothing the second time, they would begin a third time. Kirillov frowned, bargained a little about the third time, but, having bargained unsuccessfully, agreed, on condition, however, that "three times was possible, but four absolutely not." This they conceded. And so, at two o'clock in the afternoon, the meeting took place at Brykovo, that is, a little woods outside town, between Skvoreshniki on one side and the Shpigulins' factory on the other. Yesterday's rain had stopped entirely, but it was wet, damp, and windy. Low, dull, broken clouds raced quickly across the cold sky; the trees rustled densely and rollingly at their tops, and creaked on their roots; the morning was very melancholy.

Gaganov and Mavriky Nikolaevich arrived at the place in a jaunty char-à-banc and pair, driven by Artemy Pavlovich; they had a servant with them. At almost the same moment, Nikolai Vsevolodovich and Kirillov appeared, not in a carriage but on horseback, and also accompanied by a mounted servant. Kirillov, who had never mounted a horse before, sat bold and straight in the saddle, clutching in his right hand the heavy pistol box, which he would not entrust to the servant, and with his left hand, for want of skill, constantly twisting and pulling at the reins, causing the horse to toss its head and display a desire to rear, which, however, did not frighten the rider in the least. The insecure Gaganov, who took offense quickly and deeply, considered this arrival on horseback a new offense to himself, implying that his enemies therefore hoped for success, since they did not even assume the need for a carriage in case a wounded man had to be transported. He got down from his char-à-banc all yellow with anger, and felt his hands trembling, of which he informed Mavriky Nikolaevich. He did not respond at all to Nikolai Vsevolodovich's bow and turned away. The seconds cast lots: the lot fell on Kirillov's pistols. The barriers were measured out, the adversaries were placed, the carriage and horses were sent with the servants about three hundred paces off. The weapons were loaded and handed to the adversaries.

It is a pity the story must move on more quickly and there is no time for descriptions; but it is impossible to do without observations entirely. Mavriky Nikolaevich was melancholy and preoccupied. Kirillov, on the other hand, was perfectly calm and indifferent, very precise in the details of the duty he had assumed, but without the least fussiness, and almost without curiosity as to the fatal and so imminent outcome of the affair. Nikolai Vsevolodovich was paler than usual, dressed rather lightly in an overcoat and a white beaver hat. He seemed very tired, frowned from time to time, and did not find it at all necessary to conceal his unpleasant mood. But the most remarkable one at that moment was Artemy Pavlovich, so that it is altogether impossible not to say a few words about him quite separately.

II

WE HAVE HAD no occasion as yet to mention his appearance. He was a man of large stature, white-skinned, well-fed, as simple folk say, almost flabby, with thin blond hair, some thirty-three years old, and perhaps even handsome of feature. He had retired as a colonel, and had he attained the rank of general, he would have looked even more imposing as a general, and it may well be that a good combat general would have come out of him.

One cannot omit, in characterizing the man, that the main reason for his retirement was the thought of his family disgrace, which haunted him long and painfully after the offense inflicted on his father four years ago in the club by Nikolai Stavrogin. In all conscience, he considered it dishonorable to continue in the service, and was inwardly convinced that he was a blot on his regiment and his comrades, though none of them even knew of the event. True, once before he had also wanted to leave the service, way back, long before the offense, and for a totally different reason, but he kept hesitating. Strange though it is to write it, this initial intention, or, better, impulse, to retire came from the manifesto of February nineteenth on the emancipation of the peasants. Artemy Pavlovich, the wealthiest landowner of our province, who did not even lose very much after the manifesto, who, moreover, was himself capable of being convinced of the humaneness of the measure and almost of understanding the economic advantages of the reform, suddenly, after the appearance of the manifesto, felt himself personally offended, as it were. This was something unconscious, like a sort of feeling, but all the stronger the more unaccountable it was. Before his father's death, however, he did not decide to undertake anything decisive; but in Petersburg he became known for his "noble" way of thinking to many notable persons with whom he assiduously maintained connections. This was a man withdrawn, closed up in himself. Another trait: he was one of those strange but still surviving Russian noblemen who greatly value the antiquity and purity of their noble lineage and are all too seriously interested in it. At the same time he could not bear Russian history, and regarded all Russian customs in general as somewhat swinish. Already in his childhood, in that special military school for wealthier and more aristocratic pupils in which he had the honor of beginning and ending his education, certain poetic attitudes took root in him: he became fond of castles, medieval life, the whole operatic side of it, chivalry; even then he all but wept for shame that in the time of the Muscovite kingdom the tsar could corporally punish a Russian boyar,[2] and he blushed at the comparison. This taut, extremely strict man, who knew his service and discharged his duties remarkably well, in his soul was a dreamer. It was maintained that he could speak at meetings and had the gift of eloquence; yet he had kept silent in himself for all his thirty-three years. He bore himself with remarkable arrogance even in that grand Petersburg milieu in which he had moved of late. His meeting in Petersburg with Nikolai Vsevolodovich, who had just returned from abroad, almost drove him out of his mind. At the present moment, standing at the barrier, he was in terrible anxiety. He kept fancying that the thing might somehow not take place after all, and the slightest delay sent tremors through him. His face bore a pained expression when Kirillov, instead of giving the signal for the battle to begin, suddenly began to speak, for the sake of form, true, as he himself declared for all to hear:

"Just for the sake of form; now that pistols have been taken and the command must be given, for the last time, do you care to reconcile? The duty of a second."

As if on purpose, Mavriky Nikolaevich, who until then had been silent, but had been suffering inwardly since the previous day for his compliance and connivance, suddenly picked up Kirillov's thought and also spoke:

"I subscribe completely to Mr. Kirillov's words . . . the notion that it's impossible to reconcile standing at the barrier is a prejudice fit for Frenchmen . . . Be it as you will, but I do not understand what the offense is and have long wanted to say . . . because all kinds of apologies are being offered, aren't they?"

He blushed all over. Rarely had he chanced to speak so much and in such agitation.

"I again confirm my offer to present all possible apologies," Nikolai Vsevolodovich picked up with great haste.

"How is this possible?" Gaganov cried out furiously, turning to Mavriky Nikolaevich and frenziedly stamping his foot. "Do explain to this man, if you are my second and not my enemy, Mavriky Nikolaevich" (he jabbed his pistol in the direction of Nikolai Vsevolodovich) "that such concessions only add to the offense! He does not find it possible to be offended by me! . . . He does not find it a disgrace to walk away from a duel with me! Who does he take me for after that, in your eyes . . . and you are my second! You're simply irritating me so that I'll miss." He stamped his foot again; spittle sprayed from his lips.

"Negotiations are over. I ask you to listen for the command!" Kirillov shouted as loudly as he could. "One! Two! Three!"

At the word *three*, the adversaries began walking towards each other. Gaganov raised his pistol at once and fired at the fifth or sixth step. He stopped for a second and, ascertaining that he had missed, walked quickly to the barrier. Nikolai Vsevolodovich walked up, too, raised the pistol, but somehow very high, and fired almost without aiming.

Then he took out his handkerchief and wrapped it around the little finger of his right hand. Only now did they see that Artemy Pavlovich had not quite missed, but the bullet had only grazed the fleshy part of the finger without touching the bone; the scratch was insignificant. Kirillov at once announced that if the adversaries were not satisfied, the duel would continue.

"I declare," Gaganov croaked (his throat was dry), again turning to Mavriky Nikolaevich, "that this man" (he again jabbed in Stavrogin's direction) "fired into the air on purpose . . . deliberately . . . Another offense! He wants to make the duel impossible!"

"I have the right to fire any way I want, as long as it is according to the rules," Nikolai Vsevolodovich declared firmly.

"No, he hasn't! Explain to him, explain!" Gaganov cried.

"I subscribe completely to Nikolai Vsevolodovich's opinion," proclaimed Kirillov.

"Why does he spare me?" Gaganov raged, not listening. "I despise his sparing . . . I spit on it . . . I . . ."

"I give you my word that I had no wish at all to insult you," Nikolai Vsevolodovich said with impatience. "I fired high because I don't want to kill anyone anymore, neither you nor anyone else, it has nothing to do with you personally. It's true that I do not consider myself offended, and I'm sorry that it makes you angry. But I will not allow anyone to interfere with my rights."

"If he's so afraid of blood, then ask him why he challenged me!" Gaganov yelled, still addressing Mavriky Nikolaevich.

"How could he not challenge you?" Kirillov mixed in. "You wouldn't listen to anything, how else could he get rid of you!"

"I will note just one thing," said Mavriky Nikolaevich, who discussed the affair painfully and with effort. "If an adversary announces beforehand that he will fire high, then the duel really cannot continue . . . for reasons which are delicate and . . . clear . . ."

"I have by no means declared that I will fire high every time!" Stavrogin cried out, now losing all patience. "You have no idea what is in my mind or how I am going to fire now . . . I am not hindering the duel in any way."

"In that case the match may continue," Mavriky Nikolaevich said to Gaganov.

"Take your places, gentlemen!" Kirillov commanded.

Again they advanced towards each other, again Gaganov missed, and again Stavrogin fired high. There might have been a dispute about his firing high: Nikolai Vsevolodovich might have affirmed directly that he had fired properly, if he himself had not confessed to missing deliberately. He did not aim the pistol directly at the sky or a tree, but still as if at his adversary, though all the same a couple of feet above his hat. The second time he aimed even lower, even more plausibly; but now nothing could reassure Gaganov.

"Again!" he gnashed his teeth. "Never mind! I have been challenged, and I am exercising my right. I want to fire a third time . . . at all costs."

"You have every right," Kirillov cut off. Mavriky Nikolaevich said nothing. They were placed for the third time, the command was given; this time Gaganov walked right up to the barrier, and from there, from twelve paces, began taking aim. His hands were trembling too much for a good shot. Stavrogin stood with his pistol lowered and motionlessly waited for him to fire.

"Too long, you're aiming too long!" Kirillov shouted impatiently. "Fire! Fi-i-ire!"

But the shot rang out, and this time the white beaver hat flew off Nikolai Vsevolodovich's head. The shot had been quite well aimed, the crown of the hat was pierced very low down; half an inch lower and all would have been over. Kirillov picked it up and handed it to Nikolai Vsevolodovich.

"Fire, don't keep your adversary waiting!" Mavriky Nikolaevich cried in terrible agitation, seeing that Stavrogin seemed to have forgotten to fire as he examined the hat with Kirillov. Stavrogin gave a start, looked at Gaganov, turned away, and this time without any delicacy fired off into the woods. The duel was over. Gaganov stood as if crushed. Mavriky Nikolaevich went up to him and started to say something, but the man seemed not to understand. Kirillov, as he was leaving, doffed his hat and gave a nod to Mavriky Nikolaevich; but Stavrogin forgot his former politeness; after firing into the woods, he did not even turn towards the barrier, but thrust his pistol at Kirillov and hastily made for the horses. There was spite in his face; he was silent. Kirillov, too, was silent. They mounted their horses and set off at a gallop.

III

"WHY ARE YOU silent?" he called impatiently to Kirillov, not far from home.

"What do you want?" the latter answered, almost slipping off his horse, which reared up.

Stavrogin restrained himself.

"I didn't mean to offend that . . . fool, and here I've offended him again," he said softly.

"Yes, offended again," Kirillov cut off, "and, besides, he's not a fool."

"Still, I did all I could."

"No."

"What should I have done?"

"Not challenge him."

"Take another slap in the face?"

"Yes, take a slap."

"I'm beginning not to understand anything!" Stavrogin said spitefully. "Why does everyone expect something of me that they don't expect of others? Why should I take what no one else takes, and invite burdens that no one else can bear?"

"I thought you yourself were seeking a burden?"

"I'm seeking a burden?"

"Yes."

"You . . . saw that?"

"Yes."

"Is it so noticeable?"

"Yes."

There was a minute's silence. Stavrogin had a very preoccupied look, was almost struck.

"I didn't shoot at him because I didn't want to kill—there was nothing else, I assure you," he said, hastily and anxiously, as if justifying himself.

"You shouldn't have offended him."

"And what should I have done?"

"You should have killed him."

"You're sorry I didn't kill him?"

"I'm not sorry about anything. I thought you really wanted to kill him. You don't know what you're seeking."

"I'm seeking a burden," laughed Stavrogin.

"You didn't want blood, why would you let him kill?"

"If I hadn't challenged him, he'd have killed me anyway, without a duel."

"Not your business. Maybe he wouldn't have."

"And would just have beaten me up?"

"Not your business. Bear the burden. Otherwise there's no merit."

"I spit on your merit, I'm not seeking that from anyone!"

"I thought you were," Kirillov concluded with terrible equanimity. They rode into the courtyard.

"Want to come in?" Nikolai Vsevolodovich offered.

"No, home. Good-bye." He got off the horse and took his box under his arm.

"You at least are not angry with me?" Stavrogin gave him his hand.

"Not at all!" Kirillov turned back to shake hands with him. "If the burden is light for me because of my nature, then maybe the burden is heavier for you because of your nature. Nothing to be much ashamed of, only a little."

"I know I'm a worthless character, but I'm not trying to get in with the strong ones."

"Don't; you're not a strong man. Come for tea."

Nikolai Vsevolodovich entered the house greatly perturbed.

IV

HE LEARNED at once from Alexei Yegorovich that Varvara Petrovna, very pleased with Nikolai Vsevolodovich's going out—the first time after eight days of illness—for a ride on horseback, ordered a carriage to be readied and drove off alone, "after the pattern of former days, to take a breath of fresh air, for in these eight days she has forgotten what it means to breathe fresh air."

"Did she go alone or with Darya Pavlovna?" Nikolai Vsevolodovich interrupted the old man with a quick question, and frowned deeply on hearing that Darya Pavlovna "declined to accompany her, being unwell, and is now in her rooms."

"Listen, old man," he said, as if suddenly making up his mind, "keep an eye out for her all day today, and if you see her coming to me, stop her at once, and tell her that at least for a few days I'll be unable to receive her . . . that I myself ask it of her . . . and that I'll send for her when the time comes—do you hear?"

"I'll tell her, sir," Alexei Yegorovich said, with anguish in his voice, lowering his eyes.

"But not before you see clearly that she's coming to me herself."

"Do not worry, if you please, sir, there will be no mistakes. Up to now the visits have taken place through me; my assistance has always been called upon."

"I know. But, still, not before she comes herself. Bring me some tea, quickly, if you can."

As soon as the old man went out, at almost the same moment, the same door opened and Darya Pavlovna appeared on the threshold. Her eyes were calm, but her face was pale.

"Where did you come from?" Stavrogin exclaimed.

"I was standing right here, waiting for him to come out so that I could come in. I heard the order you gave him, and when he came out just now, I hid around the corner to the right, and he didn't notice me."

"I've long meant to break it off with you, Dasha . . . meanwhile . . . for the time being. I couldn't receive you last night, despite your note. I wanted to write back to you, but I'm no good at writing," he added with vexation, even as if with disgust.

"I myself thought we should break it off. Varvara Petrovna is too suspicious of our relations."

"Well, let her be."

"No, she shouldn't worry. And so, that's it now, until the end?"

"You're still so certainly expecting an end?"

"Yes, I'm sure of it."

"Nothing in the world ever ends."

"Here there will be an end. Call me then; I'll come. Now, good-bye."

"And what sort of end will it be?" Nikolai Vsevolodovich grinned.

"You're not wounded, and . . . haven't shed blood?" she asked, without answering his question about the end.

"It was stupid; I didn't kill anyone, don't worry. However, you'll hear all about it this very day from everyone. I'm a bit unwell."

"I'll leave. The marriage won't be announced today?" she added irresolutely.

"Not today; not tomorrow; about the day after tomorrow I don't know, maybe we'll all die, and so much the better. Leave me, leave me, finally."

"You won't ruin the other woman . . . the insane one?"

"I won't ruin the insane ones, neither the one nor the other, but it seems I will ruin the sane one: I'm so mean and vile, Dasha, that it seems I really will call you 'in the final end,' as you say, and you, despite your sanity, will come. Why are you ruining yourself?"

"I know that finally I alone will remain with you, and . . . I'm waiting for that."

"And what if I don't finally call you, but run away from you?"

"That cannot be. You will call."

"There's much contempt for me there."

"You know it's not just contempt."

"So there is still contempt?"

"I didn't put it right. God be my witness, I wish very much that you should never have need of me."

"One phrase is worth another. I also wish not to ruin you."

"Nothing you do can ever ruin me, and you know it better than anyone else," Darya Pavlovna said quickly and firmly. "If it's not you, I'll become a sister of mercy, or a sick-nurse, or a book-hawker and sell Gospels. I've decided it so. I can't be anyone's wife; I can't live in a house like this either; that's not what I want . . . You know all that."

"No, I never could discover what you wanted; it seems to me that you're interested in me in the same way as certain antiquated sick-nurses for some reason take an interest in some one patient as opposed to all the others, or, better still, the way certain pious old women who

hang about at funerals prefer certain nice little corpses that are come-
lier than the others. Why are you looking at me so strangely?"

"Are you very sick?" she asked sympathetically, looking at him in
some special way. "Oh, God! And this man wants to do without me!"

"Listen, Dasha! I keep seeing ghosts now. Yesterday, on the bridge,
one little demon offered to put a knife into Lebyadkin and Marya
Timofeevna for me, to do away with my lawful marriage and cover
the traces. He asked for three roubles down, but let me know plainly
that the whole operation would cost not less than fifteen hundred.
There's a calculating demon for you! A bookkeeper! Ha, ha!"

"But you're quite certain it was a ghost?"

"Oh, no, it wasn't a ghost at all! It was simply Fedka the Convict,
a robber who escaped from hard labor. But that's not the point: what
do you think I did? I gave him all the money I had in my wallet, and
now he's quite certain I've given him his down payment."

"You met him at night, and he made you such an offer? But don't
you see that you're all entangled in their net!"

"Well, never mind them. You know, you've got a question on the
tip of your tongue, I can see by your eyes," he added, with a spiteful
and irritated smile.

Dasha became frightened.

"There isn't any question, and there aren't any doubts whatever,
you'd better keep still!" she cried anxiously, as if waving his question
away.

"So you're sure I won't go shopping at Fedka's?"

"Oh, God!" she clasped her hands, "why do you torment me so?"

"Well, forgive me my stupid joke, I must be acquiring their bad
manners. You know, since last night I've wanted terribly to laugh, to
laugh all the time, constantly, long, loud. It's as if I'm charged with
laughter . . . Sh! Mother's come back; I can tell the clatter of her
carriage when it stops at the porch."

Dasha seized his hand.

"May God preserve you from your dark spirit, and . . . call me, call
me soon!"

"Oh, he's no dark spirit! He's simply a nasty, scrofulous little demon
with a runny nose, a failure. And you, Dasha, again there's something
you don't dare say?"

She looked at him with pain and reproach, and turned towards the door.

"Listen!" he shouted after her with a spiteful, twisted smile. "If . . . well, in short, *if* . . . you understand, well, even if I did go shopping, and called you after that—would you still come, after that shopping?"

She went out without turning or answering, covering her face with her hands.

"She'll come even after that shopping!" he whispered, having thought a moment, with a look of scornful disgust. "A sick-nurse! Hm! . . . However, that may be just what I need."

4

All in Expectation

I

THE IMPRESSION produced in our whole society by the story of the duel, which quickly became public, was especially remarkable for the unanimity with which everyone hastened to declare himself unconditionally for Nikolai Vsevolodovich. Many of his former enemies resolutely proclaimed themselves his friends. The main reason for such an unexpected turnabout in public opinion was a few words, spoken aloud with unusual aptness by a certain person who until then had not spoken, which all at once gave the event a significance that greatly interested our vast majority. This is how it happened: the very next day after the event, the whole town gathered to celebrate the name day of the wife of our provincial marshal of nobility. Yulia Mikhailovna was also present, or, rather, presided, having arrived with Lizaveta Nikolaevna, who shone with beauty and a special gaiety, which this time many of our ladies at once found especially suspicious. Incidentally, there could no longer be any doubts about her engagement to Mavriky Nikolaevich. That evening, to the jocular question of one retired but important general, of whom more will be said later, Lizaveta Nikolaevna herself answered directly that she was engaged. And what do you think? Decidedly none of our ladies wanted to believe in this engagement. They all stubbornly continued to suppose some romance, some fatal family secret that had taken place in Switzerland, and for some reason necessarily with Yulia Mikhailovna's participation. It is hard to say why all these rumors, or even, so to speak, dreams, held out so stubbornly, or precisely why it was so necessary to drag Yulia Mikhailovna into it. As soon as she entered, everyone turned to her with strange looks, overflowing with expectations. It must be noted that in view of the recentness of the event and certain accompanying circumstances, it was still being spoken of somewhat cautiously that evening, and not aloud. Besides, nothing was known yet about the orders of the authorities.[1] Neither duelist, as far as anyone knew, had been inconvenienced. Everyone knew, for example, that Artemy Pavlovich had gone to his Dukhovo estate early in the morning without any hindrance. Meanwhile, everyone was certainly longing for someone to be the first to speak out and thereby open the door for public impatience. They placed their hopes precisely in the above-mentioned general, and were not mistaken.

This general, one of the stateliest members of our club, a landowner of no very great wealth but of an incomparable turn of mind, an old-fashioned dangler after young ladies, was, among other things, extremely fond of speaking out in large gatherings, with a general's weightiness, precisely about things which everyone was still speaking of in cautious whispers. It was as if this constituted his specific role, so to speak, in our society. In doing so, he drew his words out especially, with a sugary enunciation, a habit he had probably borrowed from Russians traveling abroad, or from those formerly wealthy Russian landowners who had been most ruined by the peasant reform. Stepan Trofimovich even noted once that the more ruined a landowner was, the more sugarily he lisped and drew out his words. He himself, however, had the same sugary drawl and lisp, without noticing it in himself.

The general began speaking as a man of competence. Besides the fact that he was some sort of distant relation of Artemy Pavlovich's, though on bad terms and even at law with him, he had, moreover, fought two duels in the past, for one of which he had even been exiled to the ranks in the Caucasus. Someone mentioned Varvara Petrovna, that it was two days now since she had begun going out "after an illness," or not her, properly speaking, but the excellent match of her gray four-in-hand, from the Stavrogins' own stud. The general suddenly remarked that he had met "young Stavrogin" on horseback that day . . . Everyone fell silent at once. The general smacked his lips and suddenly declared, twiddling in his fingers a gold presentation snuffbox:

"I regret that I wasn't here a few years ago—I mean, that I was in Karlsbad . . . Hm. I'm very interested in this young man, of whom I then found so many rumors. Hm. And what, is it true that he's crazy? Someone said so at the time. Suddenly I'm told that some student here insulted him in the presence of his cousins, and that he hid from him under the table; then yesterday I heard from Stepan Vysotsky that Stavrogin fought with this . . . Gaganov. And solely with the gallant purpose of offering his forehead to an enraged man; just to get rid of him. Hm. That's the style of the Guard in the twenties. Does he call on anyone here?"

The general fell silent, as if waiting for an answer. The door for public impatience had been opened.

"What could be simpler?" Yulia Mikhailovna suddenly raised her voice, annoyed by the fact that everyone, as if on command, turned their eyes towards her. "How can there be anything surprising in Stavrogin fighting with Gaganov and not responding to a student? Could he challenge his own former serf to a duel?"

Portentous words! A clear and simple thought which, however, had so far not occurred to anyone. Words with extraordinary consequences. Everything scandalous and gossipy, everything petty and anecdotal, was immediately pushed into the background; a different meaning was set forth; a new person was brought forth, in whom everyone had been mistaken, a person of an almost ideal strictness of notions. Mortally offended by a student—that is, by an educated man and no longer a serf—he scorns the insult, because the offender is his former serf. Noise and gossip in society; frivolous society looks with scorn on the man who has been slapped in the face; he scorns the opinion of society, which has not yet attained to real notions and yet talks about them.

"And yet you and I, Ivan Alexandrovich, sit and talk about correct notions, sir," one little old clubman observes to another, with the noble vehemence of self-accusation.

"Yes, Pyotr Mikhailovich, yes, sir," the other yesses him delightedly, "talk about the young folk after that."

"The young folk aren't the point, Ivan Alexandrovich," a third turns up and observes. "This isn't a question of the young folk; this is a star, sir, not one of the young folk; that's how it should be understood."

"And that's just what we need; there's a dearth of such people."

The main thing here lay in the fact that the "new man," besides having shown himself an "unquestionable nobleman," was moreover the wealthiest landowner in the province, and therefore could not but come forth as a helper and an active figure. However, I have already referred in passing to the moods of our landowners.

They would even become vehement:

"Not only did he not challenge the student, he even put his hands behind his back—make special note of that, Your Excellency," one of them put forth.

"And he didn't haul him into the new courts," another added.

"Though the new courts would adjudge him fifteen roubles for a nobleman's *personal* offense, sir, heh, heh, heh!"

"No, I'll tell you, here's the secret of our new courts," the third would get frantic. "Suppose a man steals or cheats and gets caught and clearly exposed—so, run home quickly, while there's still time, and kill your mother. You'll be acquitted instantly, and the ladies will wave their cambric handkerchiefs from the gallery—it's unquestionably true!"[2]

"True, true!"

There was no doing without anecdotes. Nikolai Vsevolodovich's connections with Count K. were recalled. The stern, solitary opinions of Count K. concerning the recent reforms were well known. Well known, too, was his remarkable activity, which had ceased somewhat of late. And now suddenly it became unquestionable for everyone that Nikolai Vsevolodovich was engaged to one of Count K.'s daughters, though nothing gave any precise grounds for such a rumor. As far as certain wondrous Swiss adventures and Lizaveta Nikolaevna were concerned, even the ladies ceased mentioning them. We may mention, incidentally, that just at that time the Drozdovs succeeded in paying all the visits they had failed to pay so far. Everyone now found Lizaveta Nikolaevna unquestionably a most ordinary girl who was "making a show" of her bad nerves. They now explained her swoon on the day of Nikolai Vsevolodovich's arrival simply by her fright at the student's outrageous act. They even emphasized the prosaicness of the very thing they had previously been at such pains to endow with some fantastic coloring; and they finally forgot all about the poor lame girl; they were even ashamed to recall it. "Let there be a hundred lame girls—we were all young once!" They drew attention to Nikolai Vsevolodovich's deference to his mother, sought out various virtues in him, spoke benevolently of his learning, acquired during four years in German universities. Artemy Pavlovich's act was finally declared tactless—"their own knew not their own"—and Yulia Mikhailovna was finally acknowledged as a woman of supreme perceptivity.

Thus, when Nikolai Vsevolodovich himself appeared at last, everyone met him with the most naïve earnestness; one could read the most impatient expectations in all the eyes turned to him. Nikolai Vsevolodovich at once withdrew into the most strict silence, which certainly satisfied everyone far more than if he had talked a whole cartload. In a word, he succeeded in everything, he was in fashion. In provincial society, once a person makes his appearance, there is no way he can hide. Nikolai Vsevolodovich began, as before, to follow all the provincial rules to the point of finesse. He was not found cheerful: "The man has suffered, the man is not like everyone else, there are things on his mind." Even his pride and that squeamish unapproachability for which he had been so hated among us four years earlier, were now respected and liked.

Varvara Petrovna was most triumphant of all. I cannot say whether she grieved much over her collapsed dreams concerning Lizaveta Nikolaevna. Of course, family pride was a help here. One thing was strange: Varvara Petrovna suddenly believed in the highest degree that Nicolas had indeed "made his choice" at Count K.'s, but, strangest of all, she believed it from rumors that came to her, as to everyone else, on the wind. She was afraid to ask Nikolai Vsevolodovich directly. Some two or three times, however, she could not help herself and chided him gaily and slyly for not being more open with her; Nikolai Vsevolodovich smiled and went on being silent. The silence was taken as a sign of assent. And just think: for all that, she never forgot about the poor lame girl. The thought of her lay on her heart like a stone, like a nightmare, tormented her with strange phantoms and forebodings, and all that together and simultaneously with her dreams about

Count K.'s daughters. But more of that later. To be sure, in society Varvara Petrovna was once again treated with extreme and deferential respect, but she made little use of it and went out extremely rarely.

She did, however, pay a solemn visit to the governor's wife. To be sure, no one had been more charmed and captivated by the above-mentioned portentous words of Yulia Mikhailovna's at the evening for the wife of the marshal of nobility: they had lifted much anguish from her heart, and at once resolved much of what had so tormented her since that unfortunate Sunday. "I had not understood the woman!" she uttered, and directly, with her customary impetuousness, she announced to Yulia Mikhailovna that she had come to *thank* her. Yulia Mikhailovna was flattered, but bore herself independently. At that time she had already begun to feel her own worth, perhaps even a bit too much. She announced, for example, in the middle of the conversation, that she had never heard anything about the activity or learning of Stepan Trofimovich.

"I receive young Verkhovensky, of course, and indulge him. He's reckless, but then he's still young; of considerable education, however. In any case he's not some former retired critic."

Varvara Petrovna at once hastened to observe that Stepan Trofimovich had never been a critic, but, on the contrary, had lived all his life in her house. And he was famous for the circumstances of his early career, "known only too well to the whole world," and, lately, for his works on Spanish history; he also intended to write something about the present situation in German universities and, it seemed, something about the Dresden Madonna as well. In short, Varvara Petrovna did not want to surrender Stepan Trofimovich to Yulia Mikhailovna.

"The Dresden Madonna? You mean the Sistine Madonna?[3] *Chère* Varvara Petrovna, I sat for two hours in front of that painting and went away disappointed. I understood nothing, and was greatly surprised. Karmazinov also says it's hard to understand. No one now, Russian or English, finds anything in it. All this fame was just the old men shouting."

"So there's a new fashion?"

"And I think our young people shouldn't be neglected either. They shout that they're communists, but in my opinion they should be spared and appreciated. I read everything now—all the newspapers, communes, natural sciences—I subscribe to everything, because one should finally know where one lives and whom one is dealing with. One cannot live all one's life on the heights of one's fantasy. I have arrived at the conclusion and accepted it as a rule to indulge young people and thereby keep them on the brink. Believe me, Varvara Petrovna, only we of society, by our beneficial influence and, namely, by indulgence, can keep them from the abyss they are being pushed into by the intolerance of all these old codgers. However, I'm glad to have learned from you about Stepan Trofimovich. You've given me an idea: he could be useful at our literary reading. You know, I am organizing a whole day of entertainment by subscription for the benefit of the poor governesses of our province. They're scattered all over Russia; there are about six from our district alone; then there are two telegraph girls, two are studying at the academy, the rest would like to but have no means. The lot of the Russian woman is terrible, Varvara Petrovna! They're now making it a university question, and there has even been a meeting of the state council.[4] In our strange Russia one can do whatever one likes. And therefore, again, just by indulgence and by the direct, warm participation of all society, we could guide this great common cause onto the right path. Oh, God, do we really have so many shining lights! There are a few, of course, but they're scattered. Let us join together and be stronger. In short, I'll have a literary morning first, then a light luncheon, then an intermission, and a ball that same evening. We wanted to start the evening with tableaux vivants, but it seems the expenses would be too great, so for the public there will be one or two quadrilles in masks and character costumes representing famous literary trends. This playful idea was suggested by Karmazinov; he is a great help to me. You know, he's going to read his last thing here, as yet unknown to anyone. He's laying down his pen and will not write anymore; this last article is his farewell to the public. A lovely little thing called *Merci*. The title is French, but he finds it more playful and even more subtle. So do I—it was even I who suggested it. I think Stepan Trofimovich could also read, if it's short and . . . not really too learned. It seems Pyotr Stepanovich and someone else will read something or other. Pyotr Stepanovich will run by and tell you the program; or, better still, allow me to bring it to you."

"And you also allow me to put my name on your subscription list. I will tell Stepan Trofimovich and ask him myself."

Varvara Petrovna returned home utterly enchanted; she stood like a rock for Yulia Mikhailovna, and for some reason was now thoroughly angry with Stepan Trofimovich; and he, poor man, sat at home and did not even know anything.

"I'm in love with her, I don't understand how I could have been so mistaken about this woman," she said to Nikolai Vsevolodovich and to Pyotr Stepanovich, who ran by that evening.

"But you still ought to make peace with the old man," Pyotr Stepanovich proposed, "he's in despair. You've exiled him to the kitchen altogether. Yesterday he met your carriage, bowed, and you turned away. You know, we'll bring him forward; I have some designs on him, and he can still be useful."

"Oh, he's going to read."

"That's not all I meant. And I also wanted to run by and see him today myself. So shall I tell him?"

"If you wish. I don't know how you'll arrange it, though," she said irresolutely. "I intended to talk with him myself and wanted to fix a day and place." She frowned deeply.

"Well, no point in fixing a day. I'll simply tell him."

"Please do. Add, however, that I'll be sure to fix a day. Be sure to add that."

Pyotr Stepanovich ran off, grinning. Generally, as far as I recall, he was somehow especially angry at that time and even allowed himself extremely impatient escapades with almost everyone. Strangely, everyone somehow forgave him. Generally, the opinion became established that he should be looked upon somehow specially. I will observe that he was extremely angry about Nikolai Vsevolodovich's duel. It caught him off guard; he even turned green when he was told. Perhaps his vanity suffered here: he learned of it only the next day, when everybody knew.

"But you really had no right to fight," he whispered to Stavrogin five days later, meeting him by chance in the club. Remarkably, they had not met anywhere during those five days, though Pyotr Stepanovich ran by Varvara Petrovna's almost every day.

Nikolai Vsevolodovich looked at him silently, with a distracted air, as if not understanding what it was about, and went on without stopping. He was going through the big hall of the club towards the buffet.

"You've also been to see Shatov . . . you want to publish Marya Timofeevna," he went running after him and somehow distractedly seized his shoulder.

Nikolai Vsevolodovich suddenly shook his hand off and quickly turned to him with a menacing frown. Pyotr Stepanovich looked at him, smiling a strange, long smile. It all lasted only a moment. Nikolai Vsevolodovich walked on.

II

H E RAN OVER to the old man straight from Varvara Petrovna's, and if he hurried so, it was from sheer spite, to take revenge for a previous offense of which I had no idea until then. The thing was that at their last meeting—namely, a week ago Thursday—Stepan Trofimovich, who, incidentally, had started the argument himself, ended by driving Pyotr Stepanovich out with a stick. He concealed this fact from me then; but now, as soon as Pyotr Stepanovich ran in with his usual smirk, so naïvely supercilious, and with his unpleasantly curious eyes darting into every corner, Stepan Trofimovich at once gave me a secret sign not to leave the room. Thus their real relations were disclosed to me, for this time I listened to the whole conversation.

Stepan Trofimovich was sitting stretched out on the sofa. He had grown thin and yellow since that Thursday. Pyotr Stepanovich sat down next to him with a most familiar air, tucking his legs under him unceremoniously, and taking up much more space on the sofa than respect for a father demanded. Stepan Trofimovich silently and dignifiedly moved aside.

On the table lay an open book. It was the novel *What Is to Be Done?*[5] Alas, I must admit one strange weakness in our friend: the fancy that he ought to emerge from his solitude and fight a last battle was gaining more and more of a hold on his seduced imagination. I guessed that he had obtained and was *studying* the novel with a single purpose, so that in the event of an unquestionable confrontation with the "screamers," he would know their methods and arguments beforehand from their own "catechism," and, being thus prepared, would solemnly refute them all in *her eyes*. Oh, how this book tormented him! At times he would throw it aside in despair and, jumping up from his seat, pace the room almost in a frenzy.

"I agree that the author's basic idea is correct," he said to me feverishly, "but so much the more horrible for that! It's our same idea, precisely ours; we, we were the first to plant it, to nurture it, to prepare it—and what new could they say on their own after us! But, God, how it's all perverted, distorted, mutilated!" he exclaimed, thumping the book with his fingers. "Are these the conclusions we strove for? Who can recognize the initial thought here?"

"Getting yourself enlightened?" Pyotr Stepanovich grinned, taking the book from the table and reading the title. "It's about time. I'll bring you something better if you like."

Stepan Trofimovich again dignifiedly kept silent. I was sitting in the corner on a sofa.

Pyotr Stepanovich quickly explained the reason for his coming. Of course, Stepan Trofimovich was struck beyond measure, and listened in fear, mixed with extreme indignation.

"And this Yulia Mikhailovna is counting on me to come and read for her!"

"I mean, it's not that they need you so much. On the contrary, it's to indulge you and thereby suck up to Varvara Petrovna. But, needless to say, you won't dare refuse to read. And you yourself would even like to, I suppose," he grinned. "You old fogies are all infernally ambitious. Listen, though, it mustn't be too dull. What have you got there, Spanish history or something? Give it to me to look over a few days ahead, otherwise you may put them all to sleep."

The hasty and all too naked rudeness of these barbs was plainly deliberate. He made as if it were impossible to speak with Stepan Trofimovich in any other, more refined language or concepts. Stepan Trofimovich staunchly continued to ignore the insults. But the events he was being informed of produced a more and more staggering impression on him.

"And she herself, *herself*, said this should be told to me by . . . *you*, sir?" he asked, turning pale.

"I mean, you see, she wants to arrange a day and place for a mutual talk with you, the leftovers of your sentimentalizing. You've been flirting with her for twenty years and have got her used to the funniest ways. But don't worry, it's all different now; she herself keeps saying that she's only now beginning 'to have her eyes re-opened.' I explained to her straight out that this whole friendship of yours is just a mutual outpouring of slops. She's told me a lot, friend; pah, what a lackey position you've been in all this time. Even I blushed for you."

"I, in a lackey position?" Stepan Trofimovich could not restrain himself.

"Worse, you've been a sponger, meaning a voluntary lackey. Too lazy to work, but with an appetite for a spot of cash. All this she now understands; anyway, what she tells about you is simply terrible. No, friend, I really had a good laugh over your letters to her; shameful and disgusting. But you're all so depraved, so depraved! There's something eternally depraving in alms—you're a clear example of it!"

"She showed you my letters!"

"All of them. I mean, of course, there was no way I could read them. Pah, how much paper you wasted, there must be more than two thousand letters there . . . And you know, old man, I think there was a moment between you two when she was ready to marry you. It was most stupid of you to let it slip! I'm speaking from your viewpoint, of course, but still it would have been better than now when you almost married 'someone else's sins,' like a clown, a laughingstock, for money."

"For money! She, she says it was for money!" Stepan Trofimovich cried out in pain.

"And what else? Come now, I'm the one who had to defend you. That's the only way you could justify yourself. She understood that you needed money like everyone else, and that from that point perhaps you were right. I proved to her like two times two that you'd been living for your mutual profit: she as a capitalist, and you as her sentimental clown. By the way, she's not angry about the money, though you've been milking her like a nanny goat. She's just mad because she believed you for twenty years, because you hoodwinked her so much with nobility and made her lie for so long. That she herself was lying she will never admit, but you're going to catch it twice over for that. I don't understand how you never figured out that you'd have to settle accounts one day. You did have some sense after all, didn't you? I advised her yesterday to send you to an almshouse—a decent one, don't worry, nothing to complain of; it seems that's just what she'll do. Remember your last letter to me in Kh—— province, three weeks ago?"

"You mean you showed it to her?" Stepan Trofimovich jumped up, horrified.

"But, what else? First thing. The one in which you informed me that she exploited you because she was jealous of your talent—well, and also about 'someone else's sins.' Really, though, friend, how vain you are, incidentally! I laughed my head off. Generally, your letters are quite dull; your style is terrible. I often didn't read them at all, and there's one lying around unopened even now; I'll send it to you tomorrow. But this, this last letter of yours—it's the peak of perfection! How I laughed, how I laughed!"

"Monster! Monster!" Stepan Trofimovich cried out.

"Pah, the devil, one can't even talk with you. What, are you offended again, like last Thursday?"

Stepan Trofimovich drew himself up menacingly.

"How dare you speak to me in such language?"

"What language? Simple and clear?"

"But tell me finally, monster, are you my son or not?"

"You should know better than I. Of course, fathers always tend to be blind in such cases . . ."

"Silence! Silence!" Stepan Trofimovich was shaking all over.

"See, you shout at me and abuse me, as you did last Thursday, you were going to wave your stick at me, but I did find that document then. I spent the whole evening rummaging in my suitcase out of curiosity. True, there's nothing certain, you can be comforted. It's just my mother's note to that little Polack. But judging by her character . . ."

"One word more and I'll slap your face."

"Look at these people!" Pyotr Stepanovich suddenly turned to me. "See, we've been at it since last Thursday. I'm glad at least that you're here today and can settle it. First the fact: he reproaches me for speaking this way about my mother, but wasn't it he who suggested this very thing into my head? In Petersburg, when I was still at school, didn't he wake me up twice in the night, embracing me and weeping like a woman, and what do you think he told me those nights? These same non-lenten anecdotes about my mother! He was the first I heard them from."

"Oh, that was in the loftiest sense! Oh, you didn't understand me! Nothing, you understood nothing."

"But, still, it comes out meaner your way than mine, meaner, admit it. You see, it's all the same to me, if you like. I mean, from your point. From my viewpoint, don't worry: I don't blame mother; if it's you, it's you, if it's the Polack, it's the Polack, it makes no difference to me. It's not my fault if it came out so stupidly with you in Berlin. As if anything smarter could have come out with you. So, aren't you funny people after that! And does it make any difference to you whether I'm your son or not? Listen," he turned to me again, "he didn't spend a rouble on me all his life, he didn't know me at all till I was sixteen, then he robbed me here, and now he shouts that his heart has ached for me all his life, and poses in front of me like an actor. Really, I'm not Varvara Petrovna, for pity's sake!"

He got up and took his hat.

"I curse you henceforth in my name!" Stepan Trofimovich, pale as death, stretched his hand out over him.

"My, my, what foolishness a man can drive himself into!" Pyotr Stepanovich was even surprised. "Well, good-bye, old man, I'll never come to you again. Send your article ahead of time, don't forget, and try to do it without any humbug, if you can: facts, facts, facts, and, above all, make it short. Good-bye."

III

HOWEVER, there was also the influence of unrelated causes here. Pyotr Stepanovich indeed had certain designs on his parent. In my opinion, he meant to bring the old man to despair and thus push him into some outright scandal of a certain sort. He needed this for some further, unrelated purposes, of which we shall speak later. At that time he accumulated a great multitude of such diverse designs and calculations—almost all of them fantastic, of course. Besides Stepan

Trofimovich, he had in mind yet another martyr. Generally, he had not a few martyrs, as it turned out afterwards; but he was especially counting on this one, and it was Mr. von Lembke himself.

Andrei Antonovich von Lembke belonged to that favored (by nature) tribe which in Russia, according to the records, numbers several hundred thousand, and which is itself perhaps unaware that within her, by its sheer mass, it constitutes a strictly organized union. Not an intentional or invented union, to be sure, but one existing of itself for the entire tribe, without words or agreements, as something morally obligatory, and consisting in the mutual support of all members of this tribe by each other, always, everywhere, and in whatever circumstances. Andrei Antonovich had the honor of being educated in one of those higher Russian institutions filled with young men from families well endowed with connections or wealth. The students of this institution were intended, almost immediately upon finishing their studies, to occupy rather significant positions in one of the departments of the government service. Andrei Antonovich had one uncle who was a lieutenant colonel in the engineers, and another who was a baker; yet he wormed his way into this higher school and met there quite a few similar tribesmen. He was a merry companion; quite dull as a student, but everyone liked him. And when, in the upper grades, many of the young men, predominantly Russians, learned to talk about rather lofty contemporary questions, and with an air as if they had only to wait till graduation and then they would resolve them all—Andrei Antonovich continued to occupy himself with the most innocent schoolboy pranks. He made everyone laugh, true, though only with quite unsophisticated escapades, cynical at most, but he set that as his goal. One time he would blow his nose somehow remarkably when the teacher addressed a question to him during a lecture—making both his comrades and the teacher laugh; another time he would present some cynical tableau vivant in the dormitory, to general applause; or he would play, solely on his nose (and quite skillfully), the overture to *Fra Diavolo*. [6] He was also distinguished by his deliberate slovenliness, which for some reason he found witty. In his very last year he took to scribbling little Russian verses. His own tribal language he knew quite ungrammatically, like many of his tribe in Russia. This propensity for verse brought him together with a schoolmate, gloomy and as if downtrodden by something, the son of some poor general, one of the Russians, who was regarded at the institute as a great future writer. The latter treated him patronizingly. But it so happened that three years after graduation, this gloomy comrade, who had abandoned his career for the sake of Russian literature and, as a consequence, was already parading around in torn boots, his teeth chattering from the cold, wearing a summer coat in the depths of autumn, unexpectedly met by chance, near the Anichkov Bridge, his former protégé "Lembka," as everyone, by the way, had called him at school. And what do you think? He did not even recognize him at first sight and stopped in surprise. Before him stood an impeccably dressed young man, with wonderfully tended side-whiskers of a reddish hue, wearing a pince-nez, patent-leather boots, the freshest gloves, in a full-cut over-coat from Charmeur's, and with a briefcase under his arm. Lembke treated his comrade benignly, gave him his address, and invited him to call on him some evening. It also turned out that he was no longer "Lembka," but von Lembke. The comrade did call on him, however, if only out of spite. At the stairway, rather unattractive, and certainly not the main one, though laid with red baize, he was met and questioned by a doorkeeper. A bell rang out upstairs. But instead of the riches the visitor expected to meet, he found his "Lembka" in a side room, a very small one, dark and decrepit-looking, divided in two by a large dark green curtain, furnished with very decrepit, though soft, dark green furniture, and with dark green shades on its narrow and high windows. Von Lembke lodged with some very distant relative, a general, whose protégé he was. He met his guest amiably, was serious and gracefully polite. They also talked of literature, but within decent limits. A servant in a white tie brought some weakish tea with small, round, dry biscuits. The comrade, out of spite, asked for seltzer water. It was served, but with some delay, and Lembke seemed embarrassed at calling the servant an extra time and giving him an order. However, he himself asked whether the visitor wanted a bite to eat, and was obviously pleased when the latter declined and finally left. The simple fact was that Lembke was starting his career and was sponging on the general, a fellow tribesman, but an important one.

At that time he was sighing after the general's fifth daughter, and this seemed to be reciprocated. Nevertheless, when the time came,

Amalia was given in marriage to an old German factory owner, an old comrade of the old general's. Andrei Antonovich did not weep much, but glued together a theater made of paper. The curtains rose, the actors came out, made gestures with their hands; the audience sat in their boxes, the orchestra mechanically moved their bows across their fiddles, the conductor waved his baton, and in the stalls gentlemen and officers clapped their hands. It was all made of paper, all designed and assembled by von Lembke himself; he sat over this theater for half a year. The general purposely organized an intimate little evening, the theater was brought out for display, all five of the general's daughters, the newly wedded Amalia included, her factory owner, and many young girls and women with their Germans, attentively examined and praised the theater; then there was dancing. Lembke was very pleased and soon consoled.

Years passed and his career got established. He always served in prominent places, and always under his tribesmen's command, and in the end he served his way up to quite a significant rank, compared with his age. He had long wanted to marry, and had long been cautiously on the lookout. In secret from the authorities, he sent a novella to a magazine, but it was not published. To make up for that he glued together an entire railway station with a train, and again it came out as a most successful little thing: people left the station with suitcases and bags, children and dogs, and got into the cars. Conductors and porters walked about, the bell rang, the signal was given, and the train started on its way. He sat for a whole year over this clever piece. But all the same he had to get married. The circle of his acquaintances was quite wide, primarily in the German world; but he also moved in Russian spheres, through his superiors, of course. Finally, when he had already turned thirty-eight, he also received an inheritance. His uncle, the baker, died and left him a bequest of thirteen thousand. Now it was just a matter of the right position. Mr. von Lembke, despite the rather high cut of the sphere in which he served, was a very modest man. He would have been quite satisfied with some independent little government post, with being in charge of the delivery of government firewood, or some such plum, and that for the rest of his life. But here, instead of some anticipated Mina or Ernestina, all at once Yulia Mikhailovna turned up. His career immediately rose another degree in prominence. The modest and precise von Lembke felt that he, too, was capable of ambition.

Yulia Mikhailovna owned two hundred souls, by the old way of reckoning, and, besides that, brought big connections with her. Von Lembke, on the other hand, was handsome, and she was already past forty. Remarkably, he did really fall in love with her little by little, as he felt himself more and more a fiancé. On the morning of their wedding day he sent her some verses. She liked it all very much, even the verses: forty is no joke. Soon he was awarded a certain rank and a certain decoration, and then he was appointed to our province.

In preparation for coming to our town, Yulia Mikhailovna worked assiduously on her husband. In her opinion, he was not without abilities, knew how to make an entrance and show himself, knew how to listen with a grave air and say nothing, had picked up a few quite decent poses, could even make a speech, even had some odds and ends of ideas, and had picked up the gloss of the latest indispensable liberalism. But all the same it troubled her that he was somehow none too receptive, and, after his long, eternal search for a career, was decidedly beginning to feel a need for peace. She wanted to pour her ambition into him, and he all of a sudden began gluing together a German church: the pastor came out to preach the sermon, the faithful listened, their hands piously clasped before them, one lady wiping away tears with her handkerchief, one little old man blowing his nose; towards the end a little organ rang out—it had been specially ordered and had already arrived from Switzerland, expense notwithstanding. Yulia Mikhailovna, even with some sort of fright, took the whole work from him as soon as she found out about it, and locked it away in her drawer; she allowed him to write a novel instead, but on the quiet. Since then she began to rely directly on herself alone. The trouble was that there was a fair amount of frivolity in all this, and little measure. Fate had kept her too long among the old maids. Idea after idea now flashed in her ambitious and somewhat fretted mind. She nursed designs, she decidedly wanted to rule the province, dreamed of being surrounded at once, chose her tendency. Von Lembke even got somewhat frightened, though he quickly figured out, with his official's tact, that there was no reason at all for him to be afraid of governorship as such. The first two or three months even passed quite satisfactorily. But then

Pyotr Stepanovich turned up, and something strange began to happen.

The thing was that from the very first step the young Verkhovensky showed a decided disrespect for Andrei Antonovich, and assumed some strange rights over him, and Yulia Mikhailovna, always so jealous of her husband's significance, simply refused to notice it; at least she attached no importance to it. The young man became her favorite, ate, drank, and all but slept in the house. Von Lembke set about defending himself, called him "young man" in public, patted him patronizingly on the shoulder, but made no impression: Pyotr Stepanovich went on laughing in his face, as it were, even while apparently talking seriously, and said the most unexpected things to him in public. Once, on returning home, he found the young man in his study, asleep on the sofa, uninvited. The latter explained that he had stopped by and, finding no one home, had "caught himself a good nap." Von Lembke was offended and again complained to his wife; laughing at his irritability, she remarked caustically that it was he who seemed unable to put himself on a real footing; at least with her "this boy" never allowed himself any familiarity, and, in all events, he was "naïve and fresh, though outside the bounds of society." Von Lembke pouted. On that occasion she got them to make peace. Pyotr Stepanovich did not really apologize, but got off with some coarse joke which in other circumstances could have been taken as a new insult, but in the present case was taken as repentance. The weak point lay in Andrei Antonovich's having made a blunder at the very beginning—namely, by imparting his novel to him. Fancying him to be a fervent young man of poetry, and having long dreamed of a listener, one evening, still in the first days of their acquaintance, he read two chapters to him. He listened with unconcealed boredom, yawned impolitely, uttered not a word of praise, but on leaving asked Andrei Antonovich for the manuscript so as to form an opinion at home at his leisure, and Andrei Antonovich gave it to him. Since then, though he ran by every day, he had not returned the manuscript, and laughed in answer to inquiries; finally he announced that he had lost it then and there in the street. When she learned of it, Yulia Mikhailovna became terribly angry with her husband.

"And did you tell him about your little church, too?" she fluttered, almost frightened.

Von Lembke decidedly took to pondering, and pondering was bad for him and was forbidden by his doctors. Aside from the fact that there turned out to be much trouble with the province, of which we shall speak later, there was another matter here, and he even suffered in his heart, not merely in his official pride. On entering into marriage, Andrei Antonovich had by no means envisioned the possibility of future family strife and discord. This was not what he had always imagined in his dreams of Mina and Ernestina. He felt himself unable to endure family storms. Yulia Mikhailovna finally had a frank talk with him.

"You can't be angry at this," she said, "if only because you are three times more sensible and immeasurably higher on the social ladder. There are many leftovers of former freethinking ways in the boy—just mischief, in my opinion—but one must be gradual, not sudden. We should cherish our young people; my way is to indulge them and keep them on the brink."

"But he says the devil knows what," objected von Lembke. "I can't be tolerant when he asserts publicly and in my presence that the government purposely gets the people drunk on vodka so as to brutalize them and keep them from rebelling. Imagine my role when I'm forced to listen to that in front of everyone."

As he said this, von Lembke recalled a conversation he had had recently with Pyotr Stepanovich. With the innocent aim of disarming him with his liberalism, he had shown him his own private collection of all sorts of tracts, from Russia and abroad, which he had been carefully collecting since the year 'fifty-nine, not really as an amateur, but merely out of healthy curiosity. Pyotr Stepanovich, having guessed his aim, stated rudely that there was more sense in one line of some tracts than in certain whole chanceries, "perhaps not excluding your own."

Lembke cringed.

"But with us it's too early, much too early," he said almost pleadingly, pointing to the tracts.

"No, it's not too early; see, you're afraid, so it's not too early."

"But, all the same, here, for example, is an invitation to destroy churches."

"And why not? You're an intelligent man and, of course, not a believer yourself, but you understand only too well that you need belief in order to brutalize the people. Truth is more honest than lying."

"I agree, I agree, I fully agree with you, but for us it's too early, too early . . ." von Lembke kept wincing.

"And what sort of government official are you after that, if you yourself agree to destroy churches and march with cudgels to Petersburg, and the only difference is when to do it?"

So rudely caught up, Lembke was sorely piqued.

"It's not that, not that," he was getting carried away, his amour-propre more and more chafed. "Being a young man and, above all, unfamiliar with our goals, you are mistaken. You see, my dearest Pyotr Stepanovich, you call us officials of the government? Right. Independent officials? Right. But, may I ask, how do we act? The responsibility is on us, and as a result we serve the common cause the same as you do. We merely hold together that which you are shaking apart, and which without us would go sprawling in all directions. We're not your enemies, by no means. We say to you: go forward, progress, even shake—all that's old, that is, and has to be remade—but when need be, we will keep you within necessary limits, and save you from yourselves, for without us you will only set Russia tottering, depriving her of a decent appearance, while our task consists precisely in maintaining her decent appearance. Realize that you and we are mutually necessary to each other. In England, the Whigs and Tories are also mutually necessary to each other. So, then, we are the Tories and you are the Whigs, that's precisely how I see it."

Andrei Antonovich even waxed enthusiastic. Ever since Petersburg, he had enjoyed talking intelligently and liberally, and here, furthermore, no one was eavesdropping. Pyotr Stepanovich was silent and bore himself somehow with unusual gravity. This egged the orator on even more.

"Do you know that I, the 'master of the province,' " he went on, pacing the study, "do you know that I, owing to the multitude of my duties, am unable to fulfill even one of them, and, on the other hand, it would be just as correct to say that there is nothing for me to do here. The whole secret is that here everything depends on the views of the government. Suppose the government even establishes a republic, say, out of politics, or to restrain passions, and on the other hand, parallel with that, suppose it strengthens the power of the governors—then we governors will swallow up the republic; not just the republic, we'll swallow up whatever you like, I at least feel I am ready . . . In short, if the government sends me a telegram declaring *activité dévorante,* * then I'll give them *activité dévorante.* I said here, right in their faces: 'My dear sirs, for the balancing and flourishing of all provincial institutions, one thing is necessary—an increase of the governor's power.' You see, all these institutions, whether local or legislative, ought, so to speak, to live a double life—that is, they ought to exist (I agree that this is necessary), well, and on the other hand, they ought at the same time not to exist. All depending on the government's view. If the notion should arise that these institutions suddenly seem necessary, I immediately have them available. If the necessity passes, no one will find them anywhere in my province. That is how I understand *activité dévorante,* and it cannot exist without an increase of the governor's power. We are talking privately. You know, I've already applied to Petersburg about the necessity for a special sentry at the door of the governor's house. I'm awaiting an answer."

"You need two," said Pyotr Stepanovich.

"Why two?" von Lembke stopped in front of him.

"I don't think one will be enough to earn you respect. You surely need two."

Andrei Antonovich made a wry face.

"You . . . you allow yourself God knows what, Pyotr Stepanovich. You take advantage of my kindness to make caustic remarks and play some sort of *bourru bienfaisant* † . . ."

"Well, that's as you like," Pyotr Stepanovich muttered, "but all the same you're paving the way for us and preparing our success."

"That is, which 'us' and what success?" von Lembke stared at him in surprise, but received no answer.

Yulia Mikhailovna, after hearing a report of the conversation, was very displeased.

"But, really," von Lembke defended himself, "I cannot behave

---

*"insatiable activity"
†"benevolent curmudgeon"

as a superior towards your favorite, especially when we're in private . . . I might have let something slip . . . from the goodness of my heart."

"From all too much goodness. I didn't know you had a collection of tracts, kindly show it to me."

"But . . . but he asked to take it for a day."

"And once again you gave it!" Yulia Mikhailovna became angry. "What tactlessness!"

"I'll send someone now to take it back from him."

"He won't give it back."

"I'll insist!" von Lembke boiled over, and even jumped up from his place. "Who is he to be so feared, and who am I not to dare to do anything?"

"Sit down and calm yourself," Yulia Mikhailovna interrupted. "I will answer your first question: he came to me with excellent recommendations, he has abilities, and occasionally says extremely intelligent things. Karmazinov assured me that he has connections almost everywhere and is extremely influential with the youth of the capital. And if through him I can attract them and gather them all around me, I can divert them from ruin by showing a new path for their ambition. He is devoted to me with his whole heart and heeds me in everything."

"But while we're indulging them, they can do . . . devil knows what. Of course, it's an idea . . ." von Lembke vaguely defended himself, "but . . . but now I hear that some tracts have appeared in the ———— district."

"But we heard that rumor already in the summer—tracts, false banknotes, and whatnot—yet nothing has been brought in. Who told you?"

"I heard it from von Blum."

"Ah, spare me your Blum, and do not dare to mention him again!" Yulia Mikhailovna boiled over and for about a minute was even unable to speak. Von Blum was an official from the governor's office whom she especially hated. Of that later.

"Please don't worry about Verkhovensky," she concluded the conversation. "If he had participated in any mischief, he wouldn't talk the way he does with you and with everyone here. Phrase-mongers are not dangerous, and I would even say that if something were to happen, I would be the first to learn of it through him. He is fanatically, fanatically devoted to me."

I will note, anticipating events, that had it not been for Yulia Mikhailovna's self-importance and ambition, perhaps none of the things these bad little people managed to do here would have taken place. Much of it is her responsibility!

5

Before the Fête

I

THE DAY of the fête conceived by Yulia Mikhailovna as a subscription benefit for the governesses of our province had already been fixed and canceled several times. Constantly fluttering around her were Pyotr Stepanovich; the little clerk Lyamshin, serving as errand boy, who once upon a time used to visit Stepan Trofimovich but suddenly came into favor in the governor's house for his piano playing; Liputin, partly, whom Yulia Mikhailovna planned to make the editor of a future independent provincial newspaper; a few ladies and young girls; and finally even Karmazinov, who, though he did not flutter, nevertheless announced aloud and with a satisfied air that he was going to give everyone a pleasant surprise when the quadrille of literature began. A great many subscribers and donors turned up, all select town society; though the most non-select were also admitted, as long as they came with money. Yulia Mikhailovna observed that sometimes the mixing of ranks even ought to be allowed, "otherwise who will enlighten them?" An unofficial home committee was formed at which it was decided that the fête should be a democratic one. The extravagant subscription list tempted them to spend; they wanted to do something wonderful—which was why it kept being postponed. They still could not decide where to organize the evening ball: at the huge house of the marshal of nobility's wife, which she had offered for the day, or at Varvara Petrovna's in Skvoreshniki. Skvoreshniki would be a bit far, but many of the committee insisted that it would be "freer" there. Varvara Petrovna herself was only too anxious to have it take place there. It is hard to understand why this proud woman almost fawned on Yulia Mikhailovna. She probably liked it that the woman, in her turn, almost demeaned herself before Nikolai Vsevolodovich and paid court to him as to no one else. I will repeat once more: Pyotr Stepanovich, all the time and unceasingly, in whispers, continued to cultivate in the governor's house an idea he had set going even earlier, that Nikolai Vsevolodovich was a man who had the most mysterious connections in a most mysterious world, and that he must have come on some assignment.

Strange was the state of people's minds at that time. A certain frivolity emerged especially in the ladies' society, and one could not say little by little. Several extremely casual notions spread as if on the wind. Something light and happy-go-lucky came about, which I will not say was always pleasant. A certain disorderliness of mind became fashionable. Afterwards, when it was all over, the blame fell on Yulia Mikhailovna, her circle and influence; but it hardly all originated with Yulia Mikhailovna alone. On the contrary, a great many vied with one another in praising the new governor's wife for knowing how to bring society together, and for making things suddenly more cheerful. Several scandalous incidents even took place which were not Yulia Mikhailovna's fault at all; but at the time everyone merely laughed loudly and disported themselves, and there was no one to stop them. True, a considerable group of persons stood firmly aside, having their own special view of the course of events then; but even they did not grumble at the time; they even smiled.

I remember that at that time a rather wide circle had formed, somehow of itself, whose center may indeed have been in Yulia Mikhailovna's drawing room. In this intimate circle that crowded around her—among the young people, of course—all sorts of mischief was allowed and even accepted as a rule, some of it really quite free and easy. The circle included several even very charming ladies. The young people arranged picnics, parties, sometimes rode all around town, in a whole cavalcade, in carriages and on horseback. They sought adventures, even purposely invented some, concocting them themselves, solely for the sake of a merry joke. They treated our town as some sort of Foolsbury.[1] They were called sneerers and jeerers, because there was little they scorned to do. It so happened, for example, that one local lieutenant's wife, still a very young little brunette, though wasted from her husband's ill-keeping, thoughtlessly sat down at a party to play a high-staked hand of whist, hoping to win enough to buy a mantilla, but instead of winning, she lost fifteen roubles. Fearing her husband, and having no money to pay, she decided, recalling her former boldness, to borrow some money on the quiet, right there at the party, from our mayor's son, a very nasty boy, dissipated beyond his years. He not only refused her but also went guffawing to tell her husband. The lieutenant, who indeed lived poorly on nothing but his salary, took his wife home and gave her what for to his heart's content, though she screamed, yelled, and begged forgiveness on her knees. This outrageous story evoked only laughter everywhere in town, and though the poor woman did not belong to the society that surrounded Yulia Mikhailovna, one of the ladies of the "cavalcade," a perky and eccentric character who somehow knew the lieutenant's wife, stopped by her place and quite simply carried her off to her own house. There she was seized upon at once by our pranksters, who petted her, showered her with presents, and kept her for some four days without returning her to her husband. She lived in the perky lady's house, spending whole days driving around town with her and the rest of that frolicsome society, taking part in their merrymaking and dances. Everyone egged her on to haul her husband into court, to start a scandal. She was given assurances that they would all support her and appear as witnesses. The husband was silent, not daring to fight. The poor woman finally grasped that she was up to her ears in trouble, and on the fourth day, at nightfall, half dead with fear, she fled from her protectors to her lieutenant. It is not known precisely what took place between the spouses, but the two shutters of the low wooden house in which the lieutenant rented his lodgings did not open for two weeks. Yulia Mikhailovna was a bit angry with the pranksters when she learned about it all, and was quite displeased with the perky lady's behavior, though the lady had introduced the lieutenant's wife to her on the first day of the abduction. However, it was soon forgotten.

Another time a petty clerk, to all appearances a respectable family man, gave away his daughter, a girl of seventeen and a beauty known to the whole town, to a young man who came to town from another district. Word suddenly went around that on their wedding night the young man dealt rather uncivilly with the beauty, in revenge for his injured honor. Lyamshin, who all but witnessed the affair, because he got drunk at the wedding and stayed in the house overnight, ran around at first light bringing everyone the merry news. Instantly a company of about ten men was formed, all of them on horseback, some on hired Cossack horses, like Pyotr Stepanovich, for example, or Liputin, who, despite his gray hairs, took part at the time in almost all the scandalous adventures of our flighty youth. When the young couple appeared outside in a droshky-and-pair to go around paying calls, as our custom invariably demands on the day after a wedding, mishaps notwithstanding—the whole cavalcade surrounded the droshky, laughing merrily, and accompanied them around town all morning. True, they did not go into the houses, but waited on horseback at the gates; they refrained from any particular insults to the bride and groom, yet they still caused a scandal. The whole town began talking. Of course, everyone laughed heartily. But here von Lembke got angry and again had a lively scene with Yulia Mikhailovna. She, too, got extremely angry, and momentarily intended to deny her house to the pranksters. But the very next day she forgave everyone, after admonitions from Pyotr Stepanovich and a few words from Karmazinov. The latter found the "joke" quite witty.

"These are local ways," he said. "Anyhow it's characteristic and . . . bold; and, look, everyone's laughing, you alone are indignant."

But there were some pranks that were intolerable, with a certain tinge.

An itinerant book-hawker appeared in town selling Gospels, a respectable woman, though of tradesman's rank. She was talked about, because the metropolitan newspapers had just published some curious reports on her kind.[2] Again that same rogue, Lyamshin, with the help of some seminarian who was loafing about waiting for a teaching post in the school, while pretending to buy books from her, quietly slipped into her bag a whole bundle of enticing, nasty photographs from abroad, specially donated for the occasion, as was found out later, by a quite venerable old man whose name I shall omit, who had an important decoration around his neck, and who loved, as he put it, "healthy laughter and a merry joke." When the poor woman began taking out her sacred books in the shopping arcade, the photographs spilled out with them. There was laughter, murmuring; the crowd closed in, there was swearing, it would have gone as far as blows if the police had not come in time. The book-hawker was put in the lockup, and only that evening, through the efforts of Mavriky Nikolaevich, who had learned with indignation the intimate details of this vile story, was she freed and sent out of town. This time Yulia Mikhailovna decidedly chased Lyamshin out, but that same evening our entire company brought him to her with the news that he had invented a special new trick on the piano, and talked her into hearing it at least. The trick indeed turned out to be amusing, with the funny title of "The Franco-Prussian War." It began with the fearsome sounds of the "Marseillaise":

> *Qu'un sang impur abreuve nos sillons!**

A bombastic challenge was heard, the intoxication of future victories. But suddenly, together with masterfully varied measures from the anthem, somewhere from the side, down below, in a corner, but very close by, came the vile little strains of "Mein lieber Augustin."[3] The "Marseillaise" does not notice them, the "Marseillaise" is at the peak of her intoxication with her own grandeur; but "Augustin" is gaining strength, "Augustin" is turning insolent, and now the measures of "Augustin" somehow unexpectedly begin to fall in with the measures of the "Marseillaise." She begins to get angry, as it were; she finally notices "Augustin," she wants to shake him off, to chase him away like an importunate, worthless fly, but "Mein lieber Augustin" holds on tight; he is cheerful and confident; he is joyful and insolent; and the "Marseillaise" somehow suddenly becomes terribly stupid; she no longer conceals that she is annoyed and offended; these are cries of indignation, these are tears and oaths, with arms outstretched to providence:

> *Pas un pouce de notre terrain, pas une pierre de nos forteresses!†*

But now she is forced to sing in time with "Mein lieber Augustin." Her strains somehow turn most stupidly into "Augustin," she is

*"That impure blood should flood our furrows!"
†"Not an inch of our ground, not a stone of our fortresses!"

drooping, dying out. Only an occasional outburst, *"qu'un sang impur . . ."* is heard again, but it jumps over at once, in a most vexing way, to the vile little waltz. She is thoroughly humbled: it is Jules Favre weeping on Bismarck's bosom and giving away everything, everything[4] . . . But then "Augustin" turns ferocious: one hears hoarse sounds, senses measureless quantities of beer being drunk, a frenzy of self-advertisement, demands for billions, slender cigars, champagne, and hostages; "Augustin" turns into a furious bellowing . . . The Franco-Prussian War is over. Our group applauds, Yulia Mikhailovna smiles and says: "Well, how can one chase him out?" Peace is made. The scoundrel did indeed have a bit of talent. Stepan Trofimovich once tried to convince me that the loftiest artistic talents can be the most terrible scoundrels, and that the one does not exclude the other. Rumor later had it that Lyamshin stole this little piece from a certain talented and modest young man, a visiting acquaintance of his, who remained unknown; but that is an aside. This blackguard, who for several years fluttered around Stepan Trofimovich, portraying on demand at his parties various little Jews, the confession of a deaf woman, or the birth of a child, now at Yulia Mikhailovna's produced killing caricatures, among them one of Stepan Trofimovich himself, entitled "A Liberal of the Forties." Everyone rocked with laughter, so that by the end it was decidedly impossible to chase him out; he had become too necessary a person. Besides, he fawned servilely on Pyotr Stepanovich, who, in his turn, had by that time acquired a strangely strong influence over Yulia Mikhailovna . . .

I would not have begun speaking in particular about this scoundrel, and he would not be worth dwelling upon, but at that time a certain outrageous incident occurred in which, it was asserted, he also took part, and this incident I can by no means omit from my chronicle.

One morning the news swept through town of an ugly and outrageous blasphemy. At the entrance to our vast marketplace stands the decrepit church of the Nativity of the Mother of God, which is a notable antiquity in our ancient town. Long ago a large icon of the Mother of God had been built into the wall behind a grating near the gates of the enclosure. And so, one night the icon was robbed, the glass of the frame was knocked out, the grating was broken, and a few stones and pearls were taken from the crown and setting, whether very valuable ones or not I do not know. But the main thing was that besides the theft a senseless, jeering blasphemy was committed: behind the broken glass of the icon a live mouse was said to have been found in the morning. It is known positively now, four months later, that the crime was committed by the convict Fedka, but for some reason Lyamshin's participation has also been added to it. At the time no one mentioned Lyamshin and he was not suspected at all, but now everyone insists that it was he who let in the mouse. I remember all our authorities being somewhat at a loss. People had been crowding around the scene of the crime since morning. There was a constant crowd standing there, though not a very big one, but still about a hundred people. Some came, others left. Those who came crossed themselves and kissed the icon; there were donations, a collection plate appeared, and a monk beside it, and it was three o'clock in the afternoon before the authorities realized that they could order people not to stand in a crowd, but to move on after praying, kissing, and donating. This unfortunate incident produced a very gloomy effect on von Lembke. As I am told Yulia Mikhailovna put it afterwards, from that sinister morning on she began to notice that strange despondency in her husband which never left him afterwards up to the very day of his departure from our town, two months ago, for reasons of ill health, and seems to be accompanying him now in Switzerland as well, where he continues to rest after his brief career in our province.

I remember stopping in the square then, at one o'clock in the afternoon; the crowd was silent, the faces significantly somber. A merchant, fat and sallow, drove up in a droshky, climbed out, bowed to the ground, planted a kiss, donated a rouble, clambered back, groaning, into the droshky, and drove off again. A carriage also drove up with two of our ladies, accompanied by two of our pranksters. The young men (one of whom was no longer so young) got out of the vehicle as well and forced their way through the crowd to the icon, rather negligently pushing people aside. Neither of them took his hat off, and one placed a pince-nez on his nose. There was murmuring among the people, dull but disagreeable. The fine fellow in the pince-nez took a brass kopeck from a purse chock-full of bills and threw it into the dish; laughing and talking loudly, they both went back to the carriage. At that moment Lizaveta Nikolaevna, accompanied by Mavriky Nikolaevich, suddenly rode up. She jumped from the horse, handed the bridle to her companion, who on her orders remained mounted, and went up to the icon precisely at the moment when the kopeck was thrown. A flush of indignation covered her cheeks; she took off her round hat, her gloves, fell on her knees before the icon, right on the dirty sidewalk, and reverently bowed three times to the ground. Then she took out her purse, but as there were only a few ten-kopeck pieces in it, she instantly removed her diamond earrings and put them on the plate.

"May I? May I? To ornament the setting?" she asked the monk, all agitated.

"It is permissible," the monk replied, "every gift is good."

The people were silent, showing neither reproach nor approval; Lizaveta Nikolaevna mounted her horse in her soiled dress and rode off.

II

Two days after the incident just described, I met her in a numerous company, setting out for somewhere in three carriages surrounded by men on horseback. She beckoned to me with her hand, stopped the carriage, and demanded insistently that I join their party. Space was found for me in the carriage, and she laughingly introduced me to her companions, magnificent ladies, and explained to me that they were all setting out on an extremely interesting expedition. She laughed loudly and seemed somehow happy beyond measure. In the most recent time she had become gay to the point of friskiness. The undertaking was indeed an eccentric one: they were all going across the river, to the house of the merchant Sevostyanov, in whose wing, for about ten years now, our blessed man and prophet Semyon Yakovlevich, famous not only among us but in the neighboring provinces and even in the capitals, had been living in retirement, in ease and comfort. Everyone visited him, especially those from out of town, trying to get a word from the holy fool, venerating him, and leaving donations. The donations, sometimes significant ones, unless Semyon Yakovlevich disposed of them at once, were piously conveyed to God's church, mainly to our Bogorodsky monastery; for this purpose a monk

sent from the monastery was constantly on duty at Semyon Yakovlevich's. They were all looking forward to having great fun. No one
in the group had yet been to see Semyon Yakovlevich. Lyamshin alone
had visited him once before, and now insisted that he had ordered him
driven out with a broom and with his own hand had sent two big
boiled potatoes flying after him. Among the riders I noticed Pyotr
Stepanovich, again on a hired Cossack horse, which he sat rather
poorly, and Nikolai Vsevolodovich, also on horseback. On occasion
the latter did not shun the general amusement, and at such times was
always of decently cheerful mien, though he spoke as little and as
seldom as ever. When the expedition, descending to the bridge, came
opposite the town hotel, someone suddenly announced that in one of
the rooms of the hotel they had just found a guest who had shot
himself, and that they were awaiting the police. At once the idea was
voiced of having a look at the suicide. The idea met with support: our
ladies had never seen a suicide. I remember one of them saying aloud
right then that "everything has become so boring that there's no need
to be punctilious about entertainment, as long as it's diverting." Only
a few stood and waited by the porch; the rest went trooping down the
dirty corridor, and among them, to my surprise, I noticed Lizaveta
Nikolaevna. The room of the man who had shot himself was not
locked, and, naturally, they did not dare to keep us from going in. He
was a young boy, about nineteen, certainly not more, who must have
been very pretty, with thick blond hair, a regular oval face, a pure,
beautiful brow. He was already stiff, and his white face looked as if it
were made of marble. On the table lay a note, in his handwriting,
saying no one was to blame for his death, and that he was shooting
himself because he had "caroused away" four hundred roubles. The
phrase "caroused away" stood just so in the note: in its four lines there
were three grammatical errors. A fat landowner, who seemed to be his
neighbor and was staying in another room on business of his own,
sighed over him especially. From what he said it turned out that the
boy had been sent to town from their village by his family, his widowed mother, his sisters and aunts, to purchase, under the supervision
of a female relation who lived in town, various things for the trousseau
of his eldest sister, who was getting married, and to bring them home.
Those four hundred roubles, saved up in the course of decades, had

been entrusted to him with fearful sighs and endless admonishing exhortations, prayers, and crosses. The boy had hitherto been modest and trustworthy. Having come to town three days before, he did not go to his relation, he put up at the hotel and went straight to the club—hoping to find somewhere in a back room some traveling gambler, or at least a game of cards. But there was no card game that day, nor any gambler. Returning to his room at around midnight, he asked for champagne, Havana cigars, and ordered a dinner of six or seven courses. But the champagne made him drunk, the cigar made him throw up, so that when the food was brought he did not touch it, but went to bed almost unconscious. He woke up the next day fresh as an apple, went at once to a Gypsy camp in a village across the river, which he had heard about in the club the day before, and did not return to the hotel for two days. Finally, yesterday at five in the afternoon, he arrived drunk, went to bed at once, and slept until ten o'clock in the evening. On waking up, he asked for a cutlet, a bottle of Château d'Yquem,⁵ and grapes, some notepaper, ink, and the bill. No one noticed anything special about him; he was calm, quiet, and gentle. He must have shot himself at around midnight, though strangely, no one heard the shot, and his absence was noticed only today, at one in the afternoon, when, after knocking in vain, they broke down the door. The bottle of Château d'Yquem was half empty; about half a plate of grapes was also left. The shot had come from a small three-chambered revolver, straight into his heart. There was very little blood; the revolver had fallen from his hand onto the carpet. The youth himself was half reclined on a sofa in the corner. Death must have occurred instantly; no mortal agony showed on his face; his expression was calm, almost happy, he need only have lived. Our people all stared with greedy curiosity. Generally, in every misfortune of one's neighbor there is always something that gladdens the outsider's eye—and that even no matter who you are. Our ladies stared silently, their companions distinguished themselves by sharpness of wit and a supreme presence of mind. One of them observed that this was the best solution and that the boy even could not have come up with anything smarter; another concluded that he had lived well, if only for a moment. A third suddenly blurted out: "Why have we got so many people hanging or shooting themselves—as if we'd jumped off our roots, as if the floor had slipped from under everyone's feet?" The *raisonneur* was given unfriendly looks. Then Lyamshin, who drew honor from his role of buffoon, filched a little bunch of grapes from the plate; another, laughing, followed his example, and a third reached out for the Château d'Yquem as well. But he was stopped by the police chief, who arrived and even ordered them to "clear the room." Since everyone had already had their fill of looking, they went out at once without argument, though Lyamshin did try to badger the police chief about something. For the remaining half of the way, the general merriment, laughter, and brisk chatter became almost twice as lively.

We arrived at Semyon Yakovlevich's at exactly one o'clock in the afternoon.[6] The gates of the rather large merchant's house stood wide open, giving access to the wing. We learned at once that Semyon Yakovlevich was having his dinner, but was still receiving people. Our whole crowd went in together. The room in which the blessed man received and dined was quite spacious, with three windows, and was divided into two equal parts by a waist-high wooden railing from wall to wall. Ordinary visitors remained outside the railing, but the lucky ones were admitted, on the blessed man's instructions, through the gate of the railing into his part, and there he seated them, if he so desired, on his old leather chairs and sofa; while he invariably installed himself in an ancient, shabby Voltaire armchair. He was a rather big, puffy, sallow-faced man of about fifty-five, blond and bald, with thin hair, a clean-shaven chin, a swollen right cheek, and a mouth somewhat twisted, as it were, with a big wart near his left nostril, narrow little eyes, and a calm, solid, sleepy expression on his face. He was dressed German-fashion in a black frock coat, but with no waistcoat or tie.[7] A rather coarse, though white, shirt peeped out from under the frock coat; on his feet, which I believe were ailing, he wore slippers. I have heard that he was once an official and had some rank. He had just finished dining upon a light fish soup and begun his second course—jacket potatoes with salt. This was all he ever dined upon; he also drank lots of tea, of which he was a great fancier. Three servants, kept by the merchant, scurried about him; one of them wore a tailcoat, the second looked like a shop foreman, the third like a beadle. There was also a lad of about sixteen, quite a frisky one. Besides the servants there was present a venerable gray-haired monk, a bit too corpulent, holding a tin cup. On one of the tables an enormous samovar was boiling, and there stood a tray with as many as two dozen glasses. On another table, across the room, offerings had been placed: several loaves and packets of sugar, about two pounds of tea, a pair of embroidered slippers, a foulard, a length of broadcloth, a piece of linen, and so on. Almost all the money that was donated went into the monk's tin cup. The room was crowded, the visitors alone numbering about a dozen, of whom two sat beyond the railing with Semyon Yakovlevich—one a gray-haired little old man, a pilgrim from "simple folk," the other a small, dry monk from elsewhere who sat decorously and looked down. The rest of the visitors stood on this side of the railing, and they, too, were all mainly from simple folk, except for a fat merchant who came from a district town, a bearded fellow and dressed in Russian style, though he was known to be worth a hundred thousand; an elderly and woebegone noblewoman, and one landowner. They were all awaiting their happiness, not daring to begin speaking. Some four of them were on their knees, but it was the landowner who attracted the most attention, a fat man of about forty-five, who knelt right up against the railing where everyone could see him, and waited reverently for a benevolent glance or word from Semyon Yakovlevich. He had already been kneeling there for an hour or so, and the man had still paid him no notice.

Our ladies crowded up to the railing with gay and giggly whispers. The kneeling ones and all the other visitors were pushed aside or screened from view, except for the landowner, who stubbornly kept himself in full view and even grabbed the railing with his hands. Gay and greedily curious eyes turned towards Semyon Yakovlevich, as did lorgnettes, pince-nez, and even opera glasses; Lyamshin at least was observing through opera glasses. Semyon Yakovlevich calmly and lazily glanced around with his small eyes.

"Fairlooks! Fairlooks!" he deigned to utter, in a hoarse bass, with a slight exclamation.

Our people all laughed: "Fairlooks? What does it mean?" But Semyon Yakovlevich lapsed into silence and went on eating his potatoes. At last he wiped his mouth with a napkin and was served tea.

He usually did not take tea alone, but also had it served to his visitors, though by no means to all of them, usually pointing out himself those upon whom happiness would be bestowed. His instructions were always striking in their unexpectedness. He sometimes passed over rich men and dignitaries and ordered tea served to some peasant or some decrepit little lady; at other times he would pass over the beggarly folk and serve some one fat, wealthy merchant. The way the tea was served also varied: some got it with sugar in it, others with sugar on the side, still others with no sugar at all. This time happiness was bestowed upon the little monk in the form of a glass of tea with sugar in it, and on the old pilgrim, who was served tea without any sugar. But the fat monk with the tin cup from the monastery was for some reason not served at all, though up to then he had had his glass every day.

"Semyon Yakovlevich, say something to me, I've desired to make your acquaintance for so long," the magnificent lady from our carriage sang out, smiling and narrowing her eyes, the same lady who had observed earlier that there was no need to be punctilious about entertainment, as long as it was diverting. Semyon Yakovlevich did not even glance at her. The kneeling landowner sighed audibly and deeply, like a big bellows going up and down.

"With sugar in it!" Semyon Yakovlevich pointed suddenly to the hundred-thousand-rouble merchant; the man came forward and stood beside the landowner.

"More sugar for him!" Semyon Yakovlevich ordered, when the glass had already been poured. They added another helping. "More, more for him!" More was added a third time, and then finally a fourth. The merchant unobjectingly began to drink his syrup.

"Lord!" people whispered and crossed themselves. The landowner again sighed audibly and deeply.

"My father! Semyon Yakovlevich!" the voice of the woebegone lady, who had been pressed back against the wall by our people, suddenly rang out, a rueful voice, but so sharp one would scarcely have expected it. "For a whole hour, my dear, I have been waiting for your grace. Speak your word to me, an orphan, make your judgment."

"Ask her," Semyon Yakovlevich made a sign to the servant-beadle. He went up to the railing.

"Did you do what Semyon Yakovlevich told you last time?" he asked the widow in a soft and even voice.

"Really, father Semyon Yakovlevich, how could I, how could I do it with such people!" the widow wailed. "The cannibals, they're filing a petition against me in the district court, they're threatening to go to the Senate[8]—against their own mother! . . ."

"Give it to her!" Semyon Yakovlevich pointed to a sugarloaf. The lad sprang over, seized the loaf, and lugged it to the widow.

"Oh, father, great is your mercy. What am I to do with so much?" the poor widow began to wail.

"More, more!" Semyon Yakovlevich bestowed.

Another loaf was lugged over. "More, more," the blessed man ordered; a third and finally a fourth loaf was brought. The poor widow was surrounded on all sides with sugar. The monk from the monastery sighed: it all might have gone to the monastery that same day, as previous instances had shown.

"But what shall I do with so much?" the poor widow kept sighing obsequiously. "By myself I'll just get sick! . . . Isn't it some prophecy, father?"

"That's it, a prophecy!" someone said in the crowd.

"Another pound, another!" Semyon Yakovlevich would not let up.

There was one whole sugarloaf left on the table, but Semyon Yakovlevich had indicated a pound, and so the widow was given a pound.

"Lord, lord!" people sighed and crossed themselves. "A visible prophecy."

"Sweeten your heart beforehand with kindness and mercy, and then come to complain against your own children, bone of your bone—that, one may suppose, is what this emblem signifies," the fat but tea-bypassed monk from the monastery said softly but smugly, in a fit of wounded vanity, taking the interpretation upon himself.

"But really, father," the poor widow suddenly snarled, "they dragged me into the fire on a rope when the Verkhishins' place burned down. They put a dead cat in my trunk—I mean, no matter what the atrocity, they're ready . . ."

"Out, out!" Semyon Yakovlevich suddenly waved his arms.

The beadle and the lad burst from behind the railing. The beadle took the widow under the arm, and she, having quieted down, trailed to the door, glancing at the awarded sugarloaves which the lad dragged after her.

"One back, take one back!" Semyon Yakovlevich ordered the shop foreman, who had stayed by him. He rushed after the departing group, and all three servants returned shortly bringing the once given and now retrieved sugarloaf; the widow, however, went off with three.

"Semyon Yakovlevich," someone's voice came from the back, just by the door, "I saw a bird in a dream, a jackdaw, he flew out of water and into fire. What is the meaning of this dream?"⁹

"Frost," said Semyon Yakovlevich.

"Semyon Yakovlevich, why won't you answer me anything, I've been interested in you for so long," our lady tried to start again.

"Ask!" Semyon Yakovlevich, not listening to her, suddenly pointed to the kneeling landowner.

The monk from the monastery, who had been ordered to ask, gravely approached the landowner.

"What is your sin? And were you told to do anything?"

"Not to fight, not to be so quick-fisted," the landowner replied hoarsely.

"Have you done it?" asked the monk.

"I can't, my own strength overpowers me."

"Out, out! The broom, use the broom!" Semyon Yakovlevich was waving his arms. The landowner, without waiting to be punished, jumped up and rushed from the room.

"He left a gold piece behind," the monk declared, picking up a florin from the floor.

"To that one!" Semyon Yakovlevich jabbed his finger towards the hundred-thousand-rouble merchant. The hundred-thousand-rouble merchant did not dare refuse, and took it.

"Gold to gold," the monk from the monastery could not help himself.

"To that one, with sugar in it," Semyon Yakovlevich pointed to Mavriky Nikolaevich. The servant poured tea and offered it by mistake to the fop in the pince-nez.

"To the long one, the long one," Semyon Yakovlevich corrected.

Mavriky Nikolaevich took the glass, gave a military half-bow, and began to drink. I do not know why, but our people all rocked with laughter.

"Mavriky Nikolaevich," Liza suddenly addressed him, "that gentleman on his knees has left, go and kneel in his place."

Mavriky Nikolaevich looked at her in perplexity.

"I beg you, it will give me the greatest pleasure. Listen, Mavriky Nikolaevich," she suddenly began in an insistent, stubborn, ardent patter, "you absolutely must kneel, I absolutely want to see you kneeling. If you won't kneel, don't even come to call on me. I absolutely insist, absolutely! . . ."

I do not know what she meant by it; but she demanded insistently, implacably, as if she were having a fit. Mavriky Nikolaevich, as we shall see further on, attributed these capricious impulses in her, especially frequent of late, to outbursts of blind hatred for him, not really from malice—on the contrary, she honored, loved, and respected him, and he knew it himself—but from some special, unconscious hatred which, at moments, she was utterly unable to control.

He silently handed his cup to some little old lady standing behind him, opened the gate in the railing, stepped uninvited into Semyon Yakovlevich's private side, and knelt in the middle of the room, in view of everyone. I think he was deeply shaken in his delicate and simple soul by Liza's coarse, jeering escapade in view of the whole company. Perhaps he thought she would be ashamed of herself on seeing his humiliation, which she had so insisted on. Of course, no one but he would venture to reform a woman in such a naïve and risky way. He knelt there with his look of imperturbable gravity, long, awkward, ridiculous. But our people were not laughing; the unexpectedness of the act produced a painful effect. Everyone looked at Liza.

"Unction, unction!" muttered Semyon Yakovlevich.

Liza suddenly went pale, cried out, gasped, and rushed behind the railing. There a quick, hysterical scene took place: with all her might she began lifting Mavriky Nikolaevich from his knees, pulling at his elbow with both hands.

"Get up, get up!" she kept crying out, as if beside herself. "Get up now, now! How dared you kneel?"

Mavriky Nikolaevich rose from his knees. She gripped his arms above the elbows and stared fixedly in his face. There was fear in her eyes.

"Fairlooks! Fairlooks!" Semyon Yakovlevich repeated again.

She finally pulled Mavriky Nikolaevich back outside the railing; a great stir went through our whole crowd. The lady from our carriage, probably wishing to dispel the impression, inquired of Semyon Yakovlevich a third time, in a ringing and shrill voice, and, as before, with a coy smile:

"Now, Semyon Yakovlevich, won't you 'utter' something for me as well? I was counting on you so."

"F—— you, f—— you!" Semyon Yakovlevich, turning to her, suddenly used an extremely unprintable little word. The phrase was spoken ferociously and with horrifying distinctness. Our ladies shrieked and rushed out headlong, the gentlemen burst into Homeric laughter. And that was the end of our visit to Semyon Yakovlevich.

And yet it was at this point, they say, that another extremely mysterious event took place, and, I confess, it was rather for the sake of it that I have referred to this visit in such detail.

They say that when everyone trooped out, Liza, supported by Mavriky Nikolaevich, suddenly, in the doorway, in the crowd, ran into Nikolai Vsevolodovich. It should be mentioned that since that Sunday morning and the swoon, though the two had met more than once, they had not approached each other or exchanged a single word. I saw them run into each other in the doorway: it seemed to me that they stopped for a moment and looked at each other somehow strangely. But it is possible that I did not see very well in the crowd. It was asserted, on the contrary, and quite seriously, that Liza, having looked at Nikolai Vsevolodovich, quickly raised her hand, right up to the level of his face, and would certainly have struck him if he had not managed to draw back. Perhaps she did not like the expression on his face or some smirk of his, especially then, after such an episode with Mavriky Nikolaevich. I confess I did not see anything, but on the other hand everyone asserted that they did see it, though certainly not everyone could have seen it in that turmoil, even if some did. Only I did not believe it at the time. I remember, however, that for the whole way back Nikolai Vsevolodovich looked somewhat pale.

III

A LMOST AT THE SAME TIME, and precisely on the very same day, there at last took place the meeting between Stepan Trofimovich and Varvara Petrovna, which she had long had in mind and had long since announced to her former friend, but for some reason kept putting off. It took place at Skvoreshniki. Varvara Petrovna arrived at her country house all abustle: it had finally been determined the day before that the forthcoming fête would be given at the house of the marshal's wife. But Varvara Petrovna, with her quick mind, saw at once that no one could prevent her, after the fête, from giving a separate fête of her own, this time at Skvoreshniki, and again inviting the whole town out. Then everyone could satisfy themselves as to whose house was better, and who knew better how to receive and how to give a ball with greater taste. Generally, it was hard to recognize her. She seemed transformed and changed from the former inaccessible "high lady" (Stepan Trofimovich's expression) into a most ordinary featherbrained society woman. However, it may only have seemed so.

Having arrived at the empty house, she made the round of the rooms accompanied by the faithful and ancient Alexei Yegorovich and Fomushka, a man who had seen the world and was an expert in interior decoration. Counsels and considerations began: what furniture to transfer from the town house; what objects, paintings; where to put them; how best to manage with the conservatory and the flowers; where to hang new draperies, where to set up the buffet, one buffet or two, and so on and so forth. And then, in the heat of the bustle, she suddenly decided to send the carriage for Stepan Trofimovich.

The latter had long since been informed, and was prepared, and was every day expecting precisely such a sudden invitation. As he got into the carriage, he crossed himself; his fate was to be decided. He found his friend in the great hall, on a small settee in a niche, by a small marble table, with a pencil and paper in her hands: Fomushka was measuring the height of the galleries and windows, and Varvara Petrovna herself was writing down the numbers and making marginal notes. Without interrupting her work, she nodded her head in Stepan Trofimovich's direction and, when he muttered some greeting, hastily gave him her hand and pointed, without looking, to the place beside her.

"I sat and waited for about five minutes, 'repressing my heart,'" he told me later. "The woman I saw was not the one I had known for twenty years. The fullest conviction that all was over gave me a strength that amazed even her. I swear she was surprised by my steadfastness in that final hour."

Varvara Petrovna suddenly put her pencil down on the table and quickly turned to Stepan Trofimovich.

"Stepan Trofimovich, we must talk business. I'm sure you have prepared all your magnificent words and various little phrases, but it would be better if we got straight to business, right?"

He flinched. She was in too much of a hurry to set her tone—what would come next?

"Wait, keep still, let me speak, then you can, though I really don't know what you'd be able to say in reply," she went on in a quick patter. "The twelve hundred of your pension I regard as my sacred duty as long as you live; or, why a sacred duty, simply an agreement, that will be much more real, right? If you like, we can put it in writing. In case of my death, special arrangements have been made. But, beyond that, you now get lodgings, servants, and your full keep from me. Translated into money, that makes fifteen hundred roubles, right? I will add another three hundred roubles for emergencies, that makes it a full three thousand. Will that suffice you for a year? Doesn't seem too little? In extreme emergencies I'll add to it, however. So, take the money, send me back my servants, and live on your own, wherever you like, in Petersburg, in Moscow, abroad, or here, only not with me. Understand?"

"Not long ago a different demand was conveyed to me by those same lips just as urgently and as quickly," Stepan Trofimovich said slowly and with sad distinctness. "I resigned myself and . . . danced the little Cossack[10] to please you. *Oui, la comparaison peut être permise. C'était un petit cosaque du Don, qui sautait sur sa propre tombe.** Now . . ."

"Stop, Stepan Trofimovich. You are terribly verbose. You did not dance, but you came out to me in a new tie and shirt, wearing gloves, pomaded and perfumed. I assure you that you yourself would have liked very much to marry; it was written on your face, and, believe me, the expression was a most inelegant one. If I did not remark upon it then and there, it was solely out of delicacy. But you wished it, you wished to marry, despite the abominations you wrote privately about

---

*"Yes, the comparison is permissible. It was like a little Don Cossack, jumping upon his own grave."

me and about your bride. Now it's not that at all. And what do you mean by a *cosaque du Don* on some grave of yours? I don't understand the comparison. On the contrary, don't die but live, live as much as you can, I shall be very glad."

"In the almshouse?"

"In the almshouse? One doesn't go to the almshouse with an income of three thousand. Ah, I remember," she grinned. "Indeed, Pyotr Stepanovich once got to joking about the almshouse. Bah, but that was indeed a special almshouse, which is worth considering. It's for the most respectable persons, there are colonels there, one general even wants to go there. If you got in there with all your money, you'd find peace, satisfaction, servants. You could occupy yourself with your studies and always get up a game of preference . . ."

"*Passons.*"

"*Passons?*" Varvara Petrovna winced. "But, in that case, that's all; you've been informed; from now on we live entirely separately."

"And that's all? All that's left of twenty years? Our final farewell?"

"You're terribly fond of exclaiming, Stepan Trofimovich. It's not at all the fashion nowadays. They talk crudely but plainly. You and these twenty years of ours! Twenty years of reciprocal self-love, and nothing more. Your every letter to me was written not for me but for posterity. You're a stylist, not a friend, and friendship is merely a glorified word, essentially a mutual outpouring of slops . . ."

"God, all in other people's words! Learned by rote! So they've already put their uniform on you, too! You, too, are in joy, you, too, are in the sun; *chère, chère,* for what mess of pottage[11] have you sold them your freedom!"

"I am not a parrot to repeat other people's words," Varvara Petrovna boiled up. "Rest assured that I've stored up enough words of my own. What did you do for me in these twenty years? You denied me even the books which I ordered for you and which, if it weren't for the binder, would have been left uncut. What did you give me to read when I asked you, in the first years, to be my guide? Capefigue, nothing but Capefigue.[12] You were even jealous of my development, and took measures. And meanwhile everyone laughs at you. I confess I've always regarded you as merely a critic, you are a literary critic, and that is all. When I announced, on the way to Petersburg, that I intended to publish a magazine and dedicate my whole life to it, you at once gave me an ironic look and suddenly became terribly haughty."

"It was not that, not that . . . we were afraid of persecutions then . . ."

"It was just that, and you could by no means have been afraid of persecutions in Petersburg. Remember how afterwards, in February, when the news swept over,[13] you suddenly came running to me all in a fright and started demanding that I at once give you a certificate, in the form of a letter, that the proposed magazine had no relation to you at all, that the young people had come to see me and not you, that you were only a tutor who lived in the house because you were still owed some salary, right? Do you remember that? You have distinguished yourself superbly throughout your life, Stepan Trofimovich."

"That was only a moment of faintheartedness, an intimate moment," he exclaimed ruefully. "But can it be, can it really be that we will break up because of such petty impressions? Can it be that nothing else has been preserved between us from all those long years?"

"You are terribly calculating; you keep wanting to make it so that I am still indebted to you. When you returned from abroad, you looked down your nose at me and wouldn't let me utter a word, and when I myself came and spoke with you later about my impressions of the Madonna, you wouldn't hear me out and began smiling haughtily into your tie, as if I really could not have the same feelings as you."

"It was not that, probably not that . . . *J'ai oublié.*"*

"No, it was just that, and there was nothing to boast of before me, because it's all nonsense and merely your invention. No one, no one nowadays admires the Madonna anymore or wastes time over it, except for inveterate old men. This has been proved."

"Proved, really?"

"She serves absolutely no purpose. This mug is useful, because water can be poured into it; this pencil is useful, because everything can be written with it, but here you have a woman's face that's worse than all faces in nature. Try painting an apple and put a real apple next to it—which would you take? I'll bet you wouldn't make any mistake.

---

*"I've forgotten."

This is what your theories boil down to, once the first ray of free analysis shines on them."[14]

"So, so."

"You grin ironically. And what you said to me about charity, for example? And yet the pleasure of charity is an arrogant and immoral pleasure, a rich man's pleasure in his riches, his power, and in the comparison of his significance with the significance of a beggar. Charity corrupts both him who gives and him who takes, and, moreover, does not achieve its goal, because it only increases beggary. Sluggards who do not want to work crowd around those who give like gamblers around the gaming table, hoping to win. And yet the pitiful half-kopecks that are thrown to them are not even a hundredth part enough. How much have you given in your life? Eighty kopecks, if that, go on, use your memory. Try to remember when was the last time you gave anything—about two years ago, maybe all of four. You shout and it only hinders the cause. Charity should be forbidden by law, even in our present society. In the new order there will be no poor at all."

"Oh, what an outpouring of other people's words! So it's even gone as far as the new order? God help you, unhappy woman!"

"Yes, it has, Stepan Trofimovich; you carefully concealed from me all the new ideas that are now known to everyone, and you were doing it solely out of jealousy, so as to have more power over me. Now even this Yulia is a hundred miles ahead of me. But I, too, have now opened my eyes. I've defended you, Stepan Trofimovich, as far as I could; absolutely everyone accuses you."

"Enough!" he made as if to get up from his seat, "enough! And what else shall I wish you, if not indeed repentance?"

"Sit down for a minute, Stepan Trofimovich, there is still something I want to ask you. You have received an invitation to read at the literary matinée; that was arranged through me. Tell me, what precisely will you read?"

"Why, precisely about that queen of queens, that ideal of humanity, the Sistine Madonna, who in your opinion is not worth a glass or a pencil."

"Not from history, then?" Varvara Petrovna was ruefully surprised. "But they won't listen to you. You and your Madonna, really! Who wants it, if you just put everyone to sleep? I assure you, Stepan Trofimovich, I am speaking solely in your interest. How different if you'd take some brief but amusing little medieval court story from Spanish history, or, better, some anecdote, and pad it out with more anecdotes and witticisms of your own. They had magnificent courts there; there were such ladies, poisonings. Karmazinov says it would be strange if you couldn't at least find something amusing from Spanish history."

"Karmazinov, that written-out fool, hunts up a topic for me!"

"Karmazinov, that all but statesmanly mind! You have too bold a tongue, Stepan Trofimovich."

"Your Karmazinov is a written-out, spiteful old woman! *Chère, chère,* how long have you been so enslaved by them, oh, God!"

"I still cannot stand him for his self-importance, but I do justice to his intelligence. I repeat, I've defended you with all my strength, as far as I could. And why must you so necessarily show yourself as ridiculous and dull? On the contrary, come out on the stage with a venerable smile, as the representative of a past age, and tell three anecdotes, with all your wittiness, as only you sometimes know how to do. So you're an old man, so you belong to a bygone age, so you've fallen behind them, finally; but you can confess all that with a smile in your preface, and everyone will see that you are a dear, kind, witty relic . . . In short, a man of the old stamp, and sufficiently advanced to be able to set the right value on all the scandalousness of certain notions he used to follow. Do give me that pleasure, I beg you."

"*Chère,* enough! Don't beg me, I cannot. I will read about the Madonna, but I will raise a storm that will either crush them all, or strike me alone."

"Most likely you alone, Stepan Trofimovich."

"Such is my lot. I will tell of that mean slave, that stinking and depraved lackey, who will be the first to clamber up a ladder with scissors in his hand and slash the divine face of the great ideal in the name of equality, envy, and . . . digestion. Let my curse thunder out, and then, then . . ."

"To the madhouse?"

"Perhaps. But in any case, whether I emerge defeated or victorious, that same evening I shall take my bag, my beggar's bag, leave all my belongings, all your presents, all pensions and promises of boons to come, and go off on foot to end my life as a merchant's tutor, or die of hunger somewhere in a ditch. I have spoken. *Alea jacta est!*"[15]

He again rose slightly.

"I've been sure," Varvara Petrovna rose, flashing her eyes, "for years I've been sure that you lived precisely so that in the end you might disgrace me and my house with slander! What do you mean to say by this tutoring in a merchant's house or dying in a ditch? Spite, slander, and nothing more!"

"You have always despised me; but I will end as a knight faithful to his lady, for your opinion has always been dearest of all to me. From this minute I shall accept nothing, but revere disinterestedly."

"How stupid that is!"

"You have always not respected me. I may have had a myriad of weaknesses. Yes, I was grubbing off you—I speak the language of nihilism—but grubbing was never the highest principle of my actions. It happened just so, of itself, I don't know how . . . I always thought that something else remained between us, higher than food, and— never, never have I been a scoundrel! And so, on our way, to set things right! A late way, for it is late autumn outside, mist lies over the fields, the chill hoarfrost of old age covers my future path, and wind howls about the imminent grave . . . But on our way, our new way:

> Filled with love that's pure
> And true to the sweet dream . . .[16]

Oh, my dreams, farewell! Twenty years! *Alea jacta est!*"

His face was splashed with the tears that suddenly burst through; he took his hat.

"I don't understand Latin," said Varvara Petrovna, holding herself back with all her might.

Who knows, perhaps she also wanted to cry, but indignation and caprice once again got the upper hand.

"I know only one thing, that this is all pranks. You will never be able to carry out your threats, so filled with egoism. You will not go anywhere, not to any merchant, but will end up quite contentedly on my hands, getting a pension and holding Tuesday gatherings of your friends, who bear no resemblance to anything. Farewell, Stepan Trofimovich."

"*Alea jacta est!*" he bowed deeply to her and returned home half dead with agitation.

6

Pyotr Stepanovich Bustles About

I

THE DAY of the fête had been finally fixed, yet von Lembke was growing more and more sad and pensive. He was full of strange and sinister forebodings, and this worried Yulia Mikhailovna greatly. True, all was not well. Our soft former governor had left the administration in some disorder; at the present moment cholera was approaching; there had been a great loss of cattle in some parts; fires had raged all summer in towns and villages, and among the people a foolish murmuring about arson was more and more taking root. Robbery had increased twice over the previous scale. All of this would, of course, have been more than ordinary had there not been other, weightier reasons which disrupted the peace of the hitherto happy Andrei Antonovich.

What struck Yulia Mikhailovna most was that he was becoming taciturn and, strangely, more secretive every day. And what, she wondered, did he have to be secretive about? True, he rarely opposed her, and for the most part was perfectly obedient. On her insistence, for example, two or three highly risky and all but illegal measures were passed with a view to strengthening the governor's power. Several sinister connivances took place with the same aim; people deserving of the courts and Siberia, for example, were put up for awards solely at her insistence. It was decided to leave certain complaints and inquiries systematically unanswered. All this was found out afterwards. Lembke not only signed everything, but did not even discuss the question of the extent of his wife's participation in the fulfillment of his duties. Instead, at times he would suddenly bridle at "perfect trifles," which surprised Yulia Mikhailovna. Naturally, he felt a need to reward himself for days of obedience with little moments of rebellion. Unfortunately, Yulia Mikhailovna, for all her perspicacity, was unable to understand this noble refinement of a noble character. Alas! she could not be bothered, and that was the cause of many misunderstandings.

It is not for me to tell of certain things, nor would I be able to. To discuss administrative errors is not my business either, and so I shall also omit entirely the whole administrative side. In beginning this chronicle, I set myself other tasks. Besides, much will be uncovered by the investigation that has now been ordered in our province, one need only wait a bit. However, we still cannot avoid certain explanations.

But to continue with Yulia Mikhailovna. The poor lady (I feel very sorry for her) might have attained all that so attracted and beckoned to her (fame and the rest) quite without such strong and eccentric moves as she set herself from the very first. But either from an excess of poetry, or from the long, sad failures of her early youth, she felt suddenly, with the change in her lot, that she was somehow even all too especially called, almost anointed, one "o'er whom this tongue of flame blazed up,"[1] and it was in this tongue that the trouble consisted; after all, it is not a chignon that can go on any woman's head. But there is nothing more difficult than to convince a woman of this truth; on the contrary, anyone who chooses to yes her will succeed, and they all vied with one another in yessing her. The poor woman suddenly found herself the plaything of the most various influences, at the same time fully imagining herself to be original. Many artful dodgers feathered their own nests and took advantage of her simpleheartedness during the brief term of her governorship. And what a hash came of it, under the guise of independence! At the same time she liked large-scale landholding, and the aristocratic element, and the strengthening of the governor's power, and the democratic element, and the new institutions, and order, and freethinking, and little social ideas, and the strict tone of an aristocratic salon, and the all but pot-house casualness of the young people that surrounded her. She dreamed of *giving happiness* and reconciling the irreconcilable, or, more exactly, of uniting all and sundry in the adoration of her own person. She also had her favorites; she was very fond of Pyotr Stepanovich, who acted, incidentally, through the crudest flattery. But she also liked him for another reason, a most wondrous one and most characteristically revealing of the poor lady: she kept hoping he would point her to a whole state conspiracy! Difficult as it is to imagine, this was so. It seemed to her, for some reason, that there must be a state conspiracy lurking in the province. Pyotr Stepanovich, by his silence in some cases and his hints in others, contributed to the rooting of her strange idea. Whereas she imagined him to be connected with everything revolutionary in Russia, yet at the same time devoted to her to the point of adoration. Uncovering a conspiracy, earning the gratitude of Petersburg, furthering one's career, influencing the youth by "indulgence" so as to keep them on the brink—all this got along quite well in her fantastic head. After all, she had saved, she had won over Pyotr Stepanovich (of this she was for some reason irrefutably certain), and so she would save others. Not a one, not a one of them would perish, she would save them all; she would sort them out; and thus she would report on them; she would act with a view to higher justice, and even history and all of Russian liberalism would perhaps bless her name; and the conspiracy would be uncovered even so. All profits at once.

But, even so, it was necessary that Andrei Antonovich be a bit brighter for the fête. He absolutely had to be cheered up and reassured. She sent Pyotr Stepanovich to him on this mission, in hopes that he might influence his despondency in some reassuring way known only to himself. Perhaps even with some information delivered, so to speak, at first mouth. She trusted entirely to his adroitness. It was long since Pyotr Stepanovich had been in Mr. von Lembke's study. He flew in precisely at a moment when the patient was in a particularly tense mood.

II

A CERTAIN COMBINATION had occurred which Mr. von Lembke was simply unable to resolve. In one district (the same one in which Pyotr Stepanovich had recently been feasting) a certain sub-lieutenant had been subjected to a verbal reprimand by his immediate commander. This had happened in front of the whole company. The sub-lieutenant was still a young man, recently come from Petersburg, always sullen and taciturn, with an air of importance, but at the same time short, fat, red-cheeked. He could not endure the reprimand and suddenly charged at his commander with some sort of unexpected shriek that astonished the whole company, his head somehow savagely lowered; struck him and bit him on the shoulder as hard as he could; they were barely able to pull him away. There was no doubt that he had lost his mind; in any case it was discovered that he had been noted lately for the most impossible oddities. For example, he had thrown two icons belonging to his landlord out of his apartment, and chopped one of them up with an axe; and in his room he had placed the works of Vogt, Moleschott, and Büchner[2] on stands like three lecterns, and before each lectern kept wax church candles burning. From the number of books found in his place it could be concluded that he was a well-read man. If he had had fifty thousand francs, he might have sailed off to the Marquesas Islands like that "cadet" mentioned with such merry humor by Mr. Herzen in one of his works.[3] When he was taken, a whole bundle of the most desperate tracts was found in his pockets and in his lodgings.

Tracts are an empty affair of themselves, and in my opinion not at all worrisome. As if we haven't seen enough of them. Besides, these were not even new tracts: exactly the same ones, it was said later, had been spread recently in Kh—— province, and Liputin, who had been in the district capital and the neighboring province about a month and a half earlier, insisted that he had already seen exactly the same leaflets there. But what chiefly struck Andrei Antonovich was that just at the same time the manager of the Shpigulin factory turned in to the police two or three bundles of exactly the same leaflets as the sub-lieutenant's, which had been left at the factory during the night. The bundles had not even been undone yet, and none of the workers had had time to read even one. The fact was silly, but Andrei Antonovich fell to pondering strenuously. The affair appeared unpleasantly complicated to him.

In this factory of the Shpigulins there was just beginning that very "Shpigulin story" which caused so much shouting among us and was then passed on with such variations to the metropolitan newspapers. About three weeks previously a worker there had fallen ill and died of Asian cholera; then several more people fell ill. Everyone in town got scared, because cholera was approaching from the neighboring province. I will note that all possibly satisfactory sanitary measures were taken in our town to meet the uninvited guest. But the factory of the Shpigulins, who were millionaires and people with connections, was somehow overlooked. And so everyone suddenly started screaming that it was there that the root and hotbed of disease lay and that the uncleanliness of the factory itself, and especially of the workers' quarters, was so inveterate that even if there had been no cholera, it would have generated there of itself. Naturally, measures were taken at once, and Andrei Antonovich vigorously insisted that they be carried out immediately. The factory was cleaned up in about three weeks, but then for some reason the Shpigulins closed it. One of the Shpigulin brothers resided permanently in Petersburg, and the other, after the order from the authorities about the cleaning, left for Moscow. The manager began paying off the workers and, as it now turns out, was brazenly cheating them. The workers began to murmur, wanted their rightful pay, were foolish enough to go to the police, though without making a great noise or really causing much trouble. It was just at this time that the tracts were turned in to Andrei Antonovich by the manager.

Pyotr Stepanovich flew into the study unannounced, like a good friend and familiar, and with an errand from Yulia Mikhailovna besides. Seeing him, von Lembke scowled sullenly and stopped inimically by his desk. Before then he had been pacing the study, discussing something in private with his chancery official Blum, an extremely awkward and sullen German whom he had brought from Petersburg over the most strenuous opposition of Yulia Mikhailovna. When Pyotr Stepanovich entered, the official retreated to the door, but did not leave. It even seemed to Pyotr Stepanovich that he somehow exchanged significant looks with his superior.

"Oho, caught you this time, you cagey burgomaster!" Pyotr Stepanovich cried out, laughing, and he placed the flat of his hand over the tract lying on the table. "Adding to your collection, eh?"

Andrei Antonovich flared up. Something suddenly became as if distorted in his face.

"Leave off, leave off at once!" he cried, starting with wrath, "and do not dare . . . sir . . ."

"What's the matter with you? You seem angry?"

"Allow me to tell you, my dear sir, that henceforth I by no means intend to suffer your *sans-façon,** and I ask you to recall . . ."

"Pah, the devil, he really means it!"

"Be still, be still!" von Lembke stamped his feet on the carpet, "and do not dare . . ."

God knows what it might have come to. Alas, there was one further circumstance here, besides all the rest, which was quite unknown both to Pyotr Stepanovich and even to Yulia Mikhailovna herself. The unhappy Andrei Antonovich had reached a point of such distress that lately he had begun to be secretly jealous about his wife and Pyotr Stepanovich. Alone, especially at night, he had endured some most unpleasant moments.

"And I thought that if a man reads you his novel for two days running, in private, past midnight, and wants your opinion, then he's at least beyond these officialities . . . Yulia Mikhailovna receives me on a friendly footing; who can figure you out?" Pyotr Stepanovich pronounced, even with some dignity. "Here's your novel, by the way," he placed on the desk a large, weighty notebook, rolled into a tube and entirely wrapped in dark blue paper.

Lembke blushed and faltered.

"Where did you find it?" he asked cautiously, with a flood of joy that he could not contain and that he tried nevertheless to contain with all his might.

"Imagine, it fell behind the chest of drawers, rolled up just as it was. I must have tossed it carelessly on the chest as I came in. It was found only two days ago, when they were scrubbing the floors—and what a job you gave me, really!"

Lembke sternly lowered his eyes.

"Thanks to you I haven't slept for two nights running. They found it two days ago, but I kept it, I've been reading it, I have no time during the day, so I did it at night. Well, sir, and—I'm not pleased: can't warm up to the idea. Spit on it, however, I've never been a critic, but—I

*"informality"

couldn't tear myself away, my dear, even though I'm not pleased! The fourth and fifth chapters are . . . are . . . are . . . the devil knows what! And so crammed with humor, I laughed out loud. No, you really know how to poke fun *sans que cela paraisse*!* Well, but the ninth, the tenth, it's all about love, not my thing; makes an effect, however; and I almost started blubbering over Igrenev's letter, though you present him so subtly . . . You know, there's feeling there, and at the same time you want to present him as if with a false side, right? Have I guessed, or not? Well, and for the ending I'd simply thrash you. What is it you're pushing there? Why, it's the same old deification of family happiness, of the multiplying of children, and capital, and they lived happily ever after, for pity's sake! You'll charm the reader, because even I couldn't tear myself away, but so much the worse. Readers are as stupid as ever, intelligent people ought to shake them up, while you . . . But enough, though. Good-bye. Next time don't be angry; I had a couple of important little words to say to you; but you seem somehow . . ."

Andrei Antonovich meanwhile took his novel and locked it up in the oak bookcase, having managed in the meantime to wink at Blum to efface himself. The latter vanished with a long and sad face.

"I do not *seem somehow*, I'm simply . . . nothing but troubles," he muttered, scowling, though no longer wrathfully, and sitting down at the desk. "Sit down and tell me your two little words. I haven't seen you for a long time, Pyotr Stepanovich, only in future don't come flying in with that manner of yours . . . sometimes, when one is busy, it's . . ."

"I always have the same manners . . ."

"I know, sir, and I believe it is unintentional, but sometimes, amidst all this bustle . . . Sit down now."

Pyotr Stepanovich sprawled on the sofa and immediately tucked his legs up.

*"without letting it show!"

III

"A ND WHAT IS all this bustle—you can't mean these trifles?" he nodded towards the tract. "I can drag in as many of these leaflets as you like, I already made their acquaintance in Kh—— province."

"You mean, when you were living there?"

"Well, naturally, not when I wasn't. There's a vignette, a drawing of an axe, at the top.[4] Excuse me" (he picked up the tract), "ah, yes, here's the axe; it's the same one, exactly."

"Yes, an axe. See—an axe."

"And what, are you afraid of the axe?"

"Not of the axe . . . and not afraid, sir, but this matter is . . . such a matter, there are circumstances here."

"Which? That they were turned in from the factory? Heh, heh. You know, you'll soon have the workers at that factory writing tracts themselves."

"How's that?" von Lembke stared sternly.

"Just so. With you looking on. You're too soft, Andrei Antonovich; you write novels. What's needed here are the old methods."

"What do you mean, the old methods, what sort of advice is that? The factory has been cleaned up; I gave orders, it was cleaned up."

"Yet there's rioting among the workers. They all ought to be whipped, and there's an end to it."

"Rioting? Nonsense, I gave orders and it was cleaned up."

"Eh, what a soft man you are, Andrei Antonovich!"

"In the first place, I am by no means so soft, and in the second . . ." von Lembke felt stung again. He forced himself to talk with the young man out of curiosity, on the chance that he might tell him a little something new.

"Ahh, again an old acquaintance!" Pyotr Stepanovich interrupted, sighting another sheet of paper under the paperweight, also looking like a tract, apparently of foreign imprint, but in verse. "Why, this one I know by heart, it's 'The Shining Light.' Let me see: yes, so it is, 'The

Shining Light.' I've been acquainted with this light ever since I was abroad. Where did you dig it up?"

"You say you saw it abroad?" von Lembke roused himself.

"Sure thing, about four months ago, or even five."

"You saw quite a lot abroad, however," von Lembke glanced at him subtly. Pyotr Stepanovich, without listening, unfolded the paper and read the poem aloud:

The Shining Light

> A man of high birth he was not,
> Among the people he cast his lot.
> Hounded by the wrath of tsars,
> The jealous malice of boyars,
> He from suffering drew not back,
> From torment, torture, nor the rack,
> But firm before the people stood,
> For liberty, equality, and brotherhood.
>
> And when rebellion once was sparked,
> He then for foreign lands embarked,
> Escaping thus the tsar's redoubt,
> The tongs, the hangman, and the knout,
> While the people, cursing empty skies,
> Against harsh fate prepared to rise,
> And from Smolensk to far Tashkent
> Awaited only the studént.
>
> All were awaiting his return
> So they could go without concern
> To rid themselves of cruel boyars,
> To rid themselves of greedy tsars,
> To hold all property as one,
> And take their just revenge upon
> Marriage, church, and family ties—
> Evils in which the old world lies.[5]

"You must have taken it from that officer, eh?" Pyotr Stepanovich asked.

"So you have the honor of knowing that officer as well?"

"Sure thing. I feasted with them there for two days. He was bound to lose his mind."

"Perhaps he never did lose his mind."

"You mean since he started biting?"

"But, I beg your pardon, if you saw this poem abroad, and then, it turns out, here at this officer's . . ."

"What, intricate? I see, so you're examining me, Andrei Antonovich? You see, sir," he began suddenly, with unusual importance, "of what I saw abroad I already gave my explanations to certain persons on my return, and my explanations were found satisfactory, otherwise I would not have bestowed the happiness of my presence upon this town. I think that my affairs in that sense are done with, and that I do not owe any reports. Done with, not because I am an informer, but because I was unable to act otherwise. Those who wrote to Yulia Mikhailovna, knowing the situation, said I was an honest man . . . Well, and that's all, devil take it, because I came to tell you something serious, and it's a good thing you sent that chimney sweep of yours away. The matter is important for me, Andrei Antonovich; I have an extraordinary request to make of you."

"A request? Hm, please do, I'm waiting, and, I confess, with curiosity. And generally I will add that you rather surprise me, Pyotr Stepanovich."

Von Lembke was in some agitation. Pyotr Stepanovich crossed his legs.

"In Petersburg," he began, "I spoke candidly about many things, but certain other things—this, for instance" (he tapped "The Shining Light" with his finger), "I passed over in silence, first, because it wasn't worth speaking about, and second, because I answered only what I was asked. I don't like getting ahead of myself in that sense; here I see the difference between a scoundrel and an honest man, who quite simply was overtaken by circumstances . . . Well, in short, let's set that aside. Well, sir, and now . . . now that these fools . . . well, now that this has come out and is in your hands and, I see, will not be concealed from you—because you are a man with eyes, and you can't be second-guessed, whereas these fools are still going on with it—I . . . I . . . well, yes, in short, I've come to ask you to save one man, one more fool, a madman perhaps, in the name of his youth, his misfortunes, in the name of your own humaneness . . . It can't be that you're so humane only in novels of your own fabrication!" he suddenly broke off his speech impatiently and with rude sarcasm.

In short, one beheld a direct man, but an awkward and impolitic one, owing to an excess of humane feeling and a perhaps unnecessary ticklishness—above all, a none-too-bright man, as von Lembke judged at once with extreme subtlety, and as he had long supposed him to be, especially during the last week, alone in his study, especially at night, when he privately cursed him with all his might for his inexplicable successes with Yulia Mikhailovna.

"For whom do you make this request, and what does it all signify?" he inquired imposingly, trying to conceal his curiosity.

"It's . . . it's . . . ah, the devil . . . Am I to blame for believing in you? Am I really to blame for considering you a most noble man and, above all, a sensible one . . . that is, capable of understanding . . . ah, the devil . . ."

The poor fellow was apparently unable to control himself.

"Do finally understand," he went on, "do understand that by giving you his name, I'm really betraying him to you; I'm betraying him, right? Right?"

"But how am I to guess, however, if you can't bring yourself to say it?"

"That's just it, you always chop it down with that logic of yours, the devil . . . so, the devil . . . this 'shining light,' this 'studént'—it's Shatov . . . so, there it is!"

"Shatov? That is, how is it Shatov?"

"Shatov, he's the 'studént,' the one that's mentioned. He lives here, the former serf, well, the one who gave that slap."

"I know, I know!" Lembke narrowed his eyes. "But, excuse me, what in fact is he accused of, and, most chiefly, what are you interceding for?"

"I'm asking you to save him, do you understand! I've known him since eight years ago, you might say we used to be friends," Pyotr Stepanovich was turning himself inside out. "Well, I really don't owe you any reports on my former life," he waved his hand. "It's all insignificant, all just three men and a half, and with the ones abroad it wouldn't even make ten, and the main thing is that I was counting on your humaneness, your intelligence. You'll understand and you yourself will show the matter in the right way, not as God knows what, but as the foolish dream of a madcap . . . from misfortunes, mind you, from long misfortunes, and not as devil knows what sort of unprecedented state conspiracy! . . ."

He was almost breathless.

"Hm. I see he's to blame for the tracts with the axe," Lembke concluded almost majestically, "but, excuse me, if he's alone, how could he have spread them both here and in other districts, and even in Kh—— province, and . . . and, finally, the main thing is— where'd he get them?"

"But I'm telling you there are apparently five of them in all, or maybe ten, how should I know?"

"You don't know?"

"But how should I know, devil take it?"

"You did know, however, that Shatov was one of the accomplices?"

"Ehh!" Pyotr Stepanovich waved his arm, as if warding off the overwhelming perspicacity of the inquirer. "Well, listen, I'll tell you the whole truth: I know nothing about the tracts, I mean nothing whatsoever, devil take it, do you understand what nothing means? . . . Well, of course, that sub-lieutenant, and someone else besides, and someone else here . . . well, and maybe Shatov, well, and someone else besides, well, that's all, trash and measliness . . . but I came to plead for Shatov, he must be saved, because this poem is his, he wrote it, and it was published abroad through him; that much I know for sure, but I know nothing whatsoever about the tracts."

"If the verses are his, then most likely the tracts are, too. On what grounds, however, do you suspect Mr. Shatov?"

Pyotr Stepanovich, with the air of a man who has finally lost all patience, snatched his wallet from his pocket, and from it took a note.

"Here are the grounds!" he cried, throwing it on the desk. Lembke unfolded it; the note, as it turned out, had been written about half a year before, from here to somewhere abroad; it was a short note, a couple of words:

Am unable to print "The Shining Light" here; that or anything else; print it abroad.

Iv. Shatov

Lembke stared fixedly at Pyotr Stepanovich. Varvara Petrovna correctly referred to his having something of a sheep's gaze, especially at times.

"I mean, this is what it is," Pyotr Stepanovich lurched ahead. "That he wrote these verses here, half a year ago, but couldn't print them here, well, on some secret press—and so he asks for them to be printed abroad . . . that seems clear?"

"Yes, it's clear, sir, but whom is he asking?—that still isn't clear," Lembke remarked, with the most cunning irony.

"But, Kirillov, finally; the note was written to Kirillov abroad . . . Didn't you know? What's annoying is that you may only be pretending with me, and knew about these verses a long, long time ago, that's the thing! How else would they turn up on your desk? They did get there somehow! So why are you tormenting me?"

He convulsively wiped the sweat from his brow with a handkerchief.

"I am perhaps informed about certain things . . ." Lembke dodged adroitly, "but who is this Kirillov?"

"Well, so, he's this visiting engineer, acted as Stavrogin's second, a maniac, a madman; your sub-lieutenant may indeed just have brain fever, but this one is totally mad—totally, I guarantee it. Ehh, Andrei Antonovich, if the government only knew what sort of people they are, the lot of them, they wouldn't raise a hand against them. They're all ripe for Bedlam as it is; I saw enough of them in Switzerland and at congresses."

"From where they direct the movement here?"

"Yes, and who is directing it?—three men and another half. One just gets bored looking at them. And what is this movement here? These tracts, or what? And look who they've recruited—brain-sick sub-lieutenants and two or three students! You're an intelligent man, here's a question for you: Why don't they recruit more significant people, why is it always students and twenty-two-year-old dunces? And how many are there? They must have a million bloodhounds out searching, and how many have they found in all? Seven men. I'm telling you, one gets bored."

Lembke listened attentively, but with an air that seemed to say: "You can't catch an old bird with chaff."

"Excuse me, however, you were pleased to insist just now that the note was addressed abroad; but there's no address here; how is it known to you that the note was addressed to Mr. Kirillov, and, finally, abroad, and . . . and . . . that it was in fact written by Mr. Shatov?"

"But just get Shatov's handwriting and check. Some signature of his is bound to turn up in your chancery. And as for its being to Kirillov, it was Kirillov himself who showed it to me right then."

"So you yourself . . ."

"Well, yes, of course, so I myself. They showed me all kinds of things there. And about these verses, it was supposedly the late Herzen who wrote them for Shatov while he was still wandering abroad, supposedly in memory of their meeting, as praise, as a recommendation—ah, well, the devil . . . so Shatov is spreading it among the young people. Herzen's own opinion of me, he says."

"Tsk, tsk, tsk," Lembke finally figured it all out, "and here I was thinking: the tracts I understand, but why the verses?"

"But how could you not understand? And devil knows why I'm spilling it all out to you! Listen, you give me Shatov, and the devil take all the rest, even with Kirillov, who has now locked himself up in Filippov's house, where Shatov also lives, and is lying low. They don't like me, because I've gone back . . . but promise me Shatov and I'll bring you all the rest of them on a platter. I'll prove useful, Andrei Antonovich! I reckon the whole pitiful crew numbers nine—maybe ten—people. I'm keeping an eye on them myself, for my own part, sir. Three are already known to us: Shatov, Kirillov, and that sublieutenant. The rest I'm still *making out* . . . not that I'm all that nearsighted. It's like it was in Kh—— province; two students, one high-school boy, two twenty-year-old noblemen, one teacher, and one retired major of about sixty, stupefied with drink, were seized there with tracts—that's all, and believe me, that was all; they were even surprised that that was all. But I'll need six days. I've already worked it out on the abacus; six days, and not before. If you want to get any results, don't stir them up for another six days, and I'll tie them all into a single knot for you; stir them up before then, and the nest will scatter. But give me Shatov. I'm for Shatov . . . And best of all would be to summon him secretly and amiably, why not here to this study, and examine him, after lifting the veil for him . . . And he'll probably throw himself at your feet and weep! He's a nervous man, an unhappy man; his wife goes about with Stavrogin. Coddle him a bit and he'll reveal everything himself, but I need six days . . . And the main thing, the main thing—not even half a word to Yulia Mikhailovna. A secret. Can we keep it a secret?"

"What?" Lembke goggled his eyes. "You actually haven't . . . revealed anything to Yulia Mikhailovna?"

"To her? Save me and have mercy on me! Ehh, Andrei Antonovich! You see, sir: I greatly value her friendship and highly respect . . . well, and all that . . . but I wouldn't make such a blunder. I don't contradict her, because to contradict her, you know yourself, is dangerous. It's possible I did drop a hint or two, because she likes that, but to give away names or anything to her, as I just did to you—ehh, my dear! And why am I turning to you now? Because you are, after all, a man, a serious person, with solid, old-style experience in the service. You've seen it all. I suppose you already know every step in such matters by heart from Petersburg cases. And if I were to tell her these two names, for example, she'd just start banging the drums . . . Because she'd really love to astonish Petersburg from here. No, she's too hot-headed, that's the thing, sir."

"Yes, she does have something of that fougue," Andrei Antonovich muttered, not without pleasure, at the same time regretting terribly that this ignoramus should dare to express himself quite so freely about Yulia Mikhailovna. But Pyotr Stepanovich probably thought it was still too little, and that he must put on more steam so as to flatter and completely subdue "Lembka."

"Fougue, precisely," he agreed. "Granted she may be a genius, a literary woman, but—she'll scare the sparrows away. She couldn't hold out for six hours, much less six days. Ehh, Andrei Antonovich, don't ever lay a six-day term on a woman! You will acknowledge that I do have some experience, in these matters, I mean; I do know a thing or two, and you yourself know that I'm capable of knowing a thing or two. I'm asking you for six days not to play around, but for serious business."

"I've heard . . ." Lembke hesitated to voice his thought, "I've heard that on your return from abroad you expressed something like repentance . . . in the proper quarters?"

"Well, or whatever it was."

"And I, naturally, have no wish to go into . . . but I kept thinking that up to now you've talked in quite a different style here, about the Christian faith, for example, about social structures, and, finally, about the government . . ."

"I've said all kinds of things. I say the same things now, too, only these ideas shouldn't be pursued the way those fools do it, that's the point. What's this biting the shoulder? You agreed with me yourself, only you were saying it was too early."

"I was not, in fact, speaking about that when I agreed but said it was too early."

"You just hang every word on a hook, though—heh, heh!—you cautious man!" Pyotr Stepanovich suddenly remarked gaily. "Listen, dear heart, I did have to get acquainted with you, after all, that's why I've been speaking to you in this style of mine. It's not only you, I make many acquaintances this way. Maybe I had to figure out your character."

"And what would you need my character for?"

"Well, how should I know what for?" (he laughed again). "You see, my dear and much respected Andrei Antonovich, you are cunning, but it hasn't come to *that* yet, and most likely it won't, understand? You understand, perhaps? Though I did give explanations in the proper quarters on my return from abroad, and I really don't see why a person of certain convictions shouldn't act for the benefit of his genuine convictions . . . but no one *there* has ordered your character yet, and I have not yet taken upon myself any such orders from *there*. Try to realize: it was quite possible for me not to disclose these two names to you first, but to shoot straight over *there*—I mean, where I gave my original explanations; and if I were exerting myself on account of finances, or for some profit, then, of course, it would be a miscalculation on my part, because now they'll be grateful to you and not to me.

It's solely for the sake of Shatov," Pyotr Stepanovich added, with a noble air, "for Shatov alone, out of past friendship . . . well, and maybe when you take up your pen to write *there*, well, you can praise me, if you wish . . . I won't object, heh, heh! *Adieu*, however, I've stayed too long and babbled more than I should have!" he added, not without affability, and got up from the sofa.

"On the contrary, I'm very glad things are beginning to take shape, so to speak," von Lembke got up, too, also with an affable air, apparently influenced by the last words. "I accept your services with gratitude, and, rest assured, everything, for my part, concerning references to your zeal . . ."

"Six days, that's the main thing, give me six days, and make no move for those six days, that's what I need!"

"Very well."

"Naturally, I'm not tying your hands, and wouldn't dare to. You can't really not keep an eye out; only don't frighten the nest ahead of time, this is where I'm counting on your intelligence and experience. And I bet you must have all sorts of hounds and bloodhounds of your own ready, heh, heh!" Pyotr Stepanovich blurted out gaily and thoughtlessly (like a young man).

"Not quite," Lembke dodged affably. "It's a prejudice of youth that there's so much ready . . . But, incidentally, allow me one word: if this Kirillov was Stavrogin's second, then Mr. Stavrogin, too, in that case . . ."

"What about Stavrogin?"

"I mean, if they're such friends?"

"Ah, no, no, no! You're way off the mark, though you are cunning. And you even surprise me. I thought you were not uninformed with regard to that . . . Hm, Stavrogin is something totally the opposite—I mean, totally . . . *Avis au lecteur.*"*

"Indeed! But, can it be?" Lembke uttered mistrustfully. "Yulia Mikhailovna told me that, according to her information from Petersburg, he is a man with certain, so to speak, instructions . . ."

"I know nothing, nothing, nothing at all. *Adieu. Avis au lecteur!*" Pyotr Stepanovich suddenly and obviously dodged.

---

*"Reader take notice."

He flew to the door.

"Allow me, Pyotr Stepanovich, allow me," cried Lembke, "one other tiny matter—I won't keep you."

He pulled an envelope from his desk drawer.

"Here's one little specimen of the same category, and with this I prove that I trust you in the highest degree. Here, sir, what is your opinion?"

There was a letter in the envelope—a strange letter, anonymous, addressed to Lembke, and received only the day before. To his great vexation, Pyotr Stepanovich read the following:

Your Excellency,

For by rank you are so. I herewith announce an attempt on the life of the persons of generals and the fatherland; for it leads straight to that. I myself have constantly been spreading them for a multitude of years. And godlessness, too. A rebellion is in preparation, there being several thousand tracts, and a hundred men will run after each one with their tongues hanging out, if not taken away by the authorities beforehand, for a multitude is promised as a reward, and the simple people are stupid, and also vodka. People considering the culprit are destroying one and another, and, fearing both sides, I repented of what I did not participate in, for such are my circumstances. If you want a denunciation to save the fatherland, and also the churches and icons, I alone can. But, with that, a pardon by telegraph from the Third Department,[6] immediately, to me alone out of all of them, and the rest to be held responsible. As a signal, every evening at seven o'clock put a candle in the doorkeeper's window. Seeing it, I will believe and come to kiss the merciful hand from the capital, but, with that, a pension, otherwise what will I live on? And you will not regret it, because you will get a star. It has to be on the quiet, or else there will be a neck wrung.

Your Excellency's desperate man.

At your feet falls

the repentant freethinker, Incognito

Von Lembke explained that the letter had turned up a day ago in the doorkeeper's room, while no one was there.

"So what do you think?" Pyotr Stepanovich asked almost rudely.

"I should suppose that this is an anonymous lampoon, a mockery."

"Most likely that's what it is. You're not to be hoodwinked."

"Mainly because it's so stupid."

"And have you received other lampoons here?"

"I have, twice, anonymously."

"Well, naturally they're not going to sign them. In different styles? Different hands?"

"Different styles and different hands."

"And clownish, like this one?"

"Yes, clownish, and you know . . . extremely vile."

"Well, since there have been some already, it's probably the same now."

"And mainly because it's so stupid. Because those people are educated and probably wouldn't write so stupidly."

"Ah, yes, yes."

"But what if someone indeed wants to make a denunciation?"

"Impossible," Pyotr Stepanovich cut off dryly. "What's this telegram from the Third Department? And the pension? An obvious lampoon."

"Yes, yes," Lembke felt ashamed.

"You know what, why don't you let me keep it. I'll find out definitely for you. Even before I find out the others."

"Take it," von Lembke agreed, though with a certain hesitation.

"Have you shown it to anyone?"

"No, how would I, not to anyone."

"I mean, to Yulia Mikhailovna?"

"Ah, God forbid, and for God's sake don't you show it to her!" Lembke cried out in fright. "She'll be so shocked . . . and terribly angry with me."

"Yes, you'll be the first to catch it, she'll say you had it coming, if they write to you like that. We know women's logic. Well, good-bye. I may even present this writer to you within three days. Above all, our agreement!"

IV

PYOTR STEPANOVICH was perhaps not a stupid man, but Fedka the Convict rightly said of him that he "invents a man and then lives with him." He went away from von Lembke quite certain that he had set him at ease for at least six days, and he needed the time badly. But this notion was a false one, and it all rested on his having invented Andrei Antonovich as a perfect simpleton, from the very start, once and for all.

Like every morbidly insecure man, Andrei Antonovich, each time he emerged from uncertainty, was for the first moment extremely and joyfully trustful. The new turn of affairs presented itself to him at first in a rather agreeable way, despite certain newly emerging, troublesome complications. The old doubts, at least, were reduced to dust. Besides, he had grown so tired in the last few days, felt himself so worn out and helpless, that his soul involuntarily longed for peace. But, alas, once again he was not at peace. Long life in Petersburg had left indelible traces on his soul. He was rather well informed of the official and even the secret history of the "new generation"—he was a curious man and collected tracts—but he never understood the first word of it. And now he was as if in a forest: all his instincts told him that there was something utterly incongruous in Pyotr Stepanovich's words, something outside all forms and conventions—"though devil knows what may go on in this 'new generation,' and devil knows how things are done among them!" he pondered, losing himself in reflections.

And here, as if by design, Blum again stuck his head into the room. Throughout Pyotr Stepanovich's visit, he had bided his time not far away. This Blum was even a relation of Andrei Antonovich's, but a distant one, carefully and timorously concealed all his life. I ask the reader's pardon for granting at least a few words here to this insignificant person. Blum belonged to the strange breed of "unfortunate" Germans—not at all owing to his extreme giftlessness, but precisely for no known reason. "Unfortunate" Germans are not a myth, they really exist, even in Russia, and have their own type. All his life Andrei

Antonovich had nursed a most touching sympathy for him, and wherever he could, as he himself succeeded in the service, kept promoting him to subordinate positions within his jurisdiction, but the man had no luck anywhere. Either the position would be abolished, or the superior would be replaced, or else he was once almost put on trial along with some others. He was precise, but somehow excessively, needlessly, and to his own detriment, gloomy; red-haired, tall, stooping, doleful, even sentimental, yet, for all his downtroddenness, stubborn and persistent as an ox, though always at the wrong time. He and his wife, with their numerous children, nursed a long-standing and reverential affection for Andrei Antonovich. Except for Andrei Antonovich, no one had ever loved him. Yulia Mikhailovna discarded him at once, but proved unable to overcome her husband's tenacity. This was their first family quarrel, and it took place just after their wedding, in the very first honey days, when Blum suddenly came to light, after having been carefully hidden from her, along with the offensive secret of his being her relation. Andrei Antonovich entreated her with clasped hands, recounted feelingly the whole story of Blum and of their friendship from very childhood, but Yulia Mikhailovna considered herself disgraced forever and even resorted to swooning. Von Lembke did not yield an inch to her and declared that he would not abandon Blum for anything in the world, nor distance him from himself, so that she was finally surprised and was forced to permit Blum. Only it was decided that their relation must be concealed still more carefully than before, if that were possible, and that Blum's name and patronymic would be changed, because for some reason he, too, was named Andrei Antonovich. Among us Blum made no acquaintances, except with the German pharmacist, paid no calls, and, as was his wont, lived his niggardly and solitary life. He had long known, too, about Andrei Antonovich's literary peccadilloes. He was mainly summoned to listen to his novels in secret, intimate readings, would sit it out like a post for six hours on end; sweated, exerted all his strength to smile and not fall asleep; on coming home would lament, together with his long-legged and lean-fleshed wife, over their benefactor's unfortunate weakness for Russian literature.

Andrei Antonovich looked with suffering at the entering Blum.

"Leave me alone, Blum, I beg you," he began in an alarmed patter, obviously wishing to deflect any renewal of their previous conversation, interrupted by Pyotr Stepanovich's arrival.

"And yet it could be arranged in the most delicate way, quite privately; you do have full authority," Blum respectfully but stubbornly insisted on something, hunching his shoulders and approaching Andrei Antonovich more and more closely on small steps.

"Blum, you are devoted to me and obliging to such a degree that I get beside myself with fear each time I look at you."

"You always say sharp things and sleep peacefully feeling pleased with what you've said, but you do yourself harm that way."

"Blum, I've just become convinced that it's not that, not that at all."

"Is it from the words of this false, depraved young man whom you yourself suspect? He won you over by his flattering praise of your talent for literature."

"Blum, you understand nothing; your project is an absurdity, I tell you. We won't find anything, and there will be a terrible outcry, then laughter, and then Yulia Mikhailovna . . ."

"We will unquestionably find everything we are looking for," Blum took a firm step towards him, placing his right hand on his heart. "We will make the inspection suddenly, early in the morning, observing all delicacy regarding the person, and all the prescribed strictness of legal form. The young men, Lyamshin and Telyatnikov, insist all too much that we will find everything we want. They have visited there many times. No one is attentively disposed towards Mr. Verkhovensky. The general's widow Stavrogin has clearly denied him her patronage, and every honest man, if there be such in this rude town, is convinced that there has always been concealed there a source of disbelief and social teaching. He keeps all the forbidden books, Ryleev's *Ponderings,*[7] all of Herzen's works . . . I have an approximate catalogue just in case . . ."

"Oh, God, everyone has those books; how simple you are, my poor Blum!"

"And many tracts," Blum went on without heeding the reproof. "We will certainly finish by finding the trail of actual local tracts. This young Verkhovensky I find quite, quite suspicious."

"But you're mixing up the father and the son. They're not on good terms; the son laughs openly at the father."

"That is just a mask."

"Blum, you're sworn to be the death of me! Think, he's a notable person here, after all. He used to be a professor, he's a well-known man, he'll make an outcry, and there will be jeering all over town, and the whole thing will go amiss . . . and think what will happen with Yulia Mikhailovna!"

Blum barged ahead without listening.

"He was just an assistant professor, just only an assistant professor, and is only a mere retired collegiate assessor in rank,"[8] he kept beating his breast, "he has no distinctions, he was fired from his post on suspicion of plotting against the government. He was under secret surveillance, and no doubt still is. And in view of the newly discovered disorders, your duty no doubt obliges you. And yet you, on the contrary, are letting your distinction slip, by conniving with the real culprit."

"Yulia Mikhailovna! Get ou-u-ut, Blum!" von Lembke suddenly cried, hearing his spouse's voice in the next room.

Blum gave a start, but did not yield.

"Permit me, do permit me," he edged forward, pressing both hands still more tightly to his breast.

"Get ou-u-ut!" Andrei Antonovich gnashed. "Do what you like . . . later . . . Oh, my God!"

The portière was raised, and Yulia Mikhailovna appeared. She stopped majestically on seeing Blum, looked him over haughtily and offendedly, as if the man's very presence there were an insult to her. Blum silently and respectfully made her a low bow and, stooping with respect, went to the door on tiptoe, his hands spread slightly.

Whether he indeed took Andrei Antonovich's last hysterical exclamation as direct permission to act as he had requested, or whether he played it false in this case for the direct good of his benefactor, being only too certain that the end would crown the affair—in any case, as we shall see below, this conversation between the superior and his subordinate produced a most unexpected result, which made many laugh, became publicly known, aroused the bitter wrath of Yulia Mikhailovna, and with all that left Andrei Antonovich finally bewildered, having thrown him, at the hottest moment, into the most lamentable indecision.

V

FOR PYOTR STEPANOVICH the day proved a bustling one. From von Lembke he quickly ran over to Bogoyavlensky Street, but going down Bykov Street, past the house where Karmazinov was lodging, he suddenly halted, grinned, and went into the house. "You are expected, sir," he was told, which highly intrigued him, because he had given no notice of his coming.

But the great writer was indeed expecting him, and had been even yesterday, and the day before. Three days earlier he had handed him the manuscript of his *Merci* (which he wanted to read at the literary matinée on the day of Yulia Mikhailovna's fête), and had done so as a favor, quite certain that he would pleasantly flatter the man's vanity by letting him acquaint himself with the great work beforehand. Pyotr Stepanovich had long ago noticed that this gentleman, conceited, spoiled, and insultingly unapproachable for the non-elect, this "all but statesmanly mind," was quite simply fawning on him, even eagerly so. I believe the young man finally realized that the older one considered him, if not the ringleader of everything covertly revolutionary in the whole of Russia, at least one of those most deeply initiated into the secrets of the Russian revolution and with an unquestionable influence on the young. The state of mind of "the most intelligent man in Russia" interested Pyotr Stepanovich, but up to now, for certain reasons, he had avoided any explanations.

The great writer lodged in the house of his sister, a court chamberlain's wife and a landowner; the two of them, husband and wife, stood in awe of their famous relation, but, to their great regret, during his present visit they were both in Moscow, so that the honor of receiving him went to a little old lady, a very distant and poor relation of the chamberlain's, who lived in their house and had long looked after all the housekeeping. With the arrival of Mr. Karmazinov, the household all began to go around on tiptoe. The little old lady notified Moscow almost daily of how he had reposed and upon what he had been pleased to dine, and once sent a telegram with the news that he had been obliged, after a formal dinner at the mayor's, to take a spoonful of a certain medication. She rarely ventured into his room, though he treated her politely, if dryly, and spoke with her only if there was some need. When Pyotr Stepanovich entered, he was eating his little morning cutlet with half a glass of red wine. Pyotr Stepanovich had visited him before and always found him over this little morning cutlet, which he went on eating in his presence without ever offering him anything. After the little cutlet, a small cup of coffee was served. The valet who brought the food wore a tailcoat, soft inaudible boots, and gloves.

"Ahh!" Karmazinov rose from the sofa, wiping his mouth with a napkin, and with an air of the purest joy came at him with his kisses—a habit characteristic of Russians if they are indeed so famous. But Pyotr Stepanovich recalled from previous experience that while he would come at you with his kisses, he would then let you have his cheek, and so this time he did the same; the two cheeks met.[9] Karmazinov, without showing that he had noticed it, sat down on the sofa and affably pointed Pyotr Stepanovich to the armchair facing him, in which the latter proceeded to sprawl.

"You wouldn't . . . Would you care for some lunch?" the host asked, abandoning his habit this time, but, of course, with an air that clearly prompted a polite refusal. Pyotr Stepanovich at once did care to have lunch. A shadow of hurt amazement darkened his host's face, but only for a moment; he nervously rang for the servant and, in spite of all his good breeding, raised his voice squeamishly as he ordered a second lunch to be served.

"What will you have, a cutlet or coffee?" he inquired once more.

"A cutlet and coffee, and have them bring more wine, I'm hungry," Pyotr Stepanovich replied, studying his host's attire with calm attention. Mr. Karmazinov was wearing a little quilted jerkin, a sort of jacket, with little mother-of-pearl buttons, but much too short, and which was not at all becoming to his rather well fed tummy and the solidly rounded beginnings of his legs; but tastes vary. The checkered woolen plaid on his knees unfolded to the floor, though the room was warm.

"Are you sick or something?" Pyotr Stepanovich remarked.

"No, not sick, but afraid of becoming sick in this climate," the writer replied in his sharp voice, though with a pleasantly aristocratic lisp, lovingly scanning each word. "I expected you yesterday."

"But why? I didn't promise."

"No, but you do have my manuscript. Have you . . . read it?"

"Manuscript? What manuscript?"

Karmazinov was terribly surprised.

"But, anyhow, you did bring it with you?" he suddenly grew so alarmed that he even left off eating and looked at Pyotr Stepanovich with frightened eyes.

"Ah, this *Bonjour* you mean . . ."

"*Merci.*"

"Well, all right. I completely forgot, and I haven't read it, I have no time. I don't know, really, it's not in my pockets . . . must be on my desk. Don't worry, it'll turn up."

"No, better if I send to your place for it now. It may disappear, or get stolen, finally."

"But, who needs it! And why are you so frightened? Yulia Mikhailovna says you always have several copies stashed away, one abroad with a notary, another in Petersburg, a third in Moscow, then you send one to the bank, or whatever."

"But Moscow can also burn down, and my manuscript with it. No, I'd better send right now."

"Wait, here it is!" Pyotr Stepanovich took a bundle of writing paper from his back pocket. "It got a bit crumpled. Imagine, it's been there in my back pocket all this time, along with my handkerchief, just as I took it from you then; I forgot."

Karmazinov greedily snatched the manuscript, carefully looked it over, counted the pages, and placed it respectfully beside him for the time being, on a special little table, but so as to keep it in view at all times.

"It seems you don't read so much," he hissed, unable to restrain himself.

"No, not so much."

"And in the line of Russian belles lettres—nothing?"

"In the line of Russian belles lettres? Let me see, I did read something . . . *On the Way* . . . or *Make Way* . . . or *By the Wayside*, [10] possibly—I don't remember. I read it long ago, five years or so. I have no time."

Some silence ensued.

"I assured them all, as soon as I arrived, that you are a great mind, and now it seems they've all lost their minds over you."

"Thank you," Pyotr Stepanovich replied calmly.

Lunch was brought. Pyotr Stepanovich fell upon the little cutlet with great appetite, ate it instantly, drank the wine, and gulped down the coffee.

"This ignoramus," Karmazinov studied him pensively out of the corner of his eye as he finished the last little morsel and drank the last little sip, "this ignoramus probably understood all the sharpness of my phrase just now . . . and he certainly read the manuscript eagerly and is just lying with something in mind. Yet it may also be that he's not lying, but is quite genuinely stupid. I like it when a man of genius is somewhat stupid. Isn't he really some sort of genius hereabouts? Devil take him, anyway."

He got up from the sofa and began pacing the room slowly, from corner to corner, for exercise—something he performed every day after lunch.

"Leaving soon?" Pyotr Stepanovich asked from the armchair, having lighted a cigarette.

"I came to sell my estate, actually, and am now entirely dependent on my manager."

"But it seems you came because an epidemic was expected there after the war?"

"N-no, it wasn't quite that," Mr. Karmazinov continued, scanning his words benignly, and kicking his right leg out briskly, though only slightly, each time he turned back from a corner. "Indeed," he grinned, not without venom, "I intend to live as long as possible. There is something in the Russian gentry that very quickly wears out, in all respects. But I want to wear out as late as possible, and am now moving abroad for good; the climate is better there, and they build in stone, and everything is stronger. Europe will last my lifetime, I think. What do you think?"

"How should I know?"

"Hm. If their Babylon is indeed going to collapse, and great will be its fall[11] (in which I fully agree with you, though I do think it will last my lifetime), here in Russia there is nothing to collapse, comparatively speaking. We won't have stones tumbling down, everything will dissolve into mud. Holy Russia is least capable in all the world of resisting anything. Simple people still hang on somehow by the Russian God; but the Russian God, according to the latest reports, is rather unreliable and even barely managed to withstand the peasant reform; anyway he tottered badly. And what with the railroads, and what with your . . . no, I don't believe in the Russian God at all."

"And in the European one?"

"I don't believe in any. I've been slandered to the Russian youth. I've always sympathized with every movement of theirs. I was shown these local tracts. They're regarded with perplexity because everyone is frightened by the form, but everyone is nonetheless certain of their power, though they may not be aware of it. Everyone has long been falling, and everyone has long known that there is nothing to cling to. I'm convinced of the success of this mysterious propaganda even owing to this alone, that Russia now is preeminently the place in the whole world where anything you like can happen without the least resistance. I understand only too well why the moneyed Russians have all been pouring abroad, more and more of them every year. It's simple instinct. If a ship is about to sink, the rats are the first to leave it. Holy Russia is a wooden country, a beggarly and . . . dangerous one, a country of vainglorious beggars in its upper strata, while the vast majority live in huts on chicken legs.[12] She'll be glad of any way out, once it has been explained to her. The government alone still wants to resist, but it brandishes its cudgel in the dark and strikes its own. Everything is doomed and sentenced here. Russia as she is has no future. I've become a German and count it an honor."

"No, but you began about the tracts; tell me everything, how do you look at them?"

"Everyone is afraid of them, which means they're powerful. They openly expose deceit and prove that we have nothing to cling to and nothing to lean on. They speak out, while everyone is silent. The most winning thing about them (despite the form) is this hitherto unheard-of boldness in looking truth straight in the face. This ability to look truth straight in the face belongs only to the Russian generation. No, in Europe they are still not so bold: theirs is a kingdom of stone, they still have something to lean on. As far as I can see and am able to judge, the whole essence of the Russian revolutionary idea consists in a denial of honor. I like the way it is so boldly and fearlessly expressed. No, in Europe they still won't understand it, but here it is precisely what they will fall upon. For the Russian, honor is simply a superfluous burden. And it has always been a burden, throughout his history. He can be all the sooner carried away by an open 'right to dishonor.'[13] I am of the old generation and, I confess, still stand for honor, but only from habit. I simply like the old forms, say it's from faintheartedness; I do have to live my life out somehow."

He suddenly paused.

"I talk and talk, however," he thought, "and he says nothing and keeps an eye on me. He came so that I'd ask him a direct question. And I will ask it."

"Yulia Mikhailovna asked me to trick you somehow into telling what this surprise is that you're preparing for the ball the day after tomorrow," Pyotr Stepanovich said suddenly.

"Yes, it will indeed be a surprise, and I will indeed amaze . . ." Karmazinov assumed a dignified air, "but I won't tell you what the secret is."

Pyotr Stepanovich did not insist.

"There's some Shatov here," the great writer inquired, "and, imagine, I haven't seen him."

"A very nice person. So?"

"That's all. He's talking about something. Was he the one who slapped Stavrogin in the face?"

"Yes."

"And what do you think of Stavrogin?"

"I don't know—some sort of philanderer."

Karmazinov had come to hate Stavrogin, because he made a habit of taking no notice of him.

"This philanderer," he said, tittering, "will probably be the first to be hung from a limb, if what's preached in those tracts ever gets carried out."

"Maybe even sooner," Pyotr Stepanovich said suddenly.

"And so it should be," Karmazinov echoed, not laughing now, but somehow all too serious.

"You already said that once, and, you know, I told him so."

"What, you really told him?" Karmazinov laughed again.

"He said if it was hanging from a limb for him, a whipping would be enough for you, only not an honorary one, but painful, the way they whip a peasant."

Pyotr Stepanovich took his hat and got up from his place. Karmazinov held out both hands to him in farewell.

"And what," he peeped suddenly, in a honeyed little voice and with some special intonation, still holding his hands in his own, "what if all . . . that's being planned . . . were set to be carried out, then when . . . might it happen?"

"How should I know?" Pyotr Stepanovich replied, somewhat rudely. They gazed intently into each other's eyes.

"Roughly? Approximately?" Karmazinov peeped still more sweetly.

"You'll have time to sell the estate, and time to clear out as well," Pyotr Stepanovich muttered, still more rudely. They both gazed at each other still more intently.

There was a minute of silence.

"It will begin by the beginning of next May, and be all over by the Protection,"[14] Pyotr Stepanovich said suddenly.

"I sincerely thank you," Karmazinov said in a heartfelt voice, squeezing his hands.

"You'll have time, rat, to leave the ship!" Pyotr Stepanovich thought as he came outside. "Well, if even this 'all but statesmanly mind' is inquiring so confidently about the day and the hour, and thanks one so respectfully for the information received, we cannot doubt ourselves after that." (He grinned.) "Hm. And he's really not stupid, and . . . just a migratory rat; that kind won't inform!"

He ran to Bogoyavlensky Street, to Filippov's house.

VI

Pyotr Stepanovich went first to Kirillov. He was alone, as usual, and this time was doing exercises in the middle of the room—that is, he was standing with his legs apart, whirling his arms above his head in some special way. A ball was lying on the floor. The morning tea, already cold, had not been cleared from the table. Pyotr Stepanovich paused on the threshold for a minute.

"You take good care of your health, though," he said loudly and gaily, stepping into the room. "What a nice ball, though; look how it bounces! Is this also for exercise?"

Kirillov put his jacket on.

"Yes, also for health," he muttered dryly, "sit down."

"It's just for a minute. Still, I'll sit down. Health is health, but I've come to remind you of our agreement. Our time, sir, is 'in a certain sense' approaching," he concluded with an awkward twist.

"What agreement?"

"You ask, what agreement?" Pyotr Stepanovich got fluttered up, even frightened.

"It's not an agreement, or a duty, I'm bound by nothing, there's a mistake on your part."

"Listen, what is this you're doing?" Pyotr Stepanovich jumped all the way up.

"My will."

"Which is?"

"The same."

"I mean, how am I to understand that? You're still of the same mind?"

"I am. Only there is not and was not any agreement, and I'm bound by nothing. There was just my will, and now there is just my will."

Kirillov was talking abruptly and squeamishly.

"I agree, I agree, let it be your will, as long as this will doesn't change," Pyotr Stepanovich settled down again with a satisfied air. "You get angry at words. You've somehow become very angry lately;

that's why I've avoided visiting. I was completely sure, by the way, that you wouldn't change."

"I dislike you very much; but you can be completely sure. Though I do not recognize changes and non-changes."

"You know, though," Pyotr Stepanovich got fluttered up again, "why don't we talk it all over properly, so as not to be confused. The matter requires precision, and you disconcert me terribly. Am I permitted to speak?"

"Speak," Kirillov said curtly, looking into the corner.

"You resolved long ago to take your own life . . . I mean, you did have such an idea. Have I put it right? Is there any mistake?"

"I have such an idea now, too."

"Wonderful. And note, also, that no one has forced you into it."

"To be sure; how stupidly you talk."

"All right, all right, so I put it very stupidly. No doubt it would be very stupid to force such things. To go on: you were a member of the Society under the old organization, and it was then that you confided it to one member of the Society."

"I did not confide it, I simply told it."

"All right. It would be ridiculous to 'confide' such a thing—what sort of confession is it? You simply told it. Wonderful."

"No, not wonderful, because you maunder so. I don't owe you any accounting, and you're not capable of understanding my thoughts. I want to take my own life because I have this thought, because I do not want the fear of death, because . . . because there's nothing here for you to know . . . What is it? Want some tea? It's cold. Let me get you another glass."

Indeed, Pyotr Stepanovich had grabbed the teapot and was looking for an empty receptacle. Kirillov went to the cupboard and brought a clean glass.

"I just had lunch with Karmazinov," the visitor observed, "listened to him talk, got sweaty, then ran here and again got sweaty, I'm dying of thirst."

"Drink. Cold tea is good."

Kirillov sat down on his chair again, and again stared into the corner.

"A thought occurred in the Society," he went on in the same voice, "that I could be useful if I killed myself, and that one day when you got into some kind of mischief and they were looking for culprits, I could suddenly shoot myself and leave a letter that I had done it all, so that they wouldn't suspect you for a whole year."

"Or at least a few days; even one day is precious."

"Very well. In that sense I was told to wait if I liked. I said I would, until I was told the time by the Society, because it makes no difference to me."

"Yes, but remember you pledged that when you wrote the dying letter it would not be without me, and that on my arrival in Russia you would be at my . . . well, in short, at my disposal, that is, for this occasion alone, of course, and in all others you are certainly free," Pyotr Stepanovich added, almost courteously.

"I did not pledge, I consented, because it makes no difference to me."

"Wonderful, wonderful, I don't have the slightest intention of dampening your pride, but . . ."

"This is not pride."

"But remember that a hundred and twenty thalers were collected for your trip, so you took money."

"Not at all," Kirillov flared up, "not for that. One does not take money for that."

"Sometimes one does."

"You're lying. I declared in a letter from Petersburg, and in Petersburg I paid you a hundred and twenty thalers, handed them to you . . . and they were sent there, unless you kept them."

"Very well, very well, I'm not disputing anything, they were sent. The main thing is that you're of the same mind as before."

"The same. When you come and say 'it's time,' I'll fulfill everything. What, very soon?"

"Not so many days . . . But remember, we compose the note together, that same night."

"Or day, even. You say I must take the blame for the tracts?"

"And something else."

"I won't take everything on myself."

"What won't you take?" Pyotr Stepanovich got fluttered up again.

"Whatever I don't want to; enough. I don't want to talk about it anymore."

Pyotr Stepanovich restrained himself and changed the subject.

"Here's another thing," he warned. "Will you join us this evening? It's Virginsky's name day, that's the pretext for the gathering."

"I don't want to."

"Do me a favor and come. You must. You must, to impress them with numbers, and with your face . . . Your face is . . . well, in short, you have a fatal face."

"You find it so?" laughed Kirillov. "Very well, I'll come. Only not for my face. When?"

"Oh, earlyish, half past six. And, you know, you can come in, sit down, and not speak to anyone, however many there are. Only, you know, don't forget to bring a pencil and paper with you."

"What for?"

"It makes no difference to you anyway; and it's my special request. You'll just sit without speaking to anyone at all, listen, and from time to time make as if you're taking notes; well, you can draw something."

"Nonsense, what for?"

"Since it makes no difference to you; you do keep saying that it makes no difference to you."

"No, but what for?"

"Because that member of our Society, the inspector, got stuck in Moscow, and I announced to someone or other here that the inspector might visit us; so they'll think the inspector is you, and since you've been here for three weeks already, they'll be all the more surprised."

"Flimflam! You have no inspector in Moscow."

"Well, suppose I haven't, devil take him, is that any business of yours? And why is it so hard for you to do it? You are a member of the Society."

"Tell them I'm the inspector; I'll sit and be silent, but the pencil and paper I don't want."

"But why?"

"I don't want it."

Pyotr Stepanovich became angry, even turned green, but again restrained himself, got up, and took his hat.

"Is *he* here?" he suddenly said in a half-whisper.

"Yes."

"Good. I'll have him out soon, don't worry."

"I don't worry. He just spends nights here. The old woman is in the hospital, the daughter-in-law died; for two days I've been alone. I showed him a place in the fence where a board can be removed; he gets in, no one sees him."

"I'll take him away soon."

"He says he has many places to spend the night."

"That's a lie, they're looking for him, and here so far it's inconspicuous. Do you really get to talking with him?"

"Yes, all night. He says very bad things about you. I read him the Apocalypse at night, with tea. He listened hard; even very, all night."

"Ah, the devil, you'll convert him to the Christian faith!"

"He's of Christian faith as it is. Don't worry, he'll use his knife. Whom do you want to put a knife into?"

"No, that's not what I'm keeping him for; he's for something else . . . And does Shatov know about Fedka?"

"I don't talk and never see Shatov."

"Is he angry, or what?"

"No, we're not angry, we just turn away. We spent too long lying together in America."

"I'll go to him now."

"As you like."

"Stavrogin and I may also come to you from there, somewhere around ten o'clock."

"Come."

"I have to talk with him about an important . . . You know, why don't you give me your ball? What do you need it for now? I, too, for exercise. I'll even pay money for it."

"Just take it."

Pyotr Stepanovich put the ball in his back pocket.

"And I won't give you anything against Stavrogin," Kirillov muttered behind him, letting his visitor out. The latter looked at him in surprise, but did not respond.

Kirillov's last words confused Pyotr Stepanovich greatly; he still had not had time to make sense of them, but going up the stairs to see

Shatov he tried to recompose his displeased look into a benign physiognomy. Shatov was at home and slightly ill. He was lying on his bed,
though dressed.

"What bad luck!" Pyotr Stepanovich cried out from the threshold.
"Are you seriously ill?"

The benign expression on his face suddenly vanished; something
spiteful flashed in his eyes.

"Not in the least," Shatov jumped up nervously, "I'm not ill at all,
my head is a little . . ."

He was even at a loss; the sudden appearance of such a visitor
decidedly frightened him.

"The matter I've come on is such that it would be better not to be
sick," Pyotr Stepanovich began quickly and as if peremptorily. "Allow
me to sit down" (he sat down), "and you sit back down on your cot,
so. Today some of our people are getting together at Virginsky's,
under the pretense of his birthday; there will be no other tinge—that's
been seen to. I'll come with Nikolai Stavrogin. I certainly wouldn't
drag you there, knowing your present way of thinking . . . I mean, in
the sense of not wanting to torment you there, and not because we
think you'd inform. But it turns out that you'll have to go. You'll meet
those people there with whom we will finally decide the manner of
your leaving the Society, and to whom you will hand over what you
have. We'll do it inconspicuously; I'll lead you to some corner; there
will be a lot of people, and there's no need for everyone to know. I
confess I did have to exercise my tongue on your behalf; but now it
seems that they, too, agree, with the understanding, of course, that you
hand over the press and all the papers. Then you can go to the four
winds."

Shatov listened frowningly and spitefully. His recent nervous fright
had left him altogether.

"I do not acknowledge any obligation to give an accounting to the
devil knows whom," he stated flatly. "No one can set me free."

"Not quite so. A lot was entrusted to you. You had no right to break
it off so directly. And, finally, you never announced it clearly, so you
led them into an ambiguous position."

"As soon as I came here I announced it clearly in a letter."

"No, not clearly," Pyotr Stepanovich disputed calmly. "For instance, I sent you 'The Shining Light' to print here, and to keep the copies somewhere here with you until called for; and two tracts as well. You sent it all back with an ambiguous letter that meant nothing."

"I directly refused to print it."

"Yes, but not directly. You wrote: 'Am unable,' but did not explain for what reason. 'Unable' doesn't mean 'unwilling.' It could be supposed that you were unable simply for material reasons. In fact, they took it that way, and supposed that you still agreed to continue your connection with the Society, and so they might have entrusted you with something again, and thus have compromised themselves. Here they say you simply wanted to deceive, so that, having obtained important information, you could then denounce them. I defended you all I could, and showed your two-line written reply as a document in your favor. But I myself had to admit, on rereading it, that those two lines are vague and lead one into deception."

"And you've preserved this letter so carefully?"

"That I've preserved it is nothing; I have it even now."

"Who the devil cares! . . ." Shatov cried out furiously. "Let your fools think I denounced them, it's not my business! I'd like to see what you can do to me."

"You'd be marked out and hanged at the first success of the revolution."

"That's when you seize supreme power and subjugate Russia?"

"Don't laugh. I repeat, I stood up for you. One way or another, I'd still advise you to come today. Why waste words because of some false pride? Isn't it better to part amicably? Because you'll have to hand over the press and the type and the old papers in any case, so we can talk about that."

"I'll come," Shatov growled, hanging his head in thought. Pyotr Stepanovich studied him out of the corner of his eye from where he sat.

"Will Stavrogin be there?" Shatov suddenly asked, raising his head.

"Quite certainly."

"Heh, heh!"

Again they were silent for about a minute. Shatov was grinning squeamishly and irritably.

"And that vile 'Shining Light' of yours, which I didn't want to print here, did it get printed?"

"It did."

"To persuade schoolboys that Herzen himself wrote it into your album?"

"Herzen himself."

Again they were silent for about three minutes. Shatov finally rose from the bed.

"Get out of here from me, I don't want to sit with you."

"I'm going," Pyotr Stepanovich said, even somehow gaily, rising at once. "Only one word: it seems Kirillov is all by himself in the wing now, without any maid?"

"All by himself. Get out, I can't stay in the same room with you."

"Well, aren't you in a fine state now!" Pyotr Stepanovich reflected gaily as he was going out, "and so you will be in the evening, and that's precisely how I want you now, I could wish for nothing better, nothing better! The Russian God himself is helping out!"

VII

HE PROBABLY BUSTLED about a good deal that day on various little errands—and it must have been with success—which reflected itself in the smug expression of his physiognomy when in the evening, at six o'clock sharp, he appeared at Nikolai Vsevolodovich's. But he was not shown in to him at once; Mavriky Nikolaevich had just shut himself up with Nikolai Vsevolodovich in the study. This news instantly worried him. He sat down right by the door of the study to wait until the visitor came out. The conversation could be heard, but he was unable to catch the words. The visit did not last long; soon there was noise, an unexpectedly loud and sharp voice was heard, then the door opened and out came Mavriky Nikolaevich with a completely pale face. He did not notice Pyotr Stepanovich and quickly walked past. Pyotr Stepanovich at once ran into the study.

I cannot avoid a detailed account of this extremely brief meeting of the two "rivals"—a meeting seemingly impossible under the circumstances, but which nonetheless took place.

It happened like this. Nikolai Vsevolodovich was dozing after dinner on the sofa in his study when Alexei Yegorovich reported the
arrival of an unexpected visitor. On hearing the name announced, he
even jumped up from his place and would not believe it. But soon a
smile flashed on his lips—a smile of haughty triumph and at the same
time of a certain dull, mistrustful amazement. The entering Mavriky
Nikolaevich seemed struck by the expression of this smile; at least he
paused suddenly in the middle of the room as if undecided whether
to go on or turn back. The host at once managed to change his face,
and with a look of earnest perplexity stepped forward to meet him.
The man did not take the proffered hand, moved a chair out awkwardly, and, not saying a word, sat down even before the host, without
waiting to be invited. Nikolai Vsevolodovich sat himself down sideways on the sofa and, scrutinizing Mavriky Nikolaevich, waited
silently.

"If you can, then marry Lizaveta Nikolaevna," Mavriky Nikolaevich suddenly offered, and, what was most curious, it was quite
impossible to tell by the tone of his voice whether it was a request, a
recommendation, a concession, or an order.

Nikolai Vsevolodovich continued to be silent; but the visitor had
evidently said all he had come for, and was staring at him point-blank,
awaiting an answer.

"Unless I'm mistaken (though it's all too true), Lizaveta Nikolaevna
is already engaged to you," Stavrogin said at last.

"Betrothed and engaged," Mavriky Nikolaevich firmly and clearly
confirmed.

"You've . . . quarreled? . . . Excuse me, Mavriky Nikolaevich."

"No, she 'loves and respects' me—the words are hers. Her words are
more precious than anything."

"There's no doubt of that."

"But you should know that if she were standing right at the altar,
and you were to call her, she would drop me and everyone and go
to you."

"From the altar?"

"And after the altar."

"You're not mistaken?"

"No. From behind her ceaseless, genuine, and most complete hatred for you, love flashes every moment, and . . . madness . . . the most genuine and boundless love and—madness! On the contrary, from behind the love she feels for me, also genuinely, hatred flashes every moment—the greatest hatred! I could never have imagined all these . . . metamorphoses . . . before."

"But still it surprises me, how could you come and dispose of Lizaveta Nikolaevna's hand? Do you have the right to do that? Or did she authorize you?"

Mavriky Nikolaevich frowned and cast down his head for a moment.

"These are only just words on your part," he said suddenly, "vengeful and triumphant words: I'm sure you understand what's been left unspoken between the lines, and is there any place here for petty vanity? Aren't you satisfied enough? Is there really any need to smear it around, to dot all the *i*'s? As you wish, I will dot them, if you need my humiliation so much: I have no right, no authorization is possible; Lizaveta Nikolaevna doesn't know about anything, and her fiancé has lost his last wits and is fit for the madhouse, and to crown it all he comes himself to report it to you. You alone in the whole world can make her happy, and I alone—unhappy. You contend for her, you pursue her, but, I don't know why, you will not marry her. If it's some lovers' quarrel that happened abroad, and I must be sacrificed to end it—sacrifice me. She is too unhappy, and I cannot bear it. My words are not a permission, not a prescription, and so there is no insult to your pride. If you wanted to take my place at the altar, you could do it without any permission on my part, and there was certainly no point in my coming to you with my madness. Especially as our marriage is no longer possible at all after this step of mine. I can't lead her to the altar when I'm a scoundrel. What I am doing here and my handing her over to you, perhaps her most implacable enemy, is in my view the act of a scoundrel, which I, of course, will never be able to endure."

"Will you shoot yourself as we're getting married?"

"No, much later. Why stain her wedding garment with my blood. Maybe I won't shoot myself at all, either now or later."

"You probably wish to set me at ease by saying so?"

"You? What could one more splash of blood mean to you?"

He turned pale and his eyes flashed. A minute of silence followed.

"Excuse me for the questions I've put to you," Stavrogin began again. "Some of them I had no right to put, but to one of them it seems to me I have every right: tell me what facts led you to conclude about my feelings for Lizaveta Nikolaevna? I mean with regard to the degree of those feelings, the certainty of which allowed you to come to me and . . . risk such a suggestion."

"What?" Mavriky Nikolaevich even gave a slight start. "But haven't you been seeking after her? You were not seeking and do not want to seek after her?"

"In general, I cannot speak aloud about my feelings for this or that woman to a third person, or to anyone at all except that one woman. Excuse me, it's an oddity of my organism. But instead of that I'll tell you the whole rest of the truth: I am married, and it is no longer possible for me to marry or 'to seek after.' "

Mavriky Nikolaevich was so amazed that he recoiled against the back of his armchair, and for a while stared fixedly at Stavrogin's face.

"Imagine, I somehow didn't think of that," he muttered. "You said then, that morning, that you weren't married . . . and so I believed you weren't married . . ."

He was growing terribly pale; suddenly he banged his fist on the table with all his might.

"If after such a confession you do not leave Lizaveta Nikolaevna alone, and keep making her unhappy, I'll kill you with a stick like a dog in a ditch!"

He jumped up and quickly walked out of the room. Pyotr Stepanovich, running in, found the host in a most unexpected frame of mind.

"Ah, it's you!" Stavrogin guffawed loudly; he seemed to be guffawing only at the figure of Pyotr Stepanovich, who ran in with such impetuous curiosity.

"You were eavesdropping at the door? Wait, what is it you've arrived with? I promised you something, I know . . . Aha! I remember: to go to 'our' people! Let's go, I'm very glad, and you couldn't have thought of anything more appropriate right now."

He grabbed his hat, and the two men left the house without delay.

"You're laughing ahead of time at seeing 'our' people?" Pyotr Stepanovich fidgeted gaily, now trying to keep in stride with his companion on the narrow brick sidewalk, now even running down into the roadway, right into the mud, since his companion was completely unaware that he was walking in the very middle of the sidewalk and thus occupying the whole of it with his own person.

"Not laughing in the least," Stavrogin answered loudly and gaily, "on the contrary, I'm sure you've got some serious folk there."

" 'Gloomy dullards,' as you were pleased to put it once."

"There's nothing gayer than certain gloomy dullards."

"Ah, you mean Mavriky Nikolaevich! I'm sure he came just now to give up his fiancée to you, eh? Imagine, it was I who set him onto that, indirectly. And if he doesn't give her up, we'll take her ourselves—eh?"

Pyotr Stepanovich knew, of course, the risk of allowing himself such flourishes, but when he was excited he preferred sooner to risk everything than to leave himself in ignorance. Nikolai Vsevolodovich merely laughed.

"And you still count on helping me?" he asked.

"If you call me. But, you know what, there's one way that's best."

"I know your way."

"Ah, no, so far it's a secret. Only remember, secrets cost money."

"I even know how much," Stavrogin growled under his breath, but checked himself and fell silent.

"How much? What did you say?" Pyotr Stepanovich fluttered up.

"I said: to hell with you and your secret! Better tell me who you've got there. I know we're going to a name-day party, but who, namely, will be there?"

"Oh, all sorts of things, in the highest degree! Even Kirillov."

"All members of circles?"

"Devil take it, you rush so! Not even one circle has taken place here yet."

"Then how did you manage to spread so many tracts?"

"Where we're going only four of them are members of the circle. The rest, while they wait, are spying on each other as hard as they can and bringing everything to me. Trustworthy folk. It's all material for us to organize, and then we clear out. However, you wrote the rules yourself, there's no need to explain to you."

"So, what, the going's hard? Got stuck?"

"The going? Easy as could be. This'll make you laugh: what first of all affects them terribly is a uniform. There's nothing stronger than a uniform. I purposely invent ranks and positions: I have secretaries, secret stool pigeons, treasurers, chairmen, registrars, their adjuncts— it's all very much liked and has caught on splendidly. Then the next force, naturally, is sentimentality. You know, with us socialism spreads mostly through sentimentality. But the trouble here is with these biting lieutenants; you get burned every so often. Then come the out-and-out crooks; well, they can be nice folk, very profitable on occasion, but they take up a lot of time, require constant surveillance. Well, and finally the main force—the cement that bonds it all—is shame at one's own opinion. There is a real force! And who was it that worked, who was the 'sweetie'[15] that labored so that there isn't a single idea of one's own left in anyone's head! They consider it shameful."

"But if so, why are you bustling about like this?"

"But if it's just lying there gaping at everybody, how can one help filching it! As if you don't seriously believe success is possible? Eh, the belief is there, it's the wanting that's needed. Yes, precisely with their sort success is possible. I tell you, I can get them to go through fire, if I just yell at them that they're not liberal enough. Fools reproach me for having hoodwinked everyone here with my central committee and 'numerous branches.' You yourself once reproached me with that, but where is there any hoodwinking: the central committee is you and me, and there can be as many branches as they like."

"And all with these dregs!"

"It's material. They, too, will come in useful."

"And you're still counting on me?"

"You are the chief, you are the force; I'll just be at your side, a secretary. You know, we shall board our bark, and her oars will be of maple, and her sails of silk, and in the stern there sits a beautiful maiden, the fair Lizaveta Nikolaevna . . . or how the devil does the song go . . ."[16]

"Muffed it!" Stavrogin burst out laughing. "No, I'd better give you the refrain. Here you're counting off on your fingers what forces make up a circle? All this officialdom and sentimentality—it's good glue, but there's one thing better still: get four members of a circle to bump off a fifth on the pretense of his being an informer, and with this shed blood you'll immediately tie them together in a single knot.[17] They'll become your slaves, they won't dare rebel or call you to accounts. Ha, ha, ha!"

"You, though . . . you're going to pay for those words, my friend," Pyotr Stepanovich thought to himself, "and even this very night. You allow yourself too much."

Thus, or almost thus, Pyotr Stepanovich must have reflected. However, they were already coming up to Virginsky's house.

"You've no doubt presented me there as some sort of member from abroad, connected with the Internationale, maybe an inspector?" Stavrogin suddenly asked.

"No, not an inspector; the inspector won't be you; you are a founding member from abroad who knows the most important secrets—that's your role. You are, of course, going to speak?"

"What gives you that idea?"

"You're obliged to speak now."

Stavrogin even stopped in surprise in the middle of the street, not far from a streetlamp. Pyotr Stepanovich met his gaze boldly and calmly. Stavrogin spat and walked on.

"And are you going to speak?" he suddenly asked Pyotr Stepanovich.

"No, I'd rather listen to you."

"Devil take you! In fact, you're giving me an idea!"

"What idea?" Pyotr Stepanovich popped up.

"Maybe I will speak there, in fact, but then I'm going to give you a beating, and a good one, you know."

"By the way, I told Karmazinov about you this morning, that you supposedly said about him that he ought to get a whipping, and not just an honorary one, but painful, the way they whip a peasant."

"But I never said that, ha, ha!"

"Never mind. *Se non è vero . . .*"[18]

"Well, thanks, I'm sincerely grateful."

"You know what else Karmazinov says? That essentially our teaching is a denial of honor, and that it's easiest of all to carry the Russian man with us by an open right to dishonor."

"Excellent words! Golden words!" Stavrogin cried. "He's put his finger on it! The right to dishonor—and everyone will come running to us, no one will stay there! Listen, Verkhovensky, you're not from the higher police, eh?"

"Whoever has such questions in his mind doesn't voice them."

"I understand, but we're among ourselves."

"No, so far I'm not from the higher police. Enough, we're here. Concoct your physiognomy, Stavrogin; I always do when I come to them. Add some extra gloom, that's all, no need for anything else; it's quite a simple thing."

7

With Our People

I

VIRGINSKY LIVED in his own house, that is, in his wife's house, on Muravyiny Street. It was a one-story wooden house, and there were no other lodgers in it. Under the pretense of the host's birthday about fifteen guests had gathered; but the party in no way resembled an ordinary provincial name-day party. From the very beginning of their cohabitation, the Virginsky spouses mutually resolved once and for all that to invite guests for one's name day was perfectly stupid, and besides "there's nothing at all to be glad about." In a few years they had somehow managed to distance themselves completely from society. He, though a man of ability, and by no means a "poor sort," for some reason seemed to everyone an odd man who loved solitude and, moreover, spoke "arrogantly." While Madame Virginsky herself, who practiced the profession of midwife, by that alone stood lowest of all on the social ladder, even lower than the priest's wife, despite her husband's rank as an officer. As for the humility befitting her station, this could not be observed in her at all. And after a most stupid and unforgivably open liaison, on principle, with a certain crook, one Captain Lebyadkin, even the most lenient of our ladies turned away from her with remarkable disdain. Yet Madame Virginsky took it all as if it were just what she wanted. Remarkably, the very same severe ladies, should they happen to be in an interesting condition, turned if possible to Arina Prokhorovna (Virginsky, that is), bypassing the other three *accoucheuses* of our town. She was summoned even by country landowners' wives—so great was everyone's belief in her knowledge, luck, and adroitness in critical cases. The end was that she began to practice solely in the wealthiest houses; and she loved money to the point of greed. Having fully sensed her power, she finally stopped restraining her character altogether. Perhaps it was even on purpose that, while working in the most distinguished houses, she would frighten a nervous woman in childbed with some unheard-of nihilistic forgetting of decency, or, finally, with her mockery of "all that's holy," precisely at moments when "the holy" might have been most useful. Our army doctor, Rozanov, an *accoucheur* himself, bore positive witness that once, when a woman in labor was howling in pain and calling on the almighty name of God, it was precisely one of these freethinking outbursts from Arina Prokhorovna, sudden "like a rifle shot," that, by affecting the patient with fright, contributed to a most speedy delivery. But, though a nihilist, in case of necessity Arina Prokhorovna would not shrink at all, not only from social, but even from age-old, most prejudiced customs, if they could be of use to her. Not for anything would she miss, for example, the baptism of a baby she had delivered, and she would appear wearing a green silk dress with a train, and with her chignon combed into curls and ringlets, while at all other times she reached the point of reveling in her own slovenliness. And though she always maintained "a most insolent air" during the performance of the sacrament, to the embarrassment of the clergy, once the rite had been performed, it was she who unfailingly brought out the champagne (this was why she came, and got so dressed up), and woe to anyone who tried to take a glass from her without paying something "into the pot."

The guests who gathered at Virginsky's this time (almost all men) had some sort of accidental and urgent look.[1] There were no refreshments or cards. In the middle of the big drawing room, papered with supremely old blue wallpaper, two tables had been moved together and covered with a big tablecloth, not quite clean, incidentally, and on them two samovars were boiling. A huge tray with twenty-five glasses and a basket of ordinary French bread cut up into many slices, somewhat as in upper-class male and female children's boarding schools, occupied the end of the table. Tea was poured by a thirty-year-old maiden lady, the hostess's sister, browless and pale-haired, a silent and venomous being, but who shared in the new views, and of whom Virginsky, in his domestic existence, was terribly afraid. All together there were three ladies in the room: the hostess herself, her browless sister, and Virginsky's sister, the young Miss Virginsky, who had just got in from Petersburg. Arina Prokhorovna, an imposing lady of about twenty-seven, not bad-looking, somewhat unkempt, in a non-festive woolen dress of a greenish shade, was sitting and looking over her guests with a dauntless gaze, as if hastening to say with her eyes: "See how I'm not afraid of anything at all." The visiting Miss Virginsky, also not bad-looking, a student and a nihilist, well fed and well packed, like a little ball, with very red cheeks, and of short stature, had placed herself next to Arina Prokhorovna, still almost in her traveling clothes, with some bundle of papers in her hand, and was studying the guests with impatient, leaping eyes. Virginsky himself was somewhat unwell that evening, but he nevertheless came out and sat in an armchair at the tea table. The guests were all sitting down as well, and this decorous disposition on chairs around a table gave the suggestion of a meeting. Obviously they were all waiting for something, and, while waiting, engaged each other in loud but as if irrelevant conversation. When Stavrogin and Verkhovensky appeared, everything suddenly became hushed.

But I will allow myself some comments by way of clarification.

I believe that all these gentlemen had indeed gathered then in the pleasant hope of hearing something especially curious, and had been so informed before they gathered. They represented the flower of the most bright red liberalism in our ancient town and had been quite carefully selected by Virginsky for this "meeting." I will also note that some among them (though very few) had never visited him before. Of course, the majority of the guests had no clear notion of why they had been so informed. True, at that time they all took Pyotr Stepanovich for a visiting foreign emissary with plenary powers; this idea had somehow immediately taken root and, naturally, was flattering. And yet in this bunch of citizens gathered under the pretense of a name-day celebration, there were some to whom certain proposals had already been made. Pyotr Verkhovensky had managed to slap up a "fivesome" in our town, similar to the one he already had going in Moscow and also, as it now turns out, among the officers in our district. They say he had one in Kh—— province as well. These five elect were now sitting at the general table and managed to feign quite skillfully the look of the most ordinary people, so that no one could recognize them. These were—since it is no longer a secret—first, Liputin, then Virginsky himself, long-eared Shigalyov (Mrs. Virginsky's brother), Lyamshin, and, finally, a certain Tolkachenko—a strange character, already a man of forty, and famous for his vast study of the people, predominantly crooks and robbers, for which purpose he frequented the pot-houses (not only to study the people, however), and who flaunted among us his bad clothing, tarred boots, squintingly sly look, and frilly folk expressions. Lyamshin had already brought him once or twice to Stepan Trofimovich's evenings, where, however, he had produced no special effect. He would appear in town every so often, mostly when he was out of a job, and he used to work for the railroad. All five of these activists made up this first crew in the warm belief that it was just one unit among hundreds and thousands of fivesomes of the same sort scattered all over Russia, and that they all depended on some central, enormous, but secret place, which in turn was organically linked with Europe's world revolution. But, unfortunately, I must confess that even then there had begun to be discord among them. The thing was that though they had been expecting Pyotr Verkhovensky since spring, as had been announced to them first by Tolkachenko and then by the newly arrived Shigalyov, though they were expecting extraordinary miracles from him, and though they had all come at once, without the slightest criticism and at his first call, to join the circle, yet they had no sooner made up the fivesome than they all at once became offended, as it were, and precisely, I suppose, because of the quickness of their consent. They had joined, of course, out of a magnanimous sense of shame, so that no one could say later that they had not dared to join; but, still, Pyotr Verkhovensky ought really to have appreciated their noble deed and at least have told them some foremost anecdote as a reward. But Verkhovensky did not have the slightest wish to satisfy their legitimate curiosity, and would not tell them anything unnecessary; generally, he treated them with remarkable sternness and even casualness. This was decidedly irritating, and member Shigalyov was already instigating the others "to demand an accounting," but, of course, not now, at Virginsky's, where so many outsiders had gathered.

Speaking of outsiders, I also have an idea that the above-named members of the first fivesome were inclined to suspect that among Virginsky's guests that evening there were members of other groups unknown to them, also started in town from the same secret organization, and by the selfsame Verkhovensky, so that in the end all of those gathered suspected each other, and assumed various postures in front of each other, which indeed lent the whole gathering a rather incoherent and even partly romantic appearance. However, there were also people there who were beyond any suspicion. Such, for example, was one active army major, Virginsky's close relative, a completely innocent man, who had not even been invited, but had come on his own to celebrate the name day, so that it was simply impossible not to receive him. But anyhow Virginsky was not worried, because the major "simply could not denounce them"; for, despite all his stupidity, he had been fond throughout his life of scurrying around all those places where extreme liberals are to be found; did not sympathize himself, but liked very much to listen. Moreover, he had even been compromised once: it so happened that in his youth whole warehouses of *The Bell*[2] and various tracts had passed through his hands, and though he had been afraid even to unfold them, he would still have regarded the refusal to disseminate them as perfect baseness—and there are some Russians of his sort even to this day. The remainder of the guests represented either the type of noble amour-propre crushed to the point of bile, or the type of the first and noblest impulse of fervent youth. These were two or three teachers, one of whom was lame, already about forty-five, an instructor in the high school, an extremely venomous and remarkably vain man, and two or three officers. Of the latter, one was a very young artillerist who had arrived just the other day from some military school, a silent boy who had not yet had time to make acquaintances, and who now suddenly turned up at Virginsky's with a pencil in his hand and, almost without taking part in the conversation, kept jotting things down in his notebook. Everyone saw this, but for some reason everyone tried to make it seem as if they had not noticed. There was also the loaf-about seminarian who together with Lyamshin had slipped the vile photographs into the book-hawker's bag, a big fellow with a free and easy but at the same time mistrustful manner, with a perpetually accusatory smile, and along with that a calm look of triumphant perfection contained within himself. There was, I have no idea why, also the son of our mayor, that same nasty boy, dissipated beyond his years, whom I have already mentioned while telling the story of the lieutenant's little wife. He was silent all evening. And finally, in conclusion, there was a high-school student, a very hot-headed and disheveled boy of about eighteen, who sat with the glum look of a young man whose dignity has been insulted, and suffered visibly on account of his eighteen years. This mite of a lad was already the head of an independent crew of conspirators formed in the upper grade of the high school, which fact was discovered afterwards to general amazement. I have not mentioned Shatov: he was sitting right there at the far corner of the table, his chair moved slightly out of line; he looked down, was gloomily silent, refused tea and bread, and would not let go of his peaked cap all the while, as if wishing thereby to declare that he was not a guest but had come on business, and could get up and leave whenever he liked. Not far from him sat Kirillov, also quite silent, though he did not look down but, on the contrary, examined each speaker point-blank with his fixed, lusterless stare, and listened to everything without the least emotion or surprise. Some of the guests who had never seen him before studied him stealthily and pensively. It is not known whether Madame Virginsky herself knew anything about the existence of the fivesome. I suppose she knew everything, and precisely from her husband. The girl student, of course, did not participate in any way, but she had her own concern: she intended to stay only for a day or two, and then go on farther and farther, to all the university towns, to "share the suffering lot of the poor students and arouse them to protest." She was bringing with her several hundred lithographed copies of an appeal— of her own composition, it would seem. Remarkably, the high-school boy hated her from first sight almost to the point of blood vengeance, though it was the first time he had seen her in his life, and she him. The major was her uncle, and met her that day for the first time in ten years. When Stavrogin and Verkhovensky entered, her cheeks were as red as cranberries: she had just had a spat with her uncle over their views of the woman question.

II

VERKHOVENSKY sprawled himself with remarkable casualness on a chair at the upper corner of the table, greeting almost no one. His look was squeamish, and even arrogant. Stavrogin politely made his bows, but, despite the fact that everyone had been waiting only for them, everyone, as if on command, pretended that they had scarcely noticed them. The hostess sternly addressed Stavrogin as soon as he sat down.

"Stavrogin, you want tea?"

"Thanks," he replied.

"Tea for Stavrogin," she commanded the pouring woman, "and what about you?" (this was now to Verkhovensky).

"Of course I do, what a thing to ask a guest! And give me cream, too. You always serve such vileness instead of tea—and for a name-day party at that."

"What, you also recognize name days?" the girl student suddenly laughed. "We were just talking about that."

"It's old hat," the high-school boy grumbled from the other end of the table.

"What is old hat? To forget prejudices, innocent though they may be, isn't old hat but, on the contrary, to everyone's shame, is so far still new," the girl student instantly declared, simply lunging forward from her chair. "Besides, there are no innocent prejudices," she added bitterly.

"I just wanted to state," the high-school boy became terribly excited, "that although prejudices are, of course, old and need to be wiped out, yet concerning name days everybody already knows they're stupid and too old hat to waste precious time on, which has been wasted by the whole world even without that, so as to use one's wits for some object more in need of . . ."

"Too dragged out, can't understand a thing," the girl student shouted.

"It seems to me that everybody has the right to speak equally with everybody else, and if I wish to state my opinion, like anybody else, then . . ."

"No one is taking away your right to speak," the hostess herself now cut in sharply, "you are simply being invited to stop maundering, because no one can understand you."

"Allow me to observe, however, that you do not respect me; if I was unable to finish my thought, it's not from having no thoughts, but rather from an excess of thoughts . . ." the high-school boy muttered, all but in despair, and became finally confused.

"If you don't know how to talk, shut up," the girl student swatted.

The high-school boy even jumped on his chair.

"I just wished to state," he shouted, all burning with shame, and afraid to look around, "that you just wanted to pop up with your cleverness because Mr. Stavrogin came in—that's what!"

"Your thought is dirty and immoral, and indicates the utter insignificance of your development. I beg you not to advert to me again," the girl student rattled out.

"Stavrogin," the hostess began, "they were shouting about family rights just before you came—this officer here" (she nodded at her relative, the major). "And I'm most certainly not going to be the one to bother you with such old, long-disposed-of nonsense. All the same, where on earth could family rights and duties have come from, in the sense of the prejudice in which they now appear? That's the question. Your opinion?"

"What do you mean, where on earth?" Stavrogin asked in turn.

"That is, we know, for instance, that the prejudice about God originated in thunder and lightning," the girl student suddenly ripped out again, all but leaping on Stavrogin with her eyes. "It is known only too well that original mankind, being scared of thunder and lightning, deified the invisible enemy, feeling their weakness before him. But how did the prejudice about the family arise? Where on earth could the family itself have come from?"

"That is not quite the same . . ." the hostess tried to stop her.

"I suppose the answer to such a question would be immodest," Stavrogin answered.

"How's that?" the girl student lunged forward.

But a tittering came from the teachers' group, echoed at once from the other end by Lyamshin and the high-school boy, and followed by the husky guffaw of the major-relative.

"You should write vaudevilles," the hostess remarked to Stavrogin.

"That adverts all too little to your honor, whatever your name is," the girl student cut off in decided indignation.

"And you shouldn't pop up!" the major blurted out. "You are a young lady, you should behave modestly, and it's as if you're sitting on pins."

"Kindly keep still, and do not dare to address me familiarly with your nasty comparisons. It's the first time I've seen you and I care nothing about our family connection."

"But I'm your uncle! I used to tote you around in my arms when you were still an infant!"

"What do I care what you used to tote around. I didn't ask you to tote me around, which means, mister impolite officer, that you got pleasure from it. And allow me to remark that you dare not use a familiar tone with me, unless it's from civic feeling, and that I forbid it once and for all."

"They're all like that!" the major banged his fist on the table, addressing Stavrogin, who was sitting opposite him. "No, sir, excuse me, I like liberalism and modernity, and I like listening to intelligent conversation, but—mind you—from men. From women, from these modern dithery things—no, sir, it pains me! Don't you fidget!" he cried to the girl student, who was hopping up and down on her chair. "No, I demand to speak, too; I have been offended, sirs."

"You only hinder others, and can't say anything yourself," the hostess grumbled indignantly.

"No, I will have my say," the excited major addressed Stavrogin. "I'm counting on you, Mr. Stavrogin, as one who has only just arrived, though I do not have the honor of knowing you. Without men they'll perish like flies—that is my opinion. This whole woman question of theirs is just merely a lack of originality. I assure you that this whole woman question was invented for them by men, out of foolishness, and it has blown up in their faces—thank God I'm not married! Not the least diversity, sir, they cannot even invent a simple pattern; men even invent their patterns for them! Look here, sir, I used to carry her in my arms, danced the mazurka with her when she was ten years old, she came in today, naturally I flew to embrace her, and she announces to me from the second word that there is no God. If it had been from the third word, not from the second—but no, she's in a hurry! Well, suppose intelligent people don't believe, but that's from intelligence, and you, I say, squirt that you are, what do you understand about God? You were taught by some student, and if he'd taught you to light icon lamps, you'd do it."

"That's all lies, you are a very wicked man, and I conclusively expressed your groundlessness to you just now," the girl student replied disdainfully, as if scorning too many explanations with such a man. "I precisely told you just now that we were all taught by the catechesis: 'If you honor your father and your parents, you'll live a long life and be granted wealth.' It's in the ten commandments.[3] If God found it necessary to offer a reward for love, it means your God is immoral. These are the words in which I gave you my proof today, and not from the second word, but because you declared your rights. Whose fault is it if you're dumb and don't understand even now. You feel offended and you're angry—that's the whole clue to your generation."

"Ninny!" said the major.

"And you are a nincompoop."

"Go on, abuse me!"

"I beg your pardon, Kapiton Maximovich, but didn't you tell me that you yourself don't believe in God?" Liputin peeped from the other end of the table.

"What if I did, it's a different matter with me! Maybe I do believe, but not quite. Though I don't fully believe, still I'm not going to say that God should be shot. Back when I was serving with the hussars, I kept reflecting about God. It's an accepted fact in all poems that a hussar drinks and carouses; so, sir, maybe I did drink, but, would you believe, I used to jump out of bed in the middle of the night, just in my socks, and start crossing myself in front of the icon, asking God to send me faith, because even then I couldn't be at peace: is there God, or not? I really had a hot time of it! In the morning I'd get distracted, of course, and faith would seem to disappear again, and generally I've noticed that faith always disappears somewhat during the day."

"You wouldn't happen to have a deck of cards?" Verkhovensky, with a gaping yawn, addressed the hostess.

"I am altogether, altogether in sympathy with your question!" the girl student ripped out, aglow with indignation at the major's words.

"Precious time is being wasted listening to stupid talk," the hostess cut off, looking demandingly at her husband.

The girl student drew herself up.

"I wanted to declare to the meeting about the suffering and protest of the students, but since time is being wasted on immoral talk . . ."

"There's no such thing as moral or immoral!" the high-school boy could not bear it, once the girl student started.

"I knew that, mister high-school student, way before you were taught such things."

"And I maintain," the boy flew into a frenzy, "that you are a child come from Petersburg to enlighten us all, when we know it ourselves. About the commandment: 'Honor thy father and mother,' which you didn't know how to recite, and its being immoral—since Belinsky everyone in Russia has known that."

"Will this never end?" Madame Virginsky said determinedly to her husband. As hostess, she blushed at the worthlessness of the talk, especially when she noticed a few smiles and even some perplexity among the first-time visitors.

"Gentlemen," Virginsky suddenly raised his voice, "if anyone wished to begin on something more pertinent, or has something to state, I suggest he set about it without wasting time."

"I venture to make a question," the lame teacher, who had hitherto been silent and was sitting especially decorously, gently said. "I should like to know whether we here and now constitute some sort of meeting, or are a gathering of ordinary mortals who have come as guests? I ask more for the sake of order, and so as not to be in ignorance."

This "cunning" question produced its effect; everyone exchanged glances, each apparently expecting another to answer, and suddenly, as if on command, they all turned their eyes to Verkhovensky and Stavrogin.

"I simply suggest we vote on how to answer the question: 'Are we a meeting, or not?'" said Madame Virginsky.

"I join fully in the suggestion," echoed Liputin, "though it is somewhat vague."

"I join, too." "So do I," came other voices.

"And it seems to me there would indeed be more order," Virginsky clinched.

"So, then, let's vote!" the hostess announced. "Lyamshin, I ask that you sit down at the piano: you can give your vote from there, when the voting starts."

"Again!" cried Lyamshin. "I've banged enough for you."

"I urgently ask you, sit down and play; don't you want to be of use to the cause?"

"But I assure you, Arina Prokhorovna, no one is eavesdropping. It's just your fantasy. And the windows are high, and, besides, who'd understand anything even if he was eavesdropping?"

"We don't understand what it's about ourselves," someone's voice grumbled.

"And I tell you that precaution is always necessary. It's in case there are spies," she turned to Verkhovensky with her interpretation, "let them hear from the street that we're having a party and music."

"Eh, the devil!" Lyamshin swore, sat down at the piano, and started banging out a waltz, striking the keys randomly and all but with his fists.

"I suggest that those who wish it to be a meeting raise their right hand," Madame Virginsky suggested.

Some raised their hand, others did not. There were some who raised it and then took it back. Took it back and then raised it again.

"Pah, the devil! I didn't understand a thing," one officer shouted.

"I don't either," shouted another.

"No, I understand," a third one shouted, "hand up if it's *yes.*"

"Yes, but what does *yes* mean?"

"It means a meeting."

"No, not a meeting."

"I voted a meeting," the high-school boy shouted, addressing Madame Virginsky.

"Then why didn't you raise your hand?"

"I kept looking at you, you didn't raise yours, so I didn't either."

"How stupid, it's because I made the suggestion, that's why I didn't raise mine. Gentlemen, I suggest we do it again the other way round: whoever wants a meeting can sit and not raise his hand, and whoever doesn't, raise his right hand."

"Whoever doesn't?" the high-school boy repeated.

"Are you doing it on purpose, or what?" Madame Virginsky shouted wrathfully.

"No, excuse me, is it whoever wants or whoever doesn't—because it needs to be defined more precisely," came two or three voices.

"Whoever does not, does *not.*"

"Very well, but what should one do, raise it or not raise it, if one does *not* want?" shouted an officer.

"Ehh, we're not really used to a constitution yet," the major observed.

"Mr. Lyamshin, if you don't mind, you're pounding so that no one can hear anything," observed the lame teacher.

"But, by God, Arina Prokhorovna, nobody's eavesdropping," Lyamshin jumped up. "I simply don't want to play! I came here as a guest, not a banger on pianos!"

"Gentlemen," Virginsky suggested, "answer by voice: are we a meeting, or not?"

"A meeting, a meeting!" came from all sides.

"If so, there's no point in voting, it's enough. Is it enough, gentlemen, or need we also vote?"

"No need, no need, we understand!"

"Maybe there's someone who doesn't want a meeting?"

"No, no, we all want it."

"But what is a meeting?" shouted a voice. It went unanswered.

"We must elect a president," the shout came from all sides.

"Our host, certainly, our host!"

"If so, gentlemen," the elected Virginsky began, "then I suggest my original suggestion from earlier: if anyone wished to begin on something more pertinent, or has something to state, let him set about it without wasting time."

General silence. The eyes of all again turned to Stavrogin and Verkhovensky.

"Verkhovensky, do you have anything to state?" the hostess asked directly.

"Precisely nothing," he stretched himself, yawning, on his chair. "I would like a glass of cognac, though."

"Stavrogin, what about you?"

"Thanks, I don't drink."

"I'm asking whether or not you wish to speak, not about cognac."

"Speak? About what? No, I don't wish to."

"You'll get your cognac," she answered Verkhovensky.

The girl student stood up. She had already tried to jump up several times.

"I came to declare about the sufferings of the unfortunate students and about arousing them everywhere to protest . . ."

But she stopped short; at the other end of the table another competitor had appeared, and all eyes turned to him. Long-eared Shigalyov, with a gloomy and sullen air, slowly rose from his seat and melancholically placed a fat notebook, filled with extremely small writing, on the table. He remained standing and was silent. Many looked at the notebook in bewilderment, but Liputin, Virginsky, and the lame teacher seemed pleased with something.

"I ask for the floor," Shigalyov declared sullenly but firmly.

"You have it," Virginsky permitted.

The orator sat down, was silent for about half a minute, then said in an important voice:

"Gentlemen . . ."

"Here's the cognac!" the relative who had been pouring tea chopped off squeamishly and scornfully, returning with the cognac and now setting it in front of Verkhovensky, along with a glass which she brought in her fingers without a tray or plate.

The interrupted orator paused with dignity.

"Never mind, go on, I'm not listening," cried Verkhovensky, filling his glass.

"Gentlemen, addressing myself to your attention," Shigalyov began again, "and, as you will see further on, requesting your assistance on a point of paramount importance, I must pronounce a preface."

"Arina Prokhorovna, have you got scissors?" Pyotr Stepanovich suddenly asked.

"What do you want scissors for?" she goggled her eyes at him.

"I forgot to cut my nails, it's three days now I've been meaning to cut them," he uttered, serenely studying his long and none-too-clean nails.

Arina Prokhorovna flushed, but Miss Virginsky seemed to like something.

"I think I saw them here on the windowsill earlier." She got up from the table, went, found the scissors, and brought them back with her at once. Pyotr Stepanovich did not even glance at her, took the scissors, and began pottering with them. Arina Prokhorovna realized that this was actually a method, and was ashamed of her touchiness. The gathering silently exchanged glances. The lame teacher spitefully and enviously watched Verkhovensky. Shigalyov began to go on:

"Having devoted my energy to studying the question of the social organization of the future society which is to replace the present one, I have come to the conclusion that all creators of social systems from ancient times to our year 187– have been dreamers, tale-tellers, fools who contradicted themselves and understood precisely nothing of natural science or of that strange animal known as man. Plato, Rousseau, Fourier, aluminum columns[4]—all this is fit perhaps for sparrows, but not for human society. But since the future social form is necessary precisely now, when we are all finally going to act, so as to stop any further thinking about it, I am suggesting my own system of world organization. Here it is!" he struck the notebook. "I wanted to explain my book to the gathering in the briefest possible way; but I see that I will have to add a great deal of verbal clarification, and therefore the whole explanation will take at least ten evenings, according to the number of chapters in my book." (Laughter was heard.) "Besides that, I announce ahead of time that my system is not finished." (More laughter.) "I got entangled in my own data, and my conclusion directly contradicts the original idea from which I start. Starting from unlimited freedom, I conclude with unlimited despotism. I will add, however, that apart from my solution of the social formula, there can be no other."

The laughter was increasing more and more, but it was mostly the young and, so to speak, less initiated guests who laughed. The faces of the hostess, Liputin, and the lame teacher expressed a certain vexation.

"If you yourself weren't able to hold your system together, and arrived at despair, what are we supposed to do?" one officer observed cautiously.

"You're right, mister active officer," Shigalyov turned abruptly to him, "and most of all in having used the word 'despair.' Yes, I kept arriving at despair; nevertheless, everything expounded in my book is irreplaceable, and there is no other way out; no one can invent anything. And so I hasten, without wasting time, to invite the whole society, having heard my book in the course of ten evenings, to state its opinion. And if the members do not want to listen to me, let us break up at the very beginning—the men to occupy themselves with state service, the women to go to their kitchens, for, having rejected my book, they will find no other way out. None what-so-ever! And by losing time, they will only harm themselves, because later they will inevitably come back to the same thing."

People began to stir. "Is he crazy, or what?" voices asked.

"So it all comes down to Shigalyov's despair," Lyamshin concluded, "and the essential question is whether he is to be or not to be in despair?"

"Shigalyov's proximity to despair is a personal question," the high-school boy declared.

"I suggest we vote on how far Shigalyov's despair concerns the common cause, and along with that, whether it's worth listening to him or not," the officer gaily decided.

"That's not the point here," the lame man finally mixed in. Generally, he spoke with a certain mocking smile, as it were, so that it might have been difficult to tell whether he was speaking sincerely or joking. "That's not the point here, gentlemen. Mr. Shigalyov is all too seriously devoted to his task, and, what's more, is too modest. I know his book. He suggests, as a final solution of the question, the division of mankind into two unequal parts. One tenth is granted freedom of person and unlimited rights over the remaining nine tenths.[5] These must lose their person and turn into something like a herd, and in unlimited obedience, through a series of regenerations, attain to primeval innocence, something like the primeval paradise—though, by the way, they will have to work. The measures proposed by the author for removing the will from nine tenths of mankind and remaking them into a herd, by means of a re-educating of entire generations—are quite remarkable, based on natural facts, and extremely logical. One may disagree with certain conclusions, but it is difficult to doubt the author's intelligence and knowledge. It's a pity the stipulation of ten evenings is totally incompatible with the circumstances, otherwise we might hear a great many interesting things."

"Are you really serious?" Madame Virginsky turned to the lame man even somewhat alarmed. "If this man, not knowing what to do about the people, turns nine tenths of them into slavery? I've long suspected him."

"Your own dear brother, you mean?" the lame man asked.

"Family ties? Are you laughing at me or not?"

"And, besides, to work for the aristocrats and obey them as if they were gods is vileness!" the girl student observed furiously.

"What I propose is not vileness but paradise, earthly paradise, and there can be no other on earth," Shigalyov concluded imperiously.

"Instead of paradise," Lyamshin shouted, "I'd take these nine tenths of mankind, since there's really nothing to do about them, and blow them sky-high, and leave just a bunch of learned people who would then start living happily in an educated way."[6]

"Only a buffoon could talk like that," the girl student flared up.

"He is a buffoon, but he's useful," Madame Virginsky whispered to her.

"And that might be the best solution of the problem," Shigalyov turned hotly to Lyamshin. "You, of course, don't even know what a profound thing you've managed to say, mister funny fellow. But since your idea is almost unrealizable, we must limit ourselves to the earthly paradise, if that's what we're calling it."

"That's a lot of nonsense, however!" escaped, as it were, from Verkhovensky. Nevertheless he went on cutting his nails with complete indifference and without raising his eyes.

"Why nonsense, sir?" the lame man picked up at once, as if he had just been waiting for his first word in order to seize upon it. "Why nonsense precisely? Mr. Shigalyov is somewhat of a fanatic in his love of mankind; but remember that in Fourier, in Cabet, and even in Proudhon himself,[7] there are many quite despotic and fantastic pre-resolutions of the problem. Mr. Shigalyov perhaps resolves the matter even far more soberly than they do. I assure you that after reading his book, it is almost impossible to disagree with some things. He is perhaps least distant of all from realism, and his earthly paradise is almost the real one, the very one mankind sighs for the loss of, if indeed it ever existed."

"Well, I just knew I was letting myself in for it," Verkhovensky muttered again.

"Excuse me, sir," the lame man was seething more and more, "conversations and judgments about the future social organization are an almost imperative necessity of all modern thinking people. Herzen spent his whole life worrying about just that. Belinsky, as I know for certain, passed whole evenings with his friends debating and pre-resolving beforehand even the pettiest kitchen details, so to speak, in the future social arrangement."

"Some even lose their minds," the major suddenly remarked.

"Still, it's possible to agree on something at least, rather than sit looking like dictators and say nothing," Liputin hissed, as if finally daring to begin an attack.

"When I said it was nonsense, I didn't mean Shigalyov," mumbled Verkhovensky. "You see, gentlemen," he raised his eyes a bit, "I think all these books, these Fouriers, Cabets, all these 'rights to work,' Shigalyovism[8]—it's all like novels, of which a hundred thousand can be written. An aesthetic pastime. I understand that you're bored in this wretched little town, so you fall on any paper with writing on it."

"Excuse me, sir," the lame man was twitching on his chair, "though we are provincials, and are most certainly deserving of pity for that, nevertheless we know that so far nothing so new has happened in the world that we should weep over having missed it. Now it is being suggested to us, through various strewn-about leaflets of foreign manufacture, that we close ranks and start groups with the sole purpose of universal destruction, under the pretext that however you try to cure the world, you're not going to cure it, but by radically lopping off a hundred million heads, thereby relieving ourselves, we can more assuredly jump over the little ditch. A beautiful thought, no doubt, but one at least as incompatible with reality as 'Shigalyovism,' to which you adverted just now with such disdain."

"Well, I really didn't come here for discussions," Verkhovensky let slip this significant little phrase and, as if not noticing the slip at all, moved the candle towards him to have more light.

"It's a pity, sir, a great pity, that you didn't come here for discussions, and a great pity that you're so occupied now with your toilette."

"And what is my toilette to you?"

"A hundred million heads are as hard to realize as remaking the world by propaganda. Maybe even harder, especially if it's in Russia," Liputin ventured again.

"It's Russia they've now set their hopes on," an officer said.

"We've heard about those hopes, too," the lame man picked up. "It is known to us that the mysterious *index* is pointed at our beautiful fatherland as the country most capable of fulfilling the great task. Only here's the thing, sir: in the event of a gradual resolution of the task by propaganda, I at least gain something personally, well, even if it's just pleasant chitchat, and I might indeed get a promotion from the authorities for services to the social cause. But in the other event—that is, this quick resolution by means of a hundred million heads—what in fact will be my reward? Once you start propagandizing, you may well have your tongue cut off."

"Yours will certainly be cut off," said Verkhovensky.

"You see, sir. And since under the most favorable circumstances it would take fifty, or, say, thirty years to finish such a slaughter, because they're not sheep, they may not just let themselves be slaughtered— isn't it better to pack bag and baggage and move somewhere beyond the peaceful seas to some peaceful islands and there serenely close your eyes? Believe me, sir," he tapped the table significantly with his finger, "you'll only provoke emigration with such propaganda, and nothing else, sir!"

He finished, visibly triumphant. Here was one of the powerful intellects of the province. Liputin was smiling insidiously, Virginsky was listening somewhat glumly, the rest followed the argument with great attention, especially the ladies and officers. Everyone realized that the agent of a hundred million heads had been driven into a corner, and waited to see what would come of it.

"That was well put, by the way," Verkhovensky mumbled with still greater indifference than before, and even as if with boredom. "Emigration is a good idea. But if, in spite of all the obvious disadvantages you anticipate, there are still more and more soldiers coming to the common cause every day, then it can do without you. Here, my dear, a new religion is on its way to replace the old one, that's why so many fighters are coming, and this is a big thing. Go ahead and emigrate! And, you know, I'd advise you to go to Dresden, not to any peaceful islands. First, it's a city that has never seen an epidemic, and you, being a developed man, are surely afraid of death; second, it's close to the Russian border, so that one can the sooner receive one's income from the beloved fatherland; third, it contains so-called treasures of art, and you are an aesthetic man, a former teacher of literature, I believe; well, and, finally, it contains its own pocket Switzerland—this now is for poetic inspiration, because you surely must scribble verses. In short, a treasure in a snuffbox!"

There was movement; the officers especially stirred. Another moment and everyone would start talking at once. But the lame man irritably fell upon the bait:

"No, sir, perhaps we won't leave the common cause yet! This must be understood, sir . . ."

"What, you mean you'd really join a fivesome if I offered it?" Verkhovensky suddenly blurted out and laid the scissors down on the table.

Everyone started, as it were. The mysterious man had suddenly disclosed himself too much. Had even spoken directly about a "fivesome."

"Everyone feels himself an honest man and will not shirk the common cause," the lame man went all awry, "but . . ."

"No, sir, it's not a matter of any *but*," Verkhovensky interrupted imperiously and curtly. "I declare to you, gentlemen, that I want a direct answer. I understand only too well that, having come here and gathered you all together myself, I owe you explanations" (again an unexpected disclosure), "but I cannot give you any before I know what way of thinking you hold with. Talking aside—for we can't babble for another thirty years as we've been babbling for the past thirty—I ask you which is dearer to you: the slow way that consists in the writing of social novels and the bureaucratic predetermining of human destinies on paper for thousands of years to come, with despotism meanwhile gobbling up the roasted hunks that are flying into your mouths of themselves, but that you let go past your mouths; or do you hold with a quick solution, whatever it may consist in, which will finally untie all hands and give mankind the freedom to organize socially by itself, and that in reality, not on paper? 'A hundred million heads,' they shout, and maybe that's just a metaphor, but why be afraid of them if, with these slow paper reveries, despotism in some hundred years will eat up not a hundred but five hundred million heads? Note, too, that the incurable patient is not going to be cured anyway, no matter what prescriptions are given it on paper, and, on the contrary, if there's a delay, it will turn so rotten that it will infect us as well, and corrupt all the fresh forces which can still be counted on now, so that we'll all finally go under. I fully agree that babbling liberally and eloquently is extremely pleasant, while acting is a bit rough . . . Well, anyhow, I'm not a good speaker; I came here with communications, and therefore I ask the whole honorable company not even to vote but to declare directly and simply which is more fun for you: a snail's pace through the swamp, or full steam across it?"

"I'm positively for steaming across!" the high-school boy shouted in rapture.

"Me, too," echoed Lyamshin.

"There is certainly no doubt about the choice," one officer muttered, and another after him, and someone else after that one. Above all, everyone was struck that Verkhovensky had "communications" and had himself promised to speak presently.

"Gentlemen, I see that you almost all decide in the spirit of the tracts," he said, scanning the company.

"All, all," came a majority of voices.

"I confess I rather adhere to a humane solution," the major said, "but since it's all, I'll be with all the rest."

"So it turns out that you're not against it either?" Verkhovensky addressed the lame man.

"It's not that I . . ." the latter seemed to blush somewhat, "but if I do agree with you all now, it's solely so as not to disrupt . . ."

"You're all like that! The man is ready to argue for half a year for the sake of liberal eloquence, and then winds up voting with all the rest! Consider, however, gentlemen: is it true that you are all ready?" (Ready for what?—his question was a vague but terribly tempting one.)

"Of course, all . . ." declarations were heard. They all nevertheless kept glancing at each other.

"And maybe afterwards you'll be offended for having agreed so quickly? Because that's almost always what happens with you."

There was agitation of various sorts, great agitation. The lame man flew at Verkhovensky.

"Allow me to observe to you, however, that the answers to such questions depend on certain things. Even if we've given a decision, observe all the same that a question asked in such a strange way . . ."

"What strange way?"

"A way in which such questions are not asked."

"Teach me, please. And, you know, I was just sure you'd be the first to get offended."

"You dragged an answer out of us about readiness for immediate action, but what right did you have to do so? On what authority do you ask such questions?"

"You should have thought of asking that earlier! Why did you answer, then? First you consent, and now you repent."

"And in my opinion the light-minded frankness of your main question gives me the idea that you have no authority or rights, but were just curious for yourself."

"But what is this, what is this?" Verkhovensky cried, as if he were beginning to be greatly alarmed.

"It's that recruiting, whatever it is, is in any case done in private, and not in an unknown company of twenty people!" the lame man blurted out. He spoke his mind, but he was much too irritated. Verkhovensky quickly turned to the company with a superbly feigned look of alarm.

"Gentlemen, I consider it my duty to announce to you all that this is all foolishness and our talk has gone too far. I have not yet recruited anyone whatsoever, and no one has the right to say of me that I am recruiting, when we were simply talking about opinions. Right? But, whether it's right or not, you alarm me greatly," he again turned to the lame man. "I never thought one had to speak of such all but innocent things in private here. Or are you afraid someone will inform on you? Can it be that there's an informer among us?"

Extreme agitation set in; everyone started talking.

"If it were so, gentlemen," Verkhovensky continued, "I would be the most compromised of all, and therefore I propose that you answer one question—if you wish, of course. You're all entirely free."

"What question? what question?" everyone squawked.

"The sort of question after which it will become clear whether we stay together, or silently put on our hats and go our separate ways."

"The question, the question?"

"If any of us knew of a planned political murder, would he go and inform, foreseeing all the consequences, or would he stay home and await events? Views may differ here. The answer to the question will tell clearly whether we are to separate or stay together, and for much longer than this one evening. Allow me to address you first," he turned to the lame man.

"Why me first?"

"Because you started it all. Kindly don't evade, dodging won't help here. However, as you wish; you are entirely free."

"Excuse me, but such a question is even offensive."

"No, no, be more precise please."

"I've never been an agent of the secret police, sir," the man went even more awry.

"Kindly be more precise, don't keep us waiting."

The lame man was so angry he even stopped answering. Silently, with spiteful eyes, he stared point-blank at his tormentor from behind his spectacles.

"Yes or no? Would you inform or would you not?" Verkhovensky shouted.

"I certainly would *not* inform!" the lame man shouted twice as loudly.

"And no one would inform, of course, no one would," came many voices.

"Allow me to address you, mister Major, would you inform?" Verkhovensky continued, "and note that I'm addressing you on purpose."

"I won't inform, sir."

"Well, and if you knew that someone wanted to kill and rob someone else, an ordinary mortal, you would inform and give warning?"

"Of course, sir, but that would be a civil case, while here it's a political denunciation. I've never been a secret police agent, sir."

"And no one here has ever been," voices came again. "An empty question. We all have the same answer. There are no informers here!"

"Why is that gentleman getting up?" shouted the girl student.

"It's Shatov. Why did you get up, Shatov?" shouted the hostess.

Shatov had indeed gotten up; he was holding his hat in his hand and looking at Verkhovensky. It seemed he wanted to tell him something, but hesitated. His face was pale and spiteful, but he controlled himself, did not say a word, and silently started out of the room.

"Shatov, this is not to your advantage!" Verkhovensky shouted after him mysteriously.

"But it is to yours, spy and scoundrel that you are!" Shatov shouted at him from the doorway and left altogether.

Again shouts and exclamations.

"So that's the test!" shouted a voice.

"Proved useful!" shouted another.

"But didn't it prove useful too late?" observed a third.

"Who invited him? Who let him in? Who is he? Who is this Shatov? Will he inform or won't he?" the questions came pouring out.

"If he was an informer he'd have pretended, but he just spat and left," someone observed.

"Now Stavrogin's getting up, too; Stavrogin hasn't answered the question either," shouted the girl student.

Stavrogin indeed got up, and together with him, from the other end of the table, Kirillov also rose.

"Excuse me, Mr. Stavrogin," the hostess addressed him sharply, "all of us here have answered the question, while you're leaving without a word?"

"I see no need to answer the question that interests you," Stavrogin muttered.

"But we've compromised ourselves, and you haven't," several voices shouted.

"What do I care if you've compromised yourselves?" Stavrogin laughed, but his eyes were flashing.

"What? He doesn't care? He doesn't care?" exclamations came. Many jumped up from their chairs.

"Excuse me, gentlemen, excuse me," the lame man shouted, "but Mr. Verkhovensky also didn't answer the question, he only asked it."

The observation produced a striking effect. They all exchanged glances. Stavrogin laughed loudly in the lame man's face and walked out, followed by Kirillov. Verkhovensky ran out after them to the entryway.

"What are you doing to me?" he murmured, seizing Stavrogin's hand and clenching it as hard as he could in his own. The latter silently jerked it free.

"Go to Kirillov's now, I'll come . . . It's necessary for me, it's necessary!"

"It's not necessary for me," Stavrogin cut him short.

"Stavrogin will," Kirillov put an end to it. "Stavrogin, it is necessary for you. I'll show you there."

They left.

8

Ivan the Tsarevich

THEY LEFT. Pyotr Stepanovich first rushed back to the "meeting" in order to quiet the chaos, but, probably considering it not worth the trouble, abandoned everything and in two minutes was already flying down the road after the departing men. As he ran he recalled a lane which was a closer way to Filippov's house; sinking to his knees in mud, he started down the lane and in fact arrived at a run the very moment Stavrogin and Kirillov were going through the gate.

"Here already?" Kirillov remarked. "That is well. Come in."

"How is it you said you lived alone?" asked Stavrogin, passing through the entryway where a samovar had been prepared and was already beginning to boil.

"You'll see now who I live with," Kirillov muttered, "come in."

As soon as they entered, Verkhovensky at once pulled out the anonymous letter he had taken earlier from Lembke and placed it in front of Stavrogin. All three sat down. Stavrogin silently read the letter.

"Well?" he asked.

"The scoundrel will do as he says," Verkhovensky explained. "Since he's at your disposal, instruct me how to act. I assure you he may go to Lembke tomorrow."

"Well, let him."

"How, let him? Especially since there are ways to avoid it."

"You're mistaken, he's not dependent on me. And anyway I don't care; he's no danger to me, only to you."

"You, too."

"I don't think so."

"But others may not spare you, don't you understand? Listen, Stavrogin, this is just playing with words. Can you be sorry about the money?"

"So there's a need for money?"

"Certainly, about two thousand, or a minimum of fifteen hundred. Give it to me tomorrow, or even today, and by tomorrow evening I'll have sent him packing off to Petersburg for you, and that is precisely what he wants. If you wish, with Marya Timofeevna—mark that."

There was something completely thrown off in him, he spoke somehow imprudently, ill-considered words escaped him. Stavrogin was watching him in surprise.

"I have no need to send Marya Timofeevna away."

"Maybe you don't even want to?" Pyotr Stepanovich smiled ironically.

"Maybe I don't."

"In short, will there be money or won't there be?" he shouted at Stavrogin in spiteful impatience and as if peremptorily. The latter looked him over seriously.

"There'll be no money."

"Eh, Stavrogin! Do you know something, or have you done something already? You're—on a spree!"

His face became distorted, the corners of his mouth twitched, and he suddenly burst into somehow altogether pointless laughter, inappropriate to anything.

"You got money from your father for the estate," Nikolai Vsevolodovich observed calmly. "Maman gave you about six or eight thousand for Stepan Trofimovich. So you can pay fifteen hundred of your own. I don't want, finally, to pay for other people, I've given out a lot as it is, it makes me feel bad . . ." he grinned at his own words.

"Ah, you're beginning to joke . . ."

Stavrogin rose from his chair, and Verkhovensky instantly jumped up as well and mechanically turned his back to the door, as if blocking the way out. Nikolai Vsevolodovich had already made a motion to push him away from the door and go out, but he suddenly stopped.

"I won't let you have Shatov," he said. Pyotr Stepanovich gave a start; the two men stood looking at each other.

"I told you earlier why you need Shatov's blood," Stavrogin flashed his eyes. "You want to stick your crews together with that muck. You drove Shatov out superbly just now: you knew very well he wouldn't have said, 'I won't inform,' and he would have regarded it as baseness to lie in front of you. But me, what do you need me for now? You've been pestering me almost since abroad. The way you've been explaining it to me all along is just sheer raving. And yet what you're driving at is that by giving fifteen hundred to Lebyadkin, I would thus be giving Fedka an occasion for putting a knife into him. I know you've got the notion that I'd like to have my wife killed at the same time. By binding me with a crime you think, of course, you'll be getting power over me, right? What do you want that power for? Why the devil do you need me? Take a good look once and for all: am I your man? And leave me alone."

"Did Fedka come to you on his own?" Verkhovensky asked, short of breath.

"Yes, he did; his price is also fifteen hundred . . . But he'll confirm it himself, he's standing right here . . ." Stavrogin reached out his arm.

Pyotr Stepanovich quickly turned around. On the threshold, out of the darkness, a new figure emerged—Fedka, in a sheepskin jacket, but without a hat, as if at home. He stood and chuckled, baring his white, even teeth. His black eyes with their yellow cast darted cautiously around the room, watching the gentlemen. There was something he could not understand; he had obviously just been brought by Kirillov, and it was to him that his questioning eyes turned; he stood on the threshold but would not come into the room.

"You stashed him away here so he could listen to our bargaining, or even see the money in our hands, right?" asked Stavrogin, and without waiting for a reply, he walked out of the house. Verkhovensky caught up with him at the gate, nearly crazy.

"Stop! Not another step!" he cried, seizing him by the elbow. Stavrogin jerked his arm, but did not jerk it free. Fury came over him: seizing Verkhovensky by the hair with his left hand, he flung him down on the ground with all his might and went through the gate. But before he had walked even thirty steps, the man caught up with him again.

"Let's make peace, let's make peace," he whispered to him, in a convulsive whisper.

Nikolai Vsevolodovich heaved his shoulders, but did not stop or turn around.

"Listen, I'll bring you Lizaveta Nikolaevna tomorrow, do you want that? No? Why don't you answer? Tell me what you want and I'll do it. Listen, I'll give you Shatov, do you want that?"

"So it's true you've decided to kill him?" Nikolai Vsevolodovich cried.

"But what do you want Shatov for? What for?" the frenzied man went on in a breathless patter, running ahead all the time and seizing Stavrogin's elbow, probably without even noticing it. "Listen, I'll give him to you, let's make peace. You've run up a big account, but . . . let's make peace!"

Stavrogin finally glanced at him and was struck. This was not the same look, not the same voice as always, or as in the room just now; he saw almost a different face. The intonation of the voice was not the same: Verkhovensky was imploring, beseeching. This was a man still stunned because his most precious thing was being, or had already been, taken away.

"But what's the matter with you?" Stavrogin cried. The other did not answer, but kept running after him, looking at him with the same imploring and yet inexorable eyes.

"Let's make peace!" he whispered once more. "Listen, I've got a knife stashed in my boot, just like Fedka, but I'll make peace with you."

"But what the devil do you need me for, finally!" Stavrogin cried out, decidedly wrathful and amazed. "Is there some mystery in it, or what? What sort of talisman have you got me for?"

"Listen, we're going to stir up trouble," the other muttered quickly and almost as if in delirium. "You don't believe we're going to stir up trouble? We'll stir up such trouble that everything will go off its foundations. Karmazinov is right that there's nothing to cling to. Karmazinov is very intelligent. Just another ten crews like that all over Russia, and I'm uncatchable."

"Of the same sort of fools?" reluctantly escaped from Stavrogin.

"Oh, be a bit stupider, Stavrogin, be a bit stupider yourself! You know, you're not at all so smart that one should wish you that: you're afraid, you don't believe, you're frightened of the scale. And why are they fools? They're not such fools; nowadays nobody's mind is his own. Nowadays there are terribly few distinct minds. Virginsky is a most pure man, ten times purer than the likes of us; well, good for him, in that case. Liputin is a crook, but I know one point in him. There's no crook who doesn't have his point. Only Lyamshin doesn't have any, but he's in my hands to make up for it. A few more such crews, and I'll have passports and money everywhere, how about that alone? Just that alone? And safe places, and then let them search. They'll root out one crew but flub the next. We'll get trouble going . . . Do you really not believe that the two of us are quite enough?"

"Take Shigalyov, and let me in peace . . ."

"Shigalyov is a man of genius! Do you know he's a sort of genius like Fourier, but bolder than Fourier, but stronger than Fourier; I'm going to concern myself with him. He's invented 'equality'!"

"He's in a fever, and he's raving; something's happened to him, very peculiar," Stavrogin thought, looking at him once more. Both men walked on without stopping.

"He's got it all down nicely in his notebook," Verkhovensky continued. "He's got spying. He's got each member of society watching the others and obliged to inform. Each belongs to all, and all to each. They're all slaves and equal in their slavery. Slander and murder in extreme cases, but above all—equality. First, the level of education, science, and talents is lowered. A high level of science and talents is accessible only to higher abilities—no need for higher abilities! Higher abilities have always seized power and become despots. Higher abilities cannot fail to be despots and have always corrupted rather than been of use; they are to be banished or executed. Cicero's tongue is cut off, Copernicus's eyes are put out, Shakespeare is stoned—this is Shigalyovism! Slaves must be equal: there has never yet been either freedom or equality without despotism, but within a herd there must be equality, and this is Shigalyovism! Ha, ha, ha, so you find it strange? I'm for Shigalyovism!"

Stavrogin tried to quicken his pace and get home more quickly. "If the man is drunk, where did he manage to get drunk?" kept occurring to him. "Can it be the cognac?"

"Listen, Stavrogin: to level the mountains is a good idea, not a ridiculous one. I'm for Shigalyov! No need for education, enough of science! There's sufficient material even without science for a thousand years to come, but obedience must be set up. Only one thing is lacking in the world: obedience. The thirst for education is already an aristocratic thirst. As soon as there's just a tiny bit of family or love, there's a desire for property. We'll extinguish desire: we'll get drinking, gossip, denunciation going; we'll get unheard-of depravity going; we'll stifle every genius in infancy. Everything reduced to a common denominator, complete equality.[1] 'We've learned a trade, and we're honest people, we don't need anything else'—that was the recent response of the English workers. Only the necessary is necessary—henceforth that is the motto of the whole globe. But there is also a need for convulsion; this will be taken care of by us, the rulers. Slaves must have rulers. Complete obedience, complete impersonality, but once every thirty years Shigalyov gets a convulsion going, and they all suddenly start devouring each other, up to a certain point, simply so as not to be bored. Boredom is an aristocratic sensation; in Shigalyovism there will be no desires. Desire and suffering are for us; and for the slaves—Shigalyovism."

"You exclude yourself?" again escaped from Stavrogin.

"And you. You know, I thought of handing the whole world over to the Pope. Let him come out on foot, unshod, and show himself to the mob, as if to say: 'Look what I've been driven to!'—and everyone will swarm after him, even the army. The Pope on top, us around him, and under us—Shigalyovism. It's only necessary that the Internationale agree to the Pope; but it will. And the old codger will instantly agree. Besides, he has no other choice, so remember my words, ha, ha, ha, stupid? Tell me, is it stupid, or not?"

"Enough," Stavrogin muttered in vexation.

"Enough! Listen, I'm dropping the Pope! To hell with Shigalyovism! To hell with the Pope! We need actuality, not Shigalyovism, because Shigalyovism is a piece of jewelry. It's an ideal, it's for the future. Shigalyov is a jeweler and as stupid as every philanthropist. We need dirty work, and Shigalyov despises dirty work. Listen, the Pope will be in the West, and we, we will have you!"

"Leave me alone, drunk man!" Stavrogin muttered, and quickened his pace.

"Stavrogin, you are beautiful!" Pyotr Stepanovich cried out, almost in ecstasy. "Do you know that you are beautiful! The most precious thing in you is that you sometimes don't know it. Oh, I've studied you! I've often looked at you from the side, from a corner! There's even simpleheartedness and naïvety in you, do you know that? There is, there still is! You must be suffering, and suffering in earnest, from this simpleheartedness. I love beauty. I am a nihilist, but I love beauty. Do nihilists not love beauty? They just don't love idols, but I love an idol! You are my idol! You insult no one, yet everyone hates you; you have the air of being everyone's equal, yet everyone is afraid of you—this is good. No one will come up and slap you on the shoulder. You're a terrible aristocrat. An aristocrat, when he goes among democrats, is captivating! It's nothing for you to sacrifice life, your own or someone else's. You are precisely what's needed. I, I need precisely such a man as you. I know no one but you. You are a leader, you are a sun, and I am your worm . . ."

He suddenly kissed his hand. A chill ran down Stavrogin's spine, and he jerked his hand away in fright. They stopped.

"Madman!" whispered Stavrogin.

"Maybe I'm raving, maybe I'm raving!" the other went on in a patter. "But I've thought up the first step. Shigalyov could never think up the first step. The Shigalyovs are many! But one man, only one man in Russia has invented the first step and knows how to do it. That man is me. Why are you staring at me? It's you I need, you, without you I'm a zero. Without you I'm a fly, an idea in a bottle, Columbus without America."

Stavrogin stood looking fixedly into his insane eyes.

"Listen, first we'll get trouble going," Verkhovensky was hurrying terribly, and kept seizing Stavrogin by the left sleeve every moment. "I've already told you: we'll penetrate among the people themselves. Do you know that we're already terribly strong now? Ours aren't only the ones who knife and burn, or perform classic pistol shots, or bite people. That kind only gets in the way. I can conceive of nothing without discipline. I'm a crook, really, not a socialist, ha, ha! Listen, I've counted them all up: the teacher who laughs with children at their God and at their cradle, is already ours. The lawyer who defends an educated murderer by saying that he's more developed than his victims and couldn't help killing to get money, is already ours. Schoolboys who kill a peasant just to see how it feels, are ours. Jurors who acquit criminals right and left, are ours. The prosecutor who trembles in court for fear of being insufficiently liberal, is ours, ours. Administrators, writers—oh, a lot of them, an awful lot of them are ours, and they don't know it themselves! On the other hand, the docility of schoolboys and little fools has reached the highest point; their mentors all have burst gallbladders; everywhere there is vanity in immeasurable measure, appetites beastly, unheard-of . . . Do you know, do you know how much we can achieve with little ready-made ideas alone? When I left, Littré's thesis that crime is insanity was raging; I come back—crime is no longer insanity but precisely common sense itself, almost a duty, at any rate a noble protest: 'But how can a developed murderer not murder, if he needs money!'[2] And this is just the fruit. The Russian God has already folded in the face of 'rotgut.' The people are drunk, mothers are drunk, children are drunk, the churches are empty, and in the courts it's 'two hundred strokes, or fetch us a pot.' Oh, just let this generation grow up! Only it's a pity there's no time to wait, otherwise they could get themselves even drunker! Ah, what a pity there are no proletarians! But there will be, there will be, we're getting there . . ."

"It's also a pity we've grown more stupid," Stavrogin muttered, and moved on his way.

"Listen, I myself saw a six-year-old child leading his drunken mother home, and she was swearing at him in foul language. You think I'm glad of that? When it's in our hands, we may even cure it . . . if need be we'll drive them into the desert for forty years[3] . . . But one or two generations of depravity are necessary now, an unheard-of, mean little depravity, that turns men into vile, cowardly, cruel, self-loving slime—that's what's needed! And with a bit of 'fresh blood' to boot, for the sake of habit. Why are you laughing? I'm not contradicting myself. I'm only contradicting the philanthropists and Shigalyovism, not myself. I'm a crook, not a socialist. Ha, ha, ha! It's just a pity there's so little time. I promised Karmazinov I'd start in May and be done by the Protection. Too soon? Ha, ha! Do you know what I'm going to tell you, Stavrogin: so far there's been no cynicism in the Russian people, though they swear in foul language. Do you know that the enslaved serf had more self-respect than Karmazinov? He got flogged, but he upheld his gods, and Karmazinov did not."

"Well, Verkhovensky, I'm listening to you for the first time, and listening in amazement," said Nikolai Vsevolodovich. "So you're really not a socialist, but some sort of political . . . climber?"

"A crook, a crook. You're concerned about who I am? I'll tell you presently who I am, that's what I'm driving at. It was not for nothing that I just kissed your hand. But we need the people also to believe that we know what we want, and that the others are merely 'brandishing their cudgel and striking their own.' Eh, if only there was time! That's the one trouble—no time. We'll proclaim destruction . . . why, why, again this little idea is so captivating! But we've got to limber up. We'll get fires going . . . We'll get legends going . . . Here every mangy 'crew' will be of use. I'll find such zealots for you in these same 'crews' as would be ready for any kind of shooting and would even be grateful for the honor. Well, sir, so the trouble will start! Such a heaving will set in as the world has never seen . . . Russia will be darkened with mist, the earth will weep for the old gods . . . Well, sir, and then we'll bring out . . . whom?"

"Whom?"

"Ivan the Tsarevich."[4]

"Wh-o-om?"

"Ivan the Tsarevich—you, you!"

Stavrogin thought for a minute or so.

"An impostor?"[5] he suddenly asked in profound surprise, looking at the frenzied man. "Eh! so this at last is your plan."

"We'll say he's 'in hiding,' " Verkhovensky said softly, in a sort of amorous whisper, as if he were indeed drunk. "Do you know what this little phrase—'he is in hiding'—means? But he will appear, he will appear. We'll get a legend going better than the castrates'.[6] He exists, but no one has seen him. Oh, what a legend we can get going! And mainly—a new force is on the way. And this is what's needed, this is what the people are weeping for. What is there in socialism: it destroyed the old forces, but didn't bring any new ones. And here we have a force, and such a force, unheard-of! We need it just this once as a lever, to raise up the earth. Everything will rise!"

"So you've seriously been counting on me?" Stavrogin grinned maliciously.

"Why do you laugh, and so maliciously? Don't scare me. I'm like a child now, I can be scared to death by just one such smile. Listen, I won't show you to anybody, not to anybody: it must be that way. He exists, but no one has seen him, he's in hiding. And, you know, it's even possible to show you, for example, to some one person out of a hundred thousand. And it will start spreading all over the earth: 'We've seen him, we've seen him.' Even with Ivan Filippovich God-of-Sabaoth, they saw how he ascended to heaven in a chariot in front of the people, saw it with their 'own' eyes. And you're no Ivan Filippovich; you're beautiful, proud as a god, seeking nothing for yourself, with the halo of a victim, 'in hiding.' The main thing is the legend! You'll win them over, you'll look and win them over. He's bringing the new truth and is 'in hiding.' And here we'll get two or three judgments of Solomon going.[7] These crews, these fivesomes—no need for the newspapers! If just one petition in ten thousand is granted, everyone will come with petitions. In every village, every peasant will have heard tell that there exists somewhere this hollow in a tree where petitions are to be put. And the earth will groan a great groan: 'A new, just law is coming,' and the sea will boil up and the whole showhouse will collapse, and then we'll see how to build up an edifice of stone. For the first time! *We* will do the building, we, we alone!"

"Frenzy!" said Stavrogin.

"Why, why don't you want it? Afraid? But that's why I seized upon you, because you're afraid of nothing. Is it unreasonable, or what? But so far I'm a Columbus without an America; is a Columbus without an America reasonable?"

Stavrogin was silent. Meanwhile they had come right up to the house and stopped at the entrance.

"Listen," Verkhovensky bent towards his ear, "I'll do it for you without money; I'll end it tomorrow with Marya Timofeevna . . . without money, and by tomorrow I'll bring you Liza. Want Liza tomorrow?"

"Has he really gone crazy?" Stavrogin thought, smiling. The front doors opened.

"Stavrogin, is America ours?" Verkhovensky seized his hand one last time.

"What for?" Nikolai Vsevolodovich said seriously and sternly.

"No desire, I just knew it!" the other cried out in a burst of frenzied spite. "You're lying, you rotten, lascivious, pretentious little squire, I don't believe you, you've got a wolf's appetite! . . . Understand, you've run up too big an account now, I really can't renounce you! There's no one else in the world like you! I've been inventing you since abroad; inventing you as I looked at you. If I hadn't been looking at you from a corner, nothing would have come into my head! . . ."

Stavrogin went up the steps without answering.

"Stavrogin!" Verkhovensky shouted after him, "I'll give you a day . . . or, say, two days . . . three days; more than three I can't do, and then—your answer!"

9

Stepan Trofimovich Perquisitioned

M EANWHILE we had an adventure which surprised me and shocked Stepan Trofimovich. In the morning, at eight o'clock, Nastasya came running to me from him with the news that her master had been "perquisitioned." At first I could understand nothing: all I got was that he had been "perquisitioned" by officials, who had come and taken papers, and a soldier had tied them into a bundle and "carted them away in a wheelbarrow." It was wild news. I hastened at once to Stepan Trofimovich.

I found him in a surprising state: upset and greatly agitated, but at the same time with an unquestionably triumphant air. On the table, in the middle of the room, the samovar was boiling and there stood a full but untouched and forgotten glass of tea. Stepan Trofimovich was dawdling around the table and going into all the corners of the room, not conscious of his movements. He was wearing his usual red dressing jacket, but, seeing me, hastened to put on his waistcoat and frock coat—something he had never done before when any close friend found him in his dressing jacket. He seized me at once and ardently by the hand.

"*Enfin un ami!*"* (He drew a deep breath.) "*Cher,* I sent only to you,

---

*"At last a friend!"

and no one knows anything. Nastasya must be ordered to lock the door and let no one in, except *them,* of course . . . *Vous comprenez?"**

He looked at me worriedly, as if waiting for a reply. Of course, I fell to questioning him and learned somehow from his incoherent speech, full of interruptions and unnecessary additions, that at seven o'clock in the morning a governor's official had "suddenly" come to him . . .

"Pardon, j'ai oublié son nom. Il n'est pas du pays, but I believe Lembke brought him here, *quelque chose de bête et d'allemand dans la physionomie. Il s'appelle Rosenthal."†*

"Not Blum?"

"Blum. Precisely the name he gave. *Vous le connaissez? Quelque chose d'hébété et de très content dans la figure, pourtant très sévère, roide et sérieux. ‡* A police figure, the obedient sort, *je m'y connais. §* I was still asleep, and, imagine, he asked 'to have a glance' at my books and manuscripts, *oui, je m'en souviens, il a employé ce mot. ‖* He didn't arrest me, only books . . . *Il se tenait à distance, ¶* and when he began explaining his visit to me, he looked as though I . . . *enfin, il avait l'air de croire que je tomberai sur lui immédiatement et que je commencerai à le battre comme plâtre. Tous ces gens du bas étage sont comme ça, *** when they're dealing with a decent man. Needless to say, I understood everything at once. *Voilà vingt ans que je m'y prépare. ††* I unlocked all the drawers for him, and gave him all the keys; I personally handed them over, I handed everything over. *J'étais digne et calme. ‡‡* Of the books, he took foreign editions of Herzen, a bound volume of *The Bell,* four copies

---

*"You understand?"

†"Excuse me, I've forgotten his name. He's not from around here . . . something stupid and German in his physiognomy. His name is Rosenthal."

‡"You know him? Something dull and very self-satisfied in his face, but at the same time very severe, stiff, and serious."

§"I know the type."

‖"yes, I remember it, he used that word."

¶"He kept his distance"

***"anyhow, he seemed to believe I was going to fall on him at once and start beating him to a pulp. All these low-class people are like that"

††"It's twenty years that I've been preparing for it."

‡‡"I was dignified and calm."

of my poem, *et, enfin, tout ça.* * Then papers and letters *et quelques-unes de mes ébauches historiques, critiques et politiques.* † All this they carried off. Nastasya says a soldier carted it away in a wheelbarrow, and they covered it with an apron, *oui, c'est cela,* ‡ with an apron."

It was all raving. Who could understand any of it? Once again I showered him with questions: had Blum come alone or not? on whose behalf? by what right? how dared he? did he explain?

"*Il était seul, bien seul,* § though there was someone else *dans l'anti-chambre, oui, je m'en souviens, et puis* ‖ . . . Though there did seem to be someone else, and a guard was standing in the entryway. We must ask Nastasya; she knows it all better. *J'étais surexcité, voyez-vous. Il parlait, il parlait . . . un tas de choses;* ¶ though he talked very little, it was I who kept talking . . . I told him my life, from that point of view only, of course . . . *J'étais surexcité, mais digne, je vous l'assure.* ** I'm afraid, though, that I seem to have wept. The wheelbarrow they got from a shopkeeper next door."

"Oh, God, how could all this have happened! But, for God's sake, speak more precisely. Stepan Trofimovich, this is a dream, what you're telling me!"

"*Cher,* I'm as if in a dream myself . . . *Savez-vous, il a prononcé le nom de Teliatnikoff,* †† and I think it was he who was hiding in the entry-way. Yes, I recall he suggested the prosecutor, and it seems Dmitri Mitrych . . . *qui me doit encore quinze roubles de* pinochle *soit dit en passant. Enfin, je n'ai pas trop compris.* ‡‡ But I outwitted them, and what do I care about Dmitri Mitrych. I think I even started begging him very much to conceal, begging him very much, very much, I'm even afraid I humiliated myself, *comment croyez-vous? Enfin, il a con-*

---

*"and, anyhow, all that."
†"and some of my historical, critical, and political sketches."
‡"yes, that's right"
§"He was alone, quite alone"
‖"in the entryway, yes, I remember that, and then"
¶"I was overexcited, you see. He talked, he talked . . . a pile of things"
**"I was overexcited, but dignified, I assure you of it."
††"You know, he uttered the name of Telyatnikov"
‡‡"who still owes me fifteen roubles from [pinochle], be it said in passing. Anyhow, I didn't understand very well."

senti. * Yes, I recall it was he himself who asked that it would be better if it were concealed, because he only came 'to have a glance,' *et rien de plus,* † and nothing more, nothing . . . and that if they found nothing, then there'd be nothing. So that we ended it all *en amis, je suis tout-à-fait content.* "‡

"But, for pity's sake, he was offering you guarantees and the order proper in such cases, and you yourself refused!" I cried in friendly indignation.

"No, it's better this way, without any guarantees. And who needs a scandal? Let it be *en amis* for the time being . . . You know, in this town, if they find out . . . *mes ennemis . . . et puis à quoi bon ce procureur, ce cochon de notre procureur, qui deux fois m'a manqué de politesse et qu'on a rossé à plaisir l'autre année chez cette charmante et belle* Natalia Pavlovna, *quand il se cacha dans son boudoir. Et puis, mon ami,* § don't contradict me, or discourage, I beg you, because nothing is more unbearable when a man is unhappy than for a hundred friends to come right then and point out to him how stupid he's been. Sit down, anyway, and have some tea, I confess I'm very tired . . . oughtn't I to lie down and put some vinegar to my head, what do you think?"

"Absolutely," I cried out, "and maybe even ice. You're very upset. You're pale, your hands are trembling. Lie down, rest, and wait to tell me. I'll sit here and wait."

He could not get himself to lie down, but I insisted. Nastasya brought vinegar in a bowl, I wetted a towel and put it to his head. Then Nastasya climbed on a chair and set about lighting an icon lamp in front of the icon in the corner. I noticed it with surprise; besides, there had never even been any icon lamp, and now one had suddenly appeared.

"It was I who ordered it today, just after they left," Stepan Trofimo-

---

*"what do you think? Anyhow, he consented."
†"and nothing more"
‡"in a friendly way, I am thoroughly pleased."
§"my enemies . . . and then what good is this prosecutor, our pig of a prosecutor, who has been impolite to me twice and who got such a fine thrashing the other year at that charming and beautiful [Natalia Pavlovna's,] when he hid in her boudoir. And then, my friend"

vich muttered, glancing slyly at me. "*Quand on a de ces choses-là dans sa chambre et qu'on vient vous arrêter,* * it makes an impression, and they really must report that they've seen . . ."

Having finished with the icon lamp, Nastasya planted herself in the doorway, put her right hand to her cheek, and began looking at him with a lamentable air.

"*Éloignez-la* † under some pretext," he beckoned to me from the sofa, "I can't stand this Russian pity, *et puis ça m'embête.*"‡

But she left on her own. I noticed that he kept glancing back at the door and listening towards the entryway.

"*Il faut être prêt, voyez-vous,* " he gave me a significant look, "*chaque moment* § . . . they'll come, take, and ffft!—a man disappears!"

"Lord! Who will come? Who will take you?"

"*Voyez-vous, mon cher,* I asked him directly as he was leaving: What will they do to me now?"

"You might as well have asked where they'll exile you to!" I cried out in the same indignation.

"That's what I implied when I asked the question, but he left without answering. *Voyez-vous,* as regards underwear, clothing, warm clothing especially, that's up to them, if they tell me to take it, well and good, or else they may send me in a soldier's greatcoat. But thirty-five roubles" (here he suddenly lowered his voice, glancing back at the door through which Nastasya had left), "I've quietly slipped through a tear in my waistcoat pocket—here, feel it . . . I think they won't take my waistcoat off, and I left seven roubles in my purse, to pretend 'this is all I have.' You know, there's some change and a few coppers on the table, so they won't guess where I've hidden the money, and they'll think this is all. For God knows where I shall have to spend this night."

I hung my head at such madness. Obviously, it was not possible to make an arrest or a search in the way he was saying, and he was most certainly confused. True, it all happened in those days, before the present latest laws. True, too, he had been offered (according to his own words) a more regular procedure, but had *outwitted* them and

*"When one has such things in one's room and they come to arrest you"
†"Send her away"
‡"and besides it annoys me."
§"One must be ready, you see . . . every moment"

refused . . . Of course, before—that is, still quite recently—a governor could, in extreme cases . . . But, again, what sort of extreme case could this be? That was what baffled me.

"Most likely there was a telegram from Petersburg," Stepan Trofimovich suddenly said.

"A telegram? About you? You mean on account of Herzen's writings and your poem? You're out of your mind, what's there to arrest you for?"

I simply got angry. He made a face and was apparently offended—not at my yelling at him, but at the thought that there was nothing to arrest him for.

"Who can tell these days what he might be arrested for?" he muttered mysteriously. A wild and most absurd idea flashed through my mind.

"Stepan Trofimovich, tell me as a friend," I cried out, "as a true friend, I won't betray you: do you belong to some secret society, or do you not?"

And now, to my surprise, even here he was not certain whether he was or was not a participant in some secret society.

"But that depends, *voyez-vous* . . ."

"How does it 'depend'?"

"When one belongs wholeheartedly to progress, and . . . who can vouch for it: you think you don't belong, and then, lo and behold, it turns out you do belong to something."

"How can that be? It's either yes or no."

"*Cela date de Pétersbourg*,* when she and I wanted to found a magazine there. That's the root of it. We slipped away then and they forgot us, but now they've remembered. *Cher, cher,* but don't you know!" he exclaimed painfully. "In our country they can take you, put you in a kibitka, and march you off to Siberia for good, or else forget you in some dungeon . . ."

And he suddenly burst into hot, hot tears. Tears simply poured out of him. He covered his eyes with his red foulard and sobbed, sobbed for a good five minutes, convulsively. I cringed all over. This was the man who for twenty years had been prophesying to us, our preacher,

*"This dates from Petersburg"

mentor, patriarch, Kukolnik, holding himself so loftily and majestically over us all, before whom we bowed so wholeheartedly, considering it an honor—and now suddenly he was sobbing, sobbing like a
naughty little boy waiting for a birching from the teacher who has just
gone to fetch the rod. I felt terribly sorry for him. He obviously
believed as much in the "kibitka" as in the fact that I was sitting beside
him, and expected it precisely that morning, that very minute, and all
because of Herzen's writings and some sort of poem of his own! Such
full, such total ignorance of everyday reality was both moving and
somehow disgusting.

He finally stopped weeping, got up from the sofa, and began pacing
the room again, continuing our conversation, but glancing out the
window every moment and listening towards the entryway. Our conversation continued disjointedly. All my assurances and reassurances
were like sand against the wind. He scarcely listened, and yet he
needed terribly for me to reassure him, and talked nonstop to that end.
I saw that he could no longer do without me, and would not let me
go for anything in the world. I stayed, and we sat for something over
two hours. In the course of the conversation, he recalled that Blum had
taken with him two tracts he had found.

"What tracts!" I was fool enough to get scared. "Did you really . . ."

"Eh, ten copies were passed off on me," he replied vexedly (he spoke
with me now vexedly and haughtily, now terribly plaintively and
humbly), "but I had already taken care of eight, so Blum got hold of
only two . . ."

And he suddenly flushed with indignation.

"*Vous me mettez avec ces gens-là!** Do you really suppose I could be
in with those scoundrels, with tract-mongers, with my boy Pyotr
Stepanovich, *avec ces esprits-forts de la lâcheté!*† Oh, God!"

"Hah, haven't they somehow mixed you up with . . . Nonsense,
though, it can't be!" I observed.

"*Savez-vous,*" suddenly escaped him, "I feel at moments *que je ferai
là-bas quelque esclandre.* ‡ Oh, don't go away, don't leave me alone! *Ma*

---

*"You're putting me in with those people!"
†"with those freethinkers of cowardice!"
‡"You know . . . that I'll make some sort of scandal there."

carrière est finie aujourd'hui, je le sens. * I, you know, I will perhaps rush at someone there and bite him, like that sub-lieutenant . . ."

He gave me a strange look—frightened and at the same time as if wishing to frighten. He was indeed growing more and more vexed at someone and at something as time went by and the "kibitkas" failed to come; he was even angry. Suddenly Nastasya, who had gone from the kitchen to the entryway for something, brushed against the coat-rack there and knocked it over. Stepan Trofimovich trembled and went dead on the spot; but when the matter was clarified, he all but shrieked at Nastasya and, stamping his feet, chased her back into the kitchen. A minute later he said, looking at me in despair:

"I'm lost! *Cher,*" he suddenly sat down by me and gazed pitifully, so pitifully, into my eyes, "*cher,* it's not Siberia I'm afraid of, I swear to you, oh, *je vous jure*"† (tears even came to his eyes), "I am afraid of something else . . ."

I could tell from his look alone that he wished finally to tell me something extraordinary, meaning something he had refrained from telling me so far.

"I am afraid of disgrace," he whispered mysteriously.

"What disgrace? But quite the contrary! Believe me, Stepan Trofimovich, it will all be explained this very day and will end in your favor . . ."

"You're so certain I'll be pardoned?"

"But what is this 'pardoned'! Such words! What is it you've done? I assure you you haven't done anything!"

"*Qu'en savez-vous;* ‡ all my life has been . . . *cher* . . . They'll recall everything . . . and even if they find nothing, *so much the worse,*" he suddenly added unexpectedly.

"How, so much the worse?"

"Worse."

"I don't understand."

"My friend, my friend, so, let it be Siberia, Arkhangelsk, stripping of rights—if I'm lost, I'm lost! But . . . I'm afraid of something else" (again a whisper, a frightened look, and mysteriousness).

*"My career is finished as of today, I feel it."
†"I swear to you"
‡"What do you know about it"

"But of what, of what?"

"Flogging," he uttered, and gave me a helpless look.

"Who is going to flog you? Where? Why?" I cried out, afraid he was losing his mind.

"Where? Why, there . . . where it's done."

"And where is it done?"

"Eh, *cher,*" he whispered almost into my ear, "the floor suddenly opens under you, and you're lowered in up to the middle . . . Everybody knows that."

"Fables!" I cried, once I understood. "Old fables! And can it be that you've believed them all along?" I burst out laughing.

"Fables! But they must have started somewhere, these fables; a flogged man doesn't talk. I've pictured it ten thousand times in my imagination!"

"But you, why you? If you haven't done anything?"

"So much the worse, they'll see I haven't done anything, and they'll flog me."

"And you're convinced you'll be taken to Petersburg for that?"

"My friend, I've already said I do not regret anything, *ma carrière est finie.* From that hour in Skvoreshniki when she said farewell to me, I've had no regret for my life . . . but the disgrace, the disgrace, *que dira-t-elle,** if she finds out?"

He glanced at me despairingly, poor man, and blushed all over. I, too, looked down.

"She'll find out nothing, because nothing's going to happen to you. It's as if I were talking to you for the first time in my life, Stepan Trofimovich, you've surprised me so much this morning."

"But, my friend, this is not fear. Let them even pardon me, let them even bring me back here and do nothing—it's here that I am lost. *Elle me soupçonnera toute sa vie†* . . . me, me, the poet, the thinker, the man she worshiped for twenty-two years!"

"It won't even occur to her."

"It will," he whispered with profound conviction. "She and I talked of it several times in Petersburg, during the Great Lent, before we left,

*"what will she say"
†"She will suspect me all her life"

when we were both afraid . . . *Elle me soupçonnera toute sa vie* . . . and how undeceive her? It will come out as improbable. And who in this paltry town will believe it, *c'est invraisemblable* . . . *et puis les femmes** . . . She'll be glad. She'll be very upset, very, genuinely, like a true friend, but secretly—she'll be glad . . . I'll have given her a weapon against me for my whole life. Oh, my life is lost! Twenty years of such complete happiness with her . . . and now!"

He covered his face with his hands.

"Stepan Trofimovich, why don't you let Varvara Petrovna know at once?" I suggested.

"God forbid!" he gave a start and jumped up from his place. "Not for anything, never, after what was said at our farewell in Skvoreshniki, nev-er!"

His eyes began to flash.

We sat there, I think, for another hour or more, still waiting for something—anyway, that was the idea. He lay down again, even closed his eyes, and lay for about twenty minutes without saying a word, so that I even thought he was asleep or oblivious. Suddenly he rose up impetuously, tore the towel from his head, sprang from the sofa, dashed to the mirror, with trembling fingers tied his tie, and in a thundering voice summoned Nastasya, ordering her to bring him his coat, his new hat, and his stick.

"I can bear it no longer," he said, in a breaking voice, "I cannot, I cannot! . . . I am going myself."

"Where?" I, too, jumped up.

"To Lembke. *Cher*, I must, I am obliged to. It is my duty. I am a citizen and a human being, not a chip of wood, I have rights, I want my rights . . . For twenty years I never demanded my rights, all my life I've criminally forgotten them . . . but now I will demand them. He must tell me everything, everything. He received a telegram. He dare not torment me, otherwise arrest me, arrest me, arrest me!"

He exclaimed this with some shrieking and stamping of feet.

"I approve," I said on purpose, as calmly as I could, though I was very afraid for him. "Indeed, it is better than to sit in such anguish; but I do not approve of your mood—just look at yourself and in what

*"it's improbable . . . and then, women"

state you'll be going there. *Il faut être digne et calme avec Lembke.* * You
may really rush at someone and bite him."

"I am giving myself up. I am walking straight into the lion's maw ..."

"And I'm going with you."

"I expected nothing less of you, I accept your sacrifice, the sacrifice
of a true friend, but as far as the house, only as far as the house: you
must not, you have no right to compromise yourself further by as-
sociating with me. *Oh, croyez-moi, je serai calme!*† I am aware of being
at this moment *à la hauteur de tout ce qu'il y a de plus sacré*‡ ..."

"I might even go into the house with you," I interrupted him.
"Yesterday I was informed by their stupid committee, through Vysotsky, that they're counting on me and inviting me to this fête tomorrow as one of the ushers, or whatever they're called ... these six young
men appointed to look after the trays, take care of the ladies, show the
guests to their seats, and wear a bow of white and crimson ribbons on
their left shoulder. I intended to refuse, but why don't I go into the
house now on the pretext of talking with Yulia Mikhailovna herself ... And that way you and I can go in together."

He listened, nodding, but it seems he understood nothing. We were
standing on the threshold.

"*Cher,*" he stretched out his arm towards the icon lamp in the
corner, "*cher,* I have never believed in this, but ... so be it, so be it!"
(He crossed himself.) "*Allons!*"

"Well, that's better," I thought, going out to the porch with him.
"The fresh air on the way will help, we'll calm down a bit, come back
home, and retire to bed ..."

But I was reckoning without my host. Precisely on the way, an
adventure occurred which gave Stepan Trofimovich an even greater
shock and finally determined his course ... so that, I confess, I never
expected as much pluck from our friend as he suddenly showed that
morning. Poor friend, good friend!

*"One must be dignified and calm with Lembke."
†"Oh, believe me, I will be calm!"
‡"at the height of all that is most sacred"

10

Filibusters. A Fatal Morning

I

THE EVENT that occurred on our way was also of a surprising sort. But I must tell everything in order. An hour before Stepan Trofimovich and I went out, a crowd of people, workers from the Shpigulin factory, about seventy of them, maybe more, moved through town and was noticed with curiosity by many. They moved decorously, almost silently, in purposeful order. It was afterwards asserted that these seventy were delegates chosen from all the factory workers, of whom the Shpigulins had up to nine hundred, to go to the governor and, in view of the owners' absence, seek justice from him against the owners' manager, who, while closing down the factory and dismissing the workers, had brazenly cheated them all—a fact no longer open to any doubt. Others among us deny to this day that they were delegates, insisting that seventy people would be too many for a delegation, and that the crowd simply consisted of the most resentful ones, who came to plead only for themselves, so that there never had been any general factory "riot" such as later caused so much clamor. A third group passionately affirms that these seventy men were not simple rioters, but decidedly political ones—that is, that being some of the most violent ones to begin with, they had been further aroused by none other than the anonymous leaflets. In short, whether or not there was any influence or instigation is still not known precisely. My personal opinion is that the workers had not read any anonymous leaflets, and that even if they had, they would not have understood a word of them, for the sole reason that those who write them, for all the baldness of their style, write extremely obscurely. But since the factory men really were in bad straits—and the police, to whom they had appealed, did not want to enter into their grievance—what could be more natural than their idea of going in a crowd "to the general himself," if possible, even with a petition on their head, lining up decorously in front of his porch, and, the moment he appeared, all falling on their knees and crying out as if to providence itself? To my mind there is no need here either for a riot, or even for delegates, because this is an old, historical method; from time immemorial the Russian people have loved having a talk with "the general himself," for the sheer pleasure of it, in fact, and even regardless of what the end of such a talk might be.

And that is why I am fully convinced that although Pyotr Stepanovich, Liputin, perhaps someone else as well, perhaps even Fedka, had been shuttling among the factory workers earlier (since there exist quite firm indications of this circumstance) and had talked with them, it was certainly with no more than two or three, or say five, only as a trial, and that nothing came of this talk. As regards rioting, even if the factory workers did understand anything of their propaganda, they must certainly have stopped listening at once, seeing it was a stupid matter and altogether unsuitable. Fedka was another matter: it seems he had far better luck than Pyotr Stepanovich. In the town fire that followed three days later, as has now been indisputably revealed, two factory workers did indeed take part along with Fedka, and afterwards, a month later, three more former factory workers in our district were seized, also for robbery and arson. But if Fedka had actually managed to lure them over to direct, immediate action, it was again only these five, because nothing of the sort was heard about any of the others.

Be that as it may, the whole crowd of workers finally arrived at the little square in front of the governor's house, and lined up decorously and silently. Then they gaped at the porch and started waiting. I was told that as soon as they installed themselves, they immediately took off their hats, that is, perhaps half an hour before the arrival of the master of the province, who, as if by design, happened to be away from home at the moment. The police made their appearance at once, first as isolated phenomena, then in the fullest possible complement; they began threateningly, of course, with an order to disperse. But the workers stood there like a flock of sheep at a fence, and answered laconically that they wanted "the general hisself"; firm resolve was evident. The unnatural shouting ceased; it quickly yielded to pondering, mysteriously whispered instructions, and a stern, worried preoccupation that furrowed the official brow. The police chief preferred to wait for the arrival of von Lembke himself. It is nonsense that he came flying at full speed with a troika and supposedly started fighting before he got out of his droshky. Our governor did indeed fly and liked to fly around in his droshky with its yellow back, and as his "outrunners driven to debauchery" got wilder and wilder, to the delight of all the merchants in the shopping arcade, he would stand up in his droshky, rise to his full height, holding on to a special strap attached to the side, and, stretching his right arm into space like a monument, would thus survey the town. But in the present case he did not start fighting, and though he really could not do without strong language as he came flying off his droshky, he did it solely so as not to lose popularity. It is still greater nonsense that soldiers with bayonets were brought in, and that a message was sent somewhere by telegraph about dispatching artillery and Cossacks: these are tales that their inventors themselves no longer believe. It is also nonsense that barrels of water were brought from the firehouse and used to drench the people. Quite simply, Ilya Ilyich shouted hot-headedly that no one would escape without getting his feet wet; this must have been turned into barrels, which thus made their way into the reports of the metropolitan newspapers. The most correct version, one must suppose, was that the crowd was first surrounded by all the policemen who happened to be on hand, and a messenger was then sent to Lembke, an officer from the first precinct, who proceeded to fly down the road to Skvoreshniki in the police chief's droshky, knowing that von Lembke had set out for there half an hour earlier in his carriage . . .

But, I confess, an unresolved question still remains for me: how did it come about that a mere, that is, an ordinary crowd of petitioners—seventy men, it's true—should be turned, right from the first go, from the first step, into a riot that threatened to shake the foundations? Why did Lembke himself seize on this idea when he arrived twenty minutes later, following the messenger? I would suppose (but again this is a personal opinion) that Ilya Ilyich, who was chummy with the manager, even found it profitable to present the crowd to von Lembke in this light, precisely so as not to bring on a real investigation into the matter; and it was Lembke himself who had given him this idea. Over the past two days he had had two mysterious and exceptional talks with him—quite confused talks, incidentally—from which Ilya Ilyich had nevertheless made out that the front office was firmly set on the idea of the tracts, and of the Shpigulin workers being incited by someone to social rioting, and set on it to such a degree that they themselves might regret it if this inciting turned out to be nonsense. "He wants to distinguish himself somehow in Petersburg," thought our cunning Ilya Ilyich as he was leaving von Lembke. "Well, that plays right into my hands."

But I am convinced that poor Andrei Antonovich would not have wished for a riot even for the sake of distinguishing himself. He was an extremely responsible official, who until his marriage had dwelt in innocence. And was it his fault if, instead of innocent government firewood and a likewise innocent Minchen, a forty-year-old princess had raised him to herself? I know almost positively that it was after this same fatal morning that the first traces became manifest of the condition which is said to have sent poor Andrei Antonovich to a certain special institution in Switzerland, where he is now supposed to be gathering new strength. But if one can merely allow that, precisely after that morning, the manifest facts of *anything* became apparent, then it is possible, in my opinion, to allow that manifestations of similar facts could already have occurred the day before as well, though not so manifestly. It is known to me from rumors of a most intimate sort (well, suppose that later on Yulia Mikhailovna, no longer triumphant, but *almost* repentant—for a woman is never *wholly* repentant—told me a particle of this story herself)—it is known to me that Andrei Antonovich came to his wife on the eve of that day, late at night, past two o'clock, woke her up, and demanded that she listen to "his ultimatum." The demand was so insistent that she was obliged to get up from her bed of rest, in indignation and in curlers, and, sitting on the couch, had to listen, albeit with sarcastic disdain. Only then did she realize for the first time how far gone her Andrei Antonovich was, and she was inwardly horrified. She ought finally to have come to her senses and relented, but she concealed her horror and insisted even more persistently than before. She had (as every wife seems to have) her special way with Andrei Antonovich, already tested not a few times, and which more than once had driven him to frenzy. Yulia Mikhailovna's way consisted of scornful silence, for an hour, for two hours, for a day, for nearly three days—silence at whatever cost, whatever he might say, whatever he might do, even if he climbed out the window to throw himself from the third floor—a way intolerable for a sensitive man! Whether Yulia Mikhailovna was punishing her husband for his recent blunders and his jealous envy, as governor, of her administrative abilities; or was indignant at his criticizing her behavior with the young people and our whole society, without understanding her subtle and farsighted political goals; or was angry at his dumb and senseless jealousy of Pyotr Stepanovich—in any case, she decided not to relent even now, despite the hour of the clock and the unprecedented agitation of Andrei Antonovich. Pacing, beside himself, up and down and in all directions over the carpets of her boudoir, he laid before her everything, everything, quite disconnectedly, it's true, but still *everything* that was seething inside him, for—"it has gone beyond all limits." He began by saying that everyone was laughing at him and "leading him by the nose." "I spit on the phrase," he shrieked at once, catching her smile, "let it be 'by the nose,' but it's true! . . . No, madam, the moment has come; let me tell you that this is no time for laughter and women's coquetries. We are not in a mincing lady's boudoir; we are, as it were, two abstract beings in a balloon, who have met in order to speak out the truth." (He was muddled, of course, and unable to find the right forms for his—incidentally correct—thoughts.) "It is you, madam, who took me out of my former state, I accepted this post only for you, for your ambition . . . You smile sarcastically? Don't be triumphant, don't be hasty. Let me tell you, madam, let me tell you that I could, that I would be able to manage this post, and not just this one post but ten such posts, because I do have the ability; but with you, madam, in your presence—it's impossible for me to manage; because in your presence I do not have the ability. Two centers cannot exist, and you have set up two—one is mine, the other is in your boudoir— two centers of power, madam, but I will not allow it, I will not!! In the service, as in marriage, there is one center, and two are impossible . . . How have you repaid me?" he proceeded to exclaim. "Our marriage has consisted of nothing but you proving to me all the time, every hour, that I am worthless, stupid, and even mean, and I have been obliged, every hour and humiliatingly, to prove to you that I am not worthless, not at all stupid, and that I astound everyone with my nobility—now, is that not humiliating on both sides?" Here he began quickly and rapidly stamping the carpet with both feet, so that Yulia Mikhailovna was obliged to rise with stern dignity. He soon calmed down, but then passed over to sentimentality and started sobbing (yes, sobbing), beating himself on the breast for almost a whole five minutes, getting more and more beside himself from Yulia Mikhailovna's most profound silence. Finally, he committed the ultimate blunder and let slip that he was jealous of Pyotr Stepanovich. Realizing that this was foolish beyond all measure, he became ferociously furious and shouted that "he would not allow the denial of God"; that he would break up her "shameless salon of faithlessness"; that the burgomaster was even obliged to believe in God, "and so his wife is, too"; that he would not suffer any young men; that "you, madam, you, from your own dignity, ought to have cared for your husband and to have stood up for his intelligence, even if he was a man of poor abilities (and I am by no means of poor abilities!), whereas you are the reason why everyone here despises me, it is you who have put them up to it! . . ." He shouted that he would abolish the woman question, that he would smoke out that little spirit, that he would forbid this absurd subscription fête for the governesses (devil take them!) and break it up first thing tomorrow; that first thing tomorrow he would chase any governess he met out of the province "with a Cossack, ma'am!" "On purpose, on purpose!" he kept shrieking. "Do you know, do you know," he shouted, "that it is your scoundrels who are inciting the men at the factory, and that I am informed of it? Do you know that tracts are being distributed on purpose, on pur-pose, ma'am! Do you know that I am informed of the names of four of these scoundrels, and that I am losing my mind, losing it finally, finally!!! . . ." But here Yulia Mikhailovna suddenly broke her silence and sternly declared that she had long known about criminal designs, and that it was all foolishness, he was taking it too seriously, and with regard to pranksters, she knew not only those four, but all of them (she lied); and that she had no intention of losing her mind from all that, but, on the contrary, trusted in her mind more than ever, and hoped to lead everything to a harmonious ending: to encourage the youth, to bring them to reason, to prove to them suddenly and unexpectedly that their designs were known, and then show them to new goals for a reasonable and brighter activity. Oh, what came over Andrei Antonovich in that moment! On learning that Pyotr Stepanovich had hoodwinked him again and made fun of him so crudely, that he had revealed much more and much earlier to her than to him, and, finally, that Pyotr Stepanovich was himself perhaps the chief instigator of all the criminal designs—he flew into a frenzy. "Know, witless but venomous woman," he exclaimed, suddenly bursting all bonds, "know that I shall arrest your unworthy lover at once, put him in fetters, and dispatch him to the fortress, or—or I myself, right now, in your eyes, will jump out the window!" At this tirade, Yulia Mikhailovna, green with spite, immediately burst into laughter, long, resounding, with little peals and gales, exactly as in the French theater when a Parisian actress, invited for a hundred thousand to play coquettes, laughs in her husband's face for daring to be jealous of her. Von Lembke rushed for the window, but suddenly stopped as if rooted to the spot, folded his arms across his chest, and, pale as a corpse, gave the laughing woman an ominous look. "Do you know, do you know, Yulia . . ." he said in a suffocating, imploring voice, "do you know that I, too, can do something?" But at the new, still stronger outburst of laughter that followed his last words, he clenched his teeth, moaned, and suddenly rushed—not for the window—but at his spouse, raising his fist over her! He did not bring it down—no, three times no; but instead he perished right there on the spot. Not feeling the legs under him, he ran to his study, threw himself just as he was, fully clothed, facedown on the prepared bed, wrapped himself convulsively, head and all, in the sheet, and lay that way for about two hours—not sleeping, not thinking, with a lead weight on his heart, and dull, unmoving despair in his soul. Every once in a while he shuddered all over with a tormenting, feverish shiver. All sorts of unconnected things recalled themselves to him, which did not go with anything: now he thought, for example, of an old wall clock he had had in Petersburg about fifteen years ago, which had lost its minute hand; now of the jolly official Millebois and of how the two of them had once caught a sparrow in Alexandrovsky

Park, and only then recalled, laughing for the whole park to hear, that one of them was already a collegiate assessor. I think he fell asleep at around seven in the morning, not realizing it himself, and slept delightedly, with lovely dreams. Awakening at ten o'clock, he suddenly jumped wildly out of bed, remembered everything all at once, and gave himself a hearty smack on the head with his palm: no breakfast, no Blum, no police chief, no official come to remind him that the members of the ——— committee were expecting his chairmanship that morning—he received none of them, he listened to nothing, nor did he wish to understand, but raced like a lunatic to Yulia Mikhailovna's half. There Sofia Antropovna, a little old lady of gentle birth who had long been living with Yulia Mikhailovna, explained to him that his wife had set out at ten o'clock, with a large company, in three carriages, for Varvara Petrovna Stavrogin's, at Skvoreshniki, to look over the site for the future fête, the second one, planned for two weeks later, and that this had already been arranged three days ago with Varvara Petrovna herself. Stunned by the news, Andrei Antonovich went back to his study and impetuously ordered horses. He was even hardly able to wait. His soul yearned after Yulia Mikhailovna—only to look at her, to be near her for five minutes; perhaps she would look at him, notice him, smile as she used to, forgive—ohh! "But what's with those horses?" Mechanically, he opened a thick book that was lying on the table (he sometimes did divinations this way, by a book, opening it at random and reading on the right-hand page, three lines from the top). It came out: *"Tout est pour le mieux dans le meilleur des mondes possibles"**—*Voltaire, *Candide.* [1] He spat and ran to get into the carriage: "To Skvoreshniki!" The coachman told afterwards how the master kept urging him on all the way, but as soon as they began to approach the main house, he suddenly gave the order to turn around and drive back to town: "Faster, please, faster." Before they reached the walls of the town, "he ordered me to stop again, got out of the carriage, and went across the road into a field; from some sort of weakness, I thought; but he stopped and began examining little flowers, and stood that way for some while, really strangely, so as I felt thoroughly doubtful." Thus the coachman testified. I recall the weather that morn-

---

*"Everything is for the best in the best of all possible worlds."

ing: it was a cold, clear, but windy September day; spread before Andrei Antonovich, who had left the road, lay a stern landscape of bare fields from which the bread had been harvested long before; the howling wind swayed some pitiful remnants of dying yellow flowers . . . Did he wish to compare himself and his lot with stunted flowers beaten down by autumn and the frost? I don't think so. I even think it was certainly not so, and that he did not remember anything at all about the little flowers, despite the testimony of the coachman and the officer from the first precinct, who drove up at that moment in the police chief's droshky, and later affirmed that he had indeed found the front office with a bunch of yellow flowers in his hand. This police officer—an ecstatically administrative person, Vassily Ivanovich Filibusterov—was still a newcomer to our town, but had already distinguished himself and been noised abroad for his boundless zeal, a certain swoop in all his ways along the executive line, and an innate unsobriety. Leaping from the droshky, and not hesitating in the least at the sight of the front office's occupation, looking crazy but convinced, he fired off the report that "there's unrest in town."

"Eh? What?" Andrei Antonovich turned to him with a stern face, but without the least surprise or any recollection of the carriage or the coachman, as if he were in his own study.

"Officer of the first precinct Filibusterov, Your Excellency. There's a riot in town."

"Filibusters?" Andrei Antonovich repeated ponderingly.

"That's right, Your Excellency. The Shpigulin men are rioting."

"The Shpigulin men! . . ."

Something came back to him, as it were, at the mention of "the Shpigulin men." He even gave a start and raised his finger to his forehead: "The Shpigulin men!" Silent, but still pondering, he went unhurriedly to the carriage, got in, and gave orders for town. The officer in the droshky followed after.

I imagine that on his way he vaguely pictured many quite interesting things, on many themes, but he hardly had any firm idea or any definite intention on entering the square in front of the governor's house. But the moment he caught sight of the lined-up and firmly standing crowd of "rioters," the row of policemen, the powerless (and perhaps intentionally powerless) police chief, and the general expecta-

tion directed at him, all the blood rushed to his heart. Pale, he stepped
from the carriage.

"Hats off!" he said, breathlessly and barely audibly. "On your
knees!" he shrieked unexpectedly—unexpectedly for himself, and it
was in this unexpectedness that the whole ensuing denouement of the
affair perhaps consisted. It was like coasting down a hill at the winter
carnival; can a sled that is already going down stop in the middle of
the hillside? As ill luck would have it, Andrei Antonovich had been
distinguished all his life by the serenity of his character and had never
shouted or stamped his feet at anyone; and such men are far more
dangerous if it once happens that their sled for some reason shoots off
downhill. Everything went whirling around in front of him.

"Filibusters!" he screamed, in an even more shrill and absurd way,
and his voice cracked. He stood, still not knowing what he was going
to do, but knowing and sensing with his whole being that he was now
certainly going to do something.

"Lord!" came from the crowd. Some fellow began to cross himself;
three or four men indeed made as if to kneel, but the rest moved in
a mass about three steps forward, and suddenly they all began to
squawk at once: "Your Excellency . . . the deal was for forty . . . the
manager . . . don't you go telling us," etc., etc. Nothing could be made
of it.

Alas! Andrei Antonovich was unable to make anything out: the
flowers were still in his hand. The riot was as evident to him as the
kibitkas had been earlier to Stepan Trofimovich. And amid the crowd
of "rioters" who stood goggling at him, Pyotr Stepanovich kept darting about in front of him, "agitating" them—he who had not left him
for a moment since the day before, Pyotr Stepanovich, the detested
Pyotr Stepanovich . . .

"Birch rods!" he cried, still more unexpectedly.

A dead silence ensued.

This was how it went at the very beginning, judging by the most
precise information and my own conjectures. But on what followed
the information becomes less precise, as do my conjectures. There are,
however, certain facts.

First, the birch rods appeared somehow all too hastily; they had
apparently been readied in advance by the quick-witted police chief.

However, only two men were punished in all, I think, not even three; I insist on that. That all the men, or at least half of them, were punished, is sheer invention. It is also nonsense that some poor but noble lady was supposedly seized as she was passing by and promptly thrashed for some reason; and yet I later read about this lady myself in a report in one of the Petersburg newspapers. Many people here were talking about a woman from the cemetery almshouse, a certain Avdotya Petrovna Tarapygin, who, as she was crossing the square on her way back to the almshouse, supposedly pushed her way through the spectators, out of natural curiosity, and on seeing what was happening, exclaimed: "Shame on 'em!"—and spat. For this she was supposedly picked up and also "attended to." Not only was this case printed, but a subscription for her benefit was set up here in town on the spur of the moment. I myself donated twenty kopecks. And what then? It turns out that there never was any such almshouse Tarapygin woman in our town at all! I went myself to inquire at the almshouse by the cemetery: they had never even heard of any Tarapygin woman; moreover, they got quite offended when I told them the rumor. In fact, I mention this nonexistent Avdotya Petrovna only because the same thing that happened with her (if she had existed in reality) almost happened with Stepan Trofimovich; it may even be on account of him that this whole absurd rumor about Tarapygin got started—that is, the gossip in its further development simply went and turned him into some Tarapygin woman. First of all, I do not understand how he gave me the slip as soon as we came to the square. Having a presentiment of something none too good, I wanted to take him around the square right to the governor's porch, but I became curious myself and stopped just for a moment to question some first passer-by, when suddenly I saw that Stepan Trofimovich was no longer beside me. Following my instinct, I rushed at once to look for him in the most dangerous place; for some reason I had a presentiment that his sled had also shot off downhill. And indeed I found him already at the very center of the event. I remember seizing him by the arm; but he calmly and proudly gave me a look of boundless authority:

"*Cher,*" he pronounced, in a voice in which some strained string vibrated. "If all of them here, in the square, in front of our eyes, are ordering people around so unceremoniously, what then are we to expect, say, from *this one* ... if he should happen to act independently."

And, trembling with indignation and with a boundless wish for defiance, he transferred his threatening, exposing finger to Filibusterov, who was standing two steps away goggling his eyes at us.

"*This one!*" he exclaimed, and everything went dark before his eyes. "Which this one? And who are you?" he stepped closer, clenching his fists. "Who are you?" he bellowed furiously, morbidly, and desperately (I will note that he knew Stepan Trofimovich's face perfectly well). Another moment and he would surely have grabbed him by the scruff of the neck; but, fortunately, Lembke turned his head at the shout. Perplexed, he nevertheless looked intently at Stepan Trofimovich, as if trying to figure something out, and suddenly waved his hand impatiently. Filibusterov was cut short. I dragged Stepan Trofimovich out of the crowd. It may be, however, that by then he himself wished to retreat.

"Home, home," I insisted, "if we weren't beaten, it's certainly thanks to Lembke."

"Go, my friend, I am to blame for subjecting you. You have a future and a career of some sort, while I—*mon heure a sonné.*"*

He firmly mounted the steps to the governor's house. The doorkeeper knew me; I announced that we had both come to see Yulia Mikhailovna. In the reception room we sat down and began to wait. I did not want to abandon my friend, but I found it unnecessary to say anything more to him. He had the look of a man who has doomed himself to something like a certain death for the fatherland. We seated ourselves not next to each other but in different corners—I nearer the entrance, he on the far side opposite, his head pensively inclined, leaning lightly with both hands on his cane. He held his wide-brimmed hat in his left hand. We sat like that for about ten minutes.

II

LEMBKE SUDDENLY came in with quick steps, accompanied by the police chief, glanced at us distractedly and, paying no attention,

*"my hour has struck."

turned right to go to his study, but Stepan Trofimovich stood in front of him and blocked his way. The tall figure of Stepan Trofimovich, quite unlike any other, produced its impression; Lembke stopped.

"Who is this?" he muttered in perplexity, as if asking the police chief, not turning his head towards him in the least, however, but continuing to examine Stepan Trofimovich.

"Retired collegiate assessor Stepan Trofimovich Verkhovensky, Your Excellency," Stepan Trofimovich replied, augustly inclining his head. His Excellency continued to peer at him, though with a quite dumb look.

"What about?" And with the laconism of authority he squeamishly and impatiently turned his ear to Stepan Trofimovich, taking him finally for an ordinary petitioner with some written request.

"I was subjected today to a house search by an official acting on Your Excellency's behalf; therefore I wish . . ."

"Name? Name?" Lembke asked impatiently, as if suddenly realizing something. Stepan Trofimovich repeated his name still more augustly.

"Ahh! It's . . . it's that hotbed . . . My dear sir, you have presented yourself from such an angle . . . You're a professor? A professor?"

"I once had the honor of delivering several lectures to the youth of ———— University."

"Yo-o-outh!" Lembke seemed to jump, though I wager he still had little understanding of what it was about, and even, perhaps, of whom he was talking with. "That, my very dear sir, I will not allow," he suddenly became terribly angry. "I do not allow youth. It's all these tracts. It's a swoop upon society, my dear sir, a seafaring swoop, filibusterism . . . What is your request, if you please?"

"On the contrary, your wife has requested of me that I read tomorrow at her fête. I myself have no requests, but have come seeking my rights . . ."

"At the fête? There will be no fête. I will not allow your fête, sir! Lectures? Lectures?" he cried furiously.

"I wish very much that you would speak more politely with me, Your Excellency, and not stamp your feet or shout at me as at a boy."

"You understand, perhaps, with whom you are talking?" Lembke flushed.

"Perfectly well, Your Excellency."

"I shield society with myself, while you destroy it. Destroy it! You . . . I remember about you, however: was it you who were tutor in the house of General Stavrogin's widow?"

"Yes, I was . . . tutor . . . in the house of General Stavrogin's widow."

"And in the course of twenty years you have been a hotbed of all that has now accumulated . . . all the fruit . . . I believe I saw you in the square just now. Beware, however, my dear sir, beware: the direction of your thinking is known. You may be sure I have it in mind. Your lectures, my dear sir, I cannot allow, I cannot, sir. Address no such requests to me."

He again made as if to pass by.

"I repeat, you are mistaken, Your Excellency: it is your wife who has requested that I read—not a lecture, but something literary, at tomorrow's fête. But I myself decline to read now. My humble request is that you explain to me, if possible, how, why, and wherefore I was subjected to today's search? Some books, papers, private letters quite dear to me, were taken from me and carted through town in a wheelbarrow . . ."

"Who did the search?" Lembke fluttered up, coming fully to his senses, and suddenly blushed all over. He turned quickly to the police chief. At that same moment the stooping, long, gawky figure of Blum appeared in the doorway.

"This very same official," Stepan Trofimovich pointed to him. Blum stepped forward with a guilty but by no means capitulating look.

"*Vous ne faites que des bêtises,*"* Lembke hurled at him with vexation and spite, and was suddenly transformed, as it were, and all at once regained his consciousness. "Excuse me . . ." he babbled in extreme confusion and blushing for all he was worth, "this was all . . . this was probably all just simply a blunder, a misunderstanding . . . just simply a misunderstanding."

"Your Excellency," Stepan Trofimovich observed, "in my youth I witnessed a certain characteristic incident. Once, in a theater, in the corridor, a man quickly went up to another and, in front of the whole public, gave him a resounding slap. Perceiving immediately that the victim was not at all the person for whom the slap was intended, but

---

*"You make nothing but blunders"

someone completely different who merely resembled him slightly, the man said angrily and hurriedly, like one who cannot waste precious time, exactly what Your Excellency just said: 'I made a mistake . . . excuse me, it was a misunderstanding, nothing but a misunderstanding.' And when the offended man nevertheless went on shouting and feeling offended, he observed to him in extreme vexation: 'But I tell you it was a misunderstanding, why are you still shouting!' "

"That . . . that is, of course, very funny . . ." Lembke smiled crookedly, "but . . . but don't you see how unhappy I am myself?"

He almost cried out and . . . and, it seemed, wanted to hide his face in his hands.

This unexpected, painful outcry, almost a sob, was unbearable. It was probably his first moment since the previous day of full and vivid awareness of all that had been happening—and then at once of despair, full, humiliating, surrendering; who knows, another minute and he might have begun sobbing for the whole room to hear. Stepan Trofimovich first gazed wildly at him, then suddenly inclined his head and in a deeply moved voice said:

"Your Excellency, trouble yourself no more over my peevish complaint, and simply order my books and letters returned . . ."

He was interrupted. At that very moment, Yulia Mikhailovna and her whole attendant company noisily came in. But this I would like to describe in as much detail as possible.

III

FIRST OF ALL, everyone from all three carriages came crowding into the reception room at once. There was a separate entrance to Yulia Mikhailovna's rooms, straight from the porch to the left; but this time everyone made their way through the reception room—precisely, I suspect, because Stepan Trofimovich was there, and because everything that had happened to him, as well as everything to do with the Shpigulin men, had been announced to Yulia Mikhailovna as she drove back to town. Lyamshin, who had been left behind for some offense and had not taken part in the excursion, had thus learned everything before anyone else and was able to announce it to her. With malicious glee he raced down the road to Skvoreshniki on a hired Cossack nag to meet the returning cavalcade with the merry news. I suppose Yulia Mikhailovna, in spite of all her lofty resolution, was still a bit embarrassed on hearing such a surprising report; though probably only for a moment. The political side of the question, for instance, could not worry her: Pyotr Stepanovich had already impressed it upon her at least four times that the Shpigulin ruffians all ought to be flogged, and Pyotr Stepanovich had indeed some time since become a great authority for her. "But . . . all the same I'll make him pay for it," she must have thought to herself, and the *him* referred, of course, to her husband. I will note in passing that this time, as if by design, Pyotr Stepanovich also did not take part in the general excursion, and no one had seen him anywhere since that morning. I will also mention, incidentally, that Varvara Petrovna, after receiving her visitors, returned with them to town (in the same carriage with Yulia Mikhailovna), in order to take part without fail in the final meeting of the committee for the next day's fête. She, too, must of course have been interested in the news conveyed by Lyamshin about Stepan Trofimovich, and may even have become worried.

The reckoning with Andrei Antonovich began at once. Alas, he felt it from the first glance at his lovely spouse. With a candid air, with a bewitching smile, she quickly approached Stepan Trofimovich, offered him her charmingly begloved hand, and showered him with the most flattering greetings—as if her only care that whole morning had been to hasten to rush up and shower kindnesses upon Stepan Trofimovich for seeing him at last in her house. Not a single hint at the morning search; just as though she still knew nothing. Not a single word to her husband, not a single glance in his direction—as though he were not even in the room. Moreover, she at once imperiously confiscated Stepan Trofimovich and led him off to the drawing room—just as if he had not been discussing anything with Lembke, or, if he had been, it was not worth continuing. Again I repeat: it seems to me that despite all her high tone, Yulia Mikhailovna here again made a great blunder. In this she was helped especially by Karmazinov (who had taken part in the excursion at Yulia Mikhailovna's special request, and who thus, albeit indirectly, did finally pay a visit to Varvara Petrovna, by which she, in her faintheartedness, was perfectly delighted). While still in the doorway (he came in later than the others), he cried out on seeing Stepan Trofimovich and made for him with his embraces, even getting in the way of Yulia Mikhailovna.

"It's been ages, ages! At last . . . *Excellent ami.*"

He set about kissing and, of course, offered his cheek. The flustered Stepan Trofimovich was obliged to plant a kiss on it.

"*Cher,*" he said to me that evening, recalling everything from the past day, "at that moment I thought: which of us is the meaner? He who is embracing me so as to humiliate me right there, or I who despise him and his cheek and yet kiss it right there, though I could turn away . . . pah!"

"So, tell me, tell me everything," Karmazinov mumbled and lisped, as though it were possible just to up and tell him one's whole life over twenty-five years. But this silly frivolity was in "high" tone.

"Remember, you and I last saw each other in Moscow, at a dinner in honor of Granovsky,[2] and twenty-four years have passed since then . . ." Stepan Trofimovich began, quite reasonably (and therefore not at all in high tone).

"*Ce cher homme,*" Karmazinov interrupted shrilly and familiarly, squeezing his shoulder much too amiably with his hand, "but do take us quickly to your rooms, Yulia Mikhailovna, he'll sit down there and tell us everything."

"And yet I've never been on close terms with that irritable old woman," Stepan Trofimovich went on complaining the same evening, shaking with anger. "We were still almost boys, and even then I was beginning to hate him . . . and he me, of course . . ."

Yulia Mikhailovna's salon filled up quickly. Varvara Petrovna was in an especially excited state, though she tried to appear indifferent; two or three times I caught her glancing hatefully at Karmazinov or wrathfully at Stepan Trofimovich—wrathful beforehand, wrathful out of jealousy, out of love: if Stepan Trofimovich were somehow to muff it this time and allow Karmazinov to cut him down in front of everyone, it seemed to me she would jump up at once and give him a thrashing. I forgot to mention that Liza was also there, and I had never seen her more joyful, carelessly gay, and happy. Of course, Mavriky Nikolaevich was there, too. Then, in the crowd of young ladies and half-licentious young men who constituted Yulia Mikhailovna's usual retinue, among whom this licentiousness was taken for gaiety and a pennyworth cynicism for intelligence, I noticed two or three new faces: some visiting and much mincing Pole; some German doctor, a hale old fellow who kept laughing loudly and with pleasure at his own witzes;[3] and, finally, some very young princeling from Petersburg, a mechanical figure, with the bearing of a statesman and a terribly long collar. But one could see that Yulia Mikhailovna greatly valued this visitor and was even anxious for her salon . . .

"*Cher monsieur Karmazinoff,*" Stepan Trofimovich began to speak, sitting himself down picturesquely on the sofa, and suddenly beginning to lisp no worse than Karmazinov, "*cher monsieur Karmazinoff,* the life of a man of our former time and of certain convictions, even over a span of twenty-five years, must appear monotonous . . ."

The German burst into a loud and abrupt guffaw, like a whinny, apparently thinking that Stepan Trofimovich had said something terribly funny. The latter looked at him with affected amazement, which failed, however, to produce any effect. The prince also looked, turning with all his collar towards the German and aiming his pince-nez at him, though without the least curiosity.

". . . Must appear monotonous," Stepan Trofimovich deliberately repeated, drawing each word out as lengthily and unceremoniously as possible. "Such, too, has my life been for this whole quarter of a century, *et comme on trouve partout plus de moines que de raison,* * and since I fully agree with that,[4] the result is that for this whole quarter of a century I . . ."

"*C'est charmant, les moines,*"† Yulia Mikhailovna whispered, turning to Varvara Petrovna, who was sitting next to her.

Varvara Petrovna responded with a proud look. But Karmazinov could not bear the success of the French phrase, and quickly and shrilly interrupted Stepan Trofimovich.

"As for me, I am at ease in that regard, and it's seven years now that I've been sitting in Karlsruhe. And when the city council decided last year to install a new drainpipe, I felt in my heart that this Karlsruhian

---

*"and as one finds more monks than reason everywhere"
†"That's charming, the monks"

drainpipe question was dearer and fonder to me than all the questions of my dear fatherland . . . during all the time of these so-called reforms here."

"I am forced to sympathize, though it is counter to my heart," Stepan Trofimovich sighed, inclining his head significantly.

Yulia Mikhailovna was triumphant: the conversation was acquiring both profundity and direction.

"You mean a sewer pipe?" the doctor inquired loudly.

"A drainpipe, doctor, a drainpipe, and I even helped them to draw up the plan."

The doctor gave a splitting guffaw. Many followed him, but this time in the doctor's face, who did not notice it and was terribly pleased that everyone was laughing.

"Allow me to disagree with you, Karmazinov," Yulia Mikhailovna hastened to put in. "Karlsruhe is one thing, but you love to be mystifying, and this time we shall not believe you. Who among Russians, among writers, has put forth so many of the most modern types, divined so many of the most modern questions, indicated precisely those modern points of which the type of the modern activist is composed? You, you alone, and no one else. Just try and convince us after that of your indifference to your motherland and your terrible interest in the Karlsruhian drainpipe! Ha, ha!"

"Yes, of course," Karmazinov lisped, "I did put forth in the type of Pogozhev all the flaws of the Slavophils, and in the type of Nikodimov all the flaws of the Westerners . . ."

"*All*, indeed," Lyamshin whispered softly.

"But I do it offhand, just to kill ineluctable time somehow and . . . to satisfy all these ineluctable demands of my compatriots."

"It is probably known to you, Stepan Trofimovich," Yulia Mikhailovna went on rapturously, "that tomorrow we shall have the delight of hearing the charming lines . . . one of Semyon Yegorovich's very latest, most gracious artistic inspirations, it is entitled *Merci*. In this piece he announces that he will write no more, not for anything in the world, even if an angel from heaven, or, better to say, all of high society should beg him to alter his decision. In short, he lays down his pen for the rest of his life, and this graceful *Merci* is addressed to the public in gratitude for the constant rapture with which it has accompanied for so many years his constant service to honest Russian thought . . ."

Yulia Mikhailovna was at the height of bliss.

"Yes, it will be my farewell; I'll say my *Merci* and leave, and there . . . in Karlsruhe . . . I shall close my eyes," Karmazinov gradually started going to pieces.

Like many of our great writers (and we have very many great writers), he could not resist praise, and would begin to go soft at once, despite his wit. But I think this is pardonable. They say one of our Shakespeares blurted right out in private conversation that "for us *great men* it is impossible to do otherwise," etc., and, what's more, did not even notice it.

"There, in Karlsruhe, I shall close my eyes. For us great men, all that's left once our work is done is to hasten to close our eyes, without seeking a reward. I shall do the same."

"Give me the address, and I'll come to visit your grave in Karlsruhe," the German guffawed boundlessly.

"Nowadays they even send dead people by train," one of the insignificant young men said unexpectedly.

Lyamshin simply squealed with delight. Yulia Mikhailovna frowned. Nikolai Stavrogin entered.

"And I was told you'd been taken to the police station," he said loudly, addressing Stepan Trofimovich first of all.

"No, just my *stationery*," Stepan Trofimovich punned.

"But I hope it will not have the slightest influence upon my request," Yulia Mikhailovna picked up again, "I hope that, notwithstanding this unfortunate annoyance, of which I still have no idea, you will not disappoint our best expectations and deprive us of the delight of hearing your reading at the literary matinée."

"I don't know, I . . . now . . ."

"Really, I'm so unfortunate, Varvara Petrovna . . . and imagine, precisely when I so desired to quickly make the personal acquaintance of one of the most remarkable and independent Russian minds, and now Stepan Trofimovich suddenly expresses his intention of withdrawing from us."

"Your compliment was spoken so loudly that I, of course, ought to turn a deaf ear to it," Stepan Trofimovich rapped out, "but I do not believe that my poor person was so necessary for your fête tomorrow. However, I . . ."

"No, you're going to spoil him!" Pyotr Stepanovich cried, running quickly into the room. "I've just taken him in hand, and suddenly, in one morning—a search, an arrest, a policeman grabs him by the scruff of the neck, and now the ladies are cooing over him in the burgomaster's salon! Every little bone in him is aching with delight now; he's never dreamed of such a gala performance. Wait and see how he starts denouncing the socialists now!"

"That cannot be, Pyotr Stepanovich. Socialism is too great an idea for Stepan Trofimovich not to be aware of it," Yulia Mikhailovna interceded energetically.

"The idea is great, but those who profess it are not always giants, *et brisons-là, mon cher,*"* Stepan Trofimovich concluded, addressing his son and rising handsomely from his place.

But here a most unexpected circumstance occurred. Von Lembke had already been in the salon for some time, but had gone as if unnoticed by anyone, though everyone had seen him come in. Yulia Mikhailovna, still set on her former idea, continued to ignore him. He placed himself by the door and, with a stern look, gloomily listened to the conversation. On hearing the morning's events alluded to, he began looking around somehow uneasily, fixing his stare first on the prince, apparently struck by the thrust of his heavily starched collar; then he suddenly seemed to give a start, hearing the voice of Pyotr Stepanovich and seeing him run in, and, as soon as Stepan Trofimovich managed to utter his maxim about the socialists, he suddenly went up to him, knocking on the way into Lyamshin, who jumped aside at once with an exaggerated gesture of surprise, rubbing his shoulder and pretending he had been badly hurt.

"Enough!" said von Lembke, energetically grabbing the frightened Stepan Trofimovich's hand and squeezing it as hard as he could in his own. "Enough, the filibusters of our time are ascertained. Not a word more. Measures have been taken . . ."

He uttered it loudly, for the whole room to hear, concluding ener-

*"and let's break off there, my dear"

getically. The impression produced was painful. Everyone sensed that something was not well. I saw Yulia Mikhailovna turn pale. The effect was crowned by a silly accident. After announcing that measures had been taken, Lembke turned around sharply and started quickly out of the room, but after two steps he tripped on the rug, lurched nose downwards, and nearly fell. He stopped for a moment, looked at the place where he had tripped, and, having said aloud, "Change it," walked out the door. Yulia Mikhailovna ran after him. Her exit was followed by an uproar in which it was difficult to make anything out. Some said he was "deranged," others that he was "susceptible." A third group pointed their fingers to their foreheads; Lyamshin, in the corner, put two fingers above his forehead. There were hints at some domestic events, all in a whisper, of course. None of them took their hats, but all were waiting. I do not know what Yulia Mikhailovna managed to do, but she came back in about five minutes trying as hard as she could to appear calm. She answered evasively that Andrei Antonovich was slightly agitated, but that it was nothing, that he had had it since childhood, that she knew "far better," and that tomorrow's fête would certainly cheer him up. There followed a few flattering words to Stepan Trofimovich, but solely for the sake of decency, and a loud invitation to the committee members to open the meeting right then, at once. Only now did those not participating in the committee start preparing to go home; but the painful adventures of that fatal day were not yet over . . .

At the very moment when Nikolai Vsevolodovich entered, I noticed that Liza looked quickly and intently at him, and for a long time afterwards did not take her eyes off him—so long that in the end it aroused attention. I saw that Mavriky Nikolaevich bent over her from behind and, it seemed, wanted to whisper something to her, but evidently changed his intention and quickly straightened up, looking around at everyone like a guilty man. Nikolai Vsevolodovich, too, aroused curiosity: his face was paler than usual, and his gaze uncommonly distracted. After tossing his question at Stepan Trofimovich on entering, it was as if he forgot about him at once, and indeed, it seems to me, he even forgot to approach the hostess. He never once glanced at Liza—not because he did not want to, but, I maintain, because he did not notice her at all either. And suddenly, after some silence following Yulia Mikhailovna's invitation to open the last meeting without further delay—suddenly there came Liza's ringing, deliberately loud voice. She called to Nikolai Stavrogin.

"Nikolai Vsevolodovich, some captain who calls himself your relation, your wife's brother, a man by the name of Lebyadkin, keeps writing indecent letters to me, complaining in them about you, offering to reveal to me certain secrets concerning you. If he really is your relation, do forbid him to offend me and rid me of this unpleasantness."

A terrible challenge could be heard in these words, everyone understood that. The accusation was obvious, though perhaps unexpected even for her. She was like someone closing her eyes and throwing herself off a roof.

But Nikolai Stavrogin's answer was even more astounding.

First of all, it was strange enough that he was in no way surprised and listened to Liza with the most calm attention. His face reflected neither embarrassment nor wrath. Simply, firmly, even with an air of complete readiness, he answered the fatal question:

"Yes, I have the misfortune to be this man's relation. I am the husband of his sister, née Lebyadkin, soon now it will be for five years. Rest assured that I will convey your demands to him in the nearest future, and I will answer for his not troubling you anymore."

I will never forget the horror that was expressed on Varvara Petrovna's face. With an insane look she rose from her chair, holding her right hand up in front of her as if to defend herself. Nikolai Vsevolodovich looked at her, at Liza, at the spectators, and suddenly smiled with boundless haughtiness; unhurriedly, he walked out of the room. Everyone saw how Liza jumped up from the sofa as soon as Nikolai Vsevolodovich turned to leave and made an obvious move to run after him, but caught hold of herself and did not run but walked out quietly, also without saying a word to anyone or looking at anyone, accompanied, of course, by Mavriky Nikolaevich, who rushed after her . . .

Of the uproar and talk in town that evening I will not even make mention. Varvara Petrovna locked herself in her town house, and Nikolai Vsevolodovich, it was said, drove straight to Skvoreshniki without seeing his mother. Stepan Trofimovich sent me to *"cette chère amie"* in the evening to beg permission for him to come to her, but I was not received. He was terribly struck; he wept. "Such a marriage!

Such a marriage! Such horror in the family," he repeated all the time. However, he also kept recalling Karmazinov and abused him terribly. He was preparing energetically for the next day's reading and—the artistic nature!—preparing in front of the mirror, recalling all his witticisms and little puns over the course of his life, specially written down in a notebook, so as to introduce them into the next day's reading.

"My friend, this is for the sake of a great idea," he said to me, apparently justifying himself. "*Cher ami,* I have moved from my place of twenty-five years and suddenly set out—where, I do not know, but I have set out . . ."

PART THREE

PART THREE

1

The Fête. First Part

I

THE FÊTE TOOK PLACE, all the perplexities of the previous "Shpigulin" day notwithstanding. I think that even if Lembke had died that same night, the fête would still have taken place in the morning—so much of some special significance did Yulia Mikhailovna connect with it. Alas, until the final moment she remained blind and did not understand the mood of society. No one towards the end believed that the great day would go by without some colossal adventure, without a "denouement," as some put it, rubbing their hands in anticipation. Many, it is true, tried to assume a most frowning and political look; but, generally speaking, the Russian man is boundlessly amused by any socially scandalous commotion. True, there was among us something rather more serious than the mere thirst for scandal; there was a general irritation, something unappeasably spiteful; it seemed everyone was terribly sick of everything. Some sort of general, muddled cynicism had come to reign, a forced, as if strained, cynicism. Only the ladies were not to be muddled, and that only on one point: their merciless hatred of Yulia Mikhailovna. In this all the ladies' tendencies converged. And she, poor woman, did not even suspect; until the final hour she remained convinced that she was "surrounded" and still the subject of "fanatical devotion."

I have already hinted at the fact that various trashy sorts of people had appeared among us. Always and everywhere, in a troubled time of hesitation or transition, various trashy sorts appear. I am not speaking of the so-called "vanguard," who always rush ahead of everyone else (their chief concern) and whose goal, though very often quite stupid, is still more or less definite. No, I am speaking only of scum. This scum, which exists in every society, rises to the surface in any transitional time, and not only has no goal, but has not even the inkling of an idea, and itself merely expresses anxiety and impatience with all its might. And yet this scum, without knowing it, almost always falls under the command of that small group of the "vanguard" which acts with a definite goal, and which directs all this rabble wherever it pleases, provided it does not consist of perfect idiots itself—which, incidentally, also happens. It is said among us now, when everything is already over, that Pyotr Stepanovich was controlled by the Internationale,[1] that Pyotr Stepanovich controlled Yulia Mikhailovna, and that she, at his command, directed all sorts of scum. Our most solid minds are now marveling at themselves: how could they suddenly have gone so amiss then? What our troubled time consisted of, and from what to what our transition was—I do not know, and no one, I think, knows—except perhaps certain visitors from outside. And yet the trashiest people suddenly gained predominance and began loudly criticizing all that's holy, whereas earlier they had not dared to open their mouths, and the foremost people, who until then had so happily kept the upper hand, suddenly began listening to them, and became silent themselves; and some even chuckled along in a most disgraceful way. Some sort of Lyamshins, Telyatnikovs, landowner Tentetnikovs, homegrown milksop Radishchevs,[2] little Jews with mournful but haughty smiles, jolly passing travelers, poets with a tendency from the capital, poets who in place of a tendency and talent had peasant coats and tarred boots, majors and colonels who laughed at the meaninglessness of their rank and were ready, for an extra rouble, to take off their swords at once and slink away to become railroad clerks; generals defecting to the lawyers; developed dealers, developing little merchants, countless seminarians, women who embodied in themselves the woman question—all this suddenly and fully gained the upper hand among us, and over whom? Over the club, over venerable dignitaries, over generals on wooden legs, over our most strict and inaccessible ladies' society. If even Varvara Petrovna, right up to the catastrophe with her boy, was all but running errands for all this scum, then some of our Minervas can be partially forgiven for their befuddlement at the time. Now everything is imputed, as I have already said, to the Internationale. The idea has grown so strong that even all the visiting outsiders have been informed along these lines. Just recently Councillor Kubrikov, sixty-two years old and with a Stanislav round his neck,[3] came without any summons and declared in a heartfelt voice that during the whole three months he had undoubtedly been under the influence of the Internationale. And when, with all due respect for his age and merits, he was asked to explain himself more satisfactorily, though unable to present any documents except that he "felt it with all his senses," he nevertheless stuck firmly to his declaration, so that he was not questioned further.

I will repeat once again. Among us there was also preserved a small group of prudent persons who had secluded themselves at the very beginning and even locked themselves in. But what lock can stand against a law of nature? In the same way, even in the most prudent families, young ladies grow up who have a need to go dancing. And so all these persons, too, ended up by subscribing for the governesses. And the ball promised to be so magnificent, boundless; wonders were being told; rumors spread about visiting princes with lorgnettes, about ten ushers, all young cavaliers, with bows on their left shoulders; about Petersburg movers of some sort; about Karmazinov consenting to augment the collection by reading *Merci* in the costume of a governess from our province; about the planned "quadrille of literature," also all in costume, with each costume representing some tendency. Finally, also in costume, some sort of "honest Russian thought" would perform a dance—which in itself was a complete novelty. How could one not subscribe? Everyone subscribed.

II

ACCORDING to the program, the festive day was divided into two parts: the literary matinée, from noon till four, and then the ball, from nine o'clock on through the night. But this arrangement itself concealed germs of disorder. First, from the very beginning a rumor established itself among the public about a luncheon right after the literary matinée, or even during it, with a break especially arranged for that purpose—a free luncheon, naturally, as part of the program, and with champagne. The enormous price of the ticket (three roubles) contributed to this rumor's taking root. "Because why should I subscribe for nothing? The fête is supposed to go on round the clock, so they'll have to feed us. People will get hungry"—thus the reasoning went. I must admit that it was Yulia Mikhailovna herself who planted this pernicious rumor through her own light-mindedness. About a month earlier, still under the initial enchantment of the grand design, she had babbled about her fête with whoever happened along, and about the fact that toasts would be proposed she had even sent a notice to one of the metropolitan newspapers. She had been seduced mainly by these toasts then: she wanted to propose them herself, and kept devising them in anticipation. They were to explain our chief banner (what banner? I bet the poor dear never devised anything), to be passed on in the form of reports to the metropolitan newspapers, to touch and charm the higher authorities, and then to go winging over all the provinces, arousing astonishment and imitation. But for toasts champagne was necessary, and since one could not really drink champagne on an empty stomach, a luncheon, of itself, also became necessary. Later, when through her efforts a committee had been formed and they got down to business more seriously, it was proved to her at once and clearly that if one were dreaming of banquets, very little would be left for the governesses, even with the most abundant collection. The question thus presented two solutions: either a Belshazzar's feast[4] with toasts and about ninety roubles left for the governesses, or the realization of a significant collection, with the fête being, so to speak, only for form. The committee only wanted to give her a scare, however, and, of course, came up with a third solution, conciliatory and sensible—that is, quite a proper fête in all respects, only without champagne, and thus with quite a decent sum as a balance, much more than ninety roubles. But Yulia Mikhailovna did not agree; her character despised the philistine middle. She resolved then and there, since the first idea was unfeasible, to rush immediately and entirely to the opposite extreme—that is, to realize a colossal collection that would be the envy of all the provinces. "For the public must finally understand," she concluded her fiery committee speech, "that the achievement of universal human goals is incomparably loftier than momentary physical pleasures, that the fête is essentially only a proclamation of the great idea, and therefore one must be content with the most economical little German ball, solely as an allegory, since it's impossible to do without this obnoxious ball altogether!"—so much did she suddenly hate it. But she was finally calmed down. It was then, for example, that they thought up and suggested the "quadrille of literature" and other aesthetic things to replace physical pleasures. It was then, too, that Karmazinov finally agreed to read *Merci* (until then he had only hemmed and hawed), and thereby annihilate even the very idea of food in the minds of our incontinent public. In this way the ball was again becoming a most magnificent festivity, though no longer of the same sort. And so as not to go soaring off completely into the clouds, it was decided that at the beginning of the ball they would serve tea with lemon and little round cookies, then orgeat and lemonade, and lastly even ice cream, but that was all. For those who, always and everywhere, inevitably feel hungry and, above all, thirsty—a special buffet would be opened at the far end of the suite of rooms, to be taken charge of by Prokhorych (the head cook at the club), who—though under strict supervision by the committee—would serve whatever anyone liked, but for a separate price, and to that end a written announcement would be posted at the door of the reception hall that the buffet was outside the program. But for the matinée they decided not to open the buffet at all, so as not to interfere with the reading, even though the buffet would be located five rooms away from the white hall in which Karmazinov had consented to read *Merci*. Curiously, it seems this event—that is, the reading of *Merci*—was seen by the committee as being all too colossally significant, and even by the most practical people. As for the more poetical people, the wife of the marshal of nobility announced to Karmazinov, for instance, that after the reading she would at once order a marble plaque to be fixed to the wall of her white hall with an inscription in gold saying that on such-and-such a day and year, here, on this spot, the great Russian and European writer, as he laid down his pen, read *Merci* and thus for the first time bade farewell to the Russian public in the persons of the representatives of our town, and that everyone would be able to read this inscription at the ball, that is, only five hours after *Merci* was read. I know for certain that it was chiefly Karmazinov who demanded that there be no buffet at the matinée, while he was reading, on any account whatsoever, despite the remarks of some committee members that this was not quite our way of doing things.

Thus matters stood, while in town people still went on believing in a Belshazzar's feast—that is, in the committee buffet; they believed in it to the last hour. Even the young ladies dreamed of quantities of candies and preserves and other unheard-of things. Everyone knew that the collection realized was abundant, that the whole town would be storming the doors, that people were coming in from the country, and there were not enough tickets. It was also known that beyond the fixed price there had also been considerable donations: Varvara Petrovna, for example, had paid three hundred roubles for her ticket and provided all the flowers from her greenhouse to decorate the hall. The marshal's wife (a committee member) provided her house and the lighting; the club provided the music and servants, and released Prokhorych for the whole day. There were other donations, though not such big ones, so that there was even a thought of lowering the original ticket price from three roubles to two. The committee indeed feared at first that the young ladies would not come for three roubles, and suggested arranging family tickets somehow—namely, by asking each family to pay for just one young lady, while all other young ladies of the same name, even an edition of ten, would come free. But all fears proved groundless: on the contrary, it was precisely the young ladies who did come. Even the poorest officials brought their girls, and it was only too clear that if they had not had girls, it would never have occurred to them to subscribe. One most insignificant secretary brought all seven of his daughters, not to mention his wife, of course, and also his niece, and each of these persons held a three-rouble entrance ticket in her hand. One can imagine, however, what a revolution went on in town! Take merely the fact that the fête was divided into two parts, and thus for each lady two costumes were necessary—a morning gown for the reading, and a ball gown for the dancing. Many of the middle class, it turned out later, pawned everything for that day, even the family linen, even their sheets and almost their mattresses, to the local Jews, who, over the past two years, as if on purpose, had been settling in terrible quantities in our town, and keep coming more and more. Almost all the officials took an advance on their salaries, and some landowners sold much-needed cattle, and all this just so as to bring their young ladies looking like real marquises, and to be no worse than others. The magnificence of the costumes this time was, considering the place, unheard-of. Two weeks beforehand the town was already stuffed with family anecdotes, all of which were immediately carried to Yulia Mikhailovna's court by our witlings. Family caricatures were passed around. I myself saw several drawings of this sort in Yulia Mikhailovna's album. All this became only too well known there where the anecdotes originated; that, it seems to me, is why such hatred for Yulia Mikhailovna had built up lately in these families. Now they all curse and gnash their teeth when they recall it. But it was clear beforehand that if the committee should fail to please in some way, were the ball to go amiss somehow, there would be an unheard-of outburst of indignation. That is why everyone was secretly expecting a scandal; and if it was so expected, how then could it not take place?

At noon precisely the orchestra struck up. Being one of the ushers, that is, one of the twelve "young men with a bow," I saw with my own eyes how this day of infamous memory began. It began with a boundless crush at the entrance. How did it happen that everything went amiss from the very first, beginning with the police? I do not blame the real public: fathers of families not only were not crowding each other or anyone else, even despite their rank, but, on the contrary, are said to have been abashed while still in the street at the sight, unusual for our town, of the shoving mob that was besieging the entrance and trying to force it, instead of simply going in. Meanwhile, carriages kept driving up and finally blocked the street. Now, as I write, I have solid grounds for affirming that some of the vilest scum of our town were simply brought in without tickets by Lyamshin and Liputin, and perhaps also by someone else who, like me, was one of the ushers. Anyway, even completely unknown persons appeared, who came from other districts and elsewhere. The moment these savages entered the hall, they would go at once to inquire, in the same words (as if they had been prompted), where the buffet was, and on learning that there was no buffet, would begin swearing without any politics and with a boldness hitherto unusual among us. True, some of them came drunk.

Some were struck, like savages, by the magnificence of the marshal's wife's reception hall, since they had never seen anything like it, and, on entering, would become hushed for a moment and gaze around openmouthed. This big White Hall, despite its already decrepit structure, was indeed magnificent: of huge dimensions, with windows on both sides, with a ceiling decorated in the old manner and trimmed with gold, with galleries, with mirrors between the windows, with red and white draperies, with marble statues (such as they were, still they were statues), with heavy old furniture of the Napoleonic era, gilt white and upholstered in red velvet. At the moment described here, a high platform rose up at the end of the hall for the writers who were to read, and the entire room was completely filled with chairs, like the parterre of a theater, with wide aisles for the public. But after the first moments of astonishment, the most senseless questions and declarations would begin. "Maybe we don't even want any reading . . . We paid money . . . The public has been brazenly deceived . . . We're the masters, not the Lembkas! . . ." In a word, as though it were for just this that they had been let in. I recall particularly one confrontation in which yesterday's visiting princeling distinguished himself, the one who had been at Yulia Mikhailovna's the previous morning, in his standing collar, and looking like a wooden doll. He, too, at her relentless request, had agreed to pin a bow to his left shoulder and become our fellow usher. It turned out that this mute wax figure on springs knew, if not how to speak, then at least, after a fashion, how to act. When one pockmarked, colossal retired captain, supported by a whole crew of various scum crowding at his back, began to pester him about "where to get to the buffet"—he winked to a policeman. The directive was promptly fulfilled: in spite of his swearing, the drunken captain was dragged out of the hall. Meanwhile, the "real" public also began finally to appear and in three long lines threaded its way down the three aisles between the chairs. The disorderly element began to quiet down, but the public, even the "cleanest" part of it, had a displeased and amazed look; some of the ladies were quite simply frightened.

Finally all were seated; the music also died down. People began blowing their noses, looking around. They were altogether too solemnly expectant—which is always a bad sign in itself. But the "Lembkas" were still not there. Silks, velvets, diamonds shone and sparkled on all sides; fragrance permeated the air. The men were wearing all their decorations, and the old men were even wearing their uniforms. Finally, the marshal's wife also appeared, together with Liza. Never before had Liza been so dazzlingly lovely as that morning, or so magnificently attired. Her hair was done up in curls, her eyes flashed, a smile shone on her face. She produced a visible effect; she was looked over, whispered about. People said she was seeking Stavrogin with her eyes, but neither Stavrogin nor Varvara Petrovna was there. I did not then understand the expression of her face: why was there so much happiness, joy, energy, strength in this face? I kept recalling yesterday's event, and was nonplussed. The "Lembkas," however, were still not there. This was indeed a mistake. I learned afterwards that Yulia Mikhailovna had waited till the last minute for Pyotr Stepanovich, without whom she could not take a step lately, though she never admitted it to herself. I will note in parenthesis that at the last committee meeting, the previous day, Pyotr Stepanovich had refused the usher's bow, which had upset her very much, even to tears. To her surprise, and afterwards to her great embarrassment (which I announce beforehand), he disappeared for the whole morning and did not come to the literary reading at all, so that no one met him until that same evening. Finally, the public began to show obvious impatience. No one appeared on the platform, either. In the back rows people began clapping as in a theater. Old men and ladies were frowning: the "Lembkas" were obviously giving themselves too many airs. Even among the best part of the public an absurd whispering began, that perhaps the fête would indeed not take place, that perhaps Lembke himself was indeed quite unwell, and so on and so forth. But, thank God, the Lembkes finally appeared, he leading her by the arm—I confess, I myself was terribly worried about their appearance. But the fables thus were falling, and truth was claiming its own. The public seemed relieved. Lembke himself, apparently, was in perfect health, as I recall everyone else also concluded, for one can imagine how many eyes were turned on him. I will note as characteristic that generally very few people in our higher society supposed that Lembke was somehow not quite well; and his deeds were found perfectly normal, so much so that even the previous day's episode in the square was received with approval. "Should've done it that way from the start," the dignitaries said. "But no, they come as philanthropists and end up with the same thing, without noticing that it's necessary for philanthropy itself"—so at least they reasoned in the club. They only blamed him for getting into a temper over it. "One has to keep cool, but after all the man is new at it," the connoisseurs said. With equal greediness all eyes turned to Yulia Mikhailovna as well. Of course, no one has the right to demand of me as a narrator too detailed an account of one point: here is mystery, here is woman; but one thing I do know: the previous evening she had gone into Andrei Antonovich's study and was with him till well past midnight. Andrei Antonovich was forgiven and consoled. The spouses agreed in all things, everything was forgotten, and when at the end of their talk von Lembke did go on his knees all the same, remembering with horror the main concluding episode of the previous night, the lovely little hand, and after it the lips, of his spouse blocked the fiery outpouring of penitent speeches of a man chivalrously delicate, yet weakened by tenderness. Everyone saw happiness on her face. She walked with a candid air and in a splendid dress. It seemed she was at the summit of her desires, the fête—the goal and crown of her politics—was realized. As they proceeded to their places just in front of the platform, both Lembkes were bowing and responding to others' bows. They were surrounded at once. The marshal's wife rose to meet them . . . But here a nasty misunderstanding occurred: the orchestra, out of the blue, burst into a flourish—not some sort of march, but simply a dinnertime flourish, as at table in our club, when they drink someone's health during an official banquet. I know now that this was owing to the good services of Lyamshin, in his capacity as usher, supposedly to honor the entrance of the "Lembkas." Of course, he could always make the excuse that he had done it out of stupidity or excessive zeal . . . Alas, I did not yet know that by then they were no longer worried about making excuses, and that that day was to put an end to everything. But the flourish was not the end of it: along with the vexatious bewilderment and smiling of the public, suddenly, from the end of the hall and from the gallery there came a *hurrah,* also as if in honor of the Lembkes. The voices were few, but I confess they lasted for some time. Yulia Mikhailovna turned red; her eyes flashed. Lembke had stopped by his place and, turning in the direction of those who were shouting, was grandly and sternly surveying the hall . . . He was quickly seated. I noticed with fear that same dangerous smile on his face with which he had stood yesterday morning in his wife's drawing room and looked at Stepan Trofimovich before going up to him. It seemed to me that now, too, there was some ominous expression on his face, and, worst of all, a slightly comical one, the expression of a being who is offering himself—oh, very well— as a sacrifice, only to play up to the higher aims of his wife . . . Yulia Mikhailovna hastily beckoned me to her and whispered that I should run to Karmazinov and beg him to begin. No sooner had I turned around than another abomination occurred, only much nastier than the first one. On the platform, on the empty platform, to which till that moment all eyes and all expectations had been turned, and where all that could be seen was a small table, a chair before it, and on the table a glass of water on a little silver tray—on this empty platform suddenly flashed the colossal figure of Captain Lebyadkin in a tailcoat and white tie. I was so struck that I did not believe my eyes. The captain, it seems, became abashed and halted at the rear of the platform. Suddenly, from amid the public, a shout was heard: "Lebyadkin! you?" The captain's stupid red mug (he was totally drunk) spread at this cry into a broad, dumb smile. He raised his hand, rubbed his forehead with it, shook his shaggy head, and, as if venturing all, stepped two steps forward and— suddenly snorted with laughter, not loud but long, happy, rippling, which sent his whole fleshy mass heaving and made his little eyes shrink. At the sight of this, nearly half the public laughed, twenty people applauded. The serious public gloomily exchanged glances; all this, however, lasted no more than half a minute. Suddenly Liputin with his usher's bow and two servants ran out on the platform; they carefully took the captain under both arms, while Liputin did a bit of whispering in his ear. The captain frowned, muttered "Ah, well, in that case," waved his hand, turned his enormous back to the public, and disappeared with his escort. But a moment later Liputin again jumped out on the platform. On his lips was the sweetest of his perennial smiles, which usually resembled vinegar and sugar, and in his hands was a sheet of writing paper. With small but rapid steps he came to the edge of the platform.

"Ladies and gentlemen," he addressed the public, "by oversight a comical misunderstanding took place, which has been removed; but I, not without hope, have taken upon myself a charge and a profound, most respectful request from one of our local town bards . . . Moved by a humane and lofty goal . . . in spite of his looks . . . the very same goal which has united us all . . . to dry the tears of the poor educated girls of our province . . . this gentleman—that is, I mean to say, this local poet . . . while wishing to preserve his incognito . . . very much wished to see his poem read before the start of the ball . . . that is, I meant to say—the reading. Although this poem is not on the program and doesn't figure . . . because it was delivered only half an hour ago . . . yet it seemed to *us*" (us who? I am citing this abrupt and muddled speech verbatim) "that with its remarkable naïvety of feeling, combined with as remarkable a gaiety, the poem could be read—that is, not as something serious, but as something suited to the festivities . . . To the idea, in short . . . Moreover, these few lines . . . and so I wanted to ask permission of the benevolent public."

"Read it!" barked a voice from the end of the hall.

"Shall I read it, then?"

"Read it, read it!" came many voices.

"I'll read it, with the public's permission," Liputin twisted himself up again, with the same sugary smile. It seemed as if he still could not make up his mind, and I even had the impression that he was worried. These people sometimes stumble, for all their boldness. However, a seminarian would not have stumbled, and Liputin did, after all, belong to the old society.

"I warn you—I mean, I have the honor of warning you—that all the same this is not really the kind of ode that once used to be written for festive occasions, this is almost, so to speak, a joke, but combining indisputable feeling and playful gaiety, and with, so to speak, the realmost truth."

"Read it, read it!"

He unfolded the piece of paper. Of course, no one had time to stop him. Besides, he was there with an usher's bow. In a ringing voice he declaimed:

"To the fatherland's governess of local parts from a poet at the fête.

"I give you greetings grand and grander,
Governess! Be triumphant now,

Retrograde or true George-Sander,
Be exultant anyhow!"

"But that's Lebyadkin's! It is, it's Lebyadkin's!" several voices echoed. There was laughter and even applause, though not widespread.

"You teach our snot-nosed children French
From an alphabetic book,
The beadle even, in a pinch,
For marriage you won't overlook!"

"Hoorah! hoorah!"

"But now, when great reforms are flowering,
Even a beadle's hard to hook:
Unless, young miss, you've got a 'dowering,'
It's back to the alphabetic book."

"Precisely, precisely, that's realism, not a step without a 'dowering'!"

"Today, however, with our hosting
We have raised much capital,
And while dancing here we're posting
A dowry to you from this hall.

Retrograde or true George-Sander,
Be exultant anyhow!
Governess by dower grander,
Spit on the rest and triumph now!"

I confess, I did not believe my ears. Here was such obvious impudence that it was impossible to excuse Liputin even by stupidity. And, anyway, Liputin was far from stupid. The intention was clear, to me at least: they were as if hastening the disorder. Some lines of this idiotic poem, the very last one, for example, were of a sort that no stupidity would allow. Liputin himself seemed to feel that he had taken on too much: having accomplished his great deed, he was so taken aback by his own boldness that he did not even leave the platform, but went on standing there as if wishing to add something. He must have supposed it would come out somehow differently; but even the bunch of hooligans who had applauded during the escapade suddenly fell silent, as if they, too, were taken aback. Stupidest of all was that many of them took the whole escapade in a pathetic sense—that is, not as lampoonery, but indeed as the real truth concerning governesses, as verse with a tendency. But these people, too, were finally struck by the excessive license of the poem. As for the rest of the public, the entire hall was not only scandalized but visibly offended. I am not mistaken in conveying the impression. Yulia Mikhailovna said afterwards that she would have fainted in another moment. One of the most venerable little old men helped his little old lady to her feet, and they both left the hall, followed by the alarmed eyes of the public. Who knows, the example might have carried others along as well, if at that moment Karmazinov himself had not appeared on the platform, in a tailcoat and white tie, and with a notebook in his hand. Yulia Mikhailovna turned rapturous eyes to him, as to a deliverer . . . But by then I had already gone backstage; I was after Liputin.

"You did it on purpose!" I said, indignantly seizing him by the arm.

"By God, I had no idea," he cowered, immediately starting to lie and pretend to be miserable, "the verses were just brought, and I thought as a merry joke . . ."

"You never thought any such thing. Can you possibly find that giftless trash a merry joke?"

"Yes, sir, I do."

"You're simply lying, and it wasn't just brought to you. You wrote it yourself, together with Lebyadkin, maybe yesterday, to cause a scandal. The last line is certainly yours, and the part about the beadle as well. Why did he come out in a tailcoat? It means you were preparing to have him read, if he hadn't gotten drunk?"

Liputin looked at me coldly and caustically.

"What business is it of yours?" he asked suddenly, with a strange calm.

"What? You're wearing one of these bows, too . . . Where is Pyotr Stepanovich?"

"I don't know, somewhere around. Why?"

"Because I see through it now. This is simply a conspiracy against Yulia Mikhailovna, to disgrace the day . . ."

Liputin again looked askance at me.

"And what is that to you?" he grinned, shrugged, and walked off.

I felt as if stricken. All my suspicions were justified. And I had still hoped I was mistaken! What was I to do? I thought of discussing it with Stepan Trofimovich, but he was standing in front of the mirror, trying on various smiles, and constantly consulting a piece of paper on which he had made some notes. He was to go on right after Karmazinov and was no longer in any condition to talk with me. Should I run to Yulia Mikhailovna? But it was too soon for her: she needed a much harsher lesson to cure her of the conviction of her "surroundedness" and the general "fanatical devotion." She would not believe me and would regard me as a dreamer. And how could she be of help? "Eh," I thought, "really, what business is it of mine? I'll take the bow off and go home, *once it starts.*" I actually said "once it starts," I remember that.

But I had to go and listen to Karmazinov. Taking a last look around backstage, I noticed that there were quite a few outsiders, and even women, darting about, coming and going. This "backstage" was quite a narrow space, totally screened off from the public by a curtain and connected through a corridor in back with other rooms. Here our readers waited their turns. But I was particularly struck at that moment by the lecturer who was to follow Stepan Trofimovich. He, too, was some sort of professor (even now I do not know exactly what he was), who had voluntarily retired from some institution after some student incident and had turned up in our town for one reason or another just a few days earlier. He, too, had been recommended to Yulia Mikhailovna, and she had received him with reverence. I know now that he had visited her only on one evening prior to the reading, had spent the whole evening in silence, had smiled ambiguously at the jokes and tone of the company that surrounded Yulia Mikhailovna, and had made an unpleasant impression on everyone by his air—arrogant and at the same time touchy to the point of timorousness. It was Yulia Mikhailovna herself who had recruited him to read. Now he was pacing from corner to corner and, like Stepan Trofimovich, was whispering to himself as well, but looking at the ground, not in the mirror. He did not try on any smiles, though he smiled frequently and carnivorously. Clearly it was not possible to talk with him, either. He was short, looked about forty, was bald front and back, had a grayish little beard, and dressed decently. But most interesting was that at each turn he raised his right fist high, shook it in the air above his head, and suddenly brought it down as if crushing some adversary to dust. He repeated this trick every moment. It gave me an eerie feeling. I ran quickly to listen to Karmazinov.

III

AGAIN SOMETHING wrong was hovering in the hall. I declare beforehand: I bow down to the greatness of genius; but why is it that at the end of their illustrious years these gentlemen geniuses of ours sometimes act just like little boys? So what if he is Karmazinov and comes out with all the bearing of five court chamberlains? Is it possible to hold a public like ours for an entire hour with one article? Generally, I have observed that at a light, public literary reading, even the biggest genius cannot occupy the public with himself for more than twenty minutes with impunity. True, the entrance of the great genius was met with the utmost respect. Even the sternest old men expressed approval and curiosity, and the ladies even a certain rapture. The applause, however, was a bit brief, somehow not general, disconcerted. Yet there was not a single escapade from the back rows until Mr. Karmazinov actually began to speak, and even then it was nothing so especially bad, just a misunderstanding, as it were. I have already mentioned that his voice was rather shrill, even somewhat feminine, and with a genuine, highborn, aristocratic lisp besides. He had uttered no more than a few words when someone suddenly permitted himself to laugh loudly—probably some inexperienced little fool, who had never seen anything of the world and, besides, was naturally given to laughter. But there was nothing in the least demonstrative in it; on the contrary, the fool was hissed and he obliterated himself. But then Mr. Karmazinov, mincing and preening, announced that "he had flatly refused to read at first" (much he needed to announce that!). "There are lines," he said, "which so sing themselves from a man's heart as cannot be told,[5] and such a sacred thing simply cannot be laid before the public" (why was he laying it, then?); "but as he had been prevailed upon, so he was laying it, and as he was, moreover, putting down his pen forever, and had sworn never to write again for anything, then, so be it, he had written this last thing; and as he had sworn never, for anything in the world, to read anything in public, then, so be it, he would read this last article to the public," etc., etc., all in the same vein.

But all this would still have been nothing, and who does not know what authors' prefaces are like? Though I will note that, given the scanty education of our public and the irritability of the back rows, all this might have had an influence. So, would it not have been better to read a little tale, a tiny story, of the sort he once used to write—that is, polished, mincing, but occasionally witty? That would have saved everything. But no, sir, nothing doing! An oration commenced![6] God, what wasn't in it! I will say positively that even a metropolitan public would have been reduced to stupor, not only ours. Imagine some thirty printed pages of the most mincing and useless babble; what's more, the gentleman was reading somehow superciliously, ruefully, as if for a favor, so that it even came out offensive to our public. The theme . . . But, who could make out the theme? It was some sort of account of some sort of impressions, some sort of recollections. But of what? But what about? No matter how furrowed our provincial brows were through the first half of the reading, they could get none of it, so that they listened through the second half only out of courtesy. True, much was said about love, about the genius's love for some person, but I confess it came out rather awkwardly. The short, fattish little figure of the writer of genius somehow did not go very well, in my opinion, with the story of his first kiss . . . And, which again was offensive, these kisses occurred somehow not as with the rest of mankind. Here the inevitable furze is growing all around (it is inevitably furze or some such plant, which has to be looked up in botany). At the same time there is inevitably some violet hue in the sky which, of course, no mortal has ever noticed—that is, everyone has seen it, but failed to notice it, "while I," he says, "I looked and am now describing it to you fools as a most ordinary thing." The tree under which the interesting couple sits is inevitably of some orange color. They are sitting somewhere in Germany. Suddenly they see Pompey or Cassius on the eve of battle,[7] and both are pierced by the chill of ecstasy. Some mermaid peeps in the bushes. Gluck begins playing a fiddle among the reeds.[8] The piece he plays is named *en toutes lettres*, * but is not known to anyone, so it has to be looked up in a musical dictionary. Then mist comes billowing, billowing and billowing, more like a million pillows than any mist. And suddenly it all disappears, and the great genius is crossing the Volga in winter, during a thaw. Two and a half pages on the crossing, and he falls through a hole in the ice anyway. The genius is drowning—do you think he drowns? It never occurred to him; all this was so that when he was already quite drowned and choking, there should flash before him a piece of ice, a piece of ice tiny as a pea, but pure and transparent "like a frozen tear," and in this tear Germany was reflected, or, better say, the sky of Germany, and with its iridescent play the reflection reminded him of that same tear which, "remember, rolled from your eye, as we sat beneath the emerald tree, and you exclaimed joyfully: 'There is no crime!' 'Yes,' said I through my tears, 'but, if so, there are also no righteous men.' We wept and parted forever." She somewhere to the seacoast, he to some caves; and so he descends, and descends, for three years he descends beneath the Sukharev Tower in Moscow, and suddenly in the very depths of the earth he finds, in a cave, an icon lamp, and before the icon lamp—a monk. The monk is praying. The genius bends to a tiny barred window and suddenly hears a sigh. You think it was the monk who sighed? Much need he has for your monk! No, sir, it is simply that this sigh "reminded him of her first sigh, thirty-seven years ago," when, "remember, in Germany, we were sitting under the agate tree, and you said to me: 'Why love? Look, ochre is growing all around, and I am in love, but the ochre will stop growing, and I will cease to love.' " Here again mist billowed, Hoffmann appeared, the mermaid whistled something from Chopin, and suddenly, out of the mist, wearing a laurel wreath, over the roofs of Rome appeared Ancus Marcius.[9] "The chill of ecstasy ran down our spines, and we parted forever," etc., etc. In short, I may not be telling it right and perhaps cannot, but the sense of the blather was precisely of that sort. And, finally, what is this disgraceful passion of our great minds for punning in a higher sense! The great European

*"in full"

philosopher, the great scholar, the inventor, the laborer and martyr—all these who labor and are heavy-laden[10]—are for our Russian great genius decidedly like cooks in his kitchen. He is the master and they come to him, chef's hat in hand, waiting for orders. True, he also smiles haughtily at Russia, and he likes nothing better than to proclaim Russia's bankruptcy in all respects before the great minds of Europe, but as regards himself—no, sir, he has already risen above these great minds of Europe; they are all only material for his puns. He takes another man's idea, weaves its own antithesis into it, and the pun is ready. There is crime, there is no crime; there is no right, there are no righteous men; atheism, Darwinism, Moscow bells . . . But, alas, he no longer believes in Moscow bells; Rome, laurels . . . but he does not even believe in laurels . . . Then comes a conventional fit of Byronic anguish, a grimace from Heine, something from Pechorin,[11] and—off it goes, off it goes, the engine whistling . . . "But praise me anyway, praise me, I do love it terribly; I'm just saying that I'm putting down my pen; wait, I'll wear you out three hundred times over, you'll get tired of reading it . . ."

Of course, the end was none too good; but the bad thing was that everything started with it. Long since there had begun the shuffling, nose-blowing, coughing, and all else that occurs at a literary reading when the writer, whoever he may be, keeps the public longer than twenty minutes. But the writer of genius did not notice any of it. He went on lisping and mumbling, totally oblivious of the public, so that everyone began to be perplexed. Then suddenly, in the back rows, a lonely but loud voice was heard:

"Lord, what rubbish!"

This popped out inadvertently and, I am sure, without any demonstrativeness. The man simply got tired. But Mr. Karmazinov paused, looked mockingly at the public, and suddenly lisped with the bearing of an offended court chamberlain:

"It seems, ladies and gentlemen, that you are rather bored with me?"

And here is where he was at fault, in having spoken first; for in thus provoking a response, he gave all sorts of scum an opportunity to speak as well, and even legitimately, as it were, while if he had refrained, they would have blown their noses a little longer, and it would all have gone over somehow . . . Perhaps he expected applause in response to his question; but there was no applause; on the contrary, everyone became as if frightened, shrank down, and kept still.

"You never saw any Ancus Marcius, that's all just style," came one irritated, even as if pained, voice.

"Precisely," another voice picked up at once, "there are no ghosts nowadays, only natural science. Look it up in natural science."

"Ladies and gentlemen, such objections were the last thing I expected," Karmazinov was terribly surprised. The great genius had grown totally unaccustomed to his fatherland in Karlsruhe.

"In our age it's shameful to read that the world stands on three fishes," a young girl suddenly rattled out. "You couldn't have gone down to some hermit in a cave, Karmazinov. Who even talks about hermits nowadays?"

"What surprises me most, ladies and gentlemen, is that it's all so serious. However . . . however, you are perfectly right. No one respects real truth more than I do . . ."

Though he was smiling ironically, all the same he was greatly struck. His face simply said: "I'm not the way you think, I'm for you, only praise me, praise me more, as much as possible, I like it terribly . . ."

"Ladies and gentlemen," he cried at last, now completely wounded, "I see that my poor little poem got to the wrong place. And I think I myself got to the wrong place."

"Aimed at a crow and got a cow," some fool, undoubtedly drunk, shouted at the top of his lungs, and of course he ought to have been ignored. True, there was irreverent laughter.

"A cow, you say?" Karmazinov picked up at once. His voice was becoming more and more shrill. "Concerning crows and cows, ladies and gentlemen, I shall allow myself to refrain. I have too much respect even for any sort of public to allow myself comparisons, however innocent; but I thought . . ."

"Anyhow, dear sir, you'd better not be so . . ." someone shouted from the back rows.

"But I supposed that, as I was putting down my pen and saying farewell to the reader, I would be heard . . ."

"No, no, we want to listen, we do," several voices, emboldened at last, came from the front row.

"Read, read!" several rapturous ladies' voices picked up, and at last some applause broke through, though scant and thin, it's true. Karmazinov smiled wryly and rose from his place.

"Believe me, Karmazinov, everyone even regards it as an honor . . ." even the marshal's wife could not restrain herself.

"Mr. Karmazinov," a fresh, youthful voice suddenly came from the depths of the hall. It was the voice of a very young teacher from the district high school, an excellent young man, quiet and noble, still a recent arrival in town. He even rose slightly from his place. "Mr. Karmazinov, if I had the good fortune to love as you have described to us, I really wouldn't put anything about my love into an article intended for public reading . . ."

He even blushed all over . . .

"Ladies and gentlemen," Karmazinov cried, "I have ended. I omit the ending and I withdraw. But permit me to read just the six concluding lines.

"Yes, friend and reader, farewell!" he began at once from the manuscript and now without sitting down in his chair. "Farewell, reader; I do not even much insist that we should part friends: why, indeed, trouble you? Abuse me even, oh, abuse me as much as you like, if it gives you any pleasure. But it will be best of all if we forget each other forever. And if all of you, readers, should suddenly be so good as to fall on your knees and entreat me with tears: 'Write, oh, write for us, Karmazinov—for the fatherland, for posterity, for the wreaths of laurel—even then I would answer you, having thanked you, of course, with all courtesy: 'Ah, no, we have had enough of bothering each other, my dear compatriots, *merci*! It is time we parted ways! *Merci, merci, merci.*' "

Karmazinov bowed ceremoniously and, all red as though he had been boiled, made for backstage.

"Nobody's going down on his knees—a wild fancy."

"What conceit!"

"It's just humor!" someone a bit more sensible corrected.

"No, spare us your humor!"

"This is impudence, anyhow, gentlemen."

"He's finished now, at least."

"What a heap of boredom!"

But all these ignorant exclamations from the back rows (though not only from the back rows) were drowned by the applause of the other part of the public. Karmazinov was called back. Several ladies, Yulia Mikhailovna and the marshal's wife at their head, crowded up to the platform. In Yulia Mikhailovna's hands there appeared a magnificent wreath of laurel, on a white velvet cushion, inside another wreath of live roses.

"Laurels!" Karmazinov said with a subtle and somewhat caustic grin. "I am moved, of course, and accept this wreath, prepared beforehand but as yet unwithered, with lively emotion; but I assure you, *mesdames,* I have suddenly become so much of a realist that I consider laurels in our age rather more fitting in the hands of a skillful cook than in mine . . ."

"Except that cooks are more useful," cried that same seminarian who had attended the "meeting" at Virginsky's. The order was somewhat disrupted. People from many rows jumped up to see the ceremony with the laurel wreath.

"I'd add three more roubles for a cook," another voice picked up loudly, even too loudly, insistently loudly.

"So would I."

"So would I."

"But do they really have no buffet here?"

"Gentlemen, it's sheer deception . . ."

However, it must be admitted that all these unbridled gentlemen were still very afraid of our dignitaries, and also of the police officer who was there in the hall. After about ten minutes everyone settled down again anyhow, but the former order was not restored. And it was into this burgeoning chaos that poor Stepan Trofimovich stepped . . .

IV

I RAN TO HIM backstage one last time, however, and managed to warn him, beside myself as I was, that in my opinion it had all blown up and he had better not come out at all, but go home at once, excusing himself with his cholerine if need be, and that I, too, would tear off my bow and come with him. At this moment he was already heading for the platform, suddenly stopped, haughtily looked me up and down, and solemnly pronounced:

"Why, my dear sir, do you consider me capable of such baseness?"

I stepped back. I was as sure as two times two that he would not get out of there without a catastrophe. As I was standing in utter dejection, there again flashed before me the figure of the visiting professor, whose turn it was to go out after Stepan Trofimovich, and who earlier kept raising his fist and bringing it down with all his might. He was still pacing back and forth in the same way, absorbed in himself and muttering something under his nose with a wily but triumphant smile. Somehow almost without intending to (what on earth possessed me?), I went up to him as well.

"You know," I said, "based on many examples, if a reader keeps the public longer than twenty minutes, they cease to listen. Even a celebrity can't hold out for half an hour . . ."

He suddenly stopped and even seemed to tremble all over at the offense. A boundless haughtiness showed in his face.

"Don't worry," he muttered contemptuously, and walked by. At that moment came the sound of Stepan Trofimovich's voice in the hall.

"Eh, confound you all!" I thought, and ran to the hall.

Stepan Trofimovich sat down in the chair amid the still lingering disorder. He apparently met with ill-disposed looks from the front rows. (They had somehow stopped liking him in the club of late, and respected him much less than before.) However, it was good enough that they did not hiss. I had had this strange idea ever since yesterday: I kept thinking he would be hissed off at once, as soon as he appeared. Yet he was not even noticed right away, owing to the lingering disorder. And what could the man hope for, if even Karmazinov was treated in such a way? He was pale; it was ten years since he had appeared before the public. By his agitation and by all that I knew only too well in him, it was clear to me that he himself regarded his present appearance on the platform as the deciding of his fate, or something of the sort. That was what I was afraid of. So dear the man was to me. And what I felt when he opened his mouth and I heard his first phrase!

"Ladies and gentlemen!" he said suddenly, as if venturing all, and at the same time in an almost breaking voice. "Ladies and gentlemen! Only this morning there lay before me one of those lawless papers recently distributed here, and for the hundredth time I was asking myself the question: 'What is its mystery?' "

The entire hall instantly became hushed, all eyes turned to him, some in fear. Yes, indeed, he knew how to get their interest from the first word. Heads were even stuck out from backstage; Liputin and Lyamshin listened greedily. Yulia Mikhailovna waved her hand to me again:

"Stop him, at any cost, stop him!" she whispered in alarm. I merely shrugged; how was it possible to stop a man who has *ventured all*? Alas, I understood Stepan Trofimovich.

"Aha, it's about the tracts!" was whispered among the public; the whole hall stirred.

"Ladies and gentlemen, I have solved the whole mystery. The whole mystery of their effect lies—in their stupidity!" (His eyes began to flash.) "Yes, ladies and gentlemen, were it an intentional stupidity, counterfeited out of calculation—oh, that would even be a stroke of genius! But we must do them full justice: they have not counterfeited anything. This is the shortest, the barest, the most simplehearted stupidity—*c'est la bêtise dans son essence la plus pure, quelque chose comme un simple chimique.* * Were it just a drop more intelligently expressed, everyone would see at once all the poverty of this short stupidity. But now everyone stands perplexed: no one believes it can be so elementally stupid. 'It can't be that there's nothing more to it,' everyone says to himself, and looks for a secret, sees a mystery, tries to read between the lines—the effect is achieved! Oh, never before has stupidity received so grand a reward, though it has so often deserved it . . . For,

---

*"it is stupidity in its purest essence, something like a chemical simple."

en parenthèse, stupidity, like the loftiest genius, is equally useful in the destinies of mankind . . ."

"Puns from the forties!" came someone's, incidentally quite modest, voice, but after it everything seemed to break loose; there was loud talking and squawking.

"Hurrah, ladies and gentlemen! I propose a toast to stupidity!" Stepan Trofimovich cried, now in a perfect frenzy, defying the hall.

I ran to him as if on the pretext of pouring him some water.

"Stepan Trofimovich, leave off, Yulia Mikhailovna begs . . ."

"No, you leave off with me, idle young man!" he fell upon me at the top of his voice. I ran away. *"Messieurs!"* he went on, "why the excitement, why the shouts of indignation that I hear? I have come with an olive branch. I have brought you the last word, for in this matter the last word is mine—and then we shall make peace."

"Away!" shouted some.

"Quiet, let him speak, let him have his say," another part yelled. Especially excited was the young teacher, who, having once dared to speak, seemed no longer able to stop.

"Messieurs, the last word in this matter is all-forgiveness. I, an obsolete old man, I solemnly declare that the spirit of life blows as ever and the life force is not exhausted in the younger generation. The enthusiasm of modern youth is as pure and bright as in our time. Only one thing has happened: the displacing of purposes, the replacing of one beauty by another! The whole perplexity lies in just what is more beautiful: Shakespeare or boots, Raphael or petroleum?"[12]

"Is he an informer?" grumbled some.

"Compromising questions!"

"Agent provocateur!"

"And I proclaim," Stepan Trofimovich shrieked, in the last extremity of passion, "and I proclaim that Shakespeare and Raphael are higher than the emancipation of the serfs, higher than nationality, higher than socialism, higher than the younger generation, higher than chemistry, higher than almost all mankind, for they are already the fruit, the real fruit of all mankind, and maybe the highest fruit there ever may be! A form of beauty already achieved, without the achievement of which I might not even consent to live . . . Oh, God!" he clasped his hands, "ten years ago I cried out in the same way from a platform in Petersburg, exactly the same things and in the same words, and in exactly the same way they understood nothing, they laughed and hissed, as now; short people, what more do you need in order to understand? And do you know, do you know that mankind can live without the Englishman, it can live without Germany, it can live only too well without the Russian man, it can live without science, without bread, and it only cannot live without beauty, for then there would be nothing at all to do in the world! The whole secret is here, the whole of history is here! Science itself would not stand for a minute without beauty—are you aware of that, you who are laughing?—it would turn into boorishness, you couldn't invent the nail! . . . I will not yield!" he cried absurdly in conclusion, and banged his fist on the table with all his might.

But while he was shrieking without sense or order, the order in the hall was also breaking up. Many jumped from their places, some surged forward, closer to the platform. Generally, it all happened much more quickly than I am describing, and there was no time to take measures. Perhaps there was no wish to, either.

"It's fine for you, with everything provided, spoiled brats!" the same seminarian bellowed, right by the platform, gleefully baring his teeth at Stepan Trofimovich. He noticed it and leaped up to the very edge:

"Was it not I, was it not I who just declared that the enthusiasm of the younger generation is as pure and bright as it ever was, and that it is perishing only for being mistaken about the forms of the beautiful? Is that not enough for you? And if you take it that this was proclaimed by a crushed, insulted father, how then—oh, you short ones—how then is it possible to stand higher in impartiality and tranquillity of vision? . . . Ungrateful . . . unjust . . . why, why do you not want to make peace! . . ."

And he suddenly burst into hysterical sobs. He wiped away the flood of tears with his fingers. His shoulders and chest were shaking with sobs . . . He forgot everything in the world.

The public was decidedly seized with fright, almost everyone rose from their places. Yulia Mikhailovna also jumped up quickly, seized her husband's arm, and pulled him from the chair . . . The scandal was going beyond bounds.

"Stepan Trofimovich!" the seminarian bellowed joyfully. "Here in

town and in the vicinity we've now got Fedka the Convict, an escaped
convict, wandering around. He robs people, and just recently committed a new murder. Allow me to ask: if you had not sent him to the army
fifteen years ago to pay off a debt at cards—that is, if you had not quite
simply lost him in a card game—tell me, would he have wound up at
hard labor? Would he go around putting a knife in people, as he does
now, in his struggle for existence? What have you got to say, mister
aesthete?"

I refuse to describe the ensuing scene. First, there was furious applause. Not everyone applauded, only some fifth part of the hall, but
they applauded furiously. The rest of the public surged towards the
exit, but since the applauding part of the public was still crowding
towards the platform, there was general confusion. Ladies cried out,
some young girls started weeping and begged to be taken home.
Lembke, standing by his seat, kept glancing around wildly and
quickly. Yulia Mikhailovna was quite lost—for the first time during her
career among us. As for Stepan Trofimovich, for the first moment he
was, it seemed, literally crushed by the seminarian's words; but suddenly he raised both arms, as if stretching them out over the public,
and screamed:

"I shake off the dust from my feet[13] and curse you . . . The
end . . . the end . . ."

And, turning, he ran backstage, waving and threatening with his
arms.

"He has insulted society! . . . Verkhovensky!" the furious ones
bellowed. They even wanted to rush in pursuit of him. To calm them
was impossible, at least for the moment, and—suddenly the final catastrophe crashed down like a bomb on the gathering, and exploded in
its midst: the third reader, that maniac who kept waving his fist backstage, suddenly ran out on the platform.

He looked utterly mad. With a broad, triumphant smile, full of
boundless self-confidence, he gazed around the agitated hall and, it
seemed, was glad of the disorder. He was not embarrassed in the least
at having to read in such turmoil, on the contrary, he was visibly glad.
This was so obvious that it attracted attention at once.

"What on earth is this?" questions were heard, "who on earth is this?
Shh! What does he want to say?"

"Ladies and gentlemen!" the maniac shouted with all his might, standing at the very edge of the platform, and in almost the same shrilly feminine voice as Karmazinov, only without the aristocratic lisp. "Ladies and gentlemen! Twenty years ago, on the eve of war with half of Europe, Russia stood as an ideal in the eyes of all state and privy councillors. Literature served in the censorship; the universities taught military drill;[14] the army turned into a ballet, and the people paid taxes and kept silent under the knout of serfdom. Patriotism turned into the gouging of bribes from the living and the dead. Those who did not take bribes were considered rebels, for they disrupted the harmony. Whole birch groves were destroyed to maintain order. Europe trembled . . . But never, in all the thousand witless years of her life, did Russia reach such disgrace . . ."

He raised his fist, waving it ecstatically and menacingly over his head, and suddenly brought it down furiously, as if crushing his adversary to dust. Frenzied yelling came from all sides, deafening applause broke out. This time almost half the hall applauded; they were most innocently carried away: Russia was being dishonored before all eyes, publicly—how could one not roar in ecstasy?

"That's the business! Now we're getting to business! Hurrah! No, this is none of your aesthetics!"

The maniac went on ecstatically:

"Since then twenty years have passed. Universities have been opened and multiplied. Drill has turned into a legend; we're thousands short of the full complement of officers. Railroads have eaten up all the capital and covered Russia like spiderwebs, so that perhaps in another fifteen years or so one may even be able to take a ride somewhere. Bridges burn only rarely, while towns burn down regularly, in established order, by turns, during the fire seasons. In the courts there are judgments of Solomon, and jurors take bribes solely in the struggle for existence, when they're going to die of hunger. The serfs are free and whack each other with birch rods instead of their former landowners. Seas and oceans of vodka are drunk to support the budget, and in Novgorod, opposite the ancient and useless Sophia, a colossal bronze ball has been solemnly erected to commemorate a millennium of already elapsed disorder and witlessness.[15] Europe is frowning and beginning to worry again . . . Fifteen years of reforms! And yet never, even in the most caricaturish epochs of her witlessness, has Russia reached . . ."

The last words could not even be heard over the roar of the crowd. He could be seen raising his hand again and once more bringing it down victoriously. The ecstasy went beyond all bounds: people were yelling, clapping their hands, some of the ladies even shouted: "Enough! You couldn't say anything better!" It was like drunkenness. The orator let his eyes wander over them all and was as if melting in his own triumph. I caught a glimpse of Lembke, in inexpressible agitation, pointing something out to someone. Yulia Mikhailovna, all pale, was hurriedly saying something to the prince, who had run up to her . . . But at that moment a whole crowd of about six more or less official persons rushed out on the platform from backstage, laid hold of the orator, and drew him backstage. I do not understand how he could have torn free of them, but he did tear free, leaped up to the very edge again, and still managed to shout with all his might, waving his fist:

"But never before has Russia reached . . ."

But he was already being dragged away again. I saw about fifteen men, perhaps, rush backstage to free him, not across the platform but from the side, smashing the flimsy partition so that it finally fell down . . . I saw later, not believing my eyes, how the girl student (Virginsky's relative) jumped up on the platform with that same bundle of hers under her arm, dressed in the same clothes, her face the same red, with the same well-fed cheeks, surrounded by two or three women and two or three men, and accompanied by her mortal enemy, the high-school boy. I even managed to catch the phrase:

"Ladies and gentlemen, I have come to proclaim the sufferings of unfortunate students and rouse them to protest everywhere."

But I fled. I hid my bow in my pocket and, by various back passages known to me, got myself out of the house to the street. First of all, of course, I went to Stepan Trofimovich.

2

The End of the Fête

I

HE DID NOT receive me. He had locked himself in and was writing. To my repeated knocking and calling, he answered through the door:

"My friend, I have finished it all, who can demand more of me?"

"You didn't finish anything, you just contributed to the general collapse. For God's sake, Stepan Trofimovich, let's do without punning; open up. We must take measures; they may come here and insult you . . ."

I considered I had the right to be especially stern and even exacting. I feared he might undertake something still more insane. But to my surprise I met with an extraordinary firmness.

"Don't you be the first to insult me, then. I thank you for all that's past, but, I repeat, I have finished it all with people, both good and wicked. I am writing a letter to Darya Pavlovna, whom I have so unpardonably forgotten until now. Deliver it tomorrow, if you like, and now '*merci*.' "

"Stepan Trofimovich, I assure you the matter is more serious than you think. You think you smashed someone there? You didn't smash anyone, but you yourself broke like an empty glass" (oh, I was rude and impolite; it grieves me to remember!). "There is decidedly no reason for you to write to Darya Pavlovna . . . and what's going to become of you now without me? What do you understand of practical things? You must be plotting something else? You'll just perish another time if you're plotting something again . . ."

He rose and came right up to the door.

"You have not spent so long a time with them, yet you have been infected by their language and tone, *Dieu vous pardonne, mon ami, et Dieu vous garde.* * But I have always noticed the germs of decency in you, and perhaps you will still think better of it—*après le temps,* † of course, like all of us Russians. As for your remark about my impracticality, I shall remind you of a long-standing thought of mine: that in our Russia a vast number of people occupy themselves with nothing else but attacking other people's impracticality, fiercely and with special persistence, like flies in summer, accusing all and sundry of it, and excluding only themselves. *Cher,* remember that I am agitated and do not torment me. Once more, *merci* for everything, and let us part from each other as Karmazinov did from his public—that is, forget each other with all possible magnanimity. He was being sly when he begged his former readers so very much to forget him; *quant à moi,* ‡ I am not so vain and trust most of all in the youth of your innocent heart: are you likely to remember a useless old man for long? 'Live more,' my friend, as Nastasya wished me on my last name day *(ces pauvres gens ont quelquefois des mots charmants et pleins de philosophie).* § I do not wish you much happiness—it would bore you; I do not wish you trouble either; but, following the people's philosophy, I will simply repeat: 'Live more' and try somehow not to be too bored; this useless wish I am adding on my own. Now, farewell, and a serious farewell. And don't stand by my door, I won't open it."

He walked away, and I achieved nothing further. In spite of the "agitation," he had spoken evenly, unhurriedly, with weight, and obviously trying to impress. Of course, he was somewhat vexed with me and was indirectly taking revenge on me, let's say, perhaps still for yesterday's "kibitkas" and "opening floorboards." And this morning's public tears, despite a certain sort of victory, had placed him, he

*"God forgive you, my friend, and God keep you."
†"afterwards"
‡"as for me"
§"the sayings of these poor folk are often charming and full of philosophy"

knew, in a somewhat comical position, and there was no man more concerned with beauty and strictness of form in his relations with friends than Stepan Trofimovich. Oh, I do not blame him! But it was this scrupulousness and sarcasm, which held out in him despite all shocks, that set me at ease then: this man who had apparently changed so little as compared to usual was certainly not disposed at that moment towards anything tragic or extraordinary. So I reasoned then, and, my God, how mistakenly! I had lost sight of too many things . . .

Anticipating events, I will quote the first few lines of this letter to Darya Pavlovna, which she in fact received the next day.

"Mon enfant, my hand is trembling, but I have finished everything. You were not present at my final combat with people; you did not come to this 'reading,' and you did well. But you will be told that in our character-impoverished Russia one courageous man stood up and, despite the deadly menace pouring from all sides, told those little fools their truth—that is, that they are little fools. *O, ce sont des pauvres petits vauriens et rien de plus, des petits* little fools—*voilà le mot!** The die is cast; I am leaving this town forever, whither I do not know. Everyone I loved has turned away from me. But you, you, a pure and naïve being, you, a meek one, whose fate was almost joined with mine by the will of one capricious and tyrannical heart, you, who perhaps in disdain watched me shed fainthearted tears on the eve of our unrealized marriage; you who, whatever you may be, cannot look on me in any other way than as a comical person, oh, to you, to you goes the last cry of my heart, to you is my last duty, to you alone! I cannot possibly leave you forever to think of me as an ungrateful fool, boor, and egoist, as is probably affirmed to you day after day by one ungrateful and cruel heart, which, alas, I cannot forget . . ."*

And so on and so forth, four big pages in all.

Having pounded on the door three times with my fist in response to his "I won't open it," and having shouted after him that he would still send Nastasya for me three times that same day, but that I would not come, I abandoned him and ran to Yulia Mikhailovna.

---

*"Oh, they are poor little good-for-nothings and nothing more, little [little fools]—that's the word!"

II

THERE I FOUND myself witness to an outrageous scene: the poor woman was being deceived right to her face, and I could do nothing. Indeed, what could I tell her? I had had time to come to my senses somewhat and to realize that all I had were just certain feelings, suspicious presentiments, and nothing more. I found her in tears, almost in hysterics, with eau de Cologne compresses and a glass of water. Before her stood Pyotr Stepanovich, who was talking nonstop, and the prince, who was as silent as though he were under lock and key. With tears and little cries she was reproaching Pyotr Stepanovich for his "apostasy." It struck me at once that she ascribed the whole failure, the whole disgrace of this matinée, everything, in short, to Pyotr Stepanovich's absence alone.

As for him, I noticed one important change: he was almost serious, as if preoccupied with something. Ordinarily he never seemed serious, always laughed, even when he was angry, and he was often angry. Oh, he was angry now, too, spoke rudely, carelessly, with vexation and impatience. He assured her that he had been sick with a headache and vomiting at Gaganov's, where he had chanced to stop early that morning. Alas, the poor woman still wanted so much to be deceived! The main question I found on the agenda was whether or not the ball—that is, the whole second half of the fête—was to take place. Yulia Mikhailovna would not agree for anything in the world to appear at the ball after "today's insults"; in other words, she wished with all her might to be compelled to go, and by absolutely no one else but him, Pyotr Stepanovich. She looked upon him as an oracle, and it seemed that if he had left then, she would have taken to her bed. But he had no intention of leaving: he himself needed with all his might that the ball take place that day, and Yulia Mikhailovna absolutely had to be there . . .

"So, what's there to cry about! You absolutely must have a scene? Vent your anger on someone? Go ahead, vent it on me, only make it quick, because time is passing and we've got to decide. We messed it up with the reading; we'll smooth it over with the ball. The prince here is of the same opinion. Yes, ma'am, if it hadn't been for the prince, where would it all have ended?"

The prince had been against the ball at first (that is, against Yulia Mikhailovna's appearance at the ball; the ball itself had anyhow to take place), but after two or three such references to his opinion, he gradually began to grunt in token of consent.

I was also surprised by the altogether extraordinary impoliteness of Pyotr Stepanovich's tone. Oh, I indignantly reject the base gossip spread later about some supposed liaison between Yulia Mikhailovna and Pyotr Stepanovich. There was not and could not have been anything of the sort. He got the upper hand with her only by yessing her with all his might from the very beginning in her dreams of influencing society and the ministry; by entering into her plans, devising them for her, acting through the crudest flattery, he entangled her from head to foot, and became as necessary to her as air.

Seeing me, she cried out, flashing her eyes:

"Ask him! He, too, never left my side all the while, like the prince. Tell me, isn't it obvious that it's all a conspiracy, a base, cunning conspiracy, to do all possible evil to me and to Andrei Antonovich? Oh, they arranged it! They had a plan. There's a party, a whole party of them!"

"That's overshot, as usual with you. There's some poem eternally running through your head. I'm glad, however, to see Mr. . . . ." (he pretended to have forgotten my name), "he'll tell us his opinion."

"My opinion," I hastened, "agrees entirely with Yulia Mikhailovna's opinion. The conspiracy is all too obvious. I've brought you these ribbons, Yulia Mikhailovna. Whether the ball does or does not take place—is, of course, none of my business, since the power is not mine; but my role as an usher is at an end. Forgive my heat, but I cannot act to the detriment of common sense and conviction."

"You hear! You hear!" she clasped her hands.

"I hear, ma'am, and this is what I shall tell you," he turned to me. "I think you all must have eaten something that has made you all delirious. In my opinion, nothing has happened, precisely nothing, that never happened before and could not always have happened in this town here. What conspiracy? It came out ugly, stupid to the point of disgrace, but where is the conspiracy? You mean against Yulia Mikhailovna, against her who indulged them, protected them, forgave them right and left for all their pranks? Yulia Mikhailovna! What have I been hammering into you this whole month nonstop? What have I been warning you about? So, what, what did you need all these people for? You just had to deal with this trash! Why? What for? To unite society? But can they possibly unite, for pity's sake?"

"When did you ever warn me? On the contrary, you approved, you even demanded . . . I confess, I am so surprised . . . You yourself brought many strange people to me."

"On the contrary, I argued with you, I did not approve, and as for bringing—I did bring them, but not until they themselves came swarming by dozens, and that only recently, to make up the 'quadrille of literature,' since there was no way of doing without these boors. Only I'll bet a dozen or two more of the same boors were brought in today without tickets."

"Quite certainly," I confirmed.

"See, you already agree. Remember the tone we've had here lately, I mean, in this whole wretched town? It's all turned into nothing but insolence, shamelessness; it's been a scandal with a ceaseless ringing of bells. And who encouraged them? Who shielded them with her authority? Who got everyone muddled? Who infuriated all the small-fry? In your album all the local family secrets are reproduced. Wasn't it you who patted your poets and artists on the head? Wasn't it you who held out your hand for Lyamshin to kiss? Wasn't it in your presence that a seminarian swore at an actual state councillor and ruined his daughter's dress with his monstrous tarred boots? Why are you surprised, then, that the public is set against you?"

"But that's all you, you yourself! Oh, my God!"

"No, ma'am, I kept warning you; we quarreled, do you hear, we quarreled!"

"You're lying to my face!"

"Ah, yes, of course, it costs nothing to say a thing like that. You need a victim now, someone to vent your anger on; go ahead, vent it on me, as I told you. I'd better address myself to you, Mr. . . . ." (He still could not recall my name.) "Let's count up on our fingers: I maintain that, apart from Liputin, there was no conspiracy, none what-so-ever! I'll prove it, but let's first analyze Liputin. He came out with that fool

Lebyadkin's verses—was that, in your opinion, a conspiracy? But, you know, Liputin might simply have thought it was witty. Seriously, seriously, witty. He simply came out with the aim of making everybody laugh and have fun, his patroness Yulia Mikhailovna first, that's all. You don't believe it? Why, isn't it in tone with everything that's been going on here this whole month? And, if you wish, I'll say all: by God, under other circumstances it might even have gone over! A crude joke, well, yes, salacious or whatever, but funny, funny, right?"

"What! You consider Liputin's act witty?" Yulia Mikhailovna cried out in terrible indignation. "Such stupidity, such tactlessness, so base, so vile, so deliberate—oh, you're saying it on purpose! It means you yourself are in conspiracy with him!"

"Oh, certainly, sitting in back, hiding, moving the whole little mechanism! But if I had taken part in any conspiracy—understand this at least!—it wouldn't have ended just with Liputin! So, according to you, I also arranged with papa that he should purposely produce such a scandal? Well, ma'am, whose fault was it that father was brought in to read? Who tried to stop you yesterday, just yesterday, yesterday?"

"*O, hier il avait tant d'esprit,* * I was counting on him so much, and, besides, he has manners: I thought he and Karmazinov . . . and now look!"

"Yes, ma'am, and now look. But in spite of all that *tant d'esprit,* papa mucked it up, and if I'd known beforehand that he was going to muck it up so badly, being part of the indubitable conspiracy against your fête, I would undoubtedly not have started persuading you yesterday to keep the bull out of the china shop, right, ma'am? And yet I did try to talk you out of it yesterday—I did, because I had a presentiment. It was, of course, impossible to foresee everything: he himself probably didn't know, a minute before, what he was going to fire off. These nervous old codgers don't even resemble human beings! But you can still salvage it: tomorrow, for the public's satisfaction, send two doctors to him by administrative order, with all the trimmings, to inquire after his health—you could even do it today—and then straight to the hospital, for cold compresses. At least everyone will laugh and see that there's nothing to be offended at. I'll make an announcement about it

*"Oh, yesterday he was so witty"

tonight at the ball, since I'm the son. Karmazinov's another matter, he came out like a green ass and stretched his article for a whole hour— now there's one who must surely be in conspiracy with me! As if he said, 'Why don't I muck it up, too, just to harm Yulia Mikhailovna!' "

"Oh, Karmazinov, *quelle honte*!* I was burning, burning with shame for our public!"

"Well, ma'am, I wouldn't have burned, but I'd have roasted him. The public was right. And who, again, is guilty of Karmazinov? Did I foist him on you, or didn't I? Did I take part in adoring him, or didn't I? Ah, well, devil take him, but that third maniac, the political one, that's another question. Here everybody went amiss, it's not just my conspiracy."

"Ah, don't speak of it, it's terrible, terrible! I, I alone, am guilty of that!"

"Of course, ma'am, but here I'm going to vindicate you. Eh, who can keep track of these sincere ones! They can't guard against them even in Petersburg. Because he was recommended to you; and how he was! You'll agree, then, that it's even your duty now to appear at the ball. Because it's an important thing, because you yourself put him up on the rostrum. You must precisely declare in public now that you are not solidary with this, that the fine fellow is already in the hands of the police, and that you were deceived in some inexplicable way. You must declare indignantly that you were the victim of a mad person. Because he is a madman and nothing else. That's how he must be reported. I can't stand these biters. I may talk even worse myself, but not from the rostrum. And right now they're shouting about a senator."

"What senator? Who is shouting?"

"You see, I don't understand anything myself. You, Yulia Mikhailovna, do you know anything about some senator?"

"Senator?"

"You see, they're convinced that a senator has been appointed here, and that you are being replaced from Petersburg. I've heard it from many people."

"I've heard it, too," I confirmed.

*"what shame!"

"Who said so?" Yulia Mikhailovna flushed all over.

"You mean, who first started talking? How should I know. They're just talking. The mass is talking. They were talking yesterday especially. Everybody's somehow much too serious, though it's impossible to make anything out. Of course, those who are a bit more intelligent and competent—are not talking, but even among them some are listening to it."

"How mean! And . . . how stupid!"

"Well, so you must appear precisely now and show the fools."

"I confess, I myself feel it's even my duty, but . . . what if there's another disgrace awaiting us? What if they don't attend? Because no one's going to come, no one, no one!"

"Such ardor! They won't come, eh? And what about all those dresses made, what about the girls' costumes? No, after this I give up on you as a woman. Such human insight!"

"The marshal's wife won't come, she won't!"

"But what, finally, has happened here? Why won't they come?" he suddenly cried out with spiteful impatience.

"Infamy, disgrace—that's what has happened. There was, I don't know what, but something, after which it's impossible for me to enter."

"Why? But what, finally, are you to blame for? Why go taking the blame on yourself? Isn't it rather the public, your venerable elders, your fathers of families, who are to blame? It was for them to restrain the scoundrels and wastrels—because all we have here are wastrels and scoundrels, nothing serious. In no society anywhere is it possible to manage with the police alone. Here with us every person, on entry, demands that a special little cop be detailed to protect him. They don't understand that society protects itself. And what do our fathers of families, our dignitaries, wives, maidens, do in such circumstances? Keep mum and sulk. There's not even enough social initiative to restrain the pranksters."

"Ah, that is a golden truth! They keep mum, sulk, and . . . glance around."

"And if it's true, it's for you to speak it out here, aloud, proudly, sternly. Precisely to show that you're not crushed. Precisely to the little old men and the mothers. Oh, you'll find a way, you have the gift, when your head is clear. You'll draw them into a group—and speak aloud, aloud. Then a report to the *Voice* and the *Stock Exchange*. Wait, I'll take it in hand myself, I'll arrange it all for you. Of course, more attentiveness and a good eye on the buffet—ask the prince, ask Mr. . . . You cannot possibly leave us, *monsieur*, precisely when we must start all over again. Well, and finally, you arm in arm with Andrei Antonovich. How is Andrei Antonovich's health?"

"Oh, how unjustly, how wrongly, how offensively you have always judged that angelic man!" Yulia Mikhailovna cried out suddenly, on an unexpected impulse, and almost in tears, bringing her handkerchief to her eyes. For the first moment, Pyotr Stepanovich even faltered:

"For pity's sake, I . . . but what did I . . . I've always . . ."

"You never, never! Never did you do him justice!"

"Never can one understand a woman!" Pyotr Stepanovich grumbled, with a crooked smile.

"He is the most truthful, the most delicate, the most angelic man! The most kindly man!"

"For pity's sake, but as for his kindness, what have I . . . as for his kindness, I've always . . ."

"Never! But leave that. I defend him much too awkwardly. Today that Jesuit, the marshal's wife, also dropped a few sarcastic hints about yesterday."

"Oh, she won't be bothered now with hints about yesterday—she's got today. And why are you so worried that she won't come to the ball? Of course she won't, now that she's come into such a scandal. Maybe she's not to blame, but still there's her reputation; she got her little hands dirty."

"What? I don't understand: how are her hands dirty?" Yulia Mikhailovna looked at him in perplexity.

"I mean, I don't insist on it, but the bells are already ringing in town that it was she who did the matchmaking."

"What? Matchmaking whom?"

"Eh, so you still don't know?" he cried out in surprise, superbly feigned. "Why, Stavrogin and Lizaveta Nikolaevna!"

"How! What!" we all cried out.

"So you really don't know? Whew! There have been tragic novels going on here: Lizaveta Nikolaevna was so good as to get out of the marshal's wife's carriage and straight into Stavrogin's, and to slip away with 'the latter' to Skvoreshniki in broad daylight. Just an hour ago, not even that."

We were dumbfounded. Of course, we hastened to inquire further, but, surprisingly, though he himself had "inadvertently" been a witness, he nevertheless could tell us nothing in detail. The thing seemed to have happened like this: when the marshal's wife brought Liza and Mavriky Nikolaevich from the "reading" to the house of Liza's mother (whose legs were still ailing), someone's carriage was waiting not far from the entrance, about twenty-five steps off to one side. When Liza jumped out at the entrance, she ran straight to this carriage; the door opened, slammed shut; Liza called out "Spare me!" to Mavriky Nikolaevich—and the carriage flew at top speed to Skvoreshniki. To our hurried questions: "Was there some arrangement? Who was sitting in the carriage?"—Pyotr Stepanovich replied that he knew nothing; that there must certainly have been an arrangement, but that he had not made out Stavrogin himself in the carriage; it might have been the valet, old Alexei Yegorovich, who was sitting there. To the question: "And how did you turn up there? And why do you know for certain that she went to Skvoreshniki?"—he replied that he chanced to be there because he was passing by, and on seeing Liza even ran up to the carriage (and yet did not make out who was in the carriage, and with his curiosity!), and that Mavriky Nikolaevich not only did not set off in pursuit, but did not even try to stop Liza, and with his own hand even held back the marshal's wife, who was shouting at the top of her voice: "She's gone to Stavrogin, she's gone to Stavrogin!" Here I suddenly got beside all patience and shouted furiously at Pyotr Stepanovich:

"You set it up, you scoundrel! You killed the whole morning on it. You helped Stavrogin, you came in the carriage, you put her into it . . . you, you, you! Yulia Mikhailovna, he is your enemy, he will ruin you, too! Beware!"

And I rushed precipitously from the house.

To this day I do not understand and marvel myself at how I could have shouted that to him then. But I had guessed perfectly: it had all happened almost exactly the way I said, as turned out afterwards. In the first place, the obviously false way in which he reported the news was all too noticeable. He did not tell it as soon as he entered the house, as a first and extraordinary piece of news, but pretended that we already knew without him—which was impossible in so short a time. And if we had known, we could not in any case have kept silent about it until he started to speak. He also could not have heard of any "bells ringing" in town about the marshal's wife, because again the time was too short. Besides, as he was telling about it, he smiled a couple of times somehow meanly and flippantly, probably regarding us by then as utterly deceived fools. But I could no longer be bothered with him; the main fact I did believe, and I ran out of Yulia Mikhailovna's beside myself. The catastrophe struck me to the very heart. It pained me almost to tears; perhaps I was actually weeping. I did not know at all what to undertake. I rushed to Stepan Trofimovich, but the vexatious man again would not open the door. Nastasya assured me in a reverent whisper that he had retired to bed, but I did not believe it. At Liza's house I was able to question the servants; they confirmed the flight, but knew nothing themselves. The house was in alarm; the ailing mistress was having fainting fits, and Mavriky Nikolaevich was with her. I did not think it possible to call Mavriky Nikolaevich away. When I inquired about Pyotr Stepanovich, it was confirmed that he had been darting about the house during the past few days, sometimes even twice a day. The servants were sad, and spoke of Liza with some special reverence; she was loved. That she was ruined, utterly ruined, I did not doubt, but I was decidedly unable to comprehend the psychological side of the matter, especially after her scene the day before with Stavrogin. To run around town and inquire of acquaintances, in gloating houses, where the news, of course, had already spread, seemed disgusting to me and humiliating for Liza. But, strangely, I did run by to see Darya Pavlovna, where, however, I was not received (no one had been received in the Stavrogins' house since the previous day); what I could have said to her, and why I ran by, I do not know. From her I made my way to her brother. Shatov listened to me glumly and silently. I will note that I found him in an unprecedentedly dark mood; he was terribly thoughtful and, it seemed, had to force himself to listen to me. He said almost nothing and began walking back and forth from corner to corner of his closet, stomping more than usual with his boots. But when I was already on my way down the stairs, he shouted after

me that I should go to Liputin: "You'll find out everything there." Yet
I did not go to Liputin, but, well on my way, turned back again to
Shatov, and, half opening the door, without going in and without any
explanations, suggested to him laconically: wouldn't he be going to see
Marya Timofeevna today? At that Shatov cursed, and I left. I set down
here, so as not to forget, that that same evening he went especially to
the outskirts of town to visit Marya Timofeevna, whom he had not
seen for quite a while. He found her in reasonably good health and
spirits, and Lebyadkin dead drunk, asleep on the sofa in the front room.
This was at exactly nine o'clock. He told it to me himself the next day,
meeting me hotfoot in the street. And I decided after nine o'clock to
go to the ball, but not now as a "gentleman usher" (besides, my bow
had stayed with Yulia Mikhailovna), but from an irresistible curiosity
to hear (without asking questions) what people were saying in town
about all these events generally. Besides, I wanted to have a look at
Yulia Mikhailovna, if only from afar. I reproached myself very much
for the way I had run out on her earlier.

III

THE WHOLE of that night, with its almost absurd events and
ghastly "denouement" in the morning, comes back to me even
now as a hideous, nightmarish dream, and constitutes—for me at
least—the most difficult part of my chronicle. Though I came late to
the ball, I arrived towards the end of it anyway—so quickly was it
destined to end. It was already past ten when I reached the entrance
of the marshal's wife's house, where the same White Hall in which the
reading took place had, despite the shortness of time, been cleared and
made ready to serve as the main ballroom, it was supposed, for the
whole town. But however ill-disposed I had been towards the ball that
morning—even so I did not anticipate the full truth: not a single family
from higher circles came; even officials of any importance at all were
absent—and that was an extremely marked feature. As for ladies and
young girls, here Pyotr Stepanovich's (now obviously perfidious) calculations turned out to be incorrect to the highest degree: exceedingly
few had appeared; there was scarcely one lady to four men, and what

ladies! "Certain" wives of regimental officers, of various small fry from the post office and petty clerkdom, three doctors' wives with their daughters, two or three landowners of the poorer sort, the seven daughters and one niece of that secretary I mentioned somewhere above, some merchants' wives—was this what Yulia Mikhailovna had expected? Even half of the merchants did not come. As for the men, their mass was still indeed dense, despite the compact absence of all our nobility, but produced an ambiguous and suspicious impression. Of course, there were several rather quiet and respectful officers with their wives, several most obedient fathers of families, as again, for example, that same secretary, the father of his seven daughters. All these humble small potatoes came, so to speak, "out of inevitability," as one of these gentlemen put it. But, on the other hand, the mass of perky characters, and the mass, besides, of such persons as Pyotr Stepanovich and I had suspected of being let in to the matinée without tickets, seemed to have increased still more compared with the matinée. For the time being they were sitting in the buffet, and had gone straight to the buffet on arrival, as if the place had been appointed beforehand. At least it seemed so to me. The buffet was located at the end of the suite of rooms, in a spacious hall, where Prokhorych had installed himself with all the enticements of the club kitchen and with a tempting display of snacks and drinks. I noticed several personages there in all but torn frock coats, in the most dubious and utterly un-ball-like outfits, who had obviously been sobered up with boundless effort and for a short time only, and had been fetched from God knows where, perhaps from out of town. I knew, of course, that in accordance with Yulia Mikhailovna's idea it had been suggested to arrange a most democratic ball, "not refusing even tradesmen, if any such should happen to pay for a ticket." She could bravely utter these words in her committee, knowing perfectly well that it would not occur to any of our town tradesmen, all of them destitute, to buy a ticket. But anyway I doubted that these gloomy, all but tattered frock-coaters ought to have been let in, despite all the democratism of the committee. Who, then, had let them in, and with what purpose? Liputin and Lyamshin had been deprived of their ushers' bows (though they were present at the ball, as participants in the "quadrille of literature"); but Liputin's place had been taken, to my surprise, by that same seminarian who more than anyone else had made a scandal of the "matinée" by his skirmish with Stepan Trofimovich, and Lyamshin's by Pyotr Stepanovich himself; what, then, could be expected in such a case? I tried to listen in on conversations. Some opinions were striking in their wildness. It was maintained in one group, for example, that the whole story of Stavrogin and Liza had been fixed up by Yulia Mikhailovna, who had taken money from Stavrogin for it. The amount was even quoted. It was maintained that she had even arranged the fête for that purpose; and that was why, when they learned what was going on, half the town stayed away, and Lembke himself was so jolted that his "reason got deranged," and she was now "leading him about" insane. There was also much guffawing, hoarse, savage, and sly. Everyone criticized the ball terribly and abused Yulia Mikhailovna without any ceremony. Generally, the babble was disorderly, fragmentary, drunken, and agitated, so that it was difficult to grasp or infer anything. Simple merrymakers also found refuge in the buffet, and there were even several ladies of the sort that can no longer be surprised or frightened by anything, most jolly and amiable, mainly officers' wives, with their husbands. They settled in groups at separate tables and had an extremely merry time drinking tea. The buffet turned into a snug haven for nearly half the assembled public. And yet in a short time this whole mass was to come pouring into the ballroom; it was terrible even to think of it.

And meanwhile in the White Hall three skimpy little quadrilles had been formed, with the prince's participation. The young ladies were dancing, and their parents were rejoicing over them. But here, too, many of these respectable persons were already thinking of how, after letting their girls have fun, they could clear out in time, and not be there "once it starts." Decidedly everyone was certain that it was inevitably going to start. It would be difficult for me to describe the state of mind of Yulia Mikhailovna herself; I did not speak with her, though I came quite close to her. She did not respond to my bow on entering, because she did not notice me (really did not notice). Her face was pained, her glance haughty and disdainful, yet wandering and anxious. She was controlling herself with visible suffering—for what and for whom? She ought certainly to have left, and, above all, to have taken her husband away, yet she stayed! One could tell just by the look of her that her eyes had been "fully opened" and she had nothing more to wait for. She did not even call Pyotr Stepanovich over to her (he seemed to be avoiding her himself; I saw him in the buffet, in an exceedingly gay mood). But nevertheless she stayed at the ball and would not let Andrei Antonovich leave her side even for a moment. Oh, to the last minute she would have rejected with genuine indignation any hint at his health, even that morning, but now her eyes were to be opened in this respect as well. As for me, it seemed to me from the first glance that Andrei Antonovich looked worse than in the morning. It seemed he was in some sort of oblivion and was not quite sure where he was. Sometimes he would suddenly look around with unexpected sternness, a couple of times at me, for example. Once he tried to talk about something, began in a loud voice, and did not finish, almost throwing a scare into one humble old official who happened to be near him. But even this humble part of the public present in the White Hall gloomily and timorously avoided Yulia Mikhailovna, at the same time casting extremely strange glances at her husband, glances all too out of harmony, in their intent candor, with the fearfulness of these people.

"It was this trait that pierced me through and made me suddenly begin to guess about Andrei Antonovich," Yulia Mikhailovna privately confessed to me afterwards.

Yes, again she was to blame! Probably earlier, when, after my flight, she and Pyotr Stepanovich had decided that the ball would be and that she would be at the ball—probably she had gone again to the study of Andrei Antonovich, now finally "shaken" at the "reading," again employed all her seductions, and thus drew him along with her. But how tormented she must have been now! And still she would not leave! Whether she was tormented by pride, or was simply lost—I do not know. For all her haughtiness, she did try with humiliation and smiles to make conversation with some of the ladies, but they at once became confused, got off with a laconic, mistrustful "yes, ma'am" or "no, ma'am," and visibly avoided her.

Of the unquestionable dignitaries of our town, only one turned up at the ball—that same important retired general I have already described once, who, at the marshal's wife's, after the duel between Stavrogin and Gaganov, had "opened the door for public impatience."

He pompously strutted about the rooms, looked and listened, and tried to make it seem as if he had come more to observe morals than for any indubitable pleasure. He ended by attaching himself wholly to Yulia Mikhailovna and would not go a step away from her, apparently trying to reassure her and calm her. He was undoubtedly a most kind man, a great dignitary, and so very old that one could even tolerate his pity. But to confess to herself that this old babbler dared to pity her and almost to patronize her, understanding that he was honoring her with his presence, was extremely vexing. And the general would not leave off but kept babbling nonstop.

"A city, they say, cannot stand without seven righteous men . . . seven, I think, I don't remember the re-com-men-ded number.[1] How many of these seven . . . indubitably righteous men of our town . . . have the honor of attending your ball, I don't know, but in spite of their presence I am beginning to feel myself unsafe. *Vous me pardonnerez, charmante dame, n'est-ce pas?** I am speaking al-le-gor-i-cally, but I went to the buffet and am glad to have come back in one piece . . . Our inestimable Prokhorych is out of place there, and it looks as though his kiosk will be pulled down before morning. I'm joking, however. I'm only waiting to see how this 'quadrille of lit-er-a-ture' turns out, and then to bed. Forgive a gouty old man, I retire early, and I'd advise you to go 'bye-bye,' too, as they say *aux enfants.* In fact, I came for the young beauties . . . whom, of course, I can meet nowhere else in such rich assortment, except in this place here . . . They're all from across the river, and I don't go there. There's the wife of one officer . . . of the chasseurs, I think . . . not bad, not bad at all, and . . . and she knows it herself. I spoke with the minx—a pert thing, and . . . well, and the girls are fresh, too; but that's about it; apart from the freshness—nothing. Still, it's a pleasure. There are some sweet little buds; only they have thick lips. Generally, the Russian beauty of women's faces has little of that regularity and . . . and comes down to something like a pancake . . . *Vous me pardonnerez, n'est-ce pas* . . . with nice eyes, however . . . pretty, laughing eyes. These little buds are cha-a-arming for about two years of their youth, even three . . . well, and then they spread out forever . . . producing in their husbands that

*"You will forgive me, charming lady, won't you?"

lamentable in-dif-fer-entism which contributes so much to the development of the woman question . . . if I understand that question correctly . . . Hm. The hall is nice; the décor isn't bad. Could be worse. The music could be much worse . . . not to say it should be. Generally, having so few ladies produces a bad impression. I o-mit all men-tion of costume. It's bad that that one in the gray trousers allows himself to can-can-ize so openly. If it's from joy, I'll forgive him, and also because he's the local apothecary . . . but before eleven is still too early even for an apothecary . . . Two men had a fight there in the buffet, and they weren't taken out. Before eleven the fighters ought to be taken out, whatever the morals of the public . . . not to say past two; there we must yield to public opinion—if this ball survives until two o'clock. Varvara Petrovna, however, didn't keep her promise and supply the flowers. Hm, she can't be bothered with flowers, *pauvre mère*! And poor Liza, have you heard? A mysterious story, they say, and . . . and Stavrogin is back in the arena . . . Hm. I'd like to go home to bed . . . I'm dropping off. And when is this 'quadrille of lit-er-ature'?"

At last the "quadrille of literature" began.[2] In town lately, whenever a conversation about the coming ball started up somewhere, it would inevitably come round to this "quadrille of literature," and since no one could imagine what it was, it aroused boundless curiosity. Nothing could have been a greater threat to its success, and—what a disappointment it turned out to be!

The side doors to the White Hall, hitherto locked, were now opened, and several maskers suddenly appeared. The public eagerly surrounded them. The entire buffet to the last man poured into the hall at once. The maskers took up their positions for the dance. I managed to squeeze to the front and settled myself just behind Yulia Mikhailovna, von Lembke, and the general. Here Pyotr Stepanovich, who had been missing so far, sprang over to Yulia Mikhailovna.

"I've been in the buffet all this time, watching," he whispered, with the air of a guilty schoolboy, assumed on purpose, however, to tease her even more. She flushed with anger.

"Stop deceiving me now, at least, you brazen man!" escaped her, almost aloud, so that it was heard in the public. Pyotr Stepanovich sprang away, extremely pleased with himself.

It would be hard to imagine a more pathetic, trite, giftless, and insipid allegory than this "quadrille of literature." Nothing less suited to our public could have been devised; and yet it was said to have been devised by Karmazinov. True, it was arranged by Liputin, with advice from that lame teacher who had been at Virginsky's party. But, all the same, Karmazinov had supplied the idea, and it was said that he even wanted to dress up himself and take some special and independent role. The quadrille consisted of six pairs of pathetic maskers—almost not even maskers, because they were wearing the same clothes as everyone else. Thus, for example, one elderly gentleman, short, in a tailcoat—dressed like everyone else, in a word—with a venerable gray beard (tied on, this constituting the whole costume), was shuffling in place as he danced, with a solid expression on his face, trotting with rapid, tiny steps, and almost without moving from his place. He was producing some sounds in a moderate but husky bass, and it was this huskiness of his voice that was meant to signify one of the well-known newspapers. Opposite this masker danced a pair of giants, X and Z, with those letters pinned to their tailcoats, but what the X and Z signified remained unclear. "Honest Russian thought" was presented as a middle-aged gentleman in spectacles, tailcoat, gloves, and—in fetters (real fetters). Under this thought's arm was a briefcase containing some "dossier." Out of his pocket peeked an unsealed letter from abroad, which included an attestation, for all who doubted it, of the honesty of "honest Russian thought." All this was filled in orally by the ushers, since it was hardly possible to read a letter sticking out of someone's pocket. In his raised right hand "honest Russian thought" was holding a glass, as if he wished to propose a toast. Close to him on either side two crop-haired nihilist girls were trotting, while vis-à-vis danced some gentleman, also elderly, in a tailcoat, but with a heavy club in his hand, supposedly representing the non-Petersburg but formidable publication: *One Swat—A Wet Spot*. But, in spite of his club, he was quite unable to endure the spectacles of "honest Russian thought" staring fixedly at him and tried to avert his eyes, and as he performed the *pas de deux*, he twisted and fidgeted and did not know what to do with himself—so greatly, no doubt, did his conscience torment him . . . However, I cannot recall all these dumb little inventions;

everything was in the same vein, so that I finally felt painfully ashamed. And precisely the same impression as if of shame showed in all the public, even on the most sullen physiognomies from the buffet. For some time everyone was silent and watched in angry perplexity. An ashamed man usually begins to get angry and is inclined to cynicism. Gradually our public began to buzz:

"What on earth is this?" muttered a buffet person in one group.

"Some sort of silliness."

"Literature of some sort. They're criticizing the *Voice.*"

"What do I care."

From another group:

"Asses!"

"No, they're not asses, we're asses."

"Why are you an ass?"

"I'm not an ass."

"If you're not an ass, I'm certainly not either."

From a third group:

"Give them all a good pasting and to hell with them!"

"Shake the whole hall up!"

From a fourth:

"Aren't the Lembkas ashamed to look?"

"Why should they be ashamed? You're not ashamed, are you?"

"I am, too, ashamed, and he's the governor."

"And you are a swine."

"Never in my life have I seen such an utterly ordinary ball," one lady said venomously right beside Yulia Mikhailovna, obviously wishing to be heard. The lady was about forty, thick-set and rouged, wearing a bright silk dress; almost everyone in town knew her, but no one received her. She was the widow of a state councillor, who had left her a wooden house and a scanty pension, but she lived well and kept horses. About two months earlier she had paid a first call on Yulia Mikhailovna, but she did not receive her.

"Exactly what one might have foreseen," she added, insolently peeking into Yulia Mikhailovna's eyes.

"If you could foresee it, why then were you so good as to come?" Yulia Mikhailovna could not help saying.

"Why, out of naïvety," the perky lady snapped at once, getting all fluttered up (she wished terribly to have a fight); but the general stepped between them.

"*Chère dame,*" he bent towards Yulia Mikhailovna, "you really ought to leave. We are only hindering them, and without us they will have excellent fun. You have fulfilled everything, you have opened the ball for them, so now let them be . . . Besides, it seems Andrei Antonovich is not feeling quite sa-tis-fac-torily . . . To avoid trouble?"

But it was too late.

Throughout the quadrille, Andrei Antonovich gazed at the dancers in some wrathful perplexity, and when the public began to comment, he began to look around uneasily. Here, for the first time, certain of the buffet personages caught his attention; his eyes expressed extraordinary surprise. Suddenly there was loud laughter over one antic of the quadrille: the publisher of the "formidable non-Petersburg publication," who was dancing with a club in his hands, feeling finally that he could no longer endure the spectacles of "honest Russian thought" fixed on him, and not knowing where to hide, suddenly, during the last figure, went to meet the spectacles walking upside down—which, incidentally, was to signify the constant turning upside down of common sense in the "formidable non-Petersburg publication." Since Lyamshin was the only one who knew how to walk upside down, he had undertaken to represent the publisher with the club. Yulia Mikhailovna was decidedly unaware that there was going to be any walking upside down. "They concealed it from me, they concealed it," she repeated to me afterwards, in despair and indignation. The guffawing of the crowd greeted, of course, not the allegory, which nobody cared about, but simply the walking upside down in a coat with tails. Lembke boiled over and started shaking.

"Scoundrel!" he cried, pointing to Lyamshin. "Seize the blackguard, turn him . . . turn his legs . . . his head . . . so his head is up . . . up!"

Lyamshin jumped back to his feet. The guffawing was getting louder.

"Throw out all the scoundrels who are laughing!" Lembke suddenly prescribed. The crowd began to buzz and rumble.

"That's not right, Your Excellency."

"Shouldn't abuse the public, sir."

"A fool yourself!" came a voice from somewhere in a corner.

"Filibusters!" someone shouted from the other end.

Lembke quickly turned at the shout and went all pale. A dull smile appeared on his lips—as if he had suddenly understood and remembered something.

"Gentlemen," Yulia Mikhailovna addressed the oncoming crowd, at the same time drawing her husband away with her, "gentlemen, excuse Andrei Antonovich, Andrei Antonovich is unwell . . . excuse . . . forgive him, gentlemen!"

I precisely heard her say "forgive." The scene went very quickly. But I decidedly remember that part of the public rushed from the hall at that same moment, as if in fright, precisely after these words of Yulia Mikhailovna's. I even remember one hysterical woman's tearful cry:

"Ah, again like before!"

And suddenly, into what was already the beginnings of a crush, a bomb struck, precisely "again like before":

"Fire! All of Zarechye's in flames!"

I only do not remember where this terrible cry first arose—whether it was in the hall, or, as it now seems, someone ran in from the front steps—but it was followed by such alarm as I cannot even begin to describe. More than half of the public assembled at the ball came from Zarechye—owners of wooden houses there, or inhabitants of them. People rushed to the windows, instantly pulled open the curtains, tore down the blinds. Zarechye was ablaze. True, the fire was still just beginning, but it was blazing in three completely different places—and that was what was frightening.

"Arson! The Shpigulin men!" came screams from the crowd.

I remember several rather characteristic exclamations:

"I just felt in my heart that they'd set fire to it, all these days I've been feeling it!"

"It's the Shpigulin men, the Shpigulin men, and no one else!"

"And they gathered us here on purpose so they could set fires over there!"

This last, most astonishing cry came from a woman—the inadvertent, involuntary cry of a burnt-out Korobochka.[3] All surged towards the exit. I will not describe the crush in the entryway as people hunted for their fur coats, shawls, and cloaks, the shrieks of frightened women, the weeping of young girls. There was hardly any theft, but it was not surprising that in such disorder some people simply left without their warm clothes, unable to find them, of which there was talk in town for a long time afterwards, with legends and embellishments. Lembke and Yulia Mikhailovna were nearly crushed by the crowd in the doorway.

"Stop them all! Let no one leave!" Lembke screamed, holding out a menacing arm to meet the crowding people. "The strictest search of every last man of them, at once!"

Strong oaths poured from the hall.

"Andrei Antonovich! Andrei Antonovich!" Yulia Mikhailovna cried out in complete despair.

"Arrest her first!" the man shouted, pointing a menacing finger at her. "Search her first! The ball was organized with the intent of arson . . ."

She gave a cry and fainted (oh, it was most assuredly a real faint). The prince, the general, and I rushed to help her; there were others who helped us in this difficult moment, even from among the ladies. We carried the unfortunate woman out of that hell and into her carriage; but she came to her senses only as we neared her house, and her first cry was again about Andrei Antonovich. With the destruction of all her fantasies, Andrei Antonovich alone remained before her. A doctor was sent for. I spent a whole hour waiting at her place, as did the prince; the general, in a fit of magnanimity (though very frightened himself), wanted not to leave "the unfortunate woman's bedside" all night, but in ten minutes had fallen asleep in the drawing room while waiting for the doctor, and we simply left him there in his armchair.

The police chief, hastening from the ball to the fire, managed to lead Andrei Antonovich out behind us and tried to put him into Yulia Mikhailovna's carriage, persuading His Excellency with all his might to "take repose." I do not understand why, but he did not prevail. Of course, Andrei Antonovich would not even hear of repose and was straining to get to the fire; but this was no reason. It ended with the police chief taking him to the fire in his droshky. He told later that Lembke kept gesticulating all the way and "was shouting out such ideas as, being extraordinary, were impossible to obey." Afterwards it was reported that in those moments His Excellency was already in a state of brain fever owing to "a suddenness of fright."

There is no point in telling how the ball ended. A few dozen carousers, and with them even a few ladies, remained in the rooms. No police. They would not let the music go, and beat up the musicians who wanted to leave. By morning "Prokhorych's kiosk" had been all pulled down, they were drinking to distraction, dancing the "komarinsky" uncensored,⁴ the rooms were filthy, and only at dawn did part of this rabble, totally drunk, arrive at the scene of the dying-down fire for new disorders . . . The other half simply spent the night in the rooms, dead drunk, with all the consequences, on velvet sofas or on the floor. In the morning, at the first opportunity, they were dragged outside by the feet. Thus ended the fête for the benefit of the governesses of our province.

IV

THE FIRE FRIGHTENED our public from across the river precisely because the arson was so obvious. Remarkably, at the first cry of "fire," there came at once the cry that it was "the work of the Shpigulin men." It is known only too well now that three Shpigulin men did in fact participate in the arson, but—that was all; the rest of the factory hands were entirely vindicated both in general opinion and officially. Aside from those three scoundrels (one of whom has been caught and has confessed, while two are still in hiding), Fedka the Convict undoubtedly participated in the arson. That is all that is so far known with certainty about the origin of the fire; surmises are quite a different matter. What led these three scoundrels, were they guided by someone, or not? It is very difficult to answer all this even now.

The fire, owing to a strong wind, to the predominantly wooden buildings of Zarechye, and, finally, to its having been set at three different points, spread quickly and covered the whole area with incredible force (incidentally, the fire should be reckoned as having been set at two points: the third was caught and extinguished almost the moment it flared up—of that later). But, even so, the reporting of our disaster in the metropolitan newspapers was exaggerated: approximately speaking, no more (and perhaps less) than a quarter of the whole of Zarechye burned down. Our fire brigade, though weak in comparison with the extent and population of the town, acted quite correctly and selflessly. But it would not have done much, even with the concerted assistance of the populace, were it not that the wind changed towards morning, ceasing just before dawn. When, just an hour after fleeing from the ball, I made my way to Zarechye, the fire was already at full force. The entire street parallel to the river was in flames. It was as bright as day. I will not describe the picture of the fire in detail: who in Russia does not know it? The lanes nearest the blazing street were bustling and crowded beyond measure. Here the fire was definitely expected, and the inhabitants were dragging out their possessions, yet still would not leave their homes, but sat expectantly on dragged-out chests and feather beds, each under his own windows. Part of the male population was working hard, ruthlessly chopping down fences and even knocking apart entire shanties that stood closer to the fire and to windward. There was only the crying of awakened children and the wailing lamentations of women who had already successfully dragged their junk out. The unsuccessful were silently and energetically dragging theirs out. Sparks and grit flew far away; they were extinguished as well as possible. At the fire itself there was a crowd of spectators who had come running from every end of town. Some helped to put it out, others gazed like admirers. A big fire at night always produces a stirring and exhilarating impression; fireworks are based on that, but there the fire is disposed along graceful, regular lines and, with all its safety, produces a playful and light impression, as after a glass of champagne. A real fire is another matter: here horror and, after all, some sense of personal danger, as it were—combined with the well-known exhilarating impression of a fire at night—produce in the spectator (not, of course, in the burnt-out inhabitant) a sort of brain concussion and a challenge, as it were, to his own destructive instincts, which, alas! lie hidden in every soul, even that of the most humble and familial titular councillor[5] . . . This gloomy sensation is almost always intoxicating. "I really do not know whether it is possible to watch a fire without a certain pleasure." This was said to me, word for word, by Stepan Trofimovich, on returning from a night fire he had chanced to witness, and still under the first impression of the spectacle. Of course, that same admirer of night fires will also rush into the fire to save a burning child or an old woman; but that is an altogether different matter.

Plodding after the curious crowd, I made my way, without any inquiries, to the most important and dangerous spot, where I finally caught sight of Lembke, whom I was looking for on instructions from Yulia Mikhailovna herself. His position was astonishing and extraordinary. He was standing on the debris of a fence; to the left of him, about thirty steps away, towered the black skeleton of a nearly burnt-down two-story wooden house, with holes instead of windows on both floors, its roof fallen in, and flames still snaking here and there over the charred beams. At the back of the courtyard, about twenty steps away from the burnt-down house, a cottage, also two-storied, was beginning to blaze, and the firemen were working on it as hard as they could. To the right, the firemen and the people were fighting for a rather large wooden building which was not yet burning, but had already caught fire several times, and was inevitably fated to burn down. Lembke was shouting and gesticulating, his face turned towards the cottage, and issuing orders which no one obeyed. I almost thought he had simply been left there and completely abandoned. At least no one in the dense and extremely diverse crowd that surrounded him, in which, along with all kinds of people, there were also some gentlemen and even the cathedral priest, though they all listened to him with curiosity and astonishment, either spoke to him or tried to lead him away. Lembke, pale, his eyes flashing, was uttering the most astonishing things; to top it off, he was without his hat, and had lost it long ago.

"It's all arson! It's nihilism! If anything's ablaze, it's nihilism!" I heard all but with horror, and though there was no longer anything to be astonished at, still manifest reality always has something shocking about it.

"Your Excellency," a policeman turned up beside him, "if you'd be so good as to try domestic repose, sir . . . the way it is, it's even dangerous for Your Excellency to be standing here."

This policeman, as I learned later, was purposely left with Andrei Antonovich by the police chief, to watch over him and try as hard as he could to take him home, and in case of danger even to act with force—a charge obviously beyond the powers of its executor.

"The tears of the burnt-out people will be wiped away, but the town will be burned. It's all four blackguards, four and a half. Arrest the blackguard! He's in it alone, and has slandered the four and a half. He worms himself into the honor of families. Governesses have been used to set houses on fire. This is mean, mean! Aie, what is he doing?" he cried, suddenly noticing a fireman on the roof of the blazing cottage, the roof already burned through under him and fire flaring up all around. "Pull him down, pull him down, he'll fall through, he'll catch fire, put him out . . . What is he doing up there?"

"Putting it out, Your Excellency."

"Unbelievable. The fire is in people's minds, not on the rooftops. Pull him down and drop it all! Better drop it, drop it! Leave it to itself somehow! Aie, who is that still crying? An old woman! An old woman is shouting, why did you forget the old woman?"

Indeed, a forgotten old woman was shouting on the bottom floor of the blazing cottage, the eighty-year-old relative of the merchant who owned the burning house. But she had not been forgotten; she had gone back into the burning house herself while it was possible, with the insane purpose of dragging her feather bed out of the still untouched corner room. Choking from the smoke and shouting from the heat, because that room, too, had caught fire, she was still trying with all her might to push her feather bed through a broken window with her decrepit hands. Lembke rushed to help her. Everyone saw him run up to the window, seize a corner of the feather bed and begin to pull it through the window with all his might. As bad luck would have it, at that very moment a broken board fell from the roof and struck the unfortunate man. It did not kill him, it merely grazed his neck with one end as it fell, but the career of Andrei Antonovich was over, at least among us; the blow knocked him off his feet, and he collapsed unconscious.

At last came a sullen, gloomy dawn. The fire dwindled; after the wind it suddenly became still, and then came a slow, drizzling rain, as if through a sieve. I was by then in another part of Zarechye, far from the spot where Lembke had fallen, and there in the crowd I heard very strange talk. A strange fact had been discovered: at the edge of the quarter, on a vacant lot beyond the kitchen gardens, not less than fifty steps away from the other buildings, there stood a small, recently built

wooden house, and this solitary house had burst into flames almost
before any of the others, at the very beginning of the fire. Even if it
had burned down, it could not have transmitted the fire to any town
buildings because of the distance, and, vice versa, if the whole of
Zarechye had burned down, this one house would have remained
untouched, whatever wind was blowing. It appeared to have caught
fire separately and independently, so there was something behind it.
But the main thing was that it had not had time to burn down, and
towards daybreak astonishing things were discovered inside it. The
owner of this new house, a tradesman who lived in the nearby quarter,
as soon as he saw his new house on fire, rushed to it and managed to
save it, with the help of some neighbors, by scattering the burning logs
that had been piled against the side wall. But there were tenants living
in the house—a captain well known in town, his sister, and with them
an elderly servingwoman, and these tenants, the captain, his sister, and
the servingwoman, had all three been stabbed to death that night and
apparently robbed. (It was here that the police chief had gone when
he had left the fire while Lembke was trying to rescue the feather bed.)
By morning the news had spread and a huge mass of all sorts of people,
even some who had been burned out in Zarechye, poured down to the
vacant lot, to the new house. It was so crowded that it was even
difficult to get through. I was told at once that the captain had been
found with his throat cut, on the bench, dressed, and that he had
probably been dead drunk when he was killed, so that he had not even
felt it, and that he had bled "like a bull"; that his sister Marya Timofeevna had been "stuck all over" with a knife, and was lying on the
floor of the doorway, so that she had probably been awake and had
struggled and fought with the murderer. The housekeeper, who probably also woke up, had her head completely smashed in. According to
the owner's story, the captain had come to see him the day before, in
the morning, had boasted and displayed a lot of money, as much as two
hundred roubles. The captain's old, worn green wallet was found
empty on the floor; but Marya Timofeevna's trunk had not been
touched, and the silver casing of her icon had not been touched either;
of the captain's clothes, everything turned out to be intact as well; one
could see that the thief had been in a hurry, and that he was a man who
was familiar with the captain's affairs, had come to take money only,

and knew where to find it. If the owner had not come running right away, the logs would have flared up and quite certainly burned the house down, "and it would have been difficult to learn the truth from charred corpses."

So ran the account of the affair. Further information was added: that the place had been rented for the captain and his sister personally by Mr. Stavrogin, Nikolai Vsevolodovich, General Stavrogin's widow's boy, that he had come personally to rent it, and had been very insistent, because the owner did not want to let it and was intending to make the house a tavern, but Nikolai Vsevolodovich had spared no expense and handed him money for a year in advance.

"There's something behind this fire," voices came from the crowd.

But the majority were silent. Their faces were gloomy, but I did not notice any great, obvious irritation. All around, however, stories went on about Nikolai Vsevolodovich, that the murdered woman was his wife, that yesterday, "in a dishonest manner," he had lured to himself a young lady from the foremost house in town, the daughter of General Drozdov's widow, that a complaint would be lodged against him in Petersburg, and that if his wife had been killed, it must have been so that he could marry the Drozdov girl. Skvoreshniki was no more than a mile and a half away, and I remember thinking: shouldn't I send word to them there? However, I did not notice anyone especially inciting the crowd, and I do not want to speak evil, though I did see flash by me two or three "buffet" mugs, who turned up at the fire by morning and whom I recognized at once. I particularly remember one tall, lean fellow, a tradesman, haggard, curly-haired, as if smeared with soot—a locksmith, as I learned later. He was not drunk, but, in contrast to the gloomily standing crowd, seemed beside himself. He kept addressing the people, though I do not remember his words. Whatever was coherent was no longer than: "What's this, brothers? Can it really be like this?"—all the while waving his arms.

3

A Finished Romance

I

FROM THE BIG reception room at Skvoreshniki (the same one in which the last meeting between Varvara Petrovna and Stepan Trofimovich had taken place), the fire was in full view. At dawn, towards six o'clock, Liza was standing at the last window on the right, looking intently at the dying glow. She was alone in the room. The dress she was wearing was the festive one from the day before, in which she had appeared at the reading—light green, magnificent, all lace, but rumpled now, hastily and carelessly put on. Suddenly noticing that the front of the dress was not tightly fastened, she blushed, hastily put it right, snatched from the armchair a red shawl left there the day before when she came in, and threw it around her neck. Her fluffy hair fell in disorderly curls onto her right shoulder from under the shawl. Her face was tired, preoccupied, but her eyes were burning from under her frowning brows. She went up to the window again and leaned her hot forehead against the cold glass. The door opened and Nikolai Vsevolodovich came in.

"I've sent a messenger on horseback," he said, "in ten minutes we'll learn everything, but meanwhile the servants are saying that part of Zarechye has burned down, nearer the embankment, to the right from the bridge. It started burning before twelve; it's going out now."

He did not go to the window, but stopped three steps behind her, yet she did not turn to him.

"By the calendar it ought to have been light an hour ago, and it's still like night," she said with vexation.

"Every calendar doth lie,"[1] he remarked with an obliging grin, but, ashamed, hastened to add: "It's boring to live by the calendar, Liza."

And he fell silent finally, vexed at the new platitude he had uttered; Liza smiled crookedly.

"You're in such a sad mood that you can't even find words with me. But don't worry, you put it appropriately: I always live by the calendar, my every step is reckoned by the calendar. Are you surprised?"

She quickly turned away from the window and sat down in an armchair.

"You sit down, too, please. We won't be together long, and I want to say whatever I like . . . Why shouldn't you, too, say whatever you like?"

Nikolai Vsevolodovich sat down beside her and gently, almost timorously, took her hand.

"What does this language mean, Liza? Where does it come from so suddenly? What is the meaning of 'we won't be together long'? This is the second mysterious phrase since you woke up half an hour ago."

"You've started counting my mysterious phrases?" she laughed. "And do you remember how yesterday, as I came in, I introduced myself as a dead person? You found it necessary to forget that. To forget or not to notice."

"I don't remember, Liza. Why a dead person? One must live . . ."

"And you stop short. You've quite lost your eloquence. I've lived my hour in the world, and enough. Do you remember Khristofor Ivanovich?"

"No, I don't," he frowned.

"Khristofor Ivanovich, in Lausanne? You got terribly sick of him. He'd open the door and always say, 'I've just come for a minute,' and he'd sit for the whole day. I don't want to be like Khristofor Ivanovich and sit for the whole day."

A pained impression came to his face.

"Liza, this broken language grieves me. This grimacing must cost you dearly. What is it for? Why?"

His eyes lit up.

"Liza," he exclaimed, "I swear I love you more now than yesterday when you came to me!"

"What a strange confession! Why this yesterday and today, these two measures?"

"You won't abandon me," he went on, almost with despair, "we'll leave together, this very day, right? Right?"

"Aie, don't squeeze my hand so painfully! Where are we going to go together this very day? To 'resurrect' somewhere again? No, enough trying . . . and it's too slow for me; and I'm not able; it's too high for me. If we're to go, it should be to Moscow, to pay calls there and receive people—that's my ideal, you know; even in Switzerland I didn't conceal from you how I am. Since it's not possible for us to go to Moscow and pay calls, because you're married, there's no point in talking about it."

"Liza! What was it yesterday, then?"

"It was what it was."

"That's impossible! That's cruel!"

"So what if it's cruel; just endure it, if it's cruel."

"You're taking revenge on me for yesterday's fantasy . . ." he muttered, grinning spitefully. Liza flushed.

"What a base thought!"

"Then why did you give me . . . 'so much happiness'? Do I have the right to know?"

"No, try doing without rights somehow; don't crown the baseness of your suggestion with foolishness. You're not doing well today. Incidentally, are you not perchance afraid of the world's opinion, and that you'll be condemned for this 'so much happiness'? Oh, if you are, for God's sake don't worry. You didn't cause anything, and you're not answerable to anyone. When I was opening your door yesterday, you didn't even know who was coming in. Here it was precisely my fantasy alone, as you just put it, and nothing more. You can look everyone boldly and triumphantly in the eye."

"Your words, this laughter, for an hour already they've been sending a chill of horror over me. This 'happiness' you're now talking about so frenziedly has cost me . . . everything. How can I lose you now? I swear I loved you less yesterday. Why then do you take everything from me today? Do you know how much it cost me, this new hope? I paid for it with life."

"Your own or someone else's?"

He got up quickly.

"What does that mean?" he said, looking at her motionlessly.

"Paid with your own life or with mine, that is what I wanted to ask. Or have you now lost all understanding entirely?" Liza flushed. "Why did you jump up so suddenly? Why are you looking at me that way? You scare me. Why are you afraid all the time? I noticed a while ago that you're afraid, precisely now, precisely at this moment . . . Lord, you're turning so pale!"

"If you know anything, Liza, I swear that *I* do not . . . and I wasn't talking about *that* just now when I spoke of paying with life . . ."

"I don't understand you at all," she said, faltering timorously.

At last a slow, pensive grin appeared on his lips. He slowly sat down, put his elbows on his knees, and covered his face with his hands.

"A bad dream and delirium . . . We were talking about two different things."

"I don't know at all what you were talking about . . . Did you really not know yesterday that I would leave you today, did you or did you not? Don't lie, did you know or did you not?"

"I did . . ." he uttered softly.

"So what do you want: you knew it, and you reserved 'the moment' for yourself. How can there be any score?"

"Tell me the whole truth," he cried out with deep suffering, "when you opened my door yesterday, did you know yourself that you were opening it for one hour only?"

She looked at him with hatred:

"Truly, the most serious man can ask the most amazing questions. And why do you worry so? Can it be out of pride that a woman left you first, and not you her? You know, Nikolai Vsevolodovich, since I've been here I've become convinced, among other things, that you are being terribly magnanimous towards me, and that is precisely what I cannot endure in you."

He got up from his place and walked several steps about the room.

"Very well, suppose it has to end this way . . . But how could it all have happened?"

"Who cares! And the main thing is that you yourself can tell it off on your own fingers and understand it better than anyone in the world and were counting on it. I am a young lady, my heart was brought up in the opera, it started there, that's the whole answer."

"No."

"There's nothing here that can gall your pride, and it's all perfectly true. It began with a beautiful moment which I could not endure. Two days ago when I 'offended' you before all the world, and you gave me such a chivalrous reply, I came home and guessed at once that you were running away from me because you were married, and not at all out of contempt for me—which is what I, being a young lady of fashion, was most afraid of. I understood that it was me, a reckless girl, that you were protecting by running away. You see how I value your magnanimity. Then Pyotr Stepanovich jumped up to me and explained it all at once. He revealed to me that you were being shaken by a great idea, before which he and I were utterly nothing, but that I still stood in your way. He included himself in it; he absolutely wanted it to be the three of us together, and said the most fantastic things about a bark and maple oars from some Russian song. I praised him, said he was a poet, and he took it for pure gold. And since I'd known for a long time, even without that, that I'd never last more than a moment, I just up and decided. So that's all, and enough, and, please, no more explanations. Otherwise we might quarrel. Don't be afraid of anyone, I take it all upon myself. I'm bad, I'm capricious, I got tempted by an operatic bark, I'm a young lady . . . But, you know, I still thought you loved me terribly. Don't despise a foolish girl or laugh at this little tear that just fell. I like terribly much to cry and 'pity myself.' Well, enough, enough. I'm not capable of anything, you're not capable of anything; two flicks, one on each side, and let that be a comfort to us. At least our pride doesn't suffer."

"Dream and delirium!" Nikolai Vsevolodovich cried out, wringing his hands and pacing the room. "Liza, poor Liza, what have you done to yourself?"

"Burned myself in a candle, that's all. Are you crying, too? Be more decent, more unfeeling . . ."

"Why, why did you come to me?"

"But don't you understand, finally, what a comical position you put yourself in before worldly opinion by asking such questions?"

"Why did you ruin yourself in such an ugly and stupid way, and what is to be done now?"

"And this is Stavrogin, the 'bloodsucker Stavrogin,' as one lady here who is in love with you calls you! Listen, I already told you: I've traded my life for a single hour, and I'm at peace. Trade yours the same way . . . though you've got no reason to; you'll still have so many different 'hours' and 'moments.' "

"As many as you have; I give you my great word, not an hour more than you have!"

He kept pacing and did not see her quick, piercing look which suddenly seemed to light up with hope. But the ray of light went out at the same moment.

"If you knew the price of my present *impossible* sincerity, Liza, if only I could reveal it to you . . ."

"Reveal? You want to reveal something to me? God save me from your revelations!" she interrupted, almost fearfully.

He stopped and waited uneasily.

"I must confess to you, ever since Switzerland the thought has settled in me that there is something horrible, dirty, and bloody on your soul, and . . . at the same time something that makes you look terribly ridiculous. Beware of revealing it to me, if it's true: I'll ridicule you. I'll laugh at you all your life . . . Aie, you're turning pale again? I won't, I won't, I'll leave at once," she jumped up from the chair with a squeamish and scornful gesture.

"Torment me, punish me, vent your spite on me," he cried out in despair. "You have every right! I knew I didn't love you, and I ruined you. Yes, 'I reserved the moment for myself'; I had a hope . . . for a long time . . . a last hope . . . I couldn't resist the light that shone in my heart when you came to me yesterday, yourself, alone, first. I suddenly believed . . . maybe I believe even now."

"For such noble sincerity I shall repay you in kind. I do not want to be your tenderhearted nurse. Suppose I do indeed become a sick-nurse, unless I incidentally manage to die this very day; still, if I do, it won't be to you, though of course you're worth anyone legless or armless. It has always seemed to me that you would bring me to some place where there lives a huge, evil spider, as big as a man, and we would spend our whole life there looking at him and being afraid.

That's how our mutual love would pass. Address yourself to Dashenka; she'll go with you wherever you like."

"And even now you can't help recalling her?"

"Poor puppy! Give her my regards. Does she know you intend her for your old age in Switzerland? What consideration! What foresight! Aie, who's there?"

At the far end of the room the door opened a tiny bit; someone's head stuck itself in and quickly hid.

"Is that you, Alexei Yegorych?" Stavrogin asked.

"No, it's only me," Pyotr Stepanovich again stuck in the upper half of himself. "Hello, Lizaveta Nikolaevna; or, anyhow, good morning. I just knew I'd find you both in this room. Absolutely for just one moment, Nikolai Vsevolodovich—I hurried here at all costs for a couple of words . . . most necessary words . . . a couple, no more!"

Stavrogin started to go, but after three steps he returned to Liza.

"If you hear anything now, Liza, know this: I am guilty."

She gave a start and looked at him timorously; but he hurriedly went out.

II

THE ROOM Pyotr Stepanovich had peeked out from was a big oval anteroom. Before he came, Alexei Yegorych had been sitting there, but he sent him away. Nikolai Vsevolodovich closed the door to the reception room behind himself and stopped in expectation. Pyotr Stepanovich looked him over quickly and inquisitively.

"Well?"

"I mean, if you already know," Pyotr Stepanovich hurried on, wishing, it seemed, to jump into the man's soul with his eyes, "then, of course, none of us is guilty of anything, and you first of all, because it's such a conjunction . . . a coincidence of events . . . in short, legally it cannot involve you, and I flew here to forewarn you."

"They're burned? Killed?"

"Killed but not burned, and that's the bad thing, but I give you my word of honor that I'm not guilty there either, however much you suspect me—because maybe you do suspect me, eh? Want the whole truth? You see, the thought did indeed occur to me—you prompted me to it yourself, not seriously, teasing me (because you wouldn't really prompt me seriously), but I didn't dare, and I wouldn't have dared for anything, not even for a hundred roubles—and there isn't any profit in it, I mean for me, for me . . ." (He hurried terribly and spoke like a rattle.) "But look what a coincidence of circumstances: I gave that drunken fool Lebyadkin two hundred and thirty roubles of my own (of my own, you hear, of my own, not a rouble of it was yours, and, moreover, you know that yourself), two days ago, already that evening—you hear, two days ago, not yesterday after the 'reading,' note that: it's a rather important coincidence, because I didn't know anything for certain then about Lizaveta Nikolaevna's going to you or not; and I gave my own money solely because two days ago you distinguished yourself by deciding to announce your secret to everyone. Well, I'm not getting into . . . it's your business . . . this chivalry . . . but, I confess, it surprised me, like a clout on the head. But since I am exceeding weary of all these tragedies—and note that I'm speaking seriously, though I'm using antiquated expressions—since it's all finally harmful to my plans, I swore to myself I'd pack the Lebyadkins off to Petersburg at all costs and without your knowledge, the more so since he was anxious to go there himself. One mistake: I gave him the money on your behalf; was it a mistake, or not? Maybe not, eh? Now listen, listen to how it all turned out . . ." In the fever of talking he moved up very close to Stavrogin and went to grab him by the lapel of his jacket (maybe on purpose, by God). Stavrogin, with a strong movement, hit him on the arm.

"What's this now . . . come on . . . you'll break my arm . . . the main thing here is how it turned out," he rattled on, not even the least surprised at being hit. "I hand him the money in the evening, so that he and his dear sister can set out the next day at dawn; I charge the scoundrel Liputin with that little business, putting them on the train and seeing them off himself. But the blackguard Liputin felt the need to pull a prank on the public—maybe you heard? At the 'reading'? So listen, listen: the two of them drink, compose verses, half belonging to Liputin; he dresses him up in a tailcoat, assures me he sent him off in the morning, all the while keeping him somewhere in a back closet, in order to push him out onto the platform. But he quickly and unexpectedly gets drunk. Then the notorious scandal, then he's brought home more dead than alive, and Liputin takes the two hundred roubles from him on the sly, leaving him some change. But, unfortunately, it turns out that he had already taken the two hundred out of his pocket in the morning, boasting and showing it where he shouldn't have. And since Fedka was just waiting for that, and had heard something at Kirillov's (remember your hint?), he decided to make use of it. That's the whole truth. I'm glad at least that Fedka didn't find the money—and he was counting on getting a thousand, the scoundrel! He was in a hurry and, it seems, was frightened by the fire himself . . . Would you believe it, that fire was a real whack on the head for me. No, it's the devil knows what! It's such high-handedness . . . Look, I won't conceal anything, since I expect so much from you: so, yes, I've had this little idea of a fire ripening in me for a long time, since it's so national and popular; but I was keeping it for a critical hour, for that precious moment when we all rise up and . . . And they suddenly decided it high-handedly and without any orders, now, precisely when they should have laid low and held their breath! No, it's such high-handedness! . . . in short, I still don't know anything, they're talking here about two Shpigulin men . . . but if *ours* were in it as well, if any one of them warmed his hands at it—woe to him! You see what it means to slacken even a little! No, this democratic scum with its fivesomes is a poor support; what we need is one splendid, monumental, despotic will, supported by something external and not accidental . . . Then the fivesomes will also put their tails of obedience between their legs, and their obsequiousness will occasionally come in handy. Anyhow, though it's being shouted in all trumpets that Stavrogin needed to burn his wife, and that's why the town got burned down, still . . ."

"They're already shouting in all trumpets?"

"I mean, not at all so far, and, I confess, I've heard nothing whatsoever, but what can you do with people, especially when they've been burned out: *Vox populi vox dei.*[2] How long does it take to blow the stupidest rumor to the four winds? . . . But as a matter of fact you have nothing whatsoever to fear. Legally, you're completely in the right, and morally, too—because you didn't want it, eh? Did you? There's no evidence, just a coincidence . . . Unless Fedka happens to recall your imprudent words that time at Kirillov's (and why did you say that then?), but that proves nothing at all, and we will cancel Fedka. I'm canceling him today . . ."

"And the bodies didn't burn at all?"

"Not a bit; that rascal couldn't arrange anything properly. But I'm glad at least that you're so calm . . . because though you're not guilty in any way, not even in thought, still, all the same. And, besides, you must agree that all this gives an excellent turn to your affairs: suddenly you're a free widower and at this very moment can marry a wonderful girl with enormous money, who, on top of that, is already in your hands. That's what a simple, crude coincidence of circumstances can do—eh?"

"Are you threatening me, foolish head?"

"Eh, enough, enough, right away I'm a foolish head! And what's this tone? Instead of being glad, you . . . I came flying especially to forewarn you sooner . . . And how am I going to threaten you? As if I need you under threat! I need your good will, and not out of fear. You are the light, the sun . . . It's I who am afraid of you with all my might, not you of me! I'm not Mavriky Nikolaevich . . . And, imagine, I'm flying here in a racing droshky, and there's Mavriky Nikolaevich by the garden fence, at the back corner of the garden . . . in his greatcoat, soaked through, must have been sitting there all night! Wonders! How people can lose their minds!"

"Mavriky Nikolaevich? Is it true?"

"True, true. Sitting by the garden fence. From here—about three hundred steps from here, I suppose. I hurried to get past him, but he saw me. You didn't know? In that case I'm very glad I didn't forget to tell you. His kind is most dangerous if he happens to have a revolver, and, finally, the night, the slush, the natural irritation—because look what situation he's in now, ha, ha! Why do you think he's sitting there?"

"Waiting for Lizaveta Nikolaevna, of course."

"Ah-ha! But why should she go out to him? And . . . in such rain . . . what a fool!"

"She will go out to him presently."

"Ehh! That's news! So then . . . But listen, her affairs are completely changed now: what need does she have for Mavriky now? When you're a free widower and can marry her tomorrow? She doesn't know yet—leave it to me, I'll take care of it right away. Where is she, I must make her happy with the news."

"Happy?"

"What else! Let's go."

"And you think she won't guess about those corpses?" Stavrogin narrowed his eyes somehow peculiarly.

"Of course she won't," Pyotr Stepanovich picked up like a decided little fool, "because legally . . . Eh, you! But even if she does guess! With women it all gets so excellently shaded in—you still don't know women! Besides, it's entirely to her profit to marry you now, because she's made a scandal of herself, after all, and, besides, I told her a pile of stuff about the 'bark': I precisely thought one could affect her with the 'bark,' so that's the caliber of the girl. Don't worry, she'll step over those little corpses all right, and la-di-da!—the more so as you're perfectly, perfectly innocent, isn't that so? She'll just stash those little corpses away so as to needle you later on, say in the second year of your marriage. Every woman on her way to the altar keeps something like that stored up from her husband's old days, but then . . . what will it be like in a year? Ha, ha, ha!"

"If you came in a racing droshky, take her now to Mavriky Nikolaevich. She said just now that she couldn't stand me and was going to leave me, and she certainly won't accept my carriage."

"Ah-ha! She's really leaving? What might have brought that about?" Pyotr Stepanovich gave a silly look.

"She guessed somehow during the night that I don't love her at all . . . which, of course, she's always known."

"But don't you love her?" Pyotr Stepanovich picked up, with a look of boundless amazement. "But in that case why did you keep her here when she came yesterday, and not inform her directly, like a noble man, that you didn't love her? That is terribly mean on your part; and what a mean position you put me in before her!"

Stavrogin suddenly laughed.

"I'm laughing at my ape," he clarified at once.

"Ah! You guessed I was clowning," Pyotr Stepanovich also burst into terribly gay laughter. "It was to make you laugh! Imagine, as soon as you came out to me, I guessed at once from your face that you'd had a 'misfortune.' Maybe even a complete fiasco, eh? Now, I'll bet," he cried, almost choking with delight, "that you spent the whole night side by side on chairs in the drawing room, and argued about some most lofty nobility the whole precious time . . . Excuse me, excuse me; what do I care: I already knew for sure yesterday that it would end with foolishness between you. I brought her to you solely to amuse you, and to prove that with me you won't be bored; I'll be useful in that line three hundred times; I generally like being pleasant with people. And if you don't need her now, which is what I was figuring on, what I came for, then . . ."

"So you brought her here only for my amusement?"

"What else?"

"And not to make me kill my wife?"

"Ah-ha, but did you kill her, really? What a tragic man!"

"It makes no difference. You killed her."

"Did I, really? I'm telling you, I didn't have a drop to do with it. However, you're beginning to worry me . . ."

"Go on. You said: 'If you don't need her now, then . . .' "

"Permit me, of course! I'll get her excellently married to Mavriky Nikolaevich, whom, incidentally, I did not plant there in your garden, don't take that into your head as well. In fact, I'm afraid of him now. In the racing droshky, you say; but I really just snicked by him . . . what if he does indeed have a revolver? . . . It's a good thing I brought mine along. Here it is" (he took a revolver from his pocket, showed it, and immediately put it back again). "I brought it along on account of the far distance . . . Anyhow, I'll fix it up for you in a second: her little heart is precisely aching for Mavriky now . . . at least it should be . . . and you know—by God, I'm even slightly sorry for her now! I'll put her together with Mavriky, and she'll immediately start remembering you—praising you to him and abusing him to his face—a woman's heart! Well, so you're laughing again? I'm terribly glad you've cheered up so much. Well, then, let's go. I'll start straight off with Mavriky, and those . . . the murdered ones . . . you know, why don't we just not mention them for now? She'll find out later anyway."

"Find out what? Who has been murdered? What did you say about Mavriky Nikolaevich?" Liza suddenly opened the door.

"Ah! you've been eavesdropping?"

"What did you just say about Mavriky Nikolaevich? Has hé been murdered?"

"Ah! so you didn't quite hear! Calm yourself, Mavriky Nikolaevich is alive and well, which you can instantly ascertain for yourself, because he's here on the roadside, by the garden fence . . . and spent the whole night there, it seems; he's soaked through, in his great-coat . . . I drove by, he saw me."

"That isn't true. You said 'murdered' . . . Who has been murdered?" she insisted, with painful mistrust.

"Only my wife, her brother Lebyadkin, and their housekeeper have been murdered," Stavrogin declared firmly.

Liza gave a start and turned terribly pale.

"A brutal case, a strange case, Lizaveta Nikolaevna, a most stupid case of robbery," Pyotr Stepanovich began rattling at once, "just rob-bery, taking advantage of the fire; it's the doing of the brigand Fedka the Convict, and that fool Lebyadkin, who was showing everyone his money . . . I came flying to tell you . . . like a smack on the head. Stavrogin could barely keep his feet when I told him. We were discuss-ing whether to tell you now or not."

"Nikolai Vsevolodovich, is he telling the truth?" Liza barely uttered.

"No, it's not the truth."

"How, not the truth!" Pyotr Stepanovich jumped. "What's this now!"

"Lord, I'm losing my mind!" Liza cried out.

"But understand, at least, that right now he is the mad one!" Pyotr Stepanovich shouted with all his might. "After all, his wife has been murdered. See how pale he is . . . Wasn't he with you all night, without leaving you for a moment, how can you suspect him?"

"Nikolai Vsevolodovich, tell me, as before God, are you guilty or not, and I swear I'll believe your word as if it were God's own, and follow you to the ends of the earth, oh, I will! I'll go like a little dog . . ."

"Why are you tormenting her, you fantastic head?" Pyotr Stepano-vich flew into a frenzy. "Lizaveta Nikolaevna, grind me in a mortar, by gosh, but he's innocent, on the contrary, he's crushed and raving, you can see that. He's not guilty of anything, not of anything, not even of the thought! . . . It's all the doing of brigands alone, who will certainly be found within a week and punished with flogging . . . Fedka the Convict and the Shpigulin men are the ones, the whole town's rattling about it, which is why I am, too."

"Is that right? Is that right?" Liza waited, all trembling, for her final sentence.

"I didn't kill them and was against it, but I knew they would be killed, and I didn't stop the killers. Leave me, Liza," Stavrogin uttered, and he turned and went into the drawing room.

Liza covered her face with her hands, turned, and went out. Pyotr Stepanovich first dashed after her, but immediately came back to the drawing room.

"So that's how you are? So that's how you are? So you're not afraid of anything?" he fell upon Stavrogin in a perfect fury, muttering incoherently, almost at a loss for words, foaming at the mouth.

Stavrogin stood in the middle of the room without answering a word. He lightly grasped a tuft of his hair with his left hand and smiled forlornly. Pyotr Stepanovich pulled him hard by the sleeve.

"Are you all there, or what? So this is what you're doing now? You'll denounce everybody and take yourself to a monastery, or to the devil . . . But I'll bump you off all the same, even if you're not afraid of me!"

"Ah, it's you rattling!" Stavrogin finally made him out. "Run," he suddenly came to his senses, "run after her, order the carriage, don't abandon her . . . Run, run! Take her home, so that no one knows, and so that she doesn't go there . . . at the bodies . . . at the bodies . . . force her to get into the carriage. Alexei Yegorych! Alexei Yegorych!"

"Stop, don't shout! She's in Mavriky's arms by now . . . Mavriky is not going to get into your carriage . . . Stop! This is more precious than the carriage!"

He snatched out the revolver again; Stavrogin gave him a serious look.

"Go ahead, kill me," he said softly, almost peaceably.

"Pah, the devil, what lies a man heaps on himself!" Pyotr Stepanovich was simply shaking. "By God, you ought to be killed! Truly, she should have spat on you! What sort of 'bark' are you; you're an old, leaky timber barge, fit to be broken up! . . . Can't you come to your senses now, at least out of spite, at least out of spite! Ehh! Does it make any difference to you, since you're asking for a bullet in the head?"

Stavrogin grinned strangely.

"If you weren't such a clown, perhaps I'd say yes now . . . If you were just a drop smarter . . ."

"I am a clown, but I don't want you, my main half, to be a clown! Do you understand me?"

Stavrogin did understand, and he alone, perhaps. For Shatov was amazed when Stavrogin told him there was enthusiasm in Pyotr Stepanovich.

"Leave me now, go to the devil, and by tomorrow I'll wring something out of myself. Come tomorrow."

"Yes? Yes?"

"How do I know! . . . To the devil, to the devil!"

And he left the room.

"Maybe it's all still for the better," Pyotr Stepanovich muttered to himself, putting the revolver away.

III

HE RUSHED to catch up with Lizaveta Nikolaevna. She had not gone very far yet, only a few steps from the house. She had been detained for a while by Alexei Yegorovich, who was still following her, a step behind, in a tailcoat, reverently inclined and hatless. He begged her persistently to wait for the carriage; the old man was frightened and almost weeping.

"Go, the master's asking for tea, there's no one to serve him," Pyotr Stepanovich pushed him away and at once took Lizaveta Nikolaevna's arm.

She did not pull her arm free, but seemed not to have quite recovered her reason, not to have come to her senses yet.

"First of all, you're not going the right way," Pyotr Stepanovich began to prattle, "we must go that way, not past the garden; and, second, in any case it's not possible on foot, it's a good two miles, and you're not dressed for it. If you'd wait a bit. I came in a droshky, the horse is here in the yard, I'll bring it in a moment, put you in, and deliver you so that no one will see."

"You're so kind . . ." Liza said tenderly.

"For pity's sake, on such an occasion any humane person in my place would also . . ."

Liza looked at him and was surprised.

"Ah, my God, and I thought that old man was still here!"

"Listen, I'm terribly glad you're taking it this way, because it's all a terrible prejudice, and since that's the way it is, why don't I order this old man to take care of the carriage, it's just ten minutes, and we'll go back and wait under the porch, eh?"

"I first want . . . where are those murdered people?"

"Ah, what a fancy! Just what I was afraid of . . . No, we'd better leave that trash alone; and there's nothing there to look at."

"I know where they are, I know that house."

"So what if you do know! The rain, the fog, for pity's sake (what a sacred duty I've heaped on myself, though!) . . . Listen, Lizaveta Nikolaevna, it's one of two things: either you come with me in the droshky, in which case stop and don't go a step farther, because another twenty steps and Mavriky Nikolaevich will certainly notice us."

"Mavriky Nikolaevich! Where? Where?"

"Well, and if you want to go with him, then perhaps I'll take you a little farther and show you where he's sitting, and then—I'm your humble servant. I don't want to get near him right now."

"He's waiting for me, oh, God!" she suddenly stopped, and color spread over her face.

"But, for pity's sake, if he's a man without prejudices! You know, Lizaveta Nikolaevna, it's all none of my business; I'm completely outside of it, and you know that yourself; but still, I do wish you well . . . If our 'bark' has failed, if it has turned out to be just an old, rotten barge, only fit to be broken up . . ."

"Ah, wonderful!" Liza cried out.

"Wonderful, and with tears pouring down. One needs courage here. One mustn't yield to a man in anything. In our day and age, when a woman . . . pah, the devil!" (Pyotr Stepanovich nearly spat). "And, mainly, there's nothing to be sorry for: maybe it will all turn out excellently. Mavriky Nikolaevich is a . . . in a word, he's a sensitive man, though not very talkative, which, however, is also good, on condition, of course, if he's without prejudices . . ."

"Wonderful, wonderful!" Liza burst into hysterical laughter.

"Ah, well, the devil . . . Lizaveta Nikolaevna," Pyotr Stepanovich was suddenly piqued, "as a matter of fact, it's for you that I . . . what is it to me . . . I did you a service yesterday when you yourself wanted it, but today . . . Well, from here you can see Mavriky Nikolaevich, there he sits, he doesn't see us. I wonder, Lizaveta Nikolaevna, have you ever read *Polinka Sachs*?"[3]

"What is it?"

"There's this novella, *Polinka Sachs*. I read it when I was still a student . . . In it some official, Sachs, with a big fortune, arrests his wife at their summer house for infidelity . . . Ah, well, the devil, spit on it! You'll see, Mavriky Nikolaevich will propose to you even before you get home. He still hasn't seen us."

"Ah, he mustn't see us!" Liza cried out suddenly, as if insane. "Let's go away, go away! To the forest, to the fields!"

And she started running back.

"Lizaveta Nikolaevna, this is real faintheartedness!" Pyotr Stepanovich ran after her. "Why don't you want him to see you? On the contrary, look him proudly and directly in the eye . . . If it's something about *that* . . . maidenly . . . it's such a prejudice, such backwardness . . . But where are you going, where? Ehh, she's running! Let's better go back to Stavrogin, get my droshky . . . But where are you going? That's a field . . . hah, she fell! . . ."

He stopped. Liza was flying like a bird, not knowing where, and Pyotr Stepanovich already lagged fifty steps behind her. She stumbled over a mound and fell. At the same moment, from in back, to one side, came a terrible cry, the cry of Mavriky Nikolaevich, who had seen her run and fall, and was running to her across the field. Pyotr Stepanovich instantly retreated through the gates of Stavrogin's house, to get quickly into his droshky.

And Mavriky Nikolaevich, terribly frightened, was already standing by Liza, who had gotten to her feet, was bending over her and holding her hand in his. The whole incredible situation of this encounter shook his reason, and tears streamed down his face. He had seen her, before whom he stood in awe, madly running across the field, at such an hour, in such weather, wearing only a dress, yesterday's magnificent dress, crumpled now, dirty from her fall . . . Unable to say a word, he took off his greatcoat and, with trembling hands, began to cover her shoulders. Suddenly he gave a cry, feeling her touch his hand with her lips.

"Liza!" he cried, "I'm no good for anything, but don't drive me away from you!"

"Oh, yes, let's leave here quickly, don't abandon me!" and taking him by the hand, she drew him after her. "Mavriky Nikolaevich," she suddenly lowered her voice fearfully, "I kept pretending I was brave in there, but here I'm afraid of death. I'll die, I'll die very soon, but I'm afraid, afraid to die . . ." she whispered, squeezing his hand hard.

"Oh, if only someone," he kept looking around in despair, "if only someone would pass by! Your feet will get wet, you'll . . . lose your reason!"

"Never mind, never mind," she reassured him, "like that, I'm less afraid with you, hold my hand, lead me . . . Where are we going now, home? No, I want to see the murdered ones first. I've heard they murdered his wife, and he says he murdered her himself; but it's not true, it's not true, is it? I myself want to see the ones who were murdered . . . for me . . . because of them he stopped loving me last night . . . I'll see and I'll know everything. Hurry, hurry, I know that house . . . there's fire there . . . Mavriky Nikolaevich, my friend, don't forgive me, dishonorable as I am! Why forgive me? What are you crying for? Slap me in the face and kill me here in the field, like a dog!"

"No one can be your judge now," Mavriky Nikolaevich said firmly, "God forgive you, and least of all will I be your judge!"

But it would be strange to describe their conversation. And meanwhile the two were walking arm in arm, quickly, hurrying, as if half crazed. They were making straight for the fire. Mavriky Nikolaevich had still not lost hope of meeting some cart at least, but no one came along. A fine drizzle pervaded all the surroundings, absorbing every sheen and every shade, and turning everything into one smoky, leaden, indifferent mass. It had long been day, yet it seemed that dawn had still not come. Then suddenly, out of this cold, smoky haze, a figure materialized, strange and absurd, walking towards them. Picturing it now, I think I would not have believed my eyes, even if I had been in Lizaveta Nikolaevna's place; and yet she cried out joyfully and recognized the approaching man at once. It was Stepan Trofimovich. How he had left, in what way the insane, cerebral notion of his flight could have been carried out—of that later. I will only mention that he was already in a fever that morning, but even illness did not stop him: he strode firmly over the wet ground; one could see that he had thought the enterprise over as best he could, alone with all his bookish inexperience. He was dressed in "traveling fashion"—that is, in a greatcoat with sleeves and a wide patent-leather belt with a buckle, as well as high new boots with his trousers tucked into them. Probably he had long pictured a traveling man in this way, and several days earlier had provided himself with the belt and the high boots with their gleaming hussar tops, in which he did not know how to walk. A wide-brimmed hat, a worsted scarf wrapped tightly around his neck, a stick in his right hand, and in his left an extremely small but exceedingly tightly packed valise, completed the outfit. There was, besides, an open umbrella in that same right hand. These three objects—the umbrella, the stick, and the valise—had been very awkward to carry for the first half mile, and simply heavy for the second.

"Can it really be you?" Liza cried out, looking him over in sorrowful surprise, which replaced her first impulse of unconscious joy.

"*Lise!*" Stepan Trofimovich also cried out, rushing to her also almost in delirium. "*Chère, chère,* can it be that you, too . . . in such fog? Do you see: a glow! *Vous êtes malheureuse, n'est-ce pas?** I see, I see, don't tell, but don't question me either. *Nous sommes tous malheureux, mais il faut les pardonner tous. Pardonnons, Lise,*† and be free forever. To settle accounts with the world and be fully free—*il faut pardonner, pardonner, et pardonner!*"

"But why are you kneeling down?"

"Because, as I am bidding the world farewell, I want to bid farewell, in your image, to the whole of my past!" He began to weep and brought both her hands to his weeping eyes. "I kneel before all that was beautiful in my life, I kiss and give thanks! I've now broken myself

---

*"You are unhappy, aren't you?"
†"We are all unhappy, but we must forgive them all. Let us forgive, Liza"

in two: there—a madman who dreamed of soaring up into the sky, *vingt-deux ans!** Here—a crushed and chilled old tutor . . . *chez ce marchand, s'il existe pourtant ce marchand*† . . . But how soaked you are, *Lise!*" he cried, jumping to his feet, feeling that his knees, too, had become soaked on the sodden ground, "and how is this possible, you, in this dress? . . . and on foot, and in this field . . . You're crying? *Vous êtes malheureuse?* Hah, I heard something . . . But where are you coming from now?" he quickened his questions, with a timorous look, glancing in deep perplexity at Mavriky Nikolaevich, "*mais savez-vous l'heure qu'il est!*"‡

"Stepan Trofimovich, did you hear anything there about murdered people . . . Is it true? Is it?"

"Those people! I saw the glow of their deeds all night. They couldn't have ended otherwise . . ." (His eyes began to flash again.) "I'm running from a delirium, from a feverish dream, running to seek Russia, *existe-t-elle la Russie? Bah, c'est vous, cher capitaine!*§ I never doubted but that I'd meet you somewhere at some lofty deed . . . But do take my umbrella and—why must you go on foot? For God's sake, at least take my umbrella, and I'll hire a carriage somewhere anyway. I'm on foot only because *Stasie* (that is, Nastasya) would have started shouting for the whole street to hear, if she'd found out I was leaving; so I slipped away as incognito as possible. I don't know, in the *Voice* they're writing about robberies everywhere, but it can't be, I thought, that the moment I get out on the road, there will be a robber? *Chère Lise*, it seems you said someone murdered someone? *O, mon Dieu*, you're not well!"

"Let's go, let's go!" Liza cried out as if in hysterics, again drawing Mavriky Nikolaevich after her. "Wait, Stepan Trofimovich," she suddenly went back to him, "wait, poor dear, let me make a cross over you. It might be better to tie you up, but I'd better make a cross over you. You, too, pray for 'poor' Liza—just so, a little, don't trouble yourself too much. Mavriky Nikolaevich, give this child back his umbrella, you must give it back. There . . . Let's go now! Let's go!"

---

*"twenty-two years!"
†"in this merchant's house, if only this merchant exists"
‡"but do you know what time it is!"
§"does Russia exist? Hah, it's you, dear captain!"

Their arrival at the fatal house occurred precisely at the moment when the thick crowd thronging in front of the house had heard a good deal about Stavrogin and how it was profitable for him to kill his wife. But still, I repeat, the great majority went on listening silently and motionlessly. Only bawling drunkards and "breaking-loose" people like that arm-waving tradesman lost control of themselves. Everyone knew him as even a quiet man, but it was as if he would suddenly break loose and fly off somewhere if something suddenly struck him in a certain way. I did not see Liza and Mavriky Nikolaevich arrive. I first noticed Liza, to my stupefied amazement, when she was already far away from me in the crowd, and in the beginning I did not even make out Mavriky Nikolaevich. It seems there was a moment when he lagged a couple of steps behind her because of the crowd, or else he was forced aside. Liza, who was tearing through the crowd without seeing or noticing anything around her, like someone in a fever, like someone escaped from a hospital, of course drew attention to herself all too quickly: there was loud talk and suddenly shouting. Then someone yelled: "That's Stavrogin's woman!" And from the other side: "They don't just kill, they also come and look!" Suddenly I saw someone's hand, above her head, from behind, raised and lowered; Liza fell. There came a terrible cry from Mavriky Nikolaevich, who tore to her aid and struck the man who was between him and Liza with all his strength. But at the same moment that tradesman seized him from behind with both arms. For some time it was impossible to make anything out in the ensuing scuffle. It seems Liza got up, but fell again from another blow. Suddenly the crowd parted and a small empty circle formed around the prostrate Liza, with the bloody, crazed Mavriky Nikolaevich standing over her, shouting, weeping, and wringing his hands. I do not remember with complete precision how things went after that; I only remember that Liza was suddenly being carried away. I ran after her; she was still alive, and perhaps still conscious. From among the crowd, the tradesman and another three men were seized. These three up to now have denied any participation in the evil-doing, stubbornly insisting that they were seized by mistake; perhaps they are right. The tradesman, though clearly exposed, being a witless man, has been unable up to now to explain coherently what happened. I, too, had to give my evidence at the investigation, as a witness, though a distant one: I declared that everything had happened to the highest degree by chance, through people who, though perhaps of a certain inclination, had very little awareness, were drunk, and had already lost the thread. I am still of that opinion.

4

The Last Decision

I

MANY SAW Pyotr Stepanovich that morning; those who did recall that he was extremely excited. At two o'clock in the afternoon he ran by to see Gaganov, who had arrived from the country just the day before, and where a whole house full of visitors had gathered who talked much and hotly about the events that had just transpired. Pyotr Stepanovich talked most of all and made himself heard. He was always regarded among us as a "garrulous student with a hole in his head," but now he was talking about Yulia Mikhailovna, and, considering the general turmoil, the topic was a gripping one. In his quality as her recent and most intimate confidant, he reported many quite new and unexpected details about her; inadvertently (and, of course, imprudently) he reported some of her personal opinions about people widely known in town, thereby instantly pricking some vanities. It all came out vague and muddled, as from a none-too-clever man who yet, as an honest person, was faced with the painful necessity of explaining all at once a whole heap of perplexities, and who, in his simplehearted awkwardness, did not know himself where to begin and where to end. He let slip, also rather imprudently, that Yulia Mikhailovna knew the whole of Stavrogin's secret and that she herself had conducted the whole intrigue. And she had also done him, Pyotr Stepanovich, a bad turn, because he himself had been in love with this unfortunate Liza, and yet he had been so "turned around" that he had *almost* taken her to Stavrogin in a carriage. "Yes, yes, gentlemen, it's all very well for you to laugh, but if only I'd known, if I'd known how it would end!" he concluded. To various anxious inquiries about Stavrogin, he declared directly that the catastrophe with Lebyadkin was, in his opinion, pure chance, and the one to blame for it all was Lebyadkin himself who displayed his money. He explained this particularly well. One of the listeners at some point observed to him that he had no business "playacting"; that he ate, drank, and all but slept in Yulia Mikhailovna's house, and was now the first to besmirch her, and that it was not at all as pretty a thing as he supposed. But Pyotr Stepanovich defended himself at once: "I ate and drank not because I had no money, and I'm not to blame if I was invited there. Allow me to judge for myself how grateful I ought to be for that."

Generally, the impression was in his favor: "Granted he's an absurd fellow and, of course, an empty one, but how is he to blame for Yulia Mikhailovna's follies? On the contrary, it appears he tried to stop her . . ."

At about two o'clock the news suddenly spread that Stavrogin, of whom there was so much talk, had unexpectedly left for Petersburg on the midday train. This was very interesting; many frowned. Pyotr Stepanovich was struck to such an extent that they say he even changed countenance and exclaimed strangely: "But who could have let him out?" He immediately left Gaganov's at a run. However, he was seen in two or three other houses.

Towards dusk he found an opportunity for penetrating to Yulia Mikhailovna, though with great difficulty, because she decidedly had no wish to receive him. I learned of this circumstance only three weeks later from the lady herself, before her departure for Petersburg. She did not go into detail, but observed with a shudder that he had "amazed her then beyond all measure." I suppose he simply frightened her with a threat of complicity in case she decided to "talk." This need to frighten was closely bound up with his designs at the time, certainly unknown to her, and only afterwards, about five days later, did she guess why he had so doubted her silence and so feared any new outbursts of indignation from her . . .

Before eight o'clock in the evening, when it was already quite dark, on the outskirts of town, in Fomin Lane, in a small lopsided house, in

the apartment of Ensign Erkel, *our* people gathered in full complement, all five of them. The place of the general meeting had been
appointed by Pyotr Stepanovich himself; but he was unpardonably
late, and the members had already been waiting an hour for him. This
Ensign Erkel was that same little visiting officer who had sat the whole
time at Virginsky's party with a pencil in his hand and a notebook in
front of him. He had arrived in town not long ago, rented a solitary
place in a secluded lane from two sisters, old tradeswomen, and was
due to leave soon; to gather at his place was most inconspicuous. This
strange boy was distinguished by an extraordinary taciturnity; he
could sit for ten evenings in a row, in noisy company and amid the
most extraordinary conversations, without saying a word himself, but,
on the contrary, with extreme attention, following the speakers with
his child's eyes and listening. His face was very pretty and even as if
intelligent. He did not belong to the fivesome; our people supposed he
had special instructions of some sort and from somewhere, purely
along executive lines. It is now known that he had no instructions, and
that he hardly even understood his position. He simply bowed down
before Pyotr Stepanovich, whom he had met not long before. Had he
met some prematurely depraved monster who under some socio-
romantic pretext egged him on to found a band of robbers and ordered
him, as a test, to kill and rob the first peasant he came upon, he would
certainly have gone and obeyed. He had a sick mother somewhere to
whom he sent half of his scanty pay—and how she must have kissed
that poor blond head, trembled for it, prayed for it! I enlarge upon him
so much because I am very sorry for him.

Our people were excited. They had been struck by the events of the
past night and, it seems, had gone cowardly. The simple but systematic
scandal in which they had so zealously taken part so far, had had an
outcome they did not expect. The night fire, the murder of the Lebyadkins, the crowd's violence over Liza—these were all surprises not
envisioned in their program. They hotly accused the hand that moved
them of despotism and disingenuousness. In short, while waiting for
Pyotr Stepanovich, they incited each other so much that they again
resolved finally to ask him for a categorical explanation, and if he
evaded once more, as had already happened, even to break up the
fivesome, but so as to found, in place of it, a new secret society for the

"propaganda of ideas," and that by themselves, on the principles of equal rights and democracy. Liputin, Shigalyov, and the knower of the people especially supported this idea; Lyamshin kept mum, though with an air of agreement. Virginsky hesitated and wished to hear out Pyotr Stepanovich first. It was resolved that they would hear out Pyotr Stepanovich; but he still did not come; such negligence added even more venom. Erkel was totally silent and merely arranged for tea to be served, which he brought with his own hands from his landladies, in glasses on a tray, without bringing in the samovar or letting the servingwoman enter.

Pyotr Stepanovich arrived only at half past eight. With quick steps he went up to the round table in front of the sofa, around which the company had placed themselves; he kept his hat in his hand and refused tea. His look was angry, stern, and haughty. He must have noticed at once by their faces that they were "rebellious."

"Before I open my mouth, you lay out your stuff, you've got yourselves all braced for it," he observed with a spiteful smile, looking around at their physiognomies.

Liputin began "on behalf of all" and, in a voice trembling with offense, announced "that if it goes on like this, one could smash one's own head, sir." Oh, they're not at all afraid to smash their heads, and are even ready to, but only for the common cause. (A general stirring and concurring.) And therefore let there be frankness with them as well, so that they would always know beforehand, "otherwise what will it come to?" (Again a stirring, some guttural sounds.) To act in this way is humiliating and dangerous . . . It's not at all because we're afraid, but if there's one who acts and the rest are mere pawns, then the one may bungle it, and all will get caught. (Exclamations: yes, yes! General support.)

"Devil take it, what do you want then?"

"And what relation to the common cause," Liputin began to seethe, "do Mr. Stavrogin's little intrigues have? Suppose he does belong in some mysterious way to the center, if this fantastic center really exists, but we don't want to know about that, sir. And meanwhile a murder has taken place, the police are aroused; by the string they'll find the ball."

"If you and Stavrogin get caught, we'll get caught, too," the knower of the people added.

"And quite uselessly for the common cause," Virginsky concluded dejectedly.

"What nonsense! The murder was a matter of chance, done by Fedka for the sake of robbery."

"Hm. A strange coincidence, though, sir," Liputin squirmed.

"And, if you wish, it came about through you."

"How, through us?"

"First of all, you, Liputin, took part in this intrigue yourself, and, second, and mainly, you were ordered to send Lebyadkin away, and money was provided, and what did you do? If you had sent him away, nothing would have happened."

"But wasn't it you who came up with the idea that it would be nice to let him out to recite poetry?"

"An idea isn't an order. The order was to send him away."

"Order. Rather a strange word . . . On the contrary, you precisely ordered the sending away to be stopped."

"You're mistaken and have shown stupidity and self-will. The murder was Fedka's doing, and he acted alone, from robbery. You heard bells ringing and believed it. You turned coward. Stavrogin isn't so stupid, and the proof is—he left at twelve noon today, after a meeting with the vice-governor; if there was anything, he wouldn't have been let out to Petersburg in broad daylight."

"But we by no means assert that Mr. Stavrogin himself did the killing," Liputin picked up venomously and unabashedly. "He may even know nothing at all, sir, just as I didn't; and you yourself know only too well that I knew nothing, sir, though I fell right into it like mutton into the pot."

"Whom are you accusing, then?" Pyotr Stepanovich gave him a dark look.

"The same ones who need to burn towns, sir."

"What's worst is that you're trying to wriggle out of it. However, kindly read this and show it to the others; it's just for your information."

He took Lebyadkin's anonymous letter to Lembke from his pocket and handed it to Liputin. He read it, was visibly surprised, and pensively handed it to the next man; the letter quickly made the circle.

"Is it really Lebyadkin's handwriting?" remarked Shigalyov.

"Yes, it's his," Liputin and Tolkachenko (that is, the knower of the people) declared.

"It's just for your information, seeing that you've waxed so sentimental over Lebyadkin," Pyotr Stepanovich repeated, taking the letter back. "Thus, gentlemen, quite by chance some Fedka rids us of a dangerous man. That is what chance can sometimes mean! Instructive, is it not?"

The members exchanged quick glances.

"And now, gentlemen, it comes my turn to ask questions," Pyotr Stepanovich assumed a dignified air. "Permit me to know why you were so good as to set fire to the town without permission?"

"What's that! We, we set fire to the town? That's really shifting the blame!" they exclaimed.

"I realize that you got caught up in the game," Pyotr Stepanovich stubbornly continued, "but this is not just some little scandal with Yulia Mikhailovna. I've gathered you here, gentlemen, to explain to you the degree of danger you have so stupidly heaped on yourselves, and which threatens all too many things besides you."

"I beg your pardon, but we, on the contrary, intended presently to declare to you the degree of despotism and inequality with which such a serious and at the same time strange measure had been taken over the members' heads," the heretofore silent Virginsky declared, almost with indignation.

"So you disclaim yourselves? Yet I insist that the burning was done by you, you alone, and no one else. Do not lie, gentlemen, I have precise information. By your self-will you have even exposed the common cause to danger. You are merely one knot in an infinite network of knots, and you owe blind obedience to the center. And meanwhile three of you incited the Shpigulin men to set the fire, not having the least instructions for that, and the fire has taken place."

"Which three? Which three of us?"

"The day before yesterday, between three and four in the morning, you, Tolkachenko, were inciting Fomka Zavyalov in the 'Forget-me-not.' "

"For pity's sake," the man jumped up, "I barely said a word, and that without any intention, but just so, because he got a whipping that morning, and I dropped it at once, I saw he was too drunk. If you hadn't reminded me, I'd never have remembered. It couldn't have caught fire from a word."

"You're like the man who is surprised that a tiny spark can blow a whole powder magazine sky-high."

"I was talking in a whisper, and in a corner, into his ear, how could you have found out?" Tolkachenko suddenly realized.

"I was sitting there under the table. Don't worry, gentlemen, I know all your steps. You're smiling craftily, Mr. Liputin? Yet I know, for example, that three days ago you pinched your wife all over, at midnight, in your bedroom, as you were going to bed."

Liputin gaped and went pale.

(Afterwards it became known that he had learned of Liputin's exploit from Agafya, Liputin's maid, whom he had paid money to spy for him from the very beginning, as came to light only later.)

"May I state a fact?" Shigalyov suddenly rose.

"State it."

Shigalyov sat down and braced himself.

"So far as I have understood, and one could hardly not understand, you yourself, at the beginning and then a second time, rather eloquently—albeit too theoretically—developed a picture of Russia covered with an infinite network of knots. For its own part, each of the active groups, while proselytizing and spreading its side-branchings to infinity, has as its task, by a systematic denunciatory propaganda, ceaselessly to undermine the importance of the local powers, to produce bewilderment in communities, to engender cynicism and scandal, complete disbelief in anything whatsoever, a yearning for the better, and, finally, acting by means of fires as the popular means par excellence, to plunge the country, at the prescribed moment, if need be, even into despair. Are these your words, which I have tried to recall verbatim? Is this your program of action, conveyed by you as a representative of the central—but hitherto completely unknown and, to us, almost fantastic—committee?"

"Correct, only you're dragging it out a lot."

"Everyone has the right to his own word. Allowing us to guess that there are now up to several hundred knots of the general net already covering Russia, and developing the suggestion that if each man does his work successfully, then the whole of Russia by the given time, at the signal . . ."

"Ah, devil take it, there's enough to do without you!" Pyotr Stepanovich turned in his armchair.

"If you prefer, I'll shorten it and end simply with a question: we have already seen the scandals, seen the discontent of the populations, been present and taken part in the fall of a local administration, and, finally, with our own eyes, we have seen a fire. What, then, are you displeased with? Isn't this your program? What can you accuse us of?"

"Of self-will!" Pyotr Stepanovich shouted furiously. "While I am here, you dare not act without my permission. Enough. The denunciation is prepared, and perhaps tomorrow, or this very night, you'll all be seized. There you have it. The information is true."

This time everyone gaped.

"You'll be seized not only as inciters to arson, but as a fivesome. The informer knows the whole secret of the network. There's your mischief-making!"

"Stavrogin, for sure!" cried Liputin.

"How . . . why Stavrogin?" Pyotr Stepanovich suddenly seemed to stop short. "Eh, the devil," he recollected himself at once, "it's Shatov! You all seem to know by now that in his time Shatov belonged to the cause. I must disclose that in keeping watch on him through persons he does not suspect, I have found out, to my surprise, that for him neither the organization of the network, nor . . . in a word, nothing is secret. To save himself from being accused of former participation, he will denounce everyone. So far he has still hesitated, and I've been sparing him. Now you've unbound him with this fire: he's shaken and no longer hesitant. By tomorrow we'll be arrested as incendiaries and political criminals."

"Is it true? How does Shatov know?"

The agitation was indescribable.

"It's all perfectly true. I have no right to declare my ways to you, or how I discovered it, but here is what I can do for you meanwhile: there is one person through whom I can influence Shatov so that he, without suspecting, will hold back his denunciation—but for no longer than a day. More than a day I can't do. So you may consider yourselves safe until the morning of the day after tomorrow."

Everyone was silent.

"Send him to the devil, finally!" Tolkachenko shouted first.

"Should've been done long ago!" Lyamshin put in spitefully, banging his fist on the table.

"But how to do it?" Liputin muttered.

Pyotr Stepanovich immediately picked up the question and explained his plan. It consisted in luring Shatov, for the handing over of the secret press in his possession, to the solitary place where it was buried, the next day, at nightfall—and "taking care of it there." He went into much necessary detail, which we omit here, and thoroughly clarified those ambiguous present relations between Shatov and the central society of which the reader already knows.

"That's all very well," Liputin observed unsteadily, "but since it's again . . . a new adventure of the same sort . . . it will strike people's minds too much."

"Undoubtedly," Pyotr Stepanovich agreed, "but that, too, has been foreseen. There exists a means of averting suspicion completely."

And with the same precision he told them about Kirillov, his intention to shoot himself, and how he had promised to wait for a signal, and to leave a note before dying taking upon himself all that would be dictated to him. (In a word, all that the reader already knows.)

"His firm intention to take his life—philosophical and, in my opinion, mad—became known *there*" (Pyotr Stepanovich went on explaining). "*There* not the slightest hair, not a speck of dust is lost; everything goes to benefit the common cause. Foreseeing the benefit and becoming convinced that his intention was perfectly serious, he was offered the means to get to Russia (for some reason he wanted without fail to die in Russia), was charged with an assignment which he pledged himself to fulfill (and did fulfill), and, moreover, they pledged him to the promise, already known to you, to put an end to himself only when he was told to. He promised everything. Note that he belongs to the cause on special terms and wishes to be beneficial; I cannot reveal any more to you. Tomorrow, *after Shatov*, I'll dictate a note to him saying that the cause of Shatov's death was himself. This will be very probable: they used to be friends and went to America together, there they quarreled, and all this will be explained in the note . . . and . . . and depending on the circumstances, it may even be possible to dictate another thing or two to Kirillov, about the tracts, for example, and maybe partly about the fire. However, I'll have to think about that. Don't worry, he has no prejudices; he'll sign anything."

Doubts were voiced. The story seemed fantastic. However, everyone had more or less heard somewhat about Kirillov; Liputin more than any of them.

"What if he suddenly changes his mind and doesn't want to," said Shigalyov. "One way or another he's still a madman, so the hope is an uncertain one."

"Don't worry, gentlemen, he will want to," Pyotr Stepanovich snapped out. "According to our arrangement, I must warn him a day ahead, meaning today. I invite Liputin to go to him with me now, to make sure, and when he comes back, gentlemen, he will tell you, today if necessary, whether or not I've been speaking the truth. However," he suddenly broke off, with extreme irritation, as if he suddenly felt it was too much of an honor to persuade and bother so over such paltry people, "however, you can act as you please. If you don't decide on it, the union is dissolved—but owing solely to the fact of your disobedience and betrayal. So, then, from that moment on we're all separate. But know that in that case, along with the unpleasantness of Shatov's denunciation and its consequences, you are drawing upon yourselves yet another little unpleasantness, which was firmly stated when the union was formed. As for me, gentlemen, I am not very afraid of you . . . Don't think I'm connected with you all that much . . . However, it makes no difference."

"No, we're decided," Lyamshin declared.

"There's no other way out," Tolkachenko muttered, "and if Liputin confirms about Kirillov, then . . ."

"I'm against it; I protest with my whole soul against such a bloody solution!" Virginsky rose from his place.

"But?" Pyotr Stepanovich asked.

"What *but?*"

"You said *but* . . . so I'm waiting."

"I don't think I said *but* . . . I simply wanted to say that if it's decided on, then . . ."

"Then?"

Virginsky fell silent.

"I think one can disregard one's own safety of life," Erkel suddenly opened up his mouth, "but if the common cause may suffer, then I think one cannot dare to disregard one's own safety of life . . ."

He became confused and blushed. Preoccupied though each of them was with his own thing, they all glanced at him in astonishment, so unexpected was it that he, too, would begin to speak.

"I am for the common cause," Virginsky said suddenly.

They all got up from their places. It was decided to exchange news once more at noon the next day, though without all getting together, and then to make final arrangements. The place where the press was buried was announced, the roles and duties were distributed. Liputin and Pyotr Stepanovich immediately set off together to Kirillov.

II

THAT SHATOV would denounce them our people all believed; but that Pyotr Stepanovich was playing with them like pawns they likewise believed. And, what's more, they all knew that they would still come in complement to the spot the next day, and that Shatov's fate was sealed. They felt they had suddenly been caught like flies in the web of a huge spider; they were angry but quaking with fear.

Pyotr Stepanovich was unquestionably guilty before them: it all could have been handled with much greater accord and *ease,* if he had only cared to brighten the reality at least a little. Instead of presenting the fact in a decent light, as something Roman and civic or the like, he had held up only crude fear and the threat to their own skins, which was simply impolite. Of course, there is the struggle for existence in everything, and there is no other principle, everybody knows that, but still . . .

But Pyotr Stepanovich had no time to stir up any Romans; he himself was thrown off his tracks. Stavrogin's flight stunned and crushed him. He lied that Stavrogin had seen the vice-governor; the thing was that he had left without seeing anyone, even his mother— and it was indeed strange that he had not even been inconvenienced.

(Afterwards the authorities had to answer especially for that.) Pyotr Stepanovich had spent the whole day making inquiries, but so far had found out nothing, and never before had he been so worried. And how could he, how could he renounce Stavrogin just like that, all at once! That was why he was unable to be very tender with our people. Besides, they kept his hands tied: he had already decided to go galloping after Stavrogin without delay, and yet Shatov detained him, the fivesome had to be finally cemented together, just in case. "I can't let it go for nothing, it might come in handy." So I suppose he reasoned.

And as for Shatov, he was quite certain that he would denounce them. What he had told *our* people about the denunciation was all lies: he had never seen this denunciation or heard of it, but he was as sure of it as two times two. It precisely seemed to him that Shatov would be unable to endure the present moment—the death of Liza, the death of Marya Timofeevna—and that precisely now he would finally decide. Who knows, perhaps he had some grounds for thinking so. It is also known that he hated Shatov personally; there had once been a quarrel between them, and Pyotr Stepanovich never forgave an offense. I am even convinced that this was the foremost reason.

Our sidewalks are narrow and made of brick, or else simply of planks. Pyotr Stepanovich was striding along the middle of the sidewalk, occupying it entirely, paying not the least attention to Liputin, who had no room left next to him, so that he had either to keep a step behind, or run down into the mud if he wanted to walk next to him and talk. Pyotr Stepanovich suddenly remembered how he had recently gone scurrying through the mud in the same way in order to keep up with Stavrogin, who, like him now, also strode down the middle, occupying the entire sidewalk. He recalled this scene and rage took his breath away.

But resentment also took Liputin's breath away. Let Pyotr Stepanovich treat *our* people as he liked, but him? He who was more *in the know* than any of our people, was closest to the cause, was most intimately connected with it, and up to now had constantly, though indirectly, participated in it! Oh, he knew that even now Pyotr Stepanovich could ruin him *as a last resort.* But he had begun hating Pyotr Stepanovich long ago, and not for the danger, but for the haughtiness of his treatment. Now, when he had to venture upon such a thing, he was more angry than all the rest of our people put together. Alas, he knew that "like a slave" he would certainly be the first on the spot tomorrow and, moreover, would bring all the rest with him, and if he could somehow have killed Pyotr Stepanovich now, before tomorrow, he would certainly have killed him.

Immersed in his feelings, he kept silent and trotted after his tormentor. The latter seemed to have forgotten about him; only every now and then he carelessly and impolitely shoved him with his elbow. Suddenly, on the most prominent of our streets, Pyotr Stepanovich stopped and went into a tavern.

"Why here?" Liputin boiled up. "This is a tavern."

"I want to have a beefsteak."

"For pity's sake, it's always full of people."

"Well, so what."

"But . . . we'll be late. It's already ten o'clock."

"One can never be late there."

"No, I'll be late! They're expecting me back."

"Well, so what; only it's stupid to go back to them. Because of all your bother, I haven't had dinner today. And with Kirillov, the later the surer."

Pyotr Stepanovich took a private room. Liputin, irate and resentful, sat down in an armchair to one side and watched him eat. Half an hour passed, and more. Pyotr Stepanovich did not hurry, ate with relish, rang, demanded a different mustard, then beer, and said not a word all the while. He was deep in thought. It was possible for him to do both things at once—to eat with relish and to be deep in thought. Liputin finally hated him so much that he could not tear himself away from him. It was something like a nervous fit. He counted every piece of steak the man sent into his mouth, hated him for the way he opened it, for the way he chewed, for the way he sucked savoringly on the fatter pieces, hated the beefsteak itself. Finally, things became as if confused in his eyes; he began to feel slightly dizzy; heat and chill ran alternately down his spine.

"You're not doing anything—read this," Pyotr Stepanovich suddenly tossed him a piece of paper. Liputin went over to a candle. The paper was covered with small writing, in a bad hand, with corrections on every line. By the time he managed to read it, Pyotr Stepanovich had already paid and was going out. On the sidewalk Liputin handed the paper back to him.

"Keep it; I'll say later. Anyhow, what do you say?"

Liputin shuddered all over.

"In my opinion . . . such a tract . . . is nothing but a ridiculous absurdity."

The anger broke through; he felt as if he were being picked up and carried.

"If we decide to distribute such tracts," he was trembling all over, "we will make ourselves despised for our stupidity and incomprehension of things, sir."

"Hm. I think otherwise," Pyotr Stepanovich strode along firmly.

"And I think otherwise; can it be that you wrote it yourself?"

"That's none of your business."

"I also think the 'Shining Light' doggerel is the trashiest doggerel possible and could never have been written by Herzen."

"Lies; the poem's good."

"I'm also surprised, for instance," Liputin raced on, leaping and playing in spirit, "that it is suggested we act so that everything fails. In Europe it is natural to want everything to fail, because there's a proletariat there, but here we're just dilettantes and, in my opinion, are simply raising dust, sir."

"I thought you were a Fourierist."

"That's not Fourier, not at all, sir."

"He's nonsense, I know."

"No, Fourier is not nonsense . . . Excuse me, but I simply cannot believe there could be an uprising in May."

Liputin even unbuttoned his coat, he was so hot.

"Well, enough, and now, before I forget," Pyotr Stepanovich switched with terrible coolness, "you will have to typeset and print this leaflet with your own hands. We'll dig up Shatov's press, and you'll take charge of it tomorrow. In the shortest possible time, you will typeset and print as many copies as you can, to be distributed throughout the winter. The means will be indicated. We need as many copies as possible, because you'll have orders from other places."

"No, sir, excuse me, I cannot take upon myself such a . . . I refuse."

"And yet take it you will. I'm acting on instructions from the central committee, and you must obey."

"And I think that our centers abroad have forgotten Russian reality and broken all connections, and are therefore simply raving . . . I even think that instead of many hundreds of fivesomes there is only our one in all Russia, and there isn't any network," Liputin finally choked.

"The more contemptible for you, that you ran after the cause without believing in it . . . and are running after me now like a mean little cur."

"No, sir, I'm not running. We have every right to leave off and to form a new society."

"Mor-ron!" Pyotr Stepanovich suddenly thundered menacingly, flashing his eyes.

The two stood facing each other for a time. Pyotr Stepanovich turned and confidently set off on his way again.

It flashed like lightning through Liputin's mind: "I'll turn and go back; if I don't turn now, I'll never go back." He thought thus for exactly ten steps, but at the eleventh a new and desperate thought lit up in his mind: he did not turn and did not go back.

They came to Filippov's house, but before reaching it went down a lane, or, better to say, an inconspicuous path by the fence, so that for some time they had to make their way along the sloping side of a ditch, where one had to hold on to the fence in order to keep one's footing. In the darkest corner of the tilting fence, Pyotr Stepanovich removed a board; an opening was formed, through which he promptly climbed. Liputin was surprised, but climbed through in his turn; then the board was put back. This was that secret way by which Fedka used to get to Kirillov.

"Shatov mustn't know we're here," Pyotr Stepanovich whispered sternly to Liputin.

III

KIRILLOV, as always at that hour, was sitting on his leather sofa having tea. He did not rise to meet them, but somehow heaved himself all up and looked with alarm at the entering people.

"You're not mistaken," said Pyotr Stepanovich, "I've come for that very thing."

"Today?"

"No, no, tomorrow . . . around this time."

And he hastily sat down at the table, observing the alarmed Kirillov somewhat anxiously. He, however, had already calmed down and looked as usual.

"These people still won't believe it. You're not angry that I brought Liputin?"

"Today I'm not, but tomorrow I want to be alone."

"But not before I come, and so in my presence."

"I'd prefer not in your presence."

"You remember you promised to write out and sign everything I dictate."

"Makes no difference to me. Will you stay long now?"

"I must see a certain person, and I have half an hour till then, so whether you want it or not, I'll stay for that half hour."

Kirillov said nothing. Liputin, meanwhile, placed himself to one side, under the portrait of a bishop. The same desperate thought was taking hold of his mind more and more. Kirillov barely paid any attention to him. Liputin had known Kirillov's theory even before and had always laughed at him; but now he was silent and looked around gloomily.

"And I wouldn't mind having some tea," Pyotr Stepanovich stirred. "I've just had a beefsteak and was hoping to find your tea ready."

"Have some."

"You used to offer it yourself," Pyotr Stepanovich observed sourishly.

"Makes no difference. Liputin can have some, too."

"No, sir, I . . . can't."

"Can't, or won't?" Pyotr Stepanovich turned quickly.

"I won't do it here, sir," Liputin refused meaningly. Pyotr Stepanovich scowled.

"Smells of mysticism—devil knows what sort of people you all are!"

No one answered him; they were silent for a full minute.

"But I know one thing," he suddenly added sharply, "that no prejudice will stop any of us from doing his duty."

"Stavrogin left?" Kirillov asked.

"Yes."

"He did well."

Pyotr Stepanovich flashed his eyes, but kept hold of himself.

"I don't care what you think, so long as each one keeps his word."

"I will keep my word."

"However, I have always been sure that you would do your duty as an independent and progressive man."

"You are ridiculous."

"So be it, I'm very glad to make you laugh. I'm always glad to be able to oblige."

"You want very much that I shoot myself, and are afraid if suddenly not?"

"I mean, you see, you yourself joined your plan with our actions. Counting on your plan, we've already undertaken something, so you simply cannot refuse, because you would let us down."

"No right at all."

"I understand, I understand, it's entirely as you will, and we are nothing, just as long as this entire will of yours gets carried out."

"And I'll have to take all your vileness on myself?"

"Listen, Kirillov, you haven't turned coward? If you want to refuse, say so right now."

"I haven't turned coward."

"It's because you're asking too many questions."

"Will you leave soon?"

"Another question?"

Kirillov looked him over with contempt.

"Here, you see," Pyotr Stepanovich went on, getting more and more angry, worried, unable to find the right tone, "you want me to leave, for solitude, in order to concentrate, but these are all dangerous

Part Three

signs for you, for you first of all. You want to think a lot. In my view, it's better not to think, but just to do it. You worry me, you really do."

"Only one thing is very bad for me, that at that moment there will be such a viper as you around me."

"Well, that makes no difference. Maybe when the time comes I'll go out and stand on the porch. If you're dying and show such a lack of indifference, then . . . this is all very dangerous. I'll go out on the porch, and you can suppose that I understand nothing and am a man immeasurably lower than you."

"No, not immeasurably; you have abilities, but there is a lot you don't understand, because you are a low man."

"Very glad, very glad. I've already said I'm glad to provide diversion . . . at such a moment."

"You understand nothing."

"I mean, I . . . anyway, I listen with respect."

"You can do nothing; even now you cannot hide your petty spitefulness, though it's unprofitable to show it. You will make me angry, and I will suddenly want half a year longer."

Pyotr Stepanovich looked at his watch.

"I've never understood a thing about your theory, but I do know that you didn't make it up for us, and so you'll carry it out without us. I also know that it was not you who ate the idea, but the idea that ate you, and so you won't put it off."

"What? The idea ate me?"

"Yes."

"Not me the idea? That's good. You have some small intelligence. Only you keep teasing, and I am proud."

"Wonderful, wonderful. That's precisely how it should be—that you should be proud."

"Enough; you've drunk, now go."

"Devil take it, I guess I'll have to," Pyotr Stepanovich stood up. "It's still early, though. Listen, Kirillov, will I find our man at Myasnichikha's, you know? Or was she lying, too?"

"You won't, because he's here, not there."

"How, here, devil take it, where?"

"He's sitting in the kitchen, eating and drinking."

"But how dared he?" Pyotr Stepanovich flushed wrathfully. "He was obliged to wait . . . nonsense! He's got no passport or money!"

"I don't know. He came to say good-bye; he's dressed and ready. He's leaving and won't come back. He said you're a scoundrel and he doesn't want to wait for your money."

"Ahh! He's afraid I'll . . . well, I might even now, if he . . . Where is he, in the kitchen?"

Kirillov opened a side door into a tiny, dark room; from this room three steps led down to the kitchen, directly into the partitioned-off closet where the cook's bed usually stood. It was here, in the corner, under the icons, that Fedka was now sitting at a bare wooden table. In front of him on the table were a small bottle, a plate with bread, and, on an earthenware dish, a cold piece of beef with potatoes. He was having a leisurely snack, and was already slightly tipsy, but had his sheepskin coat on and was apparently quite ready to set off. A samovar was beginning to boil behind the partition, but it wasn't for Fedka, though Fedka himself had made a point of lighting it and preparing it every night for a week or more, for "Alexei Nilych, sir, seeing as he's so ver-ry accustomed to having tea at night." I strongly suspect that the beef and potatoes had been roasted for Fedka that morning by Kirillov himself, for lack of a cook.

"What do you think you're doing?" Pyotr Stepanovich rolled into the downstairs. "Why didn't you stay where you were ordered to?"

And he swung and banged his fist on the table.

Fedka assumed a dignified air.

"You wait, Pyotr Stepanovich, you wait," he began to speak, jauntily emphasizing each word, "here firstly you must understand that you're at a noble visit with Mr. Kirillov, Alexei Nilych, whose boots are always there for you to polish, since he's an educated mind before you, and you're just—pfui!"

And he jauntily spat over his shoulder. One could see arrogance, resoluteness, and a certain rather dangerous, affected, calm casuistry before the first explosion. But Pyotr Stepanovich was beyond noticing any danger, which, besides, did not fit with his view of things. The events and failures of the day had him totally in a whirl . . . Liputin was peeking curiously down the three steps from the dark closet.

"Do you or do you not want to have a proper passport and good money to travel where you were told. Yes or no?"

"You see, Pyotr Stepanovich, you began deceiving me from the very first beginning, whereby you come out to me as a real scoundrel. The same as a vile human louse—that's what I count you as. You promised me big money for innocent blood, and swore an oath for Mr. Stavrogin, though what comes out is nothing but your own uncivility. I got no share of it, as I live, not a drop, to say nothing of fifteen hundred, and Mr. Stavrogin slapped your face the other day, which is already known to me. Now you're threatening me again and promising money—for what business, you won't say. And I have doubts in my mind that you're sending me to Petersburg to revenge your wickedness with whatever you've got on Mr. Stavrogin, Nikolai Vsevolodovich, trusting in my gullibility. And by that you come out as the foremost murderer. And do you know what you deserve now by this sole point that in your depravity you've ceased to believe in God himself, the true creator? The same thing as an idolater, and on the same lines as a Tartar or a Mordovian. Alexei Nilych, being a philosopher, has manifoldly explained to you the true God, the creator and maker, and about the creation of the world, and equally about the future destinies and transfiguration of every creature and every beast from the book of the Apocalypse. But you, like a witless idol, persist in your deafness and dumbness, and have brought Ensign Erkel to the same thing, like that same evildoer and seducer called the atheist . . ."

"Ah, you drunken mug! You strip icons, and then preach God!"

"You see, Pyotr Stepanovich, I'll tell you it's true that I stripped them; but I only took the pearlies off, and how do you know, maybe that same moment my tear, too, was transformed before the crucible of the Almighty, for some offense against me, since I'm just exactly that very same orphan, not even having any daily refuge. Do you know from the books that once upon some ancient times a certain merchant stoled a pearl from the nimbus of the Most Holy Mother of God with just exactly the same tearful sighing and praying, and afterwards returned the whole sum right at her feet, in public, on his knees, and our Mother and Intercessor overshadowed him with her veil before all the people, so that on this subject a miracle even came about at that time, and it was ordered by way of the authorities to write it down exactly into the state books. But you let the mouse in, and so you blasphemed against the very finger of God. And if you weren't my natural master, who I used to carry in my arms when I was still a youth, I'd do you in right now, as I live, without even moving from this spot!"

Pyotr Stepanovich became exceedingly wrathful.

"Speak, did you see Stavrogin today?"

"There's one thing you daren't ever to do—to question me. Mr. Stavrogin, as he lives, stands amazed before you, nor took part by his wishes, to say nothing of any orders or money. Me you dared."

"You'll get the money, and you'll also get the two thousand, in Petersburg, on the spot, the whole sum, and still more."

"You're lying, my gentle sir, and it's funny for me even to see such a gullible man as you are. Mr. Stavrogin stands before you like on a ladder, and you're yapping at him from below like a silly tyke, whereas he regards it as doing you a big honor even to spit on you from up there."

"And do you know," Pyotr Stepanovich flew into a rage, "that I won't let you take a step out of here, you scoundrel, and will hand you straight over to the police?"

Fedka jumped to his feet and flashed his eyes furiously. Pyotr Stepanovich snatched out his revolver. Here a quick and repulsive scene took place: before Pyotr Stepanovich could aim the revolver, Fedka instantly swerved and struck him in the face with all his might. At the same moment another terrible blow was heard, then a third, a fourth, all in the face. Crazed, his eyes goggling, Pyotr Stepanovich muttered something and suddenly crashed full-length to the floor.

"There he is, take him!" Fedka cried with a victorious flourish, instantly grabbed his cap, his bundle from under the bench, and made himself scarce. Pyotr Stepanovich lay gasping, unconscious. Liputin even thought a murder had taken place. Kirillov rushed headlong down to the kitchen.

"Water on him!" he cried, and scooping some from a bucket with an iron dipper, he poured it over his head. Pyotr Stepanovich stirred, raised his head, sat up, and looked senselessly in front of him.

"Well, how's that?" asked Kirillov.

The man went on looking at him intently and still without recognition; but catching sight of Liputin, who stuck himself out from the kitchen, he smiled his nasty smile and suddenly jumped up, snatching the revolver from the floor.

"If you decide to run away tomorrow like that scoundrel Stavrogin," he flew at Kirillov in a frenzy, all pale, stammering and articulating his words imprecisely, "I'll hang you like a fly . . . squash you . . . at the other end of the globe . . . understand!"

And he pointed the revolver straight at Kirillov's forehead; but at almost the same moment, recovering his senses completely at last, he jerked his hand back, shoved the revolver into his pocket, and, without another word, went running out of the house. And Liputin after him. They climbed through the same hole and again went along the slope holding on to the fence. Pyotr Stepanovich began striding quickly down the lane, so that Liputin could barely keep up with him. At the first intersection, he suddenly stopped.

"Well?" he turned to Liputin with a challenge.

Liputin remembered the revolver and was still trembling all over from the scene that had taken place; but the answer somehow suddenly and irrepressibly jumped off his tongue of itself:

"I think . . . I think that 'from Smolensk to far Tashkent they're not so impatiently awaiting the studént.' "

"And did you see what Fedka was drinking in the kitchen?"

"What he was drinking? He was drinking vodka."

"Well, know that he was drinking vodka for the last time in his life. I recommend that you remember that for your further considerations. And now, go to the devil, you're not needed until tomorrow . . . But watch out: no foolishness!"

Liputin rushed headlong for home.

IV

H E HAD LONG kept ready a passport in a different name. It is wild even to think that this precise little man, a petty family tyrant, a functionary in any case (though a Fourierist), and, finally, before all else, a capitalist and moneylender—had long, long ago conceived within himself the fantastic notion of readying this passport just in case, so as to slip abroad with its help *if* . . . so he did allow for the possibility of this *if!* though, of course, he himself was never able to formulate precisely what this *if* might signify . . .

But now it suddenly formulated itself, and in the most unexpected way. That desperate idea with which he had come to Kirillov's, after hearing Pyotr Stepanovich's "moron" on the sidewalk, consisted in abandoning everything tomorrow at daybreak and expatriating abroad! Whoever does not believe that such fantastic things happen in our everyday reality even now, may consult the biographies of all real Russian émigrés abroad. Not one of them fled in a more intelligent or realistic way. It is all the same unbridled kingdom of phantoms, and nothing more.

Having run home, he began by locking himself in, getting a valise, and beginning to pack convulsively. His main concern was about money, what amount and how he would be able to secure it. Precisely to secure, because, according to his notion, he could not delay even an hour, and had to be on the highway at daybreak. He also did not know how he would get on the train; he vaguely resolved to get on somewhere at the second or even third big station from town, and to get there even if by foot. In this way, instinctively and mechanically, with a whole whirl of thoughts in his head, he stood pottering over his valise and—suddenly stopped, abandoned it all, and with a deep moan stretched out on the sofa.

He clearly felt and suddenly became conscious of the fact that he might indeed be running away, but that to resolve the question of whether he was to run away *before* or *after* Shatov was now already quite beyond his power; that he was now only a crude, unfeeling body, an inert mass, but that he was being moved by some external, terrible power, and that though he did have a passport for abroad, though he could run away from Shatov (otherwise why such a hurry?), he would run away not before Shatov, not from Shatov, but precisely *after* Shatov, and that it had been thus decided, signed, and sealed. In unbearable anguish, trembling and astonished at himself every moment, groaning and going numb alternately, he somehow survived, locked in and lying on his sofa, until eleven o'clock the next morning, and it was then suddenly that the expected push came which suddenly directed his decision. At eleven o'clock, as soon as he unlocked his door and went out to his family, he suddenly learned from them that a robber, the escaped convict Fedka, who terrorized everyone, a pilferer of churches, a recent murderer and arsonist, whom our police had been after but kept failing to catch, had been found murdered that morning at daybreak, some four miles from town, at the turnoff from the highway to the road to Zakharyino, and that the whole town was already talking about it. He at once rushed headlong out of the house to learn the details, and learned first that Fedka, found with his head smashed in, had by all tokens been robbed, and second, that the police already had strong suspicions and even some firm evidence for concluding that his murderer was the Shpigulin man Fomka, the same one with whom he had undoubtedly killed and set fire to the Lebyadkins, and that a quarrel had already taken place between them on their way, because Fedka had supposedly hidden a big sum of money stolen from Lebyadkin . . . Liputin also ran to Pyotr Stepanovich's place and managed to learn at the back door, on the sly, that although Pyotr Stepanovich had returned home yesterday at, say, around one o'clock in the morning, he had been pleased to spend the whole night there quietly asleep until eight o'clock. Of course, there could be no doubt that the death of the robber Fedka contained nothing at all extraordinary in itself, and that such denouements precisely happen most often in careers of that sort, but the coincidence of the fatal words that "Fedka had drunk vodka that evening for the last time," with the immediate justification of the prophecy, was so portentous that Liputin suddenly ceased to hesitate. The push was given; it was as if a stone had fallen on him and crushed him forever. Returning home, he silently shoved his valise under the bed with his foot, and that evening, at the appointed time, was the first of them all to come to the place fixed for meeting Shatov—true, with his passport still in his pocket . . .

5

A Traveler

I

THE CATASTROPHE with Liza and the death of Marya Timofeevna produced an overwhelming impression on Shatov. I have already mentioned that I saw him that morning in passing; he seemed to me as if he were not in his right mind. He told me, incidentally, that the evening before, at around nine o'clock (that is, some three hours before the fire), he had been at Marya Timofeevna's. He went in the morning to have a look at the corpses, but as far as I know he did not give any evidence anywhere that morning. Meanwhile, towards the end of the day, a whole storm arose in his soul and . . . and I believe I can say positively that there was a certain moment at dusk when he wanted to get up, go, and—declare all. What this *all* was—he himself well knew. Of course, he would have achieved nothing, and would simply have betrayed himself. He had no proofs to expose the just-committed evildoing; and what he did have were only vague guesses about it, which for him alone were equal to full conviction. But he was ready to ruin himself just in order to "crush the scoundrels"—his own words. Pyotr Stepanovich had in part correctly divined this impulse in him and knew he was running a great risk in postponing his new, terrible design until the next day. Here, as usual, there was on his part much presumption and disdain for all this "trash," and for Shatov especially. He had long disdained Shatov for his "tearful idiocy," as he had said about him while still abroad, and firmly trusted that he could handle such an unclever man—that is, not lose sight of him all that day and stop him at the first sign of danger. And yet the "scoundrels" were spared a little longer only through a completely unexpected and, by them, totally unforeseen circumstance.

Somewhere between seven and eight in the evening (it was precisely the time when *our* people were gathered at Erkel's, waiting indignantly and anxiously for Pyotr Stepanovich), Shatov, with a headache and a slight chill, was lying stretched out on his bed, in the dark, without a candle, tormented by perplexity, angry, deciding and then unable to decide finally, and anticipating with a curse that anyhow it would all lead nowhere. Gradually he dozed off into a momentary, light sleep, and in his dreams had something like a nightmare; he dreamed he was on his bed all tangled up in ropes, bound and unable to move, and meanwhile the whole house was resounding from a terrible knocking on the fence, on the gate, on his door, in Kirillov's wing, so that the whole house was trembling, and some distant, familiar, but, for him, tormenting voice was piteously calling him. He suddenly came to his senses and raised himself on his bed. To his surprise, the knocking on the gate continued, and though it was hardly as strong as it had seemed in his dream, it was rapid and persistent, and the strange and "tormenting" voice, though not piteous but, on the contrary, impatient and irritable, still came from below at the gate, alternating with another more restrained and ordinary voice. He jumped up, opened the vent window, and stuck his head out.

"Who's there?" he called, literally going stiff with fright.

"If you are Shatov," the answer came sharply and firmly from below, "then please be so good as to announce directly and honestly whether you agree to let me in or not?"

Right enough; he recognized the voice!

"Marie! . . . Is it you?"

"It's me, me, Marya Shatov, and I assure you that I cannot keep the coachman any longer."

"Wait . . . let me . . . a candle . . ." Shatov cried weakly. Then he rushed to look for matches. The matches, as usual on such occasions, refused to be found. He dropped the candlestick and candle on the floor, and as soon as the impatient voice came again from below, he abandoned everything and flew headlong down his steep stairway to open the gate.

"Kindly hold the bag till I finish with this blockhead," Mrs. Marya Shatov met him below and shoved into his hands a rather light, cheap canvas handbag with brass studs, of Dresden manufacture. And she herself irritably fell upon the coachman:

"I venture to assure you that you are charging too much. If you dragged me for a whole extra hour around your dirty streets, it's your own fault, because it means you yourself did not know where this stupid street and asinine house were. Be so good as to accept your thirty kopecks, and rest assured that you will not get any more."

"Eh, little lady, wasn't it you who jabbed at Voznesensky Street, and this here is Bogoyavlensky: Voznesensky Lane is way over that way. You just got my gelding all in a stew."

"Voznesensky, Bogoyavlensky—you ought to know all these stupid names more than I,[1] since you're a local inhabitant, and, besides, you're wrong: I told you first thing that it was Filippov's house, and you precisely confirmed that you knew it. In any case, you can claim from me tomorrow at the justice of the peace, and now I ask you to leave me alone."

"Here, here's another five kopecks!" Shatov impetuously snatched out a five-kopeck piece from his pocket and gave it to the coachman.

"Be so good, I beg you, don't you dare do that!" Madame Shatov began to seethe, but the coachman started his "gelding," and Shatov, seizing her by the hand, drew her through the gate.

"Quick, Marie, quick . . . it's all trifles and—how soaked you are! Careful, there are steps up—sorry there's no light—the stairs are steep, hold on tighter, tighter, well, so here's my closet. Excuse me, I have no light . . . wait!"

He picked up the candlestick, but the matches took a long time to be found. Mrs. Shatov stood waiting in the middle of the room, silent and motionless.

"Thank God, at last!" he cried out joyfully, lighting up the closet. Marya Shatov took a cursory look around the place.

"I was told you lived badly, but still I didn't think it was like this," she said squeamishly, and moved towards the bed.

"Oh, I'm tired!" and with a strengthless air she sat on the hard bed. "Please put the bag down, and take a chair yourself. As you wish, however; you're sticking up in front of me. I'll stay with you for a time, until I find work, because I know nothing here and have no money. But if I'm cramping you, be so good, I beg you, as to announce it to me, which is your duty if you're an honest man. I can still sell something tomorrow and pay at the hotel, but you must be so good as to take me there yourself . . . Oh, only I'm so tired!"

Shatov simply started shaking all over.

"No need, Marie, no need for the hotel! What hotel? Why? Why?" He pressed his hands together imploringly.

"Well, if it's possible to do without the hotel, it's still necessary to explain matters. Remember, Shatov, that you and I lived maritally in Geneva for two weeks and a few days; we separated three years ago, though without any special quarrel. But don't think I've come back to resume any of the former foolishness. I've come back to look for work, and if I've come directly to this town, it's because it makes no difference to me. I did not come to repent of anything; kindly don't think of that stupidity either."

"Oh, Marie! There's no need, no need at all!" Shatov was muttering vaguely.

"And if so, if you're developed enough to be able to understand that as well, then I'll allow myself to add that if I've now turned directly to you and come to your apartment, it's partly because I've always regarded you as far from a scoundrel, and perhaps a lot better than other . . . blackguards! . . ."

Her eyes flashed. She must have endured her share of one thing and another from certain "blackguards."

"And please rest assured that I was by no means laughing at you just now when I declared that you are good. I spoke directly, without eloquence, which, besides, I can't stand. However, it's all nonsense. I always hoped you'd be intelligent enough not to be a nuisance . . . Oh, enough, I'm tired!"

And she gave him a long, worn-out, tired look. Shatov stood facing her across the room, five steps away, and listened to her timidly, but somehow in a renewed way, with some never-seen radiance in his face. This strong and rough man, his fur permanently bristling, was suddenly all softness and brightness. Something unusual, altogether unexpected, trembled in his soul. Three years of separation, three years of broken marriage, had dislodged nothing from his heart. And perhaps every day of those three years he had dreamed of her, the dear being who had once said to him: "I love you." Knowing Shatov, I can say for certain that he could never have admitted in himself even the dream that some woman might say "I love you" to him. He was wildly chaste and modest, considered himself terribly ugly, hated his face and his character, compared himself with some monster who was fit only to be taken around and exhibited at fairs. As a consequence of all that, he placed honesty above all things, and gave himself up to his convictions to the point of fanaticism, was gloomy, proud, irascible, and unloquacious. But now this sole being who had loved him for two weeks (he always, always believed that!)—a being he had always regarded as immeasurably above him, despite his perfectly sober understanding of her errors; a being to whom he could forgive everything, *everything* (there could have been no question of that, but even somewhat the opposite, so that in his view it came out that he himself was guilty before her for everything), this woman, this Marya Shatov, was again suddenly in his house, was again before him . . . this was almost impossible to comprehend! He was so struck, this event contained for him so much of something fearsome, and together with it so much happiness, that, of course, he could not, and perhaps did not wish to, was afraid to, recover his senses. This was a dream. But when she gave him that worn-out look, he suddenly understood that this so beloved being was suffering, had perhaps been offended. His heart sank. He studied her features with pain: the luster of first youth had long since disappeared from this tired face. True, she was still good-looking—in his eyes a beauty, as before. (In reality she was a woman of about twenty-five, of rather strong build, taller than average (taller than Shatov), with dark blond, fluffy hair, a pale oval face, and big dark eyes, now shining with a feverish glint.) But the former thoughtless, naïve, and simplehearted energy, so familiar to him, had given place in her to sullen irritability, disappointment, cynicism, as it were, to which she was not yet accustomed and which was a burden to her. But, above all, she was ill, he could see that clearly. Despite all his fear before her, he suddenly went up to her and took her by both hands:

"Marie . . . you know . . . perhaps you're very tired, for God's sake, don't be angry . . . If you'd accept, for instance, some tea at least, eh? Tea is very fortifying, eh? If you'd accept! . . ."

"Why ask me to accept, of course I accept, what a child you are still. Give it if you can. What a small room! How cold it is!"

"Oh, right away, firewood, firewood . . . I have some firewood!" Shatov got all stirred up. "Firewood . . . that is, but . . . tea, too, right away," he waved his hand as if with desperate resolution, and grabbed his cap.

"You're going out? So there's no tea in the house!"

"There will be, there will, there'll be everything, right away . . . I . . ." He grabbed the revolver from the shelf.

"I'll sell this revolver now . . . or pawn it . . ."

"How stupid, and it will take so long! Here, take my money, if you have nothing, there's eighty kopecks, I think; that's all. It's like a crazy house here."

"There's no need, no need for your money, I'll go now, one moment, even without the revolver . . ."

And he rushed straight to Kirillov. This was probably still two hours before Kirillov was visited by Pyotr Stepanovich and Liputin. Shatov and Kirillov, who shared the same yard, hardly ever saw each other, and when they met they did not nod or speak: they had spent much too long "lying" beside each other in America.

"Kirillov, you always have tea; have you got tea and a samovar?"

Kirillov, who was pacing the room (as was his custom, all night, from corner to corner), suddenly stopped and looked intently at the man who had run in, though without any special surprise.

"There's tea, there's sugar, and there's a samovar. But no need for the samovar, the tea is hot. Just sit down and drink."

"Kirillov, we lay beside each other in America . . . My wife has come to me . . . I . . . Give me the tea . . . I need the samovar."

"If it's a wife, you need the samovar. But the samovar later. I have two. For now take the teapot from the table. Hot, the hottest. Take everything; take sugar; all of it. Bread . . . A lot of bread; all of it. There's veal. A rouble in cash."

"Give it to me, friend, I'll pay it back tomorrow! Ah, Kirillov!"

"Is this the wife who was in Switzerland? That's good. And that you ran in like that is also good."

"Kirillov!" Shatov cried, taking the teapot under his arm and sugar and bread in both hands, "Kirillov! If . . . if you could renounce your terrible fantasies and drop your atheistic ravings . . . oh, what a man you'd be, Kirillov!"

"One can see you love your wife after Switzerland. That's good, if it's after Switzerland. When you need tea, come again. Come all night, I don't sleep at all. There'll be a samovar. Take the rouble, here. Go to your wife, I'll stay and think about you and your wife."

Marya Shatov was visibly pleased by his haste and almost greedily got down to her tea, but there was no need to run for the samovar: she drank only half a cup and swallowed just a tiny piece of bread. The veal was squeamishly and irritably rejected.

"You're ill, Marie, it's all such illness in you . . ." Shatov remarked timidly, waiting timidly on her.

"Of course I'm ill, sit down, please. Where did you get tea, if there wasn't any?"

Shatov told her about Kirillov, slightly, briefly. She had heard something about him.

"He's mad, I know; no more, please. As if there weren't enough fools! So you were in America? I heard, you wrote."

"Yes, I . . . wrote to Paris."

"Enough, and please let's talk about something else. Are you a Slavophil by conviction?"

"I . . . not that I . . . Seeing it was impossible to be a Russian, I became a Slavophil," he grinned crookedly, with the strain of a man whose witticism is inappropriate and forced.

"So you're not a Russian?"

"No, I'm not."

"Well, this is all stupid. Sit down, finally, I beg you. What's all this back-and-forth? You think I'm raving? Maybe I will be raving. You say there are just the two of you in the house?"

"Two . . . downstairs . . ."

"And both such smart ones. What's downstairs? You said downstairs?"

"No, nothing."

"What, nothing? I want to know."

"I was just going to say that there are two of us on the yard now, and before the Lebyadkins used to live downstairs . . ."

"That's the woman who was killed last night?" she suddenly heaved herself up. "I heard about it. As soon as I arrived, I heard about it. You had a fire?"

"Yes, Marie, yes, and maybe I'm a terrible scoundrel this minute, because I forgive the scoundrels . . ." He suddenly got up and began to pace the room, his arms raised as if in a frenzy.

But Marie did not quite understand him. She listened distractedly to his replies; she asked, but did not listen.

"Nice things you've got going. Oh, how scoundrelly everything is! They're all such scoundrels. But do sit down, I beg you, finally—oh, how you irritate me!" and, exhausted, she lowered her head onto the pillow.

"Marie, I won't . . . Maybe you want to lie down, Marie?"

She did not answer and strengthlessly closed her eyes. Her pale face became like a dead woman's. She fell asleep almost instantly. Shatov looked around, straightened the candle, looked anxiously at her face one more time, clasped his hands tightly in front of him, and tiptoed out of the room into the hallway. At the top of the stairs he pressed his face into a corner and stood that way for about ten minutes, silently and motionlessly. He would have stood there longer, but suddenly he heard soft, cautious footsteps from below. Someone was coming up. Shatov remembered that he had forgotten to lock the gate.

"Who's there?" he asked in a whisper.

The unknown visitor kept coming up without haste and without answering. When he reached the landing, he stopped; to make him out in the darkness was impossible; suddenly there came his cautious question:

"Ivan Shatov?"

Shatov gave his name, and immediately reached his hand out to stop him; but the man himself seized him by the hand and—Shatov gave a start, as if he had touched some horrible viper.

"Stop there," he whispered quickly, "don't come in, I can't receive you now. My wife has come back to me. I'll bring a candle out."

When he came back with the candle, there stood some young little officer; he did not know his name, but he had seen him somewhere.

"Erkel," the man introduced himself. "You saw me at Virginsky's."

"I remember; you sat and wrote. Listen," Shatov suddenly boiled up, frenziedly stepping close to him, but speaking in a whisper as before, "you gave me a sign just now with your hand, when you seized mine. But know that I could spit on all these signs! I don't acknowledge . . . I don't want to . . . I could chuck you down the stairs now, do you know that?"

"No, I don't know any of it, and I don't know at all why you got so angry," the visitor replied, mildly and almost simpleheartedly. "I only have to tell you something, and that is why I've come, wishing above all not to waste any time. You have a press that does not belong to you, and for which you are accountable, as you know yourself. I was told to demand that you hand it over tomorrow, at exactly seven o'clock in the evening, to Liputin. Furthermore, I was told to inform you that nothing else will ever be demanded of you."

"Nothing?"

"Absolutely nothing. Your request is being granted, and you are removed forever. I was told to inform you positively of this."

"Who told you to inform me?"

"Those who gave me the sign."

"Are you from abroad?"

"That . . . that, I think, is irrelevant for you."

"Eh, the devil! And why didn't you come sooner, if you were told?"

"I followed certain instructions and was not alone."

"I understand, I understand that you weren't alone. Eh . . . the devil! And why didn't Liputin come himself?"

"And so I will come for you tomorrow at exactly six o'clock in the evening, and we will go there on foot. There will be no one there except the three of us."

"Will Verkhovensky be there?"

"No, he won't. Verkhovensky is leaving town tomorrow, in the morning, at eleven o'clock."

"Just as I thought," Shatov whispered furiously and struck himself on the hip with his fist, "he ran away, the dog!"

He lapsed into agitated thought. Erkel was looking intently at him, waiting silently.

"And how are you going to take it? It can't be picked up in one piece and carried away."

"There will be no need to. You'll just point out the place, and we'll just make sure it really is hidden there. We know just the whereabouts of the place, but not the place itself. And have you pointed the place out to anyone else?"

Shatov looked at him.

"And you, and you, such a boy—such a silly boy—you, too, have gotten into it up to your neck, like a sheep? Eh, but that's what they need, such sap. Well, go! Ehh! That scoundrel hoodwinked you all and ran away."

Erkel looked at him serenely and calmly, but seemed not to understand.

"Verkhovensky ran away! Verkhovensky!" Shatov rasped furiously.

"But he's still here, he hasn't left yet. He's only leaving tomorrow," Erkel observed gently and persuadingly. "I especially invited him to be present as a witness; my instructions all had to do with him" (he confided like a young, inexperienced boy). "But, unfortunately, he did not agree, on the pretext of his departure, and he really seems to be in a hurry."

Shatov again glanced pityingly at the simpleton, but suddenly waved his hand as if thinking: "What's there to pity?"

"All right, I'll come," he suddenly broke off, "and now get out of here, go!"

"And so I'll come at exactly six o'clock," Erkel bowed politely and went unhurriedly down the stairs.

"Little fool!" Shatov could not help shouting at his back from upstairs.

"What's that, sir?" the man responded from below.

"Never mind, go."

"I thought you said something."

II

ERKEL WAS the sort of "little fool" whose head lacked only the chief sense; he had no king in his head, but of lesser, subordinate sense he had plenty, even to the point of cunning. Fanatically, childishly devoted to the "common cause," and essentially to Pyotr Verkhovensky, he acted on his instructions, given him at that moment during the meeting of *our* people when the roles for the next day were arranged and handed out. Pyotr Stepanovich, assigning him the role of messenger, managed to have about a ten-minute talk with him aside. The executive line was what was required by this shallow, scant-reasoning character, eternally longing to submit to another's will—oh, to be sure, not otherwise than for the sake of a "common" or "great" cause. But that, too, made no difference, for little fanatics like Erkel simply cannot understand service to an idea otherwise than by merging it with the very person who, in their understanding, expresses this idea. Sentimental, tender, and kindly Erkel was perhaps the most unfeeling of the murderers who gathered against Shatov, and, having no personal hatred, could be present at his murder without batting an eye. Among other things, for instance, he had been told to spy out Shatov's situation thoroughly while going about his errand, and when Shatov, receiving him on the stairs, blurted out in his heat, most likely without noticing it, that his wife had returned to him—Erkel at once had enough instinctive cunning not to show the slightest further curiosity, despite the surmise flashing in his head that the fact of the returned wife was of great significance for the success of their undertaking . . .

And so it was, essentially: this fact alone saved the "blackguards" from Shatov's intention, and at the same time helped them to "get rid" of him . . . First of all, it excited Shatov, unsettled him, deprived him of his usual perspicacity and caution. Now least of all could any sort of notion of his own safety enter his head, occupied as it was by something quite different. On the contrary, he passionately believed that Pyotr Verkhovensky was going to run away the next day: it coincided so well with his suspicions! Having returned to his room, he again sat down in the corner, leaned his elbows on his knees, and covered his face with his hands. Bitter thoughts tormented him . . .

And then he would raise his head again, get up, and go on tiptoe to look at her: "Lord! By tomorrow she'll be running a fever, by morning, it may have started already! She caught cold, of course. Unused to this terrible climate, and then the train, third class, rain and storm all around, and her cape is so light, no clothes to speak of . . . And to leave her here, abandon her without any help! Her bag, such a tiny bag, light, shriveled, ten pounds! Poor thing, how wasted, how much she's endured! She's proud, that's why she doesn't complain. But irritated, so irritated! It's the illness: even an angel would get irritated in illness. How dry, how hot her forehead must be, so dark under her eyes, and . . . and yet how beautiful the oval of her face and this fluffy hair, how . . ."

And he would hasten to look away, would hasten to get away, as if fearing the mere thought of seeing anything in her but an unfortunate, worn-out being in need of help—"what *hopes* could there be here! Oh, how low, how mean man is!"—and he would go back to his corner, sit down, cover his face with his hands, and again dream, again recall . . . and again picture hopes.

"Oh, I'm tired, so tired!" he recalled her exclamations, her weak, strained voice. "Lord! To abandon her now, and she with her eighty kopecks; she offered her purse, old, tiny! She's come to look for a position—well, what does she understand about positions, what do they understand in Russia? They're like whimsical children, all they have are their own fantasies, made up by themselves; and she's angry, poor thing, why doesn't Russia resemble their little foreign dreams! Oh, unfortunate, oh, innocent ones! . . . However, it really is cold here . . ."

He remembered that she had complained, that he had promised to light the stove. "The firewood's there, I could fetch it, as long as I don't wake her up. I could do it, however. And what do I decide about the veal? She'll get up, she may want to eat . . . Well, that can wait; Kirillov doesn't sleep all night. What shall I cover her with, she's so fast asleep, but she must be cold, ah, cold!"

And he went over yet again to look at her; her dress was turned back a little, and her right leg was half bared to the knee. He suddenly turned away, almost in fear, took off his warm coat, and, remaining in a wretched old jacket, covered the bare part, trying not to look at it.

Lighting the stove, walking on tiptoe, looking at the sleeping woman, dreaming in the corner, then looking at the sleeping woman again, took a long time. Two or three hours went by. It was during this time that Verkhovensky and Liputin managed to visit Kirillov. Finally he, too, dozed off in the corner. A groan came from her; she awoke, she was calling him; he jumped up like a criminal.

"Marie! I fell asleep . . . Ah, what a scoundrel I am, Marie!"

She raised herself, looking around in surprise, as if not recognizing where she was, and suddenly became all stirred with indignation, with wrath:

"I took your bed, I fell asleep, beside myself with fatigue; how dared you not wake me up? How dared you think I intend to burden you?"

"How could I wake you, Marie?"

"You could; you should have! There's no other bed for you here, and I took yours. You shouldn't have put me in a false position. Or do you think I came to take advantage of your charity? Be so good as to take your bed right now, and I will lie down in the corner, on some chairs . . ."

"Marie, I don't have so many chairs, or anything to make a bed from."

"Well, then simply on the floor. Otherwise you yourself will have to sleep on the floor. I want the floor, now, now!"

She got up, tried to take a step, but suddenly it was as if a most violent convulsive pain took away all her strength and all her resolve at once, and with a loud groan she fell back on the bed. Shatov ran to her, but Marie, her face buried in the pillows, seized his hand in hers and began to squeeze it and wring it with all her might. This went on for about a minute.

"Marie, darling, if you need, there's a Doctor Frenzel here, an acquaintance of mine, a very . . . I could run over to him."

"Nonsense!"

"Why nonsense? Tell me, Marie, what hurts you? How about compresses . . . on your stomach, for instance . . . That I could do without a doctor . . . Or else mustard plasters."

"What is this?" she asked strangely, raising her head and looking at him fearfully.

"What do you mean, Marie?" Shatov failed to understand. "What are you asking about? Oh, God, I'm completely lost, Marie, forgive me for not understanding anything."

"Eh, leave me alone, it's not your business to understand. And it would be very funny . . ." she grinned bitterly. "Talk to me about something. Walk around the room and talk. Don't stand over me and stare at me, that I particularly ask you for the five hundredth time!"

Shatov began to walk around the room, looking at the floor and trying as hard as he could not to glance at her.

"Here—don't be cross, Marie, I beg you—I have some veal here, not far away, and tea . . . You ate so little before . . ."

She waved her hand squeamishly and angrily. Shatov bit his tongue in despair.

"Listen, I intend to open a bookbinding shop here, on rational co-operative principles.[2] Since you live here, what do you think: will it succeed or not?"

"Eh, Marie, they don't even read books here, and there aren't any at all. And why would he suddenly go binding them?"

"He who?"

"The local reader, the local inhabitant in general, Marie."

"Well, speak more clearly, then; otherwise you say *he* and nobody knows who he is. You never learned grammar."

"It's in the spirit of the language, Marie," Shatov muttered.

"Ah, go on, you and your spirit, it's boring. Why won't the local inhabitant or reader have his books bound?"

"Because to read a book and to bind it are two whole periods of development, and enormous ones. First, he gradually gets accustomed to reading—over centuries, of course—but he tears books and throws them around, not considering them serious things. Now, binding signifies a respect for books, it signifies that he has not only come to love reading, but has recognized it as a serious thing. Russia as a whole has not yet reached this period. Europe has been binding for a long time."

"Pedantically put, but still it's not such a stupid thing to have said. It reminds me of three years ago. You were sometimes rather witty three years ago."

She uttered this as squeamishly as all her earlier capricious remarks.

"Marie, Marie," Shatov addressed her with tender emotion, "oh, Marie! If you knew how much has passed and gone in these three years! I heard later that you supposedly despised me for changing my convictions. But whom did I abandon? The enemies of living life; outdated little liberals, afraid of their own independence; lackeys of thought, enemies of the person and freedom, decrepit preachers of carrion and rot! What do they have: gray heads, the golden mean, the most abject and philistine giftlessness, envious equality, equality without personal dignity, equality as understood by a lackey or a Frenchman of the year 'ninety-three[3] . . . And scoundrels, above all, scoundrels, scoundrels everywhere!"

"Yes, there are many scoundrels," she said haltingly and painfully. She was lying stretched out, motionless and as if afraid to stir, her head thrown back on the pillow, slightly to one side, looking at the ceiling with tired but hot eyes. Her face was pale, her lips dry and parched.

"You understand, Marie, you understand!" Shatov exclaimed. She was about to shake her head, but suddenly the same convulsion came over her. Again she hid her face in the pillow, and again for a whole minute she clung painfully, with all her might, to the hand of Shatov, who rushed to her and was out of his mind with terror.

"Marie, Marie! But this may be very serious, Marie!"

"Keep still . . . I don't want it, I don't want it," she kept exclaiming, almost in fury, turning her face up again, "don't you dare look at me with your compassion! Walk around, say something, talk . . ."

Shatov, like a lost man, tried to begin muttering something again.

"What do you do here?" she asked, interrupting him with squeamish impatience.

"I go to a merchant's office. You know, Marie, if I really wanted to, I could even get good money here."

"So much the better for you . . ."

"Ah, don't think anything, Marie, I just said it . . ."

"And what else are you doing? What are you preaching? Surely you can't help preaching, with such a character!"

"I preach God, Marie."

"In whom you don't believe yourself. That's an idea I never could understand."

"Let's drop it, Marie, save it for later."

"What was this Marya Timofeevna here?"

"That, too, we can save for later, Marie."

"Don't you dare make such remarks to me! Is it true that this death can be put down to these people's . . . villainy?"

"Absolutely true," Shatov ground out.

Marie suddenly raised her head and cried out painfully:

"Don't you dare say any more to me about it, ever, ever!"

And she fell back on the bed again in a seizure of the same convulsive pain; this was the third time now, but this time her moans grew louder, turned into cries.

"Oh, unbearable man! Oh, insufferable man!" she was thrashing about, no longer sparing herself, pushing away Shatov, who was standing over her.

"Marie, I'll do whatever you like . . . I'll walk, talk . . ."

"But can't you see it's begun?"

"What's begun, Marie?"

"How do I know. Do I know anything about it? . . . Oh, curse it! Oh, curse it all beforehand!"

"Marie, if you'd say what has begun . . . otherwise I . . . what am I to understand, then?"

"You're an abstract, useless babbler. Oh, curse everything in the world!"

"Marie! Marie!"

He seriously thought she was beginning to go mad.

"But can't you finally see that I'm in labor?" she raised herself a little, looking at him with a terrible, painful spite that distorted her whole face. "Curse it beforehand, this child!"

"Marie," Shatov exclaimed, realizing at last what it was about, "Marie . . . but why didn't you tell me sooner?" He suddenly collected himself and, with energetic determination, grabbed his cap.

"How did I know when I came in? Would I have come to you? I was told it would be another ten days! Where, where are you going, don't you dare!"

"To fetch a midwife! I'll sell my revolver; money's the first thing now!"

"Don't you dare do anything, no midwife, just some peasant woman, any old woman, I have eighty kopecks in my purse . . . Village women give birth without midwives . . . And if I drop dead, so much the better . . ."

"You'll have both a midwife and a peasant woman. Only how, how can I leave you alone, Marie!"

But realizing that it was better to leave her alone now, despite all her frenzy, than leave her without help later on, he paid no attention to her moans and wrathful exclamations, and, trusting to his legs, started headlong down the stairs.

III

To Kirillov, first of all. It was already one o'clock in the morning. Kirillov was standing in the middle of the room.

"Kirillov, my wife's giving birth!"

"How's that?"

"Giving birth, to a baby!"

"You're not . . . mistaken?"

"Oh, no, no, she's having spasms! . . . I need a woman, some old woman, right now . . . Can I get one now? You used to have lots of old women . . ."

"It's a great pity that I'm not able to give birth," Kirillov answered pensively, "that is, not that I'm not able to give birth, but that I'm not able to make it so that there is birth . . . or . . . No, I'm not able to say it."

"That is, you yourself can't help in childbirth; but that's not what I mean; a woman, an old woman, I'm asking for an old woman, a nurse, a servant!"

"You'll have an old woman, only maybe not now. If you like, instead, I'll . . ."

"Oh, impossible; I'll go right now to the Virginsky woman, the midwife."

"A harpy!"

"Oh, yes, Kirillov, yes, but she's the best one! Oh, yes, it will all be without awe, without joy, squeamish, with curses, with blasphemy—this great mystery, the appearance of a new being! . . . Oh, she's already cursing it now! . . ."

"If you wish, I . . ."

"No, no, but while I'm running around (oh, I'll drag that Virginsky woman here!), you should go to my stairway every once in a while and listen quietly, but don't you dare go in, you'll frighten her, don't go in for anything, only listen . . . just in some terrible case. Well, if something extreme happens, then go in."

"I understand. There's one more rouble. Here. I wanted a chicken for tomorrow, but no more. Run quickly, run as hard as you can. There's a samovar all night."

Kirillov knew nothing about the intentions concerning Shatov, and even before he never knew the full extent of the danger that threatened him. He knew only that he had some old scores with "those people," and though he himself was partly mixed up in the affair through some instructions conveyed to him from abroad (rather superficial ones, however, for he had never participated closely in anything), he had lately dropped everything, all assignments, removed himself completely from all affairs, and in the first place from the "common cause," and given himself to a life of contemplation. Although at the meeting Pyotr Verkhovensky had summoned Liputin to Kirillov's to make sure he would take the "Shatov case" upon himself at the proper moment, nevertheless, in his talk with Kirillov he did not say a word about Shatov, not even a hint—probably regarding it as impolitic, and Kirillov even as unreliable—and had left it till the next day, when everything would already be done, and it would therefore "make no difference" to Kirillov; so, at least, Pyotr Stepanovich's reasoning about Kirillov went. Liputin also noticed very well that, despite the promise, not a word was mentioned about Shatov, but Liputin was too agitated to protest.

Shatov ran like the wind to Muravyiny Street, cursing the distance and seeing no end to it.

It would take a lot of knocking at Virginsky's: everyone had long been asleep. But Shatov started banging on the shutters as hard as he could and without any ceremony. The dog tied in the yard strained and went off into a furious barking. All the dogs down the street joined in; a clamor of dogs arose.

"Why are you knocking and what is it you want?" the soft voice of Virginsky, quite incommensurate with the "outrage," came at last from a window. The shutter opened a bit, as did the vent.

"Who's there, what scoundrel?" the female voice of the old maid, Virginsky's relative, this time fully commensurate with the outrage, angrily shrieked.

"It's me, Shatov, my wife has come back to me and is now presently giving birth . . ."

"Well, let her! Away with you!"

"I've come for Arina Prokhorovna, I won't leave without Arina Prokhorovna!"

"She can't just go to everybody. Night practice is a separate thing . . . Away with you to the Maksheev woman, and don't you dare make any more noise!" the irate female voice rattled on. One could hear Virginsky trying to stop her; but the old maid kept pushing him away and would not give in.

"I won't leave!" Shatov shouted again.

"Wait, wait!" Virginsky finally raised his voice, overpowering the maid. "I beg you, Shatov, wait five minutes, I'll wake up Arina Prokhorovna, and please don't knock or shout . . . Oh, how terrible this all is!"

After five endless minutes, Arina Prokhorovna appeared.

"Your wife has come to you?" her voice issued from the vent window and, to Shatov's surprise, was not at all angry, merely peremptory as usual; but Arina Prokhorovna could not speak any other way.

"Yes, my wife, and she's in labor."

"Marya Ignatievna?"

"Yes, Marya Ignatievna. Of course, Marya Ignatievna!"

Silence ensued. Shatov waited. There was whispering in the house.

"Did she come long ago?" Madame Virginsky asked again.

"Tonight, at eight o'clock. Please hurry."

Again there was whispering and again an apparent discussion.

"Listen, you're not mistaken, are you? Did she send for me herself?"

"No, she didn't send for you, she wants a woman, a peasant woman, so as not to burden me with the expense, but don't worry, I'll pay."

"All right, I'll come, pay or no pay. I've always thought highly of Marya Ignatievna's independent feelings, though she may not remember me. Do you have the most necessary things?"

"I have nothing, but I'll get it all, I will, I will . . ."

"So there's magnanimity in these people, too!" Shatov thought, as he headed for Lyamshin's. "Convictions and the man—it seems they're two different things in many ways. Maybe in many ways I'm guilty before them! . . . We're all guilty, we're all guilty, and . . . if only we were all convinced of it! . . ."

He did not have to knock long at Lyamshin's; surprisingly, the man instantly opened the window, having jumped out of bed barefoot, in his underwear, at the risk of catching cold—he who was so nervous and constantly worried about his health. But there was a particular reason for such sensitiveness and haste; Lyamshin had been trembling all night and was still so agitated that he could not sleep, as a consequence of the meeting of *our* people; he kept imagining visits from some uninvited and altogether unwanted guests. The news about Shatov's denunciation tormented him most of all . . . And then suddenly, as if by design, there came such terrible, loud knocking at the window! . . .

He got so scared when he saw Shatov that he immediately slammed the window and ran for his bed. Shatov started knocking and shouting furiously.

"How dare you knock like that in the middle of the night?" Lyamshin, though sinking with fear, shouted threateningly, venturing to open the window again after a good two minutes and making sure finally that Shatov had come alone.

"Here's your revolver; take it back, give me fifteen roubles."

"What, are you drunk? This is hooliganism; I'll simply catch cold. Wait, let me throw a plaid over me."

"Give me fifteen roubles right now. If you don't, I'll knock and shout till dawn; I'll break your window."

"And I'll shout for help and you'll be locked up."

"And I'm mute, am I? Do you think I won't shout for help? Who should be more afraid of shouting for help, you or me?"

"How can you nurse such mean convictions . . . I know what you're hinting at . . . Wait, wait, for God's sake, don't knock! Good heavens, who has money at night? What do you need money for, if you're not drunk?"

"My wife has come back to me. I've chopped off ten roubles for you, I never once fired it; take the revolver, take it this minute."

Lyamshin mechanically reached his hand out the window and accepted the revolver; he waited a little, and all at once, quickly popping his head out the window, started babbling, as if forgetting himself, and with a chill in his spine:

"You're lying, your wife hasn't come back to you at all. It's . . . it's that you simply want to run away somewhere."

"You're a fool, where am I going to run to? Let your Pyotr Verkhovensky run away, not me. I just left the midwife Virginsky, and she agreed at once to come to me. Ask her. My wife's in labor; I need money; give me money!"

A whole fireworks of ideas flashed in Lyamshin's shifty mind. Everything suddenly took a different turn, yet fear still prevented him from reasoning.

"But how . . . aren't you separated from your wife?"

"I'll smash your head in for such questions."

"Ah, my God, forgive me, I understand, it's just that I was flabbergasted . . . But I understand, I understand. But . . . but—will Arina Prokhorovna really go? Didn't you just say she went? You know, that's not true. See, see, see, at every step you say things that aren't true."

"She must be with my wife now, don't keep me, it's not my fault that you're so stupid."

"That's not true, I'm not stupid. Excuse me, I really can't . . ."

And, completely at a loss now, he started to close the window for the third time, but Shatov raised such a cry that he immediately stuck himself out again.

"But this is a total infringement upon a person! What are you demanding of me, well, what, what?—formulate it! And in the middle of the night, note that, note that!"

"I'm demanding fifteen roubles, muttonhead!"

"But maybe I don't wish to take the revolver back. You have no right. You bought the thing—and that's that, and you have no right. There's no way I can produce such a sum at night. Where can I get such a sum?"

"You always have money; I've taken off ten roubles for you, but you're a notorious little Jew."

"Come the day after tomorrow—do you hear, the day after tomorrow, in the morning, at twelve sharp, and I'll give you all of it, agreed?"

Shatov knocked furiously at the window for the third time:

"Give me ten roubles, and five tomorrow at daybreak."

"No, five the day after tomorrow, and tomorrow nothing, by God. You'd better not come, you'd better not come."

"Give me ten—oh, you scoundrel!"

"Why such abuse? Wait, I need a light; look, you've broken the window . . . Why such abuse in the night? Here!" he held a note out to him through the window.

Shatov grabbed the note—it was five roubles.

"By God, I can't, strike me dead, but I can't, the day after tomorrow I can give you all of it, but nothing now."

"I won't leave!" Shatov bellowed.

"Well, here, take more, you see, more, and that's it. You can shout your head off, I won't give you more, whatever happens, I won't, I won't, I won't!"

He was in a frenzy, in despair, covered with sweat. The two notes he had added were for a rouble each. Altogether, Shatov had collected seven roubles.

"Well, devil take you, I'll come tomorrow. I'll give you a beating, Lyamshin, if you haven't got eight roubles ready."

"And I won't be home, you fool!" Lyamshin thought to himself quickly.

"Wait, wait!" he called frenziedly after Shatov, who was already running off. "Wait, come back. Tell me, please, is it true what you said about your wife coming back to you?"

"Fool!" Shatov spat and ran home as hard as he could.

IV

I WILL NOTE that Arina Prokhorovna knew nothing about the intentions adopted at the previous day's meeting. Virginsky, coming home stunned and weakened, did not dare tell her the adopted decision; but even so he could not help himself and did reveal half—that is, all that Verkhovensky had reported to them about Shatov's definite intention to denounce them; but he declared at the same time that he did not quite trust this report. Arina Prokhorovna was terribly frightened. That was why, when Shatov came running to fetch her, she immediately decided to go, tired though she was from having toiled over a woman in childbirth all the night before. She had always been sure that "such trash as Shatov was capable of civic meanness"; yet the arrival of Marya Ignatievna placed the matter in a new perspective. Shatov's fright, the desperate tone of his appeals, his pleas for help, signified a turnabout in the traitor's feelings: a man who had even resolved to betray himself just so as to ruin others would, it seemed, have a different look and tone than the reality presented. In short, Arina Prokhorovna resolved to examine it all herself, with her own eyes. Virginsky remained very pleased with her resolution—as if five tons had been lifted from him! A hope was even born in him: Shatov's look seemed to him to the highest degree incompatible with Verkhovensky's supposition . . .

Shatov was not mistaken; on his return he found Arina Prokhorovna already with Marie. She had just arrived, had disdainfully chased away Kirillov, who was sticking about at the foot of the stairs; had hastily made the acquaintance of Marie, who did not recognize her as an old acquaintance; had found her "in a very bad state"—that is, angry, upset, and in "the most fainthearted despair"—and in some five minutes had decidedly gained the upper hand over all her objections.

"What's all this carping about not wanting an expensive midwife?" she was saying the very moment Shatov entered. "Sheer nonsense, false notions, from the abnormal state you're in. You'd have fifty chances of ending badly with the help of some simple old woman, some peasant granny; and then there'd be more troubles and costs than with an expensive midwife. How do you know I'm an expensive midwife? You can pay later, I won't take too much from you, and I guarantee you success; with me you won't die, I've seen lots worse cases. And I'll send the baby to the orphanage, tomorrow even, if you like, and then to the country to be brought up, and that'll be the end of that. Then you can recover, settle down to some rational work, and in a very short time reward Shatov for the lodging and expenses, which won't be all that great . . ."

"It's not that . . . I have no right to be a burden . . ."

"Rational and civic feelings, but, believe me, Shatov will spend almost nothing, if he decides to turn himself, at least a little, from a fantastic gentleman into a man of right ideas. All he has to do is not commit any follies, not beat the drum, not run around town with his tongue hanging out. If he's not tied down, he'll rouse all the doctors in town before morning; he certainly roused all the dogs on my street. There's no need for doctors, I've already said I guarantee everything. You could maybe hire an old woman to serve you, that won't cost anything. Though he himself could be of use for something besides just foolishness. He's got arms, he's got legs, he can run over to the pharmacy without insulting your feelings in any way by his charity. The devil it's charity! Isn't he the one who got you into this state? Wasn't it he who made you quarrel with the family where you were governess, with the egoistic purpose of marrying you? We heard about that . . . Though he himself just came running like a lunatic and shouting for the whole street to hear. I'm not forcing myself on anybody, I came solely for you, on the principle that our people are all bound by solidarity; I announced that to him before I left the house. If I'm unnecessary in your opinion, then good-bye; only you may be asking for trouble that could easily be avoided."

And she even got up from her chair.

Marie was so helpless, she was suffering so much, and, to tell the truth, was so afraid of what lay ahead of her, that she did not dare let her go. But the woman suddenly became hateful to her: what she was saying was not it, was not at all what was in Marie's soul! But the prophecy of possible death at the hands of an inexperienced midwife overcame her revulsion. To make up for it, she became, from that moment on, even more exacting, more merciless to Shatov. It finally reached a point where she forbade him not only to look at her but even to stand facing her. The pains were becoming worse. The curses and even profanities were becoming more violent.

"Eh, why don't we send him out," Arina Prokhorovna snapped, "he looks awful, he just frightens you, he's pale as a corpse! What is it to you, tell me please, you funny fellow? What a comedy!"

Shatov did not reply; he resolved not to reply.

"I've seen foolish fathers on such occasions; they, too, lose their minds. But at least they . . ."

"Stop it, or leave me and let me die! Nobody say a word! I don't want it, I don't want it!" Marie started shouting.

"It's impossible not to say a word, or are you out of your mind yourself? That's how I understand you in the state you're in. We have to talk business at least: tell me, do you have anything ready? You answer, Shatov, she can't be bothered with it."

"Tell me what precisely is necessary?"

"In other words, nothing's ready."

She counted off all the needful things necessary and, one must do her justice, limited herself to sheer necessities, to beggarliness. It turned out that Shatov had some things. Marie took her key and gave it to him to look in her bag. His hands were trembling and he fumbled somewhat longer than he should have in opening the unfamiliar lock. Marie lost her temper, but when Arina Prokhorovna ran to take the key from him, she refused to let her peek into the bag, and insisted with capricious cries and tears that the only one who should open the bag was Shatov.

For certain things he had to run over to Kirillov. As soon as Shatov turned to go, she immediately began calling him back frenziedly, and calmed down only when Shatov rushed madly back from the stairs and explained to her that he was leaving only for a minute, to get the most necessary things, and would come back at once.

"Well, lady, you're a hard one to please," Arina Prokhorovna laughed. "One minute he has to stand facing the wall and not dare look at you, the next he mustn't dare leave for a moment or you'll cry. He might think something this way. Now, now, don't be capricious, don't pout, I'm just laughing."

"He dare not think anything."

"Tsk, tsk, tsk, if he wasn't in love with you like a sheep, he wouldn't be running around town with his tongue hanging out, and he wouldn't have roused all the local dogs. He broke my window."

V

SHATOV FOUND KIRILLOV, who was still pacing his room from corner to corner, so distracted that he had even forgotten about the wife's arrival and listened uncomprehendingly.

"Ah, yes," he remembered suddenly, as if tearing himself away with effort, and only for a moment, from some idea that held him fascinated, "yes . . . an old woman . . . A wife or an old woman? Wait: both a wife and an old woman, right? I remember; I went; the old woman will come, only not now. Take the pillow. Anything else? Yes . . . Wait, Shatov, do you ever have moments of eternal harmony?"

"You know, Kirillov, you mustn't go on not sleeping at night."

Kirillov came to himself and—strangely—began to speak even far more coherently than he usually spoke; one could see that he had long been formulating it all, and perhaps had written it down:

"There are seconds, they come only five or six at a time, and you suddenly feel the presence of eternal harmony, fully achieved. It is nothing earthly; not that it's heavenly, but man cannot endure it in his earthly state. One must change physically or die. The feeling is clear and indisputable. As if you suddenly sense the whole of nature and suddenly say: yes, this is true.[4] God, when he was creating the world, said at the end of each day of creation: 'Yes, this is true, this is good.'[5] This . . . this is not tenderheartedness, but simply joy. You don't forgive anything, because there's no longer anything to forgive. You don't really love—oh, what is here is higher than love! What's most frightening is that it's so terribly clear, and there's such joy. If it were longer than five seconds—the soul couldn't endure it and would vanish. In those five seconds I live my life through, and for them I would give my whole life, because it's worth it. To endure ten seconds one would have to change physically. I think man should stop giving birth. Why children, why development, if the goal has been achieved? It's said in the Gospel that in the resurrection there will be no birth, but people will be like God's angels.[6] A hint. Your wife's giving birth?"

"Kirillov, does it come often?"

"Once in three days, once a week."

"You don't have the falling sickness?"

"No."

"Then you will. Watch out, Kirillov, I've heard that this is precisely how the falling sickness starts. An epileptic described to me in detail this preliminary sensation before a fit, exactly like yours; he, too, gave it five seconds and said it couldn't be endured longer. Remember Muhammad's jug that had no time to spill while he flew all over paradise on his horse?[7] The jug is those same five seconds; it's all too much like your harmony, and Muhammad was an epileptic. Watch out, Kirillov, it's the falling sickness!"

"It won't have time," Kirillov chuckled softly.

VI

THE NIGHT was passing. Shatov was sent out, abused, called back. Marie reached the last degree of fear for her life. She shouted that she wanted to live, that "she must live, she must!" and was afraid to die. "Not that, not that!" she kept repeating. Had it not been for Arina Prokhorovna, things would have been very bad. Gradually she gained complete control over the patient, who started obeying her every word, her every bark, like a child. Arina Prokhorovna used severity, not kindness, but her work was masterful. Dawn broke. Arina Prokhorovna suddenly came up with the idea that Shatov had just run out to the stairs to pray to God, and she began to laugh. Marie also laughed, spitefully, caustically, as if it made her feel better. Finally, they chased Shatov out altogether. A damp, cold morning came. He leaned his face to the wall in the corner, exactly as the evening before when Erkel came. He was trembling like a leaf, afraid to think, yet his thought clung to everything that presented itself to his mind, as happens in dreams. Reveries incessantly carried him away, and incessantly snapped off like rotten threads. Finally, it was no longer groans that came from the room, but terrible, purely animal sounds, intolerable, impossible. He wanted to stop his ears, but could not, and fell to his knees, unconsciously repeating "Marie, Marie!" And then, finally, there came a cry, a new cry, at which Shatov gave a start and jumped up from his knees, the cry of an infant, weak, cracked. He crossed himself and rushed into the room. In Arina Prokhorovna's hands a small, red, wrinkled being was crying and waving its tiny arms and legs, a terribly helpless being, like a speck of dust at the mercy of the first puff of wind, yet crying and proclaiming itself, as if it, too, somehow had the fullest right to life . . . Marie was lying as if unconscious, but after a minute she opened her eyes and gave Shatov a strange, strange look: it was somehow quite a new look, precisely how he was as yet unable to understand, but he did not know or remember her ever having such a look before.

"A boy? A boy?" she asked Arina Prokhorovna in a pained voice.

"A little boy!" she shouted in reply, swaddling the baby.

For a moment, once she had swaddled him and before laying him across the bed between two pillows, she handed him to Shatov to hold. Marie, somehow on the sly and as if she were afraid of Arina Prokhorovna, nodded to him. He understood at once and brought the baby over to show her.

"How . . . pretty . . ." she whispered weakly, with a smile.

"Pah, what a look!" the triumphant Arina Prokhorovna laughed merrily, peeking into Shatov's face. "Just see the face on him!"

"Be glad, Arina Prokhorovna . . . This is a great joy . . ." Shatov babbled with an idiotically blissful look, radiant after Marie's two words about the baby.

"What's this great joy of yours?" Arina Prokhorovna was amusing herself, while bustling about, tidying up, and working like a galley slave.

"The mystery of the appearance of a new being, a great mystery and an inexplicable one, Arina Prokhorovna, and what a pity you don't understand it!"

Shatov was muttering incoherently, dazedly, and rapturously. It was as if something were swaying in his head, and of itself, without his will, pouring from his soul.

"There were two, and suddenly there's a third human being, a new spirit, whole, finished, such as doesn't come from human hands; a new thought and a new love, it's even frightening . . . And there's nothing higher in the world!"

"A nice lot of drivel! It's simply the further development of the organism, there's nothing to it, no mystery," Arina Prokhorovna was guffawing sincerely and merrily. "That way every fly is a mystery. But I tell you what: unnecessary people shouldn't be born. First reforge everything so that they're not unnecessary, and then give birth to them. Otherwise, you see, I've got to drag him to the orphanage tomorrow . . . Though that's as it should be."

"Never will he go from me to the orphanage!" Shatov said firmly, staring at the floor.

"You're adopting him?"

"He is my son."

"Of course, he's a Shatov, legally he's a Shatov, and there's no point presenting yourself as a benefactor of mankind. They just can't do without their phrases. Well, well, all right, only I tell you what, ladies and gentlemen," she finally finished tidying up, "it's time for me to go. I'll come again in the morning, and in the evening if need be, and now, since it's all gone off so very well, I must also run to the others, they've been waiting a long time. Shatov, you've got an old woman sitting somewhere; the old woman is fine, but you, dear husband, don't you leave her either; stay by her, just in case you can be useful; and I don't suppose Marya Ignatievna will chase you away . . . well, well, I'm just laughing . . ."

At the gate, where Shatov went to see her off, she added, to him alone:

"You've made me laugh for the rest of my life: I won't take any money from you; I'll laugh in my sleep. I've never seen anything funnier than you last night."

She left thoroughly pleased. From Shatov's look and his talk, it became clear as day that the man "was going to make a father of himself, and was a consummate dishrag." She ran over to her place, though it would have been closer to go directly to her next patient, on purpose to tell Virginsky about it.

"Marie, she said you should wait and not sleep for a while, though that, I see, is terribly difficult . . ." Shatov began timidly. "I'll sit here by the window and keep watch on you, hm?"

And he sat down by the window behind the sofa so that there was no way she could see him. But before a minute had passed, she called him and squeamishly asked him to straighten her pillow. He began to straighten it. She was looking angrily at the wall.

"Not like that, oh, not like that . . . What hands!"

Shatov straightened it again.

"Bend down to me," she suddenly said wildly, trying all she could not to look at him.

He gave a start, but bent down.

"More . . . not like that . . . closer," and suddenly her left arm impetuously went around his neck, and he felt on his forehead her firm, moist kiss.

"Marie!"

Her lips were trembling, she tried to restrain herself, but suddenly she sat up and, flashing her eyes, said:

"Nikolai Stavrogin is a scoundrel!"

And strengthlessly, as if cut down, she fell with her face in the pillow, sobbing hysterically and squeezing Shatov's hand tightly in her own.

From that moment on she no longer let him leave her, she demanded that he sit by her head. She could talk little, but kept looking at him with a blessed smile on her face. It was as if she had suddenly turned into some silly fool. Everything seemed transformed. Shatov now wept like a little boy, now said God knows what, wildly, dazedly, inspiredly; he kissed her hands; she listened with rapture, perhaps not even understanding, but tenderly touching his hair with a weakened hand, smoothing it, admiring it. He talked to her of Kirillov, of how they were now going to start living "anew and forever," of the existence of God, of everyone being good . . . In rapture they again took the baby out to look at him.

"Marie," he cried, holding the baby in his arms, "an end to the old delirium, disgrace, and carrion! Let us work, and on a new path, the three of us, yes, yes! . . . Ah, yes, what name are we going to give him, Marie?"

"Him? What name?" she repeated in surprise, and a terribly rueful look suddenly came to her face.

She clasped her hands, glanced reproachfully at Shatov, and threw herself facedown on the pillow.

"Marie, what is it?" he cried out with rueful fright.

"How could you, how could you . . . Oh, you ungrateful man!"

"Marie, forgive me, Marie . . . I just asked what to name him. I don't know . . ."

"Ivan, Ivan," she raised her flushed face, wet with tears, "could you really suppose it would be some other, *terrible* name?"

"Marie, calm down, oh, you're so upset!"

"More rudeness! Why ascribe it to my being upset? I bet if I told you to give him that . . . terrible name, you'd agree at once and wouldn't even notice! Oh, ungrateful, mean, all of you, all of you!"

A minute later, of course, they made peace. Shatov convinced her to get some sleep. She fell asleep, but still without letting go of his hand; she kept waking up, looking at him as if fearing he might leave, and falling asleep again.

Kirillov sent the old woman up with "congratulations," and with hot tea, besides, some just-fried cutlets, and bouillon with white bread for "Marya Ignatievna." The patient drank the bouillon greedily, the old woman changed the baby, Marie also made Shatov eat the cutlets.

Time was passing. Shatov, strengthless, fell asleep in the chair himself, his head on Marie's pillow. Thus they were found by Arina Prokhorovna, true to her word, who cheerfully woke them up, discussed whatever was necessary with Marie, looked the baby over, and again told Shatov not to leave her side. Then, cracking a joke about the "spouses" with a shade of scorn and superciliousness, she left as well pleased as before.

It was already quite dark when Shatov woke up. He hastened to light the candle and ran for the old woman; but as soon as he started down the stairs, he was struck by someone's soft, unhurried footsteps of a man coming up towards him. Erkel came in.

"Don't come in!" Shatov whispered, and seizing him impetuously by the arm, he dragged him back to the gate. "Wait here, I'll come out right away, I totally, totally forgot about you! Oh, what a reminder!"

He began hurrying so much that he did not even run over to see

Kirillov and only called the old woman out. Marie was in despair and indignation that he "could even think of leaving her alone."

"But," he cried rapturously, "this is the very last step! And then the new path, and we'll never, ever remember the old horror!"

He somehow managed to convince her and promised to be back at nine o'clock sharp; he gave her a big kiss, kissed the baby, and quickly ran down to Erkel.

The two men set off for Stavrogin's park at Skvoreshniki, where about a year and a half earlier, in a solitary place at the very edge of the park where the pine forest already began, he had buried the printing press that had been entrusted to him. The place was wild and deserted, totally inconspicuous, quite far from the Skvoreshniki house. It was about a two-mile walk from Filippov's house, maybe even two and a half.

"Not on foot, really? I'll hire a carriage."

"I beg you very much not to," Erkel objected, "they precisely insisted on that. A driver is also a witness."

"Well . . . the devil! No matter, just to be done with it, done with it!"

They were walking very quickly.

"Erkel, you little boy, you!" Shatov cried out, "have you ever been happy?"

"And you seem to be very happy now," Erkel observed with curiosity.

6

A Toilsome Night

I

VIRGINSKY, in the course of the day, employed two hours in running around to see all *our* people and tell them that Shatov was certainly not going to denounce them, because his wife had come back to him and a child had been born, and, "knowing the human heart," it was impossible to suppose he could be dangerous at that moment. But, to his disconcertion, he found almost no one home except Erkel and Lyamshin. Erkel listened to him silently, gazing serenely into his eyes; and to the direct question: "Would he go at six o'clock or not?" replied, with the most serene smile, that "of course he would."

Lyamshin was in bed, apparently quite seriously sick, with his head wrapped in a blanket. When Virginsky came in, he got scared and, as soon as he began to speak, suddenly started waving his hands from under the blanket, pleading to be left alone. However, he listened to everything about Shatov; for some reason, the news that no one was home struck him greatly. It also turned out that he already knew (through Liputin) about Fedka's death, and hurriedly and incoherently told Virginsky about it himself, thereby striking him in his turn. And to Virginsky's direct question: "Should we go or not?" he again started pleading, waving his hands, that he was "not concerned, knew nothing, and to leave him alone."

Virginsky returned home dispirited and greatly alarmed; what made it hard for him was that he also had to conceal it from his family; he was used to revealing everything to his wife, and had it not been for a new thought, a certain new, conciliatory plan for further action which lit up in his inflamed brain at that moment, he might have taken to his bed like Lyamshin. But the new thought strengthened him; what's more, he even began waiting impatiently for the time, and set out for the gathering place even earlier than necessary.

It was a very dark place, at the end of the huge Stavrogin park. Afterwards I went there on purpose to have a look; how dismal it must have seemed on that harsh autumn evening! It was the edge of an old forest preserve; in the darkness, huge, century-old pines loomed as dark and dim shapes. It was so dark that it was almost impossible for them to make each other out from two steps away, but Pyotr Stepanovich, Liputin, and then Erkel brought lanterns with them. In time immemorial, no one knew why or when, a rather ridiculous sort of grotto had been built there from wild, unhewn stones. The table and benches inside the grotto had long since rotted and fallen apart. About two hundred paces to the right was the tip of the park's third pond. These three ponds, starting right from the house, followed one another, stretching over half a mile, right to the end of the park. It was hard to suppose that a noise, a cry, or even a shot, could reach the inhabitants of the abandoned Stavrogin house. Since Nikolai Vsevolodovich's departure the day before, and with the absence of Alexei Yegorych, there were no more than five or six inhabitants left in the whole house, of an invalid sort, so to speak. In any case, one could suppose with almost full probability that even if screams and cries for help were to be heard by one of these secluded inhabitants, they would evoke only fear, but not one of them would stir from their warm stoves and warmed-up benches to help.

At twenty minutes past six almost everyone except Erkel, who had been dispatched to bring Shatov, turned out to have gathered. This time Pyotr Stepanovich did not tarry; he arrived with Tolkachenko. Tolkachenko was scowling and preoccupied; all his affected and insolently boastful resolution had vanished. He almost never left Pyotr Stepanovich's side and seemed to have become boundlessly devoted to him; he kept coming at him, frequently and fussily, with his whisperings; but the latter scarcely replied, or vexedly muttered something to get rid of him.

Shigalyov and Virginsky arrived even somewhat earlier than Pyotr Stepanovich, and at his arrival immediately drew somewhat apart in profound and obviously deliberate silence. Pyotr Stepanovich raised his lantern and looked them over with unceremonious and insulting attentiveness. "They want to talk," flashed in his head.

"No Lyamshin?" he asked Virginsky. "Who said he was sick?"

"I'm here," Lyamshin responded, suddenly stepping from behind a tree. He was wearing a warm coat and was tightly wrapped in a plaid, so that it was hard to make out his physiognomy even with a lantern.

"So, just no Liputin?"

And Liputin silently came out of the grotto. Pyotr Stepanovich again raised the lantern.

"Why were you hiding in there, why didn't you come out?"

"I suppose we all retain the right to freedom . . . of our movements," Liputin began to mutter, though probably not quite understanding what he wished to express.

"Gentlemen," Pyotr Stepanovich raised his voice, breaking the half-whisper for the first time, which produced its effect, "you understand very well, I believe, that there's no point in us smearing it around anymore. Everything was said and chewed over yesterday, directly and definitely. But perhaps, as I can see by your physiognomies, someone would like to state something; if so, I ask you to be quick. Devil take it, we don't have much time; Erkel may bring him any moment . . ."

"He's certain to bring him," Tolkachenko put in for some reason.

"If I'm not mistaken, the handing over of the press will take place first?" Liputin inquired, again as if not understanding why he was asking the question.

"Well, of course, there's no point in losing things," Pyotr Stepanovich raised the lantern to his face. "But we did all agree yesterday that we needn't actually take it. Let him just show you the spot where he buried it; we'll dig it up later ourselves. I know it's somewhere ten paces from some corner of the grotto . . . But, devil take it, how could you forget, Liputin? It was agreed that you'd meet him alone, and we'd come out only after that . . . It's strange you're asking, or was it just so?"

Liputin kept gloomily silent. Everyone fell silent. The wind swayed the tops of the pines.

"I trust, however, gentlemen, that everyone will do his duty," Pyotr Stepanovich broke off impatiently.

"I know that Shatov's wife came and gave birth to a child," Virginsky suddenly started to speak, excitedly, hurriedly, barely enunciating the words, and gesticulating. "Knowing the human heart . . . we can be sure that he won't denounce us now . . . because he's in happiness . . . And so I called on everyone earlier and found no one home . . . and so maybe there's no need for anything now . . ."

He stopped: his breath failed him.

"If you, Mr. Virginsky, should suddenly become happy," Pyotr Stepanovich made a step towards him, "would you put off—not a denunciation, no one's talking about that, but some risky civic deed, which you had been planning before your happiness and which you considered your duty and responsibility, in spite of the risk and the loss of your happiness?"

"No, I wouldn't! I wouldn't put it off for anything!" Virginsky said, with some terribly absurd fervor, his body moving all over.

"You'd sooner wish to become unhappy again than be a scoundrel?"

"Yes, yes . . . Even completely the opposite . . . I'd rather be a complete scoundrel . . . no, I mean . . . not a scoundrel at all, but the opposite, completely unhappy, than be a scoundrel."

"Let it be known to you, then, that Shatov regards this denunciation as his civic deed, his highest conviction, and the proof is that he himself is running some risk before the government, though much will certainly be forgiven him for the denunciation. Such a man will never retract. No happiness will prevail; within a day he'll come to his senses, reproach himself, and go and do it. Besides, I don't see any happiness in the fact that his wife has come to him, after three years, to give birth to a Stavrogin child."

"But no one has seen the denunciation," Shigalyov said suddenly and emphatically.

"I have seen the denunciation," cried Pyotr Stepanovich, "it exists, and all this is terribly stupid, gentlemen!"

"And I," Virginsky suddenly boiled up, "I protest . . . I protest with all my strength . . . I want . . . This is what I want: I want, when he gets here, for us all to come out and ask him: if it's true, then make him repent, and if it's word of honor, then let him go. In any case—a trial; with a trial. And not all of us hiding and then falling on him."

"To risk the common cause on a word of honor—is the height of stupidity! Devil take it, gentlemen, now is such a stupid time for this! And what role are you assuming in the moment of danger?"

"I protest, I protest," Virginsky harped.

"Don't shout, at least, or we won't hear the signal. Shatov, gentlemen . . . (Devil take it, now is such a stupid time for this!) I've already told you that Shatov is a Slavophil—that is, one of the stupidest people . . . Ah, the devil, spit on it anyhow, it makes no difference! You just throw me off! . . . Shatov, gentlemen, is an embittered man, but since he still belonged to the society, whether he liked it or not, I hoped till the last minute that he could be of use to the common cause and be employed as an embittered man. I kept him and spared him, in spite of the most precise instructions . . . I spared him a hundred times more than he was worth! But he ended by denouncing us; well, the devil, so spit on it! . . . Only just let anyone try slipping away now! None of you has the right to abandon the cause! You can go and kiss him if you like, but you have no right to betray the common cause on a word of honor! Only swine and people bought by the government act like that!"

"Who here has been bought by the government?" Liputin filtered again.

"You, maybe. Better keep still, Liputin, you're just saying it out of habit. The bought, gentlemen, are all those who turn coward in the moment of danger. Some fool will always come along who gets scared and at the last minute runs and shouts: 'Aie, forgive me, I'll sell everybody!' But know, gentlemen, that at this point you'll no longer be forgiven for any denunciation. Even if they knock off two degrees for you legally, it's still Siberia for each of you, and, besides, there's another sword you won't escape. And that other sword is sharper than the government's."

Pyotr Stepanovich was furious and said too much. Shigalyov firmly stepped three steps towards him.

"I have thought the matter over since yesterday evening," he began, confidently and methodically as always (and I believe that if the earth had given way under him, even then he would not have raised his tone or changed one iota in the methodicalness of his statement), "and having thought it over, I have decided that the intended murder is not only a waste of precious time that could be employed in a more immediate and essential way, but represents, moreover, that pernicious deviation from the normal path which has always done most harm to the cause and has obviated its successes for decades, being subject to the influence of light-minded and predominantly political men instead of pure socialists. I came here solely to protest against the intended undertaking, for general edification, and also—to remove myself from the present moment, which you, I do not know why, call your moment of danger. I am leaving—not from fear of this danger, or from any sentimentality over Shatov, whom I by no means wish to kiss, but solely because this entire affair, from beginning to end, literally contradicts my program. As regards denunciation or being bought by the government, for my part you may be perfectly at ease: there will be no denunciation."

He turned and started walking away.

"Devil take it, he'll meet them and warn Shatov!" Pyotr Stepanovich cried, and he snatched out his revolver. There was the click of the hammer being cocked.

"You may be assured," Shigalyov turned around again, "that if I meet Shatov on my way, I may still greet him, but I will not warn him."

"And do you know that you may have to pay for this, Mr. Fourier?"

"I beg you to note that I am not Fourier. By mixing me up with that sugary, abstract maunderer, you only prove that though my manuscript has been in your hands, it is completely unknown to you. And as regards your revenge, I will tell you that you should not have cocked the hammer; at the moment it is absolutely unprofitable for you. And if you are threatening me for tomorrow or the day after tomorrow, then once again, except for some extra trouble, you won't gain anything for yourself by shooting me: you will kill me, but sooner or later you will still arrive at my system. Good-bye."

At that moment there came a whistle from about two hundred paces away, from the park, in the direction of the pond. Liputin, still following yesterday's plan, responded at once by whistling back (for which purpose, not trusting in his rather toothless mouth, he had bought a child's clay whistle for a kopeck in the market that morning). Erkel had had time on the way to caution Shatov that there would be whistling, so that he would not conceive any suspicions.

"Don't worry, I'll go around them, they won't notice me at all," Shigalyov cautioned in an imposing whisper, and then, without hurrying or quickening his pace, he finally set off through the dark park for home.

How this terrible event took place is now fully known in the smallest detail. First, Liputin met Erkel and Shatov just at the grotto; Shatov did not greet him or offer his hand, but at once said hastily and loudly:

"Well, so where's your spade, and haven't you got another lantern? Don't be afraid, there's absolutely no one here; you could fire off cannons now, they wouldn't hear a thing in Skvoreshniki. It's here, this is the place, this very spot . . ."

And he stamped his foot, ten paces indeed from the far corner of the grotto, in the direction of the forest. At that same moment Tolka-chenko rushed at his back from behind a tree, and Erkel seized him by the elbows, also from the back. Liputin threw himself at him from the front. The three of them knocked him down at once and pinned him to the ground. Here Pyotr Stepanovich sprang over with his revolver. It is said that Shatov had time to turn his head towards him and was still able to make him out and recognize him. Three lanterns lighted the scene. Shatov suddenly cried out a brief and desperate cry; but he was not to cry out again: Pyotr Stepanovich accurately and firmly put the revolver right to his forehead, hard point-blank, and—pulled the trigger. The shot, I suppose, was not very loud; at least nothing was heard at Skvoreshniki. Shigalyov, who had scarcely gone three hundred steps, heard it, of course—heard both the cry and the shot, but, as he himself later testified, did not turn or even stop. Death occurred almost instantly. Full efficiency—though not, I think, cold-bloodedness—was preserved only by Pyotr Stepanovich. Squatting down, he searched the murdered man's pockets hastily but with a firm hand. There was no money (the purse had remained under Marya Ignatievna's pillow). Two or three worthless scraps of paper were found: an office note, some book title, and an old foreign tavern bill which, God knows why, had survived in his pocket for two years.

Pyotr Stepanovich transferred the scraps of paper to his own pocket and, suddenly noticing that everyone was clustered around looking at the corpse and not doing anything, he began angrily and impolitely cursing and hustling them. Tolkachenko and Erkel, coming to their senses, ran to the grotto and instantly brought two stones put there in the morning, each weighing about twenty pounds, and already pre-pared—that is, with ropes tied tightly and securely around them. Since the intention was to carry the corpse to the nearest (the third) pond and sink it there, they began tying these stones to it, at the feet and neck. The tying was done by Pyotr Stepanovich, while Tolkachenko and Erkel merely stood holding the stones and handed them over in turn. Erkel handed over the first stone, and while Pyotr Stepanovich, grumbling and cursing, was tying the legs of the corpse together and tying this first stone to them, Tolkachenko, during all this rather long time, went on holding his stone out at arm's length, his whole body bent sharply and as if reverently forward, so as to hand it over without delay at the first asking, and never once thought of lowering his burden to the ground in the meantime. When both stones were finally tied on and Pyotr Stepanovich got up from the ground to examine the physi-ognomies of those present, a strange thing suddenly happened, which was totally unexpected and surprised almost everyone.

As has already been said, almost everyone was standing and not doing anything, with the partial exception of Tolkachenko and Erkel. Virginsky, though he had rushed to Shatov along with everyone else, had not seized him or helped to hold him. And Lyamshin got into the bunch only after the shot. Then, during the perhaps ten-minute-long pottering with the corpse, they all as if lost part of their consciousness. They grouped themselves around and, before any worry or alarm, felt as if only surprise. Liputin stood in front, just by the corpse. Virginsky was behind him, peeping over his shoulder with some particular and as if unrelated curiosity, even standing on tiptoe in order to see better. And Lyamshin hid behind Virginsky, only peeping out warily from behind him every now and then, and hiding again at once. But when the stones were tied on and Pyotr Stepanovich stood up, Virginsky suddenly started quivering all over, clasped his hands, and cried rue-fully at the top of his voice:

"This is not it, this is not it! No, this is not it at all!"

He might have added something more to his so belated exclamation, but Lyamshin did not let him finish: suddenly, and with all his might, he clasped him and squeezed him from behind and let out some sort of incredible shriek. There are strong moments of fear, for instance, when a man will suddenly cry out in a voice not his own, but such as one could not even have supposed him to have before then, and the effect is sometimes even quite frightful. Lyamshin cried not with a human but with some sort of animal voice. Squeezing Virginsky from behind harder and harder with his arms, in a convulsive fit, he went on shrieking without stop or pause, his eyes goggling at them all, and his mouth opened exceedingly wide, while his feet rapidly stamped the ground as if beating out a drum roll on it. Virginsky got so scared that he cried out like a madman himself and tried to tear free of Lyamshin's grip in some sort of frenzy, so viciously that one even could not have expected it of Virginsky, scratching and punching him as well he was able to reach behind him with his arms. Erkel finally helped him to tear Lyamshin off. But when, in fear, Virginsky sprang about ten steps away, Lyamshin, seeing Pyotr Stepanovich, suddenly screamed again and rushed at him. Stumbling over the corpse, he fell across it onto Pyotr Stepanovich and now clenched him so tightly in his embrace, pressing his head against his chest, that for the first moment Pyotr Stepanovich, Tolkachenko, and Liputin were almost unable to do anything. Pyotr Stepanovich yelled, swore, beat him on the head with his fists; finally, having somehow torn himself free, he snatched out the revolver and pointed it straight into the open mouth of the still scream-ing Lyamshin, whom Tolkachenko, Erkel, and Liputin had already seized firmly by the arms; but Lyamshin went on shrieking even in spite of the revolver. Finally, Erkel somehow bunched up his foulard and stuffed it deftly into his mouth, and thus the shouting ceased. Meanwhile, Tolkachenko tied his hands with a leftover end of rope.

"This is very strange," Pyotr Stepanovich said, studying the mad-man in alarmed astonishment.

He was visibly struck.

"I had quite a different idea of him," he added pensively.

For the time being, Erkel was left with him. They had to hurry with the dead man: there had been so much shouting that it might have been heard somewhere. Tolkachenko and Pyotr Stepanovich raised their

lanterns and picked up the corpse at the head; Liputin and Virginsky
took hold of the feet and lifted. With the two stones, it was a heavy
burden, and the distance was more than two hundred steps. Tolkachenko was the strongest of them. He tried to suggest that they walk
in step, but no one responded to him, and they went on haphazardly.
Pyotr Stepanovich walked on the right and, bent completely double,
carried the dead man's head on his shoulder, supporting the stone from
underneath with his left hand. Since Tolkachenko, for a good half of
the way, never thought of helping to carry the stone, Pyotr Stepanovich finally shouted a curse at him. It was a sudden, solitary shout; they
all went on silently carrying, and only at the very edge of the pond
did Virginsky, bending under the burden and as if weary from its
weight, suddenly exclaim again in the same loud, tearful voice:

"This is not it, no, no, this is not it at all!"

Where this third, quite large Skvoreshniki pond ended, and where
they had brought the murdered man, was one of the most deserted and
unfrequented places in the park, especially at such a late time of year.
This end of the pond, near the bank, was overgrown with reeds. They
set the lantern down, swung the corpse, and threw it into the water.
There was a dull and long sound. Pyotr Stepanovich raised the lantern;
after him they all stuck their heads out, peering curiously at how the
dead man was sinking; but by then nothing could be seen: the body
with the two stones went under at once. The big ripples that spread
over the surface of the water were quickly dying away. The matter was
ended.

"Gentlemen," Pyotr Stepanovich addressed them all, "we will now
disperse. You undoubtedly must feel that free pride which is attendant
upon the fulfillment of a free duty. And if, unhappily, you are now too
alarmed for such emotions, you will undoubtedly feel it tomorrow, by
which time it would be shameful not to feel it. As for Lyamshin's all
too shameful agitation, I agree to regard it as delirium, all the more so
in that they say he really has been sick since morning. And you,
Virginsky, one moment of free reflection will show you that, in view
of the interests of the common cause, it was not possible to act upon
a word of honor, but precisely as we have done. The consequences will
show that there had been a denunciation. I agree to forget your exclamations. As for danger, there is none to be expected. No one will even

think of suspecting any of us, especially if you yourselves know how to behave; so the main thing still depends on you yourselves and on your full conviction, which I hope will grow firm in you by tomorrow. And that, incidentally, is precisely why you united together into a separate organization of the free assembly of the like-minded, so as in the common cause to share your energy among yourselves at a given moment and, if need be, to watch over and observe each other. Each of you owes a higher accounting. You are called to renew the cause, which is decrepit and stinking from stagnation; keep that always before your eyes for encouragement. In the meantime your whole step is towards getting everything destroyed: both the state and its morality. We alone will remain, having destined ourselves beforehand to assume power: we shall rally the smart ones to ourselves, and ride on the backs of the fools. You should not be embarrassed by it. This generation must be re-educated to make it worthy of freedom. There are still many thousands of Shatovs ahead of us. We will get organized so as to seize the tendency; it is shameful not to reach out and take what is lying there idly with its mouth gaping at us. I'm now going to Kirillov, and by morning there will be a document in which he, on dying, by way of an explanation to the government, will take everything upon himself. Nothing could be more plausible than such a combination. First of all, there was enmity between him and Shatov; they lived together in America, so they had time to quarrel. It is known that Shatov changed his convictions; the enmity, then, was because of convictions and the fear of denunciation—that is, the most unforgiving kind. All this will be written down just that way. Finally, it will be mentioned that Fedka lodged with him, in Filippov's house. Thus, all this will completely remove all suspicion from you, because it will throw all those muttonheads off. Tomorrow, gentlemen, we will not see each other; I'll be away in the district capital for a very short time. But the day after tomorrow you'll have reports from me. I would advise you, in fact, to spend tomorrow at home. We will now set out by twos on different routes. You, Tolkachenko, I ask to occupy yourself with Lyamshin and take him home. You may influence him and, above all, impress upon him the extent to which he will be harming himself first of all by his faintheartedness. Your relative Shigalyov, Mr. Virginsky, I do not wish to doubt, any more than I do you yourself: he will not denounce us. His action remains regrettable; but, all the same, he has not yet announced that he is leaving the society, so it is too early to bury him. Well—quick now, gentlemen; they may be muttonheads, but there's no harm in being prudent . . ."

Virginsky went with Erkel. In handing Lyamshin over to Tolka-chenko, Erkel had managed to bring him to Pyotr Stepanovich and announce that he had come to his senses, repented, and begged forgive-ness, and did not even remember what had happened to him. Pyotr Stepanovich went off alone, choosing a way around the other side of the ponds, skirting the park. This was the longest route. To his sur-prise, Liputin overtook him almost midway.

"Pyotr Stepanovich, you know, Lyamshin's sure to denounce us!"

"No, he'll come to his senses and realize that if he denounces us, he'll be the first to go to Siberia. Nobody will denounce us now. You won't either."

"And you?"

"No question, I'll have you all tucked away the minute you make a move to betray, and you know it. But you won't betray anything. Is that why you ran more than a mile after me?"

"Pyotr Stepanovich, Pyotr Stepanovich, you know, we may never see each other again!"

"What gives you that idea?"

"Tell me just one thing."

"Well, what? I wish you'd clear off, though."

"One answer, but the right one: are we the only fivesome in the world, or is it true that there are several hundred fivesomes? I'm asking in a lofty sense, Pyotr Stepanovich."

"I can see that by your frenzy. And do you know that you are more dangerous than Lyamshin, Liputin?"

"I know, I know, but—the answer, your answer!"

"What a foolish man you are! One would think it should make no difference now—one fivesome, or a thousand."

"So it's one! I just knew it!" Liputin cried out. "I knew all along it was one, right up to this very moment . . ."

And without waiting for any other reply, he turned and quickly vanished into the darkness.

Pyotr Stepanovich pondered a little.

"No, no one will denounce us," he said resolutely, "but—the crew must remain a crew and obey, otherwise I'll . . . What trash these people are, though!"

II

HE FIRST STOPPED at his place and neatly, unhurriedly, packed his suitcase. The express train was leaving at six o'clock in the morning. This early express train came only once a week and had been scheduled very recently, just as a trial for the time being. Though Pyotr Stepanovich had warned *our* people that he was supposedly going to the district capital, his intentions, as it turned out later, were quite different. After finishing with the suitcase, he settled accounts with the landlady, whom he had notified ahead of time, and moved in a hired carriage to Erkel's place, which was near the station. And only after that, at approximately one o'clock in the morning, did he go to Kirillov's, where he again penetrated through Fedka's secret passage.

The state of Pyotr Stepanovich's mind was terrible. Apart from other discontents quite important for him (he was still unable to find out anything about Stavrogin), he had, it seems—for I cannot confirm it with certainty—received during the course of the day, from somewhere (most likely Petersburg), secret notification of a certain danger awaiting him in the near future. Of course, there are now a great many legends going around town about that time; but even if something is known with certainty, it is known only to those who ought to know of it. And I simply suppose, in my own opinion, that Pyotr Stepanovich might have had doings elsewhere than in our town, so that he might indeed have received notifications. I am even convinced, contrary to Liputin's cynical and desperate doubt, that he could indeed have had two or three fivesomes besides ours, in the capitals, for instance; or, if not fivesomes, then connections and relations—perhaps even very curious ones. No more than three days after his departure, an order from the capital was received in our town for his immediate arrest—for what actual doings, ours or some others, I do not know. The order arrived just in time to increase the staggering, almost mystical sense of fear that took possession of our authorities and our hitherto stubbornly frivolous society on the discovery of the mysterious and highly portentous murder of the student Shatov—a murder that filled the measure of our absurdities—and of the extremely enigmatic circumstances that accompanied this event. But the order came too late: Pyotr Stepanovich was already in Petersburg by then, under an assumed name, and from there, having sniffed out what was going on, he instantly slipped abroad . . . But I am getting terribly far ahead of myself.

He entered Kirillov's room with a spiteful and provocative look. As if he wished, along with the main business, also to work off something personal on Kirillov, to vent something on him. Kirillov seemed glad he had come; it was obvious that he had been waiting for him terribly long, and with morbid impatience. His face was paler than usual, the expression of his black eyes heavy and fixed.

"I thought you wouldn't come," he said heavily from the corner of the sofa, though not stirring to greet him. Pyotr Stepanovich stood in front of him and, before saying a word, peered closely into his face.

"So everything's in order, and we're not going back on our intention. Good boy!" he smiled an offensively patronizing smile. "Well, so what," he added with vile jocularity, "if I'm late, it's not for you to complain: you got a gift of three hours."

"I don't want any extra hours from you, and you can't give me gifts—fool!"

"What?" Pyotr Stepanovich jumped, but instantly controlled himself. "How touchy! We're in a rage, eh?" he rapped out with the same air of offensive superciliousness. "At such a moment one rather needs to be calm. Best of all is to regard yourself as Columbus and look at me as a mouse and not be offended at me. I recommended that yesterday."

"I don't want to look at you as a mouse."

"What's that, a compliment? Anyhow, the tea is cold, too—so everything's upside down. No, something untrustworthy is going on here. Hah! What's this I see on the windowsill, on a plate" (he went over to the window). "Oho, a boiled chicken with rice! . . . But why hasn't it been touched yet? So we were in such a state of mind that even a chicken . . ."

"I ate, and it's none of your business; keep still!"

"Oh, certainly, and besides it makes no difference. But it does make a difference to me: imagine, I had hardly any dinner at all, so if this chicken is now, as I suppose, no longer needed . . . eh?"

"Eat, if you can."

"Much obliged, and tea to follow."

He instantly settled down to the table at the other end of the sofa and with extraordinary greediness fell upon the food; but at the same time he observed his victim every moment. Kirillov, with spiteful loathing, looked fixedly at him, as if unable to tear himself away.

"However," Pyotr Stepanovich suddenly heaved himself up, continuing to eat, "however, about this business? We're not going to back out, eh? And the little note?"

"I determined tonight that it makes no difference to me. I'll write it. About the tracts?"

"Yes, also about the tracts. Anyhow, I'll dictate it. It really makes no difference to you. Can you possibly worry about the contents at such a moment?"

"None of your business."

"Of course not. Anyhow, just a few lines: that you and Shatov distributed the tracts—with the help of Fedka, incidentally, who was hiding out in your apartment. This last point about Fedka and the apartment is quite important, even the most important. You see, I'm being completely frank with you."

"And Shatov? Why Shatov? Not Shatov, not for anything."

"Come on, what is it to you? You can't harm him now."

"His wife came to him. She woke up and sent to ask me where he is."

"She sent to find out where he is from you? Hm, that's not good. She might send again; no one must know I'm here . . ."

Pyotr Stepanovich became worried.

"She won't find out, she's asleep again; the midwife is with her, Arina Virginsky."

"That's just . . . and she won't hear, I suppose? You know, why don't we lock the front door?"

"She won't hear anything. And if Shatov comes, I'll hide you in that room."

"Shatov won't come; and you are going to write that you quarreled over his betrayal and denunciation . . . this night . . . and the cause of his death."

"He died!" Kirillov cried out, jumping up from the sofa.

"Today, between seven and eight in the evening, or, rather, yesterday between seven and eight in the evening, since it's now past midnight."

"You killed him! . . . And I foresaw it yesterday!"

"How could you not foresee it! With this revolver" (he pulled out the revolver, ostensibly to show it, after which he did not put it away again, but went on holding it in his right hand, as if in readiness). "You, however, are a strange man, Kirillov, you yourself knew it would have to end this way with that foolish man. What else was there to foresee? I chewed it all over for you several times. Shatov was preparing a denunciation: I was watching him; there was no way to let it go at that. And you, too, had instructions to watch him; you told me so yourself three weeks ago . . ."

"Keep still! You did it because he spat in your face in Geneva!"

"For that, and for other things. For many other things; though without any malice. Why jump up like that? What's this posturing? Oho! So that's how we are! . . ."

He jumped up and raised the revolver in front of him. The thing was that Kirillov had suddenly snatched his revolver from the windowsill, loaded and ready since morning. Pyotr Stepanovich positioned himself and aimed his weapon at Kirillov. The latter laughed spitefully.

"Confess, scoundrel, that you took out the revolver because I'm going to shoot you . . . But I'm not going to shoot you . . . although . . . although . . ."

And again he aimed his revolver at Pyotr Stepanovich as if trying it out, as if unable to deny himself the pleasure of imagining how it would be to shoot him. Pyotr Stepanovich, still positioned, was biding, biding his time until the last moment without pulling the trigger, running the risk of getting a bullet in his own head first: one might well expect it from a "maniac." But the "maniac" finally lowered his arm, gasping and trembling, unable to speak.

"We've had our play and that's enough," Pyotr Stepanovich also lowered his weapon. "I just knew you were playing; only, you know, you were taking a risk: I might have pulled the trigger."

And he sat down rather calmly on the sofa and poured himself some tea, though with a slightly trembling hand. Kirillov put his revolver on the table and started pacing back and forth.

"I won't write that I killed Shatov and . . . I won't write anything now. There won't be any document!"

"There won't?"

"There won't."

"What meanness and what foolishness!" Pyotr Stepanovich turned green with anger. "I anticipated it, though. Let me tell you that you haven't caught me unawares. However, as you wish. If I could force you, I would. You are a scoundrel, though," Pyotr Stepanovich became more and more unable to stand it. "You asked us for money that time and made a whole cartload of promises . . . Only I still won't leave without the result, I'll still see at least how you blow your head off."

"I want you to leave here now," Kirillov stopped firmly in front of him.

"No, sir, that I won't," Pyotr Stepanovich grabbed his revolver again. "You might decide now, from spite and cowardice, to put it all off and go and denounce us tomorrow, to procure a bit of cash again—they do pay for such things. Devil take you, paltry people like you are ripe for anything! Only don't worry, I foresaw it all: I won't leave before I've blown your brains out with this revolver, like that scoundrel Shatov's, if you turn coward and put off your intention, devil take you!"

"You absolutely want to see my blood, too?"

"It's not out of malice, you understand; it makes no difference to me. It's so as not to worry about our cause. One can't rely on people, you see that yourself. I don't understand a thing about your fantasy of killing yourself. I didn't think it up for you, you did yourself even before me, and you originally announced it not to me but to the members abroad. And, notice, none of them tried to elicit anything, none of them even knew you at all, but you yourself came with your confidences, out of sentimentality. So what's to be done if, right then, on that basis, with your own consent and offer (make note of that: your offer!), a certain plan for local actions was made, which it is now quite impossible to change. You put yourself in such a position that you now know too much. If you turn tail and go tomorrow with a denunciation, that might prove rather unprofitable for us, don't you think? No, sir, you committed yourself, you gave your word, you took the money. There's no way you can deny that . . ."

Pyotr Stepanovich was greatly excited, but Kirillov had long since stopped listening. He was again thoughtfully pacing the room.

"I'm sorry for Shatov," he said, stopping in front of Pyotr Stepanovich again.

"Yes, well, maybe I'm sorry, too, but can it be . . ."

"Quiet, scoundrel!" Kirillov bellowed, making a terrible and unambiguous movement, "I'll kill you!"

"Well, well, well, so I lied, I agree, I'm not sorry at all; well, enough, enough now!" Pyotr Stepanovich jumped up apprehensively, holding out his hand.

Kirillov suddenly subsided and began pacing again.

"I won't put it off; I want to kill myself precisely now: men are all scoundrels!"

"Well, that's the idea; of course, men are all scoundrels, and since it's loathsome for a decent man to be in the world . . ."

"Fool, I am a scoundrel the same as you, as all of them, not a decent man. There has not been a decent man anywhere."

"He's finally figured it out. Can it be, Kirillov, that you, with your intelligence, have only now understood that everyone's the same, that no one's better or worse, but just smarter or stupider, and that if men are all scoundrels (which is nonsense, however), then it follows that there even oughtn't to be any non-scoundrels?"

"Ah! So you're really not laughing?" Kirillov looked at him with some surprise. "You're excited and simply . . . Can it be that your kind have convictions?"

"Kirillov, I never could understand why you want to kill yourself. I know only that it's from conviction . . . firm conviction. But if you feel a need, so to speak, to pour yourself out, I'm at your service . . . Only we must consider the time . . ."

"What time is it?"

"Oho, the stroke of two," Pyotr Stepanovich looked at his watch and lit a cigarette.

"It seems we can still come to terms," he thought to himself.

"I have nothing to tell you," Kirillov muttered.

"I remember there was something about God . . . you did explain it to me once—twice, even. If you shoot yourself, you'll become God, is that right?"

"Yes, I will become God."

Pyotr Stepanovich did not even smile; he was waiting; Kirillov gave him a subtle look.

"You are a political crook and intriguer, you want to bring me down to philosophy and ecstasy and produce a reconciliation, to disperse wrath, and, once I'm reconciled, to extort a note that I killed Shatov."

Pyotr Stepanovich answered with an almost natural simpleheartedness:

"Well, suppose I am such a scoundrel, only in these last minutes what difference does it make, Kirillov? Why are we quarreling, tell me, please: you're this sort of man, I'm that sort of man—what of it? And besides, we're both . . ."

"Scoundrels."

"Yes, scoundrels, maybe. You know these are only words."

"All my life I did not want it to be only words. This is why I lived, because I kept not wanting it. And now, too, every day I want it not to be words."

"Well, each of us seeks a better place. A bug in a rug . . . I mean, each of us seeks comfort of some sort; that's all. It's been known for an extremely long time."

"Comfort, you say?"

"Well, we're not going to quarrel over words."

"No, you said it well; let it be comfort. God is necessary, and therefore must exist."

"Well, that's wonderful."

"But I know that he does not and cannot exist."

"That's more like it."

"Don't you understand that a man with these two thoughts cannot go on living?"

"Must shoot himself, you mean?"

"Don't you understand that a man can shoot himself for that alone? You don't understand that there may be such a man, one man out of the thousands of your millions, one, who will not want it and will not endure it."

"I understand only that you seem to be hesitating . . . That's very bad."

"Stavrogin was also eaten by an idea." Kirillov, sullenly pacing the room, did not mark his remark.

"What?" Pyotr Stepanovich pricked up his ears. "What idea? Did he tell you something himself?"

"No, I myself guessed it: if Stavrogin believes, he does not believe that he believes. And if he does not believe, he does not believe that he does not believe."

"Well, Stavrogin also has other things more intelligent than that . . ." Pyotr Stepanovich muttered peevishly, watching with alarm the turn of the conversation and the pale Kirillov.

"Devil take it, he won't shoot himself," he thought. "I always suspected it; it's a kink in his brain and nothing more. What trash!"

"You're the last to be with me; I wouldn't like to part badly with you," Kirillov suddenly bestowed.

Pyotr Stepanovich did not answer at once. "Devil take it, what's this now?" he thought again.

"Believe me, Kirillov, I have nothing against you personally as a man, and I've always . . ."

"You are a scoundrel and a false mind. But I am the same as you are, and I will shoot myself, while you remain alive."

"That is, you mean to say I'm so base as to want to remain alive."

He still could not tell whether it was profitable or unprofitable for him to continue such a conversation at such a moment, and decided to "give himself up to circumstances." But Kirillov's tone of superiority and ever undisguised contempt for him had always annoyed him before, and now for some reason even more than before. Perhaps because Kirillov, who was going to die in an hour or so (Pyotr Stepanovich still kept that in mind), appeared to him as something like a half-man, something of such kind as could no longer be allowed any haughtiness.

"You seem to be boasting to me about shooting yourself?"

"I've always been surprised that everyone remains alive." Kirillov did not hear his remark.

"Hm, that's an idea, I suppose, but . . ."

"Ape! You yes me to win me over. Keep still, you won't understand anything. If there is no God, then I am God."

"Now, there's the one point of yours that I could never understand: why are you God then?"

"If there is God, then the will is all his, and I cannot get out of his will. If not, the will is all mine, and it is my duty to proclaim self-will."

"Self-will? And why is it your duty?"

"Because the will has all become mine. Can it be that no one on the whole planet, having ended God and believed in self-will, dares to proclaim self-will to the fullest point? It's as if a poor man received an inheritance, got scared, and doesn't dare go near the bag, thinking he's too weak to own it. I want to proclaim self-will. I may be the only one, but I'll do it."

"Do it, then."

"It is my duty to shoot myself because the fullest point of my self-will is—for me to kill myself."

"But you're not the only one to kill yourself; there are lots of suicides."

"For reasons. But without any reason, simply for self-will—only I."

"He won't shoot himself," flashed again in Pyotr Stepanovich.

"You know what," he observed irritably, "in your place, if I wanted to show self-will, I'd kill somebody else and not myself. You could become useful. I'll point out whom, if you're not afraid. Then maybe there's no need to shoot yourself today. We could come to terms."

"To kill someone else would be the lowest point of my self-will, and there's the whole of you in that. I am not you: I want the highest point, and will kill myself."

"Reasoned it all out for himself," Pyotr Stepanovich growled spitefully.

"It is my duty to proclaim unbelief," Kirillov was pacing the room. "For me no idea is higher than that there is no God. The history of mankind is on my side. Man has done nothing but invent God, so as to live without killing himself; in that lies the whole of world history up to now. I alone for the first time in world history did not want to invent God. Let them know once and for all."

"He won't shoot himself," Pyotr Stepanovich worried.

"Who is there to know?" he kept prodding. "There is you and me, and who—Liputin?"

"Everyone is to know; everyone will know. There is nothing hid that shall not be revealed.[1] *He* said that."

And he pointed with feverish rapture to the icon of the Savior, before which an icon lamp was burning. Pyotr Stepanovich got thoroughly angry.

"So you still believe in *Him,* and keep the little lamp lit; what is it, 'just in case' or something?"

The other was silent.

"You know what, I think you believe maybe even more than any priest."

"In whom? In *Him*? Listen," Kirillov stopped, gazing before him with fixed, ecstatic eyes. "Listen to a big idea: There was one day on earth, and in the middle of the earth stood three crosses. One on a cross believed so much that he said to another: 'This day you will be with me in paradise.'[2] The day ended, they both died, went, and did not find either paradise or resurrection. What had been said would not prove true. Listen: this man was the highest on all the earth, he constituted what it was to live for. Without this man the whole planet with everything on it is—madness only. There has not been one like *Him* before or since, not ever, even to the point of miracle. This is the miracle, that there has not been and never will be such a one. And if so, if the laws of nature did not pity even *This One,* did not pity even their own miracle, but made *Him,* too, live amidst a lie and die for a lie, then the whole planet is a lie, and stands upon a lie and a stupid mockery. Then the very laws of the planet are a lie and a devil's vaudeville. Why live then, answer me, if you're a man."

"That's another turn of affairs. It seems to me you have two different causes mixed up here; and that is highly untrustworthy. But, excuse me, what if you are God? If the lie ended and you realized that the whole lie was because there had been this former God?"

"You've finally understood!" Kirillov cried out rapturously. "So it can be understood, if even someone like you understands! You understand now that the whole salvation for everyone is to prove this thought to them all. Who will prove it? I! I don't understand how, up to now, an atheist could know there is no God and not kill himself at once. To recognize that there is no God, and not to recognize at the same time that you have become God, is an absurdity, otherwise you must necessarily kill yourself. Once you recognize it, you are king, and you will not kill yourself but will live in the chiefest glory. But one, the one who is first, must necessarily kill himself, otherwise who will begin and prove it? It is I who will necessarily kill myself in order to begin and prove it. I am still God against my will, and I am unhappy, because it is my *duty* to proclaim self-will. Everyone is unhappy, because everyone is afraid to proclaim self-will. That is why man has been so unhappy and poor up to now, because he was afraid to proclaim the chief point of self-will and was self-willed only on the margins, like a schoolboy. I am terribly unhappy, because I am terribly afraid. Fear is man's curse . . . But I will proclaim self-will, it is my duty to believe that I do not believe. I will begin, and end, and open the door. And save. Only this one thing will save all men and in the next generation transform them physically; for in the present physical aspect, so far as I have thought, it is in no way possible for man to be without the former God. For three years I have been searching for the attribute of my divinity, and I have found it: the attribute of my divinity is—Self-will! That is all, by which I can show in the main point my insubordination and my new fearsome freedom. For it is very fearsome. I kill myself to show my insubordination and my new fearsome freedom."

His face was unnaturally pale, his look unbearably heavy. He was as if delirious. Pyotr Stepanovich thought he was going to collapse right there.

"Give me the pen!" Kirillov suddenly cried quite unexpectedly, in decided inspiration. "Dictate, I'll sign everything. I'll sign that I killed Shatov, too. Dictate while I'm laughing. I'm not afraid of the thoughts of arrogant slaves! You'll see yourself that all that is hid shall be revealed! And you will be crushed . . . I believe! I believe!"

Pyotr Stepanovich snatched himself from his place and instantly gave him an inkstand, paper, and began to dictate, seizing the moment and trembling for his success.

" 'I, Alexei Kirillov, declare . . .' "

"Wait! I don't want to! Declare to whom?"

Kirillov was shaking as if in a fever. This declaration and some sudden, special thought about it seemed to have absorbed him entirely all at once, as if it were some outlet where, if only for a moment, his tormented spirit rushed precipitously:

"Declare to whom? I want to know whom!"

"To nobody, to everybody, to the first one who reads it. Why specify? To the whole world!"

"To the whole world? Bravo! And so there's no need for repentance. I don't want repentance; and not to any authorities!"

"No, no need, devil take the authorities! but write, if you're serious! . . ." Pyotr Stepanovich yelled hysterically.

"Wait! I want a face at the top with its tongue sticking out."

"Ehh, nonsense!" Pyotr Stepanovich got furious. "All that can be expressed without any drawing, just by the tone."

"The tone? That's good. Yes, by the tone, the tone! Dictate with the tone."

" 'I, Alexei Kirillov,' " Pyotr Stepanovich dictated firmly and imperiously, leaning over Kirillov's shoulder and following every letter as he traced it with a hand trembling from excitement, " 'I, Kirillov, declare that today, the –th of October, in the evening, between seven and eight, I killed the student Shatov, for betrayal, in the park, and for his denunciation about the tracts and about Fedka, who secretly lodged with the two of us in Filippov's house, and spent ten days' nights there. And I kill myself today with my revolver not because I repent and am afraid of you, but because abroad I had the intention of ending my life.' "

"Only that?" Kirillov exclaimed with astonishment and indignation.

"Not a word more!" Pyotr Stepanovich waved his hand, trying to snatch the document from him.

"Wait!" Kirillov placed his hand firmly on the paper. "Wait, that's nonsense! I want who I killed him with. Why Fedka? And the fire? I want everything, and also more abuse, in the tone, in the tone!"

"Enough, Kirillov, I assure you it's enough!" Pyotr Stepanovich almost implored, trembling lest he tear the paper up. "So that they'll believe you, you must be as obscure as possible, precisely like that, with just hints. You must show only a little corner of the truth, exactly enough to get them excited. They'll always heap up more lies for themselves, and will certainly believe themselves better than us, and that's the best thing, the best of all! Give it to me; it's splendid as it is; give it to me, give it to me!"

And he kept trying to snatch the paper away. Kirillov, his eyes popping out, listened as if trying to make sense of it, but it seemed he was ceasing to understand.

"Eh, the devil!" Pyotr Stepanovich suddenly got furious, "but he hasn't even signed it yet! Why are you popping your eyes out— sign it!"

"I want more abuse . . ." Kirillov muttered, though he did take the pen and sign. "I want more abuse . . ."

"Sign: *Vive la république,* and enough."

"Bravo!" Kirillov almost bellowed with rapture. *"Vive la république démocratique, sociale et universelle ou la mort!* . . . No, no, not that! *Liberté, égalité, fraternité ou la mort!** There, that's better, that's better," he wrote it delightedly under his signature.

"Enough, enough," Pyotr Stepanovich kept repeating.

"Wait, a little bit more . . . You know, I'll sign it again in French: *'de Kirilloff, gentilhomme russe et citoyen du monde.'*† Ha, ha, ha!"[3] he dissolved in laughter. "No, no, no, wait, I've got the best one, eureka: *gentilhomme-séminariste russe et citoyen du monde civilisé!*‡—that's better than any . . ." he jumped up from the sofa and suddenly, with a quick gesture, snatched the revolver from the windowsill, ran into the other room with it, and closed the door tightly behind him. Pyotr Stepanovich stood for a moment pondering, looking at the door.

"If it's right now, maybe he'll really shoot, but if he starts thinking— nothing will happen."

Meanwhile, he took the paper, sat down, and looked it over once more. He was pleased, again, with the wording of the declaration.

"What's needed meanwhile? What's needed is to throw them off completely for a time, and so distract them. The park? There's no park

---

*"Long live the democratic, social, and universal republic, or death! . . . Liberty, equality, fraternity, or death!"
†"de Kirillov, Russian gentleman and citizen of the world."
‡"Russian gentleman-seminarian and citizen of the civilized world!"

in town, so they'll figure out for themselves that it's Skvoreshniki. While they're figuring it out, time will pass; while they search—more time; and once they find the corpse—it means what's written here is true, and so it's also true about Fedka. And what is Fedka? Fedka is the fire, he's the Lebyadkins; so everything was coming from here, from Filippov's house, and they didn't see a thing, they overlooked it all—now, that will put them into a real whirl! It won't even enter their minds about *our* people; it's Shatov, and Kirillov, and Fedka, and Lebyadkin; as for why they killed each other—there's another little question for them. Eh, the devil, no sound of a shot yet! . . ."

Though he was reading and admiring the wording, he still kept listening every moment with tormenting alarm and—suddenly got furious. He glanced worriedly at his watch; it was a bit late; and it was a good ten minutes since the man had gone out . . . Grabbing the candle, he made for the door of the room where Kirillov had shut himself up. Just at the door it occurred to him that the candle was also burning down and in another twenty minutes would go out entirely, and there was no other. He put his hand on the latch and listened cautiously; not the slightest sound could be heard; he suddenly opened the door and raised the candle: something bellowed and rushed at him. He slammed the door with all his might and leaned on it again, but everything was already quiet—again dead silence.

For a long time he stood indecisively, candle in hand. In that second as he had opened the door, he had been able to make out very little, and yet there had been a flash of the face of Kirillov standing at the back of the room by the window, and of the beastly rage with which the man had suddenly flown at him. Pyotr Stepanovich gave a start, quickly placed the candle on the table, readied his revolver, and sprang on tiptoe to the opposite corner, so that if Kirillov were to open the door and rush at the table with his revolver, he would still have time to aim and pull the trigger ahead of him.

Pyotr Stepanovich had now lost all belief in the suicide! "He was standing in the middle of the room and thinking," went like a whirlwind through Pyotr Stepanovich's mind. "A dark, horrible room, besides . . . He bellowed and rushed—two possibilities here: either I hindered him the very second he was pulling the trigger, or . . . or he was standing and thinking about how to kill me. Yes, right, he was thinking about it . . . He knows I won't leave without killing him, if he turns coward himself—so he must kill me first, to keep me from killing him . . . And again, again the silence in there! It's even frightening: he may suddenly open the door . . . The swinishness is that he believes in God worse than any priest . . . He won't shoot himself for anything! . . . These ones that 'reason it out for themselves' have been multiplying lately! Scum! Pah, devil take it, the candle, the candle! It'll certainly burn out in a quarter of an hour . . . This has got to be finished; finished at all costs . . . Well, so I could kill him now . . . With this paper, they'll never think I killed him. I could arrange him and adjust him on the floor with the discharged revolver in his hand so they'd certainly think he himself . . . Ahh, the devil, how am I going to kill him? I'll open the door, and he'll rush again and shoot first. Eh, the devil, he's bound to miss!"

So he agonized, trembling at the necessity of the plan and at his own indecision. Finally, he took the candle and again went up to the door, his revolver raised and ready; with his left hand, in which he was holding the candle, he pressed down on the handle of the latch. But the result was clumsy: the handle clicked, there was a noise and a creak. "He'll just go ahead and shoot!" flashed in Pyotr Stepanovich. He shoved the door as hard as he could with his foot, raised the candle, and thrust out the revolver; but there was no shot, no cry . . . No one was in the room.

He gave a start. It was an end room, there was no other door, no way of escape. He raised the candle higher and peered more attentively: exactly no one. He called Kirillov in a low voice, then once more, louder; no one answered.

"Can he have escaped through the window?"

Indeed, the vent pane was open in one window. "Absurd, he couldn't have escaped through the vent." Pyotr Stepanovich walked all the way across the room right to the window: "He simply couldn't have." All at once he turned quickly, and something extraordinary jolted him.

Against the wall opposite the windows, to the right of the door, stood a wardrobe. To the right of this wardrobe, in the corner formed by the wardrobe and the wall, Kirillov was standing, and standing very strangely—motionless, drawn up, his arms flat at his sides, his head raised, the back of his head pressed hard to the wall, in the very corner, as if he wished to conceal and efface all of himself. By all tokens, he was hiding, yet it was somehow not possible to believe it. Pyotr Stepanovich was standing slightly at an angle to the corner and could observe only the protruding parts of the figure. He did not yet dare move to the left so as to make out the whole of Kirillov and understand the riddle. His heart began to pound . . . And suddenly he was possessed by utter fury: he tore from his place, shouted, and, stamping his feet, rushed fiercely at the dreadful place.

But, coming close, he stopped again as if rooted, still more struck with horror. What struck him, above all, was that the figure, despite his shout and furious lunge, did not even move, did not even stir one of its members—as if it were made of stone or wax. The pallor of its face was unnatural, the black eyes were completely immobile, staring at some point in space. Pyotr Stepanovich moved the candle from up to down and up again, lighting it from all points and studying this face. He suddenly noticed that, although Kirillov was staring somewhere ahead, he could see him out of the corner of his eye, and was perhaps even watching him. Then it occurred to him to bring the flame right up to the face of "this blackguard," to burn it, and see what he would do. Suddenly he fancied that Kirillov's chin moved and a mocking smile seemed to flit over his lips—as though he had guessed his thought. He trembled and, beside himself, seized Kirillov hard by the shoulder.

Then there occurred something so hideous and quick that afterwards Pyotr Stepanovich could never bring his recollections into any kind of order. The moment he touched Kirillov, the man quickly bent his head down, and with his head knocked the candle from his hands; the candlestick fell to the floor with a clang, and the candle went out. At the same instant, he felt a terrible pain in the little finger of his left hand. He cried out, and all he could remember was that, beside himself, he had struck as hard as he could three times with the revolver on the head of Kirillov, who had leaned to him and bitten his finger. He finally tore the finger free and rushed headlong to get out of the house, feeling his way in the darkness. Terrible shouts came flying after him from the room:

"Now, now, now, now . . ."

Ten times or so. But he kept running and had already reached the front hall when there suddenly came a loud shot. At that he stopped, in the front hall, in the dark, and for about five minutes stood reflecting; finally, he went back to the rooms again. But he had to get himself a candle. It would be no trouble finding the candlestick that had been knocked out of his hands on the floor to the right of the wardrobe; but what would he light the candle end with? Suddenly a dim recollection flashed through his mind: he recalled that the day before, when he ran down to the kitchen to fall upon Fedka, he seemed to have glimpsed in passing, in the corner, on a shelf, a big red box of matches. He groped his way left towards the kitchen door, found it, crossed the landing, and went down the stairs. On the shelf, right in the very spot he had just recalled, his hand came in the darkness upon a full, as yet unopened box of matches. Without striking a light, he hastily went back upstairs, and only near the wardrobe, on the very spot where he had hit Kirillov with the revolver as he was biting him, did he suddenly remember his bitten finger and in that same instant felt an almost unbearable pain in it. Clenching his teeth, he managed somehow to light the candle end, put it back in the candlestick, and looked around: near the window with the open vent, feet towards the right-hand corner of the room, lay the corpse of Kirillov. The shot had gone into the right temple, and the bullet had come out higher up on the left side, piercing the skull. Spatters of blood and brains could be seen. The revolver had remained in the suicide's hand, which lay on the floor. Death must have occurred instantly. After examining everything carefully, Pyotr Stepanovich stood up and tiptoed out, closed the door, set the candle on the table in the front room, thought a minute, and decided not to put it out, judging that it would not cause a fire. Glancing once more at the document lying on the table, he grinned mechanically, and only then, still tiptoeing for some reason, left the house. He again got through Fedka's passage, and again carefully closed it up behind him.

III

E XACTLY at ten minutes to six, at the railway station, along the
rather long, strung-out line of cars, Pyotr Stepanovich and Erkel
were strolling. Pyotr Stepanovich was leaving, and Erkel was saying
good-bye to him. His luggage had been checked, his bag taken to a
second-class car, to the seat he had chosen. The first bell had already
rung, they were waiting for the second. Pyotr Stepanovich looked
openly all around him, observing the passengers entering the cars. But
he did not meet any close acquaintances; only twice did he have to nod
his head—to a merchant he knew distantly, and then to a young village
priest, who was leaving for his parish two stations away. Erkel evidently would have liked to talk about something more serious during
these last moments—though perhaps he himself did not know precisely what—but he did not dare begin. He kept fancying that Pyotr
Stepanovich was as if burdened by him and was waiting impatiently
for the remaining bells.

"You look so openly at everybody," he commented with a certain
timidity, as though wishing to warn him.

"And why not? I shouldn't be hiding yet. It's too soon. Don't worry.
I'm only afraid the devil may send Liputin; he'll get wind of things and
come running."

"Pyotr Stepanovich, they're unreliable," Erkel spoke out resolutely.

"Liputin?"

"All of them, Pyotr Stepanovich."

"Nonsense, they're all bound by yesterday now. None of them will
betray us. Who would face obvious ruin, unless he's lost his mind?"

"But, Pyotr Stepanovich, they will lose their minds."

This thought apparently had already entered Pyotr Stepanovich's
head, and therefore Erkel's comment made him still more angry:

"You haven't turned coward, too, Erkel? I'm trusting in you more
than all the rest of them. I see now what each of them is worth. Tell
them everything today orally, I put them directly in your charge. Run
around and see them in the morning. Read them my written instructions tomorrow or the day after, collectively, when they've become

capable of listening again . . . but, believe me, they'll be capable by tomorrow, because they'll be terribly afraid and become obedient, like wax . . . Above all, don't you lose heart."

"Ah, Pyotr Stepanovich, it would be better if you weren't leaving!"

"But it's only for a few days; I'll be back in no time."

"Pyotr Stepanovich," Erkel uttered cautiously but firmly, "even if it's to Petersburg. Since I know you only do what's necessary for the common cause."

"I expected no less of you, Erkel. If you've guessed that I'm going to Petersburg, then you can understand that it was impossible for me to tell them yesterday, at that moment, that I was going so far, lest I frighten them. You saw for yourself how they were. But you understand that it's for the cause, for the main and important cause, for the common cause, and not to slip away, as some Liputin might think."

"But, Pyotr Stepanovich, even if it's abroad, I'd understand, sir; I'd understand that you must preserve your person, because you're—everything, and we're—nothing. I'd understand, Pyotr Stepanovich."

The poor boy's voice even trembled.

"Thank you, Erkel . . . Ow, you touched my bad finger" (Erkel had pressed his hand clumsily; the bad finger was attractively bandaged in black taffeta). "But I tell you once again positively that I'll just sniff things out in Petersburg, maybe even just overnight, and be back at once. On my return I'll stay at Gaganov's estate, for the sake of appearances. If they think there's danger anywhere, I'll be the first at their head to share it. And if I'm delayed in Petersburg, I'll let you know that same moment . . . in our usual way, and you can tell them."

The second bell rang.

"Ah, so it's five minutes to departure. You know, I wouldn't like the crew here to fall apart. I'm not afraid, don't worry about me; I have enough of these knots in the general net, and there's nothing to value especially; but an extra knot won't hurt anything. However, I'm at ease about you, though I'm leaving you almost alone with these freaks: don't worry, they won't inform, they won't dare . . . Ahh, you're going today, too?" he cried suddenly in quite a different, cheerful voice to a very young man who cheerfully came up to greet him. "I didn't know you were also taking the express. Where to, your mama's?"

The young man's mama was a very wealthy landowner of the neighboring province, and the young man was a distant relation of Yulia Mikhailovna's and had spent about two weeks visiting our town.

"No, a bit farther, to R——. I'll be living on the train for a good eight hours. Off to Petersburg?" the young man laughed.

"What makes you think right away that I'm going to Petersburg?" Pyotr Stepanovich also laughed still more openly.

The young man shook a begloved finger at him.

"Well, so you've guessed it," Pyotr Stepanovich began whispering to him mysteriously. "I have Yulia Mikhailovna's letters, and must run around and see three or four persons, you know what sort—devil take them, frankly speaking. The devil of a job!"

"But, tell me, why has she turned such a coward?" the young man also began whispering. "She didn't even let me in yesterday; in my view, she needn't fear for her husband; on the contrary, he made quite an attractive fall there at the fire, even sacrificed his life, so to speak."

"Well, so it goes," Pyotr Stepanovich laughed. "You see, she's afraid they've already written from here . . . I mean, certain gentlemen . . . In short, there's mainly Stavrogin; Prince K., I mean . . . Eh, there's a whole story here; maybe I'll tell you a thing or two on the way—no more than chivalry allows, however . . . This is my relative, Ensign Erkel, from the district capital."

The young man, who had been glancing sideways at Erkel, touched his hat; Erkel made him a bow.

"You know, Verkhovensky, eight hours on a train—it's a terrible fate. There's this Berestov going with us in first class, a very funny man, a colonel, from the estate next to mine; he's married to a Garin (née de Garine), and, you know, he's a decent sort. Even has ideas. Only spent two days here. A desperate lover of bezique. How about it, eh? I've already got my eye on a fourth—Pripukhlov, our bearded T—— merchant, a millionaire, a real one, that is, take my word for it . . . I'll introduce you, a very interesting bag of goods, we'll have a real laugh."

"Bezique, with the greatest pleasure, and I'm terribly fond of it on the train, but I'm going second-class."

"Eh, come, not a word of it! Get in with us. I'll tell them right now to shift you to first class. The head conductor does as I say. What have you got—a bag? a rug?"

"Wonderful! Let's go!"

Pyotr Stepanovich took his bag, rug, and book, and with the greatest readiness moved at once to first class. Erkel helped. The third bell sounded.

"Well, Erkel," Pyotr Stepanovich hastily, and with a busy look, held out his hand to him for the last time through the car window, "here I am sitting down to play cards with them."

"But why explain to me, Pyotr Stepanovich, I understand, I understand everything, Pyotr Stepanovich!"

"Well, so, it's been a pleasure," the latter suddenly turned away at the call of the young man, who invited him to meet his partners. And that was the last Erkel ever saw of his Pyotr Stepanovich!

He returned home quite sad. It was not that he was afraid at Pyotr Stepanovich's abandoning them so suddenly, but . . . but he had turned away from him so quickly when that young fop called him, and . . . he might have found something else to say to him besides "it's been a pleasure," or . . . or might at least have pressed his hand more firmly.

This last was the main thing. Something else was beginning to scratch at his poor little heart, something he himself did not yet understand, something connected with the previous evening.

7

The Last Peregrination of Stepan Trofimovich

I

I AM CONVINCED that Stepan Trofimovich was very much afraid as he felt the time of his insane undertaking draw near. I am convinced that he suffered very much from fear, especially the night before—that terrible night. Nastasya mentioned later that he had gone to bed late and slept. But that proves nothing; they say men sentenced to death sleep very soundly even the night before their execution. Though he started out with the light of day, when a nervous man always takes heart somewhat (the major, Virginsky's relative, even ceased believing in God as soon as the night was over), I am convinced that he could never before have imagined himself, without horror, alone on the high road and in such a situation. Of course, something desperate in his thoughts probably softened for him, in the beginning, the full force of that terrible feeling of sudden solitude in which he found himself all at once, the moment he left *Stasie* and the place he had been warming up for twenty years. But, anyhow: even with the clearest awareness of all the horrors awaiting him, he still would have gone out to the high road and gone down it! There was something proud here that he admired despite all. Oh, he could have accepted Varvara Petrovna's luxurious conditions and remained with her bounties *"comme un mere sponger"*! But he had not accepted her bounties and had not remained. And now he himself was leaving her and raising "the banner of a great idea" and going to die for it on the high road! That is precisely how he must have felt about it; that is precisely how his action must have presented itself to him.

The question also presented itself to me more than once: why did he precisely run away, that is, run with his feet, in the literal sense, and not simply drive off in a carriage? At first I explained it by fifty years of impracticality and a fantastical deviation of ideas under the effect of strong emotion. It seemed to me that the thought of traveling by post in a carriage (even with bells) must have appeared too simple and prosaic to him; pilgrimage, on the other hand, even with an umbrella, was much more beautiful and vengefully amorous. But now, when everything is over, I rather suppose that at the time it all happened in a much simpler way: first, he was afraid to hire a carriage because Varvara Petrovna might get wind of it and hold him back by force, which she would certainly have done, and he would certainly have submitted, and then—good-bye forever to the great idea. Second, in order to travel by post one must at least know where one is going. But to know this precisely constituted his chief suffering at the moment: he could not name or determine upon a place for the life of him. For if he were to decide upon some town, his undertaking would instantly become both absurd and impossible in his own eyes; he sensed that very well. What was he going to do precisely in this town and not in some other? To look for *ce marchand*?* But what *marchand*? Here again that second and now most dreadful question popped up. In fact, there was nothing more dreadful for him than *ce marchand* whom he had so suddenly set off headlong in search of, and whom he was quite certainly afraid most of all to find in reality. No, better simply the high road, just simply to go out to it and go down it and not think of anything for as long as it was possible not to think. A high road is something very, very long, which one sees no end to—like human life, like the human dream. There is an idea in the high road; and what sort of idea is there in traveling by post? Traveling by post is the end of any idea. *Vive la grande route,*† and then it's whatever God sends.

After the sudden and unexpected meeting with Liza, which I have already described, he went on in even greater self-abandon. The high

---

*"that merchant"
†"Long live the high road"

road passed within a quarter mile of Skvoreshniki, and—strangely—he
did not even notice at first how he had come upon it. Sound reasoning,
or clear awareness at the least, was unbearable to him at that moment.
A drizzling rain kept stopping and starting again; but he did not notice
the rain, either. He also did not notice how he had shouldered his bag,
and how this made it easier for him to walk. He must have gone a half
or three quarters of a mile when he suddenly stopped and looked
around. Ahead of him the old, black, and deeply rutted road stretched
in an endless thread, planted out with its willows; to the right—a bare
place, fields harvested long, long ago; to the left—bushes, and beyond
them—woods. And far away—far away the faintly noticeable line of
the railroad running obliquely, with the smoke of some train on it; but
the sound could no longer be heard. Stepan Trofimovich grew a bit
timid, but only for a moment. He sighed aimlessly, placed his bag
against a willow, and sat down to rest. As he went to sit down, he felt
a chill and wrapped himself in a plaid; then, noticing the rain, he
opened the umbrella over him. For quite a long time he went on sitting
like that, occasionally munching his lips, the handle of the umbrella
grasped tightly in his hand. Various images swept before him in feverish succession, rapidly supplanting one another in his mind. *"Lise,
Lise,"* he thought, "and *ce Maurice* with her . . . Strange people . . . But what was this strange fire there, and what were they talking
about, and who was murdered? . . . I suppose *Stasie* hasn't had time
to find anything out yet and is still waiting for me with coffee . . .
Cards? Did I ever lose people at cards? Hm . . . in our Russia, during
the time of so-called serfdom . . . Ah, my God, and Fedka?"

He started up in fright and looked around: "And what if this Fedka
is sitting here somewhere behind a bush? They say he has a whole band
of highway robbers someplace around here. Oh, God, then I . . .
then I'll tell him the whole truth, that I am to blame . . . and *that I
suffered for ten years* over him, longer than he was there as a
soldier, and . . . and I'll give him my purse. Hm, *j'ai en tout quarante
roubles; il prendra les roubles et il me tuera tout de même.*"*

In fear he closed his umbrella, who knows why, and laid it down

---

*"I have forty roubles in all; he will take the roubles and kill me all the same."

beside him. Far away, on the road from town, some cart appeared; he began peering anxiously:

"*Grace à Dieu* it's a cart, and it's moving slowly; that can't be dangerous. These broken-down local nags . . . I always talked about breeding . . . It was Pyotr Ilych, however, who talked about breeding in the club, and then I finessed him, *et puis,* but what's that behind, and . . . it seems there's a woman in the cart. A woman and a peasant—*cela commence à être rassurant.* The woman behind and the peasant in front—*c'est très rassurant.* They have a cow tied behind by the horns, *c'est rassurant au plus haut degré.*"*

The cart came abreast of him, a rather sturdy and roomy peasant cart. The woman was sitting on a tightly stuffed sack, the peasant on the driver's seat, his legs hanging over on Stepan Trofimovich's side. Behind there indeed plodded a red cow tied by the horns. The peasant and the woman stared wide-eyed at Stepan Trofimovich, and Stepan Trofimovich stared in the same way at them, but after letting them go on about twenty paces, he suddenly got up in haste and went after them. Naturally, it felt more trustworthy in the vicinity of the cart, but when he caught up with it he at once forgot about everything again and again became immersed in his scraps of thoughts and imaginings. He was striding along and certainly did not suspect that for the peasant and the woman he constituted at that moment the most mysterious and curious object one could meet on the high road.

"You, I mean, what sorts are you from, if it's not impolite my asking?" the wench finally could not help herself, when Stepan Trofimovich suddenly glanced at her distractedly. She was a wench of about twenty-seven, sturdy, black-browed, and ruddy, with kindly smiling red lips, behind which her even, white teeth flashed.

"You . . . you are addressing me?" Stepan Trofimovich muttered in doleful surprise.

"Must be from merchants," the peasant said self-confidently. He was a strapping man of about forty, with a broad, sensible face and a full, reddish beard.

---

*"this begins to be reassuring . . . this is very reassuring . . . this is reassuring to the highest degree."

"No, I'm not actually a merchant, I . . . I . . . *moi c'est autre chose,* "* Stepan Trofimovich parried anyhow, and, just in case, dropped behind a little to the rear of the cart, so that he was now walking next to the cow.

"Must be from gentlefolk," the peasant decided, hearing non-Russian words, and pulled up on the nag.

"So here, to look at you, it's as if you're out for a walk?" the wench began to pry again.

"Is it . . . is it me you're asking?"

"There's visiting foreigners come by rail sometimes, you're not from these parts with boots like that . . ."

"Military-type," the peasant put in, complacently and significantly.

"No, I'm not actually from the military, I . . ."

"What a curious wench," Stepan Trofimovich thought vexedly, "and how they're studying me . . . *mais, enfin* . . . Strange, in a word, just as if I were guilty before them, yet I'm not guilty of anything before them."

The wench whispered with the peasant.

"No offense, but we could maybe give you a lift, if only it's agreeable."

Stepan Trofimovich suddenly recollected himself.

"Yes, yes, my friends, with great pleasure, because I'm very tired, only how am I to get in?"

"How amazing," he thought to himself, "I've been walking next to this cow for such a long time, and it never occurred to me to ask if I could ride with them . . . This 'real life' has something rather character-istic about it . . ."

The peasant, however, still did not stop his horse.

"And where are you headed for?" he inquired, with some mistrust.

Stepan Trofimovich did not understand at once.

"Khatovo, must be?"

"Khatov? No, not actually to Khatov . . . And I'm not quite ac-quainted; I've heard of him, though."

"It's a village, Khatovo, a village, five miles from here."

"A village? *C'est charmant,* I do believe I've heard . . ."

*"I am something else"

Stepan Trofimovich was still walking, and they still did not let him get in. A brilliant surmise flashed in his head.

"You think, perhaps, that I . . . I have a passport, and I am a professor, that is, a teacher, if you wish . . . but a head one. I am a head teacher. *Oui, c'est comme ça qu'on peut traduire.* * I would very much like to get in, and I'll buy you . . . I'll buy you a pint for it."

"It'll be fifty kopecks, sir, it's a rough road."

"Or else we'd be getting the bad end," the wench put in.

"Fifty kopecks? Very well, then, fifty kopecks. *C'est encore mieux, j'ai en tout quarante roubles, mais . . .*"†

The peasant stopped, and by general effort Stepan Trofimovich was pulled into the cart and seated next to the woman on the sack. The whirl of thoughts would not leave him. At times he sensed in himself that he was somehow terribly distracted and not thinking at all of what he ought to be thinking of, and he marveled at that. This awareness of a morbid weakness of mind at times became very burdensome and even offensive to him.

"How . . . how is it there's a cow behind?" he himself suddenly asked the wench.

"What's with you, mister, never seen one before?" the woman laughed.

"Bought her in town," the peasant intervened. "See, our cattle all dropped dead last spring—the plague. They all died, all, not even half was left, cry as you might."

And again he whipped up his nag, who had gotten stuck in a rut.

"Yes, that happens here in Russia . . . and generally we Russians . . . well, yes, it happens," Stepan Trofimovich trailed off.

"If you're a teacher, what do you want in Khatovo? Or maybe you're going farther?"

"I . . . that is, not actually farther . . . *C'est-à-dire,* ‡ to a merchant."

"To Spasov, must be?"

"Yes, yes, precisely, to Spasov. It makes no difference, however."

"If you're going to Spasov, and on foot, it'll take you a good week in those pretty boots," the wench laughed.

* "Yes, one could translate it that way."
† "That's even better, I have forty roubles in all, but . . ."
‡ "That is to say"

"Right, right, and it makes no difference, *mes amis,* no difference at all," Stepan Trofimovich impatiently cut her short.

"Terribly curious folk; the wench speaks better than he does, however, and I notice that since the nineteenth of February[1] their style has changed somewhat, and . . . and what do they care if it's Spasov or not Spasov? Anyhow, I'm paying them, so why are they pestering me?"

"If it's Spasov, then it's by steamer-boat," the peasant would not leave off.

"That's right enough," the wench put in animatedly, "because with horses along the shore you make a twenty-mile detour."

"Thirty."

"You'll just catch the steamer-boat in Ustyevo tomorrow at two o'clock," the woman clinched. But Stepan Trofimovich remained stubbornly silent. The questioners also fell silent. The peasant kept pulling up on the nag; the woman exchanged brief remarks with him from time to time. Stepan Trofimovich dozed off. He was terribly surprised when the woman, laughing, shook him awake and he saw himself in a rather large village at the front door of a cottage with three windows.

"You dozed off, mister?"

"What's that? Where am I? Ah, well! Well . . . it makes no difference," Stepan Trofimovich sighed and got out of the cart.

He looked around sadly; the village scene seemed strange to him and in some way terribly alien.

"Ah, the fifty kopecks, I forgot!" he turned to the peasant with a somehow exceedingly hasty gesture; by now he was evidently afraid to part with them.

"Come in, you can pay inside," the peasant invited.

"It's a nice place," the wench encouraged.

Stepan Trofimovich climbed the rickety porch.

"But how is this possible?" he whispered in deep and timorous perplexity, and yet he entered the cottage. "*Elle l'a voulu,*"* something stabbed at his heart, and again he suddenly forgot about everything, even that he had entered the cottage.

It was a bright, rather clean peasant cottage with three windows and

---

*"She wanted it"

two rooms; not really an inn, but a sort of guesthouse, where passing acquaintances stopped out of old habit. Stepan Trofimovich, without embarrassment, walked to the front corner, forgot to give any greetings, sat down, and lapsed into thought. Meanwhile, an extremely pleasant sensation of warmth, after three hours of dampness on the road, suddenly spread through his body. Even the chill that kept running briefly and abruptly down his spine, as always happens with especially nervous people when they are feverish and pass suddenly from cold to warmth, all at once became somehow strangely pleasant to him. He raised his head and the sweet smell of hot pancakes, over which the mistress was busying herself at the stove, tickled his nostrils. Smiling a childlike smile, he leaned towards the mistress and suddenly started prattling:

"What's this now? Is it pancakes? *Mais . . . c'est charmant.*"

"Do you wish some, mister?" the mistress offered at once and politely.

"I do, I precisely wish some, and . . . I'd also like to ask you for tea," Stepan Trofimovich perked up.

"Start the samovar? With the greatest pleasure."

On a big plate with a bold blue pattern, pancakes appeared—those well-known peasant pancakes, thin, half wheat, with hot fresh butter poured over them—most delicious pancakes. Stepan Trofimovich sampled them with delight.

"How rich and how delicious they are! If only one could have *un doigt d'eau de vie.*"*

"You wish a little vodka, mister?"

"Precisely, precisely, just a bit, *un tout petit rien.*"†

"Five kopecks' worth, you mean?"

"Five kopecks' worth—five—five—five, *un tout petit rien,*" Stepan Trofimovich yessed her with a blissful little smile.

Ask a peasant to do something for you, and, if he can and wants to, he will serve you diligently and cordially; but ask him to fetch a little vodka—and his usual calm cordiality suddenly transforms into a sort of hasty, joyful obligingness, almost a family solicitude for you. Some-

*"a finger of vodka."
†"a tiny drop."

one going to get vodka—though only you are going to drink it, not he, and he knows it beforehand—feels all the same, as it were, some part of your future gratification . . . In no more than three or four minutes (the pot-house was two steps away), there stood on the table before Stepan Trofimovich a half-pint bottle and a large greenish glass.

"And all that for me!" he was greatly surprised. "I've always had vodka, but I never knew five kopecks' worth was so much."

He poured a glass, rose, and with a certain solemnity crossed the room to the other corner, where his companion on the sack had settled herself—the black-browed wench who had so pestered him with her questions on the way. The wench was abashed and started making excuses, but, having uttered all that decency prescribed, in the end she rose, drank politely, in three sips, as women do, and with a show of great suffering on her face handed the glass back and bowed to Stepan Trofimovich. He pompously returned her bow and went back to his table even with a look of pride.

All this happened in him by some sort of inspiration: he himself had not known even a second before that he would go and treat the wench.

"My knowledge of how to handle the people is perfect, perfect, I always told them so," he thought smugly, pouring himself the remaining drink from the bottle; though it turned out to be less than a glass, the drink produced a vivifying warmth and even went to his head a little.

"*Je suis malade tout à fait, mais ce n'est pas trop mauvais d'être malade.*"*

"Would you like to buy?" a woman's soft voice came from beside him.

He looked up and, to his surprise, saw before him a lady—*une dame et elle en avait l'air* †—now past thirty, with a very modest look, dressed town-fashion in a dark dress, and with a big gray kerchief on her shoulders. There was something very affable in her face, which Stepan Trofimovich immediately liked. She had just come back to the cottage, where she had left her things on a bench next to the place Stepan Trofimovich had taken—among them a briefcase at which, he remem-

*"I am quite sick, but it's not so bad to be sick."
†"a lady and she looked it"

bered, he had glanced curiously as he entered, and a not very large oilcloth bag. From this same bag she took two handsomely bound books with crosses stamped on the covers and brought them to Stepan Trofimovich.

"Eh . . . *mais je crois que c'est l'Évangile;* * with the greatest pleasure . . . Ah, I understand now . . . *Vous êtes ce qu'on appelle* a book-hawker;† I've read of it more than once . . . Fifty kopecks?"

"Thirty-five kopecks each," the book-hawker answered.

"With the greatest pleasure. *Je n'ai rien contre l'Évangile, et‡* . . . I've long wanted to reread . . ."

It flitted through him at that moment that he had not read the Gospel for at least thirty years, and had merely recalled a bit of it perhaps seven years ago only from reading Renan's book, *La Vie de Jésus.* [2] As he had no change, he pulled out his four ten-rouble bills—all he had. The mistress undertook to break one, and only now did he take a better look and notice that a good many people had gathered in the cottage and had all been watching him for some time and seemed to be talking about him. They also discussed the fire in town, the owner of the cart with the cow most of all, since he had just come from there. They were talking about arson, about the Shpigulin men.

"He never said a word to me about the fire while he was driving me, and yet he talked about everything," it somehow occurred to Stepan Trofimovich.

"Good sir, Stepan Trofimovich, is it you I see? I really never dreamed! . . . Don't you recognize me?" exclaimed an elderly fellow, an old-time household serf by the looks, with a shaven beard and wearing a greatcoat with long, turned-back lapels.

Stepan Trofimovich was frightened at hearing his own name.

"Excuse me," he muttered, "I don't quite remember you . . ."

"No recollection! But I'm Anisim, Anisim Ivanov. I served the late Mr. Gaganov, and saw you, sir, many a time with Varvara Petrovna at the late Avdotya Sergevna's. I used to come to you from her with books, and twice brought Petersburg candy she sent to you . . ."

*"But I believe this is the Gospel"
†"You are what they call [a book-hawker]"
‡"I have nothing against the Gospel, and"

"Ah, yes, I remember you, Anisim," Stepan Trofimovich smiled. "So you live here?"

"Near Spasov, sir, by the V—— monastery, on Marfa Sergevna's estate, that's Avdotya Sergevna's sister, you may be pleased to remember her, she broke her leg jumping out of a carriage on her way to a ball. She now lives near the monastery, and me with her, sir; and now, if you please, I'm on my way to the provincial capital, to visit my family . . ."

"Ah, yes, yes."

"I saw you and it made me glad, you were ever kind to me, sir," Anisim was smiling rapturously. "And where is it you're going like this, sir, it seems you're all alone . . . Seems you never used to go out alone, sir?"

Stepan Trofimovich looked at him timorously.

"It mightn't be to our Spasov, sir?"

"Yes, to Spasov. *Il me semble que tout le monde va à Spassof . . .*"*

"It mightn't be to Fyodor Matveevich's? Won't he be glad of you. He had such respect for you in the old days; even now he often remembers you . . ."

"Yes, yes, to Fyodor Matveevich's."

"Must be so, sir, must be so. You've got the peasants here marveling; they let on, sir, that they supposedly met you on foot on the high road. Foolish folk, sir."

"I . . . It's . . . You know, Anisim, I made a wager, as Englishmen do, that I could get there on foot, and I . . ."

Sweat stood out on his forehead and temples.

"Must be so, sir, must be so . . ." Anisim listened with merciless curiosity. But Stepan Trofimovich could not bear it any longer. He was so abashed that he wanted to get up and leave the cottage. But the samovar was brought in, and at the same moment the book-hawker, who had stepped out somewhere, came back. He turned to her with the gesture of a man saving his own life, and offered her tea. Anisim yielded and walked away.

Indeed, perplexity had been emerging among the peasants.

"Who is this man? Found walking down the road, says he's a

*"It seems to me that everyone is going to Spasov . . ."

teacher, dressed like a foreigner, reasons like a little child, answers nonsensically, as if he'd run away from somebody, and he's got money!" There was beginning to be some thought of reporting to the authorities—"since anyway things are not so quiet in town." But Anisim settled it all that same minute. Stepping out to the front hall, he told everyone who cared to listen that Stepan Trofimovich was not really a teacher, but was "himself a great scholar and occupied with great studies, and was a local landowner himself and had lived for the past twenty-two years with the full general's widow Stavrogin, in place of the chiefest man in the house, and had great respect from everyone in town. He used to leave fifty or a hundred roubles of an evening in the gentlemen's club, and in rank he was a councillor, which is the same as a lieutenant colonel in the army, just one step lower than full colonel. And that he's got money is because through the full general's widow Stavrogin he has more money than you could count," and so on and so forth.

"*Mais c'est une dame, et très comme il faut,* "* Stepan Trofimovich was resting from Anisim's attack, observing with pleasant curiosity his neighbor, the book-hawker, who, however, was drinking her tea from the saucer with sugar on the side.[3] "*Ce petit morceau de sucre ce n'est rien* † . . . There is in her something noble and independent and at the same time—quiet. *Le comme il faut tout pur,* ‡ only of a somewhat different sort."

He soon learned from her that she was Sofya Matveevna Ulitin, and actually lived in K——, where she had a widowed sister, a tradeswoman; she herself was also a widow, and her husband, a sub-lieutenant who had risen to that rank from sergeant major, had been killed at Sebastopol.[4]

"But you're so young, *vous n'avez pas trente ans.* "§

"Thirty-four, sir," Sofya Matveevna smiled.

"So, you also understand French?"

"A little, sir; I lived in a noble house for four years after that and picked it up from the children there."

*"But she is a lady, and a very respectable one"
†"This little lump of sugar is nothing"
‡"Pure respectability"
§"you're not thirty years old."

She told him that being left after her husband at the age of eighteen, she had stayed for a while in Sebastopol "as a sister of mercy," and had then lived in various places, sir, and now here she was going around selling the Gospel.

"*Mais mon Dieu,* it wasn't you who were involved in that strange, even very strange, story in our town?"

She blushed; it turned out to have been she.

"*Ces vauriens, ces malheureux!** . . ." he tried to begin, in a voice trembling with indignation; a painful and hateful recollection echoed tormentingly in his heart. For a moment he became as if oblivious.

"Hah, she's gone again," he suddenly came to himself, noticing that she was no longer beside him. "She steps out frequently and is preoccupied with something, I notice she's even worried . . . *Bah, je deviens egoïste . . .*"†

He looked up and again saw Anisim, this time in the most threatening circumstances. The whole cottage was filled with peasants, all apparently dragged there by Anisim. The proprietor was there, and the peasant with the cow, and another two peasants (they turned out to be coachmen), and some other half-drunk little man, dressed like a peasant but clean-shaven, who resembled a besotted tradesman and was talking more than anyone else. And they were all discussing him, Stepan Trofimovich. The peasant with the cow stood his ground, insisting that along the shore would be about a thirty-mile detour, and that it had to be by steamer-boat. The half-drunk tradesman and the proprietor hotly objected:

"Because, dear brother, if it's by steamer-boat, of course, His Excellency will have a closer way across the lake; that's right enough; except the way things are now, the steamer-boat may not even go."

"It will, it will, it'll go for another week," Anisim was the most excited of all.

"Maybe so! but it doesn't come on schedule, because it's late in the year, and sometimes they wait three days in Ustyevo."

"It'll come tomorrow, tomorrow at two o'clock it'll come on sched-

---

*"Those worthless fellows, those wretches!"
†"Bah, I'm turning into an egoist . . ."

ule. You'll get to Spasov still before evening, sir, right on schedule," Anisim was turning himself inside out.

"*Mais qu'est-ce qu'il a, cet homme,*"* Stepan Trofimovich trembled, fearfully awaiting his fate.

The coachmen, too, stepped up and began bargaining; they were asking three roubles to Ustyevo. Others shouted that he wouldn't be doing badly, that it was the right price, just the same price they charged all summer for going from here to Ustyevo.

"But . . . it's also nice here . . . And I don't want to," Stepan Trofimovich started mumbling.

"Right, sir, it's just as you say, right now it's really nice in Spasov, and you'll make Fyodor Matveevich so glad."

"*Mon Dieu, mes amis,* all this is so unexpected for me."

At last Sofya Matveevna came back. But she sat on the bench quite crushed and sad.

"I'm not to be in Spasov!" she said to the mistress.

"What, you're going to Spasov, too?" Stepan Trofimovich roused himself.

It turned out that a certain landowner, Nadezhda Yegorovna Svetlitsyn, had told her the day before to wait for her in Khatovo and promised to take her to Spasov, and here she had not come.

"What am I to do now?" Sofya Matveevna kept repeating.

"*Mais, ma chère et nouvelle amie,*† I, too, can take you, as well as any landowner, to this, what is it called, this village I've hired a coach to, and tomorrow—well, tomorrow we'll go to Spasov together."

"But, are you also going to Spasov?"

"*Mais que faire, et je suis enchanté!*‡ I shall be extremely glad to take you there; they want to, I've already hired . . . Which of you did I hire?" Stepan Trofimovich suddenly wanted terribly much to go to Spasov.

A quarter of an hour later they were already getting into the covered britzka: he very animated and thoroughly pleased; she with her bag and a grateful smile beside him. Anisim helped them in.

*"But what's gotten into the man"
†"But, my dear and new friend"
‡"But there's no help for it, and I am delighted!"

"Have a good trip, sir," he was bustling with all his might around the britzka, "it was such gladness you caused us!"

"Good-bye, good-bye, my friend, good-bye."

"When you see Fyodor Matveevich, sir . . ."

"Yes, my friend, yes . . . Fyodor Petrovich . . . and now good-bye."

II

"Y OU SEE, my friend—you will allow me to call you my friend, *n'est-ce pas?*"* Stepan Trofimovich began hastily, as soon as the britzka started. "You see, I . . . *J'aime le peuple, c'est indispensable, mais il me semble que je ne l'avais jamais vu de près. Stasie . . . cela va sans dire qu'elle est aussi du peuple . . . mais le vrai peuple,* † that is, the real ones, the ones on the high road, it seems to me, care only about where I'm actually going . . . But let's drop our grudges. It's as if I were straying a little, but that, it seems, is from haste."

"It seems you're unwell, sir," Sofya Matveevna was studying him keenly but respectfully.

"No, no, I just need to wrap myself up, and generally the wind is somehow fresh, even very fresh, but we'll forget that. I mainly wished to say something else. *Chère et incomparable amie,* ‡ it seems to me that I am almost happy, and the one to blame for it is—you. Happiness is unprofitable for me, because I immediately set about forgiving all my enemies . . ."

"But that is very good, sir."

"Not always, *chère innocente. L'Évangile . . . Voyez-vous, désormais nous le prêcherons ensemble,* § and I'll willingly sell your handsome books. Yes, I feel there's perhaps an idea there, *quelque chose de très nouveau dans ce genre.* ‖ The people are religious, *c'est admis,* ¶ but they

---

*"won't you?"

†"I love the people, that is indispensable, but it seems to me that I have never seen them up close. Nastasya . . . it goes without saying that she is also of the people . . . but the true people"

‡"Dear and incomparable friend"

§"dear innocent one. The Gospel . . . You see, from now on we will preach it together"

‖"something very new of the sort."

¶"granted"

still don't know the Gospel. I will expound it to them . . . In expounding it orally, it is possible to correct the mistakes of this remarkable book, which I, of course, am prepared to treat with great respect. I'll also be useful on the high road. I've always been useful, I've always said so to *them* and to *cette chère ingrate* * . . . Oh, let's forgive, forgive, let's first of all forgive all and always . . . Let's hope that we, too, will be forgiven. Yes, because we are guilty one and all before each other. All are guilty! . . ."

"That, I think, you said very well, if you please, sir."

"Yes, yes . . . I feel that I am speaking very well. I will speak very well to them, but, but what was the main thing I wished to say? I keep getting confused and don't remember . . . Will you allow me not to part from you? I feel that your eyes and . . . I'm even surprised at your manners: you're simplehearted, and you say 'sir,' and you put the cup upside down on the saucer . . . with that ugly little sugar lump; but there's something lovely in you, and I can see by your features . . . Oh, don't blush, and don't be afraid of me as a man. *Chère et incomparable, pour moi une femme c'est tout.* † I cannot live without a woman near, but simply near . . . I'm terribly, terribly confused . . . I simply cannot remember what I wished to say. Oh, blessed is he to whom God always sends a woman, and . . . and I even think I'm in some sort of ecstasy. And on the high road, too, there is a lofty thought! there—that is what I wished to say—about the thought, now I've remembered it, and I kept missing it before. But why did they take us farther on? It was nice there, too, and here—*cela devient trop froid. À propos, j'ai en tout quarante roubles et voilà cet argent,* ‡ take it, take it, I don't know how, I'll lose it, they'll take it from me, and . . . It seems to me I want to sleep; something is spinning in my head. Just spinning, spinning, spinning. Oh, how kind you are, what's that you're covering me with?"

"You must be in a real fever, sir, and I've covered you with my blanket, only about the money, sir, I'd . . ."

"Oh, for God's sake, *n'en parlons plus, parce que cela me fait mal,* § oh, how kind you are!"

*"that dear ingrate"
†"Dear and incomparable one, for me a woman is all."
‡"it's turning too cold. By the way, I have forty roubles in all and here is this money"
§"let's not speak of it any more, because it upsets me"

He somehow quickly interrupted his speaking and fell asleep extremely soon, in a feverish, shivering sleep. The country road they drove on for those ten miles was not a smooth one, and the carriage jolted cruelly. Stepan Trofimovich woke up frequently, raised himself quickly from the small pillow Sofya Matveevna had slipped under his head, seized her hand, and asked: "Are you here?"—as if he feared she might leave him. He also insisted that he had seen some gaping jaws with teeth in a dream and had found it very repulsive. Sofya Matveevna was greatly worried for him.

The coachman drove them straight up to a big cottage with four windows and wings of rooms in the yard. The awakened Stepan Trofimovich hurriedly walked in and went straight to the second room, the best and most spacious in the house. His sleepy face acquired a most bustling expression. He explained at once to the mistress, a tall and sturdy woman of about forty with very black hair and all but a moustache, that he required the whole room for himself "and that the door be shut and no one be let in, *parce que nous avons à parler.*"*

"*Oui, j'ai beaucoup à vous dire, chère amie.* † I'll pay you, I'll pay you!" he waved the mistress away.

Though he was hurrying, he moved his tongue somehow stiffly. The mistress listened with displeasure, but in token of agreement kept her silence, in which, however, one could sense a certain menace. He noticed none of this and hurriedly (he was in a terrible hurry) requested that she go and serve dinner at once as soon as possible, "without the least delay."

Here the woman with the moustache could bear it no longer.

"This isn't an inn, mister, we don't serve dinners for travelers. Some boiled crayfish or a samovar, we have nothing else. There won't be fresh fish till tomorrow."

But Stepan Trofimovich began waving his arms, repeating with wrathful impatience: "I'll pay, only be quick, be quick." They settled on fish soup and roast chicken; the landlady declared that there was not a chicken to be found in the whole village; however, she agreed

---

*"because we have to talk."
†"Yes, I have much to say to you, dear friend."

to go and look, but with an air as though she were doing an extraordinary favor.

As soon as she left, Stepan Trofimovich instantly sat down on the sofa and sat Sofya Matveevna down next to him. There were both armchairs and a sofa in the room, but of dreadful appearance. Generally, the whole room, rather spacious (with a partition behind which stood a bed), with its yellow, old, torn wallpaper, with dreadful mythological lithographs on the walls, with a long row of icons and bronze triptychs[5] in the front corner, with its strange assortment of furniture, presented an unsightly mixture of the urban and the aboriginally peasant. But he did not even glance at it all, did not even look out the window at the vast lake which began about seventy feet from the cottage.

"At last we're by ourselves, and we won't let anyone in! I want to tell you everything, everything, from the very beginning."

Sofya Matveevna stopped him, even with strong uneasiness:

"Is it known to you, Stepan Trofimovich . . ."

*"Comment, vous savez déjà mon nom?"** he smiled joyfully.

"I heard it today from Anisim Ivanovich, when you were talking with him. But this, for my part, I will be so bold as to tell you . . ."

And in a quick whisper, glancing back at the closed door to be sure no one was eavesdropping, she told him that here, in this village, there is trouble, sir. That all the local peasants, though fishermen, in fact make a business of charging summer visitors whatever price they like. The village is not on a main route, but is out of the way, and the only reason to come here is that the steamer stops here, but when the steamer does not come, as always happens the moment the weather turns bad, there will be a crowd of people waiting for several days, and then all the houses in the village will be occupied, and that is just what the owners wait for; because they triple the price for everything, and the proprietor here is proud and haughty, because he is very rich for these parts—his net alone is worth a thousand roubles.

Stepan Trofimovich looked into Sofya Matveevna's extremely animated face all but with reproach, and several times made a gesture to

*"What, you already know my name?"

stop her. But she held her own and finished: according to what she said, she had already come there in the summer with one "very noble lady, sir," from town, and had also stayed overnight waiting for the steamer to come, even two whole days, sir, and had suffered such grief that it was terrible to remember. "Now you, Stepan Trofimovich, were pleased to ask for this room for yourself alone, sir . . . It's just to warn you, sir . . . There, in the other room, there are already guests, an elderly man, a young man, and also some lady with children, and by tomorrow before two o'clock there'll be a houseful, because if there hasn't been a steamer for two days, it will surely come tomorrow. So for a separate room, and for having just asked for dinner, sir, and for making it bad for the other guests, they'll demand so much from you that it's even unheard-of in the capitals, sir . . ."

But he was suffering, truly suffering:

"*Assez, mon enfant,* I pray you; *nous avons notre argent, et après—et après le bon Dieu.* And I'm even surprised that you, with the loftiness of your notions . . . *Assez, assez, vous me tourmentez,* "* he said hysterically, "our whole future is ahead of us, and you . . . you make me fear for the future . . ."

He immediately began telling the whole story, hurrying so much that at first it was even hard to understand. It took a long time. The fish soup was served, the chicken was served, the samovar, finally, was served, and he went on talking . . . What came out was somewhat strange and morbid, but he was indeed ill. This was a sudden straining of his mental powers, which, of course—and Sofya Matveevna foresaw it with anguish throughout his story—could not but lead immediately afterwards to a great loss of strength in his already unsettled organism. He started almost from childhood, when "with fresh breast he ran over the fields"; only an hour later did he reach his two marriages and Berlin life. I would not dream of laughing, however. There was something truly lofty for him here and, to use the newest language, almost a struggle for existence. He saw before him her whom he had already pre-elected for his future path, and he was hastening to initiate her, so to speak. His genius must no longer remain a secret to her . . . Perhaps

---

*"Enough, my child . . . we have our money, and after that—after that the good Lord . . . Enough, enough, you're tormenting me"

he was greatly exaggerating with regard to Sofya Matveevna, but he had already elected her. He could not be without a woman. He himself saw clearly from her face that she hardly understood him at all, even in the most capital things.

"*Ce n'est rien, nous attendrons,* * and meanwhile she can understand by intuition . . ."

"My friend, all I need is your heart alone!" he kept exclaiming, interrupting his narrative, "and this dear, charming look with which you are gazing at me now. Oh, do not blush! I've already told you . . ."

The fogginess increased greatly for poor, trapped Sofya Matveevna when the story turned almost into a whole dissertation on the subject of how no one had ever been able to understand Stepan Trofimovich and of how "talents perish in our Russia." It was "all so very intelligent," she later reported dejectedly. She listened with obvious suffering, her eyes slightly popping out. And when Stepan Trofimovich threw himself into humor and the wittiest barbs concerning our "progressive and dominating ones," she made an attempt, from grief, to smile a couple of times in response to his laughter, but it came out worse than tears, so that in the end Stepan Trofimovich himself became abashed and struck out with even greater passion and spite at the nihilists and "new people." Here he simply frightened her, and she only got a bit of respite, though a most deceptive one, when the romance proper began. A woman is always a woman, be she even a nun. She smiled, shook her head, blushed deeply all at once and lowered her eyes, thereby sending Stepan Trofimovich into utter admiration and inspiration, so that he even added quite a lot. His Varvara Petrovna came out as a most lovely brunette ("the admiration of Petersburg and a great many European capitals"), and her husband had died, "cut down by a bullet at Sebastopol," solely because he felt unworthy of her love, giving way to his rival—that is, to the same Stepan Trofimovich . . . "Do not be embarrassed, my quiet one, my Christian!" he exclaimed to Sofya Matveevna, himself almost believing everything he was telling her. "This was something lofty, something so fine that not even once in our lives did we declare it." The reason

---

*"It's nothing, we shall wait"

for such a state of affairs turned out in the ensuing narrative to be a blonde (if not Darya Pavlovna, I really don't know whom Stepan Trofimovich meant). This blonde owed everything to the brunette and, being a distant relation, had grown up in her house. The brunette, having finally noticed the blonde's love for Stepan Trofimovich, withdrew into herself. The blonde, for her part, noticing the brunette's love for Stepan Trofimovich, also withdrew into herself. And so all three of them, languishing in mutual magnanimity, were silent like this for twenty years, withdrawn into themselves. "Oh, what a passion it was, oh, what a passion!" he kept exclaiming, gasping in the most genuine rapture. "I saw the full blossom of her (the brunette's) beauty; daily 'with a sprain in my heart' I saw her passing by me, as if ashamed of her loveliness." (Once he said: "ashamed of her portliness.") At last, he had run away, abandoning all this feverish twenty-year dream. "*Vingt ans!*" And now, on the high road . . . Then, in some sort of inflammation of the brain, he began explaining to Sofya Matveevna what must be the significance of their meeting that day, "so accidentally and so fatefully, unto ages of ages." Sofya Matveevna, in terrible embarrassment, finally got up from the sofa; he even made an attempt to go on his knees before her, at which she burst into tears. Twilight was gathering; the two had already spent several hours in the closed room . . .

"No, you'd better let me go to the other room, sir," she murmured, "or else people might think something."

She finally tore herself away; he let her go, giving his word that he would go to bed at once. As he was saying good night, he complained of a bad headache. Sofya Matveevna had left her bag and things in the first room when she came in, intending to spend the night with the proprietors; but she did not manage to get any rest.

During the night, Stepan Trofimovich had an attack of that cholerine so well known to me and to all his friends—the usual outcome with him of any nervous strain or moral shock. Poor Sofya Matveevna did not sleep all night. Since, in tending to the sick man, she had to go in and out of the cottage fairly often through the proprietors' room, the guests and the mistress who were sleeping there kept grumbling and finally even began to curse when she decided towards morning to start the samovar. Stepan Trofimovich was half oblivious throughout the attack; at times he as if fancied that the samovar was being prepared, that he was being given something to drink (raspberry tea), that something warm was being put on his stomach, his chest. But he felt almost every moment that *she* was there by him; that it was she coming and going getting him out of bed and putting him back in. By three o'clock in the morning he felt better; he sat up, lowered his legs from the bed, and, not thinking of anything, collapsed on the floor in front of her. This was no longer the former kneeling; he simply fell at her feet and kissed the hem of her dress . . .

"You mustn't, sir, I'm not worthy at all," she murmured, trying to lift him back into bed.

"My savior," he clasped his hands reverently before her. *"Vous êtes noble comme une marquise!** I—I am a blackguard! Oh, I have been dishonest all my life . . ."

"Calm yourself," Sofya Matveevna pleaded.

"What I told you earlier was all lies—for glory, for magnificence, out of idleness—all, all, to the last word, oh, blackguard, blackguard!"

The cholerine thus turned into another attack, one of hysterical self-condemnation. I have already mentioned these attacks in speaking of his letters to Varvara Petrovna. He suddenly remembered *Lise,* their meeting the previous morning: "It was so terrible and—there must have been some misfortune, and I didn't ask, I didn't find out! I thought only of myself! Oh, what happened to her, do you know what happened to her?" he besought Sofya Matveevna.

Then he swore that he "would not betray," that he would return *to her* (that is, to Varvara Petrovna). "We shall go up to her porch" (all this, that is, with Sofya Matveevna) "every day, as she's getting into her carriage to go for a morning promenade, and secretly watch . . . Oh, I wish her to strike me on the other cheek; it delights me to wish it! I'll turn my other cheek to her *comme dans votre livre*!† Now, only now do I understand what it means to . . . offer the other cheek.[6] I never understood before!"

For Sofya Matveevna there followed two of the most frightful days of her life; even now she shudders to recall them. Stepan Trofimovich

*"You are as noble as a marquise!"
†"as in your book!"

became so seriously ill that he could not go on the steamer, which this time came on schedule at two o'clock in the afternoon; to leave him alone was more than she could do, so she did not go to Spasov either. By her account, he was even very glad when the steamer left.

"Well, that's fine, that's wonderful," he muttered from the bed, "and I kept being afraid we would have to go. It's so nice here, it's better than anywhere . . . You won't leave me? Oh, you haven't left me!"

"Here," however, was not so nice at all. He did not want to know anything about her difficulties; his head was filled with nothing but fantasies. His illness he considered a fleeting thing, a trifle, and he gave no thought to it, but thought only of how they would go and sell "these books." He asked her to read him the Gospel.

"It's a long time since I've read it . . . in the original. Otherwise someone may ask and I'll make a mistake; one must also be prepared, after all."

She sat down beside him and opened the book.

"You read beautifully," he interrupted her at the very first line. "I see, I see, I was not mistaken!" he added obscurely but rapturously. And generally he was in a constant state of rapture. She read the Sermon on the Mount.[7]

"*Assez, assez, mon enfant,* * enough . . . You can't think that *that* is not enough!"

And he closed his eyes strengthlessly. He was very weak, but did not yet lose consciousness. Sofya Matveevna moved to get up, thinking he wanted to sleep. But he stopped her:

"My friend, I've been lying all my life. Even when I was telling the truth. I never spoke for the truth, but only for myself, I knew that before, but only now do I see . . . Oh, where are those friends whom I have insulted with my friendship all my life? And everyone, every-one! *Savez-vous,* † perhaps I'm lying now; certainly I'm also lying now. The worst of it is that I believe myself when I lie. The most difficult thing in life is to live and not lie . . . and . . . and not believe one's own lie, yes, yes, that's precisely it! But wait, that's all for later . . . You and I together, together!" he added with enthusiasm.

---

* "Enough, enough, my child"
† "You know"

"Stepan Trofimovich," Sofya Matveevna asked timidly, "shouldn't we send to the 'big town' for a doctor?"

He was terribly struck.

"What for? *Est-ce que je suis si malade? Mais rien de sérieux.* * And what do we need strangers for? People will find out and—what will happen then? No, no, no strangers, you and I together, together!"

"You know," he said after a silence, "read me something more, just so, don't choose, something, wherever your eye falls."

Sofya Matveevna opened and started to read.

"Wherever it opens, wherever it happens to open," he repeated.

" 'And to the angel of the church in Laodicea write . . .' "[8]

"What? What is that? From where?"

"It's from the Apocalypse."

"*O, je m'en souviens, oui, l'Apocalypse. Lisez, lisez,* † I want to divine our future by the book, I want to know what comes out; read from the angel, from the angel . . ."

" 'And to the angel of the church in Laodicea write: The words of the Amen, the faithful and true witness, the beginning of God's creation. I know your works: you are neither cold nor hot! Would that you were cold or hot! So, because you are lukewarm, and neither cold nor hot, I will spew you out of my mouth. For you say, I am rich, I have prospered, and I need nothing; not knowing that you are wretched, pitiable, poor, blind, and naked.' "

"That . . . and that is in your book!" he exclaimed, flashing his eyes and raising himself from his pillow. "I never knew that great place! Do you hear: sooner cold, sooner cold than lukewarm, than *only* lukewarm. Oh, I'll prove to them. Only don't leave me, don't leave me alone! We'll prove to them, we'll prove to them!"

"No, I won't leave you, Stepan Trofimovich, I'll never leave you, sir!" she seized his hands and pressed them in hers, bringing them to her heart, looking at him with tears in her eyes. ("I pitied him so very much at that moment," she recounted later.) His lips quivered as if convulsively.

"However, Stepan Trofimovich, what are we going to do, sir?

---

*"Am I so sick? But it's nothing serious."
†"Oh, I remember, yes, the Apocalypse. Read, read"

Shouldn't we let some one of your acquaintances know, or maybe your relations?"

But at this he became so frightened that she regretted mentioning it. He implored her, trembling and shaking, not to send for anyone, not to do anything; he made her promise, he insisted: "No one, no one! We alone, only alone, *nous partirons ensemble.*"*

Another very bad thing was that the proprietors also began to worry, grumbling and pestering Sofya Matveevna. She paid them and made sure they saw she had money; this softened them for a time; but the proprietor demanded Stepan Trofimovich's "identity." With a haughty smile the sick man pointed to his little bag; in it Sofya Matveevna found the certificate of his resignation or something of the sort, with which he had lived all his life. The proprietor would not leave off and said that "he ought to be put someplace or other, because we're not a hospital, and if he dies there might be consequences; we'd all be in for it." Sofya Matveevna tried to speak with him about a doctor, but it turned out that sending to the "big town" would be so expensive that any thought of a doctor had, of course, to be abandoned. In anguish she went back to her patient. Stepan Trofimovich was growing weaker and weaker.

"Now read me one more passage . . . about the swine," he said suddenly.

"What, sir?" Sofya Matveevna was terribly frightened.

"About the swine . . . it's there . . . *ces cochons*† . . . I remember, demons entered into the swine and they all drowned. You must read it to me; I'll tell you why afterwards. I want to recall it literally. I need it literally."

Sofya Matveevna knew the Gospel well and immediately found in Luke the same passage I have placed as an epigraph to my chronicle. I quote it here again:

"Now a large herd of swine was feeding there on the hillside; and they begged him to let them enter these. So he gave them leave. Then the demons came out of the man and entered the swine, and the herd rushed down the steep bank into the lake and were drowned. When

---

*"we will leave together."
†"those swine"

the herdsmen saw what had happened, they fled, and told it in the city and in the country. Then people went out to see what had happened, and they came to Jesus, and found the man from whom the demons had gone, sitting at the feet of Jesus, clothed and in his right mind; and they were afraid. And those who had seen it told them how he who had been possessed with demons was healed."

"My friend," Stepan Trofimovich said in great excitement, *"savez-vous,* this wonderful and . . . extraordinary passage has been a stumbling block for me all my life . . . *dans ce livre* . . . so that I have remembered this passage ever since childhood. And now a thought has occurred to me; *une comparaison.* Terribly many thoughts occur to me now: you see, it's exactly like our Russia. These demons who come out of a sick man and enter into swine—it's all the sores, all the miasmas, all the uncleanness, all the big and little demons accumulated in our great and dear sick man, in our Russia, for centuries, for centuries! *Oui, cette Russie que j'aimais toujours.* * But a great will and a great thought will descend to her from on high, as upon that insane demoniac, and out will come all these demons, all the uncleanness, all the abomination that is festering on the surface . . . and they will beg of themselves to enter into swine. And perhaps they already have! It is us, us and them, and Petrusha . . . *et les autres avec lui,* † and I, perhaps, first, at the head, and we will rush, insane and raging, from the cliff down into the sea, and all be drowned, and good riddance to us, because that's the most we're fit for. But the sick man will be healed and 'sit at the feet of Jesus' . . . and everyone will look in amazement . . . Dear, *vous comprendrez après,* but it excites me very much now . . . *Vous comprendrez après . . . Nous comprendrons ensemble."* ‡

He became delirious and finally lost consciousness. It continued thus all the next day. Sofya Matveevna sat beside him and wept, this being the third night she went almost without sleep, and avoided being seen by the proprietors, who, as she sensed, were already up to something. Deliverance followed only on the third day. That morning Stepan Trofimovich came to, recognized her, and gave her his hand. She

---

*"Yes, this Russia which I always loved."
†"and the others with him"
‡"you will understand afterwards . . . We will understand together."

crossed herself in hope. He wished to look out the window: *"Tiens, un lac,"** he said, "ah, my God, I haven't even seen it yet . . ." At that moment someone's carriage clattered at the front door and a great hubbub arose in the house.

III

I T W A S Varvara Petrovna herself, arriving in a four-place coach-and-four, with two footmen and Darya Pavlovna. The miracle had come about simply: Anisim, dying of curiosity, on his arrival in town, did after all go the next day to Varvara Petrovna's house, and blabbed to the servants that he had met Stepan Trofimovich alone in a village, that peasants had seen him on the high road, alone, on foot, and that he had set out for Spasov, by way of Ustyevo, together with Sofya Matveevna. Since Varvara Petrovna, for her part, was already terribly worried, and was searching as well as she could for her runaway friend, she was informed at once about Anisim. Having listened to him and, chiefly, to the details of the departure for Ustyevo together with some Sofya Matveevna in the same britzka, she instantly got ready and, following the still warm tracks, came rolling into Ustyevo herself. She knew nothing as yet of his illness.

Her stern and commanding voice rang out; even the proprietors quailed. She had stopped just to make inquiries and find things out, being certain that Stepan Trofimovich had long been in Spasov; learning that he was there and ill, she worriedly entered the cottage.

"Well, where is he? Ah, it's you!" she cried, seeing Sofya Matveevna, who just at that moment appeared in the doorway of the second room. "I could tell by your shameless face that it was you. Out, vile creature! Don't let a trace of her remain in the house! Drive her out, or else, my girl, I'll tuck you away in jail for good. Guard her meanwhile in another house. She already once spent time in jail in our town, and she can spend some more. And I ask you, landlord, not to dare let anyone in while I'm here. I am General Stavrogin's widow and I am taking the whole house. And you, my dearest, will account to me for everything."

*"Hah, a lake"

The familiar sounds shocked Stepan Trofimovich. He trembled. But she had already come behind the partition. Flashing her eyes, she drew up a chair with her foot and, sitting back in it, shouted to Dasha:

"Go out for a while, stay with the proprietors. What is this curiosity? And do close the door tightly behind you."

For some time she peered silently and with a sort of predatory look into his frightened face.

"Well, how are you doing, Stepan Trofimovich? Had a nice little spree?" suddenly burst from her with furious irony.

"*Chère,*" Stepan Trofimovich babbled, hardly aware of himself, "I've come to know Russian real life . . . *Et je prêcherai l'Évangile . . .*"*

"Oh, shameless, ignoble man!" she suddenly cried out, clasping her hands. "It wasn't enough for you to disgrace me, you had to get mixed up with . . . Oh, you old, shameless profligate!"

"*Chère . . .*"

His voice broke off, and he was unable to utter a sound, but only stared, his eyes popping with terror.

"What is she?"

"*C'est un ange . . . C'était plus qu'un ange pour moi,*† all night she . . . Oh, don't shout, don't frighten her, *chère, chère . . .*"

Varvara Petrovna suddenly jumped up from her chair with a clatter; her frightened cry rang out: "Water, water!" Though he came to, she was still trembling from fear and, pale, was looking at his distorted face: only here for the first time did she get some idea of the extent of his illness.

"Darya," she suddenly started whispering to Darya Pavlovna, "send immediately for the doctor, for Salzfisch; let Yegorych go at once; let him hire horses here, and take another coach from town. They must be here by nighttime."

Dasha rushed to carry out the order. Stepan Trofimovich went on staring with the same popping, frightened eyes; his white lips were trembling.

"Wait, Stepan Trofimovich, wait, my dearest," she was coaxing him

---

*"And I shall preach the Gospel . . ."
†"She is an angel . . . She was more than an angel for me"

like a child, "just wait, wait, Darya will come back and . . . Ah, my God, mistress, mistress, you come at least, my dear!"

In her impatience she ran to the mistress herself.

"Right now, this minute, *that woman* must come back. Bring her back, bring her back!"

Fortunately, Sofya Matveevna had not yet had time to get far from the house and was just going out the gate with her bag and bundle. They brought her back. She was so frightened that her legs and hands even shook. Varvara Petrovna seized her by the hand, like a hawk seizing a chicken, and dragged her impetuously to Stepan Trofimovich.

"Well, here she is for you. I didn't eat her. You must have thought I'd simply eaten her."

Stepan Trofimovich seized Varvara Petrovna by the hand, brought it to his eyes, and dissolved in tears, sobbing morbidly, fitfully.

"Well, calm yourself, calm yourself, my dear, my dearest. Ah, my God, but do ca-a-alm yourself!" she cried furiously. "Oh, tormentor, tormentor, my eternal tormentor!"

"Dear," Stepan Trofimovich finally murmured, addressing Sofya Matveevna, "stay out there, dear, I want to say something here . . ."

Sofya Matveevna hastened out at once.

"*Chérie, chérie* . . ." he was suffocating.

"Wait before you talk, Stepan Trofimovich, wait a little and rest meanwhile. Here's water. Wa-a-ait, I said!"

She sat down on the chair again. Stepan Trofimovich held her firmly by the hand. For a long time she would not let him talk. He brought her hand to his lips and began to kiss it. She clenched her teeth, looking off into a corner.

"*Je vous aimais!*"* escaped him finally. She had never heard such a word from him, spoken in such a way.

"Hm," she grunted in reply.

"*Je vous aimais toute ma vie . . . vingt ans!*"†

She remained silent—two minutes, three.

"And sprayed yourself with perfume, getting ready for Dasha . . ."

---

*"I loved you."
†"I loved you all my life . . . twenty years!"

she suddenly said in a terrible whisper. Stepan Trofimovich simply froze.

"Put on a new tie . . ."

Again about two minutes of silence.

"Remember the little cigar?"

"My friend," he began mumbling in terror.

"The little cigar, in the evening, by the window . . . in the moonlight . . . after the gazebo . . . in Skvoreshniki? Do you remember? Do you remember?" she jumped up from her place, seizing his pillow by two corners and shaking his head together with it. "Do you remember, you empty, empty, inglorious, fainthearted, eternally, eternally empty man!" she spat out in her furious whisper, keeping herself from shouting. Finally she dropped him and fell onto the chair, covering her face with her hands. "Enough!" she snapped, straightening up. "Twenty years are gone, there's no bringing them back; I'm a fool, too."

"*Je vous aimais,*" he again clasped his hands.

"Why keep at me with your *aimais, aimais!* Enough!" she jumped up again. "And if you don't go to sleep right now, I'll . . . You need rest; go to sleep, go to sleep right now, close your eyes. Ah, my God, maybe he wants to have lunch! What do you eat? What does he eat? Ah, my God, where's that woman? Where is she?"

A hubbub began. But Stepan Trofimovich murmured in a weak voice that he would indeed like to sleep for *une heure,* and then—*un bouillon, un thé . . . enfin, il est si heureux.** He lay back and indeed seemed to fall asleep (he was probably pretending). Varvara Petrovna waited a little and then tiptoed out from behind the partition.

She sat down in the proprietors' room, chased the proprietors out, and ordered Dasha to bring her *that woman.* A serious interrogation began.

"Now, my girl, tell me all the details; sit beside me, so. Well?"

"I met Stepan Trofimovich . . ."

"Wait, stop. I warn you that if you lie or hold anything back, I'll dig you up out of the ground. Well?"

"Stepan Trofimovich and I . . . as soon as I came to Khatovo, ma'am . . ." Sofya Matveevna was almost suffocating . . .

*"an hour . . . some bouillon, tea . . . anyhow, he is so happy."

"Wait, stop, be quiet; what's all this stammering? First of all, what sort of bird are you?"

The woman told her haphazardly, though in the briefest terms, about herself, beginning with Sebastopol. Varvara Petrovna listened silently, sitting straight-backed on her chair, looking sternly and steadily straight into the narrator's eyes.

"Why are you so cowed? Why do you look at the ground? I like people who look straight and argue with me. Go on."

She finished telling about their meeting, about the books, about how Stepan Trofimovich treated the peasant woman to vodka . . .

"Right, right, don't leave out the smallest detail," Varvara Petrovna encouraged her. Finally, she told of how they had set off and how Stepan Trofimovich had kept talking, "already completely sick, ma'am," and even spent several hours here telling her his whole life from the very first beginning.

"Tell me about the life."

Sofya Matveevna suddenly faltered and was completely nonplussed.

"I couldn't say anything about that, ma'am," she spoke all but in tears, "and, besides, I hardly understood anything."

"Lies—it's impossible that you understood nothing at all."

"He was telling for a long time about some black-haired noble lady, ma'am," Sofya Matveevna blushed terribly, incidentally noticing Varvara Petrovna's fair hair and her total lack of resemblance to the "brunette."

"Black-haired? What, precisely? Speak!"

"How this noble lady was very much in love with him, ma'am, all her life, a whole twenty years; but she didn't dare open her heart and was ashamed before him, because she was very portly, ma'am . . ."

"Fool!" Varvara Petrovna snapped out, pensively but resolutely.

Sofya Matveevna was now completely in tears.

"I can't tell anything right about it, because I myself was in great fear for him and couldn't understand him, since he's such an intelligent man . . ."

"It's not for a crow like you to judge his intelligence. Did he offer you his hand?"

The narrator trembled.

"Did he fall in love with you? Speak! He offered you his hand?" Varvara Petrovna yelled.

"That's nearly how it was, ma'am," she sobbed. "Only I took it all for nothing, on account of his illness," she added firmly, raising her eyes.

"What is your name, name and patronymic?"

"Sofya Matveevna, ma'am."

"Let it be known to you, then, Sofya Matveevna, that he is the paltriest, the emptiest little man . . . Lord, Lord! Do you take me for some vile creature?"

The woman goggled her eyes.

"A vile creature, a tyrant? Who ruined his life?"

"How could that be, ma'am, seeing you yourself are weeping?"

Varvara Petrovna did indeed have tears in her eyes.

"Well, sit down, sit down, don't be frightened. Look me in the eyes again, straight; why are you blushing? Dasha, come here, look at her: what do you think, is her heart pure? . . ."

And to Sofya Matveevna's surprise, and perhaps still greater fright, she suddenly patted her on the cheek.

"Only it's a pity you're a fool. Too great a fool for your years. Very well, my dear, I shall concern myself with you. I see that this is all nonsense. Stay nearby for the time being, lodgings will be rented, and I'll provide board and everything . . . till I ask for you."

The frightened Sofya Matveevna tried to peep that she must hurry.

"You don't have to hurry anywhere. I'm buying all your books, and you can stay here. Quiet, no excuses. After all, if I hadn't come, you wouldn't have left him, would you?"

"I wouldn't have left him for anything, ma'am," Sofya Matveevna said softly and firmly, wiping her eyes.

It was late at night when Dr. Salzfisch was brought. He was a rather venerable old man, and quite an experienced practitioner, who had recently lost his official position in our town as the result of some ambitious quarrel with his superiors. Varvara Petrovna had instantly begun "patronizing" him with all her might. He examined the patient attentively, asked questions, and cautiously announced to Varvara Petrovna that the "sufferer's" condition was quite doubtful, owing to the occurrence of a complication in the illness, and that one must expect "even all the worst." Varvara Petrovna, who in twenty years had grown unaccustomed even to thinking that anything serious and decisive could proceed from Stepan Trofimovich personally, was deeply shaken, and even turned pale:

"Is there really no hope?"

"How could it be that there is by no means not any hope at all, but . . ."

She did not go to bed that night and could barely wait until morning. As soon as the sick man opened his eyes and regained consciousness (he had been conscious all the while, though he was growing weaker by the hour), she accosted him with the most resolute air:

"Stepan Trofimovich, one must foresee everything. I have sent for a priest. You have to fulfill your duty . . ."

Knowing his convictions, she greatly feared a refusal. He looked at her in surprise.

"Nonsense, nonsense!" she cried out, thinking he was already refusing. "This is no time for mischief. Enough foolery."

"But . . . am I really so ill?"

He pensively agreed. And, generally, I was greatly surprised to learn afterwards from Varvara Petrovna that he was not in the least afraid of death. Perhaps he simply did not believe it and continued to regard his illness as a trifle.

He confessed and took communion quite willingly. Everyone, including Sofya Matveevna, and even the servants, came to congratulate him on receiving the Holy Sacrament. Everyone to a man wept restrainedly, looking at his pinched and worn-out face and his pale, quivering lips.

"*Oui, mes amis,* and I am only surprised that you are . . . fussing so. Tomorrow I'll probably get up and we'll . . . set off . . . *Toute cette cérémonie** . . . which, to be sure, I give all its due . . . has been . . ."

"I beg you, father, to be sure to stay with the sick man," Varvara Petrovna quickly stopped the priest, who was already taking off his

*Yes, my friends . . . This whole ceremony"

vestments. "As soon as tea has been served, I beg you to start talking immediately about things divine, to bolster his faith."

The priest started to speak; everyone was sitting or standing near the sick man's bed.

"In our sinful times," the priest began smoothly, a cup of tea in his hands, "faith in the Most High is the only refuge for mankind in all the trials and tribulations of life, as well as in the hope of eternal bliss promised to the righteous . . ."

Stepan Trofimovich grew all animated, as it were; a subtle smile flitted across his lips.

*"Mon père, je vous remercie, et vous êtes bien bon, mais . . ."**

"No, no, no *mais*, no *mais* at all!" Varvara Petrovna exclaimed, leaping from her chair. "Father," she turned to the priest, "this, this is the sort of man, the sort of man . . . he'll have to be reconfessed again in an hour. That's the sort of man he is!"

Stepan Trofimovich smiled restrainedly.

"My friends," he said, "God is necessary for me if only because he is the one being who can be loved eternally . . ."

Either he had really come to believe, or the majestic ceremony of the performed sacrament had shaken him and aroused the artistic receptivity of his nature, but he uttered firmly and, they say, with great feeling, a few words which went directly against many of his former convictions.

"My immortality is necessary if only because God will not want to do an injustice and utterly extinguish the fire of love for him once kindled in my heart. And what is more precious than love? Love is higher than being, love is the crown of being, and is it possible for being not to bow before it? If I have come to love him and rejoice in my love—is it possible that he should extinguish both me and my joy and turn us to naught? If there is God, then I am immortal! *Voilà ma profession de foi.*†

"There is God, Stepan Trofimovich, I assure you there is," Varvara Petrovna implored, "give up, drop all your silliness at least once in

*"My father, I thank you, and you are very kind, but . . ."
†"There is my profession of faith."

your life!" (It seems she had not quite understood his *profession de foi.*)

"My friend," he was growing more and more animated, though his voice broke frequently, "my friend, when I understood . . . that turned cheek, I . . . right then I also understood something else . . . *J'ai menti toute ma vie,** all, all my life! and I'd like . . . tomorrow, though . . . Tomorrow we shall all set off."

Varvara Petrovna began to weep. He was searching for someone with his eyes.

"She's here, here she is!" she seized Sofya Matveevna by the hand and brought her to him. He smiled tenderly.

"Oh, I wish so much to live again!" he exclaimed, with an extraordinary rush of energy. "Each minute, each instant of life should be blessedness for man . . . they should, surely they should! It is man's own duty to arrange it so; it is his law—a hidden but a surely existing one . . . Oh, I wish to see Petrusha . . . and all of them . . . and Shatov!"

I will note that neither Darya Pavlovna, nor Varvara Petrovna, nor even Salzfisch, the latest to come from town, knew anything yet about Shatov.

Stepan Trofimovich was growing more and more excited, morbidly so, beyond his strength.

"The one constant thought that there exists something immeasurably more just and happy than I, fills the whole of me with immeasurable tenderness and—glory—oh, whoever I am, whatever I do! Far more than his own happiness, it is necessary for a man to know and believe every moment that there is somewhere a perfect and peaceful happiness, for everyone and for everything . . . The whole law of human existence consists in nothing other than a man's always being able to bow before the immeasurably great. If people are deprived of the immeasurably great, they will not live and will die in despair. The immeasurable and infinite is as necessary for man as the small planet he inhabits . . . My friends, all, all of you: long live the Great Thought! The eternal, immeasurable Thought! For every man, whoever he is, it is necessary to bow before that which is the Great Thought. Even the stupidest man needs at least something great. Petrusha . . . Oh,

---

*"I have lied all my life"

how I want to see them all again! They don't know, they don't know that they, too, have in them the same eternal Great Thought!"

Dr. Salzfisch had not been present at the ceremony. Coming in suddenly, he was horrified and dispersed the gathering, insisting that the sick man should not be disturbed.

Stepan Trofimovich died three days later, by then completely unconscious. He somehow quietly went out, like a burnt-down candle. Varvara Petrovna, after having the funeral service performed there, transferred the body of her poor friend to Skvoreshniki. His grave is within the churchyard and is already covered with a marble slab. The inscription and railing have been left till spring.

In all, Varvara Petrovna's absence from town had lasted some eight days. Along with her, sitting beside her in the carriage, there also arrived Sofya Matveevna, who seemed to have settled with her for good. I will note that as soon as Stepan Trofimovich lost consciousness (that same morning), Varvara Petrovna immediately had Sofya Matveevna removed again, out of the cottage entirely, and tended the sick man herself, alone to the end; but the moment he gave up the ghost, she immediately summoned her. She refused to listen to any objections, terribly frightened though the woman was by her offer (her order, rather) to settle in Skvoreshniki for good.

"That's all nonsense! I myself will go around selling Gospels with you. I have no one in the world now!"

"You do have a son, however," Salzfisch attempted to observe.

"I have no son!" Varvara Petrovna snapped out—as if prophetically.

8

Conclusion

ALL THE PERPETRATED outrages and crimes were discovered extraordinarily quickly, far more quickly than Pyotr Stepanovich had supposed. It began with the unfortunate Marya Ignatievna, who woke up before dawn on the night of her husband's murder, found him missing, and became indescribably worried at not seeing him beside her. The servingwoman Arina Prokhorovna had hired then was spending the night with her. She simply could not calm her down and, as soon as day broke, went running for Arina Prokhorovna herself, assuring the sick woman that she would know where her husband was and when he would be back. Meanwhile, Arina Prokhorovna had troubles of her own: she had already learned from her husband about the night's exploit at Skvoreshniki. He had returned home past ten o'clock looking and feeling terrible; clasping his hands, he threw himself facedown on the bed and kept repeating, shaking with convulsive sobs: "This is not it, this is not it; this is not it at all!" Arina Prokhorovna accosted him and, of course, he ended by confessing everything to her—though to her alone in the whole house. She left him in bed, sternly impressing upon him that "if he wanted to blubber, he should do his howling into the pillow so that no one would hear, and that he'd be a fool if he showed any such appearance tomorrow." She did become a bit pensive and immediately began tidying things up just in case: she managed to hide or destroy completely any unnecessary papers, books, perhaps even tracts. Yet, for all that, she in fact considered that she, her sister, her aunt, the girl student, and perhaps even her lop-eared brother, had nothing much to fear. When the nurse came running for her in the morning, she went to Marya Ignatievna without hesitation. However, she wanted terribly to find out all the sooner whether it was true what her husband had told her yesterday, in a frightened and insane whisper resembling delirium, about Pyotr Stepanovich's counting, with a view to common usefulness, on Kirillov.

But she was too late in coming to Marya Ignatievnas, who, once she had sent the servant off and was left alone, was unable to stand it, got out of bed, and, throwing on herself whatever clothing came to hand, evidently something very light and inappropriate to the season, went to the wing herself to see Kirillov, figuring that he perhaps could tell her most surely about her husband. One can imagine how this woman who had just given birth was affected by what she saw there. Remarkably, she did not read Kirillov's death note, which lay in full view on the table, being so frightened, of course, as to overlook it completely. She ran to her room, seized the infant, and went with him out of the house and down the street. The morning was damp, there was mist. No passers-by were to be met on such an out-of-the-way street. She kept running, breathless, through the cold and oozy mud, and finally began knocking on house doors; at one house they did not open, at another they refused to open for a long time; she left in impatience and began knocking at a third house. This was the house of our merchant Titov. Here she raised a great clamor, shouted, insisted incoherently that "her husband had been killed." Shatov and something of his story were partly known to the Titovs; they were horror-struck that she, having, in her own words, given birth just the day before, was running around the streets in such clothes and in such cold, with a barely covered infant in her arms. At first they thought she was simply raving, the more so as they were unable to make out who had been killed— Kirillov or her husband? Realizing that they did not believe her, she rushed to run farther, but was stopped by force, and they say she cried and struggled terribly. They went to Filippov's house, and in two hours Kirillov's suicide and his death note became known to the whole town. The police accosted the new mother, who was still conscious; and here it came to light that she had not read Kirillov's note, but precisely why she had concluded that her husband had been killed as well—this they could not get out of her. She only cried that "if the other one was killed, then my husband has been killed, too; they were together!" By noon she had fallen into unconsciousness, from which she never emerged, and some three days later she died. The baby caught cold and died even before her. Arina Prokhorovna, not finding Marya Ignatievna and the infant there, and realizing that things were bad, was about to rush home, but stopped at the gate and sent the nurse "to ask the gentleman in the wing if Marya Ignatievna was there or if, perchance, he knew anything about her?" The messenger came back wildly shouting for the whole street to hear. Having convinced her not to shout or tell anyone, employing the well-known argument that "they'll have the law on you," she slipped away from the premises.

It goes without saying that she was inconvenienced that same morning, as having been the new mother's midwife; but they found out little: she recounted very sensibly and coolly everything she herself had seen and heard at Shatov's, but concerning the story that had gone on she made plain that she knew and understood nothing of it.

One can imagine what a hubbub arose all over town. A new "story," another killing! But there was something else here now: it was becoming clear that there indeed existed a secret society of killers, of arsonist-revolutionaries, of rebels. The terrible death of Liza, the murder of Stavrogin's wife, Stavrogin himself, the arson, the ball for the governesses, the licentiousness surrounding Yulia Mikhailovna . . . People even insisted on seeing some mystery in Stepan Trofimovich's disappearance. There was a great, great deal of whispering about Nikolai Vsevolodovich. Towards the end of the day they also learned of Pyotr Stepanovich's absence, and, strangely, he was talked about least of all. What was talked about most of all that day was "the senator."[1] A crowd stood almost all morning by Filippov's house. The authorities were indeed led astray by Kirillov's note. They believed both in Kirillov's killing of Shatov and in the "murderer's" suicide. However, if the authorities were at a loss, they were not entirely so. The word "park," for instance, so vaguely put into Kirillov's note, did not throw anyone off, as Pyotr Stepanovich had reckoned. The police rushed at once to Skvoreshniki, and not only because there is a park there, as there is not anywhere else in our town, but also even following some sort of instinct, since all the horrors of the recent days were either directly or partially connected with Skvoreshniki. So at least I surmise. (I will note that Varvara Petrovna had driven off to catch Stepan Trofimovich early in the morning and with no knowledge of anything.) The body was found in the pond towards evening of the same day, by certain clues; on the very spot of the murder, Shatov's peaked cap was found, forgotten with great light-mindedness by the murderers.[2] The ocular and medical inspection of the corpse, along with certain surmises, awakened from the very first a suspicion that Kirillov must have had comrades. There came to light the existence of a Shatovo-Kirillovian secret society, connected with the tracts. But who were these comrades? On that day there was as yet no thought of *our* people. It was learned that Kirillov had lived as a recluse, and so solitarily that, as the note stated, Fedka had been able to lodge with him for many days, though he was being sought everywhere . . . Chiefly, everyone was tormented by the impossibility of drawing anything general and unifying from the whole tangle that presented itself. One can hardly imagine what conclusions and what mental anarchy our society, frightened to the point of panic, might have reached, if everything had not suddenly been explained all at once, the very next day, thanks to Lyamshin.

He could not stand it. What happened to him was something that even Pyotr Stepanovich had begun to anticipate towards the end. Entrusted to Tolkachenko, and then to Erkel, he spent the whole of the next day lying in bed, apparently placid, his face turned to the wall, and without saying a word, barely answering when spoken to. He thus learned nothing throughout the day of what was happening in town. But Tolkachenko, who learned everything that was happening, took it into his head towards evening to drop his role with Lyamshin and absent himself from our town to the district capital—that is, simply to run away: truly, they lost their minds, as Erkel had prophesied about them all. I will note incidentally that Liputin also disappeared from town that same day, before noon. But with this one it somehow happened that his disappearance became known to the authorities only the next day, towards evening, when his family, all frightened by his absence but silent out of fear, were directly accosted with questions. But to continue about Lyamshin. As soon as he was left alone (Erkel, relying on Tolkachenko, had gone home even earlier), he at once ran out of the house and, of course, very soon learned how matters stood. Without even stopping at home, he took to his heels and ran wherever his legs would carry him. But the night was so dark, and the undertaking so terrible and toilsome, that having gone down two or three streets, he returned home and locked himself in for the whole night. It seems he made an attempt at suicide towards morning; but nothing came of it. He sat locked in until almost noon, however, and then—suddenly ran to the authorities. It is said that he crawled on his knees, sobbed and shrieked, kissed the floor, shouting that he was unworthy even to kiss the boots of the dignitaries who stood before him. He was calmed down and even treated benignly. The interrogation lasted, they say, about three hours. He declared everything, everything, told the innermost secrets, everything he knew, all the details; he rushed ahead of himself, hastened with his confessions, even told what was unnecessary and without being asked. It turned out that he knew quite enough and had enough sense to present it well: the tragedy of Shatov and Kirillov, the fire, the death of the Lebyadkins, etc., were all put in the background. To the forefront came Pyotr Stepanovich, the secret society, the organization, the network. To the question of why so many murders, scandals, and abominations had been perpetrated, he replied with burning haste that it was all "for the systematic shaking of the foundations, for the systematic corrupting of society and all principles; in order to dishearten everyone and make a hash of everything, and society being thus loosened, ailing and limp, cynical and unbelieving, but with an infinite yearning for some guiding idea and for self-preservation—to take it suddenly into their hands, raising the banner of rebellion, and supported by the whole network of fivesomes, which would have been active all the while, recruiting and searching for practically all the means and all the weak spots that could be seized upon." He said in conclusion that here, in our town, Pyotr Stepanovich had arranged only the first trial of such systematic disorder, the program, so to speak, for further actions, even for all the fivesomes—and that this was, in fact, his own (Lyamshin's) thought, his own surmise, and "that they must be sure to remember it, and that all this must be duly pointed out, how he had explained the matter so frankly and well-behavedly, and could therefore be very useful even in the future for services to the authorities." To the outright question: are there many fivesomes?—he answered that there was an endless multitude, that the whole of Russia was covered with a network, and, though he did not present any proofs, I think his answer was completely sincere. He presented only the printed program of the society, printed abroad, and a plan for developing a system of further actions, which, though only a rough draft, was written by Pyotr Stepanovich's own hand. It turned out that with regard to "shaking the foundations," Lyamshin had quoted the paper verbatim, not omitting even periods and commas, though he had insisted it was merely his own understanding. Of Yulia Mikhailovna he said in a surprisingly funny way, and without even being asked, but rushing ahead of himself, that "she was innocent and had simply been fooled." But, remarkably, he cleared Nikolai Stavrogin completely of any participation in the secret society, of any collusion with Pyotr Stepanovich. (Of the fond and quite ridiculous hopes Pyotr Stepanovich had in Stavrogin, Lyamshin was totally unaware.) The death of the Lebyadkins, according to him, was set up by Pyotr Stepanovich alone, with no participation from Nikolai Vsevolodovich, for the cunning purpose of drawing the latter into the crime and thus into dependence on Pyotr Stepanovich; but instead of the gratitude which Pyotr Stepanovich had undoubtedly and lightmindedly counted on, he had aroused only complete indignation and even despair in the "noble" Nikolai Vsevolodovich. He finished about Stavrogin, also hurrying and without being asked, with an obviously deliberate hint that the man was all but an extremely big wig, that there was some secret in it; that he lived among us, so to speak, incognito, that he had a commission, and that he would very possibly visit us again from Petersburg (Lyamshin was sure that Stavrogin was in Petersburg), only this time in a totally different way and in different circumstances and in the retinue of such persons as we might soon hear about, and that he had heard all this from Pyotr Stepanovich, "a secret enemy of Nikolai Vsevolodovich."

I will make a *nota bene.* Two months later, Lyamshin confessed that he had cleared Stavrogin on purpose then, hoping for his protection and that he would solicit for him a two-degree alleviation from Petersburg and supply him with money and letters of recommendation in exile.[3] From this confession one can see that he indeed had a greatly exaggerated notion of Nikolai Stavrogin.

That same day, of course, Virginsky was also arrested, and, in the heat of the moment, his whole household as well. (Arina Prokhorovna, her sister, aunt, and even the girl student, have long been free; they even say that Shigalyov, too, is supposedly sure to be released in the nearest future, since he does not fit into any category of the accused; however, this is still just talk.) Virginsky admitted his guilt at once and in everything; he was sick in bed with a fever when he was arrested. They say he was almost glad: "A weight fell from my heart," he is supposed to have said. One hears of him that he is now giving evidence frankly, yet even with a certain dignity, and has not surrendered any of his "bright hopes," though at the same time he curses the political path (as opposed to the social one) onto which he had been so accidentally and light-mindedly drawn "by a whirlwind of concurrent circumstances."[4] His behavior during the committing of the murder is explained in a mitigating way for him, and it seems that he, too, may count on a certain mitigation of his lot. So at least it is asserted among us.

But an alleviation of Erkel's fate will hardly be possible. This one, since his arrest, has either kept silent or distorted the truth as far as possible. Not one word of repentance has been obtained from him so far. And yet he has aroused a certain sympathy for himself even in the sternest judges—by his youth, by his defenselessness, by obvious indications that he was simply the fanatical victim of a political seducer; and most of all by what has been discovered about his behavior towards his mother, to whom he used to send almost half of his insignificant pay. His mother is now with us; she is a weak and ailing woman, grown old before her time; she weeps and literally grovels at their feet, pleading for her son. Come what may, there are many among us who feel sorry for Erkel.

Liputin was arrested in Petersburg, where he had already been living for two whole weeks. An almost incredible thing occurred with him, which is even difficult to explain. They say he had a passport in another name and every opportunity for successfully slipping abroad, and quite a considerable amount of money with him, and yet he stayed in Petersburg and did not go anywhere. He spent some time looking for Stavrogin and Pyotr Stepanovich, and then suddenly went on a binge and got into debauchery beyond all measure, like a man who has utterly lost all common sense and understanding of his position. And so he was arrested in Petersburg, in a house of ill fame somewhere, and none too sober. Rumor has it that he has by no means lost heart now, is lying in his testimony, and is preparing himself for the forthcoming trial with a certain solemnity and hope (?). He even intends to have some say at his trial. Tolkachenko, arrested somewhere in the district capital ten days after his flight, behaves with incomparably more politeness, does not lie, does not dodge, tells all he knows, does not justify himself, acknowledges his guilt in all modesty, but is also inclined to loquacity; he speaks much and willingly, and when it comes to a knowledge of the people and its revolutionary (?) elements, he even postures and desires to produce an effect. One hears that he, too, intends to have his say at the trial. Generally, he and Liputin are not very frightened, which is even strange.

I repeat, the affair is not yet over. Now, three months later, our society has rested, relaxed, recovered, acquired its own opinion, so much so that some even regard Pyotr Stepanovich himself almost as a genius, at least as having "abilities of genius." "Organization, sir!" they say in the club, raising a finger aloft. However, all this is quite innocent, and, besides, those who say it are not many. Others, on the contrary, do not deny him acuteness of abilities, but couple it with a total ignorance of reality, a terrible abstractedness, a dull and deformed one-sidedness of development, and, proceeding from all that, an extraordinary light-mindedness. Concerning his moral aspects everyone agrees; here there is no argument.

I really do not know who else to mention, so as not to forget anyone. Mavriky Nikolaevich has gone away somewhere altogether. The old Drozdov woman has lapsed into second childhood . . . However, there remains one more very grim story to tell. I will confine myself to facts alone.

On her arrival, Varvara Petrovna stayed at her town house. All the accumulated news poured in on her at once and shook her terribly. She shut herself up alone. It was evening; everyone was tired and went to bed early.

In the morning the maid, with a mysterious air, handed Darya Pavlovna a letter. This letter, by her account, had come the day before, but late, when everyone had already retired, so that she dared not wake her up. It had come not in the mail, but through an unknown person, to Alexei Yegorych in Skvoreshniki. And Alexei Yegorych had at once delivered it himself, yesterday evening, into her hands, and had at once gone back to Skvoreshniki.

Darya Pavlovna, her heart pounding, looked at the letter for a long time without daring to open it. She knew who it was from: it had been written by Nikolai Stavrogin. She read the inscription on the envelope: "To Alexei Yegorych, to be given to Darya Pavlovna, in secret."

Here is this letter, word for word, without correcting the least mistake in style of a young Russian squire who never fully learned Russian grammar, in spite of all his European education:

My good Darya Pavlovna,

You once wanted to be my "nurse" and made me promise to send for you when needed. I am going away in two days and will not come back. Want to go with me?

Last year, like Herzen, I registered as a citizen of canton Uri,[5] and no one knows it. I have already bought a small house there. I have twelve thousand roubles left; we'll go and live there eternally. I don't want to move anywhere ever.

The place is very dull, a ravine; the mountains cramp sight and thought. Very grim. It was because there was a small house for sale. If you don't like it, I'll sell it and buy another in another place.

I'm not well, but I hope with the local air I'll get rid of my hallucinations. Physically, that is; and morally you know all; only is it all?

I've told you a lot of my life. But not all. Even to you—not all! Incidentally, I confirm that in my conscience I am guilty of my wife's death. I have not seen you since then and so I'm confirming it. I am also guilty before Lizaveta Nikolaevna; but here you do know; here you predicted almost everything.

Better don't come. The fact that I'm calling you to me is a

terrible baseness. And why should you bury your life with me? You are dear to me, and when I was in anguish I felt good near you: only in your presence could I speak of myself aloud. Nothing follows from that. You yourself defined it as "nursing"—it's your expression; why sacrifice so much? Realize, also, that I do not pity you, since I'm calling you, and do not respect you, since I'm waiting for you to come. And yet I call and wait. In any case, I need your answer, because I must leave very soon. In such case, I'll go alone.

I have no hope from Uri; I'm simply going. I did not choose a gloomy place on purpose. Nothing binds me to Russia—everything in it is as foreign to me as everywhere else. True, I disliked living in it more than elsewhere; but even in it I was unable to come to hate anything!

I've tested my strength everywhere. You advised me to do that, "in order to know myself." This testing for myself, and for show, proved it to be boundless, as before all my life. In front of your very eyes I endured a slap from your brother; I acknowledged my marriage publicly. But what to apply my strength to—that I have never seen, nor do I see it now, despite your encouragements in Switzerland, which I believed. I am as capable now as ever before of wishing to do a good deed, and I take pleasure in that; along with it, I wish for evil and also feel pleasure. But both the one and the other, as always, are too shallow, and are never very much. My desires are far too weak; they cannot guide. One can cross a river on a log, but not on a chip. All this so that you don't think I'm going to Uri with any hopes.

As always, I do not blame anyone. I've tried great debauchery and exhausted my strength in it; but I don't like debauchery and I did not want it. You've been observing me lately. Do you know that I even looked at these negators of ours with spite, envying them their hopes? But your fears were empty: I could not be their comrade, because I shared nothing. Nor could I do it out of ridicule, for spite, and not because I was afraid of the ridiculous—I cannot be afraid of the ridiculous—but because, after all, I have the habits of a decent man and felt disgusted. Still, if I had more spite and envy for them, I might even have gone over to them. You can judge how easy it has been for me and how I've tossed about!

Dear friend, tender and magnanimous being whom I divined! Perhaps you dream of giving me so much love and of pouring upon me so much of the beautiful from your beautiful soul, that you hope in that way finally to set up some goal for me? No, you had better be more careful: my love will be as shallow as I myself am, and you will be unhappy. Your brother told me that he who loses his ties with his earth also loses his gods, that is, all his goals. One can argue endlessly about everything, but what poured out of me was only negation, with no magnanimity and no force. Or not even negation. Everything is always shallow and listless. Magnanimous Kirillov could not endure his idea and—shot himself; but I do see that he was magnanimous because he was not in his right mind. I can never lose my mind, nor can I ever believe an idea to the same degree as he did. I cannot even entertain an idea to the same degree. I could never, never shoot myself!

I know I ought to kill myself, to sweep myself off the earth like a vile insect; but I'm afraid of suicide, because I'm afraid of showing magnanimity. I know it will be one more deceit—the last deceit in an endless series of deceits. What's the use of deceiving oneself just so as to play at magnanimity? There never can be indignation or shame in me; and so no despair either.

Forgive me for writing so much. I've come to my senses, and this is accidental. This way a hundred pages are too little and ten lines are enough. To call for a "nurse," ten lines are enough.

Since I left, I've been living six stations away, in the stationmaster's house. I got to know him while I was on a spree in Petersburg five years ago. No one knows I'm living here. Write care of him. I enclose the address.

Nikolai Stavrogin.

Darya Pavlovna went at once and showed the letter to Varvara Petrovna. She read it and asked Dasha to step out so that she could read it again by herself; but she somehow very quickly called her again.

"Will you go?" she asked, almost timidly.

"I will," Dasha replied.

"Get ready! We're going together."

Dasha looked at her questioningly.

"And what is there for me to do here now? Does it make any difference? I, too, will register in Uri and live in the ravine . . . Don't worry, I won't bother you."

They quickly began getting ready, in order to catch the noon train. But before half an hour had gone by, Alexei Yegorych came from Skvoreshniki. He reported that Nikolai Vsevolodovich had "suddenly" arrived that morning, on the early train, and was in Skvoreshniki, but "in such a state that he wouldn't answer any questions, walked through all the rooms, and locked himself in his half . . ."

"I concluded on coming to report without his orders," Alexei Yegorych added, with a very imposing air.

Varvara Petrovna gave him a piercing look and asked no questions. The carriage was readied instantly. She went with Dasha. On the way, it is said, she crossed herself frequently.

All the doors in "his half" were open, and Nikolai Vsevolodovich was nowhere to be found.

"Maybe in the attic, ma'am?" Fomushka said cautiously.

Remarkably, several servants followed Varvara Petrovna into "his half"; the rest of the servants all waited in the reception room. Never before would they have allowed themselves such a breach of etiquette. Varvara Petrovna noticed it but said nothing.

They went upstairs to the attic. There were three rooms there; no one was found in any of them.

"Could he maybe have gone up there?" someone pointed at the door to the garret. Indeed, the permanently closed door to the garret was now unlocked and standing wide open. It led to a long, very narrow, and terribly steep wooden stairway that went up almost under the roof. There was a sort of little room there, too.

"I won't go up there. Why on earth would he climb up there?" Varvara Petrovna turned terribly pale, looking around at the servants. They stared at her and said nothing. Dasha was trembling.

Varvara Petrovna rushed up the stairs; Dasha followed her; but as soon as she entered the garret, she cried out and fell unconscious.

The citizen of canton Uri was hanging just inside the door. On the table lay a scrap of paper with the penciled words: "Blame no one; it was I." With it on the table there also lay a hammer, a piece of soap, and a big nail, evidently prepared in reserve. The strong silk cord upon which Nikolai Vsevolodovich had hanged himself, evidently prepared and chosen beforehand, was heavily soaped. Everything indicated premeditation and consciousness to the last minute.

Our medical men, after the autopsy, completely and emphatically ruled out insanity.

Appendix

THE ORIGINAL PART TWO, CHAPTER 9

At Tikhon's

I

NIKOLAI VSEVOLODOVICH did not sleep that night and spent the whole of it sitting on the sofa, often turning his fixed gaze towards one point in the corner by the chest of drawers. His lamp burned all night. Around seven in the morning he fell asleep sitting up, and when Alexei Yegorovich, as their custom had been established once and for all, came into his room at exactly half past nine with a morning cup of coffee, and woke him up by his appearance, he, having opened his eyes, seemed unpleasantly surprised that he could have slept so long and that it was already so late. He hastily drank his coffee, hastily dressed, and hurriedly left the house. To Alexei Yegorovich's cautious inquiry: "Will there be any orders?"—he answered nothing. He walked along the street, looking at the ground, deep in thought, and only at moments raising his head and suddenly showing now and then some vague but intense disquiet. At one intersection, still not far from his house, a crowd of men crossed his path, fifty or more; they walked decorously, almost silently, in deliberate order. By the shop near which he had to wait for about a minute, someone said they were "Shpigulin workers." He barely paid any attention to them. Finally, at around half past ten, he reached the gates of our Savior–St. Yefimi–Bogorodsky monastery,[1] on the outskirts of town, by the river. It was only here that he suddenly seemed to remember something, stopped, hastily and anxiously felt for something in his side pocket—and grinned. Entering the grounds, he asked the first server he met how to find Bishop Tikhon, who was living in retirement in the monastery. The server began bowing and led him off at once. By the porch at the end of a long, two-storied monastery building, they met a fat and gray-haired monk, who imperiously and deftly took him over from the server and led him through a long, narrow corridor, also kept bowing (although, being unable to bend down owing to his fatness, he merely jerked his head frequently and abruptly) and kept inviting him to please come in, though Stavrogin was following him even without that. The monk kept posing all sorts of questions and talked about the father archimandrite;[2] receiving no answers, he became more and more deferential. Stavrogin noticed that he was known there, though, as far as he could remember, he had come there only in childhood. When they reached the door at the very end of the corridor, the monk opened it as if with an imperious hand, inquired familiarly of the cell attendant who sprang over to him whether they could come in, and, without even waiting for an answer, flung the door wide and, inclining, allowed the "dear" visitor to pass by: then, having been rewarded, he quickly vanished, all but fled. Nikolai Vsevolodovich entered a small room, and at almost the same moment there appeared in the doorway of the adjoining room a tall and lean man of about fifty-five, in a simple household cassock, who looked as if he were somewhat ill, with a vague smile and a strange, as if shy, glance. This was the very Tikhon of whom Nikolai Vsevolodovich had heard for the first time from Shatov, and of whom, since then, he had managed to gather certain information.

The information was diverse and contradictory, but there was something common to all of it—namely, that those who loved and those who did not love Tikhon (there were such), all somehow passed over him in silence—those who did not love him, probably out of scorn, and his devotees, even the ardent ones, out of some sort of modesty, as if they wished to conceal something about him, some weakness of his, perhaps holy folly.[3] Nikolai Vsevolodovich learned that he had been living in the monastery for some six years and that he was visited by the simplest people as well as the noblest persons; that even in far-off Petersburg he had ardent admirers, chiefly lady admirers. On the other hand, he heard from one of our dignified little old "club" gentlemen, a pious gentleman himself, that "this Tikhon is all but mad, a totally giftless being in any case, and unquestionably a tippler." I will add, running ahead of myself, that this last is decidedly nonsense, that he simply had a chronic rheumatic condition in his legs and now and then some nervous spasms. Nikolai Vsevolodovich also learned that, either from weakness of character or from "an absentmindedness unpardonable and unbefitting his rank," the retired bishop had proved unable to inspire any particular respect for himself in the monastery. It was said that the father archimandrite, a stern and strict man with regard to his duties as a superior, and known, besides, for his learning, even nursed a certain hostility towards him, as it were, and denounced him (not to his face, but indirectly) for careless living and almost for heresy. The monastery brethren, too, seemed to treat the ailing bishop not so much carelessly as, so to speak, familiarly. The two rooms that constituted Tikhon's cell were also furnished somehow strangely. Alongside clumpish old-style furniture with worn-through leather stood three or four elegant pieces: a luxurious easy chair, a big desk of excellent finish, an elegantly carved bookcase, little tables, whatnots—all given to him. There was an expensive Bukhara carpet, and straw mats alongside it. There were prints of "secular" subjects and from mythological times, and right there in the corner, on a big icon stand, icons gleaming with gold and silver, among them one from ancient times with relics. The library, they say, had also been assembled in a much too varied and contrasting way: alongside the writings of great Christian hierarchs and ascetics, there were theatrical writings "and maybe even worse."

After the first greetings, spoken for some reason with obvious mutual awkwardness, hastily and even indistinctly, Tikhon led his visitor to the study, sat him down on the sofa facing the table, and placed himself next to him in a wicker armchair. Nikolai Vsevolodovich was still greatly distracted by some inner anxiety that was oppressing him. It looked as if he had resolved upon something extraordinary and unquestionable but at the same time almost impossible for him. For a minute or so he looked around the study, apparently not noticing what he was looking at; he was thinking and, of course, did not know what about. He was roused by the silence, and it suddenly seemed to him that Tikhon looked down somehow bashfully and even with some unnecessary and ridiculous smile. This instantly aroused loathing in him; he wanted to get up and leave, the more so as Tikhon, in his opinion, was decidedly drunk. But the man suddenly raised his eyes and gave him a look that was so firm and so full of thought, and at the same time so unexpected and enigmatic in its expression, that he almost jumped. He imagined somehow that Tikhon already knew why he had come, had already been forewarned (though no one in the whole world could have known the reason), and that if he did not start speaking first, it was to spare him, for fear of humiliating him.

"Do you know me?" he suddenly asked curtly. "Did I introduce myself to you when I came in? I'm rather distracted . . ."

"You did not introduce yourself, but I had the pleasure of seeing you once, four years ago, here at the monastery . . . by chance."

Tikhon spoke very unhurriedly and evenly, in a soft voice, pronouncing the words clearly and distinctly.

"I wasn't in this monastery four years ago," Nikolai Vsevolodovich objected, somehow even rudely, "I was here only as a little child, when you weren't here at all."

"Perhaps you've forgotten?" Tikhon observed cautiously and without insistence.

"No, I haven't forgotten; and it would be funny not to remember," Stavrogin insisted somehow excessively. "Perhaps you simply heard about me and formed some idea, and so you confused that with seeing me."

Tikhon held his peace. Here Nikolai Vsevolodovich noticed how a nervous twitch would occasionally pass over his face, the sign of an old nervous disorder.

"I can see only that you are not well today," he said, "and I think it will be better if I leave."

He even made as if to get up from his place.

"Yes, today and yesterday I've been feeling severe pain in my legs, and I got little sleep last night . . ."

Tikhon stopped. His visitor again and suddenly fell back into his former vague pensiveness. The silence lasted a long time, about two minutes.

"Have you been watching me?" he suddenly asked, anxiously and suspiciously.

"I was looking at you and recalling your mother's features. For all the lack of external resemblance, there is much resemblance inwardly, spiritually."

"No resemblance at all, especially spiritually. None what-so-ever!" Nikolai Vsevolodovich, anxious again, insisted unnecessarily and excessively, himself not knowing why. "You're just saying it . . . out of sympathy for my position and—rubbish," he suddenly blurted out. "Hah! does my mother come to see you?"

"She does."

"I didn't know. Never heard it from her. Often?"

"Almost every month, or oftener."

"I never, never heard. Never heard. And you, of course, have heard from her that I'm crazy," he suddenly added.

"No, not really that you're crazy. However, I have also heard this notion, but from others."

"You must have a very good memory, then, if you can recall such trifles. And have you heard about the slap?"

"I've heard something."

"Everything, that is. You have an awful lot of spare time. And about the duel?"

"And about the duel."

"You've heard quite a lot here. No need for newspapers in this place. Did Shatov warn you about me? Eh?"

"No. I do know Mr. Shatov, however, but it's a long time since I've seen him."

"Hm . . . What's that map you've got there? Hah, a map of the last war! How do you have any need for that?"

"I was checking the chart against the text. A most interesting description."

"Show me. Yes, it's not a bad account. Strange reading for you, however."

He drew the book to him and took a fleeting glance at it. It was a voluminous and talented account of the circumstances of the last war,[4] though not so much in a military as in a purely literary sense. He turned the book over in his hands and suddenly tossed it aside impatiently.

"I decidedly do not know why I've come here," he said with disgust, looking straight into Tikhon's eyes, as if expecting him to reply.

"You, too, seem to be unwell?"

"Yes, unwell."

And suddenly, though in the most brief and curt expressions, so that some things were even hard to understand, he told how he was subject, especially at night, to hallucinations of a sort; how he sometimes saw or felt near him some malicious being, scoffing and "reasonable," "in various faces and characters, but one and the same, and I always get angry . . ."

These revelations were wild and incoherent, and indeed came as if from a crazy man. But, for all that, Nikolai Vsevolodovich spoke with such strange sincerity, never before seen in him, with such simple-heartedness, completely unlike him, that it seemed the former man, suddenly and inadvertently, had vanished in him completely. He was not in the least ashamed to show the fear with which he spoke about his phantom. But all this was momentary and vanished as suddenly as it had appeared.

"This is all rubbish," he said quickly and with awkward vexation, recollecting himself. "I'll go to a doctor."

"You certainly should," Tikhon confirmed.

"You say it so affirmatively . . . Have you seen such people as I, with such visions?"

"I have, but very rarely. I remember only one such in my life, an army officer, after he lost his wife, an irreplaceable life's companion for him. The other I only heard about. They were both cured abroad . . . And how long have you been subject to this?"

"About a year, but it's all rubbish. I'll go to a doctor. It's all rubbish, terrible rubbish. It's I myself in various aspects and nothing more. Since I've just added this . . . sentence, you must be thinking I'm still doubtful and am not certain that it's I and not actually a demon?"

Tikhon gave him a questioning look.

"And . . . do you see him really?" he asked, so as to remove all doubt that it was undoubtedly a false and morbid hallucination, "do you actually see some sort of image?"

"It's strange that you should insist about it, when I've already told you I do," Stavrogin again began to grow more irritated with every word, "of course I do, I see it, just as I see you . . . and sometimes I see it and am not sure I see it, though I do see it . . . and sometimes

I'm not sure I see it, and I don't know what's true: he or I . . . it's all rubbish. And you, can't you somehow suppose that it's actually a demon?" he added, laughing, and changing too abruptly to a scoffing tone. "Wouldn't that be more in line with your profession?"

"It's more likely an illness, although . . ."

"Although what?"

"Demons undoubtedly exist, but the understanding of them can vary greatly."

"You lowered your eyes again just now," Stavrogin picked up with irritable mockery, "because you were ashamed for me, that I believe in the demon, and yet in the guise of not believing I slyly asked you the question: does he or does he not actually exist?"

Tikhon smiled vaguely.

"And, you know, lowering your eyes is totally unbecoming to you: unnatural, ridiculous, and affected, and to give satisfaction for my rudeness I will tell you seriously and brazenly: I believe in the demon, believe canonically in a personal demon, not an allegory, and I have no need to elicit anything from anyone, there you have it. You must be terribly glad . . ."

He gave a nervous, unnatural laugh. Tikhon was gazing at him with curiosity, his eyes gentle and as if somewhat timid.

"Do you believe in God?" Stavrogin suddenly blurted out.

"I do."

"It is said that if you believe and tell a mountain to move, it will move[5] . . . that's rubbish, however. But, still, I'm curious: could you move a mountain, or not?"

"If God told me to, I could," Tikhon said softly and with restraint, again beginning to lower his eyes.

"Well, but that's the same as if God moved it himself. No, you, you, as a reward for your belief in God?"

"Perhaps not."

" 'Perhaps'? That's not bad. And why do you doubt?"

"I don't believe perfectly."

"What, *you*? not perfectly? not fully?"

"Yes . . . perhaps not to perfection."

"Well! In any case you still believe that at least with God's help you could move it, and that's no small thing. It's still a bit more than the *très peu** of a certain also archbishop—under the sword, it's true.[6] You are, of course, a Christian, too?"

"Let me not be ashamed of thy cross, O Lord," Tikhon almost whispered in a sort of passionate whisper, inclining his head still more. The corners of his lips suddenly moved nervously and quickly.

"And is it possible to believe in a demon, without believing at all in God?" Stavrogin laughed.

"Oh, quite possible, it happens all the time," Tikhon raised his eyes and also smiled.

"And I'm sure you find such faith more respectable than total disbelief . . . Oh, you cleric!" Stavrogin burst out laughing. Tikhon again smiled to him.

"On the contrary, total atheism is more respectable than worldly indifference," he added, gaily and ingenuously.

"Oho, so that's how you are."

"A complete atheist stands on the next-to-last upper step to the most complete faith (he may or may not take that step), while the indifferent one has no faith, apart from a bad fear."

"However, you . . . you have read the Apocalypse?"

"I have."

"Do you remember: 'To the angel of the church in Laodicea write . . .'?"

"I do. Lovely words."

"Lovely? A strange expression for a bishop, and generally you are an odd man . . . Where is the book?" Stavrogin became strangely hurried and anxious, his eyes seeking the book on the table. "I'd like to read it to you . . . do you have a Russian translation?"

"I know it, I know the passage, I remember it very well," said Tikhon.

"You know it by heart? Recite it! . . ."

He quickly lowered his eyes, rested his two palms on his knees, and impatiently prepared to listen. Tikhon recited, recalling it word for word: "And unto the angel of the church of the Laodiceans write; These things saith the Amen, the faithful and true witness, the beginning of the creation of God; I know thy works, that thou art neither

*"very little"

cold nor hot: I would thou wert cold or hot. So then because thou art lukewarm, and neither cold nor hot, I will spue thee out of my mouth. Because thou sayest, I am rich, and increased with goods, and have need of nothing; and knowest not that thou art wretched, and miserable, and poor, and blind, and naked . . ."[7]

"Enough . . ." Stavrogin cut him short. "It's for the middling sort, for the indifferent ones, right? You know, I love you very much."

"And I you," Tikhon responded in a low voice.

Stavrogin fell silent and suddenly lapsed again into his former pensiveness. This occurred as if in fits, for the third time now. And he had said "I love you" to Tikhon also almost in a fit, at least unexpectedly for himself. More than a minute passed.

"Don't be angry," Tikhon whispered, touching his elbow just barely with his finger, and as if growing timid himself. The other gave a start and frowned wrathfully.

"How could you tell I was angry?" he said quickly. Tikhon was about to say something, but the other suddenly interrupted him in inexplicable alarm:

"What made you precisely think I was sure to get angry? Yes, I was angry, you're right, and precisely for having said 'I love you.' You're right, but you're a crude cynic, your thoughts are humiliating to human nature. There might be no anger if it was another man and not me . . . However, the point isn't about this other one, but about me. Anyhow you're an odd man and a holy fool . . ."

He was growing more and more irritated, and, strangely, no longer bothered about his words:

"Listen, I don't like spies and psychologists, at least those who try to pry into my soul. I don't invite anyone into my soul, I don't need anyone, I'm able to manage by myself. You think I'm afraid of you?" he raised his voice and looked up defiantly. "You are fully convinced that I've come to reveal some 'dreadful' secret to you and are waiting for it with all the monkish curiosity you're capable of? Well, know then that I shall reveal nothing to you, no secret, because I don't need you at all."

Tikhon looked at him steadily:

"You are struck that the Lamb loves the cold one better than the merely lukewarm one," he said. "You do not want to be *merely* lukewarm. I feel that you are in the grip of an extraordinary intention, perhaps a terrible one. If so, I implore you, do not torment yourself and tell me everything you've come with."

"And you knew for certain that I had come with something?"

"I . . . guessed it from your face," Tikhon whispered, lowering his eyes.

Nikolai Vsevolodovich was somewhat pale, his hands were trembling slightly. For a few seconds he looked motionlessly and silently at Tikhon, as if making a final decision. Finally he took some printed pages from the side pocket of his frock coat and placed them on the table.

"These are pages intended for distribution," he said in a somewhat faltering voice. "If at least one man reads them, then you should know that I am not going to conceal them, and everyone will read them. That is decided. I don't need you at all, because I've decided everything. But read it . . . While you're reading, don't say anything, and when you've finished—say everything . . ."

"Shall I read it?" Tikhon asked hesitantly.

"Read it; I've long been at peace."

"No, I can't make it out without my glasses; the print is fine, foreign."

"Here are your glasses," Stavrogin picked them up from the table, handed them to him, and leaned back on the sofa. Tikhon immersed himself in reading.

II

THE PRINT was indeed foreign—three printed pages of ordinary, small-format stationery, sewn together. It must have been printed secretly by some Russian press abroad, and at first glance the pages looked very much like a tract. The heading read: "From Stavrogin."

I introduce this document into my chronicle verbatim. One may suppose it is now known to many. I have allowed myself only to correct the spelling errors, rather numerous, which even surprised me somewhat, since the author was after all an educated man, and even a well-read one (judging relatively, of course). In the style I have made no changes, despite the errors and even obscurities. In any case, it is apparent that the author is above all not a writer.

FROM STAVROGIN

I, Nikolai Stavrogin, a retired officer, was living in Petersburg in the year 186–, giving myself over to debauchery in which I found no pleasure. For a certain stretch of time then, I had three apartments. In one of them I myself lived, in a rooming house with board and service, where Marya Lebyadkin, now my lawful wife, was then also living. My other two apartments I then rented by the month for an intrigue: in one of them I received a lady who was in love with me, and in the other her maid, and for a while I was much taken up by the intention of bringing the two together, so that the mistress and the wench should meet at my place, in the presence of my friends and the husband. Knowing both their characters, I expected to derive great pleasure from this stupid joke.

While I was leisurely preparing this meeting, I had more often to visit one of these apartments, in a large house on Gorokhovy Street, since this was where the maid used to come. I had only one room there, on the fourth floor, rented from some Russian tradespeople.[8] They themselves occupied the next room, a smaller one, so much so that the door between the two was always left open, which was just what I wanted. The husband worked in someone's office and was away from morning till night. The wife, a woman of about forty, cut up and remade new clothes out of old ones, and also frequently left the house to deliver what she had sewn. I would be left alone with their daughter, about fourteen years old, I think, but who still looked quite a child. Her name was Matryosha. The mother loved her, but used to beat her often, and yelled at her terribly, as such women have a habit of doing. This girl served me and tidied up behind my screen. I declare that I have forgotten the number of the house. Now, on inquiring, I have learned that the old house was demolished, resold, and in place of two or three former houses there stands one very large new one. I have also forgotten the family name of my tradespeople (maybe I did not know it then, either). I remember that the woman's name was Stepanida—

Mikhailovna, I think. His I don't remember. Who they were, where they came from, and what has become of them, I have no idea. I suppose if one were really to start searching and making all sorts of inquiries from the Petersburg police, one might find traces. The apartment was on the courtyard, in a corner. It all happened in June. The house was of a light blue color.

One day a penknife, which I didn't need at all and which was just lying about, disappeared from my table. I told the landlady, not even thinking she would whip her daughter. But the woman had just yelled at the child (I lived simply, and they didn't stand on ceremony with me) for the disappearance of some rag, suspecting her of filching it, and had even pulled her hair. And when this same rag was found under the tablecloth, the girl chose not to utter a word of reproach and watched silently. I noticed this, and then for the first time noticed the child's face, which before had just flitted by. She was pale-haired and freckled, an ordinary face, but with much in it that was childish and quiet, extremely quiet. The mother was displeased that the daughter did not reproach her for having beaten her for nothing, and she shook her fist at her, but did not hit her; just then my penknife came up. Indeed, there was no one there except the three of us, and only the girl had gone behind my screen. The woman went wild, because her first beating had been unjust, rushed for the broom, pulled some twigs from it, and whipped the girl so that she raised welts on her, right in front of me. Matryosha did not cry out from the birching, but somehow whimpered strangely at each stroke. And afterwards she whimpered very much, for a whole hour.

But before that here is what happened: at the same moment as the landlady was rushing to pull the twigs from the broom, I found the knife on my bed, where it had somehow fallen from the table. It immediately came into my head not to announce anything, so that she would get a birching. I decided on it instantly: such moments always take my breath away. But I intend to tell everything in the firmest words, so that nothing remains hidden any longer.

Every extremely shameful, immeasurably humiliating, mean, and, above all, ridiculous position I have happened to get into in my life has always aroused in me, along with boundless wrath, an unbelievable pleasure. Exactly the same as in moments of crime, or in moments threatening to life. If I was stealing something, I would feel, while committing the theft, intoxication from the awareness of the depth of my meanness. It was not meanness that I loved (here my reason was completely sound), but I liked the intoxication from the tormenting awareness of my baseness. In the same way, each time I stood at the barrier waiting for my adversary to shoot, I felt the same shameful and violent sensation, and once extraordinarily strongly. I confess, I often sought it out myself, because for me it is stronger than any of its sort. When I was slapped (and I have been slapped twice in my life), it was there as well, in spite of the terrible wrath. But if, for all that, the wrath can be restrained, the pleasure will exceed anything imaginable. I never spoke of it to anyone, never even hinted at it, and concealed it as a shame and a disgrace. Yet when I was badly beaten once in a pot-house in Petersburg, and dragged by the hair, I did not feel this sensation, but only unbelievable wrath, without being drunk, but just fighting. Yet if that Frenchman abroad, the *vicomte* who slapped me and whose lower jaw I shot off for it, had seized my hair and pulled me down, I would have felt intoxication and perhaps not even wrath. So it seemed to me then.

All this so that everyone will know that this feeling never subjected the whole of me, but there was always full consciousness left (and it was all based on consciousness!). And though it possessed me to the point of recklessness, it never came to the point of forgetting myself. Going as far as a perfect burning in me, I was at the same time quite able to subdue it, even to stop it at its peak. I am convinced that I could live my whole life as a monk, despite the animal sensuality I am endowed with and which I have always provoked. Giving myself with extraordinary immoderation, until the age of sixteen, to the vice confessed by Jean-Jacques Rousseau,[9] I stopped it the moment I decided I wanted to, in my seventeenth year. I am always master of myself when I want to be. And so, let it be known that I do not want to seek irresponsibility for my crimes either in the environment or in illness.

When the punishment was over, I put the knife into my waistcoat pocket, went out, and threw it away in the street, far from the house, so that no one would ever know. Then I waited for two days. The girl cried a little and became even more silent; against me, I am convinced, she had no spiteful feeling. Though there probably was some shame at having been punished in such a way in front of me, she hadn't cried out, but had only whimpered under the strokes, of course because I was standing there and saw it all. But, being a child, she probably blamed only herself for this shame. Up to then, perhaps, she had only feared me, not personally, but as a tenant, a stranger, and it seems she was very timid.

It was during those two days that I once asked myself the question whether I could drop it and walk away from my planned intention, and I felt at once that I could, could at any time and at that very moment. Around then I wanted to kill myself, from the disease of indifference; however, I do not know from what. During those same two or three days (because I absolutely had to wait until the girl forgot it all), I committed a theft in the rooming house, probably to distract myself from incessant dreaming, or just for the fun of it. This was the only theft in my life.

There were many people nesting in that rooming house. Among them was one official and his family, living in two furnished rooms; about forty years old, not all that stupid, and with a decent air, but poor. I never got close with him, and he was afraid of the company that surrounded me there. He had just received his pay, thirty-five roubles. What chiefly prompted me was that at that moment I really did need money (though four days later I received a postal money order), so that I stole as if from need and not as a joke. It was done brazenly and obviously: I simply went into his room while he and his wife and children were having dinner in their other closet. There on the chair, right next to the door, lay his folded uniform. The thought had suddenly flashed in me still in the corridor. I thrust my hand into the pocket and took out the wallet. But the official heard a rustle and peeked out of the closet. It seems he even saw at least something, but since it was not everything, of course he did not believe his eyes. I said that as I was going down the corridor I came in to glance at the time on his wall clock. "Stopped, sir," he replied, and I left.

I was drinking a lot then, and there used to be a whole crowd in my rooms, Lebyadkin among them. I threw out the wallet with the small change and kept the bills. There were thirty-two roubles, three red bills and two yellow. I broke one of the red ones immediately and sent for champagne; then I sent another red one, and then the third. About four hours later, in the evening, the official stood waiting for me in the corridor.

"Nikolai Vsevolodovich, when you came in earlier, didn't you accidentally knock my uniform off the chair . . . where it was lying by the door?"

"Not that I remember. Your uniform was lying there?"

"Yes, lying there, sir."

"On the floor?"

"First on the chair and then on the floor."

"So, did you pick it up?"

"I did."

"Well, what more do you want?"

"In that case, nothing, sir . . ."

He did not dare finish, and he did not dare tell anyone in the rooming house—so timid these people are. However, everybody in the rooming house was terribly afraid and respectful of me then. Afterwards I enjoyed meeting his eyes once or twice in the corridor. But quickly got bored.

As soon as three days passed, I went back to Gorokhovy Street. The mother was going out somewhere with a bundle; the tradesman was, of course, not there. Matryosha and I remained. The windows were open. The tenants of the house were all craftsmen, and all day long there was a tapping of hammers and singing coming from all the floors. We had been there an hour already. Matryosha sat in her closet on a low bench, back to me, pottering over something with her needle. At last she suddenly started to sing softly, very softly; she sometimes did that. I took out my watch and looked at the time—it was two. My heart was beginning to pound. But then I suddenly asked myself again: could I stop? and answered at once that I could. I got up and began stealing towards her. They had a lot of geraniums in the window, and the sun was shining terribly brightly. I quietly sat down on the floor next to her. She gave a start and at first was unbelievably frightened and jumped up. I took her hand and softly kissed it, pulling her back down onto the bench, and began looking into her eyes. The fact that I had kissed her hand suddenly made her laugh like a child, but only for one second, because she impetuously jumped up again, now so frightened that a spasm passed over her face. She looked at me with horribly fixed eyes, and her lips began to twitch, as if on the verge of tears, but all the same she did not cry out. I began to kiss her hands again and, taking her on my knees, kissed her face and her feet. When I kissed her feet, she recoiled all over and smiled as if in shame, but with some crooked smile. Her whole face flushed with shame. I kept whispering something to her. Finally, there suddenly occurred an odd thing, which I will never forget and which caused me astonishment: the girl threw her arms around my neck and suddenly began kissing me terribly herself. Her face expressed complete admiration. I almost got up and left—so unpleasant was it in such a tiny child—out of pity. But I overcame the sudden sensation of my fear and stayed.

When it was all over, she was embarrassed. I didn't try to reassure her and no longer caressed her. She looked at me, smiling timidly. Her face suddenly seemed stupid to me. Embarrassment quickly came over her more and more with every moment. At last, she covered her face with her hands and stood in the corner motionlessly, turned to the wall. I was afraid she was going to get frightened again, as she had earlier, and silently left the house.

I suppose everything that had happened finally had to appear to her as a boundless outrage, with mortal horror. Despite the Russian curses she must have been hearing since she was in diapers, and all sorts of strange conversations, I have the full conviction that she still understood nothing. Most likely it seemed to her in the end that she had committed an unbelievable crime and was mortally guilty for it—that she had "killed God."

That night I had the fight in the pot-house which I have mentioned fleetingly. But I woke up in my rooms the next morning, Lebyadkin had brought me. My first thought on waking up was of whether she had told or not; this was a moment of real fear, though not very strong yet. I was very cheerful that morning and terribly kind to everyone, and the whole crowd was very pleased with me. But I dropped them all and went to Gorokhovy Street. I met her downstairs in the entry-way. She was coming back from the shop where she had been sent to buy chicory. When she saw me, she shot up the stairs in terrible fear. When I came in, her mother had already slapped her twice in the face for having run in "headlong," which also covered the real reason for her fright. And so, for the time being everything was quiet. She hid somewhere and never came in while I was there. I stayed for about an hour and then left.

Towards evening I again felt fear, but this time it was incomparably stronger. Of course, I could deny it, but they could also expose me. I kept imagining hard labor. I had never felt any fear, and, apart from this occasion in my life, was never afraid of anything either before or since. Especially not of Siberia, though I could have been sent there more than once. But this time I was frightened and really felt fear, I do not know why, for the first time in my life—a very tormenting sensation. Besides that, in the evening, in my rooms, I came to hate her so much that I decided to kill her. My chief hatred was at the remembrance of her smile. Contempt together with boundless revulsion would spring up in me for the way she had rushed into the corner after it all and covered herself with her hands; I was seized by an inexplicable rage; then came a chill, and when fever began to set in towards morning, I was again overcome by fear, but so strong this time that I have never known a stronger torment. But I no longer hated the girl; at least it did not reach such a paroxysm as the evening before. I observed that strong fear utterly drives out hatred and vengeful feeling.

I woke up around noon, healthy and even surprised at some of yesterday's feelings. I was nonetheless in a bad humor, and again felt compelled to go to Gorokhovy Street, despite all my revulsion. I remember wanting terribly at that moment to have a quarrel with someone, only a real one. But on coming to Gorokhovy Street, I suddenly found Nina Savelyevna in my room, the maid, who had already been waiting for me for about an hour. I was not at all in love with the girl, so that she had come a bit afraid that I might be angry at the uninvited visit. But I was suddenly very glad to see her. She was not bad-looking, but modest and with the sort of manners common people like, so that my landlady had long been praising her to me. I found them together over coffee, and the landlady was greatly enjoying the pleasant conversation. In the corner of the room I noticed Matryosha. She stood and gazed fixedly at her mother and the visitor. When I came in, she did not hide as before, and did not run away. Only it seemed to me that she had become very thin and that she had a fever. I was tender with Nina and closed the door to the landlady's room, something I hadn't done for a long time, so that Nina left perfectly pleased. I myself took her out and for two days did not go to Goro-khovy Street. I was already sick of it.

I decided to finish it all, to give up the apartment and leave Peters-burg. But when I came to give up the apartment, I found the landlady worried and distressed: for three days Matryosha had been sick, lying every night in a fever and raving all night. Of course, I asked what she was raving about (we were talking in a whisper in my room). She whispered to me that she was raving "something terrible," saying "I killed God." I offered to bring a doctor at my own expense, but she did not want to: "God willing, it'll just go away, she doesn't lie down all the time, she goes out during the day, she just ran to the store." I decided to find Matryosha when she was alone, and since the landlady had let on that she had to go to the Petersburg side by five o'clock,[10] I decided to come back in the evening.

I had dinner in a tavern. Came back at exactly five-fifteen. I always let myself in with my own key. There was no one there but Matryosha. She was lying in their closet, behind the screen, on her mother's bed, and I saw her peek out; but I pretended not to notice. All the windows were open. The air was warm, it was even hot. I walked about the room and sat down on the sofa. I remember it all to the last minute. It decidedly gave me pleasure not to start talking with Matryosha. I waited and sat there for a whole hour, and suddenly she herself jumped from behind the screen. I heard her two feet hit the floor as she jumped off the bed, then rather quick steps, and then she was standing on the threshold of my room. She looked at me silently. In the three or four days since that time, during which I had never once seen her up close, she had indeed become very thin. Her face was as if dried up and her head must have been hot. Her eyes had grown big and looked at me fixedly, as if with dull curiosity—so it seemed to me at first. I was sitting on the corner of the sofa, looked at her, and did not budge. And then I suddenly felt hatred again. But very soon I noticed that she was not frightened of me at all, but was perhaps more likely delirious. But she was not delirious either. She suddenly began shaking her head rapidly at me, as people do when they reproach very much, and suddenly she raised her little fist at me and began threatening me with it from where she stood. For the first moment this gesture seemed funny to me, but I could not stand it for long; I got up and moved nearer to her. There was despair in her face, such as was impossible to see on the face of a child. She kept brandishing her little fist at me threateningly and shaking her head in reproach. I came close and cautiously began to speak, but saw that she would not understand. Then suddenly she covered her face impetuously with both hands, like before, walked over and stood by the window, back to me. I left her, returned to my room, and sat by my own window. I have no idea why I did not leave then, but stayed as if I were waiting. Soon I heard her hurrying steps again, she walked out the door onto the wooden gallery, from which a stairway went down, and I at once ran to my door, opened it a bit, and had just time to spy Matryosha going into a tiny shed, like a chicken coop, next to the other place. A strange thought flashed in my mind. I closed the door and—back to the window. Of course, it was impossible to believe a fleeting thought; "and yet . . ." (I remember everything.)

A minute later I looked at my watch and made note of the time. Evening was coming. A fly was buzzing over me and kept landing on my face. I caught it, held it in my fingers, and let it go out the window. Very loudly a cart rolled into the courtyard below. Very loudly (and for long now) an artisan, a tailor, had been singing a song in the corner of the yard, in his window. He was sitting over his work, and I could see him. It occurred to me that since no one had met me when I came through the gateway and went upstairs, so no one had better meet me going downstairs now, and I moved the chair away from the window. Then I picked up a book, threw it down again, began watching a tiny red spider on a geranium leaf, and became oblivious. I remember everything to the last moment.

I suddenly snatched out my watch. It was twenty minutes since she went out. My guess was assuming the shape of a probability. But I decided to wait another quarter of an hour. It also occurred to me that she might have come back and that I perhaps had not heard; but that could not be: there was dead silence and I could hear the whine of every little fly. Suddenly my heart began to pound. I took out my watch: three minutes to go; I sat them out, though my heart was pounding so that it hurt. Then I got up, covered myself with my hat, buttoned my coat, and glanced around the room to make sure everything was in place and there were no signs that I had come. I moved the chair closer to the window, as it had stood before. Finally, I quietly opened the door, locked it with my key, and went to the shed. The door was closed, but not locked; I knew it could not be locked, yet I did not want to open it, but got up on tiptoe and began looking through the crack. At that very moment, as I was getting up on tiptoe, I recalled that when I was sitting by the window looking at the little red spider and became oblivious, I was thinking of how I would get up on tiptoe and reach that crack with my eyes. By putting in this trifle here, I want to prove with certainty to what degree of clarity I was in possession of my mental faculties. I looked through that crack for a long time, it was dark inside, but not totally. At last I made out what I needed . . . I wanted to be totally sure.

I decided finally that I could leave, and went downstairs. I did not meet anyone. About three hours later we were all in our shirtsleeves, drinking tea in my rooms and playing a friendly game of cards. Lebyadkin was reciting poetry. Many stories were told and, as if by design, they were all successful and funny, not stupid as usual. Kirillov was also there. No one drank, and though a bottle of rum was standing there, only Lebyadkin kept nipping from it. Prokhor Malov observed that "when Nikolai Vsevolodovich is pleased and not moping, all our boys are cheerful and talk cleverly." It sank into my mind right then.

But by around eleven o'clock the caretaker's girl came running from the landlady, from Gorokhovy Street, bringing me the news that Matryosha had hanged herself. I went with the girl and saw that the landlady did not know herself why she had sent for me. She was howling and thrashing, there was turmoil, a lot of people, police. I stood in the entryway for a while and then left.

I was hardly inconvenienced, though they did ask the appropriate questions. But apart from the fact that the girl had been sick and occasionally delirious over the past few days, so that for my part I had offered a doctor at my own expense, I had decidedly nothing to give as evidence. They also asked me about the penknife; I said that the landlady had given the girl a whipping, but that it was nothing. No one found out that I had come in the evening. I heard nothing about the results of the medical examination.

For a week or so I did not go back there. I went when they had long since buried her, in order to give up the apartment. The landlady was still crying, though she was already pottering with her rags and sewing as before. "It was on account of your knife that I offended her," she said to me, but without great reproach. I paid her off on the pretext that I really could no longer remain in such an apartment and receive Nina Savelyevna in it. She praised Nina Savelyevna once more on parting. As I left I gave her five roubles on top of what I owed for the apartment.

And generally I was bored with life then, to the point of stupefaction. Once the danger was past, I all but completely forgot the incident on Gorokhovy Street, like everything else then, except that for some time I remembered spitefully how I had turned coward. I vented my spite on whomever I could. At the same time, but not at all for any reason or other, I conceived the notion of somehow maiming my life, only in as repulsive a way as possible. For a year already I had been thinking of shooting myself; something better turned up. Once, looking at the lame Marya Timofeevna Lebyadkin, who was something of a servant in those corners, not yet crazy then, but simply an ecstatic idiot, and secretly madly in love with me (as our boys spied out), I decided suddenly to marry her. The thought of Stavrogin marrying such a last being tickled my nerves. Nothing uglier could be imagined. But I will not venture to decide whether my decisiveness included at least unconsciously (of course, unconsciously!) my spite at the base cowardice that had come over me after the thing with Matryosha. I do not think so, really; but in any case I went to the altar not just because of "a bet for wine after a drunken dinner." The witnesses to the marriage were Kirillov and Pyotr Verkhovensky, who happened to be in Petersburg then; and, finally, Lebyadkin himself, and Prokhor Malov (now dead). No one else ever learned of it, and these gave their word to be silent. This silence has always seemed to me a vile thing, as it were, but so far it has not been broken, though I had the intention of announcing it; I announce it now, along with everything else.

After the wedding, I left for the province to see my mother. I went for distraction, because it was unbearable. In our town I left the idea that I was crazy—an idea not eradicated even now, and undoubtedly harmful to me, as I will explain further on. I then went abroad and stayed for four years.

I was in the East, I stood through eight-hour vigils on Mount

Athos,[11] was in Egypt, lived in Switzerland, even went to Iceland; sat out a whole yearlong course in Göttingen. During the last year I became very close with one noble Russian family in Paris and two Russian girls in Switzerland. About two years ago, in Frankfurt, passing by a stationer's shop, I noticed among the photographs on display a small picture of a girl, dressed in an elegant child's costume, but very much resembling Matryosha. I bought the picture at once and, coming to my hotel, placed it on the mantelpiece. There it stayed untouched for about a week, and I never once glanced at it; when I left Frankfurt, I forgot to take it with me.

I am setting this down precisely in order to prove the extent of my power over my memories, and how unfeeling for them I had become. I would reject them all in a mass, and the whole mass would obediently disappear each time the moment I wanted it to. I have always felt bored remembering the past, and was never able to talk about the past, as almost everyone does. As for Matryosha, I even forgot her picture on the mantelpiece.

About a year ago, in the spring, traveling through Germany, I absentmindedly missed the station where I should have changed for my direction, and got onto a different branch. They let me off at the next station; it was three o'clock in the afternoon, a bright day. It was a tiny German town. A hotel was pointed out to me. I had to wait: the next train came through at eleven o'clock at night. I was even pleased with the adventure, because I was not in any hurry. The hotel turned out to be trashy and small, but all sunk in greenery and completely surrounded with flower beds. They gave me a cramped little room. I had a nice meal, and since I had spent the whole night on the train, I fell asleep excellently after dinner, at four o'clock in the afternoon.

I had a dream which for me was totally unexpected, because I had never before had one like it. In Dresden, in the gallery, there exists a painting by Claude Lorrain—"Acis and Galatea,"[12] I think, according to the catalogue, but I always called it "The Golden Age," I do not know why myself. I had seen it before, but now, three days earlier, I had noticed it once again as I was passing through. It was this painting that I saw in my dream, though not as a painting, but as if it were some kind of verity.

A corner of the Greek archipelago; blue, caressing waves, islands and rocks, a luxuriant coastline, a magic panorama in the distance, an inviting sunset—words cannot express it. Here European mankind remembered its cradle, here were the first scenes from mythology, its earthly paradise . . . Here beautiful people lived! They rose and lay down to sleep happy and innocent; the groves were filled with their merry songs, the great abundance of their untapped forces went into love, into simplehearted joy. The sun poured down its rays upon these islands and this sea, rejoicing over its beautiful children. A wondrous dream, a lofty delusion! The most incredible vision of all that have ever been, to which mankind throughout its life has given all its forces, for which it has sacrificed everything, for which prophets have died on crosses and been killed, without which people do not want to live and cannot even die. It was as if I lived through this whole sensation in my dream; I don't know precisely what I dreamed about, but the rocks and sea, the slanting rays of the setting sun—it was as if I still saw it all when I woke up and opened my eyes, for the first time in my life literally wet with tears. A feeling of happiness, as yet unknown to me, went through my heart even till it hurt. It was already full evening; in the window of my little room, through the foliage of the flowers in the window, a whole sheaf of bright slanting rays of the setting sun was bursting and flooding me with light. I quickly closed my eyes again, as if straining to return to the departed dream, but suddenly, as if in the midst of the bright, bright light, I saw some tiny dot. It was taking some shape, and suddenly appeared distinctly to me as a tiny red spider. I recalled it at once on the geranium leaf, when the slanting rays of the setting sun had been pouring in just as they were now. It was as though something pierced me, I raised myself and sat up on the bed . . . (This was how it all happened then!)

I saw before me (oh, not in reality! and if only, if only it had been a real vision!), I saw Matryosha, wasted and with feverish eyes, exactly the same as when she had stood on my threshold and, shaking her head, had raised her tiny little fist at me. And nothing had ever seemed so tormenting to me! The pitiful despair of a helpless ten-year-old being with a still unformed mind, who was threatening me (with what? what could she do to me?), but, of course, blaming only herself! Nothing like it had ever happened to me. I sat until nightfall, not moving and forgetting about time. Is this what is called remorse of conscience or repentance? I do not know, and I cannot tell to this day. Perhaps even to this moment I do not loathe the memory of the act itself. Perhaps this remembrance even now contains something pleasurable for my passions. No—what is unbearable to me is only this image alone, and precisely on the threshold, with its raised and threatening little fist, only that look alone, only that minute alone, only that shaking head. This is what I cannot bear, because since then it appears to me almost every day. It does not appear on its own, but I myself evoke it, and cannot help evoking it, even though I cannot live with it. Oh, if only I could ever see her really, at least in a hallucination!

I have other old memories, perhaps even better than this one. I behaved worse with one woman, and she died from it. In duels I have taken the lives of two men who were innocent before me. Once I was mortally insulted and did not take revenge on my adversary. There is one poisoning to my account—intentional and successful and unknown to anyone. (If need be, I'll tell about it all.)

But why is it that none of these memories evokes anything of the kind in me? Only hatred, perhaps, and that caused by my present situation, while before I would cold-bloodedly forget it and keep it away.

After that I wandered about for almost this whole year trying to occupy myself. I know I can remove the girl even now, whenever I wish. As before, I am in perfect control of my will. But the whole point is that I have never wanted to do it, I myself do not want to and will not want to; that I do know. And so it will go on, right up to my madness.

In Switzerland, two months ago, I was able to fall in love with one girl, or, better to say, I felt a fit of the same passion, with the same sort of violent impulse, as used to happen only long ago, in the beginning. I felt a terrible temptation for a new crime—that is, to commit bigamy (since I was already married); but I fled, following the advice of another girl to whom I confided almost everything. Besides, this new crime would in no way have rid me of Matryosha.

So it is that I have decided to print these pages and bring them to Russia in three hundred copies. When the time comes, I will send them to the police and the local authorities; simultaneously, I will send them to the editorial offices of all the newspapers, requesting that they be made public, and to my numerous acquaintances in Petersburg and in Russia. They will equally appear in translation abroad. I know that legally I will perhaps not be inconvenienced, at least not considerably; I am making this statement on my own, and have no accuser; besides, there are very few if any proofs. Finally, there is the deeply rooted idea that my mind is deranged, and the efforts my family will certainly make to use this idea to stifle any legal prosecution that might be dangerous for me. I state this incidentally, to prove that I am fully in my right mind and understand my position. But there will remain for me those who know everything and who will look at me, and I at them. And the more of them the better. Whether this will make it any easier for me—I do not know. I am doing it as a last resort.

Once again: a good search through the Petersburg police records might turn something up. The tradespeople might still be in Petersburg. The house will, of course, be remembered. It was light blue. As for me, I won't be going anywhere, and for some time (a year or two) I can always be found at Skvoreshniki, my mother's estate. If I'm summoned, I'll appear anywhere.

Nikolai Stavrogin

The reading took about an hour. Tikhon read slowly and perhaps reread some passages a second time. Stavrogin sat all the while silent and motionless. Strangely, the shade of impatience, distraction, and as if delirium that had been on his face all that morning almost disappeared, giving way to calm and as if a sort of sincerity, which lent him an air almost of dignity. Tikhon removed his glasses and began first, somewhat cautiously.

"And might it be possible to make some corrections in this document?"

"What for? I wrote it sincerely," replied Stavrogin.

"To touch up the style a little."

"I forgot to warn you that all your words will be in vain; I will not put off my intention; don't bother talking me out of it."

"You did not forget to warn me of that earlier, before the reading."

"Never mind, I repeat again: no matter how strong your objections, I will not leave off my intention. Note that by this unfortunate phrase, or fortunate—think what you like—I am in no way inviting you to quickly start objecting to me and entreating me," he added, as if unable to help himself, again suddenly falling for a moment into the former tone, but he at once smiled sadly at his own words.

"I would not even be able to object or to entreat you especially to give up your intention. This thought is a great thought, and there is no way to express a Christian thought more fully. Repentance cannot go any further than the astonishing deed you are contemplating, if only . . ."

"If only what?"

"If only it is indeed repentance and indeed a Christian thought."

"These are fine points, it seems to me; does it make any difference? I wrote it sincerely."

"It is as if you purposely want to portray yourself as coarser than your heart would wish . . ." Tikhon was growing more and more bold. Obviously, the "document" had made a strong impression on him.

" 'Portray'? I tell you again: I was not 'portraying myself' and especially was not 'posturing.' "

Tikhon quickly lowered his eyes.

"This document comes straight from the need of a mortally wounded heart—do I understand correctly?" he went on insistently and with extraordinary ardor. "Yes, it is repentance and the natural need for it that have overcome you, and you have struck upon a great path, a path of an unheard-of sort. But it is as if you already hate beforehand all those who will read what is described here and are challenging them to battle. If you are not ashamed to confess the crime, why are you ashamed of repentance? Let them look at me, you say; well, and you yourself, how are you going to look at them? Certain places in your account are stylistically accentuated; as if you admire your own psychology and seize upon every little detail just to astonish the reader with an unfeelingness that is not in you. What is that if not the proud challenge of a guilty man to his judge?"

"Where is there any challenge? I eliminated all personal reasoning."

Tikhon held his peace. Color even spread over his pale cheeks.

"Let's leave that," Stavrogin brought it abruptly to a halt. "Allow me instead to make you a question: here it is already five minutes that we've been talking after that" (he nodded to the pages) "and I don't see any expression of loathing or shame in you . . . you're not squeamish, it seems! . . ."

He did not finish and grinned.

"That is, you wish I'd quickly voice my contempt for you," Tikhon rounded off firmly. "I won't conceal anything from you: I was horrified at this great idle force being spent deliberately on abomination. As for the crime itself, many people sin in the same way, and live in peace and quiet with their conscience, even regarding it as one of the inevitable trespasses of youth. There are old men who sin in the same way, even contentedly and playfully. The whole world is filled with all these horrors. But you have felt the whole depth of it, something which rarely happens to such an extent."

"You haven't taken to respecting me after these pages?" Stavrogin grinned crookedly.

"To that I shall not respond directly. But, of course, there is not and cannot be any greater and more terrible crime than your act with the maiden."

"Let's quit putting a yardstick to it. I'm somewhat surprised at your opinion about other people and the ordinariness of such a crime. Perhaps I don't suffer nearly as much as I've written here, and perhaps I've really heaped too many lies on myself," he added unexpectedly.

Tikhon once more held his peace. Stavrogin was not even thinking of leaving; on the contrary, he again began to lapse at moments into deep pensiveness.

"And this girl," Tikhon began again, very timidly, "with whom you broke off in Switzerland, is, if I may ask . . . where is she at the present moment?"

"Here."

Again silence.

"Perhaps I was indeed heaping lies on myself," Stavrogin repeated insistently once more. "However, what of it if I'm challenging them by the coarseness of my confession, since you did notice the challenge? I'll make them hate me even more, that's all. And so much the easier for me."

"That is, their hatred will evoke yours, and, hating, it will be easier for you than if you were to accept their pity?"

"You're right. You know," he suddenly laughed, "I may well be called a Jesuit and a pious hypocrite, ha, ha, ha! Right?"

"Of course, there will be such an opinion. And how soon do you hope to carry out this intention?"

"Today, tomorrow, the day after tomorrow, how do I know? Only very soon. You're right: I think what's precisely going to happen is that I'll make it public unexpectedly and precisely at some vengeful, hateful moment, when I'm hating them most of all."

"Answer one question, but sincerely, for me alone, only me: if someone forgave you for that" (Tikhon pointed to the pages), "and not someone of those you respect or fear, but a stranger, a man you will never know, silently, reading your terrible confession to himself, would this thought make it easier for you, or would it make no difference?"

"Easier," Stavrogin replied in a soft voice, lowering his eyes. "If you were to forgive me, it would be much easier for me," he added unexpectedly and in a half-whisper.

"And you me, as well," Tikhon said in a deeply moved voice.

"What for? what have you done to me? Ah, yes, it's a monastery formula?"

"For my sins both voluntary and involuntary.[13] In sinning, each man sins against all, and each man is at least partly guilty for another's sin. There is no isolated sin. And I am a great sinner, perhaps more than you are."

"I'll tell you the whole truth: I wish you to forgive me, and another with you, and a third, but the rest—the rest had better hate me. But I wish it in order to endure with humility . . ."

"And universal pity you would not be able to endure with the same humility?"

"Perhaps I wouldn't. You picked that up very nicely. But . . . why are you doing this?"

"I feel the degree of your sincerity and, of course, am much to blame for not knowing how to approach people. I've always felt it to be my greatest failing," Tikhon said sincerely and feelingly, looking straight into Stavrogin's eyes. "It's only because I fear for you," he added, "there is an almost impassible abyss before you."

"That I won't endure? that I won't endure their hatred with humility?"

"Not only their hatred."

"And what else?"

"Their laughter," escaped from Tikhon, almost as if despite himself and in a half-whisper.

Stavrogin became embarrassed; uneasiness showed in his face.

"I anticipated that," he said. "So, then, I appeared as a very comical character to you on reading my 'document,' in spite of the whole tragedy? Don't worry, don't be put out . . . I did anticipate it."

"There will be horror on all sides, and, of course, more false than sincere. People fear only what directly threatens their personal interests. I'm not speaking of the pure souls: they will be horrified and will blame themselves, but they will not be noticeable. The laughter, however, will be universal."

"Add to that the thinker's observation that there is always something pleasing in another man's calamity."

"A correct thought."

"You, however . . . you yourself . . . I'm surprised at how badly you think of people, with what loathing," Stavrogin said, looking somewhat resentful.

"And yet, believe me, I said it judging more by myself than about other people," Tikhon exclaimed.

"Really? Can there indeed be at least something in your soul that finds amusement here in my calamity?"

"Who knows, perhaps there is. Oh, perhaps there is!"

"Enough. Show me, then, precisely what makes me ridiculous in my manuscript? I know what, but I want you to point your finger to it. And say it nice and cynically, say it with all the sincerity you're capable of. And I'll also tell you again that you are a terribly odd man."

"Even the form of this truly great repentance has something ridiculous in it. Oh, do not believe that you will not win!" he suddenly exclaimed almost in ecstasy. "Even this form will win" (he pointed to the pages), "if only you sincerely accept the beating and the spitting.[14] In the end it has always been that the most disgraceful cross becomes a great glory and a great power, if the humility of the deed is sincere.

It may even be that you will be comforted in your own life-time! . . ."

"So, in the form alone, in the style, you find something ridiculous?" Stavrogin persisted.

"And in the essence. The uncomeliness will kill it," Tikhon whispered, lowering his eyes.

"What, sir? Uncomeliness? The uncomeliness of what?"

"Of the crime. There are crimes that are truly uncomely. With crimes, whatever they may be, the more blood, the more horror there is, the more imposing they are, the more picturesque, so to speak; but there are crimes that are shameful, disgraceful, all horror aside, so to speak, even far too ungracious . . ."

Tikhon did not finish.

"That is," Stavrogin picked up in agitation, "you find I made quite a ridiculous figure when I was kissing the dirty little girl's foot . . . and all that I said about my temperament and . . . well, and all the rest . . . I understand. I understand you very well. And you despair of me precisely because it is uncomely, vile, no, not really vile, but shameful, ridiculous, and you think it's this, rather than anything else, that I won't be able to endure?"

Tikhon was silent.

"Yes, you do know people, that is, you know that I, precisely I, will not be able to endure . . . I understand why you asked about the young lady from Switzerland, whether she was here."

"You're not prepared, not tempered," Tikhon whispered timidly, with lowered eyes.

"Listen, Father Tikhon: I want to forgive myself, and that is my chief goal, my whole goal!" Stavrogin said suddenly, with grim rapture in his eyes. "I know that only then will the apparition vanish. That is why I am seeking boundless suffering, seeking it myself. So do not frighten me."

"If you believe that you can forgive yourself and can attain to this forgiveness in this world, then you believe everything!" Tikhon exclaimed rapturously. "How is it that you say you do not believe in God?"

Stavrogin made no reply.

"God will forgive your unbelief, for you venerate the Holy Spirit without knowing him."

"Christ, incidentally, will not forgive," Stavrogin asked, and a light shade of irony could be heard in the tone of the question, "for it is said in the book: 'Whoso shall offend one of these little ones'—remember? According to the Gospel, there is not and cannot be any greater crime.[15] In this book!"

He pointed to the Gospel.

"I have glad tidings for you about that," Tikhon spoke with tender feeling. "Christ, too, will forgive, if only you attain to forgiving yourself . . . Oh, no, no, do not believe that I have spoken a blasphemy: even if you do not attain to reconciliation with yourself and forgiveness of yourself, even then He will forgive you for your intention and for your great suffering . . . for there are no words or thoughts in human language to express *all* the ways and reasons of the Lamb, 'until his ways are openly revealed to us.'[16] Who can embrace him who is unembraceable, who can grasp the *whole* of him who is infinite!"

The corners of his mouth twitched as before, and a barely noticeable spasm again passed over his face. He restrained himself for a moment and then, unable to stand it, quickly lowered his eyes.

Stavrogin took his hat from the sofa.

"I'll come again sometime," he said with an air of great fatigue, "you and I . . . I appreciate only too well the pleasure of the conversation and the honor . . . and your feelings. Believe me, I understand why there are some who love you so. I ask your prayers from Him whom you love so much . . ."

"And you're leaving already?" Tikhon also rose quickly, as though not at all expecting such a speedy farewell. "And I . . ." he was as if at a loss, "I was about to present you with a request of my own, but . . . I don't know how . . . and now I'm afraid."

"Ah, kindly do." Stavrogin sat down at once, his hat in his hand. Tikhon looked at this hat, at this pose, the pose of a man suddenly turned worldly, both agitated and half crazy, who was granting him five minutes to finish his business—and became still more abashed.

"My whole request is merely that you . . . now you must admit, Nikolai Vsevolodovich (that is your name, I believe?), that if you make your pages public, you will spoil your fate . . . in the sense of a career, for example, and . . . in the sense of all the rest."

"Career?" Nikolai Vsevolodovich scowled unpleasantly.

"Why should you spoil it? Why, as it seems, such inflexibility?" Tikhon concluded almost pleadingly, obviously aware of his own awkwardness. A pained impression showed on the face of Nikolai Vsevolodovich.

"I have already asked you and will ask you again: all your words will be superfluous . . . and in general all our talk is beginning to be unbearable."

He turned significantly in his chair.

"You don't understand me, hear me out and don't be annoyed. You know my opinion: your deed, if done in humility, would be the greatest Christian deed, if you could endure it. Even if you were unable to endure it, all the same the Lord would count your initial sacrifice. Everything will be counted: not a word, not a movement of the soul, not a half thought will be in vain. But I am offering you, instead of this deed, another still greater one, something unquestionably great . . ."

Nikolai Vsevolodovich was silent.

"You are in the grip of a desire for martyrdom and self-sacrifice; conquer this desire as well, set aside your pages and your intention—and then you will overcome everything. You will put to shame all your pride and your demon! You will win, you will attain freedom . . ."

His eyes lit up; he pressed his hands together pleadingly.

"You quite simply want very much to avoid a scandal, and you are setting a trap for me, good Father Tikhon," Stavrogin mumbled casually and with vexation, making as if to get up. "In short, you would like me to settle down, perhaps get married, and end my life as a member of the local club, visiting your monastery on every feast day. What a penance! Although, being a reader of human hearts, you may even foresee that this will undoubtedly be so, and the only thing now is to beg me nicely, for the sake of decency, since this is what I myself am longing for—right?"

He laughed contortedly.

"No, not that penance, I am preparing a different one!" Tikhon continued ardently, not paying the least attention to Stavrogin's laughter or remark. "I know an elder, not here, but not far from here, a hermit and monk, and of such Christian wisdom as you and I cannot even understand. He will heed my requests. I will tell him all about you. Put yourself under obedience to him, under his orders, for some five or seven years, for as long as you yourself find necessary afterwards. Make a vow to yourself, and with this great sacrifice you will buy everything that you long for, and even what you do not expect, for you cannot understand now what you will receive!"

Stavrogin heard out his last suggestion seriously, even very seriously.

"You are quite simply suggesting that I become a monk in that monastery? Much though I respect you, that is precisely what I should have expected. Well, I shall even confess to you that the thought has already flashed in me at moments of faintheartedness: to hide away from people in a monastery, at least for a time, once I had made these pages public. But I immediately blushed at such baseness. But to take monastic vows—that never entered my head even in moments of the most fainthearted fear."

"You needn't be in a monastery, you needn't take vows, just be a novice secretly, unapparently, it may even be done so that you live entirely in the world . . ."

"Stop it, Father Tikhon," Stavrogin interrupted squeamishly and rose from the chair. Tikhon rose, too.

"What's the matter with you?" he suddenly cried out, peering at Tikhon almost in fright. The man stood before him, his hands pressed together in front of him, and a painful spasm, as if from the greatest fear, passed momentarily over his face.

"What's the matter? What's the matter?" Stavrogin repeated, rushing to support him. It seemed to him that the man was about to fall over.

"I see . . . I see as in reality," Tikhon exclaimed in a soul-penetrating voice and with an expression of the most intense grief, "that you, poor, lost youth, have never stood so close to the most terrible crime as at this moment!"

"Calm yourself!" Stavrogin kept repeating, decidedly alarmed for him. "I may still put it off . . . you're right, I may not be able to endure it, and in my spite I'll commit a new crime . . . all that is so . . . you're right, I'll put it off."

"No, not after the publication, but before the publication of the pages, a day, maybe an hour before the great step, you will throw yourself into a new crime as a way out, only to *avoid* publishing these pages!"

Stavrogin even trembled with wrath and almost with fear.

"Cursed psychologist!" he broke off suddenly in a rage and, without looking back, left the cell.

Notes

For many details in the following notes we are indebted to the commentaries in the Soviet Academy of Sciences edition, volume 12 (Leningrad, 1975).

PART ONE

CHAPTER 1: *Instead of an Introduction*

1. "Exile" here means internal exile to the provinces, a measure taken in Russia against politically suspect persons.

2. Pyotr Yakovlevich Chaadaev (1794?–1856) was the author of eight *Philosophical Letters,* written in French and circulated in manuscript, which among other things were sharply critical of Russia's intellectual isolation and social backwardness. The publication in 1836 of the first letter (the only one published in Chaadaev's lifetime) has been called the "opening shot" of the Westerner-Slavophil controversy which dominated nineteenth-century Russian social thought. Chaadaev's ideas in fact influenced both the Westerners, who favored various degrees of liberal reform to bring Russia into line with developments in Europe, and the Slavophils, proponents of Russian national culture and Orthodoxy.

Vissarion Grigorievich Belinsky (1811–48) was the most influential liberal critic and ideologist of his time, an advocate of socially conscious literature. He championed Dostoevsky's first novel, *Poor Folk* (1845), but Dostoevsky soon broke with him.

Timofei Nikolaevich Granovsky (1813–55), liberal historian and professor at Moscow University, is generally regarded as the founder of the Westerners. Stepan Trofimovich was first called "Granovsky" in the early drafts of *Demons;* Dostoevsky has given him Granovsky's general intellectual profile, his love of letter writing and card playing, his taste for champagne, his tearfulness, and his religious position ("Leave me God and art. I yield Christ up to you").

Alexander Ivanovich Herzen (1812–70) was a novelist, publicist, and radical social critic. Self-exiled from Russia in 1847, he lived in London, where he edited the influential journal *The Bell (Kolokol).* He was one of an unofficial triumvirate of revolutionary émigrés, along with the anarchist Mikhail Bakunin (1814–76) and the poet and propagandist Nikolai Ogaryov (1813–77).

3. This phrase is probably a deliberate echo of an even clumsier phrase ("a whirlwind of emerged entanglements") in *Selected Passages from Correspondence with Friends* (1847), the last published work of Nikolai Gogol (1809–52).

4. "Hanseatic," pertaining to the Hansa, a medieval German merchant guild, later

a trading league of free German cities. These details of Stepan Trofimovich's career are all ironic allusions to the activities of T. N. Granovsky (see note 2 above).

5. That is, "lovers of the Slavs" (see note 2 above).

6. The journal Dostoevsky has in mind is *Fatherland Notes*, where his own first novel was published, and which in the 1840s, under the editorship of Andrei Antonovich Kraevsky (1810–89), became a major forum for the Westerners. Kraevsky published the first Russian translations of Charles Dickens (1812–70) and George Sand (pen name of the French writer Aurore Dupin, *baronne* Dudevant, 1804–76).

7. There were a number of such secret societies in nineteenth-century Russia. Dostoevsky most likely has in mind the Petrashevsky circle, which he himself frequented from 1847 until its suppression in 1849, when he and other members were arrested. The Petrashevists were particularly interested in the ideas of the French utopian socialist Charles Fourier (1772–1837). His system, known as "Fourierism," envisaged the organization of individuals into "phalansteries," or social-economic groups harmoniously composed with the aim of securing the well-being of each member through the freely accepted labor of all.

8. The second part of the grand verse drama *Faust* by the German poet Johann Wolfgang von Goethe (1749–1832) is characterized by its mystical and allegorical choruses.

9. The poet and liberal journalist Nikolai A. Nekrasov (1821–77), Dostoevsky's sometime friend and frequent ideological opponent, was referred to as a "people's poet" in his own lifetime, by Dostoevsky among others. The quotation here, somewhat rearranged, is from Nekrasov's poem "The Bear Hunt."

10. The phrase "civic grief," meaning an acute suffering over social ills and inequities, was widely used in the Russia of the 1860s; the disease itself became fashionable in Petersburg, where the deaths of some high-school students and cadets were even ascribed to it.

11. Rumors of the government's intention to liberate the serfs began to emerge as early as the 1840s. Their emancipation was finally decreed by the emperor Alexander II on 19 February 1861.

12. In 1836, the famous artist K. P. Briullov (1799–1852), leader of the Russian romantic school, made an engraving of the mediocre poet N. V. Kukolnik (1809–68), which was used as a frontispiece in editions of his poems.

13. Alexis Clérel de Tocqueville (1805–59), French politician and writer, was the author of two classic works, *Democracy in America* (1835–40) and *The Ancien Régime and the Revolution* (1856). The French writer Paul de Kock (1794–1871) was the author of innumerable novels depicting petit bourgeois life, some of them considered risqué.

14. Alexander Radishchev (1749–1802), author of *A Journey from Petersburg to Moscow*, was exiled to Siberia by the empress Catherine the Great because of his outspoken attacks on social abuses.

15. Protests against "outrageous acts" were symptomatic of the radical press of the 1860s, for instance the polemical article entitled "The Outrageous Act of *The Age*," published in the *St. Petersburg Gazette* (3 March 1861), protesting against an attack on the movement for women's emancipation in the journal *The Age*, referred to by Svidrigailov in *Crime and Punishment*.

16. All these issues were discussed in the radical press of the 1860s. The apparent hodgepodge of points from "dividing Russia" through "women's rights" was in fact

the program spelled out in one of the tracts of the time. "The Passage" was and is a shopping arcade in Petersburg which also housed a public auditorium. For Kraevsky, see note 6 above.

17. The points Stepan Trofimovich agrees with are some of those listed in the anarchist program of Mikhail Bakunin (see note 2 above), published in the first issue of his journal *The People's Cause* (Geneva, 1869). However, Stepan Trofimovich vehemently rejects the utilitarianism of such radical critics as D. I. Pisarev (1840–68), for whom poetry was a prime target, particularly that of Russia's greatest poet, Alexander Pushkin (1799–1837).

18. These are actually the first lines of some doggerel Dostoevsky himself wrote in parody of popular themes in contemporary journalism. *Vek* (*The Age*) was a Petersburg weekly; Lev Kambek was a second-rate journalist of the time.

19. *Athenian* (or *Attic*) *Nights* by the Roman writer Aulus Gellius (second century A.D.) is a collection of dialogues on various branches of knowledge. The title came proverbially to signify "orgy," but is used by Stepan Trofimovich in its original sense of a refined evening discussion.

20. The Madonna painted for the church of St. Sixtus in Piacenza by Raphael Sanzio (1483–1520), later acquired by the museum of Dresden. According to the memoirs of his wife, Anna Grigorievna, Dostoevsky placed Raphael above all painters and considered the Sistine Madonna the summit of his art.

21. The Russian saying "where Makar never drove his calves" signifies a remote place. For Stepan Trofimovich and Varvara Petrovna it evidently stood for exile to some far corner of Russia.

22. Clergy and wealthier peasants might send their sons to study in seminaries without destining them for a churchly career. Many radical writers of the 1860s were former seminarians, as Joseph Stalin was later. Dostoevsky saw them as a distinct type; in a notebook from that time he wrote: "These seminarians have introduced a special negation into our literature, too complete, too hostile, too sharp, and therefore too limited."

23. Ironically called "ancient Roman," this utterance is actually a parody of the manner of speaking favored among the characters in the novel *What Is to Be Done?* (1863), by the utilitarian communist writer, and former seminarian, Nikolai G. Chernyshevsky (1828–89). Dostoevsky parodied this same mannerism in *Crime and Punishment* through the character of Lebezyatnikov.

24. The French national anthem, originally the marching song of the Army of the Rhine in the 1792 war of the young French Republic against Austria. It was composed by a captain from Lons-le-Saunier, Claude-Joseph Rouget de Lisle (1760–1836).

25. See note 11 above.

26. A paraphrase of an anonymous poem entitled "Fantasy," published in the radical almanac *North Star* in 1861.

27. The "komarinsky" is a Russian dance-song with comical words.

28. Élisa Félix (1820–58), whose stage name was Mlle. Rachel, contributed to the revival of French classical tragedy in the nineteenth century.

29. The perfume *"Bouquet de l'impératrice"* was awarded a gold medal at the World Exposition of 1867 in Paris, and instantly became fashionable. The *impératrice* was Eugénie, wife of Napoléon III.

30. Title of a novel published in 1847 by Dmitri V. Grigorovich (1822–99), a senti-

mental depiction of peasant life praised by the critic Belinsky (see note 2 above) for political reasons. Grigorovich was a close friend of Dostoevsky's from their days in the Petersburg Military Engineering Academy.

31. Anton Petrov was a peasant from the village of Bezdna ("abyss" in Russian) who was given the task of reading the statutes of the peasant reform of 1861 to the peasants. Up to five thousand people gathered from surrounding villages to hear his explanations of the reform, causing unrest which was severely quashed by the authorities.

32. That is, St. Peter's School, a German high school in Petersburg, founded in the eighteenth century.

33. Igor Svyatoslavich (1151–1202) was prince of Novgorod-Seversk, a small town near Chernigov, in the period predating the rise of the Muscovite kingdom. Stepan Trofimovich means some mythical long-ago.

34. Anti-clerical and anti-Christian barbs are not uncommon in the poetry of Goethe (see note 8 above), particularly in his *Roman Elegies* and *Venetian Epigrams* (1786–90), written in classical forms and celebrating a certain urbane sensuality thought to be pagan in spirit.

35. See note 6 above. Stepan Trofimovich probably has in mind the novel *Lélia* (1838), which protests against the constraints put upon women by society and religion and defends freedom of feelings.

36. See note 2 above. In a famous letter to Gogol (15 July 1847), Belinsky denounced the "father of Russian prose" for turning reactionary in his last book (see note 3 above), and took the opportunity to condemn Russian tyranny, landowning, and the Church. It was for reading this letter to the Petrashevsky circle that Dostoevsky was arrested and sentenced to prison in 1849 (see note 7 above). The quotation here, however, is not from the same letter.

37. Ivan Andreevich Krylov (1769–1844), poet and fabulist, the Russian La Fontaine (whom he translated), wrote a fable entitled "The Inquisitive Man" (1814), which tells of a man who goes to a museum and notices all sorts of tiny things, but fails to notice an elephant. The phrase became proverbial.

CHAPTER 2: *Prince Harry. Matchmaking*

1. Characters from Shakespeare's history plays *Henry the Fourth, Parts I* and *II*, and, with the exception of the prince, from *The Merry Wives of Windsor* (1597–1600).

2. Victor Considérant (1808–93) was a devoted follower of Fourier (see Chapter One, note 7) who oversaw the publication of his master's writings and himself produced a three-volume systematization of Fourier's ideas entitled *La Destinée sociale* ("Social Destiny," 1834–44), popular among Russian liberals of the 1840s.

3. See Chapter One, note 7.

4. Otto von Bismarck (1815–98), called "the Iron Chancellor," was a Prussian statesman and one of the main architects of German unity; founder of the Triple Alliance (with Austria and Italy) against France.

5. Blaise Pascal (1623–62), French mathematician, physicist, and philosopher, author of the unfinished *Pensées* and of *Letters to a Provincial* (1656–57), from which the quoted phrase comes.

6. A "magnificent literary masterpiece, half poem, half oration," in the words of

Vladimir Nabokov, who translated it into English (1960), discovered around 1790 by Count Alexei Musin-Pushkin in a collection of old manuscripts, but dating back to the year 1187, narrating certain events in the life of Prince Igor (see Chapter One, note 33).

7. Before the emancipation of the serfs in 1861, Russian estates were evaluated according to the number of "souls" or adult male serfs living on them.

8. Badinguet was the name of the stonemason whose identity and clothing Louis-Napoléon Bonaparte (1808–73), the future emperor Napoléon III, borrowed for his escape from the fortress of Ham in 1846. The name was later mockingly applied to the emperor by his opponents.

CHAPTER 3: *Someone Else's Sins*

1. The portrait of Semyon Yegorovich Karmazinov in *Demons* is to a considerable extent a caricature of the Russian writer Ivan Turgenev (1818–83), with whom Dostoevsky entertained relations varying from cool friendship to bitter hostility throughout his life. In spirit and art the two writers were opposites, but in 1880, a few months before Dostoevsky's death, on the occasion of his famous speech on Pushkin (8 June), they fell into each other's arms and were briefly reconciled.

2. Jean-Baptiste Poquelin (1622–73), known as Molière, poet, playwright, actor, and director, is among the greatest of French writers. François-Marie Arouet (1694–1778), called Voltaire, wrote in many forms and was widely read in his lifetime; his philosophical tale *Candide* (1759) was one of Dostoevsky's favorite books.

3. David Teniers the Elder (1582–1649), or else David Teniers the Younger (1610–90), Flemish painters, father and son; the realistic popular scenes of village weddings and feasts painted by Teniers the Younger are perhaps better known than the works of his father.

4. *The Man Who Laughs*, a novel by Victor Hugo (1802–85), published in 1869, based on the antithesis between moral beauty and physical deformity.

5. In *Selected Passages from Correspondence with Friends*, Gogol wrote: "You trusted that I knew Russia like my five fingers; and I know precisely nothing in it." Dostoevsky has Stepan Trofimovich ironically echo these words while claiming the opposite, and with an added distortion of idiom.

6. Pechorin is the cold, aloof hero of *A Hero of Our Time* (1840), a novel by the poet Mikhail Lermontov (1814–41).

7. A kalatch is a loaf of very fine white bread shaped like a purse with a looped handle and generously dusted with flour.

8. The seaport of Sebastopol in the Crimea was besieged by French and English forces for eleven months in 1854–55, during the Crimean War (1854–56), and was eventually taken by the besiegers.

9. Korobochka ("little box") is the name of a lady landowner in Gogol's novel *Dead Souls* (1843). It became synonymous with a certain type of person—suspicious, stingy, stubborn, stupid.

CHAPTER 4: *The Lame Girl*

1. Among Dostoevsky's preliminary notes for *Crime and Punishment* we read: "*N.B.:* Nihilism is lackeyishness of thought. A nihilist is a lackey of thought." The term "nihilism," first used philosophically in German *(nihilismus)* to signify annihilation, a reduction to nothing (attributed to Buddha), or the rejection of religious beliefs and moral principles, came via the French *nihilisme* to Russian, where it acquired a political meaning, referring to the doctrine of the younger generation of socialists of the 1860s, who advocated the destruction of the existing social order without specifying what should replace it. The great nineteenth-century Russian lexicographer Vladimir Ivanovich Dahl (1801–72), normally a model of restraint, defines "nihilism" in his *Interpretive Dictionary of the Living Russian Language* as "an ugly and immoral doctrine which rejects everything that cannot be palpated." The term became current after it appeared in Turgenev's *Fathers and Sons* (1862), where it is applied to the hero Bazarov.

2. Gogol, at the beginning of the seventh chapter of *Dead Souls,* says of himself that he is "destined to look at life through laughter visible to the world and tears invisible and unknown to it."

3. An altered quotation from travel notes by P. I. Ogorodnikov entitled "From New York to San Francisco and Back to Russia," published in the journal *Zarya* (1870, No. XI).

4. Also from Ogorodnikov's travel notes.

5. Mount Athos, at the southern end of the easternmost peninsula of Chalkidiki in Macedonia, is an autonomous region which has been a monastic center since the fifth century A.D.

6. "Prophesying" as an ecstatic form of religious behavior might be condoned by the Church as a kind of "folly for Christ's sake" or might be put under penance.

7. "Kitty" (*koshechka,* diminutive of *koshka,* "female cat") is an endearing name in Russian. But the refrain "Kitty, come out to me" also occurs in Russian yuletide carols as a marriage motif (see Vladimir Nabokov's commentary to his translation of Pushkin's *Eugene Onegin,* abridged edition, Princeton, 1981, volume II, part one, pp. 496–97). Such carols might have been found in Marya Timofeevna's songbook.

8. The subject matter of this stanza, widely known in Russian folklore, is connected with the name of Eudoxia Lopukhin (to whom the words are also ascribed), the first wife of Peter the Great (1672–1725), who had her sent to a convent and made a nun.

9. An absurdly distorted but recognizable version of a well-known poem by Afanasy Fet (1820–92), "I Have Come to You with Greeting" (1843).

CHAPTER 5: *The Wise Serpent*

1. Russian banknotes had different colors depending on their denomination. A green banknote was worth three roubles.

2. General A. P. Ermolov (1772–1861) was a hero of the Napoleonic war of 1812, a brilliant military commander and diplomat. From 1817 to 1827 he served as commander-in-chief of the Russian army in the Caucasus.

3. A misquotation of a line from a poem by N. Kukolnik (see Chapter One, note 12 above), famous as a song with music by M. I. Glinka (1804–57). It should read, "Sleep, hopeless heart!"

4. The age of the universe used to be calculated according to biblical chronology. By the Hebrew calendar, creation was 5,631 years old as Lebyadkin was speaking; by the chronology of Bishop James Ussher of Dublin (1581–1656), it was 5,875 years old. Lebyadkin gives a rounded-off figure.

5. The Prince de Monbars, or Monbars l'Exterminateur (b. 1646), was a chief of the *flibustres* (French for "filibusters"). He terrorized shipping in the West Indies and in 1683 managed to capture Veracruz. Hero of several popular dramas and novels.

6. See Chapter One, note 37 above. The monument, a statue of Krylov surrounded by animals from his fables, was set up on the children's playground in the Petersburg Summer Garden in 1855, and is still there. It is known affectionately as "Grandpa Krylov."

7. Denis Vasilievich Davydov (1784–1839), himself a hussar and a hero of the Napoleonic war of 1812, wrote energetic, humorous poems which have remained very popular.

8. See Chapter Two, note 1 above.

9. The "Merchant's Yard" in old Russian, a huge shopping arcade in Petersburg, still so called.

10. According to the biblical account (Genesis 19:1–28), God destroyed Sodom because the men of the city practiced "sodomy," but in Russian use "Sodom" means a more generally disordered and outrageous kind of life. Owners of apartments used to rent out not only individual rooms but sectioned-off parts of rooms, or "corners," which inevitably led to a certain communality among the tenants.

11. The sudden death of the emperor Alexander I on 19 November 1825 was followed by a period of confusion about the succession. A conspiratorial group of officers and noblemen, opposed to imperial absolutism and favoring a constitutional monarchy or even a republican government, seized the occasion and gathered their forces in the Senate Square of Petersburg on 14 December 1825. Hence the name "Decembrists." The uprising was promptly quelled by loyal contingents of the Imperial Guard; one hundred twenty-one men were arrested, of whom five were executed and the rest exiled to Siberia. M. S. Lunin (1787–1845), one of the exiled Decembrists, was indeed famous for his fearlessness.

12. See Chapter Three, note 6. Lermontov had a venomous tongue and a cold, scornful view of life and men; he fought a number of duels and was eventually killed in one.

PART TWO

CHAPTER 1: *Night*

1. The zemstvo was an elective provincial council with powers of local government.

2. See Part One, Chapter Four, note 1.

3. The English poet George Gordon, Lord Byron (1788–1824), was himself a romantic figure, at least in the minds of his contemporaries—a citizen of the world, a lady-killer, a lover of freedom. Nozdryov, one of the landowners in Gogol's *Dead Souls*, became proverbial as the type of the feisty, interfering, obnoxious braggart, the carousing gambler, the purposeless liar and babbler. For Bazarov, see Part One, Chapter Four, note 1.

4. See Part One, Chapter One, note 20.

5. Dostoevsky himself coined the term "omni-man" *(obshchechelovek);* it appears, in the plural, at the very end of *Notes from Underground* (1864).

6. Russian borrowed the word *kipsek* ("keepsake") from English; it was the trade name of a literary annual, finely bound and illustrated, intended for gift-giving.

7. The sect of the castrates *(skoptsi),* a reform of the older sect of the flagellants, was founded in Orlov province in the second half of the eighteenth century by a peasant named Kondraty Selivanov. To combat the promiscuous behavior that generally accompanied the "zeals" (sessions) of the flagellants, he introduced the practice of self-castration. The sect was forbidden by law.

8. That is, the International Workingmen's Association, or First Internationale, founded in Geneva by Karl Marx, Bakunin, and others, in 1864.

9. Charmeur was a well-known Petersburg tailor. According to his wife's memoirs, Dostoevsky had his own suits made by Charmeur, whom he also advertised in *Crime and Punishment.*

10. Landowners had to supply a quota of recruits for the army from among their serfs, the selection being left to the landowner. Serfs had many ways of evading this hated duty, of which one of the simplest was to buy their way out. Household serfs were exempted from army service, but their masters could send them to fill such gaps in the quota. That is what Stepan Trofimovich did with Fedka.

11. Pushkin deliberately used extremely injurious language in his letter of 26 January 1837 to the Dutch diplomat Baron van Heeckeren, provoking the baron's adopted son Georges d'Anthès to a duel. (Baron van Heeckeren, surnamed Jakob Derk Burckardt Anna in family records, is called Louis by most scholars.)

12. See Revelation 10:6 (King James Version).

13. The "God-man" is Christ, "truly God and truly man," in the definition of the council of Chalcedon (451 A.D.). Notions of anthropotheism, or "man-godhood," arrived at in discussions within the Petrashevsky circle (see Part One, Chapter One, note 7) were drawn ultimately from German idealist philosophy, representing an inversion of Christianity which Kirillov carries to its final conclusion.

14. Russian casement windows normally have one pane, or part of a pane, that can be opened for ventilation when the window is sealed shut for the winter.

15. The idea of Russia as a "god-bearing" nation can be traced to the thought of the

Slavophil Nikolai Yakovlevich Danilevsky (1822–95), an idiosyncratic interpretation of the philosophy of history of the German idealists Friedrich Hegel (1770–1831) and Friedrich Schelling (1775–1854). Danilevsky's treatise in the philosophy of history, *Russia and Europe*, was published in 1871.

16. Dostoevsky lends Shatov some of his own ideas about Roman Catholicism. The announcement at the first Vatican council (1870) of the new dogma of papal infallibility deeply shocked him; he saw it as the proclaiming of a "new Christ" who represents earthly power and has thus succumbed to the third temptation of the devil (see Matthew 4:1–11, Luke 4:1–13).

17. The thought Shatov here attributes to Stavrogin had in fact been Dostoevsky's own, expressed with slightly different wording in his often-quoted letter of 1854 to N. D. Fonvizin, wife of one of the Decembrists, who had met him in Tobolsk in 1850 on his way to prison and given him a copy of the Gospels which was to be his only reading during his four years at hard labor.

18. Shatov seems to confuse two passages from the New Testament: the "rivers of living water" that appear as a metaphor of the Spirit in John 7:38 are not the same as the waters that dry up in Revelation 16:12.

19. See note 3 above (Nozdryov claimed that he actually caught a hare by the hind legs with his own hands).

20. Stepan Timofeevich ("Stenka") Razin (?–1671), a Don Cossack, led a peasant uprising in Russia (1667–71) for which he became a popular hero.

21. Donatien Alphonse François, marquis de Sade (1740–1814), novelist and theorist of the erotic, accused of practicing what he preached, was tried and sentenced to prison for rape; later he was condemned to death for sodomy and poisoning, but the sentence was lifted.

CHAPTER 2: *Night (Continued)*

1. Fedka's speech throughout is based on Dostoevsky's notes on the language of the convicts he met during his imprisonment in Omsk (1850–54).

2. Zossima here is a name for a generic hermit, not an actual person.

3. The poet is Pyotr A. Vyazemsky (1792–1878), a friend of Pushkin's; the lines, slightly adjusted by Lebyadkin, come from Vyazemsky's poem "To the Memory of the Painter Orlovsky" (1838).

4. In *Selected Passages from Correspondence with Friends*, Gogol refers to an as yet unwritten "Farewell Story" of which he says: "I swear, I did not invent or think it up; it sang itself out of my soul . . ." The story remained unwritten.

5. Gavriil Derzhavin (1743–1816) was one of the greatest Russian poets of the eighteenth century. Lebyadkin refers to his ode "God" (1784), which contains the line: "I am king—I am slave, I am worm—I am god!"

6. Grigory ("Grishka") Otrepev, known as "the False Dmitri," was a defrocked monk who claimed the Russian throne by pretending to be the lawful heir, the prince Dmitri, murdered in childhood through the intrigues of Boris Godunov (1551–1605), who thus made himself tsar. In 1605, by order of the patriarch Job, the impostor Grigory Otrepev was anathematized and cursed "in this age and the age to come" in

all the churches of Russia. The "seven councils" is a hyperbolic reference to the ecumenical councils of the Church, held between 325 and 787 A.D.

7. Dostoevsky wrote down these terms for church objects in his Omsk notebook, but without giving definitions of them. The "swinger" is probably a censer; the second item, which we translate as "swatter," remains mysterious; the "deacon's girth" is no doubt a deacon's stole or orarion, often richly decorated. Icons, as of St. Nicholas the Wonder-worker, are often covered with precious casings of silver or gold ornamented with jewels. "Similor" (originally a French word) is a yellow brass used in making cheap jewelry.

CHAPTER 3: *The Duel*

1. There is an excellent short treatise on the classical duel *à volonté* ("at will") in Vladimir Nabokov's commentary to his translation of Pushkin's *Eugene Onegin* (abridged edition, Princeton, 1981, volume II, part two, pp. 43–45).

2. Corporal punishment for all ranks of the population, including clergy and boyars (a privileged order of Russian aristocracy), existed in the Muscovite kingdom from its very beginnings in the fourteenth century.

CHAPTER 4: *All in Expectation*

1. Dueling was officially outlawed and therefore could be punished by the authorities, though they might choose to overlook it.

2. This conversation reflects certain skeptical attitudes towards the new courts established by the legal reform of 1864, which replaced the former courts, separate for each rank of society, with general courts for all ranks, open to the public, allowing for trial by jury, the use of lawyers, and free discussion in the press.

3. See Part One, Chapter One, note 20.

4. The question of women's equality emerged in Russia at the end of the 1850s. During the 1860s it was much discussed in the press. Dostoevsky saw the emancipation of women as one instance of the restoration of human dignity in general, and regarded it as very important.

5. See Part One, Chapter One, note 23.

6. *Fra Diavolo* (1830) is a comic opera by the French composer Esprit Auber (1782–1871), based on the life of an Italian brigand.

CHAPTER 5: *Before the Fête*

1. "Foolsbury" (*Glupov* in Russian) is the subject of *The History of a Certain Town*, a satirical history of Russia by M. E. Saltykov-Shchedrin (1826–89).

2. In fact, Dostoevsky based this episode with the book-hawker on an actual incident reported in the press.

3. The "Marseillaise" (see Part One, Chapter One, note 24) is a marching song, "Mein lieber Augustin" is a beer-hall waltz, in Lyamshin's musical parody symbolizing

the triumph of German philistinism over the spirit of the French Revolution. The actual Franco-Prussian War (1870–71) was started and lost by Napoléon III.

4. Jules Favre (1809–80), French politician and republican, called for the deposing of Napoléon III in 1870, and negotiated the treaty of Frankfurt (10 May 1871), which ended the Franco-Prussian War. For Bismarck, see Part One, Chapter Two, note 4.

5. Properly, Château-Yquem, the greatest of sauternes.

6. According to Anna Grigorievna, the visit to Semyon Yakovlevich in *Demons* is partly based on Dostoevsky's own visit to a well-known holy fool *(yurodivy)* in Moscow, Ivan Yakovlevich Koreisha.

7. The Russian merchant class was divided in its habits of dress; some retained the long-skirted coat and full beard of the traditional Russian merchant, others adopted so-called German fashions (frock coat, waistcoat, tie) and went clean-shaven.

8. The Senate in Petersburg was the highest judicial as well as legislative body in imperial Russia.

9. The question "What is the meaning of this dream?" is ultimately a paraphrase of a line from Pushkin's poem "The Bridegroom" (1825). In the 1860s it became a journalistic cliché applied metaphorically to various events of the day. Dostoevsky here restores it to its literal meaning, with very funny effect.

10. The "little Cossack" *(kazachok)* is a dance imitative of military steps.

11. See Genesis 25:29–34. Esau, the elder son of Isaac, sells his birthright to his brother Jacob for "a mess of pottage," that is, a bowl of lentil soup.

12. Baptiste Honoré Raymond Capefigue (1802–72) was a French historian and man of letters, author of historical compilations.

13. That is, news of the emancipation of the serfs on 19 February 1861.

14. Dostoevsky again parodies the utilitarian aesthetics of the nihilists, particularly of N. G. Chernyshevsky (see Part One, Chapter One, note 23), who declared in his university dissertation entitled *The Relations of Art to Reality* (written in 1853, defended on 10 May 1855): "Artistic creations are lower than the beautiful in reality." The public debate occasioned by Chernyshevsky's defense of his thesis was considered the first manifestation of the "intellectual trend of the sixties."

15. "The die is cast!" (Latin); words uttered by Julius Caesar when he defied the Roman Senate by bringing his legions across the Rubicon in 50 B.C. and marching on Rome.

16. Lines from Pushkin's poem "Once There Lived a Poor Knight" (1829).

CHAPTER 6: *Pyotr Stepanovich Bustles About*

1. A quotation from Pushkin's poem "A Hero" (1830).

2. Karl Vogt (1817–95), German naturalist, was a defender of the biological theory of transformism (as were Lamarck and Darwin). Jacob Moleschott (1822–93), Dutch physiologist and philosopher, was an advocate of materialism, as was the German philosopher Ludwig Büchner (1824–99), brother of the playwright Georg Büchner. Their writings were a sort of bible of the materialist worldview for young Russians of the 1860s.

3. Dostoevsky is thinking of Herzen's account of Pavel A. Bakhmetev, in a chapter on the young generation in his book *From My Life and Thoughts* (1852–55). Bakhmetev,

a wealthy young nobleman of revolutionary sympathies, supplied the émigrés with funds for propaganda, most of which went eventually to the subject of the next note.

4. Sergei Gennadievich Nechaev (1847–82), nihilist theoretician and murderer, whose activities together with the court proceedings arising from them were one of Dostoevsky's sources for the writing of *Demons,* was the founder of a revolutionary society called "The Committee of the People's Summary Justice of 19 February 1870." The society's tracts and documents bore an oval seal showing an axe with the name of the committee written around it.

5. "The Shining Light" is Dostoevsky's parody of a poem by Nikolai Ogaryov (see Part One, Chapter One, note 2), entitled "The Student." Ogaryov had originally written the poem for a friend who had died in 1867, but then he met Nechaev in Geneva two years later and was so taken with him that he added the dedication "to young friend Nechaev" when the poem was printed as a tract.

6. That is, the imperial secret police.

7. Kondraty Ryleev (1795–1826), a leading Decembrist, was one of the five who were hanged after the uprising. His *Ponderings* (1821–23) is a collection of mediocre patriotic poems on historical subjects.

8. Collegiate assessor was the eighth of the fourteen ranks in the imperial Russian civil service, equivalent to the military rank of major.

9. See Part One, Chapter Three, note 1. Dostoevsky wrote of Turgenev in a letter: "I also don't like his aristocratical and pharisaic embrace, when he comes at you with a kiss, but instead offers you his cheek." He has given Karmazinov other personal traits of Turgenev—his high voice, his manner of speaking, his practice of making multiple copies of his writings.

10. A parody of various liberal titles: *On the Eve, Who Is to Blame?, What Is to Be Done?, Nowhere to Go.*

11. This is the apocalyptic Babylon of the Hebrew prophets (Jeremiah 50, 51; Isaiah 13) and Revelation (18:2); see also Matthew 7:27.

12. The hut on chicken legs is the traditional dwelling of Baba Yaga, the witch of Russian folktales.

13. In the first publication of his new society, Nechaev wrote: "We come from the people, with hides bitten through by the teeth of the present-day setup, guided by hatred for everything not of the people, having no idea of moral obligation or honor with regard to the world that we hate and from which we expect nothing but evil." Dostoevsky later commented on this "right to dishonor" in his *Diary of a Writer* (March 1876, chapter two, part 4).

14. The Feast of the Protective Veil of the Mother of God, commonly referred to as "the Protection" (the Russian *pokrov* means both "protection" and "veil"), is celebrated on 1 October. (Nechaev had a similarly short timetable in mind for the success of his general uprising.)

15. Vera Pavlovna, heroine of Chernyshevsky's *What Is to Be Done?,* habitually addresses her husband Lopukhov as "sweetie." The Russian word immediately calls up this literary context.

16. The phrasing and details here come from a song of the Volga robbers. Further on in the song, the beautiful maiden has a dream prophesying a bad end to the robbers' enterprise. Pyotr Stepanovich will refer to it again, as will Liza.

17. In 1926, fifty-seven years after the event, Alexei Kuznetsov, a member of Ne-

chaev's society and a participant in the murder of the student Ivanov, wrote in a memoir that there had been no reason for the murder, but that Nechaev had needed it in order "to better weld us together with blood."

18. Half of the Italian saying *Se non è vero, è ben trovato* ("If it's not true, it's well invented").

CHAPTER 7: *With Our People*

1. Many details of this "meeting" at Virginsky's correspond to particulars of the Nechaev circle as they emerged at the trial of the Nechaevists in July–August 1871 (Nechaev himself was eventually arrested abroad and tried in Moscow on 8 January 1873); for example: the young Miss Virginsky with her bundle of tracts and her concern for the plight of poor students; the silent young artillerist who writes all the time and is meant to be taken for some kind of foreign inspector; the "knower of the people" and expert in pot-houses (the Nechaevist Pryzhov had written a *History of Pot-houses* in 1868, and had become an alcoholic in the course of his researches).

2. See Part One, Chapter One, note 2.

3. See Exodus 20:1–17. Miss Virginsky misquotes the fifth commandment, which reads: "Honor your father and your mother, that your days may be long in the land which the Lord your God gives you."

4. Shigalyov scornfully lumps together three very unlike authors of utopian systems: the Athenian philosopher Plato (428–347 B.C.), author of the *Republic*; the French writer Jean-Jacques Rousseau (1712–78), author of *On the Social Contract* (1762); and Charles Fourier (see Part One, Chapter One, note 7). The aluminum columns come from yet another utopian vision, the "Fourth Dream of Vera Pavlovna" in Chernyshevsky's *What Is to Be Done?*, where they adorn the crystal palace of the future phalanstery.

5. In his *Diary of a Writer* for January 1876 (chapter three, section 1), Dostoevsky strongly attacks the notion of enlightening one tenth of the people "while the remaining nine tenths serve only as the material and means to that end, continuing to dwell in darkness." Similar proportions appear in Raskolnikov's article on crime in *Crime and Punishment* (1866) and Ivan Fyodorovich's "poem" about the Grand Inquisitor in *The Brothers Karamazov* (1880).

6. Lyamshin's suggestion may owe something in spirit to the tract "Principles of Revolution" written by Nechaev in 1869, with its celebration of total destruction.

7. Étienne Cabet (1788–1856), French publicist, wrote a well-known utopian communist novel, *Voyage to Icaria* (1840). Pierre-Joseph Proudhon (1809–65), French philosopher, was one of the principal socialist theorists of the nineteenth century, advocate of a libertarian socialism opposed to Marxism; to him we owe the phrase "Property is theft."

8. The word "Shigalyovism" *(shigalyovshchina)* entered the Russian language; it denotes a form of socio-political demagogy and posturing with a tendency to propose extreme measures and total solutions.

CHAPTER 8: *Ivan the Tsarevich*

1. Pyotr Stepanovich echoes some of the points outlined in Nechaev's article "The Basic Principles of the Future Social Organization" (1869), which gives the scheme for a kind of "barracks communism" that Marx, among others, found appalling.

2. Émile Littré (1801–81), French lexicographer and positivist philosopher, is erroneously mentioned here; the idea that "crime is madness," very popular in Russia in the 1860s, came from the Belgian mathematician and statistician Adolphe Quételet (1796–1874). Dostoevsky repeatedly opposed attempts to justify crime statistically or by appeals to necessity, heredity, the environment, because they deny human freedom and dignity.

3. The period of the Jews' wandering in the desert after Moses led them out of Egypt; proverbially a period of trial and purification.

4. Ivan the Tsarevich is a figure in Russian folktales: generally the third and youngest of the tsar's sons, it is he who does the work, endures the tests, and wins throne and princess in the end.

5. The theme of the impostor has already emerged once in connection with Stavrogin (see Part Two, Chapter Two, note 6). In fact, possibly owing to the extent of the country and the unfamiliarity of the tsar's person, impostors were not unusual in Russia. There were, for instance, three other "False Dmitris" around the time of Grishka Otrepev. As recently as 1845, an impostor appeared in the Orenburg region claiming to be the grand duke Konstantin Pavlovich (brother of the emperor Alexander I, who declined the throne in November 1825, stepping aside for his younger brother Nikolai, and who died in 1831). The impostor promised to defend the peasants against oppression by nobles and officials and was greeted with great enthusiasm.

6. See Part Two, Chapter One, note 7. The castrates had many legends, among them a messianic tale of a progenitor coming from the East, mounted on "a white, spiritually reasonable horse," to unite the tribes of the castrates and "spread their teaching even to French lands in the West." In his further mythographying, Pyotr Stepanovich combines two figures from the sect of the flagellants—one who called himself Danila Filippovich God-Sabaoth, the other Ivan Timofeevich Suslov, who proclaimed himself Christ.

7. See 1 Kings 3:16–28.

CHAPTER 10: *Filibusters. A Fatal Morning*

1. This well-known sentence from Voltaire's *Candide* (see Part One, Chapter Three, note 2) is uttered by the hero's teacher, Dr. Pangloss, representative of the optimistic (German) philosophy Voltaire makes fun of in his "philosophical tale."

2. See Part One, Chapter One, note 2.

3. Dostoevsky naturalizes the German word for "joke" with a Russian plural ending; we follow suit.

4. See Part One, Chapter Two, note 5. Stepan Trofimovich repeats himself verbatim, this time with success.

PART THREE

CHAPTER 1: *The Fête. First Part*

1. See Part Two, Chapter One, note 8.

2. The landowner Tentetnikov appears in the unfinished second part of Gogol's *Dead Souls;* he is an enlightened young man, full of good intentions, who gradually falls into mental and moral lethargy and becomes an indolent sluggard. For Radishchev, see Part One, Chapter One, note 14.

3. That is, wearing the decoration of the Polish civil order of St. Stanislas ("Stanislav" in Russian). Founded in Poland in 1792, the order began to be awarded in Russia in 1831.

4. This feast, described in Daniel 5, became proverbial for its sumptuousness, though it ended unhappily for Belshazzar.

5. See Part Two, Chapter Two, note 4. Gogol's words have migrated from Lebyadkin to Karmazinov.

6. Karmazinov's *Merci* is a parody of several pieces by Turgenev: its beginning and end are suggestive of Turgenev's article "Apropos of *Fathers and Sons*" in its address to the reader; its composition calls to mind Turgenev's novella *Phantoms,* which he himself described as "a series of rather loosely connected pictures"; the crossing of the Volga in winter and the visit to the hermit's cave have correspondences in *Enough,* one of Turgenev's farewells to his public.

7. Pompey (Gnaeus Pompeius Magnus, 106–48 B.C.), Roman general, lost his dispute with Julius Caesar for absolute power in Rome at the battle of Pharsalia. Gaius Cassius Longinus (d. 42 B.C.), one of the leaders of the conspiracy to assassinate Caesar, was defeated by Mark Antony and Octavius Caesar at Philippi.

8. Christoph Willibald Gluck (1714–87), German composer, long resident in France, is best known for his opera *Orphée* (1774).

9. E. T. A. Hoffmann (1776–1822), German musician and writer, was the author of fantastic tales. Frédéric Chopin (1810–49), Polish pianist and composer, produced works of a personal, penetrating, and often melancholic character. Ancus Marcius (seventh century B.C.), grandson of Numa Pompilius, was the fourth of the legendary kings of Rome.

10. See Matthew 11:28, where the words have quite a different meaning.

11. For Byron, see Part Two, Chapter One, note 3; for Pechorin, see Part One, Chapter Three, note 6. Heinrich Heine (1797–1856), German poet, wrote poems of a lively and often biting humor.

12. Stepan Trofimovich reformulates the aesthetic controversy over boots and Pushkin (see Part One, Chapter One, note 17), intensifying his opposition to the nihilists. In the journal *The Russian Word* (1864, No. 3), the nihilist critic B. A. Zaitsev wrote: "... there is no floor-sweeper, no toilet-cleaner, who is not infinitely more useful than Shakespeare."

13. Stepan Trofimovich, though no frequenter of the Gospels, resorts to evangelic language here (see Matthew 10:14, Mark 6:11).

14. During the reign of Nicholas I (emperor from 1825 to 1855), a number of writers,

quite distinguished ones among them (Aksakov, Vyazemsky, Tyutchev, Goncharov), served for periods as government censors, winning disapproval from many of their contemporaries. In 1835 the emperor, who loved drilling and parades, introduced military order in Moscow University, requiring students to wear uniforms and swords (the latter soon abolished). A more liberal university code was introduced by Alexander II in 1863.

15. The speaker refers to the cathedral of St. Sophia in Novgorod. In 1862 a monument by the sculptor M. O. Mikeshin (1836–96) was set up near the cathedral to commemorate the thousandth anniversary of Russia.

CHAPTER 2: *The End of the Fête*

1. The general is mistaken; in Genesis 18:22–33, Abraham bargains with God for the lives of the righteous men of Sodom, and God finally agrees to spare the city if ten righteous men can be found in it.

2. Russian commentators suggest that this "quadrille of literature" is a parody of a "literary quadrille" organized by Moscow artistic circles for the costume ball in the halls of the Assembly of Nobility in February 1869.

3. See Part One, Chapter Three, note 9.

4. "Uncensored" can have two meanings here: the words to the "komarinsky" contained unprintable expressions, but several satirical and revolutionary versions of it also appeared in the 1860s.

5. Titular councillor was ninth of the fourteen ranks in the imperial civil service, a humble position immortalized by Gogol in the character of Akaky Akakievich, hero of "The Overcoat" (1842).

CHAPTER 3: *A Finished Romance*

1. Stavrogin quotes a proverbial line from the play *Woe from Wit* (1824) by Alexander Griboedov (1795–1829).

2. "The voice of the people [is] the voice of God" (Latin), a saying ultimately drawn from *Works and Days* by the Boeotian farmer-poet Hesiod (eighth century B.C.).

3. A novella by A. V. Druzhinin (1824–64), published in 1847, written under the influence of George Sand and pervaded by the ideas of women's emancipation.

CHAPTER 5: *A Traveler*

1. *Voznesensky* means "of the Ascension," *Bogoyavlensky* means "of the Epiphany." The nihilist Marya Shatov ideologically scorns such "Orthodox" street names, which in fact were quite common in Russia.

2. After the publication of Chernyshevsky's *What Is to Be Done?* in 1863, many young radicals attempted to set up co-operative enterprises on socialist principles, following the example of Vera Pavlovna, the novel's heroine. The famous revolutionary Vera Zasulich, a member of Nechaev's circle, who attempted to assassinate the

military governor of Petersburg on 24 January 1878, worked briefly with her sisters in a sewing co-operative and also made a try at bookbinding.

3. On 2 June 1793, the government of France was handed over to the dictatorship of the Committee of Public Safety, headed by Maximilien de Robespierre (1758–94), and the Reign of Terror began.

4. According to his wife's memoirs, Dostoevsky's sensations in the moments preceding an epileptic attack were much like those Kirillov describes here.

5. See Genesis 1, where God finds His creation "good" and even "very good," but never calls it "true."

6. An inexact reference to Matthew 22:30, Mark 12:25, where it is said, "they neither marry nor are given in marriage, but are like angels in heaven."

7. According to Muslim tradition, Muhammad was awakened one night by the archangel Gabriel, who in the process brushed against a jug of water with his wing. Muhammad then traveled to Jerusalem, from there rose into heaven where he spoke with angels, prophets, and Allah, visited the fiery Gehenna, and came back in time to keep the jug from spilling.

CHAPTER 6: *A Toilsome Night*

1. An inexact quotation of Matthew 10:26, Luke 12:2, which will later be misquoted in a different way. Kirillov unwittingly prophesies the novel's denouement.

2. Christ's words to the good thief crucified with him (Luke 23:43).

3. Kirillov's conflicting attitudes become quite incoherent in their final expression here. French, the "republican" language, was also the language of Russian aristocrats. After quoting the motto of the French republic ("Liberty, equality, fraternity" to which he adds "or death!"), Kirillov proceeds to give himself the *de* of a French nobleman in his signature.

CHAPTER 7: *The Last Peregrination of Stepan Trofimovich*

1. See Part One, Chapter One, note 11.

2. *The Life of Jesus* by Ernest Renan (1823–92), lapsed Catholic and rationalist religious historian, indeed appeared about seven years before the events described in *Demons*, in 1863.

3. A low-class way of drinking tea by sipping it through a lump of sugar.

4. See Part One, Chapter Three, note 8.

5. Small folding icons cast in bronze.

6. See Matthew 5:39, Luke 6:29.

7. The Sermon on the Mount (Matthew 5–6) gives the essential commandments of the Christian life.

8. See Revelation 3:14–17, which Sofya Matveevna goes on to read in a moment, and which we give in the Revised Standard Version.

CHAPTER 8: *Conclusion*

1. Earlier (Part Three, Chapter Two, section II) Pyotr Stepanovich and the narrator both allude to rumors that "some senator" had been sent from Petersburg to replace the Lembkes.

2. After the murder of the student Ivanov by Nechaev and his fivesome, Nechaev himself was flustered enough to put on Ivanov's cap and leave his own at the scene of the crime.

3. That is, in internal exile.

4. See Part One, Chapter One, note 3.

5. One of the cantons (territorial subdivisions, or states) of the Swiss Confederation.

APPENDIX: *At Tikhon's*

1. A fuller version of the name of this fictional monastery than Shatov uses at the end of Part Two, Chapter One. Monasteries were named for their patron saint, their churches, and their locale, in various combinations: this is the monastery of the Savior and St. Euphemius in Bogorodsk.

2. A monk of a higher rank in the Orthodox Church, usually the superior of a monastery.

3. "Holy folly" (*yurodstvo* in Russian) might be a kind of harmless mental infirmity or simplicity; it can also be a form of saintliness expressing itself as "folly."

4. The Crimean War (1854–56), fought in the Crimea by Russia against an alliance of France, England, Turkey, and the Piedmont.

5. See Matthew 17:20, 21:21; Mark 11:23.

6. Dostoevsky expanded on this anecdote later in his "Story of Father Nilus" (1873), describing how the archbishop of Paris during the French Revolution came out to the people and openly renounced his old, pernicious ways now that *la raison* ("reason") had come, throwing down his vestments, crosses, chalices, Gospels. " 'Do you believe in God?' one worker with a bare sword in his hand shouted to the archbishop. *'Très peu,'* said the archbishop, hoping to mollify the crowd. 'Then you're a scoundrel and have been deceiving us up to now,' the worker cried and promptly cut the archbishop down with his sword."

7. Tikhon recites from memory in a mixture of Russian and Old Slavonic (the language used in the Russian Orthodox Church), which makes his version somewhat different from the version read by Sofya Matveevna (see Part Three, Chapter Seven, note 8). We give the King James Version here.

8. Stavrogin specifies Russian tradespeople because many of the tradespeople living in Petersburg at that time were German.

9. That is, masturbation; see Book Three of Rousseau's posthumously published *Confessions* (1782).

10. A section of Petersburg between the Little Neva and the Nevka rivers, opposite the main part of the city, which is on the south bank of the Neva.

11. See Part One, Chapter Four, note 5.

12. Claude Gellée, called Le Lorrain (1600–1682), a master of sun and light, is one of the greatest French painters of landscape. Acis was a Sicilian shepherd who was loved by the nymph Galatea and whom the cyclops Polyphemus, out of jealousy, crushed under a huge rock. The cyclops in the picture makes it a bit less "golden" than Stavrogin thinks.

13. This formula occurs in all Orthodox prayers for the forgiveness of sins.

14. Treatment suffered by Christ at the hands of the high priest Caiaphas and the scribes and elders of Jerusalem, and/or from the Roman soldiers, before his crucifixion (see Matthew 26:67, 27:30; Mark 15:19).

15. Christ's words in Matthew 18:6 (King James Version): "But whoso shall offend one of these little ones which believe in me, it were better for him that a millstone were hanged about his neck, and that he were drowned in the depth of the sea."

16. No source for these words is known; they sound like a paraphrase from Revelation.

A Note on the Type

This book was set in Janson, a typeface long thought to have been made by the Dutchman Anton Janson, who was a practicing type founder in Leipzig during the years 1668–1687. However, it has been conclusively demonstrated that these types are actually the work of Nicholas Kis (1650–1702), a Hungarian, who most probably learned his trade from the master Dutch type founder Dirk Voskens. The type is an excellent example of the influential and sturdy Dutch types that prevailed in England up to the time William Caslon (1692–1766) developed his own incomparable designs from them.

Composed, printed, and bound by
The Haddon Craftsmen, Scranton, Pennsylvania

Designed by Peter A. Andersen